the infernal underground

PRISON FOR SUPERNATURAL OFFENDERS BOOK THREE

MEGAN LINSKI & ALICIA RADES

We the authors acknowledge that the United States of America is a country formed on stolen land. We respect and honor the indigenous peoples who have lived here for centuries, and we recognize there is still much work to do to make reparations and heal the damage caused to the many indigenous nations who were first here, both in the past and today.

May we remember the atrocities once committed, create a better world in the present, and look forward together for our future.

This book features characters with the following medical conditions. The information included is meant to educate readers on disabilities featured within the *Prison for Supernatural Offenders* series.

DWARFISM

Dwarfism is a shortness in height— under 4-feet 10-inches in adulthood— caused by a range of medical conditions, including genetic mutations that inhibit bone growth. Common complications include crowded teeth, poor muscle tone, hunching of the back, and bowed legs.

ONE

A year ago, I had hope of getting out of this prison alive.

Now, I had nothing. No hope. No fear. Nothing. I had too much time to think these days, so I just... didn't. I shut down. It was all too easy to go into autopilot while labeling boxes during my Work-Study hours. The Warden obviously didn't want me working in the mines anymore— not after the stunt the Villain's Club pulled last semester, when my friends and I had exposed Forevermore. I'd been reassigned to a packaging facility located in the prison wing furthest from the classrooms. The guards had shoved a label gun in my hand and had me labeling boxes eight hours a day, every day.

Box. Label. Box. Label. Box. Label.

That's all I let go through my head. It was easier to focus on the process than ponder any real problems— like how to save the Elves, or how to get over... *her.*

Tonight, though, my thoughts raced. I tried to shut them down, but they wouldn't go away.

The sound of machinery whirred around me, and the heavy scent of metal filled my nose. A box moved down the conveyor belt to my station. I felt for the corner, then pressed the label on with the gun. I could feel the noxite inside the box draining my energy. I didn't know what was actually *in* the boxes. It could be raw noxite, cuffs, darts, really anything. The guards never said, and we weren't supposed to ask.

No one spoke here in the facility, though I could hear other students shuffling around the large room, working their factory jobs. It was a dull job, but better than the mines, at least.

I hadn't been to the mines since I'd found Forevermore with Ava-Marie.

Hell, Ava.

I hadn't run into her since we'd broken up. The mere memory of her fingers gliding over my skin caused my entire form to go rigid, and my guts to twist. No magical torture could be so intense as the recollection of my hands running through her long hair. The thought of her beautiful voice, which I'd missed so much, almost dropped me to my knees. It had been months, but instead of getting better, the agony of losing her had only gotten worse. It was like my soul was being torn to shreds, hacked to bits by pieces of glass that were too fragmented for me to pull out, and I bled every time I tried.

Don't think about her.

Iron bars came down as I shut the ever-encompassing thought of *her* out of my mind. I wouldn't allow myself to go down that pit to hell. No thanks.

I had no classes over the summer, just my Work-Study credit I earned from labeling these stupid boxes. During the summer semester at the Institute, classes were suspended, and inmates were expected to work forty-hours a week— or more— on our Work-Study courses.

I was supposed to keep attending counseling sessions, but no one had seen Professor Takahashi since the Elves had fled Forevermore. I didn't know why he'd left, but I was sure it was for a good reason. What-ever it was, it was certainly more important than counseling a couple of college-aged criminals.

I took it as a blessing. The Institute hadn't found anyone to replace Takahashi, so I hadn't been forced to go to counseling and talk to *her* all summer. I'd been avoiding her as much as possible, for reasons too painful to consider.

When I wasn't labeling boxes, I was training for the fight club. I didn't really want to do it anymore. What was the point? I'd only been doing it to save money to provide for my girl when we got out of this hell hole, and she was gone now.

Although fight club certainly paid better than my garbage Work-Study job— if you could call it a *job*. I was pretty sure I made less than ten cents an hour, though no one had ever given me an official number. Prisoner wages were shit.

But I didn't need the money anymore, not now that she and I had split. Money just didn't matter. I'd lived without it before. I could do it again.

But I couldn't get out of fight club, even if I wanted to. When I'd *hinted* I wanted to quit, Captain had yanked a punching bag off its chains and threw it at me. He wasn't the kind of vampire you wanted to mess with. It was easier to fight my peers than it was to fight him. So I just took the beatings, because at least I felt *something* when I was being pummeled by a dragon shifter.

The rest of the time, I was just... numb.

Don't think. Don't feel. Just breathe.

Every breath I took felt suffocating.

My bonded partner wasn't the only person I was avoiding. I avoided the guys at fight club as much as I could, too. I put in my training hours at night, when most students were in bed. The guards left my door unlocked so I could sneak down to the training center after my late Work-Study shift. I'd train all night, then sneak back into my room before *her* cell unlocked from beside mine. I'd sleep most of the day, until my Work-Study shift started at two o'clock.

And I repeated that over and over. Like I said, it'd become too easy to fall into an autopilot routine. Any spare moment I had, I spent with Eddie searching for information about the keys to open the Elven gate on Darke Island, but we hadn't found anything.

I was prophesied to bring the Elves into paradise, by opening that Elven gate using seven keys, one from every supernatural race, and leading them on into heaven— the Blessed Haven, where the Elves belonged.

Though at this point, it felt more like I was leading them to their doom.

I'd basically given up. What was the point, anyhow? The Warden had won.

Box. Label. Box. Label.

A buzzer went off overhead, and I breathed a sigh of relief. That was the cue for the end of my shift. I shoved the label gun back in its holder at my station, then got the hell out of there, because I didn't want to stay a second longer than I had to. It was gross how the Institute used us for cheap labor, under the guise of *rehabilitating* us.

Rehabilitation, my ass. If anything, I'd gotten *worse* since I'd shown up here. I'd joined a freaking fight club, for the ancestors' sake!

She'd been right, and I should've never joined. They were using me.

But there was no going back now. I was in this until I graduated or until I fucking died here.

Right now, dying felt like the better option.

The good thing about fight club— besides the guards looking the other way when I did shit that should've earned me an infraction— was free reign to punch something whenever I wanted. After my Work-Study shift, I always needed a good punching bag to beat the shit out of. I swear, it was the only thing that kept me sane in this place.

The quickest way to get to the secret training room from the packaging facility was to cut through the prison yard, near the siren lake, rather than weave through the maze of hallways. I could always navigate the outdoors better anyway, because of my magic.

Better than that— she was hardly ever outside, and it helped me to avoid her.

I could tell it was late when I left the building, because the air was cool, and the bugs that only came out at night sang their mating calls loudly. I counted my steps as I left the building, and paid attention to landmarks throughout the prison yard, listening for the sound of my footsteps echoing off the obstacles around me. It's how I navigated the Institute as a blind guy when my Familiar, Oberi, wasn't here to guide me.

Not far from me, I could hear the waves of the lake lapping against the shore. I reached out with my magic to sense a large tree up ahead. As I approached it, I grazed my fingers against the rough bark, which was a habit now. I liked to touch my landmarks to confirm I was headed in the right direction.

Screech!

My heart lurched as a high-pitched alarm filled the prison yard. Voices began shouting, and the wind whipped around me. It wasn't my magic; it was someone else's. Instinctually, I ducked behind the tree to conceal myself from whatever the hell was going on.

"Get him!" someone shouted. The voice was rough, and belonged to a guard for sure. They were coming straight toward me. For a second, I thought they were talking about me, but curfew wasn't for another few minutes. I'd done nothing wrong.

"Get back here!" another guard shouted.

"Don't let him get away!" someone screamed.

Hell, I realized. Someone was making a break for it.

Good for them, I thought. They were braver than I. No one got out of the Institute, and if you tried, you were sent to Cellblock 9. Marcus and Kallie had tried to escape once, but they'd gotten lucky. Professor Warbright had talked down the guards for them. I wouldn't want to risk it— not after what we'd discovered about the Warden last semester.

We'd discovered that he'd been running experiments on students, trying to find a demigod for some nefarious purpose. We hadn't gotten any evidence, but I knew it was true. Any sorry sucker who got dragged off to Cellblock 9 was a victim of those experiments. I was sure of it.

There were so many footsteps racing across the prison yard that I couldn't make out how many guards were in pursuit. They were closing in fast, coming closer and closer to my hiding spot.

"Take him down by any means necessary!" one guard screamed to the others.

"My magic's gone!" another yelled back.

"Then shoot him!"

"He's an *Elf!*" the guard spat back.

I held my breath. One of the Elves was trying to escape, and if he'd managed to take a guards' magic, he was going to make it. I hoped he did. It was the first time in forever I felt *any* kind of hope.

Elves were immune to noxite. The darts wouldn't slow him down. But the fence around the property did. It was the only thing keeping the

Elves prisoner. I'd asked Eddie about it once— why he and his friends couldn't just steal the guards' magic and get the hell out of here. Hell, he could break us all out if he wanted.

But Eddie had assured me that stealing someone else's magic was difficult, something none of the Elves at the Institute had mastered yet. At least, not until tonight. As Eddie had put it, *"We may be immune to noxite, but there's still barbed wire keeping us from jumping that fence."*

There was hope. If an Elf had figured out how to overpower the guards, they could steal someone else's magic and fly out, or break straight through the gates with vampire strength.

Hell, I hoped it was Eddie, but I knew he wouldn't attempt to leave without me. He was born to protect me... psh... the *Elf prince.*

I was the grandson of the Elven Emperor. Still hadn't quite wrapped my head around it myself. And to be honest, I was still feeling a little bitter about the whole thing. I'd found my family, but then I'd lost them again.

Even worse, finding my heritage had cost me the love of my life. Nothing good ever happened to me, and if it did, it always came with a cost too high to bear.

My heart hammered as I listened closely. It felt good to *feel* something. The wind picked up around me, whipping my long hair around my face. I could hardly hear the conversation between the guards anymore. I tried to calm the wind with my elemental magic, so I could figure out what the hell was going on, but it barely died down. That meant whoever was whipping up the windstorm was nearly as strong as I was.

It was the Elf. I just knew it. He'd taken one of the Yapluma guards' Air magic and was using it to keep them away, so he could make his escape.

"I got him!" a guard shouted.

The Air around me swirled chaotically. It was as if two Elementai were warring against one another— a guard against the Elf, I was sure.

"You're not going anywhere," a guard growled across the prison yard.

The Elf laughed maniacally. "You want to bet?"

He must've given up on the Air magic, because the wind died down.

The next thing I knew, a deafening screech filled the yard. I threw my hands over my ears and curled against the tree I hid behind. It was louder than the alarm blaring overhead and made it feel as if my brain was rattling around in my skull.

When I thought it was over, I dropped my hands from my ears. All throughout the prison yard, guards groaned in agony. The Elf had stolen a siren guard's cry.

The sound of wings unfurling met my ears, and they began to flap. I could tell by the sound that they were huge and feathery, like angel wings. Most angels could only fly around the center of the prison yard. Once they got close to the noxite gates, their wings gave out.

But this guy was no angel.

"What the hell?!" a guard yelled. "He's stolen my wings!"

I smirked. Good for him!

"So long, suckers!" the Elf laughed. He flapped his newfound wings and flew directly over me. My jaw hung slack as I listened to him fly away, far above the barbed wire fence, and into the forest beyond.

Holy ancestors. He'd done it. He'd *escaped the Institute.*

I beamed. If this Elf could escape, then it meant others could as well. *I* could get out of here!

I pressed my back to the tree, where the guards couldn't see me. I was still trying to catch my breath, because I was so shocked by it all. I couldn't believe someone had gotten away. This was a big fucking deal.

"You bastard!" a guard screamed.

"*You're* the one who let him steal your wings. If you were stronger, he wouldn't have escaped."

"This is *your* fault!" another accused.

"Oh, yeah? You wanna fight about it? I'll give you a fight—" The guard must've shifted mid-sentence, because the next thing I knew, a dragon's roar filled the prison yard.

One of the guards laughed. "What do you think you're gonna do with those dull dragon claws? Half of us are vampires. I'd rip your head off and suck you dry. I don't care how filthy your blood tastes."

Hell, the guards could be worse than the inmates sometimes.

"Stop screwing around and go after him," another guard growled. "He's on an island for fuck's sake. He can't go far!"

The guards were *pissed*! They hurried off in pursuit of the Elf, but they had to go out the gate, because even the guards couldn't get past the noxite fence. The Elf had a major head start, though. I didn't think the guards would find him, even on Darke Island. If the Elf got past the ward surrounding the island somehow, he'd be home free.

I sat behind my tree a while longer, listening to the fading sounds of the guards' footsteps. When I was confident they were gone, I rushed out from behind my hiding spot and hurried into the building.

I was still reeling over what I'd just witnessed that I wasn't quite paying attention to where I was going. I quickly got lost in the maze of hallways.

Hell, where was I? I stopped to take in my surroundings. It had to be minutes from curfew by now. The halls were dead silent.

Then I heard the sound of paws padding down the hallway. My heart surged when I felt Oberi's presence through our bond.

"Hey, boy," I greeted. I knelt down and scratched him behind the ears.

I frowned when I noticed his fur was matted and felt a bit rough. It seemed Oberi hadn't been brushed all summer, which made me sad... because it meant *she* was sad. Oberi didn't ask to be groomed when my other half was feeling down.

Oberi barked and panted happily. Usually, he didn't visit me until after I got back from training. It was unusual for him to find me this late at night, since he usually spent the night with her. He must've noticed something felt off.

"It's okay, boy," I told him. "I'm safe."

I noticed your lost ass needed saving, Oberi cracked.

I frowned. He could get sassy when he wanted to. "I need to find Eddie. Can you lead me to him?"

Oberi barked. I placed my hand on his back, and he guided me through the halls. I heard voices ahead, and I figured we'd entered one of the cellblocks. Oberi slowed and guided me into what I figured had to be one of the cells.

"Charlie?" Eddie asked, sounding surprised. I wasn't so good with voices, but Eddie and I had spent a lot of time together over the summer.

I'd learned to recognize his voice easily. "What are you doing in my dorm? Curfew's in two minutes."

"Something's happened," I said breathlessly.

Eddie's bed springs squeaked as he jumped up from his bed and shut the door. He spoke in a hushed tone. "What is it? Have you found something on the keys?"

I scoffed. At this point, I wasn't sure we'd *ever* find anything. "It's not that. You heard the alarm?"

The fabric of Eddie's uniform rustled as he crossed his arms. "The whole prison heard it. Wait... you weren't involved in that, were you?"

"No, but I heard what happened. One of your buddies escaped."

"Fuck," Eddie growled under his breath. He sounded exasperated as he sat back down on his bed. "It was Gavyn, wasn't it?"

"No idea," I said. "All I know is that it was an Elf. He overpowered the guards and stole some of their powers. I thought you said none of the Elves at the Institute were strong enough for that."

"We weren't," Eddie admitted. "But Gavyn's been training with his magic all summer, in secret."

The lock on Eddie's door clicked, and I knew there was no leaving now. I was stuck in here with him all night. Not a big deal, since the guards never checked my bed anyway. I figured I might as well get comfortable. Oberi guided me to the chair beside Eddie's desk, and I sat.

"You sound upset," I remarked. "I thought you'd be happy for him. You're always talking like you want to get out of here."

"Of course I do, but not like this." Eddie sighed. "After the Elves were captured in Forevermore, we got together and talked about our options. Gavyn *always* wanted to get out. He talked about it constantly. But none of our magic was strong enough, and we knew we wouldn't *become* strong enough to get everyone out at once. We needed to practice first. We agreed to stick together, seeing as we don't know where to find the rest of the Elves. The deal was either we all go, or no one goes. Gavyn apparently did not listen."

"But if one Elf gets out, so can the rest of you," I remarked. So could *I*, since I was part Elf. For once, I actually had a spark of hope.

Unlike me, Eddie was realistic and logical. "We're still pretty young Elves, and while we can do *some* magical manipulation, it's not enough to get all of us out. That's why we agreed to stick together. Even our illusion magic is shit. Gavyn has betrayed us. Even if we did get out of the gates, we'd have to be strong enough to get off Darke Island. There's a ward around the whole island, you know."

Hell, he was right. Even though I hoped Gavyn was strong enough to overpower that somehow, too.

"One Elf escapes, and the Warden is going to come down on the rest of us," Eddie pointed out. "You just watch."

I didn't want to believe that Eddie was right. I wanted to believe we had a chance at getting the hell away from here, where the Warden couldn't run his experiments on us, and where he'd never figure out what I was— an Elf prince, and a demigod.

But it didn't take long before Eddie's suspicions were confirmed. The next morning, a letter slid under Eddie's dorm.

"*All students are required to attend an assembly in the Room of Mirrors at eight a.m. sharp,*" Eddie read aloud to me. "*Anyone not in attendance will be given an infraction, and a six-hundred-dollar fine will be charged to their account.*"

Hell, a fine that huge would put most students' accounts in the negative. Most of us made less than ten dollars a month, working the shitty Work-Study jobs they forced us into.

"Can the Warden do that?" I questioned. "Charge a fine?"

"I don't want to find out," Eddie remarked.

I didn't want to attract the Warden's attention. Once Eddie's door unlocked, we went to the cafeteria to get some food, then headed to the Room of Mirrors. It was the same room where the Warden had hosted his welcome speech my first day here, and where the Villain's Ball was held after the Darke Games every year. The vast room was used for various school functions, but it got quite crowded when the whole student body was packed inside.

Bodies pressed in on me from all angles. Oberi stayed close to my side in his husky form. He seemed calm and relaxed, which worried me, because he hadn't been this way since before *she* and I had broken up.

I realized it probably meant *she* was nearby, and he was happy we were finally in the same room together again. I listened closely to the voices around me, but I couldn't pick her out of the crowd. I hoped she was across the room and couldn't see me. I wouldn't be able to know she was approaching until she was right on top of me, as our bond had weakened considerably since we'd been apart. The magic between us was almost... gone.

Ava's three rows up, Oberi mentioned. *You should go talk to her.*

I scowled. *How many times are we going to have this conversation?*

As many as it takes.

I huffed. Oberi had been trying to talk me into getting back together with Ava all summer. Every fucking day of the week, actually.

It was never going to happen. We were bad for each other. We had made the right decision.

Or so I told myself.

"Are you okay?" Eddie leaned over and asked me.

"Yeah. I just have to deal with *his* sassy ass all day." I poked Oberi.

Better to be a sassy ass than a grumpy ass, he shot back.

I was sure that was Ava's half of our soul talking. Oberi didn't really think before he spoke.

"Welcome, students." The Warden's cool voice boomed over the room, and the student body began to quiet. A few people still made noise, because most students here had a problem with authority. On the other hand, the majority of us were scared shitless of the Warden, so it didn't take long before the room fell silent.

My guts twisted at the sound of his voice. The Warden had tortured me last semester and nearly killed me. I despised the man.

"I have called this assembly today to share news of an incident that transpired last night," the Warden said. His voice came from high up on the balcony. He made it sound like he was trying to sympathize with the students, but his attempt came across stale. He was shit at pretending like he cared about any of us. We were just numbers to him.

"Last night, a student by the name of Gavyn Woodward attempted to escape the Darke Institute," the Warden announced.

Gasps traveled around the room. I furrowed my brow, because I hadn't expected the Warden to tell the truth. The Institute was supposedly impossible to escape. I would've expected him to maintain that illusion.

"Settle down," the Warden said in a threatening tone. The whispers filling the room settled, though they didn't completely die down. "It's important that you realize this student was no ordinary supernatural. He was an *Elf.*"

He spoke the word *Elf* like it was some sort of curse. It was obvious he despised us.

"I tell you this to keep you safe," the Warden said— like he gave two shits. "What Gavyn Woodward did last night in his attempt to escape was deplorable. He created a windstorm, stole a siren's scream, and slaughtered six guards using an angel's life-force power."

People gasped again, and the whispers grew.

My eyebrows furrowed. That had never happened. Gavyn had stolen an angel's powers, but only their wings, not their life-force abilities. The only way that was true was if the guards had found Gavyn on Darke Island after he'd escaped, but I didn't know how they could've caught up with him. The Warden was twisting the truth to suit his message. It made me sick.

"Unfortunately, drastic measures had to be taken to protect everyone here at the Institute," he said. The Warden was trying to make himself seem like the *good* guy. I wasn't buying it. His voice turned sad, but I could hear how fake it was. "I am devastated to announce that Gavyn Woodward died last night in his attempt to escape."

The whispers around the room grew louder. My lips tightened at the Warden's lies. I wanted to tell everyone he was *wrong*, that Gavyn had actually escaped without killing anyone, but that was a good way to piss off the Warden.

"The safety of our students and staff is of the utmost importance," the Warden continued. "I do not take kindly to *any* threats within the Institute. Rest assured that anyone who threatens the safety of the students or guards *will* be dealt with by any means necessary."

Students murmured around me, but they seemed to *agree* with the Warden. They thought he was protecting them.

But I knew better. This speech was a threat to the Elves. To *me.*

"Know that you are safe here," the Warden said, like we were supposed to be *grateful.* "Anyone who is deemed a threat will be *punished.*"

He said it with such finality that there was no denying what he meant. Anyone who stepped out of line, or who showed too much power here at the prison, would be killed. The Warden could do anything he wanted to us, all in the name of keeping us *safe*.

And people fucking bought it. I could hear them whispering around me.

Gavyn got what he deserved.

The Warden is doing his best.

Some kids can't be saved.

My nostrils flared, and I just wanted to scream.

Stay calm. You can't tell anyone what you know, Oberi insisted.

My hands curled into fists at my sides. Oberi was right. It wasn't like exposing the Warden for his lies would change anything. He'd twist some story to make me out as a *threat* so he could run his sick experiments on me. And if he found out I was a demigod, we were all doomed.

The Warden could keep his lies.

This time.

With the Warden's threat hanging in the air, he excused us. Students filed out of the room and headed in different directions. The conversations around me were deafening.

We didn't make it far before Eddie pulled me aside, and we ducked into an empty classroom. The door shut behind us, and I felt like I could finally think in the silence. Oberi nudged against me, like he was trying to comfort me, but I was fuming.

"The Warden is lying," Eddie raged.

"I know," I agreed. "Gavyn didn't kill anyone when he escaped. I'd have heard *something*."

"Of course he didn't," Eddie insisted. "Gavyn wanted out, but he was no murderer. I know him. We grew up together. He wouldn't do what the Warden said he did."

I gritted my teeth. "The Warden is trying to scare us."

"The Elves aren't bad people," Eddie practically pleaded. "We just want peace."

"I know that. But it's not me you have to convince."

Eddie began pacing. "The Warden started a war when he raided

Forevermore. He's using Gavyn's escape to perpetuate that war. It won't stop unless we do something."

I raked my fingers through my hair. "I want to. I just don't know what we can do. I'm not totally immune to noxite like Gavyn is. I can't go up against the Warden on my own and get everyone out, even with what I am."

I made sure never to say what I was aloud— a demigod *or* the Elven prince— in case someone overheard.

Eddie stopped pacing. "You're assuming you have to do this on your own."

I huffed, then lowered my voice to a whisper. "Well, don't I? My prophecy says so."

Eddie had practically drilled the prophecy into my head. I could never forget it— it repeated like a mantra every day, a curse I could never escape.

The emperor's legacy will return, and bring light to a new dawn. A second war will break Forevermore, but it shall be restored by the power of the demigods. It is his choice to damn the realm, or save us all.

"No," Eddie clarified. "You *will* lead us to the Blessed Haven, but nowhere does the prophecy state that you must do it on your own."

I was so frustrated, I could break something. I held myself back. "Who's going to help?" I demanded. "We have no allies here."

Eddie spoke softly. "You have Ava."

When he said her name, my heart stopped. I didn't talk about Ava, not even to Oberi. I'd barely heard her name in months. It was too much to hear. I could feel my chest ripping apart, as if a wolven shifter was digging inside of it to devour my heart. I'd rather feel nothing at all.

"I don't have Ava," I spat. "We broke up. Remember?"

"That doesn't mean you can't be allies," Eddie insisted. "Your destinies are entwined, and you know it. It's time you two stopped acting like you can do this on your own. If you can't face each other, everyone will perish."

Eddie was always kind to me, but he sure had a way of making me feel guilty.

"I didn't ask for this!" I growled.

"Nobody did," Eddie said calmly. "Please stop acting like you have to go at this alone."

"I'm not alone," I argued. "I have you."

"And others! The Elves are here to help you. If we just had a little instruction, then maybe our powers would grow strong enough to save everyone. Someone like you, Charlie."

I paused for a moment to digest his suggestion. "You want me to teach the Elves how to use their powers?"

"Yes," Eddie said. "You're more powerful than any of us. This war was always going to lead to a revolution, and we need you and your friends to lead it."

I knew what he meant without him saying it. We needed *demigods*. It was part of the prophecy.

Hell, I hadn't spoken to Kallie or Marcus since we left Forevermore, either. We weren't friends anymore— none of us were. I didn't know if they'd help Eddie and me save the Elves.

Ancestors, I'd been *so lonely* since the summer had begun. I hadn't said a word to any of my old friends— not Ez, Opal, Ivy, any of them. I didn't even talk to Chancey, and he was in fight club with me, for ancestors' sake. The thought of speaking to any of them again was soul-crushing. I just wanted to be left alone, to deal with this hurt.

But Eddie was right. We hadn't gotten anywhere on our own, and if we didn't do something soon, the Elves would die, and the rest of us wouldn't be far behind. My ex-friends were the only ones who would help us.

I couldn't open the Elven gate on the island without them, anyway. Ava, Kallie, and Marcus all had a key— the Elementai, fae, and witch keys that would help open up the portal to heaven. Though who knew if they'd actually *want* to give them to me, after the destruction we'd caused last semester?

It didn't matter. If I wanted to save the Elves, I had to get the Villain's Club back together— no matter how much it hurt.

Even worse... I'd have to face Ava again.

I'd spent an entire summer feeling nothing, but once I spoke to Ava,

I was certain every emotion I'd ever had about her would come rushing back, and I'd be helpless to stop it.

Forget the Warden. I was sure that facing Ava was going to be the end of me.

ava-marie

TWO

I was really going to miss this program. It was the only distraction I'd had all summer that had made my life worthwhile.

I sighed as I woefully put away the anthropology textbooks Professor Hemlock had pulled out this morning, restacking them in rows along her classroom shelves. It was the last day of my summer internship, and I'd made it through the course. I was officially enrolled in the Institute's Anthropology major now, and it'd been hard work to pass—though I'd been grateful for every moment of it, because the tough academia was the only thing that distracted me from the ache in my heart.

Most inmates at the Institute worked full-time in their Work-Study courses all summer, until it was time to go back to regular courses in the fall. I'd gotten lucky by enrolling as Hemlock's personal intern last semester, so I didn't have to go work in the prison's factory like most of the inmates did. I'd learned so much from her about ancient supernatural societies. We'd spent day and night going over artifacts, old discoveries, and magical history. I'd endured a rigorous set of exams and papers, appreciating the one-on-one time with Hemlock and absorbing her knowledge.

But now it was all over. And there was nothing left to distract me from the pain that was quaking me from the inside out.

I heard a scuffle in the hallway. I glanced out the open classroom door. My heart twisted as I saw an Elvish girl being harassed by one of the guards. He pushed her down and pulled her hair, taunting her about her ears.

I wanted to step in, but the Elvish girl ran off. The guard stared after her with a satisfied smirk before walking in the other direction.

I forced myself to go back to what I was doing. I didn't interfere anymore... didn't try to play the hero. I'd learned my lesson with that. It was better to do nothing at all.

At least that way, I didn't make it worse.

The Elves were mistreated at the prison. I hoped wherever the rest of them were, they had hidden themselves so well that no one would ever find them.

We'd avoided studying the Elves during my internship. I didn't think Hemlock wished to cover them, after I'd gone against her advice and searched for Forevermore. I knew Hemlock was disappointed in me, and there was nothing I could say to defend myself. I'd exposed Forevermore. Now the Elves were in hiding while the supernatural world argued how to find them and what to do with them. No matter which way you spun it, I was responsible for re-igniting an entire genocide, and there was no forgiveness for that.

I swung my bag over my shoulder. The strap pressed into my bone through the fabric I was wearing, making me wince. I wore multiple layers underneath my Institute sweater. I was *so cold*. Food made me even more nervous than before. I couldn't look at a plate these days without feeling nauseous. I choked down something every now and then, to keep my body running, but I rarely ate every day— and it was all too easy to skip meals while working for Hemlock, who rarely took breaks herself.

I probably looked sick as all hell, but no one had noticed, so I didn't care, either.

I went to the prison's mailroom to check to see if I had any mail. The only letter that had arrived was another offer from *Toaqua Today*, with an even bigger cash offer this time.

I scoffed and threw away the letter the moment I passed a trash can. Ever since I'd found Forevermore, all the magazines in the supernatural world were trying to contact me, to get me to do an exclusive on the Elves and what had happened.

Prisoners can still do interviews, you know. It's not a crime, the letters reminded me. *Just a quick interview, a few pictures, and we'll make it worth your time.*

I wasn't interested. It was just another scandal they wanted to take advantage of. The papers were all abuzz over the fact that the firstborn daughter of the Water chief had made such an important discovery—and as an inmate, no less. It had gossip written all over it.

Gossip I wanted no part of. They were even sending letters to my *brother*, to try and get in contact with me. It was ridiculous.

I began my long walk down the hallway to my cell, which seemed even more lonesome than it usually did. Classes started next week, and I wasn't looking forward to getting back to them. I wished to remain in the anthropology internship, where I could lock myself away in Hemlock's classroom for hours at a time, reading about civilizations I wasn't a part of in an attempt to escape my own thoughts. I worried that once classes struck up again, I'd be forced to face... well, everyone.

I'd used the intensity of the anthropology program as an excuse, but to be honest, I'd been avoiding the people I used to consider my friends ever since the Warden had seized Forevermore. My brother was the one person I'd talked to all summer, and I'd barely said ten sentences to him in three months.

I knew. I'd counted.

I missed my friends. I missed Kallie, Marcus, Opal and Ivy. But no matter how much I missed them, I didn't allow myself to speak to them. I'd condemned a city with my most recent screw-up, and was wary of what else I could do to ruin people's lives. I'd already hurt Charlie enough.

I shook my head and forced a confident smile onto my face, though it hurt to hold.

Charlie *who*? I didn't know why he'd crossed my mind. I didn't care about him. I didn't *need* an Elf prince cutie with a quirky smile and a sculpted ass. I needed a big bank account, a shopping day, and a trip to the spa. Who wanted *men* anyhow? Certainly not me. I could be a confi-dent, badass bitch all on my own.

I'd entered into the Elementai cellblock when I almost ran into the one person I'd been thinking of— and the last person I wanted to see.

Him. Charlie stood ten feet away, looming outside his door like he was waiting for someone to walk by. Oberi sat by his feet, wagging his tail and drooling.

My eyes ran him up and down, taking in his tall frame. The sight of him was a shot to the heart. *Oh no. He was still hot.* I'd somehow hoped he'd become ugly over the summer. Or at least, not as fucking attractive.

Apparently, I existed on this Earth to be tormented, because Charlie hadn't only *remained* good-looking, his sexiness level had increased. His hair was longer, and he had this *gorgeous* beard that was only slightly longer than five o'clock shadow, scruffy and oh-so-delicious.

Wow. Did he just not care to shave, or was he *trying* to make my panties wet? The self-righteous bastard! How *dare* he!

Butterflies welled in my stomach until I felt like I should be puking out insect wings. The horrifying feelings bubbled past my middle and overfilled my heart as his presence drew near. Reluctantly, I had to admit I knew all too well what the hated *feelings* were.

Dammit!!! I was still in love with him. Fuccccckkkk.

I hoped to the ancestors he'd turn around and leave me alone, but the butterflies flew up from my stomach and started choking me as his steps grew closer, Oberi leading us together.

Shit, he was coming this way. No. No. *Nooooooo.*

Charlie stopped in front of me. Oberi barked, but I waved my hand to tell him to shut up. I kept my mouth closed and remained frozen. I struck a pose like a statue, refusing to move a single muscle. If I didn't say anything, maybe he wouldn't know I was here. Our bond was weak now. It wasn't like we could feel each other's presence like we used to.

That was my plan. He couldn't see me, so I just shut up and acted like I wasn't around. Maybe if I kept it up—

"We should talk," Charlie started, and my heart sank.

I held my breath, and Charlie ground his teeth. "Ava, I *know you're there.* Stop acting like you're invisible. I'm sure you look stupid."

My temper flared. I dropped my pose and sneered, "*You* don't tell me what to do."

Charlie gave a harsh laugh under his breath. "Yeah, you've made that clear as hell."

"Screw you," I spat. I hated him more now than I did back then. His mere presence irritated me. The fact that we had a history now made him even more nauseating. I couldn't believe I screwed around with this loser.

And kissed him...

And gave him a lap dance...

And... *oh ancestors*... his dick though...

"Ava, are you paying attention?" Charlie asked roughly. "I need to speak with you. It's important."

"Why?" I asked. "You haven't spoken to me all summer. What's the rush?"

"Things are different—" he began, but I cut him off.

"Nothing's changed," I stated. "I'm sure you want some help with your little Elf... *thing*... but I've got my own problems, so don't let the ass hit you in the door on the way— shit— I mean, don't let the door fuck you in the ass— *dammit*, you know what I mean!"

"Does me being here offend you?" Charlie seethed. "Because right now, it seems like I'm annoying you just by breathing."

"You are, so go away." I huffed and turned my back on Charlie, but he reached out and nabbed me by the shoulder.

"Unhand me, you ruffian!" I screeched, and I batted at his arm.

"*Ruffian?* Are you a hundred fucking years old?" he growled. He tugged on my arm, and I yanked back. We waged a tug-of-war that didn't do anything but stretch out my ugly-ass Institute sweater. Oberi barked madly around us and grabbed Charlie's pant-leg, pulling at it like he thought this was a game.

"Ouch! Oberi, cut it out!" Charlie said as the husky nearly yanked him off his feet with a giddy growl.

"Get him, Oberi! Good boy!" I cheered.

Charlie shook Oberi off, then grabbed my wrists. He pushed me into the wall roughly— though not as roughly as I would've liked— pinning my hands above my head.

Finally, we were getting somewhere— wait, no— fuck, Ava, make up your mind!

I was all over the place. Right now, my heart was split between choking this bastard or letting him screw me against the wall.

Both, please?

Charlie blocked me in, so I had nowhere to go. His hands were so firm, I knew any attempt to push him away would be absolutely futile. He was so close that I could feel his breath on my skin, and the heat of our bodies as they pressed together. Unlike when we'd first met, he was fed up with taking my shit and knew how to deal with me now.

I was momentarily terrified that Charlie would realize how much weight I'd lost. But he must've not noticed my bony frame through all the layers I was wearing, so at least I was spared from one lecture...

Or maybe he didn't care. Who knew?

I didn't really *mean* to, but for some reason or another, I pushed my boobs up. My breasts crushed against his chest, and Charlie breathed raggedly. "Hell, one of these days, I'm going to make you listen."

"It's not going to be today," I sneered. "So piss off."

"Goddamn you, pidge—" Charlie growled, but as he said it, he hitched a breath.

With that one word, both of our walls came crashing down in a moment of vulnerability, and a second was all it took.

Everything we'd shared. Everything we'd felt. The connection we had came rushing back. A well of love opened up inside of me, overflowing into an ocean that I couldn't hold back. The effect broke me and healed me all at once. I'd forgotten what it was like to feel our bond. It'd been blocked off on both ends for so long. I never reached out to feel Charlie's consciousness anymore, but when I did out of habit, I always hit resistance. Now that way was open, and I could feel the half of Charlie's soul reaching out for my own, like it was lonely.

Through our bond, I *experienced* Charlie's feelings. Ancestors, he was so torn up inside. His heart was shattered. I didn't think, after all this time, he still—

This was too painful. I immediately shut the bond off, and I felt Charlie do the same on his end. The effect was similar to crashing into a brick wall full-speed, and nearly as fatal. He let go of my wrists and took a few steps back, widening the gap between us. My half of our soul wept in sorrow at failing to be reunited with its twin, curling up and dying in my chest.

Charlie scratched the back of his head and said quietly, "If you don't want to come, fine. But to be honest, I need you. I can't do this without you. So are you in, or what?"

All my earlier reservations were thrown out the window when he said he needed me. I couldn't deny him. Not when he asked me like that. "Let's just get this over with. Where are we going?"

"The chapel." He said nothing more, just let Oberi lead him onward. I followed at a distance, keeping my head down.

When Charlie opened the chapel doors, my stomach plummeted even further. Kallie and Marcus were inside, sitting in separate pews on opposite sides of the chapel. I didn't think they'd talked all summer, either— all of us had been off doing our own thing.

Eddie bounced in a corner, obviously pleased with himself. "They're here, sir," Eddie said. "I gathered Kallie and Marcus, just like you asked."

"Thanks," Charlie said. "And Eddie— stop calling me sir."

"Right away, sir!"

Charlie sighed. "Can you give us some space?"

"Absolutely!" Eddie romped out like he was Charlie's personal lap dog, excited he'd gotten thrown a treat. When the door clicked shut, there was an anxious silence— made even worse by the obnoxious tapping of Marcus' shoe against the floor.

"Marcus!" Kallie snapped, throwing her hands up. "Gods, can you just chill out?"

"Sorry! I'm nervous," Marcus blurted. "I don't know why we're doing this. Why now?"

Nobody said anything, and it was clear we were waiting for Charlie. He took a breath. "Eddie and I have been doing our best to search for the remaining keys on our own, but we're not getting anywhere. We need help."

Ancestors, the *keys*. The ones that opened the Elven gate on Darke Island. We'd hid them in the Criminal Lair last summer, because it was the only place they felt safe. It was the last time I spoke to Kallie or Marcus. I hadn't given them a thought since, because the last time we'd gone looking for a key, my entire life had imploded. I honestly thought we were done with this.

"So you only talk to us when you need something. Got it," Kallie said.

"It's not like that," Charlie ground out. "Things were... they're complicated. It didn't feel right to be friends, after—"

"After we condemned a whole city to their doom?" Kallie raised an eyebrow. "Yeah, got to say, that's pretty awkward."

Charlie rubbed his face. "This is going to sound harsh, but I think it's time all of us just... got over it."

"*Got over it?*" I repeated with disdain. "You want us to get over the fact that the four of us led the Warden straight to the Elves, and set off tension between the supernatural races that just might start another war?"

"We don't have any other choice. We have to move forward," Charlie snapped.

"And how do you expect us to do that?" I crossed my arms.

"By focusing on what's ahead," Charlie said firmly. "We can't go back and reverse what we did, but we can still make things right. There are Elves out there that need our help. We can't bring back those who died, but we can rescue those who are still alive."

Could we? I wasn't sure. The Elves would've been better off if we had done nothing at all.

Charlie noticed my silence. "Did you make any headway on your own prophecy?"

I scoffed. "No."

And I didn't want to. I couldn't care less about my prophecy. The night Forevermore had been discovered, I'd stormed back to my cell and tossed the journal my Aunt Maddie had given me into my desk drawer in a fit of rage. It'd been collecting dust ever since. I didn't care about fulfilling my prophecy, finding the keys, or anything having to do with my destiny. As far as I was concerned, my prophecy had cost me everything that mattered, so I didn't wish to have anything to do with it until I was forced to face it again. I'd lost interest in finding clues, or even in discovering more about my demigod blood.

Charlie frowned. "I'd thought you'd be interested in uncovering what the other verses meant."

I gave a pitiful laugh. "Why? So more people can get hurt? I've already fulfilled one line of the prophecy: *A discovery of the ancient ones on the island of shadow will change the course of our universe.* That line came to pass, and now, Forevermore is gone. That was only *one verse,* and there are still five verses left to go— oh, wait, there's *six* now. I forgot."

My tone was bitter. Charlie hunched over, away from my voice.

"Six?" Kallie asked. "I thought—"

"There are seven verses of my prophecy, one that my Aunt Maddie kept hidden from me, but she told *Charlie,*" I said. "The last verse says; *A choice will be made by the twin of her soul, to save her and damn the realm, or curse her, and save us all. A fate worse than death is the chosen one's destiny.* Charlie's supposed to cause my greatest demise, or whatever. Like anything could be worse than languishing in this hellhole, forced to endure the Warden's every whim."

"Wow. That's rough," Marcus said, raising his eyebrows.

"Yeah. So excuse me if I don't exactly want to push forward with my own prophecy. I'd like not to destroy any more civilizations... or myself." I shrugged.

Charlie went on, in a hurry to get away from what I'd revealed. "Anyway. I know saving the Elves is my responsibility, because I'm the Elven heir. You guys don't have anything to do with this. All of you can walk away."

"Walk away?" Marcus sounded disgusted. "Do you really think we'd do that?"

"I'm asking you not to!" Charlie shouted. "I need your help!"

"You need our keys to open the gate on Darke Island, so you can lead the Elves to the Blessed Haven," Kallie clarified. "That's it."

"No." Charlie shook his head. "It's not that simple."

Charlie collapsed in a pew a few rows down from Marcus. I took a seat across the aisle away from him, waiting for him to explain.

"The Elves are being targeted at the prison," he began. "You guys already know this, but now that one of them escaped and didn't die like the

Warden said, the prison considers us a threat. Nobody knows that I have Elf blood yet, or that I'm the heir, but one day, they will. Before that day comes, I have to train the Elves at the Institute, and teach them how to fight back."

"Charlie, you have no idea what you're doing," I said. "You don't know how to steal another supernatural's powers. How can you teach the Elves something you're not sure of yourself?"

"I've been siphoning people's powers by accident since the beginning of the year. I just have to learn how to do it consciously," Charlie pointed out. "Once I do, I can teach the other Elves how to do it, too, and we'll be ready to fight when it's time."

"But the Elves have such small numbers now," Marcus said. "They won't survive another war."

"That's the point. The Elves can't hold the other races off forever," Charlie said. "Which means I have to find the keys, and lead them to the Blessed Haven, like the prophecy says I'm supposed to do. I have to do this as soon as possible, before they're wiped out. Every day that passes is another day closer to the Elves losing their chance to get to heaven and live in peace. I can't afford to waste any more time. Which is why I'm asking you guys to step in."

"Sorry, but why does this even matter?" I asked.

"What the fuck? Why does it *matter*?" Charlie asked scathingly.

"Yeah. I mean, it really sucks, but if the Elves die, doesn't that mean they get to go to the Blessed Haven anyway? That's their heaven. Why do they need *you* to lead them there?" I asked.

"They want me to lead their mortal bodies there, so they can live peacefully for eternity," Charlie protested.

"But their souls are destined for the Blessed Haven anyway, right? That's their afterlife. Maybe it would just be better if—"

"Don't say it," Charlie hissed.

"— If the Elves just died out anyway, because at least then they'd be at peace and in the Blessed Haven, and not in the middle of this stupid ass war!" I shouted.

"So you're saying it would've been better to stand back and allow them all to be slaughtered in Forevermore?" Charlie asked, completely aghast.

"I don't know, but we've condemned them to a life of suffering by letting them live!" I argued. "If we had allowed Forevermore to be conquered, and let the Elves be killed, their souls would be in the Blessed Haven right now. Instead they're here on Earth, suffering because we tried to save them."

It was a dark-ass way to think, but my mind couldn't help but go there. I wanted to wipe suffering from the world *so badly*, and make society a more just and joyful place for all.

But as I was learning quickly, my ability to end suffering, or even just stop it for a time, was very minimal, even as a demigod. Was living really worth it, if it meant living this way?

"Life matters," Charlie said firmly. "This war matters, bringing the Elves to the Blessed Haven before they die *matters*."

"Why?" I flung my hands up. "Why does any of it matter who lives and who dies? We're all going to the afterlife, anyway."

"We're here for a reason. We can't just give up," Charlie argued. "We might not know why we're doing this, why we're living, but the gods do."

"Screw the gods," I snapped. "If they wanted to give us an answer, they'd tell us. They've communicated with supernaturals before, but they don't care now, and I don't want to be a pawn for a bunch of egotistical maniacs who want to play games."

Coyote Spirit came to mind. He hadn't contacted me since the Darke Games, and he'd hardly been helpful since.

"There's a war coming, Ava! We need to stop it!" Charlie shouted. Kallie tried to shush him, and gave a quick glance at the door.

"War is pointless. There's no need for it. We'll all be at peace when we die anyway, so why bother fighting?" I said flippantly.

"You gotta be sure you're going to the right place," Kallie pointed out. "If you don't, you're fucked for literally forever."

"Who cares," I said tirelessly, tipping my head back. I was sure my soul was fated for hell, and at this point, I couldn't really give a shit. It couldn't be a worse place than where I was now.

"You sure aren't bothered by the thought of eternal damnation," Charlie grumbled.

"Because this is all so *dumb*!" I complained. "Might as well just cork off now and get to the good stuff. Or the bad stuff, anyway. At least after we die, we won't have to deal with a pointless war."

"Maybe that's not true," Marcus said nervously. "Ava, your prophecy refers to a war of gods. Maybe... maybe the afterlife isn't as peaceful as we think. Maybe war is happening there, too."

I physically felt the blood drain from my face at that horrible thought. To die on this Earth, only to go into the afterlife and have to fight there, too? Talk about eternal damnation.

"Marcus could be right," Kallie theorized. "We know not everyone has a peaceful afterlife. There are some people in hell, whatever version of hell it is. Perhaps that's where the gods will fight."

"But the Blessed Haven and the rest of heaven will be safe, right?" I asked.

"I don't know..." Marcus said slowly. "What if it isn't? What if this puts *everyone's* soul at risk?"

"Or heaven itself," Charlie commented. "We think the Ancestral Lands are a safe place of rest for Elementai souls, but what if the Ancestral Lands aren't there anymore once this war of gods is done? What if it's destroyed, along with the Blessed Haven and the rest of the heavenly planes of reality?"

I felt sick at the thought. I didn't want to consider this an actual threat, so I turned to Kallie and asked, "Fae know about interdimensional realms. Do you think our theory has any weight to it?"

My gut sank as I watched her chew her lip thoughtfully. "It's possible," she theorized. "The afterlife is another dimension, one we can only access after we die, when our souls ascend. There was war in Edinmyre long ago, in the ancestral home of the fae, and that's in another dimension. The fae afterlife exists in a part of Edinmyre itself, though one that's inaccessible to those who haven't yet died. Why can't war exist in the heavens, too?"

"If there's war in heaven, can your soul die in the afterlife? And if it does, do you just... cease to exist?" Marcus wondered aloud.

Ancestors, nobody wanted to consider that. The chapel went deathly silent at the idea.

I couldn't take the quiet, so I blurted, "What are the gods fighting about?"

"It's gotta be something big, to put the afterlife at risk," Marcus worried.

"Yes, but *why*? Why are we here?" I said desperately. I needed an answer; some sort of direction that explained what my life meant and why it mattered, and leaving the answer up to fate wasn't good enough.

"It doesn't matter what the meaning of life is. It's useless to sit here and debate about it when there's people out there that need us," Charlie insisted. "If we don't do something to stop this, we're just as bad as the Warden. And I swear to the ancestors, I'm not going to lose myself because of this. I won't become a monster because I've lost hope and don't understand what any of this means."

"I'll be damned before I become the Warden," I snarled. I *hated* him. I despised him so badly, with every inch of my being.

"Then *help me*," Charlie pleaded. "This isn't just about the Elves. This is a multi-realm war, on Earth and possibly in the afterlife. Just dying doesn't solve anyone's problem, especially if the war is still going on in heaven, too. I can't give up. *We* can't give up. So don't turn your back on me now, Ava, because I don't think I can take it."

My form went completely rigid, and a coldness crept over my skin as I heard him beg. Kallie shivered, while Marcus looked away.

Charlie was right. If I didn't do something to prevent the suffering of millions of people, whether they'd end up in heaven or not in the end, I was a monster. I might as well start calling myself Doctor Taurus, and I'd rather be in hell before I ended up like the Warden.

Or let Charlie down. That was a stupid consequence of being in love with somebody you couldn't have.

Charlie's jaw tightened. "Either way, this all begins with the Elves. We have to start somewhere if we're going to stop this. Only question is, where do we begin?"

"The Warden took forty Elves from Forevermore," I said. "Twenty of them are here, and the rest are at the adult penitentiary on the other side of the island. What does the Warden want to do with them?"

"We know the Warden was looking for demigods to experiment on," Kallie suggested. "Maybe he wants to use the Elves for the same purpose."

"But it's been three months. Shouldn't he have done that by now?" I asked.

"Maybe he started with the adults," Charlie mentioned. "And he's just now moving on to us."

That was a scary idea. I twisted a lock of hair around my finger. "We can't know for sure. There's no way of telling what he's been up to."

"We know what he's been up to," Kallie murmured, and I glanced up at her. She and Marcus shared a gaze that seemed... private, in a way.

"Before you guys showed up, Kallie and I had a minute to talk," Marcus said. "All summer, the Warden was pillaging Forevermore, looking for intel on demigods. He didn't get far— the Elves burned the records they had before they left the city— but from what I found out, the Warden is a big deal with the Celestials. The angels love him. He's a big part of the Celestial Church. He's even one of their Deacons on their ruling council."

"If that's true and he has so much power with the angels, why did he take a job at a reform school for supernaturals? Seems below his paygrade," I questioned.

"Because he's looking for demigods, and he knows if they exist, they'll end up here," Marcus said firmly. "He's not the only one who wants them. The Celestial Church is after them, too."

I shivered as I recalled how the angel professors had called the Warden *my lord* after I'd overheard their conversation about experimenting on inmates.

"And how'd you manage to get access to this information?" I asked suspiciously.

"Doesn't matter," Marcus said shortly.

"*Doesn't matter?*" Kallie asked.

"It's safer if you don't know. Trust me," Marcus said.

I scowled. Marcus was hiding something. Like we needed any more secrets around here.

Marcus sighed. "Point is, he's one of the top Deacons in the angel hierarchy, which means he's pulling the shots with the Celestials. Whatever he wants, the angels are going to give him."

"We know the Warden is looking for demigods because he wants to use their powers for his own will, probably to gain control of the other supernatural races, and open the portal to the Blessed Haven that's on Darke Island," Kallie said. "I bet he wants to make the angels the overlords of everyone, with him at the top, and he needs demigods to do it."

"Seems really extreme, even for him," I remarked.

"I found out he was a soldier during the first Great Supernatural War. He was angry the angels were humiliated in defeat, and wants his second shot to prove the angels deserve to be our overlords," Marcus said.

"Really?" I asked. The Warden seemed so young— the Great Supernatural War was a hundred years ago.

"Angels are immortal, like the Elves," Kallie reminded me. "He might be young for an angel, but not to us."

We thought on this for a moment, before I suggested, "We should assassinate the Warden."

"Ava," Charlie said tiredly.

"Why not? Kill him, and it solves all our problems!" I said.

"And how do you expect to murder a powerful angel? They're hard to kill, even with magic," Charlie said.

"I hate to say this, but Charlie is right," Kallie admitted reluctantly. "Their mastery over life-force manipulation makes them invulnerable to most attacks. The strong ones can heal themselves, and we know the Warden is strong. Even with my experience as an assassin during my vigilante days in Malovia, that's one job I wouldn't take on."

"Plus we'd get caught," Marcus pointed out. "No way we'd get away with it, not at the prison. Without a means of escape, the guards would trace it right back to us."

"Wouldn't it be worth it, if it meant stopping the war and saving the Elves?" I asked.

"Not when there are easier ways to fight back that won't get us killed," Charlie said.

I huffed. I sure thought taking out the Warden *was* the easy way.

Charlie rubbed his hands together. "You guys can do what you want. I know this isn't your fight."

"No, Charlie. This *is* our fight," Kallie said quietly. "Saving the Elves involves everyone. If we have another Great Supernatural War, Malovia will step in, and the fae are already feared and hated all around the world. The other races would jump at the chance to try and take us out, too."

"And the Miriamic Coven," Marcus added. "Some supernaturals think witches and warlocks are weak. I could see both the vampires and the angels attacking us to claim Octavia Falls for themselves. They'd want to enslave us like they did the Elves, but we won't go down without one hell of a fight."

"The Elementai won't be safe within our borders for long," I mused. "The tribe won't be able to stay out of it this time, and if our allies have already been conquered, it won't be long until we're next."

"The angels and the vampires will definitely team up," Marcus pointed out. "They hated Elves back then, and they still hate them now. Look at how the Warden talks about them. He wants to use them, then dispose of them when they no longer serve his purpose. And together, the vampires and the angels aren't anything to mess with."

"Who will the fae side with?" I asked Kallie.

Kallie shrugged. "I don't know. Malovia's history suggests they'd side with the angels, but my family is in charge now, and my dad will soon pass the throne on to my brother next spring. My entire family wants to make reparations with the other supernatural races for what we did during the last war, but not all fae see it that way. My parents could be overruled by the Circle, but at the same time, Malovia's views on the other races have somewhat changed. Maybe they'd want to help the Elves."

"That would mean the fae would have to side with the witches," Marcus pointed out.

"Yeah, I know." Kallie sighed and dropped her head. "It's never been done."

"Whatever the case, I don't want to live in a world where the Warden makes the rules, and that's going to happen if we don't get the Elves to safety and stop this war before it happens," Charlie said. "The angels and the vampires can't see an opportunity to strike before we're ready. If they do, we're all in big trouble."

Charlie held a breath. "Either way, the only way for me to protect the Elves in the meantime is to teach them how to defend themselves.

But it's not enough. I— *we*— need to start looking for those keys again. So... are you guys with me?"

Marcus stood. "I'm always with you, man. Count me in."

He shook Charlie's hand, and Kallie got up. She tossed her hair over her shoulder and said, "We wasted time by not talking over the summer. Whatever happened back then is in the past. It's over now. I'll be here for whatever you need."

Kallie and Marcus looked at me. Charlie leaned on the edge of his seat, awaiting my answer.

I stuck out my lip. "Guess I can't really say no, can I? The Elves are depending on us."

Charlie's shoulders sagged in relief.

"If we're in agreement, why don't we just break out now?" Kallie asked. "We can get to work on ending this thing before it starts."

"What about the noxite around the prison?" Marcus asked.

"We're demigods. We can overpower noxite," Kallie said. "I've been working all summer on negating its effects on me, and I'm pretty damn good at it by now. We already know it barely bothers Charlie. How about you two?"

"I've been practicing with it on morning runs," I said. "I try to get as close to the fence as possible and work on summoning my magic at the same time. Noxite doesn't bother me anymore."

"Um... I haven't practiced, but I *think* I could overpower it if I really tried," Marcus said.

"Great!" Kallie said. "What are we waiting for? Let's leave right now."

"I don't know if we can..." Marcus started. "On my way over here, I saw the guards burying something around the perimeter of the fence."

"More stuff to keep us in?" I asked.

"I think so. They're upping the magical defenses since that Elf broke out. Noxite isn't enough to keep us in anymore," Marcus said.

"So? We're demigods. Let's just smash through it and have it over with," Kallie said.

She scampered toward the door before we could protest further, so the rest of us were forced to follow. I kept my distance from Charlie as we left the prison and headed into the yard. We waited until the guards were distracted by a fist fight on the basketball court before we hurried into the forest.

Once we were sure we were far enough away from any guards, and out of the sight of the towers, Kallie said, "Okay. Time to blow this joint."

Charlie tried first. He created a tunnel out of the earth, and used it to try and dig underneath the fence. Six feet out from the fence line, the tunnel abruptly stopped, as if Charlie had commanded his magic to stop.

"My Earth magic won't go under the fence," Charlie said. "I can't dig us out of here."

"Try something else," Kallie demanded.

Charlie tried blowing the fence down with a sharp gust of wind, but that didn't work, either. It just ended up coming back at us and knocking us over. I summoned my Water and Fire magic together, merging them into a blue fireball that I tossed at the fence. It fizzled out before it even touched the chain link.

"Ugh!" I gave a cry of frustration. I tried to cast jets of water and plumes of flame over the fence, instead of going through it, but water droplets and ashes fell onto my face from above as my magic failed to ascend over the barbed wire.

Marcus tossed battle orbs at the fence before one of them bounced back and hit him in the face. It knocked him over, leaving a red welt on his cheek.

"Hey, that's the closest we've ever gotten!" I said brightly. "At least your magic touched the fence. Good job!"

Marcus rose with a scowl, rubbing the side of his face. I approached the fence warily, reaching out my hand to grasp the chainlink. As I did so, a nauseated feeling whirled in my stomach, and my knees buckled as if I might faint. I backed off. I stepped away from the fence, the feeling went away.

"The guards definitely put something new here since the Elf broke out," I said. "Whatever it is, it's making me feel sick. It's gotta be stronger than noxite."

"Nothing we try is working. We might as well give up," Marcus said in exasperation.

"Screw that! I'm done being here. See you later." Kallie summoned her wings, then fluttered upward. She sailed through the air, and I thought for sure she'd be able to fly over the fence and get out.

Then, without warning, her wings began to twitch. She staggered while hovering, dropping a few feet before she managed to reach the barbed wire.

"Kallie, you okay?" I called.

"My wings aren't working!" she cried out, before they ceased to beat at all. She gave a scream as she began to tumble through the air.

"Charlie, help her!" I shouted.

"I can't!" he replied as he flailed his hands uselessly. "My magic doesn't work this close to the fence!"

"Kallie!" Marcus yelped. He scampered below her, feebly holding his arms out. She crash-landed into him, and they both fell to the ground. He let out an *oof* when he caught her. The two of them laid in a tangled pile of limbs, moaning in pain.

"Guess that didn't work," Charlie said dryly.

"Our godsdamn powers aren't working!" Kallie snapped as she rolled off Marcus. "I don't get it! Our demigod abilities should be able to overpower this fence easy!"

"Whatever the Warden buried under the fence affects us..." I mused. "Ancestors, I hope he doesn't know."

"If he knew, we would already be in deep shit," Charlie pointed out. "But this is a sign that he suspects *somebody* at the prison is a demigod, even if he's not looking at us."

"Oh, he's looking," I stated. "Trust me."

"I guess running away is out," Marcus groaned, holding his stomach. "We're still trapped here."

"For now," Kallie growled.

I shook my head. "If we can't get out, I think we're done here. You guys want to reach out to me about prophecy stuff, you know where to find me."

I left it at that, hoping they'd assume I didn't want anything to do with them otherwise... even though I did. I wanted my friends back. I was so lonely.

But being lonely meant being safe, and I'd rather be alone than keep getting hurt.

I rushed past Charlie. I didn't shake his hand, or touch him in any way. I didn't think I could do that without breaking down. Instead, I ran out of the forest without a goodbye. Oberi followed me, giving a few quick barks as he chased me back to the Institute and into the coldness of its halls.

I ran all the way back to my cell, because I didn't think I could face anyone at the moment. Oberi slipped in through the door as I closed it behind me. I took a few deep breaths before I sank against the ground, telling myself to keep it together. With every gasp I took, it felt like my chest was being torn in two. The thought of Charlie broke into my mind again, and I swear, it nearly did me in.

I wasn't the kind of girl to throw herself on the bed and weep— I wouldn't allow myself to cry over a *guy*, for the ancestors' sake. Not after this long.

Oberi gave a whine beside me, and my feelings twisted. Who was I fooling? This *sucked*. It still sucked! Three months had done nothing to dull the hurt between Charlie and me. If anything, I only wanted him more.

And I hated how weak that made me feel. We were broken up. It was time for me to stop having feelings for him.

"What am I going to do, boy?" I asked, and I stroked Oberi's ears. "He despises me."

Oberi let out a groan, like that wasn't true. I scratched his chin and said, "Well, at least we're fixing our mistake. We're going to save the Elves. Or at least, we're going to try. There's a chance, isn't there?"

Oberi gave me a surly glance, and I knew what it meant. Whatever we tried, Oberi didn't think it would work unless Charlie and I were together.

Fat chance. The hope of us reconciling was less than zero. We couldn't even be friends.

But at the very least, we had to be enemies who agreed to work together. For the world's sake.

What other option was there?

charlie
THREE

When I died, I figured Ava-Marie would be right there in hell with me.

Not the *true* Ava. She'd made mistakes, yeah, but her heart was in the right place. She'd end up with the ancestors for sure.

No... my hell would have some copy of her, like that illusion I'd seen in the mines on our way to Forevermore. The sole purpose of this fake Ava would be to torture me.

That's what it felt like to be near her again— like hell on Earth. Touching her felt like tearing my soul in half all over again. It physically *hurt*, as if the flesh was being torn from my bones, layer after layer. Hearing her voice was agonizing. It was as beautiful as ever— that soft, yet snarky tone ate away at me bit by bit. It sounded the same, but where it once made my spirit soar, it now felt like I'd been impaled by a sword.

It hurt too much to be near her again. It was a harsh reminder of what I'd lost.

I wondered if maybe I *had* died. Perhaps the Warden had followed through on his threat in Forevermore. Maybe he'd killed me, and I hadn't known, and I'd just woken up to this new reality that *was* hell. I was, after all, stuck in a prison. I didn't know how much worse things could get.

But on the off chance that I was still alive, I couldn't let everyone else perish. I had to do *something* to save them... even when I couldn't save myself.

Ava could pretend she didn't care all she wanted, but I knew the truth. She'd felt the agony in our reunion, too.

It was obvious in the way her shoulders felt under my hands. She was nothing but skin and bones. But hell, she had to eat *something*. She was killing herself like this. I was really worried that she was willingly marching herself to a slow death.

If she didn't start eating soon, she was going to hear about it. I wouldn't stand by while she starved herself.

"Charlie, you with us?" Marcus asked, nudging my shoulder.

I swayed a little in my seat, then snapped back to attention. "I'm here."

Barely.

"I asked what you think of the spell," he said.

"Right. The spell..." I trailed off. Marcus had some sort of tracking magic he wanted to show me. He'd said it might help us find the keys.

We sat in an alchemy room at the top of a tower near the chapel. All sorts of scents wafted from the potions ingredients lined along the shelves. Marcus had accidentally knocked a couple over while gathering ingredients.

This was one of the specialty rooms on campus, designed for witches and warlocks to study in. It was stocked with potions ingredients—though only for the simplest of spells, like the ones taught in the Institute's alchemy classes. Books infused with magic fluttered around the room above our heads like birds, flying from one bookcase to another. I could feel the air coming off the pages.

We were the only ones in here, along with Rishi and Oberi, who were chasing a rat skeleton some necromancer had left running around earlier. There'd been two groups here when we arrived, including some witches who were playing with their cats in the corner and gossiping about their crystal ball and tarot readings. A couple of warlocks used their telekinetic powers to fly on brooms around the room, until one of them knocked over a cauldron onto a girl's cat. The two groups fought for a while before leaving. I was glad to finally have some peace and quiet, but I hadn't heard a word Marcus had said.

"I read the whole locator spell to you," Marcus groaned. "Did you hear anything I said?"

"Sorry." I sighed. "I was just thinking."

A heavy *thud* sounded as Marcus set his spellbook on the table in front of me. "Look, I know things are tough right now with the Villain's Club, but we agreed to work together."

I frowned. "Don't call us that. We're not *the Villain's Club* anymore."

"That's a problem if we want to work together again." Marcus huffed. "I thought you wanted my help."

"I do," I insisted. "Can you repeat what you said?"

He drew a deep breath. "Basically, I found a locator spell in one of my textbooks over the summer."

My eyebrows pressed together in skepticism. "What were you doing reading over the summer?"

Marcus sounded offended. "I read *sometimes*, you know. I've actually been working on my magic all summer, so I don't fail all my classes. The last thing I need is to get sent to the adult penitentiary because I didn't graduate."

It sounded like Marcus was making excuses... like there was something else he wasn't telling me. I couldn't figure out what it was.

"I've actually gotten better with my magic," he remarked proudly. "I can reanimate small creatures whenever I want now."

"As opposed to fifteen minutes every Tuesday?" I teased.

Marcus grunted. "Like I said, I'm getting better. Anyway, we don't learn locator spells at the Institute. I don't know why— probably because the Warden doesn't want anyone finding demigods before he does."

I felt the blood drain from my face. "Could he *use* magic to find demigods?"

"Unlikely," Marcus stated. "Demigods are too strong to be tracked. *But* I came across a spell in one of my books, and I tried it a couple of times just to see if I could do it, but the Institute doesn't have enough of the right ingredients."

"Is a locator spell even going to work? I don't think it would be powerful enough to find the keys, since they're so strong," I stated.

"If I make it, I think so."

It was clear he meant because he was a demigod. He had a point.

"The keys are calling to us. As long as I brew the potion, my magic should be strong enough to locate where they are. Do you have any idea what might be a good substitute for liverwort?" Marcus asked.

Hell if I knew.

I shrugged. "Garlic?"

"You think?" Marcus sounded intrigued. "I actually have some of that."

"No, ancestors. I'm not an alchemist. How would I know? Ava's the one who knows about potions."

"Oh, well. I just thought..." Marcus flustered.

I knew exactly what he thought. He thought Ava and I couldn't work together, so he didn't bother asking both of us to be here. Hell, maybe we couldn't, but we had to at least *try*. We were out of options.

"Ava and I are going to have to learn how to be in the same room together without killing each other," I said, even though it was hard to admit.

"Mm..." Marcus mused. "Maybe she can suggest an alternative for liverwort. Goddess knows I'm not going to figure out this locator spell without decent ingredients."

"You're not going to locate a damn thing with liverwort," a male voice piped up from across the room.

I stilled. I hadn't known anyone else was in here. How much had they overheard?

Marcus must've been shocked, too, because he leaned over to me and whispered. "I thought we were alone."

"No shit," I growled, before turning to the stranger. "Hey, if you're so good at locator spells, why don't *you* show us how to do it?"

"Is that a dare?" he growled. A chair squeaked near the crackling fireplace as he jumped out of it and landed on the floor. A cat meowed and padded beside the stranger. Something clicked against the floor as he crossed the room toward us. I didn't realize what it was until a hard, long stick smacked my leg. "What, you think just because I'm a blind, gay dwarf that I can't perform a simple spell? I may be new around here, but I know my way around an alchemy room. You want a locator spell? I'll show you a damn locator—"

"Alistair?" Marcus squeaked.

"Yeah, what's it to ya?" he snapped. "Gonna make fun of my *name*, too? This cane makes a damn good weapon if I want it to. I'll smack you good, I will."

I was stunned silent, still shocked to learn I wasn't the only blind guy at this prison. What were the odds?

Marcus laughed. "Alistair, it's me! Marcus!"

Alistair sounded about ready to fight, but his tone softened. "Marcus? By the Goddess, how the hell are you, man?"

"Surviving," Marcus said simply. "What are you *doing* here? I thought you were back in Octavia Falls."

"I *was*," Alistair replied. "But you know me and my big mouth."

"What did you *do*?" Marcus asked.

"I didn't kill anyone, if that's what you're asking," Alistair cracked, like it was supposed to be some big joke— though neither Marcus nor I found it funny, considering Marcus *was* here for unintentional manslaughter.

Alistair didn't seem to notice— or perhaps didn't care— that his joke had fallen flat. "It wasn't a big deal, really. The college brought in a visiting professor, an Astromancer who's supposed to teach one of the astrology classes. She cut in front of me in line at the Cozy Cat Cafe, so I drizzled a little farting potion on top of her cupcake. How was I supposed to know it was the visiting professor and not some rando witch? Can you expect me to know she'd have a bad reaction to the magic and be stuck with the shits for a week and end up in the hospital? Yeah, I understand dehydration and all that, and she almost *died*— yada, yada— but it's not like I did it *intentionally*."

"You, uh, *did* give her the potion," I pointed out.

"I basically gave her a whoopie cushion and her ass blew up," Alistair said nonchalantly.

Holy shit, this kid was intense.

I shifted uncomfortably. "So, uh, how do you two know each other?"

Alistair gasped dramatically. "Marcus, you haven't mentioned me? Of all the stories we share."

Marcus groaned. "That was a long time ago."

"No shit, and I had to try surviving a whole *year* without you," Alistair said. "Do you have any idea how shitty the college's drama department is compared to the one at the high school? Theater used to be *fun*, but not with oh-so-high-and-mighty Professor Glass, who I prefer to call *Professor Ass*. You know who she cast me as? A *child!* I tried out for the role of the handsome prince, and I got *one* line as *the child*. What a load of bullshit."

"Man, that's rough," Marcus said.

"Rough?" Alistair repeated. "Who is this guy? You sound so chill. You've changed."

"Changed how?" Marcus asked.

Alistair chuckled. "Well, you always used to have a stick up your ass in theater club. You used to freak out about everything."

"Believe me, that hasn't changed," I cracked.

"I *do not* have a stick up my ass!" Marcus cried. "Could we perhaps get back to the task at hand? Alistair, you know how to perform a locator spell?"

"I know a lot more than that," he said proudly. "You remember how Vincent Rhodes always picked on me in high school? I bet he couldn't tell his left ass cheek from his right, considering it didn't matter how many times I told him I'm not a *midget*, I'm a *dwarf*. The m-word is a demeaning slur, but even after I told him that time and time again, he still insisted on calling me names. He deliberately chose not to use my preferred terms. Call me a little person or a person with dwarfism. Hell, you can even call me a dwarf, but don't use the m-word. Well, I tell ya, the second I got my powers, I learned defensive magic and shield magic, so I could finally stick up for myself against that asshole."

"As a freshman?" Marcus squeaked. "That's pretty advanced magic."

"You saying I can't perform advanced magic?" Alistair demanded.

"No, it's just I-I," Marcus stammered.

"I didn't spend my childhood in and out of the hospital just to be bullied by assholes like Vincent Rhodes," Alistair said.

"I try not to care about what Vincent says," Marcus advised. "He's not very bright."

Alistair scoffed. "You're telling me. He literally thinks people with dwarfism are the same as those fantasy-type dwarves— you know, the people who have beards and axes and mine and all that corny shit? I tried to tell him that what I am is different, because I'm just a regular person with shorter stature due to my medical condition and genetics, but all he did was grunt and hobble away on his knuckles like the primitive jerk he is. Apparently, he forgot all that whenever he got the itch to start taunting me again. One battle orb to the face, and he finally left me alone for good."

Marcus laughed. "Good for you. I once saw Charlie toss a bully into the lake in the prison yard. Made me think of you a little."

"Respect, my man," Alistair said.

A long pause ensued. I nervously filled it with, "Yeah. Good for me, I guess."

"What? I don't get a high-five?" Alistair asked.

Oh, so *that's* what the awkward silence was about. He was waiting for a high-five.

"I, uh... didn't notice," I said.

"Charlie's blind, like you," Marcus told him. "Well, not *exactly* like you. He can't see any shapes and colors like you can, and he uses his magic to get around instead of a cane."

"Damn!" Alistair practically sang. "You must be pretty powerful. What kind of magic do ya got?"

I shifted uncomfortably. Alistair was a lot to take in all at once, but I guess if Marcus was friends with him, I could trust him... to a point. "I'm an Elementai. I'm a dual caster— Air and Earth magic. It's not special, really. It's like your cane— just a tool."

"It's still pretty cool," Alistair said. "All I've got is this cane and a guide cat."

"I've got a Familiar. Oberi helps me around," I offered, finally feeling less awkward. Perhaps Alistair and I could get along.

Though it's not like I needed another friend to let down, so it was probably best if I kept my distance.

"Ah, that's your dog over there?" Alistair asked. "I was wondering what kind of psycho would bring a *dog* in here. This is cat territory."

"If you ask me, you cat people are the psychos," I deadpanned.

Alistair laughed so loudly that his cat jumped and stumbled into my leg. "I like that you tell it like it is, Charlie. I think we'll get along."

"If you can help us with this locator spell, you can be my best friend," I told him.

He snorted. "Friends? Who needs 'em? But allies, I'll take."

The chair beside me screeched as Alistair pulled it back and sat in it. "So, here's the deal. Any locator spell that calls for *liverwort* is a sham. It's probably why the Warden didn't remove that spell from your book. You need an eyeball— you know, to represent *seeing* and all that— and liverwort is going to affect the integrity of the eyeball."

"A *real* eyeball?" Marcus asked, sounding nervous. Ancestors, for a necromancer who could make skeletons come back to life, he sure seemed squeamish about eyeballs.

"You think plastic is going to work?" Alistair huffed. "Yes, a *real* eyeball."

"Where are we going to get an eyeball?" I asked.

Alistair nudged me with his elbow. "We could take yours, considering you're not using them. Am I right?"

He laughed loudly, though I wasn't amused. "I'm not digging my eyeball out of my skull for a spell," I grumbled.

"That's fine," Alistair replied. "I'm sure Marcus will volunteer, if this spell is that important to you and all. What did you say you were looking for? Demigods? You wanna find them before the Warden does?"

I felt the blood drain from my face. I couldn't remember how much we'd said. I'd been so careful not to mention demigods out in the open in case someone overheard. Marcus ruined it in a simple sentence.

"We're not looking for demigods," Marcus said quickly. "We're looking for... something else."

"Huh." Alistair sounded intrigued. "I guess you haven't changed that much. You still lie like shit."

"I'm not lying," Marcus said, though his voice was several pitches higher than normal.

Alistair wasn't buying it. "And you were such a good actor in theater club. I don't get it."

"Look," I said. "You want to be our ally? You're gonna have to stop asking questions."

Alistair sighed. "Fine, but I'm only doing this because Marcus is an old friend."

"I thought we were allies, not friends," Marcus pointed out.

"It's whatever," Alistair replied nonchalantly. "We're gonna need some ingredients. Milk, honey, sea salt, pomegranates, a mirror, and an eye of a newt."

Marcus raced around the room gathering the ingredients. "Hey, I found them all."

"Not *eye of newt*, the herb," Alistair clarified. "I need an *actual* eyeball. The eye of a newt. That's why people always fuck the spell up. They never read the specifics."

"Oh, uh... here we go," Marcus said, sounding flustered. He placed the ingredients on the table. I heard one roll away, but Oberi rushed over and caught it before it could shatter on the ground.

I winced as Oberi placed the jar in my hand. "Try to be a little more careful next time, Marcus. With the limited resources at the Institute, we may not have many chances to perform this spell."

"I'm *being* careful," Marcus insisted. "Okay. What's next?"

Alistair began giving instructions on how to mix the ingredients. "Simmer the brew for fifteen minutes *exactly*," he emphasized. "One second too soon or too late could change the whole potion."

The room got quiet as Marcus turned on a burner and began stirring the cauldron, making scratching noises on the side of it with his spoon. "So, you're an Alchemist?" Marcus asked.

Alistair chuckled. "Hell, no. I just like to experiment with stuff every now and then. I'm a Mentalist."

"That's the witch Cast known for telekinesis and mind powers," Marcus explained to me.

"Remember Eliza Truman?" Alistair asked.

"Sure," Marcus replied. "She played the pumpkin in *Cinderella* freshman year."

"Yeah, she's an Alchemist now," Alistair told him. "We came up with this potion together when I lost Pig last semester."

"Pig?" I asked.

"My cat," he clarified. "Named for her tendency to pig out. I've gotta be careful in the cafeteria. She'll eat anything. Anyway, I was the brains, Eliza was the brawn, and we found Pig locked in the Vanishing Stairwell back at school. She survived, thank the Goddess."

"I would *not* want to be caught in there," Marcus remarked. "People have died."

"And you see why I was worried," Alistair said.

"So what happens with the potion after fifteen minutes?" I asked.

"We drink it," Alistair stated simply.

I paused for a moment, unsure if we could trust him. "We drink a potion... that you invented."

"What, you don't think it's strong enough?" he demanded. "It's a damn good spell, I tell ya. To create a locator spell from the simplest of ingredients is an incredible feat. I could probably make millions selling it to the coven, though I never got the chance before I was sentenced to this shithole."

"By the sounds of it, things were shittier back in Octavia Falls," I joked.

Alistair laughed. "With the shit coming out of that Astromancer's rear end, you might be right."

We all shared a laugh. It was strange to be laughing after so long of not feeling much of anything. Alistair seemed a bit abrasive, but at least I could relax around him.

As soon as fifteen minutes hit, Marcus rushed to shut off the burner, and the potion stopped bubbling. "It looks like goo," he told us, sounding disgusted.

"Well, what did you expect?" Alistair asked. "Vanilla pudding?"

The potion made glopping noises as Marcus scooped some into small cups. "If we're gonna drink it, I expected something that looked a little more appetizing than... this."

"If you're desperate enough to find whatever you're looking for, you'll do anything," Alistair said. "Bottoms up."

Marcus handed me one of the cups. I sniffed it, and it smelled like sweaty socks. I wasn't entirely convinced this was a locator spell. I wouldn't be surprised if this was one of Alistair's pranks, like he'd tried to pull on the professor he'd accidentally poisoned. But Marcus gulped his down, and he didn't start shitting his pants, so I figured it was safe. I tipped my glass back and drank the thick, bitter potion.

I didn't really know what to expect, but I certainly didn't expect the chair I was sitting in to disappear beneath me. My head spun, and I felt as if I was soaring high in the clouds. The air was cold but humid. My heart began to race, but then I felt Oberi's nose nudge against my hand.

It's a vision, Charlie, Oberi told me. *Relax.*

I calmed down and let the vision take me wherever it wanted. I focused on the keys, and felt the vision shift. I came down from the clouds, until my feet hit solid ground. I heard shouting in the distance, then the sound of gates clanging shut. I couldn't tell where I was, so I approached the noises to get a better idea of where the vision had taken me. As I neared the gates, my magic began to drain from my body. I'd become so accustomed to the feeling now that there was no denying what was ahead.

Noxite. The vision had taken me to the Institute.

The second I realized it, the vision shifted around me. I was somewhere damp and cold, a lot like the alchemy room I was *actually* sitting in. At first, I thought the vision had worn off, but the silence was deafening. No way was I sitting next to Marcus, who was always fidgeting. I couldn't make sense of where I was before the vision shifted again.

An ice-cold chill surrounded me. When I tried to breathe in, no air came. I began to panic. For an Air Elementai, losing your breath was one of our greatest fears. I couldn't figure out anything else about my surroundings before the vision changed again.

A strong force grabbed my body and whipped me through space at lightning speed. Wherever I'd just been, I was thousands of miles away now. I came to an abrupt stop and swayed on my feet. The air was chilly around me, and a shiver ran down my spine, though it wasn't because of the cold. It was more like... someone was watching me. The sounds of a bustling city welled around me, and for a second, I thought I was back in Detroit.

That was all I heard before I was whipped back into my body, gasping.

"Holy shit," I rasped, gripping on to the edge of the table for support. Oberi nuzzled his head against my arm, like he was trying to comfort me.

"What the hell was that?" Marcus demanded breathlessly.

"It's one hell of a trip, isn't it?" Alistair said proudly.

Marcus' breathing slowed. "Yeah, but I couldn't make sense of any of it."

"Did you see anything?" I asked him.

"The Institute," he replied in a chilling voice. "Then everything else was dark."

"Same," I agreed. "Though I more or less *felt* the Institute."

"Then that means..." Marcus trailed off, because he didn't want to say too much in front of Alistair.

Alistair grumbled. "Yeah, I get it. Secret Villain's Club shit and all that. How *does* one join this Villain's Club?"

"They don't," I said flatly. Ancestors, how much had Marcus' big mouth revealed?

"Fine, fine." Alistair stood, though he sounded less than pleased. "I don't know what *you* were locating, but I've located *myself* a hot date. I'll catch up with you losers later. Oh, and if I hear anything about demigods, I'll be sure to let you know. I'm quite good at gathering intel."

As Alistair and his cat started out of the room, Marcus turned to me. "One of the keys is at the Institute," he hissed.

I tapped my fingers on the tabletop. "I think *three* of them might be here, or at least on Darke Island. I felt the Institute, then the next two visions weren't far away, but the last one—"

"Felt like a thousand miles," Marcus finished for me. "A city of some kind."

"Yeah." I huffed. "I don't know how the hell we're going to find *that* key."

We were stuck here until we graduated, at least. We might be able to get around Darke Island while still at the prison, but there was no way we were getting off the island itself for a few more years.

"At least we have a starting point," Marcus encouraged. "There's for sure one key at the Institute. Once we find it, we're one step closer to opening the portal."

It was a start, at least. But I didn't feel like the locator spell had done much of anything but made us more confused.

A voice drifted through the open door. "Watch where you're going, you incompetent fool," Alistair spat from somewhere down the staircase.

"You watch it, ya fucking midget," a deep voice snapped back.

Rage flared in my veins at the vile word. Alistair had made it clear he didn't like being called that.

Alistair grunted, like he'd been shoved into a wall. I jumped to my feet to defend him, but whoever pushed him must've already moved on, because I heard several pairs of footsteps coming up the stairs.

A group of guys entered the room— three of them, I guessed, by the sound of their footsteps. They headed straight for us. I could hear Alistair mumbling curse words under his breath as he headed down the twisting staircase to the main level.

"Marcus," one of the guys practically sang, like the two were best friends.

"Big G..." Marcus stammered, sounding shocked to see him.

Big G? What a dumb name.

"Our Little Drummer Boy," Big G said in a tone that was more condescending than friendly. "How you doing?"

The guys surrounded Marcus, who didn't say a word. Beside me, Rishi growled. I could tell these guys were bad news. My hands curled into fists, ready to throw a punch if I had to.

"What's this?" I demanded. "Marcus, who are these guys?"

"No one," Marcus said quietly, before clearing his throat and speaking with more confidence. "No one you should concern yourself with."

"Us?" Big G balked. "Who are *you*?"

"He's my lab partner," Marcus answered quickly. "Thought we'd get a head start on the semester."

"Don't spend too much time studying," Big G growled. "Boss needs your sheets by tonight. If you don't got 'em..."

A *thwack* sounded, like he'd smacked his fist into his own palm. It was a threat.

"I've got them right here." Marcus fumbled with a few papers, rustling them as he shoved them into one of the guy's hands. They'd come from out of nowhere. I figured he'd just conjured them.

"Perfect." Big G sounded pleased. "Have the next ones ready by Tuesday. None of this same-day shit."

"I will," Marcus promised.

"Yeah, you will," Big G said through gritted teeth. "I'll make sure of it."

The guys shoved Marcus in a way I guessed was supposed to be friendly. It was so hard that he hit the edge of the table and sucked a breath through his teeth. The three guys laughed as they left the room with Marcus' papers.

I waited until the room had gone silent before whirling toward Marcus. "What was that? Who were those guys?"

Glass vials clinked against one another as Marcus started putting potion ingredients away. "I told you, they're not important."

"It didn't sound like it. Marcus, were those *gang* members?"

He practically raced across the room to put ingredients away. He mumbled something, but I didn't hear it.

"Was that a yes?" I demanded.

"They're just... my friends."

My nostrils flared. "Gang member friends?"

"So what if they are?" Marcus snapped. "You're acting like it's the end of the world."

"Marcus, you idiot!" I burst. "Those guys aren't your friends! They're *using* you!"

"They are not!"

"Then what were those papers? What are you doing for them? Homework? Work-Study stuff?"

"No. Even if I wanted to tell you, I can't," he snapped.

"Tell me everything, or Marcus, I swear—"

His tone got nasty. "Why? I thought we weren't friends anymore."

That hurt. More than I wanted to admit.

My shoulders fell. "Maybe... maybe we could be friends again."

Marcus seemed to calm down, because he returned to the table, and sat across from me. "Even if I wanted to tell you about the Dead Men Walking, I couldn't. I took an oath when I joined."

I'd heard about the Dead Men Walking. They were one of the Institute's biggest gangs, and the people who got involved with them usually ended up in Cellblock 9 or the prison's morgue.

I shook my head. I couldn't believe Marcus had ended up in a prison gang. And by the sounds of it, they didn't care about him. They just wanted him for whatever those papers were. I felt so bad for Marcus. I was lying to myself if I said we weren't friends anymore.

"You know why they call themselves the Dead Men Walking, don't you?" I asked, trying to talk some sense into him.

"It's creative and intimidating," he stated confidently.

"Yeah, because that's what you call a guy on death row!" I explained. "These guys want to be so evil that they end up there."

"That's ridiculous," Marcus countered.

I pressed my hand to the side of my face. "Ancestors, they've brainwashed you."

"I'm not brainwashed," Marcus spat defensively. "They're my friends."

I scoffed. "Some friends, making you do their homework."

"You don't understand," Marcus growled. "After Forevermore... after I lost the Villain's Club... I needed *someone*. I can't survive in this prison alone."

I felt the blood drain from my face. Marcus had joined a prison gang because of *me*— because I'd abandoned him. My tone softened as I realized what he must've gone through. "You joined them for protection."

"Yeah, I guess," he admitted.

I raked my fingers through my hair. Fuck, how was I going to get him out of this? This could turn bad pretty damn fast.

"How did you guess they were gang members?" Marcus asked after a beat.

I shrugged. "I don't know. They just sounded like... like people I've dealt with before."

Marcus gasped. "*You* were in a gang?"

"Not officially," I quickly clarified. "I mean, kind of... for a while.

My friend Marty taught me to never join a gang. It can get dangerous really fast. But I dealt with a lot of gangs on the streets back when I sold drugs."

"Back when you *what?*"

I don't know why I opened up to Marcus. Maybe I thought if I told him about my experience, he'd tell me more about the gang he was in, and I could somehow save him from it.

"It was a long time ago," I said. "Marty taught me how to get my hands on party drugs and sell them. It was how I survived for a few years. I didn't really *do* the drugs. I tried them a couple of times, but Marty taught me the drugs were for profit, not for myself. I was lucky enough to get out. Not everyone does. I feel pretty bad about it now. I'm not sure how many people got hurt because of me."

"Man, I'm sorry. But this is different."

"Is it?" I challenged. "Are they dealing nightshade?"

Marcus went silent, which told me all I needed to know.

I sighed. "Do you have any idea what you've done? Once you're in a gang, you can't get out. I bet they told you all this bullshit about how *we're a family* and all that."

"It's a *brotherhood*," Marcus defended.

"It's a cult," I argued. "They're never going to let you leave."

"Maybe I don't want to."

I gritted my teeth. Marcus was being stubborn. "I mean it. If things go south, you can't get out. If you move to another gang, you'll be killed. These types of guys take this stuff seriously. You know what? I don't even want to know anything about this gang, because if you tell me, they could kill you for it. I'd rather you be safe. Ancestors, Marcus. The only reason I managed to get out of the gang I was in is because everyone else ended up dead or in prison. You're already in prison. There's nowhere for these guys to go."

Marcus' voice wavered, like he was scared. "I'll be fine. I don't need a lecture from you."

"You don't sound fine. Is this why you've been working on your powers? Is this how you knew so much about the Warden?"

"I may have snuck into the Warden's office for them—" he admitted, before he caught himself.

His tone became harsh. "I thought you didn't want me to tell you anything."

My stomach sank. "This is just like fight club," I mumbled.

"What do you mean?" Marcus asked.

I scoffed. "You think I can get out of *that*? Hell, no."

"You want out?" Marcus sounded surprised. I guess I could understand, considering how much I liked it last semester. But it just wasn't worth it anymore.

"Fuck yes. It's gotten old, fast. I didn't want to admit they were using me before, but it's so obvious now." I buried my hands in my hair.

"The Dead Men Walking aren't like that," he whined.

"Yeah, right," I growled. Marcus had *no idea* what he was getting into. "Shit, we gotta get you out of there. If they're already making you their errand boy, it won't be long until they have you running nightshade. If you're caught, you'll be sent to Cellblock 9. Then the Warden will find out what you are, and we're all fucked."

Marcus drew a sharp breath, like he hadn't considered that before. He fumbled for words. "That— that's not gonna happen to me."

"You don't know that! These guys aren't your friends, and you know it. You need to get out as soon as you can."

"How?" Marcus sounded scared.

"Leverage or something. I don't know. And don't think they won't use whatever they can to manipulate you."

"What do you mean?" Marcus' voice wavered.

"The time will come when they ask you to do something you don't want to do. I guarantee it. And if you try to say no, they'll threaten Rishi to get you to do it."

"Not Rishi!" Marcus scooped up his cat, who purred against him. "I can't lose him again!"

I tilted my head. The way he said it suggested there was a deeper story there. "Again? Did the gang go after him to get you to join?"

"No," he said quickly. "I meant..."

"You meant what?" I demanded. Marcus was avoiding the story, which worried me. "Look, I get that we all have secrets around here, but I never thought *you* would keep a secret from me. If we're going to be friends again, we have to be honest with each other."

He breathed a heavy sigh. "It's not a secret per se... It's just never come up."

"Well, you sound pretty hurt by it," I pointed out. I wanted to help, the same way I wanted to get him out of that gang.

Marcus fidgeted for a few moments before finally speaking. "You might not know this, but the reason cats are so special to the Miriamic Coven is because we believe our cats are reincarnations of our deceased loved ones. They return to support us on our life journey."

"Rishi was someone you loved?" I asked carefully.

Marcus' chair squeaked as she shifted uncomfortably. "You know how an Elementai's soul resides within their Familiar?"

I stroked the top of Oberi's head. "Yeah, I'm aware."

"Well, in my culture, we believe twins are two parts of the same soul," he continued. "If one twin dies, the other can survive. It's not like if a Familiar dies. But you lose a piece of yourself. It's rough. So when one twin dies and comes back as a cat... you kind of share a soul. It's as deep of a bond as you and your Familiar."

My stomach dropped. "Marcus, are you a twin?"

"Yeah," he said sheepishly. "I had an identical twin brother."

I reeled back. I didn't know what to say to that. All I could manage to spit out was, "What... what happened?"

Marcus didn't answer the question directly, like it was too hard. "His name was Dean, not Rishi. We give our cats different names than they had in their old life. Dean died a long time ago. I don't really want to talk about it. Every time I do, I just... I don't know why *he* died and I lived."

I felt so bad for him that I didn't push it. He didn't need to tell me for me to know Dean's death had messed him up.

"Rishi's been with me my whole life," Marcus rambled. "He'll probably live just as long as me. Cats in the Miriamic Coven live longer than other animals. I can't imagine losing him again. I just can't."

"Hey," I said gently. "We'll make sure he stays safe. We'll get you out of the gang."

"I can't," he argued. "I'm already a part of it."

I couldn't tell if Marcus actually wanted to stay, or if he was just too scared to leave. It didn't matter. I knew a prison gang was nothing but bad news. One way or another, I was going to get Marcus out. I just had to figure out how.

"It doesn't matter," Marcus said, changing the subject. "We should probably start looking for those keys. I mean, if they're at the Institute and all."

My shoulders slumped. Even though we *had* narrowed it down, it seemed finding these keys was still impossible. "The Institute is pretty big. It could take years of searching this place before we found one. There's gotta be a way to narrow it down further."

"Maybe Ava or Kallie know a spell that could help," Marcus suggested as we rose from our chairs.

"Maybe... at the very least, we should probably tell them what we found. And stop talking about this shit out in the open, or someone worse than Alistair might overhear. Use code words or something."

"Okay," Marcus agreed as we headed out of the room. "What's a good code word for keys?"

"I don't know. What's something that wouldn't raise suspicion?"

"Penises," Marcus deadpanned.

"Are you freaking kidding me?"

"Ava and Kallie talk about dicks all the time!" he defended. "No one would suspect a thing."

He's not wrong, Oberi cut in.

"Get more creative, because I'm *not* talking about dicks all day," I said.

"I'll think of something," he replied thoughtfully.

We reached the bottom of the tower. I turned the corner and nearly ran into someone. His shoulder slammed into mine, and I stumbled to the side. "Watch where you're going," I growled.

"Sorry," he muttered meekly before scurrying away.

I scoffed as I turned back in the direction we were headed. "Someone must be new around here. No one apologizes at the Institute."

Marcus lowered his voice. "It was Uriel. One of the Elves."

"Oh," I said flatly. I hadn't officially met Uriel, but he worked the same shift as me at the factory, and I could hear him singing every now and then from a few stations over. Eddie had talked about him before. I kind of felt bad for snapping at him, but Marcus and I had more important things to worry about. "Where do you think we'll find the girls? We have to tell them about our vision."

"Kallie mentioned something about visiting the pool sometime," Marcus recalled. "I think she wants to hang out with Opal."

I nodded. "Okay. We'll check there."

Marcus and I had just entered the stairwell to the basement when the screaming started. We both stopped in our tracks, and Rishi ran straight into me.

"What's going on?" I asked.

"No idea." Marcus led me toward the pool, where the shouts were coming from. We crept closer to the door, and he peeked inside. "Looks like someone got busted."

"I didn't do it!" someone shouted, their voice wavering. "Please, it wasn't me!"

"Witnesses say otherwise," a gruff voice replied— one of the guards, I guessed. "Shut the hell up and quit your crying."

We snuck inside, but the second we entered, Marcus gasped. "Goddess!"

I could hear the chatter around us. Whispers traveled all around the room, though I couldn't hear anything beyond the guards' shouting.

"What's going on?" I whispered.

"There's a merman... floating in the pool." Marcus gagged a little. "He's not moving. There's... so much blood coming out of his fins. It's staining the whole pool red."

I felt the blood drain from my face. A *murder?*

"Who are they blaming?" I demanded. The person was still pleading their innocence. He didn't sound like the kind of guy who had just killed someone. He sounded terrified.

"It's Uriel," Marcus said breathlessly.

"That's impossible," I protested. "We just saw him in the hall. He couldn't have been more than thirty seconds ahead of us."

"Right. He couldn't have done this," Marcus agreed. "That looks like a vampire bite... maybe a siren."

"Uriel's half-vampire," I recalled. "Eddie told me. He grew up in Forevermore, but his mom was an Elf and his dad was a vampire."

"Which means he's the perfect person to set up," Marcus replied.

My hands curled into fists, and my blood boiled. "The Warden wants to make an example of the Elves. He just found his first target."

"Ow! You're hurting me!" Uriel screamed. "I swear, I wasn't even in the pool when it happened!"

Before I knew what I was doing, I'd stalked forward. "Hey, get off him!"

The guards didn't even acknowledge me. Instead, one of them growled at Uriel, "You want a trip to Cellblock 9? How about death row?"

"I said *get off*!" I demanded. "I'll vouch for him."

The guards must've noticed me, because they just started laughing. "You?" one of them chuckled. "You think you fight well enough to let off a murderer? How would you like to head down to Cellblock 9 with this low life?"

Hell, it was true I'd lost my last few fights at the club— I couldn't bring myself to care anymore— but I thought I still carried some weight around here.

Then again, this *was* a murder. I could be undefeated, and I wouldn't be able to save anyone from this.

"Tranquilize him," one of them said simply. I heard a *click*, and Uriel's cries died down. With vampire ancestry, he was mildly affected by noxite, at minimum. The whispers around the room grew.

"He didn't do it," I insisted. "The least you can do is investigate before arresting him."

One of the guards laughed. "Kid, he's already in prison. Get your head out of your ass and look around. Oh, that's *right*. You can't."

The guard shoved me aside so hard that I stumbled sideways. I lost my balance and crashed into the pool. Cold water surrounded me, and shock riveted through my body. My head surfaced, and I gasped for air. I flailed my arms. They smacked straight into something solid. I found my footing, then felt for what I'd hit. My fingers touched something smooth, and I realized with horror it was the scales of the merman who'd died.

A pair of hands landed on me and yanked me out of the pool. "You okay?" Marcus asked.

"Fine," I said, wiping the water from my eyes.

Very graceful, Oberi deadpanned.

"Not now, Oberi," I growled.

"Move aside," a guard snapped.

Marcus grabbed my shirt and yanked me to the edge of the room. "They're fishing the merman from the pool," he said lowly. "I can't believe someone would do this. Those fang marks are just..."

He didn't finish, and I really didn't want to know. I could only imagine what a vampire in this prison might do. And if they'd gone underwater, where no one else could see them, they could easily get away with it.

"That filthy hybrid got what he deserved, if you ask me," a deep voice boomed from nearby.

"Absolutely," his friend agreed.

I recognized the deep voice. It was hard to miss.

Mad Dog.

Wind swirled around me, and I started toward him. Marcus tried to hold me back, but I shook him off.

"It was *you*, wasn't it?" I demanded, shoving Mad Dog. "What, you get your kicks out of drinking Atlantean blood and blaming it on someone else? You set Uriel up."

"What are you gonna do about it?" Mad Dog snarled.

Marcus grabbed my shoulder and whispered in my ear. "You're outnumbered... by *a lot*. Back down, or you'll be killed next."

I didn't care. Uriel was innocent— of that, I was certain. I couldn't stand by and let the real murderer get away with this.

"Uriel wasn't in here long enough to do anything!" I screamed. "I just saw him in the hall."

Mad Dog laughed. "With what eyes, dickhead?"

That *really* pissed me off. I reacted without thinking about it. Magic swelled within me. I didn't know how I did it, but I siphoned Mad Dog's super strength from him and swung my fist. The impact was satisfying as hell. I'd hit him so hard that he stumbled into his friends. Several of them grunted as they caught him. He scrambled back to his feet, and several pairs of footsteps closed in on me.

"No!" Mad Dog boomed, stopping his cronies. "He's mine!"

I heard the snapping of knuckles, then before I knew it, something hard cracked against the side of my face. I stumbled to the ground, my ears ringing. Beside me, Marcus gasped, and Oberi barked loudly.

"You better watch what you accuse me of," Mad Dog threatened. Damn, he had one hell of a swing. I swear my jaw dislocated for a second there.

I thought Mad Dog was going to beat me up, but a guard grabbed me by the back of the shirt and yanked me to my feet.

"Save your fights for the club, Bandit," the guard growled in my ear. "That's an infraction for you. Have fun putting in double time at the factory."

Aw, fuck! Like I needed a fucking infraction.

The guard shoved me toward the door, then shouted, "*Out!* Everybody out!"

Mad Dog knew he won this fight, and he was smug about it. He spat at my feet and walked away laughing, his cronies following behind him.

Marcus helped me into the hall. "Anything broken?"

I stretched out my face to test my muscles. Mad Dog had a good swing, but my face seemed intact. "Just my pride," I answered.

"Let's get out of here," Marcus suggested. "We'll find the girls another time."

We didn't really know where we were going— just *away*. We didn't stop until we'd entered the Villain's Den. I collapsed into one of the couches, but there were other people in here, so I kept my voice low. "Uriel didn't do it."

"I know," Marcus whispered back as he sat beside me. "But it's not like we can prove that."

My shoulder sagged in defeat. "Yeah, and now I've got extra hours at the factory, so I won't be able to train. Captain's going to *love* that."

I punched the arm of the couch. "The Warden is going to use every opportunity he can to weed out the Elves and perform his sick experiments on them. This isn't right. I have to teach the Elves how to defend themselves, and how to absorb magic from other races."

Yeah, with all your experience, Oberi said flatly.

"You're not helping," I snapped at him. He jumped onto the couch next to Rishi and proceeded to ignore me.

"Do you even know *how* to teach them?" Marcus asked in a low voice.

I hesitated a moment. "Maybe. Kind of."

"You don't sound very confident."

"Well, forgive me for trying." I huffed. "I used my powers on Mad Dog, but it wasn't on purpose. I'm not totally sure how to use them yet, but I can figure it out."

"I'll be your guinea pig," Marcus offered.

I calmed a little. "You will?"

"Yeah. It's part of fulfilling the prophecy, right? And I agreed to help you with that. Plus, I'm kind of curious how it feels."

I thought of the other times I'd taken magic from other people. When I'd calmed Ava down outside Commissary last semester, I'd been holding her shoulders. I thought maybe I should start by touching Marcus, because maybe that would be easier to steal his magic. I placed a hand on his shoulder, but I didn't really know what I was doing. I felt nothing.

We sat there for several long minutes before Marcus said, "I don't feel anything."

"That's because I'm not doing anything," I stated. "With Ava, I could feel her magic. I don't feel anything with you."

"Maybe I'm too weak?" he theorized.

I snorted. "You've *got* to get over that. You've got magic for days, and you've proven it. Now get your head on straight, and maybe we can do this."

Marcus hummed for a moment. "I did a little bit of work with magic manipulation over the summer, to help me understand my Curse Breaking powers. It's not quite the same as Elf magic— not nearly as strong— but I bet the technique is similar."

"What's the technique?" I asked.

"At first, you have to reach out with your own magic," Marcus instructed. "You kind of have to weave it in with the other person's, and then you can yank it backward. Think of it like a rope. You've gotta tie your end of the rope to mine before you can pull it away from me."

"Okay..." I started with Air, manipulating the particles around him so that I could feel the resistance of his body against my powers. I didn't feel any magic, though.

"Maybe if I pushed my magic toward you, so you could feel it easier," Marcus suggested. "That way, you can see what it feels like."

"You can try."

I don't know what Marcus did, but after a moment, I felt a tingle against my Air magic. I couldn't describe it, because it wasn't like I felt it in my body. It was a different type of sensation, tied deep into my soul—wherever the hell my magic resided. It was like my magic surged for a moment, but in a way that didn't feel like my own.

"I felt it," I remarked. "Keep going."

The tingle of magic grew more intense, but when I tried to take it from him, all I did was draw my own magic back, breaking the connection.

"Let me try again," I said.

Marcus took a deep breath and relaxed, like he was willing to give me all the time in the world to figure this out. I sat there for a while, just trying to get a feel for his magic. It felt chaotic, but was somewhat soothing. I waited until the feeling became familiar to me, until I could imagine it as my own.

This time when I drew back, Marcus' magic came with mine. I was filled with a high-frequency buzz that seemed to rattle around in my chest.

This is boring as fuck, Marcus' voice sounded in my head. *Oh, shit. I know who I'd like to fuck. But like, not in a fucking way. I'd love her tenderly. I'd respect her. I think she'd like that.*

"Hey, I did it!" I cried. I'd heard Marcus' thoughts, and taken his mind-reading abilities, if only for a second. Although Marcus had told me before he could only read dirty thoughts, so I wasn't sure how useful that was going to be.

"You did?" Marcus sounded proud. "Oh, yeah, I can kind of feel it. My magic is weak. Can you cast a spell?"

"What's a good thing to start with?"

Marcus shifted, as if looking around the room. "No one's looking. Try a battle orb."

"I don't know what I'm doing, but okay..." I lifted my hand and searched for that magic that wasn't quite my own. I felt it travel down my arm like a tiny electric current. Then pain shot through my fingers, like I'd just touched a hot stove.

Hell, that hurt. I yanked my hand back on instinct, then shook it out.

"You made a spark!" Marcus cried.

I panicked for a second, then lowered my voice. "I can't do this in front of everyone. It could expose us. Also, that hurt like hell. I'm not trying that again."

"It must take some getting used to," he said thoughtfully. "We can try reading thoughts. No one will know."

I smirked. "I already can. You'd like to *love Kallie tenderly?*"

"Shit." Marcus sounded embarrassed. Meanwhile, Oberi snickered in my mind.

"Never mind that. Try it on someone else," Marcus suggested.

I listened closely to the other people in the room and honed my attention on a guy playing an old arcade game in the corner. His voice rang in my ear like he was sitting right next to me. Somehow, I could *feel* the energy of his thoughts and just *knew* they belonged to him.

It'd be like that porno I was watching when Mom walked in on me, he thought. *I'll be the pizza delivery guy, and she'll be the—*

I instantly drew back, not wanting to hear the rest of that thought. Instead, I focused on other people, but I couldn't connect with most of them. I figured they had to be thinking dirty thoughts, since those were the only ones Marcus could read, and it was *his* magic I was using.

I wonder what he looks like under those trousers, a female across the room was thinking. *I bet he's even bigger in dragon form. I'd like to get him out in the prison yard and—*

"I'm done. These people are sick," I complained. I pushed my magic outward again and severed the tie between Marcus and me. "Also, I don't need *two* voices in my head. Oberi, would you shut up?"

He couldn't stop laughing. *Don't think just because you're my Elementai you can tell me what to do, you limp biscuit.*

"Ew, Oberi. Do you have any idea what that means?" I asked.

Ava calls you that all the time, he cracked. I didn't think he was serious. Or at least, I hoped not.

"What'd he say?" Marcus questioned.

I frowned. "He called me a limp biscuit."

"I thought it was just an insult," Marcus said. "What does it mean?"

I groaned. "Ancestors, I'm *not* explaining that. Let's just say you don't want to go searching for the definition on the library computers. You'll regret it."

"Will it ruin my innocence?"

"Yes, you poor, sweet soul."

"Then we best stick with studying your magic," Marcus said.

That was all I *could* do, because I was supposed to protect the Elves. If Uriel had known how to use his magic, he could've defended himself from being taken ancestors knew where.

It was too late to save him, but maybe we could still save the others.

That is, as long as there weren't any other murders at the prison. But with how deadly the Institute was, I knew the Elves were in danger. I had to master my Elf powers— and fast.

ava-marie

FOUR

Why are you bothering with this, Ava?
Wouldn't it just be easier if it was all over with?
Aren't you tired of fighting?

I brushed back a lock of my hair as I entered the Villain's Den. It was early afternoon, when most people were at lunch, but I'd signed into the cafeteria and left immediately after without getting anything. I wanted to be alone at all points of the day, and lunch was the only time the recreation room was ever empty. I passed the crappy television mounted to the wall, where the supernatural news station was covering a story from Malovia.

"Tensions are high between the fae and the vampires," the reporter stated. "Since the former treaty expired late this summer, negotiations between the two races are developing. It appears that the Midnighters are asking for more than the standard agreement from the Arcanea, which King Ethan is refusing to honor. Rumors abound that the fae are hiding the mysterious Elves within their borders, although there is no evidence to imply..."

I ignored the news broadcast and sat down at a table to do my homework. I'd blown off all my classes last semester, but I immersed myself in them now. They were my only distraction. I was doing extra projects just to keep my mind off things.

I knew the telltale swishing of Ivy's skirt before he sat down next to me. That familiar ache of loneliness was abated as I felt him grow near.

"Sweetheart!" Ivy exclaimed as he placed a takeout box from the cafeteria on the table. He reached out to give me a hug. "Oh, how *are* you? I haven't seen you in what feels like ages."

"Hi, Ivy." I was so surprised he wanted to see me. I thought he'd forgotten all about me. I squeezed him back so tight— even tighter than I wanted to— and didn't let go for a long time.

"Babe, I've got so much to tell you. We need to *talk*," Ivy emphasized, his thick Italian accent smacking with the words. He picked up the takeout box. "Oh, I grabbed lunch from the cafeteria, but I didn't realize it's pad thai, and I don't like it. But it's *your* favorite, isn't it, Ava? Do you want it?"

Ivy shoved the takeout box into my hands.

"Okay... sure." I flipped open the lid, and the smell of peanut butter and cashews hit my nose. My stomach grumbled, and I nibbled on a couple of rice noodles as Ivy chattered on.

"My summer was *so boring*. They had me sorting and packing noxite every day in the factory." Ivy made a gagging sound before he lit up. "But Chance... by Atlantis, I can't stop thinking about him. I don't think we spent a moment apart, save for when we had to work. And maybe..."

Ivy bit his lip, and I said, "He's been sneaking out at night?"

Ivy gave a shrug. "Kinda. I don't know what he's doing, but his business is his business. I try not to pry."

So Ivy still didn't know about the fight club. That was so wrong. Chancey needed to stop lying to him. I knew Ivy hung out in the prison yard when Charlie and Chancey worked out. I wondered what excuse Chancey had given him.

"But what about you?" Ivy asked. "You must've been pretty busy, seeing as how we haven't talked in forever."

His tone was genuine, but guilt still overpowered my senses. "I'm sorry I didn't see you," I said. "I was caught up in anthropology stuff."

Ivy gave a warm smile. "I know you've been busy all summer

studying your major. And I'm *so* proud of you, being the strong, independent woman you are, working on your dreams."

Ivy reached out and took my hands. "But I can't help but feel you've been avoiding everyone not because you're busy, but because you're dying of a broken heart."

My eyes watered, and I pushed Ivy's hands away. "I don't want to talk about it."

"Precious, you can't lie to me," Ivy said, stroking my hair. "Charlie's a right bastard, doing what he did to you. I mean, how could he not want a girl like you? A true dumbass, I'd say."

I didn't bother to mention the breakup had been mutual. Even thinking about it was too painful.

"It doesn't matter. It's been a long time." I pushed the food away, and Ivy eyed me. I was surprised to notice I'd consumed almost the whole meal in a matter of moments. I'd barely realized I was eating it.

"You know what you need?" Ivy asked.

"Everything this prison doesn't offer?" I asked. A trip to the mall would cheer me right up.

"Yes, but also, some fresh air. Come on."

Ivy tossed the remainder of my food away, then hooked my arm in his. We walked outside to the prison yard, where people were taking a short walk after lunch.

As we passed, I noticed a guard was snatching magazines out of the hands of inmates and shoving them into a trash bag, looking surly. Girls whined in complaint, until the guard gave a sneer.

Chancey leaned against a wall, watching people as they passed. He always acted like someone was gonna jump him, though his cold expression immediately changed when he noticed Ivy approaching.

Ancestors. I missed when someone lit up when they realized I was nearby.

Vampires weren't allowed to drink from other inmates, but Ivy and Chancey clearly hadn't been following that rule, as Chancey's neck was bruised from the base to his chin.

Chancey caught me staring and gave a wink. His New York accent drawled as he said, "Ives is a messy eater."

"I am not!" Ivy said indignantly.

The girls' squeals grew, and I looked around. A bunch of women had collected near the basketball court, gossiping loudly.

"What's everyone talking about?" I asked.

The girls noticed me and ran over in a herd before I had a chance to react. They surrounded me on all sides, talking nonstop. None of them had ever spoken to me before, so I found it all very weird.

Velma was a vampire girl. I knew her because she was in some of my classes. She pressed herself to the front and gushed, "By the gods, Ava, your brother is such a cutie. He looks *amazing*, you know, since he bulked up and lost his baby weight."

"Uh, sure?" I said. I mean, I *guess* my brother had gotten some muscle since he'd been working in the mines, but I hadn't noticed.

"Can you introduce me?" Velma pleaded.

The rest of the girls pressed in, all shouting, "*And me!*"

So many girls were clambering in my space, I couldn't focus. I pushed through the crowd and said, "Maybe later. I need a minute."

Ivy and Chancey followed me back into the prison before I turned around and asked, "What's going on?"

"Oh, you didn't see?" Chancey asked slyly. He reached into his back pocket and handed me a rolled-up magazine. I unfurled it, and my jaw dropped. On the cover of the latest edition of *Toaqua Today* was my brother.

In his underwear.

It was a black-and-white picture of him sitting in a chair in nothing but his boxers. I'm sure to any other girl it'd look hot, but he was my *brother*, for ancestors' sake, and it creeped me out.

I gaped. Ivy and Chancey, shitheads they were, snickered at me.

"Somebody snuck a bunch of copies into the prison." Ivy laughed. "The guards have been confiscating them all morning, but apparently it's a hot commodity, especially with the ladies."

I read the headline. *All Grown Up! The son of the Water chief is imprisoned, but he's legal... and single!*

Shit. The reporters hadn't been able to get an interview with me, so they'd gone after the next best thing. I opened up the magazine and scanned through the pages until I found the main article, and oh my ancestors, it got even worse. Within the magazine were so many photos of Ez, in a variety of very promiscuous positions. He looked like a freaking underwear model.

I looked closely at the background and could tell that the photoshoot had been set up somewhere within the walls of the prison. The reporters had come here to take pictures and do an interview. What in the *hell* had possessed him to do this?

I turned the page and almost vomited at a full-page spread of Ezekiel lying on a bearskin rug in front of a fireplace. The boxers were gone this time. Everything was covered, since he was lying front-down, but the sight of his bare ass was definitely something I never wanted to observe in my lifetime.

I began reading the article, hoping to the ancestors Ezekiel hadn't told the magazine anything of importance to print.

TT: We're sitting down with Ezekiel Mitoh, the eldest son of Chief Mitoh and current inmate at the Darke Institute for Supernatural Offenders. And let me tell you, readers, when we asked to do an interview with Ezekiel— Ez, as his family calls him— he didn't hesitate to hold back the details!

EM: I don't mind being vulnerable with people. I'm an open book, really.

TT: Both you and your sister are in prison. Were there more problems in the Mitoh household than the tribe was aware of? You always seemed like such a perfect family.

EM: No. My parents were pretty cool. I had a happy childhood. It was great growing up.

TT: Then I do have to ask; you're in the Institute for an attempted murder charge, but sitting across from you, I must say you don't seem like the type.

EM: All of us have a dark side. It only takes the wrong thing to make it come out.

TT: Are you admitting you have no remorse for your crime?

EM: Not in the slightest. We all want to protect the people we love. That's all I'll say about what I did.

TT: Well, I think our readers will agree that from your photos, you should receive Toaqua Today's annual Rear of the Year award!

EM: Thanks, I guess?

TT: So, we're all dying to ask, is there a special lady in your life? Perhaps someone who has caught your eye?

EM: Uh, not really. I haven't noticed anyone. But I'm open for anything.

I rolled my eyes, then scanned the rest of the article. I found that the rest of the questions were just asking about stuff Ez liked, or trying to poke into his sex life. Gross.

I smacked the magazine into Chancey's chest. "I'm off to kill Ez. Any idea where he might be?"

"Probably getting his dick sucked by some horny girl," Ivy cracked.

I flipped Ivy off, then hurried down the hall. I didn't think Ez had a class right now, so he had to be *somewhere* roaming the grounds.

I stopped into the Arts & Crafts room, where I saw Opal washing dishes. She was cleaning up after she'd burnt a batch of cookies. She washed the dishes with force, jaw clenched, and broke one while polishing off a bit of peanut butter.

Kallie was with her, chewing on a couple of cookies that hadn't been burnt. They must've been making them together. The fae eyed me with a knowing, gloaty glance, which was vastly annoying.

I took a breath. "Opal, have you seen—?"

"No," she said shortly, throwing the broken dish onto the counter, where it cracked.

Okay... someone was in a mood. "I'd really like to talk to him."

"You're going to have to fight through a horde of sirens to get to him," Opal seethed. "Now that he's *famous* and all."

"You should be happy for Ez. He looks really great," Kallie said.

"He looked *fine* before," Opal hissed under her breath.

"I think I saw him down at the mermaid pool," Kallie said. "He went for a swim after lunch."

"Thanks," I told Kallie. I left Opal to her warpath of destruction and hurried in that direction.

Opal wasn't exaggerating. My brother was surrounded by a literal horde of sirens, who had cornered him on a pool chair.

Sirens were hideous monsters when they were in the water, but when they were outside of it, they were beautiful, with long, gossamer hair, flawless skin and perfect bodies. They were all over him— sitting on his lap and rubbing his chest and ancestors knew whatever gross shit. His hair was mussed, and he had this dazed look in his eyes that was clearly the result of siren seduction.

I'm sure this was a wet dream of his, but I was putting an end to it. "Family meeting, ladies," I told them, putting my hands on my hips. "Hit the road."

There were a couple of disappointed *aw's* and some siren hisses, but I waved them off, and they eventually left the pool area. The daze drizzled away from my brother's eyes.

"Do you mind explaining yourself?" I demanded.

"What's there to explain?" Ez got off the chair, then jumped into the water. He wiped his wet hair out of his eyes while I sat at the edge of the pool.

"Why you decided to show the supernatural world what boxers you purchase," I said dryly.

"Relax. I made the reporters promise they wouldn't ask any questions about you or the Elves," Ezekiel insisted. "It's just a feature about me."

"I can see that. But I don't understand why you agreed to do it."

"It's extra money," Ez said.

"Which you don't need."

"Is it a bad thing if I like being in the spotlight?" Ez asked. "They asked me to do an article, and I was intrigued, so I thought I'd take them up on the offer."

"And you're totally okay with being portrayed like that."

"Why not? The only girl I've ever been with is Rosary. Why can't I start playing the field? It'll be fun," he said.

"You're not that kind of guy."

"But I *could* be," he argued. "I don't want to be mean, but you kind of took up all the attention when we were younger. And still a lot now, especially since Forevermore was discovered. It's nice for people to be looking at me for once."

For the second time that day, guilt plagued my feelings. I didn't know if I'd ever get rid of it.

"And I'm assuming Mama and Daddy were just *thrilled* when they found out," I said.

"Ancestors, Mom was on the phone the minute the prison opened up calls." Ezekiel laughed. "She ran to every store in town and bought up as many magazines as she could. But it backfired, because now they're making so much money, they're doing a second printing. I guess Dad thought it was funny. She's so mad at him. You should've heard her. *Everyone in town has naughty pictures of my baby boy!*"

He grinned, and I said, "You'd think you'd feel worse about it, seeing as you're such a Mommy's Boy."

"I am not!" he yelped.

I used my magic to toss a wave at him. It pushed him under before he came back up, spitting a stream of water at me. I waved my hand, and it turned around to smack him in the face.

He shook the water out of his eyes. "Anyway, it's a good thing. All those long hours in the mines finally paid off."

"I know you're happy about being in shape now, but it's not like you're a different person."

"Yeah, but people obviously like me like *this*," he said. "So it's better."

"You don't have to change who you are to be liked," I insisted.

"Yes, I do," he snapped. "Nobody noticed me before, but since I lost weight, *everyone* compliments me and thinks I'm awesome. So what's the harm? I'm probably healthier like this, anyway."

I scowled and stood up. "Whatever makes you happy, Ez. Try not to sleep with every girl in the prison, okay?"

He smirked and ducked underwater. I left the pool and wandered back to my dorm.

I'd given up on trying to help people. It only made things worse.

I felt my heart stutter when I saw Oberi standing outside of my cell in her unicorn form. Her head hung low, and the flames on her mane and tail barely simmered. They were only an inch high, making her look bald. Her eyes were dull, and cracks ran through her hooves.

"What's going on, girl?" I ran a hand through her mane, and the flames barely licked at my fingers. "Why is your fire going out?"

She gave a low nicker, and I desperately worried. I pushed open my cell door, and she changed into a husky.

Oberi's usually bright coat was nearly void of color. I gave him a pat, and to my horror, a chunk of fur drifted to the floor.

"You're sick." I knelt by Oberi's side and examined him for any wounds, but he didn't have any. He gagged when I checked his mouth, and gave me a resentful look.

Maybe it was something he ate. He slumped to the floor and tossed a loose sock I had lying around between his paws, appearing listless.

"I know it's hard that you have to go back and forth all the time," I told him, and I stroked his ears. "You like it when Charlie and I are together."

He gave a harsh snuff, but I said, "We *can't* be together, though. It's hard for Charlie and I to be in the same room. This is just how it has to be."

Oberi hacked on the floor. I was sure him puking was a way of getting back at me for making that statement. I sighed and cleaned it up.

A knock came at my door. To my surprise, I found Kallie waiting outside.

"I thought I'd leave Opal be," Kallie said. "She's having somewhat of a tantrum right now."

"I can imagine." I let Kallie inside, and we sat on my bed.

"She's as upset over Ez as you are about— well." Kallie gave me an awkward look.

I barely allowed myself to blink. "Charlie who? I'm out here living my best life without him."

"Sure." Kallie shook out her hair. "Anyway, I came by because I thought we could take a look at that journal."

"The one my Aunt Maddie left me?"

"Yes. I know you've read it a million times, but we've never gone over it as a group," Kallie said. "I figured you could show me, and I could tell the guys, so it'd be less weird between you and You-Know-Who."

I scoffed. Charlie might as well be Voldemort, in my opinion.

"Let's check it out." I opened my desk drawer and dusted off a bit of dirt that had gathered over the journal. I set it on the bed, and we began turning pages.

"Most of the journal is just a lot of phrases and words, jumbled around drawings," I explained. I pointed to a drawing on the page of a girl walking towards a tunnel of light. The words scrawled around it said *Ancestral Lands* and *destined meeting*.

"That looks like you," Kallie said, peering closer.

"It has to be me, because I'm who the prophecy is about. Then if you look here, you'll see the two drawings are connected." I pointed to the next page, where my aunt had sketched a drawing of a phoenix. "It's a message of death and rebirth."

"Are you supposed to meet someone from the Ancestral Lands?" Kallie asked. "Or perhaps another Hawkei god? You've already seen Coyote and Whale Spirit."

"I think so. The Hawkei can summon their ancestors, and we can speak with them, but I'm not sure what the phoenix has to do with it. It's some sort of clue," I said. "Then once you turn the page..."

I did so, and Kallie gasped. On both of the next pages was a depiction of a building aflame, bodies gathered around it. Smoke was rising over the horizon and blocking out the sky.

"That looks like the Institute," Kallie whispered.

"Yeah, and it's on fire," I said. "I feel like that's pretty obvious."

"Okay, so we know something is going to happen to the school at some point, but what?" Kallie asked.

"I think it's a timeline." I shuffled back through the pages, until I came to a page with a jagged line. "I couldn't make this drawing out before. I thought it was some sort of code, until we came back from Forevermore, and I looked closer. I realized that it's the skyline of the city. So that already happened. On the page beside that, it's completely covered in black ink. You can't see anything. It's like some sort of dark pit I'm descending into... maybe a basement of some kind?"

"So this comes next," Kallie whispered. "Then your tunnel of light, then the phoenix, then the school's on fire. What happens after that?"

"It just gets more complicated," I said, flipping through the pages. "There's a drawing of another ship, like the ones Charlie and I found on the shores of Kinpago— and a page of actual blood."

"Really?" Kallie grabbed the journal from me and scanned the journal. On the pages were blood droplets streaked across the page, like someone had purposefully bled upon it.

"Yep. Gross, right?" I asked. "Then there's this twisted drawing of a face, one that's half-man, half-woman, and some sort of crystal cave, and — get this— the Institute symbol on the last page."

I turned to the final page, where there was a depiction of the Institute logo— a twisted flying snake with wings, wrapped around a key. That symbol was everywhere, carved into stone pillars all around the Institute, and on our uniforms. I saw it every day. "The rest of the journal is just filled with things like Elven symbols. It's not helpful."

"So we have to be in the right place to find keys," Kallie said. "Though it's all really vague. Are you *sure* your aunt knew what she was doing?"

"Most of this handwriting isn't hers," I said. "There are at least two other versions of script in this journal."

"Which means someone must've worked on it with her," Kallie said. "Maybe they wrote stuff down when she was having visions."

"Possibly, but who was helping her?" Who would my aunt have trusted with this kind of information? The mysterious handwriting in the journal wasn't the scrawling of anyone I knew, that was for sure. I knew my Uncle Drew's handwriting, and this wasn't it. My aunt hadn't asked her husband to help with this.

"None of this makes any sense. It's just a scramble of clues," Kallie said.

"I know," I said with a sigh. "That's why it's so hard to make out. I've tried and tried, and I'm getting nowhere. That's why I stopped reading it."

A rattling sound came from my desk. Oberi cocked his head, and his ears perked up. I opened the desk drawer and found the blue egg I'd stolen from Contraband inside. My eyes widened. I'd taken that egg almost a year ago, and it'd never moved. I thought it was some sort of jewel, or a fossil, but as the egg shook back and forth, I realized there was a creature inside.

"Holy ancestors," I breathed. I grabbed the egg and set it on the bed. It was warm to the touch, and there was a thin crack in the blue lining of the shell. "It's hatching."

"Let me hold it," Kallie said. She reached out to grab the egg. Once she sat it in her lap, the egg burst open. From within the egg emerged a fuzzy blue and white creature. It looked like a moth, with a long, thin body, six legs and fuzzy feelers. It had the biggest, most brilliant sapphire eyes and a little mouth that held teeth. The creature could fit in Kallie's hand. She reached out her fingers, and the moth waddled into Kallie's open palm, snuggling her thumb and beating her majestic wings. It was undeniably cute.

"Oh my gosh! It's a *malyludwy*— a type of faekin!" Kallie gushed. "They're little creatures that are related to my kind. They're rare to find outside of Malovia. Sometimes, they bond with faeries who they're destined to protect."

"Looks like that one bonded with you," I marveled. The faekin was *purring*, making loving sounds as it danced on Kallie's hand.

"You think so?" Kallie's eyes grew alight with wonder as the fuzzy moth took to the air. "They like to rearrange furniture and play pranks on their caretakers. If a fae bonds with one, the faekin will defend them with their life. They can be really powerful."

"Well, she needs a name," I said. "What are you going to call her?"

"I think I like the name Alette," Kallie said. "It's very faerie-like."

"Alette it is." I cleaned up the remnants of the shell. "You're going to have to hide her. If the guards see you with her, she'll get taken away."

Other races at the prison weren't allowed to have animals like Elementai and witches were, and Alette was just too cool to give up.

Alette fluttered around the room and landed on Oberi's nose. She beat her wings once or twice, giving Oberi a mask with her wings. Oberi sneezed, and Alette took to the air again, fluttering this way and that.

"Faekin are good at hiding. She'll remain concealed," Kallie said.

As if to prove it, Alette fluttered toward Kallie and landed on her shoulder. She crawled behind her neck, hiding behind Kallie's curtain of blonde hair. Her little feelers poked out, and I giggled.

"I knew stealing that egg was a good thing. Now you have a pet," I said brightly.

"Yeah, and I think her hatching gave me an idea..." Kallie mused. "You just had a gut feeling when you took Alette's egg from Contraband, right?"

"Yeah. I felt like we were just meant to have it," I said.

"That's intuition. We've been talking about it in Hemlock's class. Do you know how to use it?"

"I've heard of it, but I didn't really pay attention," I confessed. Hemlock had been lecturing on intuition last semester, but since I'd been going through a major bipolar episode at the time, I hadn't been able to concentrate on what she said.

"Intuition helps a supernatural on their life path, connecting us to our true purpose," Kallie said. "Intuition can be harnessed to help us discover which path to take or where to go next. Why don't we use intuition to figure out what we should do next with your prophecy?"

"That's a great idea. How's it done?" I asked.

"Hemlock said intuition can be accessed in a lot of different ways, but meditation is the easiest. Let's go down to the Elementai Arboretum and meditate by the waterfall. I bet we'll get somewhere."

"Brilliant. Come on."

Kallie and I hurried to the special Elementai room, and Oberi followed. Alette remained hidden in Kallie's hair, so no one would notice her. When we entered the greenhouse, I took a deep breath of fresh air. The Arboretum was beautiful, full of all kinds of incredible plants, a waterfall, and a trickling stream. It reminded me of nature, and of home. Inwardly, I ached for Kinpago. We'd trained for the Darke Games here, but I hadn't returned since. Looks like they'd fixed the broken window my friends and I had smashed when we'd collapsed a flaming, walking tree during our training.

We sat by the waterfall. Oberi leapt, and changed into a narwhal mid-jump. She landed in the pool below the waterfall and swam around, splashing water upward with her tail.

I perched on a rock. "Any instructions?"

"Just... ask your intuition a question, and maybe it'll give us the answer," Kallie said. "I don't know how long it's supposed to take."

This seemed really open-ended, but we didn't have any other ideas. I closed my eyes and focused on the sound of the rushing waterfall, taking deep breaths in order to clear my mind.

At first, it was really hard to concentrate. The voices in my head were really loud, and they were demanding that I hear them.

This is pointless, Ava.

It's so boring.

This isn't working. You might as well quit.

I didn't give up. I remained sitting, allowing the voices to wash over me until they faded into background noise alongside the rushing of the waterfall. All I could hear was the sound of Alette's tiny wings as she fluttered around, and Oberi's splashes as she swam in the pool.

I need to know where to go next with my prophecy, I thought. *What should I do?*

There came no immediate response. I felt slightly frustrated, but knew this could take time, so I didn't push for an answer. Instead, I remembered what I could of Hemlock's lecture. She'd said a supernatural's intuition was a light inside of them, the same color as their aura... the energy field around one's spirit.

A black orb came into my mind's eye. The light appeared like it was dying, flickering out bit by bit. It felt damaging to see.

I knew a person's aura color could change, so it didn't unsettle me as much as it should. I prodded at the ball of light and asked again, but didn't get an answer. It nearly withered at my touch.

By this point, I'd been sitting there for twenty minutes and my ass was getting sore. I shifted on the rock and thought, *Please. I need an answer.*

The orb in my mind faded away, and I heard a soft voice whisper, *You must discover your power to achieve your goal.*

What power was it talking about? We already knew we had more power than most supernaturals. Charlie and I were both dual-casters, and Marcus had the mark of every Cast in his coven. Kallie was the only female fae who could shift. What other powers had we yet to uncover—

I gasped, and almost fell off the rock. My eyes shot open as I exclaimed, "I got it!"

"Got what?" Kallie opened her eyes, perching her chin on her hand.

"We're demigods, but demigods have powers beyond those of regular supernaturals," I explained. "We talked about this in class last semester. In Professor Mazur's lecture on demigods, she said that they could do things *beyond* what other supernaturals could do— stuff like change reality, create energy out of nothing, and build new worlds."

"So what are you getting at?" Kallie asked.

"Since we're demigods, each of us has undiscovered powers that we aren't sure of yet, powers that aren't related to what our races can do," I said. "What if we could find out what those powers were, and harness them? I bet that would help us locate the keys."

"That's excellent. I bet you're right," Kallie said, getting to her feet. "Let's find the boys. It's time to put these powers to the test."

Kallie ran off to find the others while I waited in the Arboretum for them to arrive. She found Marcus first and sent him to the waterfall. He perched on a rock and scowled. A book sat on his lap while Rishi batted at fish in the water.

Kallie was still searching for Charlie. With every moment that passed, I got more and more nervous. I didn't want to see him. It made my stomach churn whenever he was in my line of sight.

I had to settle my anxiety, so I tried distracting myself by talking to Marcus.

"You seem like you're in a bad mood," I noted.

"Kallie put a stupid hex on my warlock textbook. Every time you open it or turn a page, it makes a sex noise," Marcus bitched. "I had to use it for an exam in my Miriamic Spells class, and it was moaning all hour."

He handed me the book. I opened it to see, and sure enough, it let out a gasp that definitely sounded sexual.

I snickered and handed him back the book. "That's hilarious."

"Not when everyone in class thinks you're a pervert! I got an infraction for *being inappropriate*. People thought *I* was making the noises!" Marcus huffed.

"You're a Curse Breaker. You can break fae magic," I pointed out. "Just remove the spell from the book."

"I don't know how!" Marcus grumbled. "I've been working on breaking wards, and it's hard!"

"As I can see from my book," Kallie noted as she returned.

"It was a mean fae trick," Marcus complained.

"One of my specialties," Kallie said proudly.

Charlie followed behind her. The sight of him caused my insides to plummet beneath the floor of the prison. Ancestors, I felt like vomiting. I was allergic to his very presence.

Oberi, who was splashing in the pool, blew a spout of water out of her blowhole. It sputtered out of the pool and landed on Charlie's shoes.

"Thanks," he said sourly. She let out a high-pitched whistle, and the narwhal waved her horn in the water.

"You didn't have to do that, Kallie. You could've played a nicer prank," Marcus complained.

"It would've been less fun," she argued.

"You're my bully," Marcus shot back at her.

"And I'm proud of it," Kallie said.

"You're so ridiculous!" The book flopped out of Marcus' lap as he stood. It landed on its spine, opening wide between Charlie and me.

The book gave a particularly loud moan, and Charlie and I both cringed. Something involuntarily flared through our bond that I didn't like, and I instantly shut it off. Charlie felt it, and he scowled.

"You should be grateful! That hex is the closest to being laid you're ever going to get. I bet you don't even know what a vagina looks like," Kallie teased.

"I know what it looks like," Marcus grumbled. "I took sex ed."

"Can we focus?" Charlie complained. "We're wasting time being here in the first place."

"Good to know you think saving the world is *wasting time*," I growled under my breath. The sound of his voice was grating on my nerves. "If you have better things to do, there's the door. In the meantime, I'm going to be saving as many lives as I can."

"What is it with you and *saving* people?" Charlie scathed. "No one's buying the self-righteous act you put on."

"Oh, I'm sorry, I thought that's what we were doing," I shot back.

Charlie's voice grew louder. "It wasn't that long ago you wanted to give up on this whole thing! Last time we talked, you wanted to let all the Elves die. Today, you want to save everyone. You're being bi—"

Charlie cut himself off at the last second, and I seethed. "I'm *being bipolar*, is that right?" I spat back.

Charlie took a short breath. "Look. We can't save everyone. That's naive and childish. We need to save the people we can and forget about the rest."

"I forgot what a *positive* outlook you have on life."

"I'm a realist. I don't fool myself with fairy tales, unlike some people," Charlie spat.

He was really trying to piss me off. Apparently, the things he'd found endearing about me before were just aggravating to him now— and vice versa.

I wasn't the only one who harbored resentment. He clearly disliked me worse than he had in the beginning.

And we'd been around each other long enough to know every button to push. Oh, *goody*. This was going to be fun.

"Cut it out, you two," Kallie said. "We're here to practice our powers, not fight. We know that the locator spell worked, and about the vision you guys had, but we've gone over what they could mean, and we've hit a dead end. So if we can't find the keys through the locator spell, why don't we try working on our demigod powers?"

"But how are we going to do that when we don't even know what they are?" Marcus asked. "They literally could be anything."

"So we're going to have to experiment," Kallie said.

Alette fluttered out from behind her hair and began buzzing from flower to flower, collecting nectar. Rishi completely forgot about the fish in the pool and locked eyes on Alette, swishing his tail back and forth.

Kallie paced back and forth. "Let's think. From our research, we know that demigods can manipulate reality, create their own energy, use more magical energy than others, and— *Rishi!*"

Rishi leapt into the air to try and catch Alette. Marcus balked, and Kallie gasped. She put up a hand instinctively, and all of a sudden— everything stopped.

The waterfall ceased to move. Sunlight froze in place, and particles hovered upon the air. All sound within the prison halted, bringing everything to a complete halt. Rishi and Alette paused in mid-air, as if stuck there. Nothing moved— except for the four of us and Oberi, who'd poked her head out of the water to see what was going on.

"What the hell?" Charlie asked. He'd noticed the abrupt halt of sound. He knelt by the edge of the pool and stuck his hand into the waterfall. It didn't rush over his hand, merely rippled around it. The water particles drifted into the air, hovering for a moment before they halted in place.

"Kallie, did you just... freeze time?" Marcus strolled around. Kallie's look was so shocked, she didn't say anything.

Abruptly, everything went back to the way it was. Time began moving again— the waterfall resumed, and noise abounded at the prison. Rishi fell out of the air, and Alette zoomed back to the safety of Kallie's shoulder.

"I think she did," I said in awe. "She stopped time."

"How's that possible?" Kallie asked in wonder.

"Professor Mazur said demigods could influence time. It was one of their powers," I said.

"But I don't think all of us could do it. The way I understand it, demigod powers are like Elven abilities. You only get one special power per demigod, beyond the magic your race already provides," Charlie said.

"Can you do it again?" Marcus asked.

Kallie snapped her fingers, and just like that, time froze. Everything halted, although the four of us, along with Oberi, could move around just fine. Rishi and Alette remained frozen, Rishi on the ground and Alette in Kallie's hair.

"Demigods must not be affected by it," I said. "We must be outside the boundaries of time. That's wicked."

"What about Oberi?" Charlie said, kneeling by the edge of the pool and stroking her smooth skin. "She's not frozen, either."

"Oberi's a *mutabeecha*. They're spiritual creatures from the afterlife, much stronger than your average Familiar," I pointed out. "It makes sense she's not affected."

Time resumed again, and Marcus stated, "I want to do an experiment. I'm going to walk out of the room and see if time freezes in the rest of the prison, or if Kallie only affects time around her."

"Good idea," Kallie said. She froze time again. This time, her shoulders slumped, as if she was getting tired.

I could understand why. This was extraordinary magic, beyond the bounds of what any supernatural alive could do.

Marcus hurried out of the Arboretum. He was gone for several moments, then came rushing back in when time resumed.

"When Kallie stops time, it looks like it freezes everywhere," Marcus said. "Wherever I walked in the prison, time wasn't moving."

"Time is a concept, an idea. In reality, time isn't a straightforward line. It's happening all at once," Kallie said. "It's very similar to illusion magic, which is why I think I can do it."

"Do you think once you enhance your powers, we could time travel?" My heartbeat picked up at the possibilities. Maybe if we could reverse time, we could go back and stop the Warden from finding Forevermore.

"I don't know. I can't hold it for more than a few seconds without feeling exhausted," Kallie said. "Traveling through time itself, if it's even possible, might kill me."

"We don't know that yet," Charlie said. "But what we can figure out is how long you can hold it for."

"Let's try again," Kallie suggested. "Marcus, go back into the hallway. I want to see if you have to be close to me to be affected, or if time will stop for all demigods anywhere."

He wandered back out again. Oberi hopped out of the pool and changed into a husky, picking up Rishi by the scruff so he didn't try to chase Alette again. Kallie stopped time, and we followed her as she maneuvered through the Arboretum.

A couple of students in the hallway were completely frozen, mouths open, still in the middle of conversation. Kallie wandered throughout the hall and experimented, shifting paintings from one wall to another. Nothing was truly *stuck*— she could grab and move objects just as she could in real time. We spotted Marcus up ahead with his back to us, bouncing on his toes and waiting for us to find him.

Kallie snuck up behind Marcus and grabbed his waistband to yank it down and pants him. Marcus gave a yelp when he felt her hands around his hips.

"Hey!" Marcus shouted, scrambling to hold up his pants.

Kallie snickered, and time resumed again. The students who had paused with the halt of time resumed their walk, acting as if nothing had happened.

"It looks like you can influence things while time is frozen," I remarked quietly. "But demigods anywhere experience the time anomaly, too."

Marcus bit his lower lip. "This could be dangerous. If there are other demigods out there, they'll realize someone else is manipulating time. We have to be careful. We don't know if other demigods will be allies or enemies."

Kallie nodded. "I'll be careful. I'll only use it when necessary."

Charlie wore a puzzled look, like he was thinking hard. The expression was endearing to me, and I found it painful to witness, so I forced myself to look down.

"We could use this," Charlie said. "What if Kallie can freeze time long enough for us to break into the Warden's office?"

"I can only hold it for ten seconds," Kallie said. "That's not enough time for us to search."

"There's also a ward on his office, which won't be easy to get around," Marcus said. "Stopping time won't be enough."

"The Warden thinks other demigods are here. Why don't we use Kallie's powers to find out for ourselves?" Charlie asked.

"How?" Kallie asked.

"It's close to dinner. Most of the inmates are going to be in the cafeteria," Charlie said. "If we freeze time there, and someone's not affected, we know they have demigod blood."

"But that's risky. Someone could be a demigod that's our enemy, and they could tell the Warden once they realize Kallie has stopped time," I said. "Plus, we just agreed Kallie would only use her power when necessary."

"This is necessary," Charlie said harshly. "We have to take risks. We can't keep sitting back hoping things will pan out on their own, because that's never worked before. Let's see if we can find any demigods before they figure out what's happening."

Before I could argue further, Kallie said, "I think we should do it. Let's go."

The cafeteria was full when we got there. I was a jumble of nerves when we snuck in, but the moment Kallie stopped time, everyone in the cafeteria froze in place. It was strange, seeing so many familiar faces frozen like statues. Marcus, Kallie and I scanned the area quickly, but no one moved except us.

I spotted our friends at a table nearby. Opal's features froze in admiration as she stared across the table at Ez. Chancey's hand lay on Ivy's leg underneath the table. He obviously thought he was being discreet about it. I spotted Eddie in the lunch line, eyeing a short warlock with a cane, who must've been new here. None of our friends moved.

I quickly scanned the cafeteria for enemies, like Deuce and Naya, but it was so crowded that I didn't spot them before activity resumed in the cafeteria again. Everyone went back to eating and chatting. Kallie swayed on her feet. Marcus immediately moved close and put his arm around Kallie's hip to hold her up.

"I have to stop," Kallie mumbled. "I think I'm going to pass out."

"That's fine. We should quit for the day," Charlie said.

"Who made you boss?" I mumbled under my breath.

"Um, everyone, since you guys voted me Captain," he replied.

"The Darke Games are over, jackass. We don't have to listen to you anymore," I bit back.

"You didn't listen to me then, either, so I don't know what the hell's the difference," he said, his voice on the verge of a yell.

"Guys," Marcus said, and he gestured to Kallie. Her eyes were lolling.

Charlie and I hesitated, and Marcus dragged Kallie closer.

"I'll take her back to her cell," Marcus offered. "She needs some rest."

Marcus walked Kallie back to her cellblock, and Rishi trailed dutifully behind. Oberi wandered between Charlie and me, giving low, impatient whines.

"What's wrong with him?" Charlie asked, leaning down to pet Oberi.

"He's not feeling well," I said. "It's like he gets worse every day."

Oberi let out a moan. "There must be something we can do," Charlie insisted.

Get along, I thought, but it wasn't like that was going to happen.

"He's just upset about... us," I said. I didn't know how else to put it, but even saying it that way felt like a knife carving my heart in two.

Charlie frowned. "Well, he's going to have to move on. It's over."

It felt like he was saying those words to *me*, and not to Oberi, and that really stung.

I stomped my foot and turned around. "You know what? He's probably just bummed out, because he spends all his time with you. He needs some fun in his life. Come on, Oberi."

I walked away, and Oberi barked as he trailed behind. I didn't know if Charlie stayed there or left, because I didn't look back to see.

I wasn't sure where I was going, but I didn't care. As long as I got away from Mister Cynical.

Kallie could stop time, but I damn sure wished she could reverse it. If so, I'd use her powers to go back in time and stop myself from ever meeting Charlie Wahkin in the first place.

But even if I erased him from my mind, and my past, I didn't know if that would help, because for some stupid reason, I couldn't get him out of my heart.

And it was killing me.

charlie

FIVE

I had to admit, Kallie's new powers were pretty badass, but it was obvious she wasn't going to perfect them anytime soon. I thought we could use them to escape the Institute, or get away with beating the shit out of the Warden, but the little bit of magic she'd used had knocked her on her ass. She hadn't been at lunch all week.

It wasn't until Friday morning that I ran into her again. Marcus and I sat in Commissary, drinking coffee just to keep ourselves awake between classes. I'd been working double shifts at the factory, as punishment for starting a fight with Mad Dog. With classes and a few hours of fight club training thrown in, I'd barely had time to sleep.

"Professor Warbright wants me to brew a transfiguration potion for my semester final," Marcus said. It was hard to hear him above all the chatter and the TV playing in the corner. "He claims I have *potential*, and that I should start studying now."

"You *do* have potential," I said. "But I thought transfiguration potions were banned. Otherwise, Alistair would be running around turning everyone into a frog."

Marcus laughed. "You're not wrong. Warbright says it's okay under teacher supervision— oh, shit."

I sighed. "What now? Don't tell me you spilled coffee on your pants *again*."

"Don't look," Marcus said quickly.

I sarcastically made a show of moving my head one way, then the other, as if I was glancing around the Commissary.

"I-I didn't mean—" Marcus stammered.

He cut off just as I heard the sound of Oberi's panting coming our way. I reached out and scratched him behind the ears, and he barked happily. The chair squeaked beside me, and Kallie plopped into it, blowing a breath. Ava's scent surrounded me as she quietly took the chair opposite Kallie.

"Hey, Kallie," I said. "Feeling better?"

She groaned. "I have one hell of a headache. Thank the gods for coffee, right?"

She started chugging her drink loudly. Beside me, Ava didn't make a sound. She hadn't brought any breakfast with her. She wasn't eating again, which concerned me and kind of pissed me off. I rested my hand on the table, and my fingers brushed against hers. My heart pitter-pattered, and she drew back quickly. I hadn't meant to touch her... or maybe I had, subconsciously.

"Oh my gods," Kallie gasped.

"What?" Marcus sounded concerned.

"Did you guys hear what the newscaster just said?" she asked. "Listen."

The chatter around Commissary turned to whispers. It seemed everyone was watching the newscast coming from the TV in the corner.

"... There are rumors of discord within the United Supernatural Union. Reports say the Union is divided on how to handle the controversy surrounding the Elves," the newscaster said. "Angel, vampire, and mermaid representatives agree that drastic measures must be taken to track down the remaining Elves. Elementals, witches, and fae suggest waiting for the Elves to reveal themselves. The Astromancers have refused to comment on their stance at this time."

The tone of the newscast shifted, as if the program had changed to a roundtable discussion.

"I think we can all agree that the angels have a point," a man said. "The Elves must be found at all costs."

"Why, though?" a woman asked. "The Elves were doing just fine for years while they were in hiding. What's the rush?"

"We don't know what they're planning," the man insisted.

"We don't know that they're *planning* anything," she replied. "We must approach the Elves peacefully and diplomatically. We can't be flushing them out with tear gas and explosives. It will only incite another war."

My stomach twisted.

"If another war is coming, then we must prepare," the man suggested. "The Elves *wanted* this war. Otherwise, why would they reveal themselves now? We must be ready to strike before they do—"

"This is bullshit," I growled under my breath. I couldn't listen to any more of this. I snatched my coffee and shot out of my chair, grabbing Oberi's scruff. I didn't care that it was Ava's turn with him. He led me out of Commissary. I paced up and down the hall, until I heard my friends' footsteps behind me.

"You okay, Charlie?" Marcus asked, sounding concerned.

"No, I'm not okay," I snapped. "And you shouldn't be, either. There's no question about whether there's going to be another war or not. It's already started. Even the United Supernatural Union is divided. The Elves are fucked, and it's all our fault."

I started pacing again, one hand fisting at my side, while the other tightened on my coffee.

Marcus grabbed my shoulder to stop me. "I know you have people you care about caught in the middle of this."

He was talking about my father and grandfather. I'd barely met them, and I'd already lost my chance at building a relationship with them. But there were more people I cared about caught in the middle of this. *Everyone* I loved was a part of this. No one was immune to this war.

"But didn't you hear the witches and the fae agree on something?" Marcus pointed out. "This is a step in the right direction for the entire supernatural community."

I shrugged him off. "Your optimism is more depressing than anything."

"We could use some optimism," Kallie said, coming to Marcus' defense. "The fact is, we can't keep rehashing what's already happened. We can only figure out what to do moving forward."

"How can you be so sure?" I asked, referencing her new-found powers.

"Because I've *tried*," Kallie emphasized. She couldn't say it out in the open, but I knew what she meant. She'd been practicing her time-bending powers, trying to turn back time so we could reverse what we'd done. It wasn't any wonder why she'd been so sick all week. "I can keep practicing, but I really don't think it's going to happen overnight."

"How often are you practicing?" I wondered. "I haven't noticed any... time anomalies."

I tried to choose my words carefully, but I didn't know how else to put it.

Kallie kept her voice low. "I think you only notice when I *stop* time. Trying to turn it back is different. I think I need portal magic to do it, though— sort of like simultension. If I combine my powers with something else, I might be able to portal back in time. But my portal powers are blocked on campus. There are too many wards. And I don't know how far back I'd be able to go, even if I could do it."

"I don't know if this is really going to work," I said. "Figuring out how to use our demigod powers could take too long."

"If you don't want to help us, you don't have to," Ava told me sternly.

"You know I want to." I was offended that she'd suggest otherwise.

"Then you need to get your shit together," she demanded.

I scoffed. "I thought we weren't allowed to tell each other what to do."

Ava huffed. "Don't you have a class to get to?"

I didn't move. "I might. Why do you care?"

"Oh, shit," Marcus said, like he'd just realized something. "I'm going to be late for class, too."

"I'll walk with you," Kallie offered.

It was obvious they were giving us our space. I was sure everyone could feel the rising tension between Ava and me, and they wanted to get the hell away from us. It was infuriating.

I pressed my fingers to my forehead, where a tension headache was forming. "I don't want to fight. I'm just sick of sitting around *talking* about this. I'm ready to do something."

"Any suggestions?" Ava asked.

Not really.

"We could get something to eat," I said, because she needed to eat *something*.

"I'm not hungry," she stated, but it sounded flat. She was obviously lying. Oberi sighed heavily and pressed his forehead into my hand, further confirming my suspicions. If Oberi was concerned, so was I.

"You should eat something," I pressed.

"I said *I'm fine*," she insisted. She could be so stubborn sometimes.

I pursed my lips. "Oberi, is she fine?"

She doesn't want me to tell you, he admitted. *You're both fools, if you ask me.*

"Oberi says you're lying," I stated firmly.

"Oberi!" she objected. "That's not fair."

What's not fair is how you two have been treating each other, Oberi said in a snarky tone.

How have I been treating her? I demanded of Oberi in my mind. *Like I care?*

I know you do, he said. *Might as well admit it.*

I'm not admitting anything, I growled at him.

"What are you two talking about?" Ava demanded. "It's not fair that you two can have private conversations. I'm bonded to Oberi, too."

"I'm not the one who knows how this bonding thing works," I said. "I don't know why Oberi can talk to me and not to you."

She's jealous, Oberi told me.

Of course she is, I replied. *Why don't you just talk to her?*

It's not that easy. She has to let me in.

"What's Oberi saying?" Ava asked again.

"He says you need to stay healthy." I shoved my coffee toward her. "Drink up."

Ava's took a step back. "You know I can't drink anything from Commissary. You remember what happened last time I did."

Yeah, Naya had fucked up Ava's drink on purpose, and it'd messed with her meds. Naya wasn't working the counter today, though, and there was nothing magical about the drink I'd ordered.

"It's plain coffee. Just drink it," I said.

Ava huffed. "You can't tell me what to do."

"You'd rather starve to death?" I challenged. "As the other half of your soul, I think I get a say in whether you kill yourself or not."

"Just because we're working together again doesn't mean you know a damn thing about me," Ava spat.

I huffed. It was like I cared more about her than she cared herself, and that drove me nuts. All I wanted was for her to eat something, and she took it as some sort of attack. I was getting irritated with her pretty quickly. "I know you're not eating. You're wasting away."

"You just happen to know that because we share a plate every meal?" Ava said sarcastically.

Something twinged through our bond, and I wasn't sure if it'd come from me or from her. She'd hit a nerve without realizing it, because that's *exactly* what we used to do— back when we were together.

"Maybe we *need* to share, so you don't starve to death," I shot at her. "I felt it when I touched you. You've lost weight."

"Now you're analyzing my body?" She sounded offended.

"Ancestors, no. I'm just watching out for you."

"You don't have to," Ava huffed. "You want me to drink your coffee? Here's what I think of it."

She grabbed the coffee from my hands, then stomped over to a nearby garbage can. A *thud* sounded as she tossed the remainder of the coffee into the trash.

I gaped at her. "Are you serious right now?"

"No one tells me what to do," she said proudly. "Especially not you, Charlie Wahkin."

I didn't know what that was supposed to mean. Oberi quickly translated for me. *She's just mad because she knows you're right. She'll eat when she's ready.*

She'll eat when we start sharing a plate again, I told Oberi sarcastically, but the suggestion sent a pang through my heart. Did I really think we could ever do that again? Sharing food had been our special thing before, and we hadn't done it in months.

"I'll get you to eat one way or another," I threatened.

"I'd like to see you try," she challenged.

I raked my hands through my hair. It was obvious Ava wasn't going to do a damn thing she didn't want to do. Fighting was the last way to get through to her. I had to try another way.

My tone softened as I suggested, "Can we compromise?"

She hesitated a moment. My sudden shift in tone must've caught her off guard. "What did you have in mind?"

I wasn't entirely sure. All I knew was that I couldn't keep having these fights. They were killing both of us.

I caved. "Just... tell me how I can support you. I'm worried about you. I care. Please, let me help."

Ava tapped her foot, like she was thinking hard. "I guess we could sit together at lunch again," she offered. "I'm sick of sitting alone."

My heart surged. "And we can share food?" I questioned.

"I want to eat off my own plate," she said hastily. It was obvious why — so that I couldn't tell as easily how much she actually ate. But at least it was *something*.

"I can agree to that," I said. "But you have to have something in front of you. You can't just sit there with an empty plate."

"That's agreeable, I guess," she said. "So... I'll see you at lunch tomorrow?"

"I'll be there," I promised.

"You really should get to class," Ava suggested gently. "You're going to be late."

I left feeling like Ava and I were actually getting somewhere. We may not be any closer to the keys, but we were on track to solve one problem, at least.

Oberi led me to Supernatural Government, where I slid into a seat beside Eddie. Chatter buzzed around the room, though I ignored it.

"Something's bothering you," Eddie stated. It wasn't a question.

I slumped in my chair. "Ava-Marie and I just had a... weird encounter."

"Good or bad?" he asked.

"Both?" I answered.

"Eh, women," Eddie said nonchalantly. "What are you gonna do?"

"Fuck 'em." A guy who'd overheard us laughed as he passed by on his way to his desk.

My hands curled into fists, and I shot out of my chair. "You think that's funny? I'll fuck *you* up."

"Oh, yeah? You wanna go?" he challenged.

Eddie put a hand on my arm and tugged. "He's not worth it."

Oberi growled. Just then, Professor Woolly called the class to attention. "Calm down, everyone. Mister Wahkin, Mister Perry, I suggest you take a seat, or I'll have the guards escort you out of my classroom."

"We'll finish this another time," the guy growled. "And I'm not gonna tell you again, old man. The name's Bones."

Bones. I hadn't had the pleasure of fighting him in the ring yet, but I'd heard his stats were pretty amazing. He was a warlock with one hell of a temper. Rumor had it, he'd killed his first opponent when he'd joined the fight club last semester. I hadn't seen the fight, thank the ancestors.

"Ah, yes, Mister Bones," Professor Woolly said coolly. "Have a seat and pay attention."

Professor Woolly was kind and gentle at times, but he knew how to keep the class in order. He didn't take anyone's shit. He paced at the front of the room and began his lecture. "Based on last week's essay questions, I see that we need to review the structure of the Supernatural Union. For some reason, quite a few of you thought that *gods* were members of the Supernatural Union. I believe one of you even listed your *cat* as a representative. A few people mentioned angelic Deacons and the Arcanean king."

"Yeah, and you marked the answer wrong, too," someone at the front of the room said, sounding upset.

"That's because it is," Professor Woolly stated bluntly. "The United Supernatural Union is a level of government that deals with interracial treaties and laws. These laws are put in place and enforced by a council, which is made up of a representative from each of the major supernatural races. Your answers to the essay questions suggested most of you believed that chiefs and monarchs serve on this council, but that's simply not the case."

Pages rustled as Professor Woolly flipped through a book. "If you'll turn to page fifty-six in your textbook, you'll see a diagram of the hierarchy in supernatural government, with the United Supernatural Union at the top. Chiefs, priestesses, monarchs, and the like are at the top of *their* government, as you can see in the chart, but their power lies only among their own people. They, of course, do have some influence as advisors to the Union representatives, but since participating on the Union council is a full-time job, no chief or king could run the Union *and* their own race."

"So who runs it, then?" a girl asked.

"That's exactly what I wanted to discuss," Professor Woolly said. "Each member of the Union council is appointed by his or her people. In some cultures, the decision is left up to the highest reigning monarch, such as in fae culture. Others, like the Elementai, vote on their representative. There is, of course, a process to undergo— background checks and the like— before a new representative can join the Union council. It's important for you to know who your representatives are."

Professor Woolly began listing out all the representatives. "Remember these names, as you'll be tested on them: Amber Lee, elemental; Onyx Foxe, witch; Theodore Antov, fae; Lazarus Gray, angel; Vilas Blackwell, vampire; Merida Sharpe, mermaid; and Orion Themis, Astromancer."

I noticed he hadn't mentioned an Elf representative. I bet they weren't even thinking of having one on the council. That was shitty and unfair.

"We'll be diving into their background and qualifications over the next two class periods. We'll cover representatives for the elementals, witches, and fae today, and follow up with the others on—" Professor Woolly's lecture stopped dead when heavy footsteps came into the room. It sounded like the heavy boots of a guard. I instantly froze, sensing something wasn't right.

"May I help you?" Professor Woolly asked.

The guard began listing off names. "Brianna Thomas, Cain Flores, and Eugene Perry— you're all to come with me to the infirmary."

"Ha! Eugene," someone cracked.

"The name's *Bones*!" he snapped. "Call me that again, and I'll rip your head off."

"What's wrong?" the girl sitting ahead of me squeaked. Her fae wings fluttered.

"You've been randomly selected for a blood test," the guard said. "Let's get a move on."

"What lame-ass test is this?" Bones demanded. "I haven't been doing drugs. Who told you I had? Was it Big G?"

The guard must've grabbed Bones, because he yelled, "Get your goddamn hands off of me! I don't go anywhere I don't want to."

"It's not a drug test," the guard growled. "But I'll make sure they test you for every drug on the list if you don't come with me now."

That must've scared Bones, because he didn't protest any further. The guard dragged the students out of the room, though Bones could still be heard muttering curses under his breath as he left.

The room fell silent. Everyone was in complete shock.

"As I was saying—" Professor Woolly started, but a girl cut him off.

"Professor, if I can ask, what are they blood testing for?" she asked.

"I— I can't say for sure..." He sounded a bit apprehensive.

"If they're testing at random, we deserve to know," she insisted.

Professor Woolly sighed. He was one of the few professors who actually cared about our rehabilitation. He was willing to get real with us and treat us like adults. "I guess you're right, considering it's likely you'll *all* be tested eventually."

My mouth went dry. Did this have something to do with the Warden's experiments?

"Tested for what?" the girl pressed.

"It's a DNA test, ordered by the Warden," Professor Woolly admitted. "Several incidents have occurred this semester involving the Elves and Elf-hybrids. The Warden just wants to make sure everyone's magical ancestry is well documented, to ensure the safety of the students at the Institute."

My stomach dropped from my abdomen. I couldn't believe the injustice. Beside me, Eddie shifted in his chair, and his shoes squeaked against the floor.

"The Elves haven't done anything wrong!" I blurted. My hands shook. I *couldn't* get tested. The Warden would find out what I was.

"Well, that depends which side of the story you've heard," Professor Woolly said, dismissing my comment. "Rest assured, you all have nothing to worry about. It is simply procedure and will improve security on campus."

Even Professor Woolly didn't sound like he believed it. It was more like he was repeating whatever speech the Warden had given to the professors.

I was fuming by the time class let out. "This has to be a violation of our rights," I said to Eddie. "Why didn't you say anything? Why didn't you stick up for yourself?"

"I-I," Eddie stammered. "I didn't know what *to* say. It's not like the Elves can fight back. Not yet."

I raked my fingers through my hair as Oberi guided me through the halls. I lowered my voice and hissed, "You know what this means, don't you? *I'm* going to get tested."

"We'll figure it out," Eddie assured me, but I wasn't confident.

Oberi led us out into the prison yard. He must've sensed I needed to get the hell out of the building. My magic was starting to get away from me, and the ground shook beneath us.

I gritted my teeth. "That's not good enough. We can't sit around passively like we've been doing for months. We have to *do* something."

"What do you want me to do, Charlie?" Eddie practically begged. "Just tell me, and it's done."

Hell if I knew. "I'd just like to see you stand up for yourself every now and then."

Truth was, Eddie was a quiet guy. He'd kept his head down ever since he came to the Institute. He might've been born to defend me, but I wasn't sure he actually knew how to face conflict. He'd grown up in Forevermore, a paradise on Earth. I'd be surprised to hear an insult come off his tongue, let alone witness him in a brawl.

My shoulders dropped. "It's not your fault. I'm just pissed at the Warden, and I'm taking it out on you. It's unfair."

"I get it," Eddie said kindly. "Things are tough right now. You have every right to be mad."

I needed to take it easy on him. Eddie may not be able to speak up in class, but he was a good friend.

I was still walking across the prison yard when my foot caught a branch, and I went tumbling into the grass. A cat screeched as I landed on top of it, and Eddie gasped.

"Hey, watch it," someone growled. The voice had a unique twang to it, so it was easy to recognize.

"Alistair?" I asked. I realized then that I hadn't tripped over a branch. It'd been Alistair's cane.

"Who's asking?" he demanded.

I stood and dusted myself off. "It's Charlie."

Alistair's tone became friendly. "Ah, Charlie. Sorry, didn't see ya there."

I snickered at the lame joke. "Same. Eddie or Oberi could've warned me."

Oberi huffed. *Someone needs to knock you on your ass every once in a while.*

"Eddie, huh?" Alistair said. "You're an Elf, aren't you? You friend or foe?"

"Friend," Eddie stated proudly.

"Ah, good. We could all use some around here. The people in this place are bat-shit crazy. Am I right?" Alistair babbled. "And don't get me started on the professors. This bitch Professor Mazur caught me reading the braille signs outside the bathrooms and chastised me for *trying to snatch a peek inside the ladies' room*. Please, like I'd want to see *her* ugly ass."

"You know braille?" I asked.

"Yeah. You don't?"

"Never had the chance to learn."

Alistair sounded disappointed. "Stupid education system. It's like it's set up to fail us. But if you want, I'll teach you, Charlie."

"Really?" My voice brightened. "That would be great."

I'd been interested in learning braille, but no one had ever offered to teach me. This could be another tool I could use to navigate my world. I couldn't wait to get started on it.

"Charlie!" a voice growled as a man approached. I didn't recognize the voice at first, but he sounded angry.

I sighed and turned toward him. "Hell, what now?"

"My sister's pissed. What did you say to her?" he demanded.

I realized then that it was Ezekiel. Great. More drama to deal with.

"Nothing," I said. "What happened?"

"I don't know, you tell me," he demanded. "I walked in on her crying."

Ouch. If that didn't twist me up inside, nothing did.

"We just talked about her eating," I confessed, but Ez apparently didn't like that.

"You don't think before you talk, do you!?" he accused. "You can't say that kind of stuff to my sister. You know she's struggled with eating disorders."

"Yeah, and I was trying to *help*," I emphasized.

"Ava doesn't want your help," he spat.

I gaped. "Did she say that?"

"She won't say it, but I know the truth," he accused. "She's not eating because of *you*. You broke my sister's heart!"

My hands curled into fists. He didn't know shit. If he didn't know I was broken up about this, too, he was clueless.

I was about to give Ez a piece of my mind and tell him the breakup was mutual, but he got up in my face and spat, "You don't get a say in anything she does. I think it's time someone teaches you a lesson."

"What are you gonna do, Ez? *Beat me up?*"

Oberi panted happily, like he was encouraging the fight. He thought this was funny.

"Look, we're friends, and I don't want to hurt you, but I've gotta fight for my sister's honor." Ez rocked his weight between his feet, and I felt it with my Earth magic. "Put 'em up!"

I groaned. "Are you serious, man? Ez, I could knock you out in under two seconds. You don't want to fight me."

"He looks pretty serious," Eddie mentioned. "Do you want *me* to fight him for you?"

"No, he's just pissed," I said. "Ez is the furthest thing from a threat."

"You're just scared," Ez accused.

Beside me, Alistair tried to hold back a laugh.

"I've bulked up," Ez pointed out. "You don't know what I'm capable of. Look, I'll even make it fair. I'll close my eyes."

That statement pissed me the fuck off. "This is ridiculous!" I protested. "I'm not making negotiations, and I'm certainly not fighting you!"

Ez didn't know a thing about fight club. He had no idea what I could actually do to him. The poor kid would end up unconscious in the infirmary.

Then again, he *had* tried to murder John to avenge Ava, and he'd put him in the hospital. The kid was ruthless when it came to his sister.

But I wasn't anything like John. I cared about Ava-Marie more than anybody.

"The rest of you better back up," Ez threatened. "I'm not joking. Let's get this over with."

This whole thing was comical, at best. "Ez, stop it. I didn't break Ava's heart. It was mutual."

"Oh, yeah? Then how come Chancey told me you're the one who broke up with her?" he demanded.

Irritation flitted through me at Chancey. The idiot needed to get his story straight, and stop gossiping about me. "Chancey doesn't know a thing," I said.

"If that's true, why aren't *you* upset about the break-up?"

The accusation broke me. The fact that anyone could assume I wasn't hurt by what happened between Ava and me was ludicrous. It was as if Ez was denying everything Ava and I had been through, claiming none of it had been real. It was the realest thing I'd ever experienced— every breath, every heartbeat was seared into my memory like the brand from a hot iron. I thought about her every second of every day, and it ripped me to shreds that I'd let her go, even though I knew it was the right thing for both of us. To even *suggest* I didn't care was an insult of the highest degree.

I couldn't handle it. So, I snapped.

My fist cracked against the side of Ez's face, but it didn't faze him like I expected. Ez slammed his fist into my nose three times in quick succession. Blood spurted everywhere.

My head was spinning. Damn, he hit harder than I thought he could. Ez tackled me to the ground with a roar, and he managed to punch me a few more times before I kicked him off of me. I got back on my feet again and felt him coming with my Air magic. I ducked his final blow, then landed an uppercut to his jaw. He fell flat on his back.

Ez made no sound for a second, and I thought for sure I'd knocked him out. Alistair roared in laughter, but he wasn't the only one. We caught the attention of other groups around the yard.

A moment later, Ez came to. His words were slurred, like he'd bit his tongue. "You gonna pay for that!"

Ez jumped to his feet and swung his fist in my direction. I ducked, and the air whooshed above me as he missed. The laughter around the yard grew.

"Stop, Ez," I said. "You're making a fool out of yourself."

"I'd rather be a fool than stand around doing nothing," he shot back, before taking another swing at me. I dodged that one, too.

Nearby, someone laughed loudly. "What a pathetic loser! The Bandit's blind, and Ez can't even hit him!"

My hands curled into fists, and I whirled toward the asshole. Even though he was being a jackass right now, *nobody* made fun of Ez. He was Ava's brother, and my buddy on top of it, despite him acting really stupid at the moment.

"What did you just say?" I growled. "You think *you* can fight me? Come on, let's go. Leave the kid out of this."

The guy cracked his knuckles. "Hell yeah, I can beat you. I've been dying to get in the ring with you, Bandit."

"Oh, so you've heard of me?" I snapped.

"Charlie, it's *Bones*," Eddie said under his breath.

Great. This loser. "Aw, fuck," I groaned. "I thought he was getting blood tested."

"He must be finished," Eddie said.

Alistair pushed past us. His cat meowed and followed dutifully behind him.

"If any of you pieces of shit want to fight someone, you've gotta go through me," Alistair said. "So, what's it gonna be? You gonna fight, or walk? I suggest you walk."

"Holy mushrooms!" Eddie squeaked. "Alistair is quite bold."

Bones laughed so loudly, I bet he could be heard all the way across the prison yard. His band of cronies chuckled alongside him. "You think I'm scared of you, munchkin? You're like, three feet tall!"

"Four-foot-two, thank you very much," Alistair said proudly. "Maybe get creative with your insults. I've heard the munchkin one before."

"Oh, I've got plenty for you, you little—" Bones started, but he never got a chance to finish.

A blast sounded throughout the prison yard, and I felt the electric sizzle of magic as something exploded through the air. Bones and his cronies screamed, their yells echoing through the yard as they were sent flying several feet away from where they'd just been.

"HEY!" The deep voices of several guards sounded across the yard.

My jaw dropped. "Did Alistair just—?"

"Attack with a battle orb?" Eddie finished for me. He sounded totally shocked— and a little starstruck. "That was so badass."

"You're gonna *die*, you filthy motherfucker!" Bones roared.

Another blast sounded, and I could only guess Bones had conjured a battle orb of his own. I reacted before I could think about it, and I thrust my Air power outward. Bones' magic smashed into mine, sizzling out. Oberi barked loudly, and the ground began to shake.

Noxite darts flew toward us, but my magic threw them off course. Guards shouted as they raced in our direction.

"You call that a battle orb?" Alistair teased Bones.

"We gotta run!" Ez said at the same time.

A little late, kid, Oberi grumbled.

"You're all gonna die!" Bones screamed. "Get 'em!"

Footsteps charged toward us, but we stood our ground. I didn't know how many guys Bones had on his side, but there had to be nearly a half dozen of them. We were outnumbered.

I shoved Ez. "Go!"

He had to get out of here before he got hurt. I wasn't giving him a choice. Ez scurried behind me toward the trees. I threw my arms upward, controlling the dirt in the prison yard. Chunks of gravel flew upward, knocking Bones' men on their ass.

That's the best you got? Oberi teased me. Bits of dirt sprayed across my face as Oberi tossed up more earth with his own magic. I could feel the ground move as he created miniature hills to slow the gang down.

Beside me, Eddie breathed heavily, like he was pissed. He grabbed my arm and yanked me backward, throwing himself in front of me like a shield. "Stand back, Charlie! I'll protect you."

Before I could protest, Eddie sprinted forward. I heard the *thud* as he slammed into Bones, tackling him to the ground. *Thud! Thwack! Crack!* The sounds of Eddie's fist smashing in Bones' face was both sickening and satisfying.

I raced after him, intent on doing some damage myself, but I didn't reach Bones or his friends before the guards got to us. Someone grabbed my arm before I even realized he was there. He grabbed so hard and fast that it nearly yanked my arm out of the socket. Judging by the strength of the grip, it was a vampire.

"You're all coming with us!" the guard growled. "Captain's orders."

My shoulders sagged. If I didn't want to get in trouble, I had to follow them. Answering to Captain was a hell of a lot better than facing the Warden.

Oberi, go find Ez. Make sure he's okay, I instructed.

I'm going with you, he objected.

No, you're not! I snapped in my mind. I hadn't let Oberi get involved with the fight club yet. I wasn't about to start inviting him along.

Oberi huffed, but he raced off before the guards could grab hold of him.

"Dear Goddess!" Alistair exclaimed with a gleeful laugh as a guard dragged him away. "Your friend is *hot*, Charlie! I'd eat Elf ass for that man."

"You were quite impressive yourself," Eddie replied shyly, before a guard told him to shut up.

Ancestors, these two had a crush. I already couldn't deal with them.

The guards dragged my friends and me into the building. I didn't know what they planned to do with Bones and his band of assholes, but I guessed they'd let them off with a warning, considering Bones' status in fight club. My stats had fallen quite a bit over the summer, since I just didn't care anymore. I didn't get the same privileges I used to.

Which meant I was going to get my ass chewed out. A door creaked open, and the guards shoved us into a small room. I guessed it was Captain's office.

"These three started a fight in the prison yard," a guard said. "This Elf here broke Bones' nose."

"That's impressive." Captain's deep voice sounded approving. "I'd like to have a little chat. Come in."

The guards left us there and shut the door behind us, though not before tossing Alistair's cat into the room like a ragdoll. The cat hissed as it landed hard on the ground.

"Please, take a seat," Captain said kindly. The man could go from being your best friend to your worst nightmare in two-point-five seconds, but I'd gotten used to it.

Almost.

Eddie guided me into a chair, and Alistair sat on the other side of him.

"What's the deal, princess?" Alistair asked boldly. "You gonna give us an infraction, or what?"

Captain laughed, and the chair behind his desk squeaked as he leaned back in it. "I may be head of security, but I didn't invite you in here to deal out a punishment. I want to make you an offer. You two intrigue me— an Elf and a blind dwarf. It'd be a great show."

Aw, fuck. The last thing I wanted was for Eddie and Alistair to get wrapped up in fight club.

"You're offering us a place in the fight club," Alistair guessed.

My jaw fell. "How'd you know about fight club?" Alistair had barely been here a month.

"Eh," he said. "I've got my ways."

"There's a fight club?" Eddie squeaked, pretending like he had no idea. Of course, I'd been obligated to tell him, after he'd seen all the bruises on me.

"Yes, and I want you two on board," Captain said.

"You can't take the deal!" I blurted.

"Why not? This sounds great!" Alistair protested.

"Just trust me," I insisted. "Fight club isn't a place for either of you."

"Oh, come on now, Charlie," Captain practically sang. "You can't truly believe it's *that* bad. You love it!"

My lips tightened. Captain didn't take well to requests to leave the fight club. I'd really liked him at first, but I was starting to see him for the manipulative bastard he was. He'd made it pretty clear that nothing I said would get me out— and he'd pit me up against the toughest guys in the league if I said anything more. It could literally get me killed to keep pushing him.

So I said the only thing I could to save my friends. "To be honest, Captain, I don't think they have what it takes."

"Hey!" Alistair protested. "You wanna see what I've got? I'll *show* you what I've got!"

Captain laughed, like my attempt to save my friends was comical. "That's up to them, Bandit. Should you two take this offer, you'll be provided extra privileges on campus, and be rewarded monetarily."

"And if we don't?" Eddie asked warily. I already knew he wouldn't join— not if I told him so.

"You'll receive a memory-wiping potion and forget this meeting ever happened," Captain said. "But should you get into a second fight, you won't get another opportunity to join. You'll answer to the Warden next time. This is your one and only chance."

"I can do it," Alistair stated confidently. "Let me at those jerks, and I'll show them what my battle orbs are made of."

"That's the thing, Alistair," I told him. "You can't use magic in fight club."

"What?" he balked. "No magic? You expect me to fight with just my fists? No thank you, old man. Those vampires will turn me into a pretzel."

"Hm," Captain huffed. He was trying to hide his emotions, but it was obvious he was very displeased with the answer. "And you, Elf?"

Eddie hesitated, then turned to me. "If I was in the fight club with you, we could train together. I could learn how to defend myself here."

"No," I stated. "Take the potion, Eddie."

I wasn't giving him a choice. As my guard, he was magically bound to do what I said.

"Okay. I'll take the potion," Eddie agreed automatically. His answer was a little too bright for Captain's taste, and I heard him make a dangerous noise.

"Are you sure?" Captain pressed. "This is your one and only shot. Perhaps I can convince you with numbers—"

"They said no," I snapped. "Give them the potion and be done with it."

Captain drummed his fingers on his desk, as if waiting for one of them to change their mind. Nobody spoke.

Finally, Captain drew a breath and said, "Very well."

Slowly, he stood from his desk and opened the door. He called one of his guards outside. "Ender! Get in here!"

"What is it, Cap?"

Captain sounded less than pleased. "Take these boys and get them the memory-wiping potion. We're done here."

"Very well, Captain."

Eddie and Alistair stood, and I started to follow. Before I got out of the room, though, Captain shoved an arm in front of me, nearly clothes-lining me. "Not you, Bandit. Let's chat."

My stomach dropped from my abdomen as Captain swung the door shut, leaving only the two of us in the room.

"I'll meet you in your cellblock!" Eddie called before the door shut. I wasn't sure if he'd remember after he took the potion.

My knees quivered as Captain took a step toward me. I retreated until my back was pressed against the wall. The ex-military head of security loomed over me, his hot, angry breath brushing against my cheek. I thought for sure the vampire was going to pummel me, but he just stood there, letting the adrenaline pump through my blood. I wasn't scared of most people in this prison, but this man was intimidating as hell.

Captain must've had enough with the silence, because he smacked me upside the head— which fucking *hurt*.

"Ow!" I cried. I resisted the urge to cradle the side of my head, because you couldn't show weakness around Captain.

"What the hell is your problem, Bandit?!" he roared. His nose was barely an inch from mine, and spittle flew into my face. "You just cost me two fighters! Those bets could've bought you a mansion if you wanted it, with the recruitment commission!"

To hell with it. I wouldn't let my friends join for all the money on Darke Island.

"Maybe if you let people leave, I'd have encouraged them to join," I snapped. "They're already prisoners in this place. I'm not letting them become *your* prisoner, too."

I was too pissed to hold it all back. I didn't care how badly Captain punished me for talking back to him. It felt pretty damn good, considering how hard he'd been pushing me these past few months. I hated that I ever fell for his charm and joined the fight club in the first place.

Captain grabbed me by the shirt and shoved me against the wall so hard it knocked the wind out of me. "You think you're so *cool*, don't you, Bandit?" he taunted. "You think you're in control. Well, get it out of your head right now!"

He smacked me again, and I gritted my teeth.

"You knew what you were getting into when you joined my team," he growled. "I can't have you running off spreading rumors about the club, and I sure as hell can't wipe your memory of the past six months."

"If you let me out, I won't say a damn thing," I promised. It seemed like a fair trade.

"It don't work like that, Bandit. You want out, you're gonna have to prove yourself."

"Then tell me what to do, because I'm done."

Captain scoffed, then dropped me. "That's been obvious for months. Is that why you didn't fill your hours this week?"

"I'm working extra shifts at the factory," I reminded him. "I told you that when I got the infraction."

"That's your own damn fault!" he snapped. "If I didn't know better, I'd say you were rigging the fights just to piss me off."

I scoffed. "Believe me, I wouldn't care enough to put in the effort."

He paced several feet away, then whirled back toward me. "Well, someone's fixing the fights! My best fighters are losing. I've been training in combat all my life. I know what a fake knock-out looks like. These fights have turned into sissy wars— nothing but a bunch of pussies. I need action, or the whole club goes bottom-up. The stats don't add up, and I'm losing bet money. I'm sick and tired of it!"

Captain swiped his hand through the air, and something made of glass flew off his desk and shattered. "I need this guy caught, and I need him caught now. Tell you what, Bandit. You want to leave so badly, I'll make you a deal."

My heart lifted. If there was a chance to get out, I'd take it. I just hoped he wasn't asking me to kill someone or something. I *did* have a moral code, albeit a loose one.

"Here's the deal. You catch this guy who's fixing the fights, and I'll let you walk," he offered.

My breath caught, but I tried not to let it show. It was a pretty good deal, but I worried there was a catch. "And if I don't catch him?"

"Then you're mine for good," he threatened. "Need I remind you that things aren't looking good for you right now? You've missed a week of training. As punishment, I've scheduled you to fight three dragon shifters."

"I've beat dragon shifters before," I stated.

"Not three at once."

"*What?*" I gaped. "That will kill me!"

Captain chuckled, like the idea amused him. "That's too damn bad. You agree to investigate who's fixing the fights, and I'll forgive your missed training sessions. I'll take that fight off the schedule. As soon as you catch the bastard that's rigging the ring, you're done. You can walk."

"Really?" It seemed too easy.

And that's exactly what I was worried about.

"What?" he snapped. "Is it too hard a task for you?"

"No. I can do it," I said quickly. But it wasn't good enough for me. "If I catch him, you let Chancey and Ghost go, too."

Captain laughed. "You think you're in a place to negotiate?"

I cocked an eyebrow. "Aren't I? Last semester, Ghost was promised two more fights before he could leave, yet he's still in. The man wants out, and I'm taking him with me, or I'm not investigating."

Captain went quiet for a few moments before saying, "I suppose I can let Ghost go with the deal, but Chancey won't want to leave."

The least I could do was *try* to save my friend. "Then I guess we'll give him the choice. I won't settle for anything less. Chancey may be your best recruiter, but your whole operation will crumble if someone keeps rigging those fights. You need him gone, and I'll make sure to get rid of him as long as you let me, Chancey, and Ghost all go free once he's caught."

My heart hammered as I awaited Captain's response. Certainly, I was asking for too much.

I was shocked when Captain finally answered, "You've got yourself a deal, Bandit. But you'd better deliver results. If you don't, you won't like what I decide to do with you. So figure out exactly what's going on here. Otherwise... you're mine."

ava-marie

SIX

I scowled as I read the newest comments on my vlogging page, which had been posted only a few days ago. The quiet sounds of the prison library rattled in my ears as I scanned the computer screen, feeling worse with each word.

Where'd she go?

She ditched us again, I bet.

We want more songs!

I hadn't made any new content on my vlog since we'd found Forevermore, and my fans had clearly noticed. I thought they'd give up and find someone else to follow, but apparently, they really liked my music and wanted to know what the hold-up was in making another video.

They weren't the only ones.

"You need to get back to producing," Ezekiel said, and he leaned closer to me. "Three months is a long time without something new."

He'd dragged me down here and forced me to check my vlog, which I'd all but ignored in the past three months. I'd made a post in the spring telling everyone I'd be too busy this summer with my internship to post anything, but now it was the fall, and my fans were wondering where I was and why I hadn't delivered any new songs.

"I'm not a fucking performing monkey. I can't just spit out content because everyone's tired of waiting for me," I complained.

"But you can't abandon your fans because you're feeling depressed, either," Ez insisted. "It's bad for your brand, and you aren't the kind of person that doesn't keep promises to their subscribers. This could be an option for you after you graduate, Ava. Don't throw it away because of Charlie."

I wrinkled my nose. "I'm not *depressed*, especially not because of that dick. I'm just not feeling *creatively inclined*. And by the way, I'm very thankful that you punched Charlie for me, but not at the expense of possibly getting thrown into Cellblock 9."

Overall, I thought the fight was pretty stupid once I'd heard about it, but I was still sad I hadn't been there, because I bet it had been entertaining.

"Look, Charlie had it coming, and now everyone's even. Now we can get back to being friends, right?"

Ez was pretty much begging me to come back and hang with the entire group again, like we used to. He didn't get that wasn't going to happen.

I opened my mouth to make up some excuse, but before I could, Ez unexpectedly lolled forward. He nearly toppled out of his chair, and I had to reach out to keep him upright.

"Whoa," I said, pushing him back in his seat. He looked dizzy. Panic flooded through me as I realized that he was warm underneath my hands. "Ez, you're burning up."

"I don't have a fever," he said, somewhat out of it.

Because immunocompromised people can't get them, I thought angrily.

Ez reached for a cup from Commissary he'd placed on the desk, and drank deeply from it. As he did, a sharp, sweet scent rose past my nose. I knew it, because I'd used the root quite a few times in my Alchemy class.

"That's a magical drink," I accused. I recognized the recipe. It was a smoothie with all kinds of magical ingredients that were supposed to help boost your immune system. Ez wasn't fooling anybody.

"So? They don't affect me like they do you," Ez said before he took another drink. "They give me energy."

"You're trying to supplement what you don't have. You can't keep self-medicating. They'll help in the short term, but overall they're just going to make you sicker," I insisted.

"Who said anything about self-medicating? I feel... better than ever." He took a deep breath, as if it hurt to breathe.

"Getting in shape has nothing to do with how well your body actually functions," I argued. "You can look fine on the outside and be wasting away on the inside."

Ez scoffed. "I thought we were talking about you, not me."

I sensed this conversation was quickly going to revert to me not eating, and I didn't want to go there. I sighed and hefted my bag onto my shoulder. "I'll make another video next week, I promise. You'll be on guitar. I wrote a couple of songs over the summer. We'll film something this Friday."

"Okay." Ez swept a couple of black strands out of his eyes. He looked so tired.

Worry tumbled through my gut as I left the library. My brother couldn't keep doing this to himself. It'd kill him. But what could I do to stop it? Absolutely nothing. I felt as powerless to change his denial as he probably did about my weight.

I wanted both of us to get better, but I didn't know how. It seemed as simple as just making a decision, but neither of us wanted to. I felt as helpless over my own condition as I did Ezekiel's.

At some point, everything was going to boil over.

On my way to the lunchroom, I saw Ivy, Opal and Kallie sitting in Commissary. Ivy waved me over, and I sat beside him. All of my friends had various meals placed in front of them, which they'd grabbed from the cafeteria.

Ivy peeked at the wrap he'd gotten. "Ugh. It's turkey. I *hate* turkey, but I don't want it to go to waste. Ava, would you eat it?"

"Sure." I grabbed the wrap from Ivy and took a bite. Mayonnaise filled my mouth, and I chewed lightly.

"We have to go to therapy this afternoon," Kallie said. "I heard we have a new counselor."

Disgust churned in my gut at the thought of going to a therapy session with my ex. Sounded about as pleasurable as a cactus up the ass. I didn't want— or trust— a new therapist. No one was as good as Professor Takahashi.

But it was a mandated part of our sentence, so it wasn't like we had a choice but to show up. "Do you know anything about the new social worker?" I asked.

"No." Kallie shook her head. "Apparently, she was a last-minute hire."

"She had to be, if she wants to work here," Ivy said disdainfully. "She has no idea what she's getting into, counseling a bunch of kids with criminal records and bad tattoos."

"Ugh, don't remind me," I moaned. I gave another distasteful glance at Charlie's name scrawled across my skin. You know what was worse than splitting up with the love of your life? Having their stupid name tattooed on your wrist, and being forced to look at it every day. Charlie got off easy.

"Hey precious, we've all made bad decisions with men. Yours is just permanent," Ivy joked.

"I want this ugly thing gone. It was a terrible decision at the time," I said.

"You could ask Marcus to cover it up," Kallie suggested.

"Or I could put *is an asshole* after his name," I said with a shrug. "Either works."

Ivy and Kallie laughed, but Opal didn't even crack a smile. She was being really quiet.

Kallie nudged her. "What's up? You seem bummed."

Opal poked at her salad. "Ez can't keep anything down," she muttered. "Every time he eats something, it comes right back up. All he consumes now is those magical drinks, because it's the only thing his stomach can handle."

"How do you know about it?" Ivy asked suspiciously.

"He tells me everything," Opal said. "He doesn't hide stuff from me."

Well, he was certainly hiding stuff from the rest of us. Anxiety knotted in my chest as Ivy let out a sarcastic noise. "Girl, you need to ask him out already."

"I do not!" Opal blushed so red that her cheeks became more vibrant than a rose.

"Well, you obviously care about him, or you wouldn't be telling us this," Kallie pointed out.

Opal's mouth twisted. "It's just... it's really bad now. He's worse than before. I was holding his hand yesterday morning as he threw up in the men's room. I was worried he'd start coughing up blood."

Images of Opal sitting on the bathroom floor as my brother vomited into a toilet assaulted my mind. This had gone too far. My chair screeched as I stood up from the table. "I gotta go. See you guys later."

I tossed the empty takeout container box into the trash— I'd actually finished my meal— and stormed down to the prison phones. I paid the guard for extra time, then yanked the receiver off the holder as I dialed my father's office number.

He picked up almost immediately. "Hel—"

"Daddy, you need to talk to Ez." I cut him off before he could even say a greeting.

His voice took on a brusk tone. "Your brother is an adult. He can speak to me whenever he wants."

Frustration welled up in me. This was more important than any stupid argument the two of them had been carrying out over the past few months. I didn't care if they were still pissed off and holding grudges about whatever had been said when Ez had committed his crime. This had to end.

"He *needs* you, Daddy," I insisted. "He's really sick."

The other end went silent, and I continued on. "He's been throwing up every day, and he's really weak. He's always getting some kind of infection. He nearly passed out this morning! He's not getting any better."

Daddy's voice was sad. "There isn't much I can do."

"You have to convince him to go get help!" I burst. "He'll listen to you!"

"He's not ready," Daddy said gently. "And he needs to be, if he's going to face this."

"He's going to die." I sniffed and rubbed my face. Fuck, I was so tired of crying all the time. It was really getting old.

"We all accept our illness in our own time. You can drag him to the doctor, but you can't force him to get treatment," Daddy said. "As terrible as this disease is, it's *his*. His to deal with, his to decide how to handle. All we can do is support him."

It was the same conversation I'd had with Opal last semester, and nothing had changed. I wanted things to be different.

"But you know how bad it can be," I insisted. "How can you just... watch him go through this and accept it?"

"Because I know how it feels, and it's hell, Ava, to put it bluntly," Daddy said. "Forcing him to face the obvious is just going to put him through more pain, and his body isn't giving him a choice, so we have to."

"This denial is going to make his condition worse unless we do something," I said.

"He doesn't want to admit it, and I understand why." Daddy's voice was heavy with guilt.

"Don't blame yourself. It's not your fault." I tugged on the phone cord anxiously. "All you can do is convince him what he's doing is stupid and could get him killed."

"I'll try to intercede, but I don't know if he'll take my call. We haven't spoken in... months, really."

"What about Mama? She can do something," I pleaded.

"I don't know, Ava. Ez is scared. We all are."

I shared his fear, yet I wasn't about to give in. I knew this was terrifying, but we had better treatment options for Combined Magical Suppression Syndrome now than we did for my dad when he was young. If we caught it early, we could deter some of the damage that the condition did to Ezekiel's body, before it was too late. He didn't have to live with the same pain that Daddy did— but he had to start treatment now.

I was silent for too long, and Daddy said, "Peanut, are you doing okay?"

My lip wobbled— damn me. "I don't want to get into it."

"You know you can always talk to me."

"What's there to talk about? I— I broke up with him."

Wasn't exactly truthful, but admitting the alternative was too agonizing, so I didn't.

"Breakups still hurt, even if you're the one who made the call," Daddy said. "Even your mother and I have disagreements sometimes."

I scoffed. I didn't want to be reminded of my parents' incredible love story. I bet *they'd* never broken up. It made me feel bitter. "Sure you do."

"There's more to our past than you know," Daddy reassured me. "I can understand how you feel better than you think. You just have to tell me how you feel."

I took in a harsh breath. "The truth is... I'm angry, and I hate him, and I never want to see him again, but I'm stuck here, so I'm forced to. It wasn't going to work out, anyway. What else is there to say?"

"Are you sure you two didn't talk yourselves out of it?" Daddy asked gently. "There might be another way."

"We condemned a whole race, Daddy. We started a genocide all over again." I rubbed my temple.

"You can't blame yourself for what happened to the Elves, peanut. Prophecy stuff is hard, and destiny would've led you there whether you wanted it to or not. Sometimes, things happen, and you don't have any control over it. But I promise, even with the bad things, it all works out for a greater purpose. You have to trust in that."

"I bet," I mumbled. I didn't believe him— not right now.

The line *pinged*, telling me my time was up. Before I hung up, Daddy said, "Just don't deny your feelings, peanut. Stuffing it down isn't going to help you feel better. And if it gets really bad, I want you to call me straight away, do you understand?"

I bit my lip. "Okay. Bye, Daddy."

I hung up the phone, then turned on my heel, feeling like the conversation hadn't gone anywhere. I resolved to deal with this myself. I wasn't giving Ez any more time. If he didn't recover soon, I'd drag him to the infirmary myself. I couldn't stand aside and watch my brother suffer. Not when there could be a way to stop it.

By the time I got done with the conversation, it was time for my much-dreaded therapy session. I dragged my ass to the counseling tower and hoped this wouldn't turn into a major shit show.

When I got there, I had to stop to look around. The room had been totally redecorated. Takahashi kept things clean, straightforward, and minimalist, but now there were all kinds of motivational posters decorating the walls, as well as a variety of plants, such as Venus flytraps. I passed a type of plant we grew in Kinpago that only ate meat, and recoiled when the petals snapped out at me like jaws.

The others were already here, sitting in our usual circle and seeming wary. Oberi didn't bark like he usually did when I arrived. His dark eyes lingered on the woman at the head of the group, and he let out a low, subdued growl.

I observed our new therapist. She was a small woman with a long, blonde braid that fell down her back. Large, obnoxious eyeglasses that perched on a thin nose, hiding green eyes. She looked to be a little older than my parents.

Something about her seemed oddly familiar, but I couldn't place what. I was sure I hadn't met her before, so I didn't know where the connection came from. I shook it off to coincidence and took a cautious seat beside Charlie.

"Where were you at lunch? I waited for you," Charlie asked.

"I didn't break my promise," I said. "I ate with Ivy, a whole turkey wrap."

Charlie nodded, as if he thought that was an acceptable trade. The counselor observed me with a greedy gaze, as if she'd been excited for my arrival.

The blonde gave a big, annoying smile. "Hello, students. My name is Jaymin Vengier, but you may call me Professor Jaymin. Unlike the other teachers here at this school, I think it's very important that we get to know each other on a first-name basis, as I want you to see me as your *friend*, not someone in authority," she cooed. "I am an Elementai of the Earth House. Like you, Charlie."

Her attempt to connect with Charlie fell flat, and he said nothing. Professor Jaymin wriggled in her chair and said, "I've taken a look at your files, and I must say, what bright students you all are. Each of you is very talented, and I'm honored to be your new counselor. I'm sure we all have a lot to share."

We still didn't talk. It was hard enough getting us to open up to

Professor Takahashi, and he'd been kind. This lady seemed faker than a spray tan.

She cleared her throat. "Since this is the group that discovered Forevermore, I thought we might talk about your methods of investigation. Mainly, how you found the city in the first place. I understand this isn't a subject that's been breached by any of your teachers, or even the Warden, but this is a *therapy session*, and I think it's a good idea for the four of you to talk about your experiences last semester. Perhaps to alleviate the guilt?"

Kallie completely blanched, and Marcus hunched his shoulders. "I'm sorry, Professor Vengier—"

"Professor *Jaymin*," she snapped, nearly in irritation. "This is a casual gathering, Marcus. I am your ally, after all."

Marcus gulped before he said, "We don't feel comfortable talking about all that. It was somewhat traumatizing."

"But that's why you're here!" Jaymin exclaimed. "I can assure you that anything you say will be confidential."

Bullshit. More like anything we say can and will be used against us, I thought.

Charlie shifted forward. "We'd like to talk about something else, if you don't mind."

"Very well," Jaymin said. I swear, I saw her eyebrow twitch. "Let's move on. Since the four of you are so clever, you must be working on some sort of special project this semester. Tell me, what are you all doing in your free time?"

She's trying to get answers out of us, I realized. The Warden had put her up to learning what we were doing. Charlie stiffened beside me, and Oberi let out another growl.

"Uh, I started a new painting," Marcus stuttered. I nodded encouragingly at him, telling him to keep talking. "It's an imitation of Rembrandt."

"And I joined the prison football team," Kallie added hastily. "I mean, we don't really play against anyone but ourselves, but it's nice to get some aggression out, and they might even make me the quarterback—"

"I see," Jaymin said blandly, cutting Kallie off. Clearly, those weren't the answers she was looking for.

Her attention rounded on me like a venomous snake. "What about *you*, Ava? I've heard so much about you, from the Warden and others. You must be researching something new. You always are."

If this bitch found out about my journal, she'd tell the Warden, and I'd lose it immediately. She wouldn't accept that I wasn't researching anything, so I lied.

"I'm investigating Atlantean shipwrecks," I bluffed. "It's fascinating."

"Hm." Jaymin scribbled something down on her clipboard. "Very interesting."

Yeah, go ahead and research that dead end. Hopefully it would mislead her and the Warden for a few weeks, at least.

"What have you learned?" Jaymin asked, breaking me out of my relief. "Anything useful?"

"Um—" I started. I was a bit rusty on mermaid lore. I tried to gather my thoughts, but Jaymin cut me off.

"You're the subject of a prophecy, aren't you? A chosen one. The Warden told me about that," Jaymin said cheerily. "You must be doing something to investigate what it means."

My entire body went cold, and I forced an impassive look on my face. "I've been leaving it up to fate, mostly. I don't care to keep looking into it, seeing as how it caused an entire city to go up in smoke."

Jaymin gave a bemused smile. "But there must be *something* you know. One tiny piece you've worked out?"

This woman wasn't going to stop pressing. I tried to think up excuses, but Charlie broke in before I had to come up with another lie.

"Aren't we supposed to be talking about our feelings?" he asked. "I mean, that's what therapy is, right?"

"Therapy is whatever you want it to be, Charlie," Jaymin said, scribbling more down on her clipboard. She was ignoring Charlie entirely, like she didn't think he mattered. It was ableist, but her discrimination was also a benefit. She didn't think a blind person was capable of anything extraordinary, and thought the only avenues worth pursuing were the three of us. Her ignorance would help disguise the fact that Charlie had Elf blood that much longer, buying us time.

Rishi meowed. He crawled toward Jaymin's high heel, sniffing it like he smelled something rotten. He batted at the toe, yowling at Marcus.

Jaymin reached down to try and shove Rishi off her, but the cat didn't move. "The point of these sessions is— ugh! Get off me, you ugly thing."

Jaymin kicked Rishi across the circle. The cat hissed. Marcus bent down to pick him up, looking horrified.

Jaymin took a quick breath. "As I was saying, the point of these sessions is to lift the burden from your shoulders. You know you've done wrong, and that you *deserve* to be here. Think of me as a diary, one you can tell your deepest, darkest thoughts to without any fear of consequences."

"Gods, lady, we're criminals, that doesn't mean we have to feel bad about everything we do," Kallie said. She'd let her thoughts slip. Kallie immediately flattened her lips together once she'd realized her mistake.

Jaymin blinked. Her voice was cool as she replied, "Be that as it may, you all know, deep down, that your punishment is justified. I think you may even *want* it. And maybe, just maybe, we can turn you into a good person again, one whom people can love and accept. That is, if you're willing to confess to whatever bad you might still be doing. With a little hard work, anything's possible, hm?"

The guilt trip wasn't going to work with this group. Most of us already figured we were too far gone, and those that hadn't didn't care for acceptance either way, because we knew we weren't going to get it. We didn't owe this woman anything.

I think Jaymin realized that, because she switched tactics. "I'm sure, like the other inmates, the integration of the Elves into the student body has uprooted your lives. Is there anyone acting strangely among you, someone who just might sympathize with these new arrivals?"

"Why does that matter?" Charlie spat. He crossed his arms, clearly losing his temper. As painful as it was, I reached across our bond and nudged him, telling him to calm down.

"Because the Elves are a lower supernatural race, who need to be taught how to integrate into modern society," Jaymin replied, as if she was explaining something simple to a child. "They've been gone for a hundred years. They don't understand the ways of civilized culture. It's up to us to teach them. We don't need anyone telling them that their ways of being are acceptable in today's supernatural world."

"What are you talking about? The Elves are the most powerful supernatural race there is. They can take magic from others and break bonds. They had the most valuable city in the world, until the Warden took it over," Charlie responded.

He was dangerously close to exposing himself. Kallie, Marcus and I looked between each other, not knowing what to do, before Jaymin responded, "The Elves earned their wealth and power through criminal ways. They stole everything they gained and manipulated others to do it. They have to be trained."

"Trained?" Charlie asked, disgusted.

"Of course. Everyone knows that the average Elf brain is much smaller than any other supernatural's, even a merperson's," Jaymin replied. "It's common knowledge."

Charlie's mouth had fallen open in shock, and Jaymin took that as an excuse to keep talking. "The most highly spiritual and powerful individuals were able to be masters over the Elves, because the Great Spirit and the other gods made it so. Their sin is even shown in their ears, which are pointed like a devil's, and different from all the rest."

Marcus put a hand over his mouth, like he couldn't believe how offensive Jaymin was being. Kallie had ducked her head, as if she was embarrassed the fae had treated Elves so poorly.

I could feel the rage pouring off Charlie as he fumed, "That's a lie."

"You can't ignore history, Charlie. When the Elves were enslaved during the Great Supernatural War a hundred years ago, it was a good economic stabilizer. It created wealth for the other races to share. Slavery is a just punishment for lower supernatural life forms, which the Elves are," Jaymin replied.

"There's no excuse for slavery, ever," Charlie argued.

Jaymin gave a tittering, cruel laugh. "Elves cannot take care of *themselves*. They're inferior beings, who will always resort to crime if they are not controlled. They're happier if their lives are run by someone else.

This is the way of things in nature— weaker beings serve the higher ones. It is the order of the universe."

"That was the same premise the Hawkei Civil War was fought on," I said. "My parents fought against the idea that the weak have to serve the strong, and it shouldn't apply here."

"The Hawkei are different," Jaymin said, as if she was insulted I'd compare an Elementai to an Elf.

"It doesn't matter. Slavery in the supernatural world is illegal. It was outlawed after the Great Supernatural War," Marcus said nervously.

Jaymin lifted an eyebrow and said coolly, "For now."

I heard Charlie's knuckles crack as he tightened his hands into fists. He was going to explode any moment. I had to do something, before Charlie lost his shit and said something that put us all in jeopardy.

This was a therapy session. She had to talk about our mental health if we asked for help, right? It had to be a legal requirement of the job or *something*. Anything to get us off the topic of the Elves.

"My bipolar is getting unmanageable," I blurted. Kallie and Marcus glanced at me, and Charlie went still.

"Really. How so?" Jaymin crossed her legs and stared at me.

I swallowed. "I'm not happy. My condition is contributing to that."

"That's odd," Jaymin said. "When I looked at your file, it said you were on a new medication, and that you haven't experienced any major mood swings or psychotic episodes since the previous semester."

"Yes, my moods are stable. I haven't experienced any highs or bad lows in the last few months. The medication is helping with that. I'm not on the rollercoaster anymore."

I took a breath. "But I am still struggling. I haven't been eating. And I've been more depressed than usual, though I hate to admit it. It's not that I don't *want* to, I just... I don't understand how to make it stop. I need help to understand it. And get it under control."

Everything I said hadn't been a lie, either. I *did* want help. I was tired of starving myself and feeling sad. I wanted a change, and I'd do anything to make the nightmares in my head stop.

"Well, you're just going to have to get over it," Jaymin replied snidely. "The world doesn't revolve around you, Ava. It's something we all have to realize one day. I know you're a chronic liar, but you don't need to keep making up stories to get attention."

My stomach dropped to the floor. I'd had a lot of therapists in my day, and some shitty ones, but none of them had been so cruel as to say *that* to me.

I wished Professor Takahashi was here. He cared. He would've helped me figure out how to eat, how to look at things a different way, and how to feel better.

But he was gone. And in his place was this dirtbag.

I started to tear up. I got really quiet, but where I was silenced, Charlie was more than willing to be my voice. His chair clattered backward as he got up, and Oberi let out a snarl.

"Are you fucking kidding me? You think she's *making it up?*" Charlie sneered.

"Do not use that kind of language with me, Charlie. In Ava's file, it is stated that she's been known to over-exaggerate," Jaymin replied. "I am simply not willing to indulge in her fantasies, as all her enablers have. I'm sure with some positive thinking, she could learn to control her mind. She just doesn't want to."

What kind of a therapist didn't believe in mental illness? It was insane.

Kallie went to say something, but her words turned into a scream as Charlie threw his chair across the room. It went sailing in Jaymin's direction before it smashed through a window. Jaymin's mouth dropped open, looking at the window Charlie had broken.

"Charlie!" I jumped up and grabbed his arm. I held on to it tightly. It was the first time I'd touched him in... ancestors, I didn't know how long. The physical contact made Fire and Water pulse through my veins, and was so intoxicating. But I couldn't let myself be distracted, because we were in big trouble, if more wasn't coming. Oberi jumped to all fours, ready to pounce on Jaymin at Charlie's say-so.

"I'm giving you an infraction for attacking a professor!" Jaymin screeched. "If you don't want to be taken to Cellblock 9 this instant, I suggest you *back down.*"

"Don't," I whimpered. Charlie's body slackened as my grip tightened on his arm. Marcus got up and grabbed his other elbow. Charlie let us lead him away, although I could feel his body shake under my hand.

Jaymin rose, her lip in a snarl. "It's clear our session is over for today. You children obviously don't want to divulge your nasty little secrets, but we'll try again next time. I pray next week you'll be more cooperative."

I didn't know what she would do if we weren't. The four of us hurried to the staircase, our animals following behind.

Charlie's face was still stone-cold. I was sure if some asshole decided to try his patience, he wouldn't hesitate to pummel their face in, and now that he had one infraction on his record, he couldn't get another.

"We need to go somewhere private," I said.

Kallie and Marcus nodded. We hadn't dared to go to the Lair since we'd found Forevermore. We were too worried with the Warden following us around, it'd be discovered. But it was the only place I knew where Charlie could let off some steam without consequence.

"I'll make sure nobody follows," Kallie suggested. "Meet you there in a minute."

Kallie changed into a wolf and took off. Marcus and I kept hold of Charlie and didn't let him go until we were a good way into the woods.

Charlie was still fuming. He punched and kicked boulders that were in our path, and at his Earth magic, they burst into rubble. Oberi changed into a Fire unicorn and led the way until we came to the massive stone monument. The sight of it was nearly comforting, like coming home after a time spent too long away.

We walked into the Lair, which I saw with disappointment was covered with dust. We'd abandoned this place like we had everything else. The discarded Elven bow lay in the corner, and all the extra stuff we'd brought to hide lay in discarded piles.

Once we entered, the ground started shaking. Oberi stomped her hoof on the floor and tossed her head as Charlie trembled just like the earth did.

"Dude, don't bring this place down," Marcus said. "Chill out for a second."

Charlie took a few long, deep breaths. "Don't listen to her, pidge."

My heart twisted at the old name, but I knew Charlie only said it as a show of comfort. "It doesn't mean anything," I said quietly. "People have accused me of worse."

"Well, fuck them and fuck her," Charlie said. "You're not lying about that shit."

"Of course I'm not, Charlie." I'd say anything to calm him down right now. He was seconds away from causing an earthquake and sinking us down with it.

I heard a shifter morphing in the stone hallway. Kallie came into view, Alette hovering on her shoulder.

"All clear," Kallie said. "No strange scents or followers. We're still safe here."

"Thank the ancestors," I muttered. I couldn't stand losing this place, too.

"She's a joke," Charlie said hatefully, clearly referring to Jaymin.

"No shit! She's like, the worst therapist ever!" Marcus exclaimed.

"And now we're stuck with her," Kallie said glumly. "Great."

"If she's an elemental like us, where's her Familiar? I didn't see one," I said.

"She has to be hiding it somewhere," Kallie replied.

"Well, she must hate animals, because she kicked Rishi!" Marcus said. Rishi gave another yowl, and Marcus bent down to pet him.

"What do you think Rishi was smelling on her?" I asked.

Charlie paused for a moment before he said, "I don't know, but Oberi said she smelled it too. Said it resembled a corpse."

Oberi bobbed her head.

Kallie's face twisted in confusion. "I couldn't smell it. My shifter senses should've enabled me to."

"She has to be under some kind of ward, then, or a spell masking it, so students don't notice," Marcus said.

"Why is she here? She was asking a lot of weird questions during that counseling session," Kallie asked.

"I bet the Warden hired her to help root out anyone who's got Elf blood," Charlie said. "Along with figuring out what we're up to."

"I don't know why she's working for the Warden. She's an Elemental, like us," I said. "Wouldn't she want to be on the Elves' side?"

"Not if she's racist," Kallie piped up.

Charlie huffed. "I mean, she thinks Elves are devil people, so..."

"That's not enough to be here," I insisted. "There must be something else in it for her. The Warden is promising her something the Hawkei tribe can't provide."

"And we have to talk to her every week," Kallie moaned. "How are we going to come up with enough lies to keep her satisfied? She's just gonna feed whatever we say straight back to the Warden."

"We just have to give her what she wants, and make her think we're telling the truth," I said. "Let her think she's brainwashing us about the Elves. As long as we don't tell her anything about what we're actually doing, she can't use it to hurt us."

"The Warden isn't going to fall for that," Charlie objected.

"It's the best we can do," I said, nearly in defeat. "We'll just have to make it up as we go."

That was all we were doing lately, and it was so frustrating. I rubbed my eyes. "We should go back. We can't be missing for too long. Someone will notice, with the way we're being followed."

Grim notes of acknowledgement rose from the group, and we left the Lair. Kallie had football practice, so she said goodbye the moment we got to the prison yard. Marcus went to the witch alchemy lab to get catnip for Rishi, to make up for Jaymin hurting him.

That left me alone with Charlie. As much as I'd disliked being in his presence before, since the encounter with Jaymin, I didn't want to leave his side. He made me feel safe, which was a feeling all too rare at the Institute.

"Thanks for sticking up for me." I hugged my torso. "You didn't have to."

"Of course I did. Why wouldn't I?" He stuck his hands in his pockets. I curled even farther inward than I already was.

"I don't know. Things are different between us now."

"Maybe not as much as we think," Charlie offered.

I hated that feeling he created in me. Hope. Like things between us could ever get better.

I shivered as a cold autumn wind passed me by. "I hate it here," I said, looking around the prison yard. "Too many people."

Oberi nudged Charlie with her nose, and he said, "Let's go to the chapel. It's quiet there."

I wandered after Charlie and Oberi. I expected us to go into the pews, but instead, he took us to the loft, where the organ was. The dusty old instrument hadn't been touched since the last time Charlie and I had been up here, which felt like forever ago.

We'd confessed our deepest, darkest secrets in this loft. Even now, the place held a sort of reverence for us. It was better than the balcony above the prison, which was tainted now with the memory of what had happened there.

Charlie sat down at the bench and began to play. Dust particles rose off the keys as he made the organ sing, and it made a smile come to my face.

He played when he got nervous. The music helped the both of us relax. I disliked the close quarters, but Oberi pushed me forward, and I stumbled onto the bench beside Charlie.

"Ez told me you were making a new video next week," Charlie said.

I scowled. My brother and his big mouth. I was sure he had ulterior motives. "Yeah. What about it?"

"Do you want me in it?"

"What?" I nearly fell off the bench. "Um, why?"

Charlie scowled. I sensed he was going to yell at me, before he changed tactics and said, "Maybe we could make music together again. I mean, what's the harm, right? Your subscribers are going to expect me to be there."

I was about to say no, before I realized we'd never really clarified in any of the videos what Charlie and I were. It wasn't like we had to announce our breakup. My fans wouldn't know any better. As far as they knew, he was just the guy who played piano.

"Why would you want to?" I asked. I didn't get him. He'd all but implied that we shouldn't hang out, unless it was about prophecy stuff. Now he wanted to spend time with me. What was his deal? I wanted him to make up his mind.

"Because..." Charlie sighed. He stopped playing and shifted on the bench so he was closer to me. "I think it's pretty obvious that avoiding each other isn't working. We've got Oberi, who isn't healthy or happy unless we're getting along, and we're trying to save the world together, which makes things pretty awkward as it is. I think it'd be easier if we at least *tried* to do friend stuff. Clearly, we can't have a clean break."

No, we couldn't. Things were too complicated. Because of Oberi, and our prophecies, Charlie would always be in my life, and in a big way. We shared a soul bond. It wasn't like I could forget about him, like every other guy.

A bit of my unease slipped through our bond, and Charlie balked. "Never mind. It was a stupid idea."

"It's not," I said. "We should make a music video again. It'll help things feel... normal, I guess."

Whatever the hell normal was, anyway.

Charlie went to put his fingers on the keys again, but I grabbed his wrists when I heard the doors of the chapel open behind us. I wasn't sure who it was, but I had a gut feeling whoever was coming in wasn't up to any good. I'd been working on my intuition lately, and I wasn't about to doubt it now.

"Get down," I hissed. I dragged Charlie to the floor, and we scampered past the balcony and behind a wall. Oberi scrambled behind us, ducking into cover just as the door slammed shut.

On the floor below, I could hear several footsteps. I dared to peek around the banister. A lump rose in my throat as I caught sight of the Warden marching into the chapel, Professor Cusak trailing nervously behind.

"What do you mean the girl's mother is investigating? I told you to get rid of her!" the Warden hissed.

Cusak's voice trembled as he replied, "She's been difficult to exterminate. A strong succubus like her isn't easy to destroy."

"I don't care what methods you employ, just do it," the Warden demanded. "We can't have this going public!"

"But my lord, the other parents are already asking questions—"

"Then get rid of them as well," the Warden replied coolly. "You have a variety of resources at your disposal to make them seem like accidents. We can't have these families discovering the truth. It'll be a catastrophe for the Institute."

I shivered. Oberi's breath across my cheek was hot as she listened closely to what the Warden had to say.

"They'll want answers," Cusak whimpered. "If they learn of the Infernal Underground and our plans—"

My eyes widened. The Infernal Underground? What was that?

A slapping noise echoed throughout the chapel, and I realized with horror the Warden had *hit* Professor Cusak. "I've told you never to whisper that name," the Warden seethed. "It's forbidden."

"I'm sorry, my lord," Professor Cusak replied. "It's only— the inmates in Cellblock 9—"

"We've all but exhausted our resources there. We know there isn't a demigod in Cellblock 9. We've already tried to find one," the Warden replied. "Those degenerates are useless. What we're looking for is within the student body."

"Why not take the ones you've already suspected?" Cusak asked meekly. "The Mitoh girl, perhaps, or the people she associates herself with?"

I nearly choked when he said my name. Charlie slapped a hand over his mouth to keep from crying out.

"Do you think it is that *easy?*" the Warden thundered. "Ava-Marie Mitoh, though a chosen one and extremely promising, is the daughter of a chieftain, who will certainly raise war if she goes missing. Her little friends are no different. The fae girl is the daughter of a king, and the warlock boy comes from one of the most powerful families in the Miriamic Coven. Use your head, Cusak. We cannot ignite a war before we are prepared to fight it. We'll take the Mitoh girl once we've perfected the spell, and not before."

Spell? What spell was he talking about? This was getting worse by the second.

"What about the blind one? We could try him," Cusak offered. "He has no family, no one who will speak out."

There was a long silence, and I knew the Warden was greedily considering the idea. I trembled with fear as I thought of Charlie being taken. Charlie sank down against the wall, nearly to the floor.

Then the Warden spoke. "I already have Jaymin Vengier investigating. We make our move at the proper time."

Cusak gave a tiny mew of fear, and the Warden said, "You've disappointed me, Cusak. You need to be punished."

I heard a gargling sound, then an array of terrifying screams. The cries of agony grew in intensity, nearly shaking the walls.

Oh my ancestors! He was *torturing* Professor Cusak!

Charlie grabbed me and dragged me close, like he thought he could protect me from whatever was going on down there. I felt Charlie's heartbeat quicken as Cusak's screams rose throughout the chapel. Involuntarily, I buried my head in Charlie's sweater, trying to block out the noise.

A *thump* sounded as Cusak's body fell to the floor, and the Warden sneered, "You don't want to disappoint me again. You are all too easily replaced, and I have no trouble disposing of you in order to find someone who can do the job. You have until the end of the year to correct this, Cusak. Otherwise, you force my hand."

The Warden walked out, his sharp shoes slapping against the hard floor. A few moments afterward, we heard Cusak give a couple of sobs. I dared to peek out again, and saw that Cusak had used a couple of the pews to drag himself to his feet. He shuffled warily out of the chapel, head bowed and looking meek.

Charlie and I didn't dare to speak until both of them were long gone. He was still holding on to me, and I didn't want him to let me go. This was fucked up.

"They're doing everything they can to trap us," Charlie said.

"Yes, but we have our parents, so we're safe for now," I insisted.

"I don't," Charlie said hollowly. "They'll come for me first."

"Then we'll stop them, Charlie. We won't let this happen."

There was another long stretch of silence, which Oberi broke with a nicker. I cleared my throat and said, "So what's the Infernal Underground?"

"It sounded like code to me. It must be a movement of some kind, a group of people the Warden uses to hurt students," Charlie theorized.

"The Underground must be connected to the experiments the Warden is performing to find demigods," I said.

"Absolutely. It sounds like there are a lot of people involved."

Charlie opened his arms, and I finally felt safe enough to climb out of them.

I crossed my legs underneath me as I faced Charlie. "We know Jaymin is working for the Warden now, for sure. She must be part of the Underground. She's looking for an excuse to have the Warden take you."

"And I just threw a chair at her." Charlie rubbed his face. "That was fucking stupid."

"It's too late to go back now. Whatever the case, we need to outsmart her. And we need to stop the Warden from capturing us *before* it happens."

"And how do you plan on doing that?"

I smirked. "By doing what the Warden is most afraid of. Finding out what the Underground's plans are, and exposing them to the world."

"Figure that'll work?"

"It's our only shot."

My endless curiosity overwhelmed my fear as I considered all the questions before me. What exactly were the Warden's plans? And how could we stop the Infernal Underground before it was too late?

I was determined to find out.

charlie

SEVEN

The Infernal Underground.

The phrase repeated in my mind long after we'd overheard the Warden speak it. What exactly was this secret society hiding?

Our friends didn't seem to have any clue, and no one had overheard anything since we'd told them about it. I remained alert in the following weeks, waiting for a guard to jump me and cart me off to Cellblock 9 for something I didn't do— just like they'd done to Uriel. I kept my head down during my factory shifts, and I didn't speak to anyone during fight club. I was so on edge that I barely processed anything in my classes.

I thought the guards might kidnap me when I was alone, mopping the cafeteria floors as my second infraction punishment. But every night was more silent than the last. In my dorm, I lay in bed practicing my Elven magic when no one was around. I thought they might burst in at any moment, but the door remained untouched.

Nothing happened, which was almost even more terrifying. It meant the Warden was waiting for something. But waiting for what? He spoke of a spell, but what kind of magic was he planning on using?

"How many can you get, Charlie?" Alistair asked, snapping me back to attention.

"What?" I'd spaced out again.

We sat in the library after lunch. It was one of the rare moments of free time I got these days. Alistair sat beside me, and Eddie wasn't far, perusing the books in the aisle next to us. He claimed he'd tagged along to make sure I stayed safe, but I knew it was just to check out Alistair.

The warlock pushed a sheet of braille paper toward me. Pig, his pet cat, laid on the paper, before he shooed him off.

"Pop quiz," Alistair announced. "How many letters do you know?"

I ran my fingers over the bumps and frowned. "Easy. They're in alphabetical order."

"Ah, so you *have* been paying attention," Alistair said snidely. "I thought I lost you there for a minute."

I pressed my fingers to the side of my head. "I'm sorry. You've taught me a lot in our lessons, but I just can't process any of it today."

"Stressed out?" he asked, taking the braille paper back. "I hear ya. I've got some relationship problems of my own."

"It's not *relationship problems*. Not this time, at least."

I didn't want to talk about my issues, but Alistair could be a good distraction at times, so I asked, "What relationship problems are you dealing with?"

He lowered his voice. "There's this guy I like, but I don't know how to tell him."

"It's Eddie," I stated bluntly.

"What?" Alistair squeaked. "No! It's... yeah, it's Eddie. How'd you know?"

"You two shared a moment," I said, before realizing Alistair's memory of our fight in the prison yard must've been a bit fuzzy after he'd taken that memory-wiping potion. Eddie, on the other hand, had remembered the whole thing. Memory-wiping potions were apparently like noxite— a supernatural restraint that didn't work on Elves— because Eddie had met me at my dorm like he'd promised after my meeting with Captain. He remembered the whole thing, though he'd never let the guards catch on to that.

"What moment?" Alistair demanded. "Did Eddie say we shared *a moment*? Because if we did, I'm totally clueless, and I want in on it. I want *a moment*."

I smirked. "You'll have one. I'm sure of it."

Alistair leaned forward and whispered. "Eddie's gay, right? Has he said anything about me?"

I shrugged. "Why don't you ask him?"

Alistair squealed a little. "Should I? I should, shouldn't I? I can't."

He was practically begging for me to call Eddie over. I guess I could play along.

"Hey, Eddie." I whistled lowly, and Eddie slammed a book shut and hurried over to us.

"Yes, sir— I mean, Charlie?"

Beside me, Alistair practically bounced in his seat. He was so excited.

"Alistair has a question for you," I told him.

"Oh?" Eddie sounded intrigued. "Ask me anything."

Alistair fidgeted with the edge of the table, making scratching noises with his fingernail. "Are you— do you... do you like cats?"

Pig meowed and padded across the table toward Eddie. She started purring.

"I love cats," Eddie said kindly. "They're gentle companions. Always wanted one myself."

"Really?" Alistair squeaked a few pitches higher than normal. He was obviously starstruck.

It was clear our braille lesson was over, and to be honest, I wasn't into it today anyway. I had a lot on my mind, along with another fight tonight to prepare for. Not like I wanted to sit here and listen to these two flirt.

"I've got class in a bit," I announced as I stood. "You guys have fun."

Neither of them heard me as I excused myself from the library. I really hoped it worked out between them, because as much as I enjoyed Eddie's company, I appreciated a moment to myself every now and then. If I wasn't with Oberi, Eddie was following me around like a puppy. And he could really loosen up a bit. He was always so proper, with the *sir* and everything. I thought Alistair would be good for him.

It was the one good thing that happened all day. It was nice to know that somewhere in the Institute, something was going right for *someone*. Because it certainly wasn't me.

I sat in the locker room at the fight club that night, my shoulders slumped. Chancey bounced on his toes across the room, grunting as he threw practice punches into the air. Crowds cheered from outside, but I barely heard them. It was the only way to deal with fight club these days — to deal with *anything*, really. I had to dissociate. My body was here, but my mind wasn't.

"Whatcha sitting there for, Charlie?" Chancey asked, pulling my attention to the present. "You're in the ring next. You've gotta warm up."

I sighed. "What's the point? I'm sure Captain's gonna pit me against one of the toughest guys in the league. I'll lose anyway."

"Don't say that," Chancey insisted. "You're gonna go out there and win this fight, no matter *who* you're up against, you hear?"

"I'm sick of fighting," I admitted. "And not just in the ring, either. Every day of my life is one battle after another. I don't know how much longer I can go on like this."

Chancey froze. "You're not saying that you want to...?"

"No, I don't want to kill myself," I practically growled. "I want to *live*. I'm just sick of fighting for the chance to survive, you know? It gets fucking old. Don't you ever want to get out of here?"

Chancey sighed and sat beside me on the bench. "Yeah, of course I do. I'm sick of lying about fight club to Ives. I can't keep going behind his back like this. I'm going to help you find who's rigging the fights, and we'll both get out of here."

Chancey knew about my deal with Captain, because he'd been the first person I'd approached about it. Chancey took bets for the league, so if anyone had heard whispers of who was behind it, I figured Chancey would be the first to know. Unfortunately, Chancey knew as much about the rigging as I did.

"But until we catch this guy, do you want to tell me what's really going on?" Chancey asked.

"I'm pretty sure the Warden wants to harvest my organs," I said flatly.

Chancey chuckled. "Everything but your eyes."

I smirked. "Of course."

His laughter died, and his tone turned serious. "How can I help?"

"You haven't heard any whispers about the rigged fights since I last asked, have you?"

"I haven't heard a damn thing," he said regrettably. "If I do, you'll be the first to know. I hate seeing you get your ass kicked."

I nudged him in the side. "You just want me out because my bets are shit."

Chancey didn't sound amused. "Your bets are shit because Captain's punishing you. He never would've pit you against that vamp last week under normal circumstances."

I pressed my fingers to the tender bruises I still had above my eye. The vampire I'd fought had pummeled me so freaking hard, I'd gone unconscious. "No kidding. I'm not looking forward to whatever flavor of poison he's cooked up for me tonight."

I'd found out nothing about the fights, and Captain was getting impatient.

"Rumor has it I'm up against Flames tonight," Chancey said. "I hear he's a little cheat who throws punches with a bit of Fire power behind them. Your bruises turn into burns, so that'll be fun."

"Suck a little life force out of him," I suggested, only half-joking. "I'm sure that'll slow him down."

Chancey snorted. "I wish I could do that. Someday, maybe. But they're not gonna teach me as long as I'm in this hellhole."

Chancey couldn't fool me. He *loved* the Institute. He'd once let it slip that it was the only place that had ever felt like home. If he didn't end up in the adult penitentiary after he left here, it was only because he was smart and cunning, not because he'd changed his ways. He was a criminal through and through.

Though maybe that was changing now that he was with Ivy. His boyfriend was the only reason he wanted out of fight club, I was sure.

The crowd erupted outside, and an announcement boomed over the speakers.

Chancey clapped me on the shoulder. "Sounds like you're up. Good luck out there. I hope to see you win."

"Even though the bets are stacked against me?" I asked.

"It's nice to keep things interesting."

The door to the locker room burst open, and the last two fighters stormed inside, cursing up a storm at each other.

"Chancey, Bandit, you're up!" Captain growled.

Chancey shot to his feet when his name was called, but he froze beside me.

"Both of us?" I gaped. "I thought Chancey was up against Flames."

Captain didn't sound happy at all. "There's been a change to the roster. You two are in the ring. *Now!*"

For a moment, I couldn't think. I couldn't move. I realized this was a punishment, to get back at me for not figuring out who was rigging the fights. Captain expected answers by now, and because I didn't have them, he was making me fight my *friend*— as if that was supposed to motivate me. The asshole was going to punish me in every possible way until I caught this guy.

"Charlie, come on," Chancey prodded. He grabbed my arm and tried dragging me to my feet, but my legs felt like noodles.

"I'm *not* fighting you," I protested, jerking my arm away.

Chancey leaned down and hissed, "Would you rather he put Sharptooth and Steele in the ring to beat you two-to-one? Because you know he will."

Aw, fuck. I knew he was right. If I refused to fight Chancey, Captain would put me in a worse fight, where I'd be outnumbered. I'd be beaten to a pulp for sure— that is, if I made it out of the fight alive.

And yet that almost sounded like a better option than punching my buddy.

"Get your asses out here now, or you'll be cleaning blood off the ring with your tongue at the end of the night!" Captain threatened.

Chancey yanked on my arm and dragged me toward the door. He spoke in rushed whispers. "Don't hold back on me, all right? Captain will punish you if you take it easy on me."

"I don't want to do this," I hissed.

"Doesn't matter. You have to," Chancey insisted. "And you have to win! If you don't, Captain will put you up against someone that'll *kill* you next time! He's not fucking around anymore. This proves it. And I ain't letting a good friend die."

"I'm not—" I started to say, but Chancey shoved me out of the locker room. The screams from the crowd drowned everything else out.

"*Chancey! Chancey!*" the crowd shouted. He was a real fan favorite.

Chancey wasn't allowed to take bets on his own fights, but I knew where I'd put my money on this fight.

An announcement boomed through the room, but I barely heard what it said because my ears were ringing. I could handle a scuffle with my friends, but these people weren't here for that. They wanted blood. One of us had to give it to them.

Someone's hands landed on me— I didn't know whose— and they shoved me into the ring. I fumbled over the ropes, but found my footing a second before the bell rang. Chancey bounced from foot to foot, circling me in the ring. His footsteps were loud, and his heavy breaths even louder. It was like he was deliberately making it easy to track his movements.

"You're going down, Bandit!"

"Kick him in the head!"

"He's blind, for crying out loud!"

This wasn't fun anymore. I didn't feel the rush of adrenaline or the excitement of the crowd. I hadn't in weeks. This was pure torture.

Chancey threw a punch, but it was sloppy. I instinctually blocked it. I realized why he'd gone for the sloppy approach. He was warming me up, trying to get my instincts to kick in.

"Come on, Bandit!" Chancey yelled. "Fight me!"

"Don't talk to me like we're enemies," I snapped.

"We need to be right now," he growled. "Fight back."

"Make me," I said. It wasn't a threat. It was a request.

Chancey knew how to make hard decisions. It was one of the reasons I liked him. Even though we were friends, he had to hit me where it hurt.

"Fuck you! You're nothing!" Chancey shouted. "You're only in this prison because no one else wanted you. Your parents abandoned your orphan ass because they didn't want you."

I swung my fist and caught his jaw, but the strength needed to do any damage wasn't behind it. He barely staggered.

"Your punch is weak, just like your magic," Chancey accused.

I held my fists up and circled him. "You're gonna have to try harder than that."

Chancey's foot connected with my ribs, and I grunted as the air whooshed from my chest. It was a good kick, but I recovered quickly. He could've caused a lot more damage if he wanted to, which meant Chancey was trying hard not to hurt me.

I swung my arm out, but Chancey dodged it, and I stumbled forward into the ropes. This fight was pathetic, and the crowd knew it, too. They were getting bored.

"*I wanna see some blood!*"

"*Show him what you've got, Chancey!*"

Captain's voice broke through the roaring crowd. "Knock him down, dammit!"

Chancey jumped me from behind, tackling me to the ground. He punched me between the shoulders, conveniently between two bruises. He sat on top of me, pressing the side of my face into the floor. I bucked him off as quickly as I could, then kicked him square in the gut before he could get to his feet. The crowd cheered. We both jumped to opposite sides of the ring as we scrambled upright.

"You're right," Chancey said. "Your magic doesn't make you weak. You know what does? Your hopeless attachment to Ava-Marie."

My temper flared immediately. "Don't cross the line," I warned him.

"Maybe I need to!" he spat over the roar of the crowd. "You need to take this fight seriously!"

I scoffed as I rocked my weight between my feet. "Your lame attempt at trash talk is starting to piss me off."

"Good," he said. "Then I'm succeeding."

I jumped at Chancey. I aimed for his face, but my fist landed on his shoulder. He cried out, but I suspected it was more for the crowd's benefit than anything. I hadn't hit him very hard.

"You're a pathetic little child who needs a woman to give you purpose," Chancey accused. "You're devastated about Ava because you're afraid no one will ever love you again. You have no idea who you truly are, because everything that was ever good about you is part of Ava now—"

I lowered my shoulder and threw myself at Chancey. My shoulder landed on his gut, and we went flying into the ropes. We bounced off of them, and he rolled across the ground, landing on his stomach. I jumped on top of him before he could move. I wrapped my arms around his leg and yanked it backward, pinning the other one under my knee. The crowd screamed in exhilaration.

"You're an asshole, you know that?" I growled.

"I'm just telling it like it is!" He laughed.

I didn't know if Chancey believed anything he'd said, but I didn't question it, either. If I did, I wasn't sure I'd be able to finish this fight.

Chancey hooked the back of his knee around my neck and flipped the both of us over, until he gained the upper hand. At this point, we were just trying to make the fight look good. He squeezed my neck tight with his legs, so much that I began gasping for air.

"That's it!" Captain shouted from outside the ring. The crowd went wild as I struggled for breath. "Get him!"

I punched Chancey a few times in the leg, but he didn't let up.

"Come on, Charlie!" he cried. "You can do better than that!"

Chancey punched me in the face, and one of my wounds from my last fight broke open. Blood trickled down my cheek and into my mouth. I spat it out, and the crowd went wild.

"Hit me harder, Charlie!" Chancey screamed. "Do it! Make me bleed!"

I panicked, because I was running out of air. I tried cheating, because I just didn't care anymore, and I forced Air into my lungs with my magic.

But it wasn't enough. Chancey had cut off my airways. He wanted me to play dirty.

And so I did.

I grabbed a handful of skin on Chancey's leg and twisted so hard I was sure he'd end up with a bruise larger than my head. Chancey cried out in pain, which sounded real this time. His hold on me let up, and I shoved him off of me, gasping for breath.

"Finish him off!" someone in the crowd screamed.

The world spun around me as I drew in greedy breaths. Chancey had nearly knocked me out, and I stumbled as I got up.

"Chase me, Charlie," Chancey taunted as he hobbled to the other end of the ring. I must've really hurt him.

I stumbled toward him and kicked, but I missed him entirely. It was more or less on purpose.

It must've pissed Chancey off, because he spat, "Why don't you channel that part of Ava you're so attached to? You're just as nutty as she is. Go psycho on me, just like your crazy-ass ex-girlfriend—"

That was the last straw. My fist connected with the side of Chancey's head, and he went down. He hit the floor so hard, I was certain he'd been knocked out instantly.

The crowd screamed so loud that my head spun. Captain stepped into the ring and announced me the winner, but I barely heard it over the roar of the crowd. All I could focus on was Chancey being hauled off to the med tent on a stretcher.

Chancey was one of my closest friends, and I'd fucked him up because he'd gotten to me about Ava. I could hardly live with myself.

"You did well, Bandit," Captain praised. "Keep fighting like that, and I'll be a little more generous in the ring."

"You're a cold-blooded snake," I seethed.

Captain laughed. "A proud snake. Hit the showers. You look disgusting."

My nostrils flared, and my hands curled into fists. *The bastard!* I jumped out of the ring, Captain's laughter echoing behind me over the crowd.

I shoved my way past the next fighters and burst through the door to the locker room. I was so pissed that I couldn't hold back. My fist slammed into the closest locker, the sound echoing through the empty room. Pain radiated through my knuckles.

"Fuck this!" I screamed.

Captain knew exactly what he was doing— knew exactly how to *motivate* me. No matter how much I enjoyed the fights, I didn't care to knock out one of my best friends. I had no interest in continuing to play this man's puppet.

I needed to get out of fight club as fast as I could. Problem was, I wasn't going anywhere without some damn answers.

Without them, I was fucked.

"CHARLES WAHKIN."

The sound of my name rattled my bones. I sat beside Eddie in Supernatural Government when a guard came in. He'd listed off a bunch of names before getting to mine. Oberi tensed at my feet, pressing his body to my legs protectively.

"Come with me," the guard demanded.

Chairs squeaked as half a dozen students rose from their chairs. No one questioned where we were going. We already knew.

They were blood testing us for Elven heritage.

The Warden must've increased demand for testing, because I'd heard people were getting pulled out of class all week. I knew they'd get to me eventually, but I'd hoped I had more time.

What the hell was I going to do?

"Charlie...?" Eddie whispered.

Get up, Oberi said. *The guard is watching you.*

My fists shook on the top of my desk. *I can't*, I told him.

You can, and you will, Oberi demanded.

The Warden will figure out what I am, I reminded him.

No, he won't. Let's go. Oberi nudged me with his wet nose, and I stood.

"What are you going to do?" Eddie hissed.

"I don't know yet," I whispered back, before Oberi nipped at me to get me moving.

The guard huffed, like he didn't like to be kept waiting, but he turned out of the room, and the rest of us followed. He started giving some speech about how this was just routine to keep everyone safe, but I was preoccupied with Oberi.

Tell me you have a plan, I begged.

Not yet, but we'll figure something out, he assured me.

You're awfully confident for a dog without a plan, I practically growled.

It's a gift, he replied in a snarky tone. *Get in line.*

Oberi guided me behind the other students as we slowed outside the infirmary. The area buzzed with chatter. I didn't know how many students they'd pulled out of class, but it must've been close to a hundred. The infirmary was so crowded that people pushed past me to get out the door.

The Warden must be getting impatient, I remarked to Oberi.

Or he perfected his testing method, he theorized. *This place is a zoo. I bet no one would notice if we left.*

Probably not, but that doesn't help us, I replied thoughtfully. *They must be keeping some sort of record. The Warden will know I wasn't tested.*

"This way!" a nurse called, and my group moved forward. "Your station just opened up over here."

Several students in other lines groaned as we went ahead of them to a new station. It was pretty obvious no one wanted to waste any time being here.

"Your name?" another nurse asked the student at the front of our line.

"Anna Davis," she replied timidly.

I heard the shuffling of papers.

"Anna Davis," the nurse said thoughtfully. "Ah, here's your record card. Hold your finger out. You'll just feel a prick. It'll all be over in a minute."

It was less than a minute, and Anna was already done. The chair squeaked as she got up, and the next person sat.

I started to panic. There couldn't have been more than five people in front of me.

Shit, I said to Oberi. *We've gotta think of something— and fast. Give me a run-down of the area.*

There's one nurse per station. They're pricking fingers and placing drops of blood into a solution. All the solutions are turning blue.

That must be a negative test, I said to Oberi. *Mine won't be blue.*

They're marking the results on a clipboard with a stamp, Oberi observed.

That's it! I realized. *Oberi, you have to get my sheet and mark it negative.*

And just how do you expect me to do that—? he started to say, but he cut off as a cry broke out in the infirmary.

At the station beside me, a girl began screaming. "No, no! I can't! I *hate* needles. Please don't make me!"

"You need to sit still, young lady," the nurse snapped. "This test was ordered by the Warden."

"I don't care!" the girl yelled. "I can't. I'm gonna pass out! I— I—" She broke off as she broke out in sobs.

"Daphne," the nurse barked. "I need help with this one!"

"I'll be right there," the nurse at my station replied hastily. A beat passed, then she rushed over to help hold the girl down. I heard the sound of a clipboard land on the ground, then noticed the flutter of pages scattering.

I shoved Oberi. *That's your cue. Go!*

Oberi darted away from me, and my heart slammed against my rib cage. I held my breath, despite my fear of ever being without air. I was so nervous.

How's it going? I asked Oberi in my mind.

Don't pressure me, he shot back.

The nurse will be back any moment. Hurry up.

I've got the stamp. I'm just looking for... aha!

Oberi didn't say anything else. Several beats passed before I heard the nurse snap, "And just what do you think *you're* doing!?"

My heart lurched. *Oberi!*

A second later, he was at my side, panting. *It wasn't me!*

The nurse exploded. "You think you can steal needles from my station! I'm reporting you to the Warden!"

"I— I— didn't," some idiot ahead of me stammered. He'd been trying to steal syringes in order to do drugs. What a moron.

"I just saw you!" the nurse snapped. "I caught you red-handed. Guards!"

Several guards hurried over and hauled the guy away, while the nurse shuffled papers back into her clipboard loudly.

Oberi shoved something that felt like paper into my hand. It was wet with slobber, but I grabbed it tightly.

Put this on your middle finger, Oberi instructed.

I realized it was a bandage. I worked as quickly and discreetly as I could, peeling back the layers and shoving them in my pocket, then wrapping it around the end of my finger. My shoulders relaxed the second it was done.

Oberi nudged me. *You're up.*

I felt for the edge of the chair and sat, giving an annoyed breath.

"Name?" the nurse asked.

"Charlie Wahkin," I told her. "But I don't get why I have to get my finger pricked *again*."

"What do you mean *again*?" she asked skeptically.

"I already got tested this morning," I lied, holding up my hand to show her the bandage. "What, was one negative test not good enough for you people? I'm an Elementai with Air magic. I don't know how many tests I have to take to prove that."

Just to drive my point home, I moved my hand through the air and sent a soft breeze through her hair.

"Hmph," she huffed, sounding displeased. "I don't know why they called you down here again... huh, that's weird."

I swallowed the lump in my throat. "What's that?"

"Your test results are in my *incomplete* file," she said, sounding confused. "I don't know how that got there, since your results have already been recorded. No wonder they called you down here."

"Great," I groaned. "Of all the mix-ups there could be, *I'm* the one whose paperwork gets put in the wrong pile. To think if it got lost and I had to do this all over again. It's bullshit."

"It's a waste of my time and resources is what it is," she said impatiently. "Either way, it's sorted now. You can get back to class."

Thank the ancestors, I thought.

I scrambled out of the chair and into the hall faster than I'd ever moved before. As soon as Oberi and I were outside the infirmary, I breathed a sigh of relief.

That was lucky, Oberi remarked.

No shit, I agreed.

I put my hand on Oberi's back, and he led me away from the infirmary. It wasn't until we'd turned several corners that I realized I didn't know where we were going.

Shouldn't we be headed back to class? I asked him.

Class is over by now, he pointed out.

Where are you taking me?

You'll see, he replied simply.

Oberi, I groaned internally. *Tell me where we're going, or I'll—*

You'll what? he challenged.

Oberi rushed ahead of me, then a door creaked open. I stopped dead when I heard the sound of an angelic voice spilling out into the hall. She sang a beautiful tune that warmed my heart.

I barely heard a second of the song before she cut off and cried, "Oberi!"

I stepped toward the music room and pushed the door open wider. Oberi had shifted, and she stomped her hooves happily.

I scowled. *What a greeeat surprise.*

Did I tell you it'd be great? she snickered.

"Charlie," Ava breathed, sounding surprised.

"Pi— Ava," I replied, catching myself before I could call her *that.*

Ava must've noticed the bandage on my finger, because she gasped. "They tested you?"

"No, thank the ancestors," I said as I ripped the bandage off. "Oberi forged some paperwork. As far as anyone knows, my test is negative."

She breathed a sigh of relief. "Thank the Great Spirit."

"It'll hold the Warden off for now, at least," I said. I didn't know if the ruse would last forever.

A beat passed, like Ava was thinking. The piano bench squeaked as she stood. "You don't look good."

My shoulder slumped. "You gonna give me a lecture?"

"I was thinking of giving you *makeup,* to cover up that black eye you're sporting," she responded. "But if you want a lecture—"

"I don't," I replied curtly. I'd been walking around with bruises for months, and Ava hadn't said anything. We'd all just ignored the topic, like fight club didn't exist. It must've looked pretty bad if Ava was bringing it up now.

Ava tugged at my arm. "Sit down. I have some makeup in my bag. I'll make you look brand new."

I groaned, but I sat anyway. "No one cares."

A case snapped open, then Ava began brushing powder over my face. "My *followers* care. I can't have you record another music video looking like that."

I froze. Ava got so close that her breath brushed across my face. Heat flared in my stomach, but I ignored it. We'd agreed to make music videos together again, but we hadn't planned a time to do it. I thought for sure it'd be one of those things we *said* we were going to do, but never actually got around to doing.

"Did you post anything new yet?" I asked, trying to keep my tone steady.

"One thing," she admitted as she dabbed makeup over my bruises. Her tone was casual, like we were old friends catching up. It hurt a little, to be honest. "Ez played guitar while I sang, but I think my followers were disappointed. They wanted to see you on piano. You were quite popular with them."

"I was?" I asked, loosening up. "I've never been popular with *anyone.*"

"That's not true," she protested. "After we came in second in the Games, all the girls wanted to fuck you. Maybe even some guys."

I chuckled lightly. "Well, there was only one girl I wanted—"

I cut off before the full confession came out, but we both knew what I was going to say. Ava's brush paused on the end of my nose, then she drew away suddenly.

She fumbled with the makeup in her bag as she spoke. "I promised them you'd be back this week," she said sheepishly. "I don't know why I said it. I never asked you when you wanted to, and... and—"

I reached out for Ava's wrists, because I could hear that she was getting flustered. Her skin was hot, but welcoming. Electricity surged between us when we touched, making my heart come alive in my chest. I should've drawn away, but I couldn't bring myself to. I was so entranced by her presence.

Ava didn't pull away, either— at least, not right away. Her breath hitched. We just sat there for a moment, as if we were addicted to the sweet tenderness of each other's touch. Neither of us wanted it to end, and so, we held on a beat longer than we should have.

Eventually, Ava dropped her hands. A chill rushed over my fingers where her skin had just been. All I wanted was to touch her again. The woman was like a drug— one hit, and I was done for.

"I— I'm sorry," I stammered. "I shouldn't have—"

"It's okay," she said softly. "I'm almost done."

Ava dabbed more powder on my face, and neither of us spoke. Oberi didn't make a sound, either. She was probably sitting over in the corner, cheering us on. The little shit.

I was deeply aware of every movement Ava made and every breath she took. It was like I had to drink her in when she was this close, because I didn't know if it'd be the last time. Thank the ancestors she couldn't hear my heart racing in my chest.

"There," she announced proudly when she'd finished. "You look hot."

My cheeks flamed, but Ava quickly corrected herself. "For my fans, I mean."

"Well, they're the ones who care," I pointed out, but it came out sounding lame.

To break the tension, I spun around on the piano bench and faced the keys, running my fingers over them lightly.

"What are we playing?" I asked. "Have you written anything new lately?"

"A few things," she said as she sat beside me. Her proximity was intoxicating. "Most of it I'm still working on, but I'm almost finished with this one."

A few papers rustled as she set them on the piano. "I just can't get the last verse right. Maybe you can help me with the chords."

"Sing it for me," I suggested.

Ava began singing, and I nearly fell off the bench, it was so beautiful. When her voice filled the room, it was like nothing else existed but that incredible tune. I hardly knew up from down.

The scent of magic fills the air
This is my ancestry
Bound up in my hair

I rediscover what was me
Reclaiming all I once had
And who I am to be.

After she finished, all I could do was sit there, letting her words echo around in my mind. They were so beautiful, I couldn't think.

"What do you think?" she asked.

"About what?" I replied lamely.

"The last verse," she replied. "It needs work, doesn't it?"

"The lyrics were perfect," I said honestly. "I think you need a key change."

I began playing chords to match the tune she'd sung, then switched them up on the key change.

"That's perfect!" Ava cried, bouncing a little on the bench. "Oh, Charlie! Our fans are going to love this!"

I stopped playing. "*Our* fans?"

"Um, well... I guess? They like us both, so I guess they're *ours*."

It was nice to have something that was *ours*— besides Oberi— though I'd never admit it.

"I think I've got a good handle on the chord progression," I said. "It repeats the same four chords until that key change. How does this sound?"

I played the chord progression a few times, throwing in an arpeggio to make it interesting.

"That sounds really good," Ava remarked. "Keep going."

I continued playing, and Ava started singing. I couldn't get over how amazing the song was, even after half an hour passed and I must've heard it a dozen times.

"I think we're ready to record something," Ava said.

"I'm set if you are," I agreed.

"Let me just get the camera set up—"

Ava's words halted as both of us felt the shift. Silence dominated the prison. The only sound I heard was our ragged breathing. It was like that for nearly ten seconds before sound resumed in the prison again, and the air ceased to be fragile.

She grabbed my hand and squeezed it. "Did you notice that?"

"Yes. Kallie stopped time," I said.

"Why?" Ava asked. "We agreed she wouldn't unless—"

Ava cut off as the door to the music room burst open. Several people stumbled inside, before the door slammed shut behind them.

"Behind the piano!" Kallie barked. A moment later, the sound of a light switch clicked. She must've turned the lights off. I heard the sound of Alette's wings flutter as she crossed the room.

Marcus whimpered and scurried behind the piano. He must've stepped on Rishi's tail, because the cat yowled. Oberi stomped her hooves, like she was worried.

"Ancestors!" Ava cried, shooting up from her seat.

"What's going on?" I demanded.

"Everybody quiet!" Kallie hissed. "Get down!"

Ava yanked on my shirt. We both ducked behind the piano beside Kallie and Marcus. I slipped on something wet when I went to hide, and I fell onto my knees. Oberi shifted into a husky and ducked beneath the bench.

Outside, I heard people shouting— which was saying something, because the music room was supposed to be soundproof.

"Where'd that motherfucker go?" someone screamed.

"This way!" someone else called.

"Marcus, what happened to your face?" Ava hissed in a low whisper.

A chill rippled through my stomach when I realized I'd slipped in blood.

"Shh!" Kallie snapped.

Nobody moved. I didn't think we breathed for a good thirty seconds. Even after the voices faded down the hall, we waited.

After at least a minute, Kallie finally stood. "I think the coast is clear."

Ava groaned as she crawled out from behind the cramped quarters. "Do you mind telling us what the hell is going on?"

Kallie walked to the other end of the room, and the light switch clicked again. "Yeah, *Marcus*," she said sternly. "Want to tell them what happened?"

Marcus sighed and plopped down on the piano bench. Oberi and I stood in the corner, awaiting an explanation.

"Some guys jumped me outside the cafeteria," he admitted, though his words were slurred. "They— ow."

Ava must've touched a wound, because Marcus sucked a breath.

"Please tell me you still have first-aid supplies," Ava begged.

"A few." He must've conjured something, because Ava ripped open a package.

"They had me surrounded," Marcus continued. "I was on the ground, and they were kicking me when Kallie..."

"When Kallie what?" I asked when he trailed off.

"When she showed up and saw what was happening," Marcus said. "She was like my own personal guardian angel."

"Don't make it out like it was romantic," Kallie said bitterly. "I had to stop time to drag Marcus out of there, but we only had a ten-second head start. I almost exposed myself to save your ass!"

"Those assholes aren't going to question it," Marcus promised.

"What if someone *saw*?" she retorted, and her voice cracked. "We have to be extra careful, and I can't do that if I have to stop time to protect you!"

Kallie made it sound like she was mad at Marcus, but it was obvious what was clearly going on. She was more upset that Marcus had the shit beat out of him. Anyone with a brain could see that.

"Charlie, can you help me?" Ava requested.

I went over to her, and she handed me a few pieces of medical tape to hold while she worked on bandaging up Marcus.

"What I want to know is *why* they were saying that stuff about you," Kallie demanded.

"What stuff?" I asked, my gut sinking. Kallie made it sound like this wasn't a random attack, which only meant one thing.

Kallie breathed heavy, angry breaths. "*You and your friends are gonna pay. You're a dead man walking.* Marcus, they were going to kill you!"

"It's not— ow! It's not like that," he insisted.

Ava took the last bits of tape from my hands, and I crossed my arms. Marcus still hadn't told the girls about what he'd been up to all summer, and it was starting to piss me off.

"Then what *is* it like?" Kallie demanded.

Silence stretched between the group, and I couldn't take it.

"Tell them, Marcus," I pressed. "Tell them, or I will."

"Tell us what?" Ava asked, sounding worried.

Marcus didn't say anything.

"We agreed to work together, and we can't keep secrets like this anymore," I said. "It could put us all in danger."

Kallie stomped her foot. "Tell us what's going on, or so help me, Marcus."

"Fine," Marcus sighed in defeat.

Ava must've finished bandaging him up, because she stepped back. Marcus drummed his fingers on the piano bench nervously.

"The truth is... uh... those guys were rivals. Last summer, I joined a gang," Marcus spat out.

"You WHAT?!" Kallie cried.

"Ancestors!" Ava gasped at the same time.

"Do you have any idea how stupid that is?" Kallie screamed.

"Yeah, yeah, I know!" Marcus shot back. "You just think I'm a stupid, pathetic loser!"

"I don't think that—" Kallie started, but Marcus cut her off.

"Yes, you do!" Marcus yelled. "You tell me that all the time."

"Because you *are* stupid!" she screamed. "Joining a gang *is* stupid, and you can't argue that!"

Marcus shot to his feet. "I joined the Dead Men Walking because I had no one else! You all stopped caring about me, and I had *nowhere else to go*! I don't need your fucking lecture, Kallie. I need your support!"

A small bout of silence stretched through the room. Kallie hiccupped, before she broke out into sobs. I nearly stumbled backward in shock. Kallie wasn't the kind of person to let other people see her cry. It made the tears that much more surprising.

"I care!" Kallie cried. "I've *always* cared! I'm a shifter, and shifters are supposed to defend their mates, regardless of whether we're together or not. You joined a gang because I wasn't there, and I— I—"

Kallie gasped, and ancestors, the tension was unbearable. Kallie never brought up that she and Marcus were bonded. Marcus didn't, either. They never talked about it, since they'd both agreed not to date.

But what she'd just said was everything. Kallie still saw Marcus as her mate, whether she admitted it or not. And it was killing her that they weren't together.

What she'd said was so similar to how I felt about Ava, and hell, it ached.

Marcus sighed heavily. It was obvious he felt really bad about upsetting her. His tone softened. "I know it was dumb to join a gang, and I'm sorry. I wish I could go back and change it, but I can't."

"It doesn't matter. We need to get you out," Kallie said.

"It hasn't been a total waste," he offered. "The Dead Men Walking know how to get through wards. I've been trying to learn how to break wards myself. With my Curse Breaker powers, I should be able to do it, but I haven't figured it out yet. And my mind-reading powers are getting me nowhere. I've been trying to use them on the Warden to uncover his secrets, but he must have some sort of protection spell blocking his mind, because I haven't heard anything from him. I have to rely on the Dead Men to get into the Warden's office if I want to uncover anything. Bones developed a potion to get past his barriers."

So *that's* how Marcus was getting into the Warden's office. I knew the Dead Men had something to do with it, but I didn't know Bones had created a potion.

"I thought Bones was an idiot," I said.

"He's smarter than you think," Marcus replied.

"The Warden's office!" Kallie exploded. "Don't tell me you went in there!"

"So what if I did?" Marcus challenged.

"Gods, Marcus!" Kallie cried. "The Warden is the most dangerous man in the world, and you're just strolling into his office like it's your grandma's house."

"My grandma's house is—" Marcus started, but Kallie cut him off.

"I thought we agreed to lie low," she continued. "This is a far cry from lying low. If you get caught, it jeopardizes everything."

"Well, I haven't been caught yet," Marcus snapped.

"How does this potion work?" Ava asked, steering the conversation away from their argument. Kallie sniffled in the corner.

Marcus sank back down onto the piano bench. "I'm not sure, exactly. Bones is an Alchemist. He developed it himself. When I drink it, it confuses the ward. It thinks I'm the Warden, so the alarm doesn't go off."

"It makes you look like the Warden?" Ava asked, sounding intrigued.

"No," Marcus said. "It must change something energetically so the ward doesn't know the difference between him and me. It only lasts a few minutes, though, and it's not very strong. I don't think it would work on a ward bigger than one room. I have to be really quick when I go in."

"What are they sending you in there for?" I asked, worry knotting in my gut.

"Bones sent me in to dig up dirt on the Warden," Marcus admitted. "He wants to blackmail the Warden to get the Dead Men Walking pardoned. I haven't found anything useful to Bones, but I *did* find something you all might be interested in."

I leaned forward, curious. "What's that?"

Marcus drew a deep breath. "The Warden has figured out the wording to your prophecy, Charlie."

My stomach dropped out of my abdomen.

"What? How?" Ava demanded.

"Forevermore, of course," Marcus said, like it was obvious. "His records indicate that the Elves burned pretty much everything before they fled Forevermore, but there must've been something left behind about the prophecy, because he has it written on a bulletin board in his office, with all these notes about the Elf Prince."

I swayed on my feet. "He doesn't know...?"

"Not yet," Marcus assured me. "I couldn't find anything that suggests he knows you're the heir. He thinks he's looking for the Emperor's son, not his grandson. Records that showed Cameron was Cassiel's son must've been burned, too, because there's nothing about your dad in there."

"Shh..." I hissed. "I know the music room is soundproof, but can we *please* be quiet when we talk about this shit?"

Marcus cleared his throat. "Right. Anyway, the Warden doesn't know who he's looking for. He's got pictures of all the Elves at the Institute on his board. He must assume the heir grew up in Forevermore. But I don't think he's gotten anywhere with the Elves. That's why he's blood testing everyone."

"So he must suspect the heir is here," Ava said thoughtfully.

"But why?" I questioned. "Thousands of Elves escaped. Why wouldn't he assume the heir escaped with them?"

"There are prophets in all types of supernatural religions," Kallie cut in. Her voice shook, like she was trying to keep the tears at bay. "Marcus' whole coven is at least a quarter Seer. I'm sure the Warden would've tried to get answers from someone. They may not be able to see clearly *who* the heir is, but someone with strong psychic abilities could've told him the heir was at the Institute."

"Fuck," I growled under my breath. "So all it takes is one prophet to lead him straight to us?"

"Psychic visions tend to be very unclear," Marcus told me. "But I think Kallie's on the right track. Regardless of how he knows, the Warden suspects the heir is here."

"Is there more?" I asked.

"I've told you everything I've learned so far," Marcus said.

Ava paced around the room, sounding thoughtful. "We need some of that potion. We have to learn more."

Marcus blew a breath. "I can't just waltz up to Bones and get an endless supply of it. It's his own brew. He's not going to just hand it over."

"Then we'll brew it ourselves," Ava said simply.

"I don't know the recipe," Marcus said.

"So we get our hands on it," Ava suggested.

"No," Kallie protested sharply. "Marcus isn't going to do anything to get himself in trouble with these people."

Marcus sighed. "Even if I wanted to, I'm not sure I could. There are some potions that are unique to their creators. I've never seen Bones brew it, but I'm guessing this is one of them. It's too unique for just anyone to brew."

"They'll keep sending you in, though, right?" Ava wondered aloud. "Can we learn more about the Warden that way?"

"I'm sure of it," Marcus said. "But I don't know what more I'll learn. The Warden only leaves so much out in the open."

"Did you find out anything about the Infernal Underground, like who might be part of it?" I asked.

"No." Marcus sighed. "That's one thing I haven't been able to figure out. The Warden is keeping any information about the Infernal Underground under tight wraps."

Kallie stepped forward. "I don't like this. Whether this gang helps us get answers or not, it puts Marcus in danger. He has to leave."

"And how do you suggest I do that?" he demanded. "You can't leave a gang once you join it. They'll hurt me. Plus, we need this. It's our key into the Warden's office, which gives us an advantage."

I frowned. "Kallie's right. This can't go on much longer. Eventually, we have to find some way to get you out of the gang. Either Bones will kill you, or those other guys will."

"I know." Marcus sounded defeated. "It's just not possible."

"I'll kill Bones in the ring," I offered.

Marcus burst out laughing, like I was joking. I wasn't. "That's a great idea. Then the rest of the Dead Men Walking can murder *you*, or even go after Ava or Oberi to get to you."

My stomach twisted. Marcus was right. I couldn't make rash decisions about this.

"We might as well give up," Marcus said in defeat. "I joined the gang, I took the oath. I'm stuck in it now, till I'm fucking dead."

"Bullshit," Kallie spat. "This isn't a death sentence."

"Yeah," Ava said. "We'll get you out of this, Marcus."

Marcus made a skeptical sound, but I agreed with the girls. I wasn't going to give up. One way or another, I was getting him out.

I just had to be smart about it— or Marcus wouldn't be the only one six feet under once the gang got done with us.

ava-marie

EIGHT

Marcus was risking his life to get us more information on the Warden and the Infernal Underground. But I wasn't sure it was worth it. Stopping the Warden was critical, but I didn't want to lose a friend.

Or *friends*, if this situation didn't turn out well. With Marcus being in a gang, all of us were at risk.

I was walking to the music room on Monday, looking to get some practice in before class, when I heard a scuffle around the corner. It sounded like a body being thrown against a wall. Oberi started, her hooves slipping against the carpet. I hurried to see what was going on, and a lump formed in my throat at the sight in front of me.

It was Ivy, and he had *Charlie* pinned up against the wall. Ivy held Charlie in place with one hand, his fingers around Charlie's neck. His fangs were on display, and his eyes were blood-red. He looked completely murderous.

Charlie didn't make a move to fight back, just grasped at Ivy's wrist and wrenched, like he was doing his best to defend himself, but couldn't.

I froze in shock. What was going on?

"Breaking Ava's heart was mistake number one. Beating the shit out of my boyfriend was mistake number two," Ivy seethed. "Tell me why I shouldn't snap your neck right here, right now."

My heart pounded against my ribcage so quickly it nearly ached. This didn't make any sense. Why would Charlie hurt Chancey? He would never. They were close. But something must've gone down; otherwise, Ivy wouldn't be losing his shit.

I instantly knew what had happened— that bastard Captain and his damn fight club. This was his doing, making friends fight each other so the guards could get a kick out of it.

Charlie didn't say anything, and Ivy slammed him against the wall again. I cringed as Charlie let out a gasp of pain.

Ivy leaned in to whisper, "You ain't gonna get away with this. You forget, I ain't your run-of-the-mill average whore."

Ivy had a reputation for being a prostitute, but I knew full well he was deadly. His grip tightened on Charlie's neck, and Charlie cringed.

Oberi lowered her horn, ready to charge at Ivy, but she was waiting on my say-so. I waved her off, telling her to stand down, before I tried to force my way between them.

"Ivy, stop it!" I demanded. I put a hand on Ivy's arm and attempted to wrench him off Charlie. It was like moving a concrete statue.

"This one's no good, precious. I say we deal with him once and for all," Ivy spat.

I was worried he would use his vampire strength to pop Charlie's head clean off his shoulders. "It wasn't his fault," I rushed to say. "He had no choice."

"I don't care what the reasons were. You should see Chance." Ivy's eyes narrowed.

"I didn't want to, Ivy." Charlie managed to choke out the words, though his shoes kicked at the floor.

"And I don't wanna be in here neither, but guess where I am." Ivy's chest heaved. I didn't think he'd hurt Charlie, not with me here, but there was a darkness inside of him that was definitely contemplating it. I could feel it.

I was terrified I wouldn't be able to stop this, until I heard someone say, "Ives, let him go."

Chancey really did look like shit. His face was swollen and bruised, and he had a nasty black eye that he could barely see out of. Charlie had done a number on him. I could hardly blame Ivy for being pissed. If things were the other way around, I'd be plucking Chancey's feathers out one by one.

Chancey put a firm hand on Ivy's arm. "You don't want to hurt him, Ives. He's our friend, remember?"

"Yeah? You gonna call him a friend after he did that to you?" Ivy challenged.

"He had to, Ives. I let him. Just back off."

Ivy glanced at me, and I figured I had to look pretty desperate. At my pleading, and at Chancey's demand, Ivy backed down. He let go of Charlie, and he fell to the floor. I knelt beside him, rubbing his back as he coughed. Oberi knelt down and sniffed his hair.

"So which one of you two palookas are gonna tell me why you felt the need to beat the shit outta each other?" Ivy said, putting a hand on his hip. "Or am I gonna have to strangle that outta you, too?"

"It... it was fight club," Chancey admitted heavily.

Oh, shit. I swear something dark flashed in Ivy's red eyes as he completely lost it. "You're in the *fucking fight club?*"

"Yeah, I'm in fight club," Chancey shot back. "And sometimes it ain't pretty, as you can see."

"You just can't stop gambling, can you? I *knew* you were doing some shit behind my back, losing money betting on fights," Ivy growled.

"I quit all that," Chancey argued. "All I do now is get in the ring."

"And get your mug turned to a pulp! Why the hell didn't you tell me?" Ivy yelled.

"Because I knew you'd react like this," Chancey shot back. "You can't beat the shit out of every shifter, vamp or elemental that kicks my ass!"

"Can't I? *Can't I?*" Ivy screeched.

"Look, Charlie and I are trying to get out of it. We gotta talk about this someplace else," Chancey said, and he put his arm around Ivy's shoulders. "You're coming with me, doll face. *Now.*"

Ivy sneered, but he let Chancey lead him off. I could hear Ivy yelling insults all the way down the hallway as Chancey dragged him in the direction of the angel cellblock.

"Are you okay?" I asked Charlie as he slumped against the wall.

"I'm fine," he said, rubbing his neck. "Ivy's got one hell of a grip, though. You were right about him being strong."

"Why didn't you defend yourself?" I demanded.

"I couldn't hit him back. I already felt bad enough about Chancey. At this point, everyone I care about is getting hurt because of me. It felt justified to let Ivy do what he wanted."

"You shouldn't be punishing yourself, or letting other people punish you." I looked closer at his neck. Ivy hadn't left any bruises, so maybe he hadn't wanted to hurt Charlie after all.

"Why not? Maybe I'll stop fucking up."

I shook my head. "Charlie, you've got to get out of fight club. At this rate, it's just as bad as Marcus' gang. It's going to kill you."

"I'm doing what I can to figure out who's fixing the fights, but I haven't gotten anywhere. All the people I've talked to say they know nothing," Charlie replied.

"Someone's lying. They have to know," I insisted.

"If they do, they aren't telling me."

I helped Charlie off the floor and brushed off his clothes. It was so natural, I didn't realize I was doing it until he was all clean, so I stopped. "I was going to the music room, but I think my creativity's been rattled out of me."

"I was actually looking for you," Charlie stated.

"Me?" My heart got that stupid fluttery feeling again, and I hated it, so I quashed it. Like a bug.

"Yeah. I think I might have made some headway on the Infernal Underground."

"Really? How?"

"Come with me."

Charlie put a hand on Oberi's back to lead him onward, and the unicorn ambled ahead. Oberi took us to the library, to a back corner that was practically deserted. Charlie skimmed his hand along the spines of books until he found one he recognized and opened it. Inside was a stack of papers. It looked like he'd tucked them away for safe-keeping.

"Alistair and I found these news articles while we were looking for books that had braille," Charlie said, and he handed the stack of papers to me. "Eddie noticed something strange about them, and read them aloud to us. I noticed one very peculiar thing about them."

I scanned the papers he gave me. They were all articles from supernatural news agencies, twenty years old or more. Most of them were dated before I was even born. "These are just articles about the experiments, from when the school was shut down the first time," I said.

"Exactly. We know the Infernal Underground is a group of people who experiments on inmates. The prison probably never stopped performing the experiments even after the Institute was caught. They just moved them to a secret location where the United Supernatural Union wouldn't notice what they were doing."

"But how does this help us?" I asked.

"Look at the articles again. They have one similarity."

Oberi nudged my shoulder, telling me to reread. I wasn't sure what I was searching for, until something clicked. "They say some sort of crystal was used to torture the inmates. But it's barely mentioned— only a sentence or two per article about them, and it never lists the name."

"Yeah, but it isn't noxite, because it doesn't have those properties," Charlie said. "Whatever crystal that was used to torture these people is something different."

I blinked. Charlie caught my silence and asked, "What is it?"

I bit my lip. "It's nothing."

"You wouldn't be so quiet if it wasn't."

"It's just..." I held a breath. "During the Hawkei Civil War, my Aunt Maddie was tortured by the Elders— one Elder specifically. His name was Elder Oleander. He wanted to control the tribe. She said he tortured her by using these strange crystals, to try and make her see visions. She never talks about it, but whenever she *did* speak of what happened to her, she always said those dark crystals Oleander used on her were odd. She'd never seen them before, and didn't know what they were."

"Do you think that she was under so much duress, she just mistook them for something uncommon?"

"My aunt is a skilled alchemist, like I am. She knows the properties of every magical substance, but she couldn't place this one." I tapped my chin. "What if the crystals used to torture my Aunt Maddie were the same ones used for the experiments at the prison, and the Institute was Oleander's supplier?"

"I bet the Warden and Oleander were buddies. They sound like they're cut from the same cloth," Charlie said disdainfully. "I'm more certain than anything Oleander asked for these crystals, and the Warden gave them to him. The Warden would love to get info out of a prophet."

"Do you think this crystal can only be found on Darke Island?"

"It has to be. Otherwise, it'd be all over the supernatural world by now, and these crystals aren't mainstream."

Oberi nickered, and I said, "So if we know what type of crystal it is that they use for the experiments..."

"It'll bring us that much closer to the Underground," Charlie finished. "Though finding out what the crystal is, or where one might be, could be complicated."

"If we can get our hands on one of those crystals, I can examine it with alchemy, use a potion to dissolve it and figure out what's in it," I said quickly. "But..."

"But what?"

I gave a tense breath. "I bet the only one who has access to one of these things is the Warden. And we'd have to ask Marcus to find one in his office and steal it in order for me to test it."

"That's too risky," Charlie immediately said. "The Warden will notice if a powerful object like that goes missing. If we're caught, we're screwed."

"I know." My shoulders slumped. "But we *have* to get our hands on one of these crystals somehow. It's the only clue we've gotten so far about the Underground, and to be honest, I don't think there are that many in the first place. The Warden is keeping this project tightly locked up. We've gotta take what we can get."

Charlie took the papers from me and shoved them back in the book before putting it on the shelf. "We need to be careful. We know the Underground is looking for demigods. Which means whatever these crystals are, they have an effect on us. I'm gonna wager whatever those crystals can do to demigods, it's not good."

I gave a curt nod. "Right. They're some kind of weapon. We have to assume that."

Charlie waited for a second. The sound of conversation rose over the shelves. "We need to get out of here. Alistair and I have been spending too much time in the library lately, and it looks weird for any Institute student to be hanging around books. If word gets back to the Warden that I brought you in here with me, he'll know we're on to something."

"Then let's get out of here." I took Charlie's arm to lead him out. My steps were quick and long, and we covered the library in half the time it would usually take us. The librarian's eyes were on us as we walked out the doors. She gave us a slight smile, which I took as a kind gesture and not a threat.

Madame Rayne was nice. She wouldn't tell on us, would she?

Wouldn't bet on it. You couldn't trust anybody in this place.

Once we got out of the library, Charlie and I didn't *need* to walk together. But my hand on his arm felt right, and to be honest, I didn't want to let it go. Oberi shook her head and let out a breath, like she found our posturing annoying. We just walked in any direction, not really going anywhere, but being together.

"So... we should probably find Kallie and Marcus and tell them what we know," Charlie started.

I went to agree, but before I could, a scream echoed down the hallway. Both Charlie and I stopped dead in our tracks, and my heart leapt into my throat.

"Help! Someone, help!" The sound came from one of the bathrooms.

"That's Opal," I said, already scared out of my mind. I grabbed Charlie's hand, and we ran down the hallway. Oberi gave a loud noise, and we followed the screams to the nearest men's room.

Opal was on her hands and knees in front of the sinks, tears streaming down her face. Beside her was my brother, lying on his back and completely still. His body was completely loose, and his complexion matched that of a ghost. His eyes had rolled to the back of his head, and his breaths were shallow.

"What happened to Ez?" I asked, falling to my knees beside him.

"He— he said he didn't feel well. I followed him in here, and he passed out." Opal wiped at her nose. "I've tried to wake him up, but he's completely out of it! I didn't want to leave him."

"Go to the infirmary, Opal," Charlie said quickly. "We have to get him help."

Opal's shoes slapped against the floor as she ran out of the bathroom. I put a hand over his chest and felt my brother's weak heartbeat. It was fading by the second. Instinctively, I knew the nurses wouldn't get here in time.

"He's *dying*." I had told my brother that avoiding treatment would kill him someday. Why hadn't he listened?

"What are you talking about, Ava? How can you tell?" Charlie demanded.

"I just *can*!" I shouted. "Don't you feel it?"

"Feel what?"

I couldn't explain what was coursing through me right now, except that I had an unknown certainty that my brother *was* dying, and if I didn't help him, he'd be dead in minutes or less. I grabbed Charlie's hand and put it onto Ezekiel's stomach.

"Take some power from me! Tell me you can't feel that!" I shouted.

I felt power ripple through our bond, and a bit of my magic left me to flood into Charlie. It only took moments, but the color drained from Charlie's face. He didn't understand what he was feeling, and neither did I, but he knew as well as I did that Ezekiel would be dead by the time Opal returned with help.

I began hyperventilating as Charlie pulled his hand away. This was like losing Monica all over again, except that it was even worse, because I was watching my little brother die. I was sobbing so hard I couldn't see straight. The room wavered and spun around me, but I forced myself to keep conscious, because I didn't know how many seconds my brother had left of life, and I wanted to spend his last moments by his side.

I pleaded with someone— anyone— to help me. There had to be a way to stop this.

Ava, you need to calm down, a soothing voice said. *Controlling your emotions is the only way to help your brother.*

I knew that voice. It resonated deep in my spirit. Charlie heard it too, and he stiffened beside me. Oberi calmly strode to my side and looked me in the eyes. Her dark pupils instantly connected with my soul, and I was certain the voice I heard in my mind was hers.

I'd waited so long for Oberi to speak to me, but I couldn't enjoy the moment, because my brother was dying. "I don't know what's wrong with him," I wept.

It's sepsis, Oberi replied. *I can smell it in his blood. Can't your magic feel it?*

Was that what I was feeling? I put my hand over Ezekiel's body again and paid attention this time. The dark, foreboding presence I'd sensed there before was more prominent this time. It tasted like metal in my mouth, and smelled like sour blood. Now that I knew what I was looking for, it wasn't hard to notice. The sepsis was pulsing through his veins like fire and shutting down his organs.

He's had it for a few days, but it's progressed quickly because of his condition. If you don't help him, he will *die,* Oberi said firmly.

I gave a loud wail, but Oberi shoved me with her head. *Ava, now isn't the time to fall apart. You can heal him. You have your mother's strength inside of you. That's how you knew he was dying. You could sense the poison in his blood, and your magic told you so.*

My breath knotted in my throat. "It's not possible. My mother has Anichi magic, but I'm only Koigni and Toaqua. I can only use Fire and Water."

You aren't a dual-caster, Ava. You're a tricaster, *the first of your kind. You have the ability to heal inside of you,* Oberi said. *It will be all right. Charlie and I will help you.*

"But I've never healed anyone!" I whimpered.

You've done this before. You just didn't know it. Trust me. Put your hands on his chest, Ava. I will teach you what to do.

I wanted to panic, but Ezekiel's breaths were getting shallower by the moment, and there wasn't any time for hesitation. I put my hands over my brother's chest and tried to concentrate. This felt all too familiar, and it made me sick.

Seek out the sepsis in his blood. Once you find it, destroy the bacteria that are causing it, Oberi instructed.

"But healing magic doesn't work that way. Anichi magic makes the body recover by forcing it to do what it naturally can on its own," I stuttered. "Ezekiel's body doesn't have the potential to fight off an infection like this. His immune system is too weak."

You are no average Anichi, and can do things others cannot. Use your Anichi magic like your Fire. Find the infection, and burn it, Oberi said sharply.

Oberi nudged Charlie's shoulder. *Charlie, you need to pull magic from me and funnel it into Ava. This is powerful magic, bringing someone back from the point of death. She can't do both at once, and this will take all our strength, all three of us.*

I didn't have any time to object. Ez was fading away by the second. I put my hands over his heart and felt its slow beat as I sought out the sepsis. It flooded through his veins, and that sour taste filled my mouth again. It made me want to gag, but I pushed past the feeling and called my Anichi magic to the surface.

I hadn't noticed it was ever there before, but now that I knew it was real, I couldn't believe I hadn't recognized it. It always sat inside me, like a quiet hum waiting to be summoned and serve. It was warm, like my Fire, and needed to be directed. I flooded my healing magic through my fingers, and a white glow began to encompass my brother's chest as my Anichi power flowed through his body. It burned like my Koigni magic, yet moved like water, washing over his systems. The combination felt familiar to me and was effortless. I felt my Anichi magic work furiously as it ate away at the infection overpowering my brother's blood.

When my Anichi powers were summoned, something strange happened with Oberi. Her horn began to glow. The light filled the entire bathroom, bathing us in a pure white hue. It was odd, but I had no time to contemplate it now.

Nerves ate away at me as I worked. Healing magic wasn't flawless. If someone was too far gone, not even Anichi magic could restore what was ruined. I doubted even if my mother was here, her Anichi powers could save Ez now.

But mine could. I *knew* they could. Despite never healing anyone on purpose before, I was stronger than my mother was, and her power ran through my veins, amplified by my demigod blood. I was going to heal my brother out of sheer will. I *refused* to let the ancestors have him.

This was a hard job. I could feel my strength ebbing away minute by minute, like I was running a marathon and had no energy left to make the last mile. Charlie's face knitted in concentration, and through our bond, I felt him funnel power from Oberi into me. Even so, his body slumped, like this was anything but easy to do.

It's working, Oberi gasped, but she sounded like she was in pain. Her knees buckled, and she hit the floor. My Anichi magic suddenly gave out.

The light died, and I gave a cry of worry. "It stopped!"

He's healed, Ava. You removed the infection from his blood, Oberi said with a tired sigh. *But it's taken all of what's in us, unfortunately.*

I didn't realize how tired I was until Oberi said those words. Immediately, a heaviness pressed in around my body, and I could no longer remain upright. I collapsed onto the floor just as the door burst open and Opal flooded in with a host of nurses.

The last thing I saw was Oberi's glowing horn, dimming into shadow before I passed out.

⛓

I HAD a headache when I woke up, but I managed to sit. I was in a private room inside the infirmary, dressed in a thin hospital gown. It was the next morning, judging by the sunlight streaming through my window.

And standing right in front of me, with his hands clasped, was the fucking Warden. He'd been here for ancestors knew how long, watching me sleep like a weirdo and waiting for me to wake up.

Great. He was the last fucking person I wanted to see.

"You've been asleep for an entire day, Miss Mitoh," the Warden said coolly. "You'll be pleased to know your brother is doing well, thanks to your quick intervention. A *tricaster.* How unique."

I narrowed my eyes. "Where's Charlie?"

"In class, with your Familiar. The two of them were worn by helping you in your endeavor, but they did not sustain the kind of exhaustion you succumbed to."

The Warden sat down in a chair by my bedside and leaned in. He looked like he wanted to devour me alive.

Ugh, go away. My body instinctively turned away from him, though I tried to remain as still as possible.

"What you did yesterday was nothing short of brilliant. I have no doubt that in time, your healing magic will become phenomenal," the Warden whispered.

"Yeah, well, don't look for me to do the same for you," I shot back. "Because if you were in my brother's place, I would've watched you die, and laughed."

The Warden's mouth twitched, like he found me amusing. It was insulting. "I have no doubt you would, Miss Mitoh."

He stood from the chair and turned his back to me. "Extraordinary again. Such a prize to have in my possession."

"I don't belong to anyone," I snarled.

The Warden smiled. He twirled a hand in the air, gesturing to the walls, the ceiling. "You're in here, aren't you?"

He left then. I was completely furious. I was already the Warden's favorite toy, and now I'd become even more interesting to him by being the first Elementai with three different powers. I'd hoped to keep my Anichi magic a secret, but the secret was already blown out of the water. I was sure the entire prison knew the news by now.

It didn't matter. It was worth it to save my brother's life.

I got up from the bed without alerting the nurses and scrambled to find my uniform. It was tucked away neatly in a cupboard by the bed, along with my shoes. I put my clothes on and hurried out of the room to find my brother.

I was certain he was in one of the private rooms, like I was. I waited until the nurses were busy with a couple of patients, then ran along the hallway until I came to the only closed door in the infirmary.

I pushed it open. Ezekiel was sitting up in bed with his arms crossed, looking out a window. He had an IV in his arm. He wasn't doing anything. Just sitting there staring. He looked like his whole world had been crushed. On his bedside, a small tray of cookies had been placed, tied with a blue seashell ribbon.

"Hey, Ez." I sat on the edge of his bed. He didn't look at me. "Are you...?"

Asking if he was okay was stupid. I scooted closer and nudged his arm. "How are you feeling?"

Ez scoffed. "Perfect, now that I know I have a life-threatening disease."

I remained silent, and he said, "I always knew, deep down. I just didn't want to admit it."

He seemed so resentful. Ez finally pulled his gaze away from the window. "I should've listened to you, Ava. You saved my life."

"I can't believe that I did," I marveled. "Anichi magic. Can you believe it, Ez?"

"Not really. You're always wowing everyone with something new," he said. "And look at me. I've got treatments scheduled every week for the rest of forever."

"I can do them," I offered. "I'll heal you."

"No, sis. You've got to save your strength for whatever the Warden's got planned, because we know there's always something," Ez stated. "Let one of the Anichi nurses here do it."

I frowned. Anichi magic could do so much— heal infections, mend bones, even stop death in its tracks... but it couldn't cure most diseases, including my brother's. "What are you feeling?"

"I don't know. Dad was more in shock than anything when he got diagnosed. I'm just *angry*. I really hoped—"

My brother's eyes watered, and he slammed his fist against the mattress. He brought his knees up to his chin and curled his arms around his legs. He put his head down, and I felt like caving inward.

"I'm sorry. This is really hard," I said.

"I'm just not ready to be sick for the rest of my life," he whispered.

"You won't be, Ez. It'll be hard, and you'll have bad days, but you'll have good ones, too," I said, rubbing his back. "This for sure feels like the end of the world, but it's not, and you know why? Because now you can get treated and start feeling better."

"I never feel better. I always feel like shit."

"That doesn't mean it'll always be that way." I brushed back his hair and wiped a couple of tears from his eyes. "I promise you that things are better now that you know, and you can do something about it. Avoiding it wasn't solving the problem. In fact, it nearly killed you. So swear to me this time you'll get help the next time you need it, and that you'll take care of yourself, before your illness spirals out of control."

Ez sniffed and nodded. He wiped his face with the back of his arm, before his eyes gravitated to the tray on his bedside. In a small voice, he asked, "Can I have a cookie?"

I laughed. "Yes, you can have a cookie." I handed him one, and he chewed on it. "Who brought them?"

"Opal. One of the nurses told me she'd been here." He'd already devoured one cookie, and had snagged another. "I guess she snuck in last night, and didn't leave until they found her here in the morning. They escorted her out before I even woke up."

Devoted. "She was really scared when you collapsed."

Ez frowned. "I know. I feel really bad doing that to her. She told me to get help, too. I guess I'm kind of stupid that way."

"Not just *that* way..." I mumbled under my breath, but Ez didn't hear me.

He shoved a third cookie in his mouth. "I'm *so* lucky she decided to make some more cookies this week in Arts & Crafts. Peanut butter is my favorite."

He shrugged. "Though I guess she hates them. Why she'd make *peanut butter* cookies if she's not going to eat them, I don't know."

"Wow, Ez." My voice was flat.

"What? Do you know something I don't?"

His face was blank. If he wasn't feeling like crap right now, I'd hit him. People liked to joke that my mother and Grandpa Elliot could be oblivious. Clearly, Ez had inherited *that* gene.

"Miss Mitoh, what are you doing here?" Lady Helga's brusque voice cut into our conversation as the door opened behind us. "You haven't yet been discharged, and your brother needs rest."

"He needs me, too," I pleaded. Lady Helga carried in a new IV bag, which she clipped on to a medical pole.

"You may return to visit tomorrow morning," Lady Helga said. "In the meantime, Mister Mitoh needs sleep. You may have healed his sepsis, but he still has a long recovery ahead of him before he returns to class next week."

"Next *week?*" Ez moaned.

"If you would've come in sooner, perhaps you wouldn't have to spend so much time here, sir," Lady Helga quipped. "Let this be a lesson not to let things go for too long."

Ez swore under his breath, and I stood. "I'll be back later, Ez. Try to get some sleep."

"This is cruel and unusual punishment," he growled.

I kissed my brother on the top of the head before I skipped out. I haggled with the nurses to let me go, and they did, though only because I pleaded.

I was off to look for Charlie and Oberi. I knew they were in class, so I had to wait for them to be excused before we could talk. I figured our cellblock was the best place to go to pass the time, so I headed there.

On the way, I noticed Ghost sweeping the floors, probably doing the job the Institute assigned him to. He had a white tomcat beside him that was batting at a dust bunny in the corner. The cat had the biggest eyes and the most crooked whiskers. The little thing constantly looked terrified. It was kind of funny.

When I passed, Ghost waved me over. I walked to his side, and he said, "I heard you healed your brother. Amazing magic, though I'm sorry the whole school knows."

"It was better than the alternative," I said, shrugging. "Though it was a real shock, discovering I have Anichi magic."

"I thought you always knew. You healed my arm in fight club, remember?" Ghost said.

A memory of the night when I'd stood up for Ghost crossed through my mind. He'd gotten hurt in a match, and didn't want to fight anymore, but the guards still made him. Me standing up for Ghost had resulted in me getting punched in the face by Tony, and Charlie nearly killing him. It'd been a crazy night.

"Barely," I said. "Are you *sure* I healed your arm?"

"Yeah. It was broken, and you mended it in a second. Didn't you know?" Ghost asked.

I hadn't. I'd felt some power go out of me when I'd touched Ghost's arm, but I didn't realize what was happening.

"You didn't tell anyone that I healed you?" I marveled.

"No. I thought it was your secret, and that I should shut up about it." He blinked.

Ghost was one of the few good people left at the Institute. I really liked him.

"Are they still making you fight?" I asked Ghost.

He sagged forward on his broom. "Yeah, but I think Captain's getting tired of me. The guards are bored watching me getting my ass kicked around. He's probably going to put me up against a group next time. I'm going to be killed eventually, to keep the crowd entertained."

"That's barbaric," I said in disgust.

"What am I gonna do? They'll never let me out. Might as well accept my fate instead of fighting the inevitable." Ghost frowned. "Anyway, I never thanked you for healing my arm, so... thanks. Not a lot of people are kind to me. It's a nice change."

Ghost hurried off, and his white tomcat ran behind. I hoped Charlie would be able to help Ghost get out once he discovered who was fixing the fights. Then again, I didn't even know if *Charlie* would be able to escape fight club, and with nowhere to go, Ghost's chances of surviving seemed slim to none.

I felt really sorry for him, but didn't know what I could do... except help Charlie find some answers. Maybe he could get leverage over Captain somehow. That would be the only thing that could save Ghost's life.

Kallie was waiting for me outside of my dormitory. She lay outside of it as a wolf, seemingly guarding it. She transformed back when I appeared.

"What's up?" I asked. "You look tense."

"Things have been weird since people have found out you're a tricaster— nice job saving Ez, by the way," she stated. "The rest of the students think you're some sort of deity or something. I overheard a couple of people whispering they should go through your stuff, figure out if you've got something boosting your magic."

"Do you think other inmates will figure out what I am, or what we are? The professors give lectures on demigods every semester," I worried.

"I don't think so. Most people in class don't pay attention. You forget that no one is an outstanding student here at the Institute. Everyone here is too dumb to figure it out."

"Not everyone. There are some smart criminals here. We aren't the only ones," I pointed out.

"It's not the majority. I don't think anyone's made a demigod connection. If they had, rumor would've traveled around the prison already, and I haven't heard anything."

Let's hope it stayed that way. I opened my cell door. It didn't look like anything had been disturbed. I was the last one here.

I heard Marcus' loud footsteps approaching long before he reached my room. He panted as he rasped, "Kallie asked me to meet you guys here..."

He trailed off, and both Kallie and I turned to look at him. His expression was flat, and his body was rigid, like he could sense something. At his feet, Rishi gave a hiss.

"What?" Kallie asked, annoyed.

Marcus began walking around the room. His eyes narrowed in concern. "Ava, how long has your cell been like this?"

"I'm sorry for the mess, but I'm kind of a disorganized slob," I apologized, kicking a shirt out of the way.

"No, not that." His lips tightened. "There's negative energy in this room. A lot of it."

"Huh?" Kallie tilted her head.

"I *mean* there's bad spirits in here. Dozens of them," Marcus said. "I can feel it."

"Bad spirits? Like, dead people?" I yelped.

"Kind of? I'm not sure. You've definitely got some negative energy attached to this place... though it could be demonic."

"What the hell? Why couldn't I notice anything?" I asked.

"You wouldn't, if they showed up over a long period of time, little by little. You'd have excuses to explain them away. Bad moods, bipolar swings," Marcus said. He conjured a bundle of cedar.

"Are you *sure* this place is stuffed with bad spirits?" Kallie asked skeptically.

"Absolutely," he said. I lit the cedar for Marcus, and he started waving it around. "I don't get it. I've been in here dozens of times, and it was fine last spring."

"They must've flooded in here over the summer when we weren't talking," I said, depressed.

"No problem. I'll clear it out now." Marcus began waving the burning cedar around the room. As the smoke lifted, my attitude improved. I couldn't feel or see the ghosts, but I could physically sense the energy in the room changing, from a heavy coat of despair to a light, airy tone of positivity. It was so significant that I couldn't believe I hadn't noticed the difference.

"Any of you ghosts want to tell me what you're here for, or do we have to do this the *hard way?*" Marcus asked. The room remained silent, but I didn't think I'd be able to listen in on whatever the spirits were saying.

"Are they saying anything?" Kallie pressed.

"No. I know they hear me. They're ignoring me." Marcus scowled. "Whatever these spirits are here for, they were sent on business."

"Business?" I asked.

"Negative entities are always looking for someone to latch on to and feed off of," Marcus said, waving the cedar around. "Though I've never seen so many in one place before. Usually, they're all around us."

"Is that common at the prison?" Kallie questioned.

"Oh, the Institute's full of that kind of shit. We've got negative energy up the ass around here. Look what the bus brings in every week. You can bet there's some evil spirits attached to some of these jerks walking around," Marcus said.

He set the burning cedar down on the edge of my table, then turned to me. "You got something to make noise?"

I had a couple of alchemy pots from class lying around. I handed them to Marcus, and he started banging them together, screaming, "COME OUT, GHOSTS! TIME TO TALK!"

"Gods, Marcus, cut it out." Kallie put her hands over her ears and winced.

"No good. They aren't responding." Marcus sighed, and let the pots clatter to the floor. It jarred my hearing.

"*That* was the hard way?" Kallie scowled.

"Hey, I still don't know what I'm doing," Marcus said with a shrug. "That's all I've got, and anyway, they're gone now. You should notice a difference, Ava."

I really did. Rishi lay on my bed and purred, like he was pleased the area had been cleared.

Charlie poked his head in my dorm. "Are you girls in here? I heard Marcus screaming from all the way down the hall and assumed it was a normal Tuesday."

"Fuck off, Charlie," Marcus snapped.

I giggled. "Kallie and I are here. How do you feel?"

"I'm fine. You sound a lot better, pidge."

It didn't hurt when he called me that, like it had before. We'd... ugh... had a *bonding* moment when we saved my brother, and now we were that much closer.

I didn't know whether to feel happy or sad about that.

"I'm doing good. And Ez will be all right, though he's taking his diagnosis really hard."

"We'll be here for him," Kallie said. "He'll be back to his happy, underwear model self in no time."

Oberi nosed his way in as a husky. He panted heavily, drooling all over my floor. *About time you woke up. You don't need that much beauty sleep.*

I patted his head. "You saved my brother's life, Oberi. You knew exactly what to do."

Well, I couldn't very well let him lie there. He makes a crappy area rug. Oberi's tongue lolled out.

"You should let me in your cell, Charlie. I found some negative entities in Ava's room, and I'm betting there's some in yours, too," Marcus said.

"Entities?" Charlie asked.

Kallie and I explained what was going on as Marcus cleared Charlie's room. He came out again a few minutes later, looking just as perturbed.

"Charlie's got some bad shit in his cell, too, though not as bad as Ava's," Marcus said. "I just cleared both of them. You guys should start feeling a lot better, physically and emotionally. It's no good when your energy's cluttered."

"This is definitely weird," Charlie said, scratching the back of his head.

"We need to check Kallie's room." Marcus started forward before the rest of us could follow, walking with purpose.

The fae cellblock was fucking loud. There were a bunch of shifters wrestling in the hallways, and balls bouncing off the walls from sorceresses playing sports. Everyone down here was absolutely obnoxious. Psh. Faeries.

Kallie opened her cell door, and Marcus walked in. Immediately after, he let out a high-pitched, awful wail that immediately made me petrified with fear. The entire fae cellblock went quiet, and everyone looked our way.

"What? What did you find?" Charlie shouted.

Marcus covered his eyes as he walked out, completely red in the face. "Kallie, can you *please* clean up your... *lady garments*?"

I peeked inside, and saw that Kallie's lace bras and dainty thongs were scattered everywhere. I let out a snicker.

"I was organizing my drawer and didn't have enough time to finish before I had to go to class! Sor-*ree!*" Kallie whined.

Everyone in the fae cellblock laughed. Kallie gathered her panties in her arms and tossed them into a drawer. It took a lot of prodding before we were able to drag Marcus back in. He was in there longer than he was in my room, as if he was doing a double sweep.

"There were bad spirits in Kallie's cell, too." Marcus looked very worried as he subconjured the ashen remains of the cedar he was carrying. "They didn't want to leave. I had to force them."

"What about your cell?" Kallie asked. She pulled Charlie and me inside her room and shut the door behind us, so no one could listen in on our conversation.

"My room is clear. I cleanse it every Sunday," Marcus said.

"Maybe you should skip it this week, and see if any baddies show up," Kallie suggested.

"Might not be a bad idea..." Marcus mused. "We could figure out if these spirits are appearing by coincidence, or on purpose."

"What's the benefit of clearing spirits?" Charlie asked. "I mean, I can tell the difference in how I feel, but what do they show up to do?"

"They can make you sick, but mostly, they're around to make you depressed. They feed off energy, especially positive vibes. They literally suck the life out of you," Marcus explained. "If these spirits were sent here by a big, bad spiritual force, it's to weaken us."

"I'm sure the Warden sent them," I spat, and Oberi gave a growl.

Marcus gave a skeptical sound. "He doesn't have control over spirits or demons. He's just an angel."

"*Is he*, though?" Kallie asked. "What if he made a deal with the... you know... *other side?*"

"This isn't a movie, Kallie," Marcus said, rolling his eyes.

"But this is the supernatural world, and we know contracts with bad forces can be done! The fae create binding magical contracts every day," Kallie said.

"But what does the Warden *really* want? And why would dark forces want to help him to achieve it?" I asked.

"I'm willing to bet my wings these bad spirits aren't just showing up in our rooms for no reason," Kallie insisted.

"The Warden, though? That's a stretch, even for him," Charlie argued. "I don't think this is his doing. These spirits are being sent by someone in the spiritual realm, and whoever they are, they have a lot of power."

"You're talking about a god, like Coyote Spirit, or Whale Spirit," I offered.

"Yes, but we know those gods are on our side," Charlie said. "Which means there have to be some gods that aren't."

Well, that was a fucking scary ass statement. I knew there were dark gods out there, trying to manipulate my life and make it so I didn't accomplish my destiny— Coyote had told me so. Yet to see the evidence right in front of me made me unable to deny his words.

"We should cleanse the Lair. There might be spirits in there, too," Charlie suggested.

"Good idea," Kallie said.

We started heading that way, before we were interrupted. A guard cried out, "Wahkin!" He jogged toward us, clutching his noxite gun.

I could physically *feel* Charlie's teeth grinding through our bond as he whirled around and growled, *"What?"*

"Captain wants you down for training. You haven't been filling your hours, and he knows you ain't got no class right now," the guard said.

"Tell him I'm busy," Charlie seethed.

"You tell him. I'm not taking the fall for your disobedience. You're showing up for training, or else."

Charlie's jaw worked, and he grumbled, "I'll see you guys later." He told Oberi to stay with me and left with the guard.

A twinge of irritation crossed through my body. "I'm getting really tired of Charlie having to answer to these pricks."

"Yeah, but what are we going to do? They're *scary*," Marcus whimpered.

Kallie's face was contemplative. "Actually, now that I think of it, if Charlie's staying behind, so should you. It looks suspicious if we all vanish at once. The four of us shouldn't go to the Lair together unless absolutely necessary."

"What should we do?" I asked.

"Marcus and I will clear it out. You stay here," Kallie said. "Let's go, string bean."

Marcus yelped as Kallie tugged at the back of his sweater. They wandered down the hall. Oberi transformed into a unicorn, giving a snort.

I need a break, Oberi said with a weary sigh. *Let's go outside. I'd like to get some sunshine.*

Oberi and I walked to the prison yard. I took a seat on one of the metal benches, while Oberi collapsed in the grass and rolled around, letting out a couple of snuffs as her coat reflected the sunlight.

A thought came to me as I watched her frolic. "How old are you, Oberi?"

So old and no older, she said, lying on her back and waving her hooves in the air.

"You must be ancient. Most Familiars are born when their Elementai get their powers, but you seem older than Charlie and me."

Ancient?! Oberi fluttered her eyelashes and huffed. *It is inappropriate to ask a unicorn her age.*

"But you aren't *really* a unicorn, are you?" I asked, wrinkling my nose.

I existed before Familiars were even conceived, and I'll exist long after Familiars are gone, Oberi replied shortly. *I am a great deal older than most creatures you can imagine, yes. I am a mutabeecha, and we are eternal beings, crafted at the beginning of time. Though you're really making me feel my wrinkles right now, girlfriend.*

"So you can't die?" I asked.

Of course I can, Oberi replied. *But my death would be different.*

"How so?" I wondered.

I can't say for certain. Much of my understanding about the universe doesn't make sense in my earthly form. It's like I've forgotten... I was not born like most beings are. I have no parents. I was spoken into being by the gods. But when I came here, I developed an earthly vessel, and much of my knowledge was lost.

"Are you really a part of the Great Spirit, like the legends say?"

Ask him yourself.

I rolled my eyes. "If you've been around since the start of creation, you must have a ton of knowledge you can offer. Maybe something that would help with my prophecy?"

Most of my existence has been spent in the Ancestral Lands, bouncing between spiritual realms. I'm not very experienced in the mortal world, or how it works. Probably why I am not much help to you here.

"Don't say that. You are helpful," I insisted.

I'm not helpful enough, Oberi mumbled. *I can't seem to get you and Charlie on the same page.*

I felt my jaw tighten. "Maybe it's better if we aren't."

You two are lying to yourselves, Oberi said, almost bored. *Charlie holds back because he has a fear of getting hurt, and you are holding back because of an asinine sense of pride. I'd thought the two of you would've given up by now, but gods, both of you are stubborn.*

"You can't make us get back together, so nah, nah." I stuck my tongue out at her.

That's fine. I'm not the only one suffering, she shot back at me. *We'll all be in misery together.*

"It's not all that bad," I said, and it wasn't so much a lie— because really, it was terrible.

I want my soul to be fused, Ava. I'm tired of being torn in half day by day. That can't happen until you and Charlie are truly one, Oberi said. *I feel as if I'm in two different places, being stretched from one side to the other. I waited many years for the two of you to come together again, and now that you finally are, you're* wasting *it. Gods, the drama.*

"What the hell are you talking about?"

I've said too much. Lessons you are not ready to learn, Oberi replied. *Perhaps another time.*

"Can you make more— ow!" I held my finger up. I'd gotten a small cut on my finger from a tear in the crappy metal bench. Blood leaked out of my finger. I tried to use my Anichi powers to mend it, summoning my powers and sending it to the cut.

Nothing happened. It kept bleeding. I tried again, and the cut didn't mend this time, either.

I felt my brow furrow. "How can I heal my brother from a deadly infection one day and not be able to heal a cut on my finger the next?"

You can't really limit what you can do to Anichi magic. Your healing powers go far beyond actual healing, *if you catch my drift.*

"Are my healing powers connected to my special abilities as a demigod?" I asked Oberi.

You're on to something, Oberi said with a nod. *Though what you could be capable of, I'm not entirely sure. This will be difficult magic, Ava, and not easy to access.*

"Like Kallie's ability to halt time."

Yes. Remember that.

I opened and closed my hand. The cut on my finger was still bleeding.

I could do more than just heal. I wasn't sure where my abilities would lead me quite yet, but I had a feeling my power to heal was different from that of my tribe. It wasn't like my mother's Anichi magic, which showed up on command. It was a part of my demigod abilities.

I wouldn't have been able to heal Ez if I was a normal Anichi. I knew that for certain. I hadn't manipulated Ez's body to heal itself, like another healer would. It was like I'd commanded my *own* power to stop Ez's sickness, and fixed him myself, out of my own will.

My healing powers were different. They were the powers of a demigod, unstoppable and able to do things other Anichi couldn't, but they were also turbulent and unreliable.

Which means they could fail if I really needed them. I hoped to the ancestors that never happened.

Though one day, it might.

charlie

NINE

Adrenaline raced through my system as I rammed my fist into a punching bag over and over again. Sweat dripped down my forehead, and I wiped it from my skin. As much as I hated fight club, I *loved* the rush of the workout.

I just wished it was under different circumstances.

Grunts filled the room as people sparred, and someone screamed from inside the boxing ring. The smell of blood was unmistakable.

Chancey slurped his water bottle loudly from beside me. "Someone piss in your cereal this morning?"

I steadied the punching bag and turned to him. "What are you on about?"

"*On about?* What are you, British?" Chancey teased. "I'm talking about the way you're punching that bag. You're about to knock it off the chains. You're angry."

"Of course I'm angry. I have to deal with your snarky ass five times a week," I jabbed.

"You should be *disappointed* you only see me five times a week," he replied with a full mouth. "Energy bar?"

"Nah, I'm good."

"Your form could use some work," he stated.

I frowned. "I don't give a shit about my form. If it does damage, that's all I care about."

"*I* thought his form looked great," a girl cut in. Velcro ripped as she yanked her gloves off. "It's *sexy* watching you work out, Charlie."

I gaped, but I didn't get a chance to say anything before Chancey spoke. "Stop it, Scarlet. You're making Charlie uncomfortable."

"Or giving him a hard on," another girl laughed as she walked by.

"Fuck off, Mistress," Scarlet snapped.

The other girl huffed, then walked away to another area of the gym.

Scarlet turned back to us. "I think the Bandit can speak for himself."

I didn't know what to say, honestly. Scarlet was a fighter in the club who was at the top of the female rankings. She was a succubus, and one of the strongest people I knew. I wouldn't want to get in the ring with her, that was for sure. Even so, we'd barely talked. I hardly knew her, aside from when we trained together every now and then.

It was weird that Scarlet was flirting with me, and it wasn't because I'd nearly won the Darke Games. The tiny high I rode after that was long over. The eye candy in this prison changed at the drop of a dime. Even Ez's fifteen minutes of fame had passed pretty quickly, after a new bus of students had arrived. All the girls seemed to talk about these days was a guy from Malovia, who was supposed to be some sort of duke or something. I hadn't really caught the gossip, and I didn't care.

Still. She acted like she was interested.

"Are you... flirting with me, Scarlet?" I asked.

She blew a breath. "I just called you sexy. Of course I'm flirting with you. I've watched you in the ring, Bandit. You really get my motor running, if you know what I mean."

Damn, this girl came on strong. Then again, she *was* a succubus. That was kind of their thing.

She came closer to me, so close that I could feel the heat coming off her body. She gently took my hands and placed them on her waist. She wore only a sports bra, so my hands landed on bare skin. I could feel that she was thin, which I found attractive. Part of me enjoyed the close contact— like I could easily crawl into bed with her for a meaningless night, if only to take my mind off things. I wanted to forget.

It was an odd survival mechanism I'd adopted. I didn't want to feel this way anymore. I didn't *want* this to be my safety net.

But that's what it had become, back when I lived on the streets. Some days, it was the only way to get food and a warm bed. Even though I had that here, the idea of being close to a woman made me feel secure in a way I couldn't understand— in a way I didn't want to feel.

Because all I wanted now was Ava. Hell, I was running my hands over Scarlet's skin, and all I could think about was my ex. Just touching Scarlet felt like a betrayal.

"You like what you feel?" she asked. This girl was desperate for the D.

"I'm—" I cut off. I almost said *taken*, before I realized that I wasn't. It'd been months since Ava and I broke up, and it still didn't feel real. There was nothing wrong with accepting Scarlet's advances. I could sleep with her a hundred times, and no one would think anything of it.

Except for me. It felt dirty, because I didn't want Scarlet.

I wanted Ava.

"You're what?" she asked curiously. "Busy tomorrow night?"

"Not really," I said, before I realized what she was asking.

"Perfect. So you'll pick me up at seven?"

"Uh... I've got factory duty," I said lamely.

"Then seven a.m. it is," she replied proudly. "You can take me out for breakfast."

"Wait. What?"

"See you then," she said, before bouncing off toward another training area.

I had no idea what had just happened. I turned to Chancey. "Did I just get a date?"

Chancey chuckled under his breath. "It sounds like you got a lot more than that."

I plopped into the seat beside him. "I don't want to sleep with Scarlet."

"Why not? She's hot. You know, if you're single."

"I'm not— I don't *want* to be single."

"Well, you are. Might as well enjoy it—" Chancey started to say, but he was cut off when the doors to the training room burst open. Several heavy pairs of footsteps marched inside, and my blood immediately turned to ice. I'd learned the beat of those footsteps all too well during my time at the Institute. It was the guards.

The guards never came down here during training. It was against Captain's policy, because he didn't want our training to influence their bets. The entire gym went silent.

"Hey!" Captain snapped, abandoning the new recruit he'd been training. "What do you think you're doing here? You know the rules!"

"Warden's orders," one of the guards said.

"What orders?" Captain barked. "The Warden don't touch fight club."

"New test results have come in," the guard stated. "There's an Elf hybrid on your roster."

If I thought my blood turned to ice a moment ago, it was nothing compared to the way I froze up then. My entire body might as well have been dumped in the arctic. I couldn't move—couldn't even breathe.

Captain scoffed. "I think I'd know if I had a kid with Elf blood among my fighters."

"Says here he's a quarter Elf," the guard said. "We're to bring him to the Warden as quickly as possible."

How the hell did they find out?

My hands began to shake as I considered the spells I might throw at the guards to get out of this. But I already knew there was no way out. There was only one entrance in and out of the gym. The only other place to go was the locker rooms, and there weren't any exits there— not even a window. The guards had me cornered.

Captain hesitated. Finally, he said, "Fine, but be quick about it. These kids have training to do."

The guards began to march in my direction, and panic set in. I grabbed Chancey's arm so hard that he drew a sharp breath.

"Chancey," I hissed. "You've gotta help me. You've gotta—"

I cut off when the guards walked straight past me and barked, "Anthony Lange, you're coming with us."

Chancey shoved me off of him. "What are *you* on about?"

I barely heard or felt him. I went as still as a statue as I heard the guards drag the Elf hybrid away.

"Me?" Anthony squeaked. "You bastards are mistaken— don't touch me!"

I leaned over to Chancey. "Who the hell is Anthony?"

"Tony," he replied. "The Dangerous Dragon."

It wasn't fair that I relaxed a little when he said that, but I did. I'd fought him last semester. Tony had been an asshole in the ring, and even worse outside of it. He'd punched Ava last semester. If it were anyone else, I'd stand up for them, but in this case, I was pleased to see Tony get dragged off to Cellblock 9. It didn't matter that we were both Elf hybrids and I *should* have stood up for my own. Tony deserved Cellblock 9 for other reasons.

"I'm no Elf!" Tony screamed. His shoes squeaked against the floor as he struggled against the guards' hold. "I'm a dragon shifter. I'm a fae!"

"Ever met your grandparents, kid?" one of the guards asked.

"What does that have to do with anything?" he demanded.

Tony sounded like he was telling the truth. Either he really didn't know of his heritage, or the Warden was manufacturing results. I recalled the conversation I'd overheard with Professor Cusak. Perhaps *he* had given Tony up as a possible demigod, to appease the Warden's timeline.

"You assholes are going to pay!" Tony shouted.

"Oof!" A guard let out a pained grunt. I assumed Tony had elbowed him in the gut and gotten free, because he scrambled across the room. The ropes surrounding the fight ring *twanged* as Tony jumped into the ring.

"You want me? You're gonna have to catch me!" Tony snarled.

What an idiot. The ring was far away from the door. There was no way he was getting out of here.

The air in the room shifted, pushing out of the way to make room for a massive beast. Something made from wood cracked. My heart leapt as a dragon's cry filled the room, and the guards began to shout. Noxite guns clicked in quick succession— dozens of them by the sound of it.

The dragon's cries faded, until he collapsed into a heap on the ground. Tony might've been a quarter Elf like me, but he wasn't prac-ticed in his powers, nor was he a demigod like I was. That much noxite was enough to knock him out for hours, if not days. He shrank back into a man, judging by the way the air expanded once again. I could hear the sound of his heels dragging on the ground as the guards pulled him out of the room.

Even after they left, the whole training room remained silent. Nobody moved as we absorbed what had happened. It had gone down so fast.

"Show's over!" Captain finally barked. "Get back to training! Scarlet. Big G. Clean up these broken bits of bench! This area's a mess."

"Where are you going, Cap?" someone asked.

"To get a drink!" he snarled. Captain marched out of the room, leaving us to ourselves.

The training area remained quiet at first, but conversation slowly returned, and people started moving again. It wasn't like before, though. Nobody punched bags or sparred. All I could hear were their whispers.

Did you know the Dangerous Dragon was an Elf?

I wonder if he had any idea.

What are they going to do with him?

Beside me, Chancey sighed. "That was... intense. What were you so scared about? You sounded worried they were coming for you."

A lump rose in my throat.

Realization dawned in Chancey's voice. "They're not going to come for you, Charlie... are they?"

His words sent a chill down my spine. Maybe I didn't care that they'd dragged Tony away, but they were coming for the Elves in this prison— all of them. It was only a matter of time before the Warden worked his way through the entire school and sent all the Elves and half-bloods to Cellblock 9. Eventually, it was going to be someone I cared about.

I'd been waiting to start training the Elves until I knew more about my powers, so I could train them properly. But the time for proper training had passed. Those Elves needed to be trained *now*— properly or not. They had to learn to defend themselves in ways Tony hadn't.

"Charlie!" Chancey shook me. "Charlie, what can I do? How can I help?"

I snapped out of my thoughts and turned to him. "You can help by talking to Ivy. We're going to need his help."

"Help with what, exactly?"

I cracked my knuckles as I stood. "He's going to help us teach the Warden a lesson."

⚭

THAT NIGHT, I stood on the stage Ivy had built in his secret nightclub, The Devil's Playground. I'd conned one of the guards to let me out of my factory hours tonight, claiming I had orders from Captain to train. Oberi was off somewhere with Ava, which was good. They didn't need to be around this if it didn't go well.

Chatter buzzed around the room as Elves began to arrive. By the bar, Ivy and Chancey whispered lowly to one another. I'd had to let them in on this because The Devil's Playground was the only place on campus we could train in secret— apart from the Lair, which I was *not* about to expose to anyone. A few more people snuck into the room, until there were a dozen Elves standing in front of me.

"I'm loving the new look, Eddie," Ivy said.

"Really? Thanks so much," Eddie replied chipperly.

"New look?" Alistair asked. "What new look?"

Eddie had suggested bringing Alistair along, so we could practice pulling magic from him, Ivy, and Chancey. I knew it was really so he could hang out with him— as his *official boyfriend*, as he'd put it. Alistair had asked him out yesterday at breakfast, and Eddie hadn't shut up about it since. This was kind of a lame first date, if you asked me.

"I, uh, spiked my hair," Eddie said sheepishly.

"Ooh, can I feel?" Alistair asked. "Mm, that's hot."

"You like it?" Eddie sounded excited.

"I like Elf ass is what I like," Alistair muttered under his breath, but Eddie must've not heard him, because Ivy had launched into a list of his favorite hair products.

I clapped my hands together, because if I had to hear about *Elf ass* one more fucking time, I was going to lose it. "Okay, let's get started. I assume Eddie has mentioned to you all why you're here tonight. We all know the potential of your magic, and that until you learn to control it, the Warden will use your weakness to control you. Gavyn learned how to defend himself and escaped this prison. I believe that each and every one of you can do the same. That said, there are some disclaimers we need to discuss before we begin. Eddie, if you would."

Eddie took center stage. He'd rehearsed a speech about how Gavyn had betrayed the Elves by escaping on his own and leaving the rest of them behind. "If we are going to do this, we must cooperate with each other," he said. "We've seen what happened since Gavyn left. The Warden has begun blood testing people. They took Uriel away. If we must act, we act together, or the rest of us will suffer."

"That also means no training outside of this room," I added. "Otherwise, we risk getting caught and deemed a threat by the Warden. The only reason he hasn't dragged any of you off yet is because he doesn't deem your powers worth his purposes yet. Once he learns how powerful you can be, he won't hesitate to hurt you."

I paused for a moment, but everyone was dead silent. They knew how truthfully frightening that statement was.

"Are we agreed, then?" Eddie asked.

Murmurs of agreement traveled around the group.

"Excellent. Then we may begin," Eddie said. "Charlie's the one who knows what he's doing, so I'll let him take it from here."

I shifted nervously as I returned to center stage. I *didn't* really know what I was doing, but the Elves didn't need to know that. What they needed right now was a leader, and as their prince, I was the best leader they were going to get.

"Eddie tells me that Elf magic matures as you age, and that most of you haven't grown into your power yet," I started. "I'm twenty-three and the oldest one here, so that's probably why my powers have started growing."

Truth be told, it probably had something to do with being a demigod, but I didn't admit this to the Elves. Not even Chancey was privy to that information, after I'd told him the truth about my heritage. Eddie had promised not to tell Alistair, either, though he'd convinced me to let him tell him the rest.

"The thing is, Gavyn wasn't much older than any of you," I continued. "I believe you *all* have what it takes to perform the magic he did.

First, I'd like to assess where you're all at. Has anyone managed to siphon power from another supernatural yet?"

I was met with nothing but silence, but I sensed someone shifting in the front row.

"If you're raising your hand, I'm going to need you to speak up," I said.

The kid cleared his throat, like he'd forgotten I was blind. "I've been working on it, and I managed to siphon wolven magic in the cafeteria last week. It wasn't much, but I got my hand to grow some fur. I've been trying to make a complete shift into a wolf, but so far, it hasn't worked."

I nodded thoughtfully. "That's a good start, but you're starting too far up the pay scale. Shifter magic is more difficult to cast than, say, warlock magic. It's even more difficult if the supernatural isn't consciously sharing their magic with you."

"Who would do that?" a girl wondered aloud.

"It's unlikely in a real-life situation," I admitted. "But it's helpful in practice. That's why I've invited some friends here to help us. We'll be starting with simple magic among willing participants. As each of your magic grows, we'll start learning more complex techniques. Alistair, if you would assist me?"

Alistair walked on stage. Pig must've hung back by Eddie, because I could hear her meowing softly.

"What are we starting with?" he asked, sounding pumped and ready to help.

"Battle orbs are your specialty?" I questioned.

He clicked his tongue. "You betcha."

I nodded firmly. "Then we'll start with that. When you feel me tug on your magic, let it flow into me, okay?"

"Gotcha. I'm ready."

I began to explain as I performed the magic. "First, you must find the magic inside the other person. It will feel like an electric buzz permeating your heart or your stomach, depending on the type. Watch for magic that twists in your gut, as that will be more unpredictable and difficult to control."

I frowned as I connected with Alistair's magic. "In Alistair's case, that would be *all* his magic. Damn, you're one angry dude."

Alistair chuckled lightly. "I've got some shit to work through. You want this magic or not?"

"I want it. Let's go."

I consciously grabbed hold of Alistair's magic. "Taking someone else's magic is like reaching out an invisible arm and latching on to it. You should be able to *feel* it, the way you would if you were actually touching the person with your hand. It's like an extra sense that can't be put into words. You'll understand it once you experience it yourself."

When I took hold of the magic, it didn't resist. Alistair's magic flowed into me, and I felt the buzz of defensive magic begging to escape. I lifted my hand, and a hot battle orb formed, warming my palm. The Elves gasped. I tossed the battle orb into the air, and it exploded, sizzling like a firework over the Elves.

"Wow, that was amazing!" one of them cried.

"Do it again!" another begged.

I cocked my head toward Chancey. "Hey, you wanna give it a try?"

"Do I have a choice?" he asked, but he was already making his way on stage as Alistair returned to the audience. He nudged me when he reached me, then whispered lowly, "I still can't believe you're part Elf."

"You better start believing it, because after this, you won't be doubting me," I said.

"You've been using it in the ring, haven't you?"

I smirked. "Just a bit."

He cracked his knuckles. "Show me your worst."

I shrugged. "You asked for it. Stand here, would you?"

I guided Chancey several feet away from me. "Angels are considered to be quite strong," I told the Elves. "Their magic is trickier, but there are different levels to it. Stealing their wings, for example, will be as complicated as stealing a shifter's magic. Siphoning their super strength, on the other hand, is pretty easy— even if the supernatural resists."

Chancey sounded intrigued. "You wanna play Tug-of-War?"

I shrugged. "You wanna get your ass kicked?"

"I wanna see what you're capable of."

"Then by all means, hold back," I invited him. "You're gonna regret this."

"Not a chance."

I found Chancey's super strength with ease and tugged on it. He resisted me, but I'd grown accustomed to this magic after all my time in the ring pulling strength from my opponents without even realizing it. I yanked on his magic, and it flowed into me. To show him just what I was made of, I spun and landed a heavy kick to his chest. Chancey went flying across the stage and landed on a chair in the crowd. By the sound of it, he'd crushed it to bits.

Ivy gasped as he scurried over to him. "Chance, you okay?"

Chancey didn't make a noise for a moment, and I feared I'd knocked him out. Then he burst into a fit of laughter, catching everyone off guard. "God, that was incredible! Charlie, you've been holding back on me!"

"Chance, you're bleeding!" Ivy protested.

Chancey didn't seem to care. He was more impressed than anything. "It's fine. I heal fast. What's next?"

"Let's split into three groups," I said. "Chancey and Ivy will work on strength magic with their groups. Alistair will work on battle orbs. I'll come around to see how everyone's doing. Our goal today is to help everyone get a sense for what someone else's magic feels like. Let's get started."

Everyone split off, and I walked around to observe.

"Wow, I feel really strong!" a guy working with Chancey exclaimed. I thought it was the same kid who said he'd stolen wolven magic.

"Wanna test it out?" Chancey asked. "Lift me above your head."

"Easy," he replied. He grabbed Chancey and lifted him up so fast that Chancey's foot nearly caught the end of my nose. Chancey hollered in laughter. He was getting a real kick out of the Elves.

After he set Chancey down, I turned to the guy. "What's your name?"

"Reid, my prince."

"Call me Charlie," I told him. "Reid, you seem to have a pretty good handle on this. Do you mind helping your group while I visit the others?"

"No problem, my prin— I mean, Charlie."

I headed to Ivy's group next and listened in.

"I don't feel anything," a girl said. "I don't really get it."

"Let me show you, Samara," her friend said.

A few moments passed before the girl sighed. "Never mind."

"Maybe I can help," I offered. "Samara, right? Have you ever cast an illusion?"

"Sure. A few," she said.

"Great. What does your magic feel like when you cast an illusion?"

"Um... it's hard to explain," she said. "It's like a sixth sense. I can just *feel* it. It kind of feels like a vibration in my chest. Like I just think about it, and it's there. I don't have to worry about conjuring it, because I just *know* it'll happen."

"Right. You're looking for a similar feeling in Ivy," I told her. "Take that vibration in your chest, and reach it outward, until it starts to change. When you feel something new, then you know you've connected with Ivy."

"Okay..." She sounded unsure. "I'll give it a try."

"It's okay, cupcake," Ivy said. "I don't bite... hard."

I frowned. "Come on, Ivy. Don't scare the poor girl."

"You're right, you're right. I'm a friend. I promise," Ivy sang.

Samara tried again. Several minutes of silence passed, and I was getting impatient, but I didn't say anything.

Finally, she gasped. "I think I feel something."

"I'm ready whenever you are," Ivy said.

Samara drew a deep breath. "I think I got some of your strength."

I held up my palms. "Test it out on me. Punch me."

"I don't want to hurt you," she said timidly.

"I've seen it all before. Show me what you've got."

Samara punched me, but there was almost no strength behind it. It felt like being hit by a wad of paper. If anything, I would've thought someone siphoned *her* strength.

She gasped and slapped a hand over her mouth. "I'm *so* sorry. Did I hurt you?"

"Not a bit," I replied in disappointment. "Keep trying. You'll get it."

The problem was, I wasn't quite sure she *would*. As I made my way around the room, it became more and more evident that these young Elves had almost no magic to speak of. They'd grown up in Forevermore, a paradise that required no aggressive training. Sure, they believed they'd be attacked *one* day, but they obviously didn't think it would happen so soon— or they thought their escape plan was foolproof— because the Elves hadn't trained their kids in anything worthwhile. A few of them could cast minor illusions, but that was it.

My teeth gritted as I thought of my dad and grandfather. It was their job to prepare the Elves to defend themselves, and they'd dropped the ball. Now I'd been left to clean up their mess. I clearly had my work cut out for me. I really wasn't sure if I could train these people.

"I did it!" Eddie squealed in excitement when I reached his group.

"I could feel it," Alistair said. "That was a pretty nice battle orb."

"Well, I have a strong warlock to draw from," Eddie cooed. Thank the ancestors I couldn't see, because I was pretty sure Eddie was batting his eyelashes right now.

"You two have been practicing in private, haven't you?" I asked.

"Just a little," Eddie admitted.

"How about we let someone else try?" I suggested.

"Sure," Eddie agreed. "Felicity, you wanna give it a go?"

"I can try," Felicity said timidly.

Several moments passed, and her breaths grew deeper in frustration. "I'm not getting it."

"Just relax," I told her. "It can take some time."

The group went silent as we waited for something to happen. Seconds turned into minutes, and Felicity just stood there, concentrating.

"Come on, sweetheart," Alistair said, breaking the silence. "I'm giving it all I've got."

"So am I. I just... I can't!" Felicity broke into tears, then bolted out of the room.

"Fel! Wait!" someone called, before running after her. I thought it was Reid.

We all just stood there in shock for a moment before Alistair opened his big mouth. "Well, she's a hopeless case."

"Nobody here is hopeless," I snapped. I knew Alistair was just trying to lighten the mood, but I didn't take it well.

The problem was, I worried he might be right, and that put me on edge. Besides Reid and Eddie, nobody managed to perform Elven magic all night. I knew it would take practice, but my ancestors, I was hoping for *something*. We were running out of time.

Another hour of training passed. I repeated myself over and over again, but none of the Elves seemed to get it. I was getting more frustrated by the moment. It wasn't until my hands curled into fists and I felt magic ripple through my arms— strength I was inadvertently drawing from Chancey— that I finally decided to call it quits.

"We'll try again another time," I announced. "It's almost curfew anyway, and it's probably best if we don't all flood back to our dorms at the same time. We'll take turns leaving."

"You look defeated," Ivy pointed out as the Elves began to leave. "You need a drink?"

I sank into one of the stools at the bar. It was rickety, and though I was certain he was making deals with guards to get supplies for his nightclub, I was pretty sure he'd pulled this stool from the garbage. "Nah. It's hard enough for you to get your hands on alcohol. Save it for paying customers."

Eddie and Chancey approached. Alistair remained across the room, talking to an Elvish girl about his cat. Eddie sat beside me, and Chancey leaned on the bar.

"Is everything all right, Charlie?" Eddie asked.

I blew a breath. "Ancestors, do I have it written across my forehead or something? I'm fine."

"You don't sound fine," Chancey pointed out. I must've been using a harsher tone than I realized.

My nostrils flared. "Maybe I'm not, but you don't have to grill me about it!"

"Someone needs a punching bag," Chancey mumbled.

"You wanna volunteer?" I growled.

"I didn't mean anything by it," Chancey said. "You've been real moody lately."

"As Alistair would say, I believe *someone* needs to take a chill pill," Eddie added.

I totally lost it. I shot out of my chair, and it toppled over. Magic rattled around inside my chest as I screamed. "What I *need* is some goddamn certainty! I wake up every day unsure if any of us will be alive by the end of it. I'm not just imprisoned here, but in the fight club— and my one chance at getting free is hopeless, because I can't find any goddamn answers! My best friend is in a gang, and I can do *nothing* to help him out of it. I'm a fucking terrible teacher, but I'm all any of you have, and it's going to get you killed!"

I pushed away from the bar and started to pace around. "Worst of all, I've ruined the *one good thing* that's ever happened to me. I gave her up, and I'm *never* going to get her back. You all act like everything's totally fine, because you've got someone to keep you company at night. I have *no one.* The only thing I'm certain of is that if I don't die in the middle of this, someone I care about will! Forgive me if I'm a little bitter about it all!"

The room went dead silent. Even the Elves who had hung around on the other side of the room, waiting for their chance to leave, didn't say a word— not even a whisper. My chest heaved. I just wanted someone to say something. *Anything.* Tell me I wasn't fucking crazy.

"Charlie," Eddie said softly. "We're not going to die."

"That's a fucking lie, and you know it!" I yelled.

Forget it. I didn't want to hear a damn thing. It only made it worse.

I couldn't stand here and hope that my friends might soothe me, because there was *nothing* they could say right now. I whirled around and stomped out of the room. My shoulder slammed into the doorway on the way out, but I didn't care. The pain felt good, because it distracted me from my emotions.

I marched down the hall, hands fisting at my sides, until I was far enough away from The Devil's Playground that I didn't think anyone would follow. I stopped in an empty hallway and leaned against the wall, heaving. I didn't know where the hell I'd ended up, but it didn't matter.

What was that? Oberi's voice cut through my mind. I could feel through the bond that he was already looking for me.

Nothing, I growled. *Go away.*

I'm not going away when you need me. You're lost. I can feel it.

Of course I was lost— and not just in the hallways of the Institute. Ever since Ava and I broke up, I had turned off my feelings. I'd pushed them down so far that I didn't even know what I felt anymore. I was bound to break at some point.

Problem was, now that it'd come spilling out, I didn't think I could shove it back inside anymore.

I was bleeding, and the only way to stop the flow was to bleed out entirely.

I WAS NOT interested in getting out of bed the following morning. I wanted to pull the covers over my head and sleep all day. But Oberi wasn't having any of it. He grabbed the covers with his teeth and yanked them off of me.

Wake up, sleepyhead.

"Go away," I growled.

You missed your shift last night at the factory. You're not missing class.

How would you know?

I know how you feel, Oberi said. It wasn't to comfort me. He was being literal— a real hard-ass. *And if you miss your shift again, the Warden is going to take notice. I'm trying to help you.*

You can help by going away.

You can help by going away, Oberi mocked in a high-pitched tone. *Fine. Ava wanted to give me a bath, anyway.*

He was trying to make me jealous, and it was working. I didn't like that he'd rather be with Ava right now than with me, but I didn't say anything.

But Oberi wasn't about to make a threat he wouldn't follow through on. When I didn't protest, he huffed and left the room.

Even though he was gone, I knew I couldn't sit in bed all day. Oberi had been right. I had to get to class. The Warden was watching me— all of us. Taking off my factory shift last night had been a bad move. I had to find another time to train the Elves.

Problem was, all my "free time" was spent in the training center, and Captain wasn't giving me much of a choice there.

I dragged my ass out of bed, showered, and dressed in my uniform. I was counting my steps to the cafeteria when someone slid up beside me, looping their arm through mine.

"Charlie!" a girl sang. "I almost thought you'd forgotten about me."

"Uh..." I had no idea who was standing next to me. All I knew was it sure as hell wasn't Ava.

"I *did* say seven a.m., but I realized that I never told you my dorm number," she gushed. "You must've been looking everywhere for me! Finally, we can head to breakfast."

"Scarlet," I said slowly as it clicked in my mind. I'd never really *agreed* to go out with her, but I could see where she thought I had.

"Yes, it's me," she said. "Were you expecting someone else?"

I might've been *hoping* for someone else...

The thought twisted my guts. To hope for Ava was futile and a waste of my energy. We could fight the Warden together, but we were never getting *back together*— not the way we used to be. It had become a major distraction, where I couldn't even teach the Elves without thinking about her. We'd broken up because we weren't safe for each other, but holding on to her was just as dangerous. It'd be better for everyone if I just got over her.

And what better way than to throw myself at the first girl who was asking?

I despised the idea, but it felt like my only option.

"No," I told Scarlet. "I wasn't expecting anyone. You just surprised me."

"I surprise a lot of people," she chuckled. "Mostly with my brains and my brawn. Shall we?"

"Sure."

Scarlet and I got takeout from the cafeteria— because it wouldn't be a real date if we actually *ate* there.

"Where are we eating?" she asked.

"Um, I don't know..." I replied.

"You're the guy, so you have to surprise me," she said.

I thought about it, but every location that came to mind reminded me of Ava. The balcony was totally off-limits. I would *never* take Scarlet there. But even the most casual locations held *some* sort of memory with Ava— Commissary, the Villain's Den, the Arboretum. Was there *anywhere* on campus that Ava and I hadn't shared a moment or two together?

"I haven't been to the Arcanea Illusions room yet," I suggested. It wasn't particularly high on my list, considering the illusions were mostly visual, from what I'd heard.

"I can't, unfortunately," Scarlet said. "It's for good behavior only, and I have an infraction on my record this semester."

"What for?"

Scarlet snickered. "If you want to find out, we can rack up a few infractions of our own."

Scarlet grabbed my ass, and I scowled. *So attractive, I'm sure.*

The thing was, I didn't *want* Scarlet to be attracted to me. I was trying to forget about Ava, to be comfortable in Scarlet's presence, but I couldn't help it when my guts twisted whenever she came near. I wanted to hurl at her touch.

But I wanted to give this a chance, too. I knew Scarlet only wanted to use me like I'd been used so many times before, but maybe I could use her, too. Maybe she'd help me forget.

"Maybe not this early in the morning," I said in a dry tone.

"Fair enough." Finally, her hand left my ass, and I felt like I could relax.

"What about the room for vampires and succubi?" I suggested. "We could go there."

"Ew," she gagged. "With all *those* assholes? No, thank you!"

"Um..." I thought about it a moment longer, but all my good ideas just didn't feel *right* with Scarlet.

"What about the cemetery?" she practically sang. "I've never had a *date* in the cemetery."

Lovely. Scarlet wanted to fuck me on someone's grave in broad daylight. I just wanted to eat my food.

"There's a cemetery on campus?" I asked. I'd never been there.

"Well, they have to bury dead inmates somewhere," Scarlet said nonchalantly. "It's just outside the chapel. Come on."

Scarlet took my hand, and I followed her. At least the cemetery wouldn't remind me of Ava, though I thought it wasn't the best place for a date. Scarlet led me outside, until I heard the clang of metal and the creak of a gate. The air was chilly, and the clouds must've been thick overhead, because I couldn't feel the sunlight on my skin.

"This is *perfect*," she said, sounding overly enthused. It was in stark contrast to my grumpy attitude, and wasn't really helping. If anything, I was just getting more annoyed.

Scarlet led me past the gate surrounding the cemetery. We walked over uneven ground, which really threw me off. I didn't know where to step to navigate through the graveyard. It was like the graves had just been forgotten. Scarlet dragged me forward, and my shin slammed into something hard.

"Fuck," I growled as I sucked a breath. I felt for what I'd walked into and realized it was a broken gravestone. The Warden obviously didn't care about this cemetery. It was probably left over from when this place was a church. I bet the Warden was banned from demolishing it, or he'd have a haunting on his hands for disrupting the graves. It obviously wasn't very sacred, since the gate had been left unlocked.

"Come on, Charlie," Scarlet said, like she hadn't noticed me stumble. "We're almost there."

Scarlet led me forward, until we came to a set of stairs. She guided me to sit. I could sense a wall ahead of us, but I couldn't tell what it was — some sort of building set in the middle of the graveyard.

"What's this?" I asked.

"It's the mausoleum," Scarlet told me. "Cool, isn't it? I've always thought it was kind of spooky."

Cool? All I could feel was the cold concrete beneath my ass. I had no idea what it looked like.

Ava would be describing the architecture to me. I felt kind of bitter that Scarlet didn't make the effort.

Whatever. I opened my take-out container, and the scent of bacon hit my nose.

"Mm…" Scarlet breathed. "That bacon smells delicious. I bet it's better than this synthetic blood they have us drinking."

"If you like it, why didn't you order some?" I asked, before popping a strip of bacon in my mouth.

"It doesn't give me energy, but the salt still gets in my blood," she said. "It's unhealthy, but it just… it smells so good."

I swear she was about to orgasm just at the smell. She was throwing herself at me, and with every attempt, it only got more irritating.

"Can I?" she asked, leaning toward me.

"Uh... sure?" I barely started speaking before Scarlet snatched a strip of bacon from my container. She moaned in pleasure, but I was far from pleased. Ava could take food off my plate all day, but when Scarlet did it, I went back to a different place. I was that kid jumping between foster homes again, always trying to save my scraps so the other kids wouldn't take them from me. There'd never been enough to go around back then, and I didn't want to share now. I set my container next to me, far away from Scarlet so she couldn't reach my food.

She was still chewing her piece, savoring every bit, when she asked, "Do you ever just sit here and wonder what it'll be like when you get outside these gates?"

I shrugged. "I used to."

She must've been staring into the forest, because she turned away from me when she spoke. "To anyone else, the forest outside the fence would look frightening, but to me, it's like home. It's right there, yet I can't reach out and touch it."

"You miss home," I remarked.

She turned back to me. "Of course I do. Don't you?"

I sighed and poked at my food. "I don't really have a home. I have nothing to go back to."

"I'm sorry about that." Scarlet sounded like she meant it, and for a moment, it felt like we were truly bonding.

The confession tumbled out of me. "I grew up in foster care. I never stayed in one place too long. Then, when I aged out of the system, I was so fucked up I never settled down. I had to do lots of tough shit just to survive."

"I suppose that's why you ended up here," she said, sounding sad about my story.

"I'm not just talking about the criminal stuff," I said, loosening up a bit. It was easier to talk about this, after I'd told Ava. "I used to sleep with women off the street, just to get a warm bed for the night. Mostly older women who took advantage of me. I don't know if they took pity on me or found me attractive or what."

"Well, you *are* sexy," Scarlet said. "I can see why they wanted to sleep with you."

"Yeah, but I just wanted to be something to *someone*, you know? Something more than just a one-night stand. I thought I found that here at the Institute, but... well, everyone knows that went down in flames."

Scarlet shifted, sounding uncomfortable. "You're talking about Ava-Marie?"

"Yeah." My shoulders slumped. "We're bonded, you know? In a weird way. I still don't totally understand it."

"I thought you guys broke up." Scarlet's tone wasn't quite as soft anymore— like she was getting annoyed.

"We did, but it's... complicated. We're not together, but we're still bonded."

"Oh. That must be hard."

"Yeah, it can be," I admitted.

Silence stretched between us for a moment. I was about to say something more, but Scarlet closed the distance between us in an instant, and her lips connected with mine. I was so shocked that I drew away just as quickly, but Scarlet must've thought it was an invitation. She jumped on top of me, pinning my body to the mausoleum staircase. The edges of the stairs dug into my back, and Scarlet's tongue slithered inside of my mouth. She worked her succubus powers on me, entrancing me to remain still as her lips moved over mine.

My magic warred against hers. I didn't know whether to shove her off of me or succumb to her. I wanted to enjoy this, but I just... didn't. Kissing her felt gross, and I wanted her *off* of me.

Betrayal twinged inside of me. I shoved at Scarlet's shoulders. At first, I thought the feeling had come from me, an innate reaction to kissing another woman. But the twinge ebbed away as quickly as it came.

I realized that it hadn't come from me at all. It'd come through our bond. Mortification swallowed me whole as I realized what had happened.

Scarlet finally drew away from me. "Whoops."

Damn it. "Ava saw, didn't she?"

Scarlet sucked a breath between her teeth. "She's on the other side of the prison yard. I didn't realize."

Oberi, I growled through the bond. *You brought her here, didn't you?*

I'm not letting you get involved with Scarlet that easily, he sneered back, sounding slightly proud of himself.

I sat up. "We should've picked somewhere more private. Maybe next time we can—"

Scarlet stood, cutting me off. "Let's take some time to think about it. I just realized I'm late for class."

I got to my feet beside her. "Well, uh, I had a good time," I lied. I wasn't sure where the words came from, because they weren't true. I was certain some of Scarlet's succubus magic had actually taken hold of me, but something had turned her off. Maybe I wasn't as easy to manipulate as her other suitors, and that bothered her.

Or maybe she didn't like that there was still another woman in the picture. "You're easy to talk to. When can I see you again?" I asked lamely.

How about never, Oberi laughed in my head.

Fuck off, I snapped.

I can't. I'm already walking toward you.

"Um, I'm not sure," Scarlet said. "I have a lot of training to do for my next fight. Rain check?"

"Yeah, sounds good. I'll see you around," I said. I heard Scarlet's footsteps as she hastily ran out of the cemetery.

Oberi cackled in my mind. *You scared her away!*

You scared her away by bringing Ava out here, I snapped.

I left the cemetery after Scarlet, and the gate creaked shut behind me. The moment I was back in the prison yard, Ava and Oberi approached. I noticed another pair of footsteps with them, along with the soft pad of paws in the grass. It must've been Marcus and Rishi.

I shoved my hands into my pockets, feeling like I'd been caught doing something bad. And I had. Succubus influence or not, I couldn't convince myself otherwise. "Hey, guys. What's up?"

Ava didn't say a thing. Though she tried to hide it, I heard her sniffle.

"Have you seen Kallie this morning?" Marcus asked. "We've been looking everywhere for her."

"No. Why?"

He sounded worried. "We were supposed to meet in the Villain's Den. She was going to quiz me on my history homework. She didn't show up."

"Maybe Oberi can sniff her out," I suggested.

"We tried that," Ava said, quite harshly. "He led us out here, but there are so many other smells that he lost track of her scent."

"Maybe she—" I started to say, but I was cut off by the sound of a blood-curdling scream coming from the forest. We all went still. The guards were currently dealing with a scuffle near the basketball court, and I didn't think they'd heard it.

"That was Kallie!" Marcus cried breathlessly.

We all knew instantly that Kallie was in trouble. We bolted toward the trees. I grabbed Oberi's fur to guide me. We hadn't made it far into the forest when he skidded to a halt beside me.

"You're going to walk away and leave him alone!" a male voice shouted. "You're not to talk to him ever again."

Something ripped, like a piece of fabric. "Ow! You're hurting me!" Kallie screamed.

I hardly had a moment to process what was going on before Marcus ran forward. "Get off of her!"

He must've shoved the guy, because I heard him stumble backward. The big guy wasn't the only one confronting Kallie, though. There were at least three others, judging by the shouting that ensued.

"Don't you *dare* touch Big G," someone growled.

"You know your place," another snapped.

"You really want to stand up for *this* bitch?" a third guy laughed, like he found it comical.

"Marcus!" Kallie cried in relief. "Thank the gods you're okay. They said you were hurt out here and asked for my help. They lured me here!"

The gang members ignored her. Heavy footsteps squished through the mud. Judging by the deep voice, it was Big G. "Do you really want to fight me, Little Drummer Boy? Or shall I leave you to Bones? He'll have one hell of a great time with this story. Poor little Marcus, sticking up for the dainty little fae girl."

"Hell yeah, I'll stick up for her," Marcus said. I'd never heard his voice come out so strong.

Big G laughed. "Wrong answer. You're one of the Dead Men Walking. You don't get to associate yourself with bitches like her anymore. You belong to *us*!"

"I belong to no one!" Marcus snapped.

"Tell that to Bones."

The gang members moved so fast that none of us could react. I heard their footsteps, then Kallie let out a cry. Marcus grunted, like he'd been punched in the gut. Rishi hissed, and Oberi barked loudly. I moved to jump in and give them a piece of my mind, but Ava grabbed my arm and yanked me back.

"They've got a shiv to Kallie's neck!" she cried.

My blood went cold. Fuck— if we made a wrong move, her life would be over.

"Stand back!" one of the gang members yelled. "Or the fae gets it!"

Whoever was holding her must've been strong, because I could hear Kallie struggling, yet she couldn't get free. I heard someone snap their fingers, and I realized Kallie must be trying to stop time. It wasn't working.

Oberi, what's happening? I demanded.

A vampire's got a hold of Kallie, he told me quickly. *The big one punched Marcus and has his arm twisted behind his back.*

Fuck, they'd gained the upper hand. If Ava or I tried anything, they could slice Kallie's throat right then. Ava's fingers trembled on my wrist. She still hadn't let me go.

"It's time to teach you a lesson," Big G growled at Marcus. "I'm going to give you a choice right here, right now. It's the Dead Men Walking, or your girlfriend. But I'm warning you, if you choose her, she'll bleed out in under a minute."

"Why do you care?" Marcus spat. "She's done nothing to you!"

"Because you took an oath!" Big G yelled. "We don't associate with people outside our own. She's nothing but a distraction. How many of our secrets have you shared with her— or your loser friends over there, for that matter?'

"None— ow!"

"How many!" Big G roared.

"None, I swear! Just let her go," Marcus begged.

"If I let her go, you're choosing us," Big G told him. "Is that what you want?"

A beat passed before Big G screamed, "IS THAT WHAT YOU WANT?"

"I... I..." Marcus' voice wavered.

The vamp holding Kallie must've pressed the shiv deeper into her neck to pressure Marcus, because she whimpered again. It was at that moment that something broke within Marcus.

"I want you to go to hell," Marcus growled.

"What did you just—?" Big G started.

"Charlie, Ava, get behind a tree! Now!" Marcus shouted.

We didn't have to question it. Ava jumped behind one tree with Oberi, and I leapt behind another with Rishi.

Boom!

An explosion sounded, making my ears ring. Air whooshed by me so strong that I would've been knocked over if I didn't have the tree for protection. Magic sizzled in the air, and my ears rang.

As my hearing returned, I noticed that the forest was silent. Slowly, Ava and I stepped out from behind our trees, and she gasped.

He's killed them. All of them, Oberi said, sounding shocked. *Including Kallie.*

My stomach bottomed out. The story of what he'd done to get sentenced here came back to me. Marcus had lost control of his powers and killed a bunch of people, including his girlfriend.

It happened again. Except this time, he'd killed his mate.

Ava took a cautious step forward. "Are they...?"

Marcus must've had a moment to absorb the shock, because he was rushing across the forest a second later. I heard him drop to his knees beside where I thought Kallie had been.

"No, not dead," he said quickly. "I only used enough power to knock them out. Unfortunately, I had to knock Kallie out to save her. Come help me."

Oberi shifted into a unicorn and hurried over. I helped him hoist Kallie onto Oberi's back. Rishi meowed softly, like he was worried.

"Get her out of here, Oberi," Marcus demanded. "I don't want her anywhere near these guys."

On it, Oberi said, even though Marcus couldn't hear her.

"I'm coming with you," Ava said immediately. "I can heal any damage the blast might've caused."

"Go, before they come around," Marcus instructed.

The girls left with Oberi. I turned back to the guys lying on the ground. "What about them? Do we kill them?"

"Kill them?" Marcus balked.

"This is our chance to get you out of the gang," I insisted. I had no second thoughts about it. Any hesitation I had to take the lives of these dickheads had flown out the window once they'd put a blade to Kallie's neck.

Marcus blew a breath. "The gang is *way* bigger than this. If I kill them, the Dead Men Walking will murder us all for certain. Besides, how would we cover this up from the Warden?"

I gave a heavy huff. "You're right, but we have to do *something*. They're going to have to come after you either way."

"I know what to do." Marcus shoved a glass vial into my hand that he must've just conjured. "Quickly, we have to give them these while they're still passed out."

"What is it?" I asked, popping the cork and giving it a good sniff.

Marcus was already on the ground, pouring liquid down Big G's throat. "Bones had me lift some memory-wiping potion from Captain's stash. I can get him more after we use this up."

"So they won't remember this?"

"Exactly," Marcus said. "I'll have to convince them I want nothing to do with Kallie. They won't remember they went after her, and hopefully they won't go after her again."

"You think this will work?" I asked.

"What other choice do I have?" Marcus begged. "This is our only option."

He was right. It wasn't a fool-proof plan. These guys would wake up in the forest and wonder what the hell happened. But hopefully they came up with an explanation that didn't involve Marcus.

"I've got some empty nightshade bottles I was supposed to return to Bones," Marcus said. "We can leave them here so they think they overdosed. They'll write off their memory loss."

I felt around for the nearest gang member, then dripped the memory potion into his mouth. "Ancestors, Marcus. Memory potion? Nightshade? What type of operation is Bones running, exactly?"

Marcus scrambled to the next gang member. "It's honestly best if you don't know."

I grabbed him and shook him. "Marcus, you need to stop this! You told me about the Warden's office. You can tell me about the rest. What's going on?"

Marcus froze for a moment, as if trying to decide how much to reveal. He didn't say a thing before yanking the memory-wiping potion from my fingers and using it on the guy beside me.

"I can't tell you. They'll find out you know," he insisted. "One wrong move, and that's it for us. They'll kill us."

"How would they find out?" I demanded. "I'm not going to tell them."

"You'll tell someone!" Marcus shouted.

"Who? Ava? Kallie? They deserve to know."

"You'll tell Captain!" Marcus snapped.

I felt the blood in my veins freeze. Marcus gasped when he realized what he'd just said.

"Are you... did you...?" I couldn't think straight.

"Fuck," Marcus muttered. "Yes, okay? It's me! I'm... I'm the one rigging the fights."

I couldn't believe it. I just sat there, frozen.

"When I joined the Dead Men Walking, I didn't just become their mole," he admitted. "I'm their strategy guy. I analyze the fight stats to predict who's going to win and who's going to lose. I tell them where to put their money so that they make the most out of it. I see the patterns, and I've studied how to fix the fights so we can win the most bets. I can figure out who's willing to be bribed to throw the fights and who won't.

What did you *think* were on the papers I gave to Big G that day in the alchemy room? Predictions for the fights!"

My jaw dropped. I couldn't believe what I was hearing.

"We can fix this," I said quickly.

"No, we can't," Marcus argued. "We're both dead anyway. Let's just do what we can to protect the girls. We'll go down fighting if we have to."

Hell, that was all we *could* do. Both of us would lay our lives down to defend Ava and Kallie, and right now, it was looking like that was exactly what we were going to do.

Marcus had been right. I wish he *hadn't* told me. Because now I had to choose.

I could stay in fight club... or I could throw Marcus to the wolves.

The answer was obvious. I had to stay. But if I did, I had no doubt that Captain would become impatient with me sooner than later. I'd never seen my life flash before my eyes so fast. In that moment, one thing became *very* certain.

I was going to die in that ring to save my best friend.

ava-marie

TEN

Charlie had been on a date. With a *fucking succubus.*

And *fucking* was the right word, because I *knew* he'd slept with her. Scarlet had a reputation at this prison for handing out pussy like it was candy. I bet he'd eaten it up, too.

Whatever. I didn't give a shit. Unfortunately, I still had to go to counseling sessions with the bastard, so I dragged my happy little ass down to the therapy tower on Friday, bitching about the situation to Oberi the entire way. She walked at my side as a unicorn as I ranted, waving my arms and all.

"Look, it's not like I *care*," I seethed, wrinkling my nose. "But I'm just saying, she's gonna dump him like a hot tomato once she gets bored, so he better be prepared to lose out on that golden vagina she's always bragging about."

I think the phrase is hot potato, Oberi objected.

I rolled my eyes. "Of course you'd be obsessed with semantics."

I understand you're hurt, but he's hurting, too, Oberi said.

I gave a loud snort. "I'm not hurt. I don't feel a damn thing. And if he was so hurt, he'd talk to me about it, instead of looking for some other girl to sink his dick into."

You're jealous.

"If I was jealous, I would say something to him, but I haven't, so I can't be bothered," I offered with a shrug.

He's just looking for comfort.

"I'm sure she's *comforting him*, all right."

Oberi gave a snuff and shook her head. Kallie was waiting at the base of the stairs. She pushed off against the wall she was leaning on as I came near. I spotted Alette's antennas peeking out from under Kallie's hair.

"Are you okay?" I asked. I hadn't seen her since the other day, when I'd used my healing powers to bring her back around after she'd been knocked out.

"I'm fine," Kallie said, and she rubbed her temple. "Though I've had a headache ever since. Marcus' magic is strong as hell."

"The other day, when the vampires had you cornered... why didn't you stop time and save yourself?" I asked her.

"I tried, but I was too afraid," she said. "Illusion magic doesn't work if you're frightened, and my demigod powers are still linked to my fae magic. I was so scared about what could have happened to Marcus..."

She trailed off, and I nodded. Kallie was a badass assassin. She might've been able to take those vamps no problem, but she was too worried about what they might've done to her mate. No wonder she rushed into the situation without using her head.

She dropped her gaze. "Have I ever told you that my powers are affected by how Marcus treats me?"

"What do you mean?" I asked.

"It has to do with the mating bond," she explained. "I'm a fae, and we're not strong without our mates, especially shifters. If Marcus and I are fighting, my powers become weaker across the board. And we haven't embraced the bond yet, so..."

"Why don't you two get together already?" I questioned. "We all know you like each other, and that you're mated."

"It's not that simple," she insisted. "He's never going to stop pushing me away, and it's *killing* me, Ava. I'm a wolf who's been rejected by her mate, and that's always going to make me vulnerable. Until he accepts me... and he never will... I won't be able to access the height of my powers."

She looked away and wiped her eyes with the back of her sleeve. "But it's no use trying to fight it. I'm a lone wolf. I always have been. I just have to figure out how to go at it alone."

I wanted to protest further, but I thought about Charlie and me. We were one soul living in two separate bodies, who were destined to be together, but we weren't. I couldn't convince Kallie there was hope for her situation when I didn't feel like there was any for my own.

"Kallie, people have figured out he's your weak spot," I warned her. "You have to be careful."

She rubbed her arms. "I know. I don't think when he's in danger. I just act."

"You can't," I argued. "If you keep doing so, it's going to get you killed someday."

Kallie turned toward the door and shifted her bag on her back. "Let's go in."

We climbed the stairs to the tower. Marcus and Charlie were already sitting in the therapy circle. With one look at Charlie, I felt my entire body flush with rage.

Ooh, I was so mad at him. Mad as hell. But I didn't have any right to be. We were both single, and we'd been broken up now for almost half a year. It was clear his attention was elsewhere. So, fine. He could walk his fine ass away. I could date other people, too.

Not like you want to, Oberi whispered.

I huffed and stomped toward my seat. Kallie and I plopped down, and nobody talked.

Well, this is awkward, Oberi commented. Rishi gave a yowl.

I was about to break the silence, until a high-pitched ringing hit my ears. It was painful— like some sort of alarm going off in the distance. It made my eardrums ache.

"Do you guys hear that?" Marcus asked, cringing.

"Ugh, it's horrible," Kallie said, covering her ears.

Charlie's countenance was grim, like the ringing bothered him at his core. "What *is* it?"

Rishi meowed, unbothered, and Alette remained tucked under Kallie's hair.

Oberi, on the other hand, bobbed her head, shaking out her mane. *It's quite awful*, she commented.

Despite the irritating ringing, we could still hear each other and the other noises in the room. The sound of Professor Jaymin's shoes tapped on the stairs.

"Act normal," I told them. Everyone straightened up and became passive, though that obnoxious ringing didn't go away.

The door opened, and once it did, a wave of nausea so strong nearly knocked me out of my chair. Marcus gagged, and Kallie put a hand over her nose. Charlie sank in his seat. Jaymin walked into the room, looking bright and peppy as ever.

"Good morning," she sang. "I hope all of you are having a pleasant day."

I caught on. All of us felt sick, and we'd all been fine before we'd walked into the counseling session. That was, until Jaymin got here. Something was off.

I studied the area, looking for something new. The buzzing was coming from Jaymin. Nothing looked out of the ordinary on her person, but I wasn't fooled by first appearances.

I studied Jaymin's clothing as she sat across from me. There was a small, pronounced lump in her jacket pocket, like one a stone would make. Just looking at it made my stomach churn.

What if that's the crystal we need? I thought. *The kind Charlie learned about in the news articles from the library that they used to experiment on people here at the Institute.*

Charlie started next to me, and it nearly made me jump. His expression looked... confused, but held a hint of confirmation.

Had he heard me? I wasn't sure. Could Charlie and I communicate telepathically, like Oberi could with us?

I didn't see why we couldn't. We shared feelings all the time. It shouldn't be that hard to share thoughts, too. Why not try it out?

Left corner pocket on Jaymin's jacket, I thought. Charlie nodded subtly, like he got the message. I could sense he was trying to say something back to me, but our bond wasn't strong enough for him to reach out to me.

Maybe it would be easier for us to communicate telepathically, if he wasn't screwing someone else.

Charlie's entire face flushed, and his jawline hardened. Oh, shit, he'd *definitely* heard that one, and it'd pissed him off. Oops. I needed to monitor my thoughts around this guy.

I mean, I was the talker between us, so it wasn't odd that I could speak to him and he couldn't reply back.

Ava, pay attention, Oberi snapped. *Jaymin's talking.*

I snapped myself out of it. Jaymin was rattling on about something—usually, our sessions were full of racist talk about the Elves that we all tried to block out, but this time, whatever she was doing seemed important.

"How do we feel today?" Jaymin asked. She glanced from one face to the other, waiting for someone to admit guilt.

I got the game. She was using the crystal to try and weaken students, get them to snap. We couldn't fall for it. If we admitted we didn't feel well, it'd tip her off to what we were.

Jaymin looked fine. Maybe she had some kind of protection from it. She blinked at us, waiting for our answer.

Kallie was trying to lightly snap her fingers in her lap, hiding the motion from Jaymin within her skirt. Marcus glanced at her, but Kallie shook her head, telling him to stay quiet.

"We feel great," Charlie stated.

"Hm." Jaymin frowned. "Well, I heard there's a bug going around the prison."

"None of us have caught it," Charlie said. "We're healthy as ever."

The four of us forced smiles, but I wasn't sure how long we could hold out the ruse. I felt more ill with every passing second.

Jaymin scribbled something down on her clipboard, stabbing the paper with her pen. "Very well. I suppose that's good news."

Didn't sound like it, from her tone. She placed her clipboard in her lap. "You've been skipping shifts at the factory, Charlie. Is the work too difficult for you? Or do you simply have better things to do?"

Charlie's eyebrow twitched, but Oberi huffed at him to stay calm. "I'm a busy guy."

"Surely," Jaymin cooed. "I don't expect that you had any drive to get a job before you got here, looking at your record for petty theft. It's sad that you're still looking to get out of work. But I suppose not all of us are born with the desire to better ourselves."

"No one would hire me back then, anyway. Most blind people live in poverty due to a failure to obtain employment," Charlie rattled off. He knew Jaymin would pick on this aspect of his life eventually and already had a comeback planned.

"Remember what we talked about last week, about not making excuses?" Jaymin asked. "I'm sorry to say the Institute can't correct laziness, though we try."

Charlie didn't react to the taunt, thank the ancestors. *Jaymin was purposefully trying to get us to flip out, but... why?*

Bet it had something to do with the crystal in her pocket.

I knew she was coming for me next, so I steadied myself as Jaymin said, "And your feelings, Ava? Are we experiencing any more... delusions?"

I didn't dare talk about my emotions, or my bipolar, when we were in therapy. I didn't want Charlie breaking any more windows.

"I'm doing fine," I said. "Meds are working, mood is steady. Nothing more to it."

"What about the voices you hear?"

"They talk. I ignore them. Like most people," I stated bluntly.

Jaymin cocked her head. "I see you've gained some weight. When we met at the start of the semester, you were skin and bones."

"Yep. I'm happy to say I'm eating three square meals a day, and finishing all of them, all thanks to you and your *incredible* counseling sessions," I said sarcastically.

Charlie laughed under his breath, and Jaymin caught it. Her eyes flashed as she added, "Yes, well, watch that waistline. Don't want to get *too* comfortable with your calories."

Charlie gasped beside me, and Oberi pawed her hoof against the floor. But I refused to let Jaymin's goading get to me.

I gave a careless shrug. "Being over or underweight is a temporary state. Being stupid, though— that's permanent, and not correctable in most people. If that's not clear enough, I'm referencing someone in this room."

Kallie and Marcus couldn't help but let out snickers. Jaymin tightened her grip on her pen as she turned in her seat to look at Kallie. "Professor Mazur notified me that you failed your exam in Flight class last week. Too tired to fly, perhaps?"

"I wasn't feeling well," Kallie said. "I flunked because I skipped class to rest... but I'm better today," Kallie added as I hastily nodded at her.

"Hm. You must be trying magic beyond your capabilities. New abilities, perhaps?" Jaymin asked.

Shit. She was close to figuring out that Kallie had demigod powers. I started to sweat, but Kallie said, "Nah, just working too hard at football practice."

Jaymin kept prodding. "Isn't it upsetting to you that you failed?"

"Yeah, but so did your daddy's condom, and that's a bigger tragedy," Kallie replied with a short shrug.

Jaymin's nose twitched, but she let that one go. Jaymin often ignored Kallie completely, if she could help it. My fae friend was a tough nut to crack, and I figured Jaymin found her too difficult to interrogate. Any attempt to get her to confess to anything just dissolved into an argument between them, wasting our counseling time.

Marcus was the easiest to get to fess up, and Jaymin had figured that out. He hadn't let anything slip during our counseling sessions, but he'd stopped himself before he'd said something incriminating one too many times, and she'd picked up on that.

Jaymin wore a harsh grin as she set her sights on Marcus. "I don't know if you noticed, but in the *Miriamic Messenger,* Octavia Fall's local newspaper, they dedicated a new park to one of the little girls you slayed in your little... accident."

"Teena Mars," Marcus said sadly. "I noticed."

"Yes. She was only six when you blew her apart. Terrible thing, really. How does that make you feel?"

This was going too far. Jaymin was a mean counselor, and yet this bordered on cruelty. I went to say something in Marcus' defense, but Kallie spoke up first.

"That's nice they're doing a memorial," Kallie said. "Good people should be remembered."

"Yes," Jaymin replied slyly. "But she wouldn't have to be remembered at all if Marcus hadn't killed her, isn't that right? She'd still be alive."

"She would be," Marcus replied back, haunted. "But she's not."

"That's too bad. I'm only disappointed you can't apply yourself at the Institute, and show the kind of potential you did during your crime," Jaymin said, in a fake-ass, disappointed tone. "Wouldn't it be nice to use that talent for good, instead of evil, like you did?"

Jaymin made a tittering sound. "Unfortunately, it just doesn't look like you have the talent."

Marcus hung his head, but Kallie wasn't going to allow that comment to slide. "That's not true," Kallie immediately broke in. "Marcus is stronger than all of us."

Jaymin let out a tinkling little laugh. "I'm sorry, but Marcus' performance in his classes has left much to be desired."

"Screw class," Kallie barked. "It's not like that matters."

"She's right, Kallie. Let it go," Marcus said quietly.

"No, Marcus!" Kallie's tone was so vibrant, it drew everyone's attention. She fisted her hands in her skirt. "You're stronger than all of us. You killed eleven people, including someone you loved. I couldn't live with the guilt if I did that. I'd die of sadness and a broken heart."

She drew herself and added, "But you *did*, Marcus. You found a way to go on and keep living your life even after losing something so precious to you. You're hated by your coven, you ruined people's lives, hell, you even lost the one person that you thought really understood you, and yet you're *still here*. None of us in this room could do that. Not a damn one of us. But you pulled through. Which makes you the best out of all of us."

I thought about how I'd feel if I accidentally killed Charlie, and immediately agreed with Kallie. I wouldn't survive that.

"Well, thanks, Kallie," Marcus said, like he was honored. "That really means a lot."

"Touching," Jaymin commented, and she tossed her clipboard on the small table beside her. She stood to open the door. "I think we're done for today. You are dismissed."

Clearly, she was frustrated we hadn't shown any weakness at whatever was in her pocket. We stood up to leave. On the way out, Charlie bumped into Jaymin, nearly knocking her over. He grabbed her shoulder to steady her while his other hand slipped into her jacket pocket. She didn't even notice.

"I'm sorry," he said quickly. "Can't see where I'm going."

Jaymin's lip curled. "Yes. I suppose we should all be more careful."

I smirked. It was the same trick Charlie had used to steal my wallet long ago. Jaymin sneered at us as we left the room, and we took the winding tower downward.

"Gods, that woman is horrid," Kallie complained when we reached the bottom stair. "It's like we go in to get bullied every week."

"Did you get the crystal?" I asked Charlie.

He opened his hand. Resting on his palm was a tiny purple gemstone. It was see-through, and at such a close distance, the ringing it emitted niggled at my brain. I wanted to pass out just looking at it.

"Do you think Jaymin will notice that you nicked it?" Marcus asked nervously.

"She has counseling sessions all day. She'll suspect us, but she'll suspect others as well," Charlie pointed out. "We just have to hope she doesn't realize it's gone until the end of the day."

"I couldn't stop time with that crystal in the room," Kallie said. "Whatever it is, it limits our demigod powers."

"Jaymin didn't seem affected by it," I pointed out. "Neither did Rishi and Alette, but Oberi was. It's the same with Kallie's powers, so it *has* to be something for demigods. I bet Jaymin's carrying it around to see who gets sick."

"I've felt this way once before," Charlie remarked. "I got the same headache when we went to the fence line and tried to escape earlier this semester. These crystals must be what the Warden buried around the perimeter of the Institute. They're why we can't break out."

I gritted my teeth as I took the gemstone from Charlie. "This thing literally burns my hand."

"Mine too," Charlie said. "It was painful to hold."

"Oh, ancestors. Does anyone have a glove?" I asked painstakingly. Touching this thing was getting more agonizing by the minute.

"Here." Charlie slipped off his sweater and handed it to me, leaving him in his white button-up. I bundled the crystal into the sweater, and the effects lessened slightly, though the thing made me nauseous to be around. It'd left a tiny mark on my skin.

"Remember the potion I talked about, Charlie?" I asked. "The one that could tell us what this thing is made of? Let's go brew it now. The stuff's in the Lair."

"I'm not going," Marcus said. "I need to leave."

"Marcus," Kallie said softly.

"I'm at the counseling session because I have to be, but as far as anything else goes, I can't be seen with you guys anymore. It's too dangerous," Marcus insisted. "I have to report back to the Dead Men. Don't try to talk to me, especially not in public. It'll only make things worse."

Marcus romped off with Rishi. Kallie's gaze dropped, and I asked, "Do you want to stay here? Charlie and I can handle this."

"Yeah," she said quietly. "See you two later."

Kallie headed off in the other direction, her hair hanging in her face. Gods, she got really depressed when Marcus wasn't around. It was so sad to see.

"Let's leave, before anyone notices us doing so," Charlie noted.

We got to the Lair as quickly as we could. I'd already stashed the ingredients we needed for the potion there after stealing them from the alchemy lab days ago. Oberi stood guard at the entrance, while I sat on the floor and got to brewing the potion. I lit a fire underneath my cauldron before I added water and started pouring ingredients in; olive oil, cinnamon, dried primrose, and faekin dust that I'd gathered from Alette's wings. The crystal sat bunched in Charlie's sweater beside me as I brewed. Even though it wasn't touching me, I could still feel the crystal's soft hum.

"What do you think is in that crystal?" Charlie asked.

"I can't be sure. We know the crystal hurts prophets and demigods," I said. "If my theory is right, this type of crystal was used on my Aunt Maddie to force her to see visions, and it obviously has a negative effect on us."

"Hopefully this potion will help us figure out why," Charlie mused.

"You should know that the potion will eat whatever is put into it. The crystal will be destroyed during the process of the potion breaking down the chemical compounds," I explained. "We won't be able to keep it once I drop it in."

"Fine. Get rid of it," Charlie demanded, like he couldn't stand to have the crystal in his presence.

I dropped the crystal into the potion. Charlie and I both sighed in relief as we felt the crystal's awful effects reside, and the ringing in our ears faded.

I stirred the concoction counterclockwise, before I stood. "We should leave this here to brew. I'll check on it before our cells are locked for the night."

Charlie nodded briskly. We got back to the prison before anyone noticed our absence. Oberi walked behind us as we roamed the Institute halls. I headed toward the Villain's Den, looking to relax for at least a bit of the afternoon. Charlie followed me, and I didn't know why.

It was annoying. I wanted to be left alone. Loneliness... it was safer. It wouldn't hurt like seeing Charlie with Scarlet had.

"I could hear your thoughts in counseling," Charlie noted. "Not everything, but bits and pieces. It was smart of you to tell me where Jaymin had hid the crystal."

"Uh huh."

Charlie's brow furrowed. "Don't you think it's cool we can communicate telepathically? It's something we should work on."

That would only bring us closer together, which was something I didn't want. "Keep your thoughts to yourself. I've got enough on my mind."

Charlie frowned. "So... you don't want to talk to me?"

"Not really." *Ugh, asswipe.*

"Did you just call me an asswipe?" Charlie snapped.

"No!" Another unfortunate slip of the brain.

"Yeah, okay. Why are you always in a mood?" Charlie said sourly.

"Oh, gee, it wouldn't have anything to do with me having a *mood disorder*, now would it?"

"This has nothing to do with your bipolar. You've been stable for months," Charlie accused.

"Maybe it has to do with the fact that *you—* what was that?"

Our bickering was cut off by the sound of arguing coming from the merperson cellblock of the prison.

Uh-oh. That didn't sound good.

Charlie and I hurried down the hall, Oberi scrambling behind. Opal stood outside of her dorm room, holding on to a blanket that had little narwhals all over it. She was trying to get it back from a huge, hulking merman, who was yanking on the blanket with a cruel laugh.

"Cut it out, Kyle!" Opal screamed. She bordered on hysterics as she tugged on the other end of the blanket, trying to get it back.

Kyle snickered. "Still need a blankie? Aren't you cute."

I knew this loser. He'd choked me out during the Darke Games, and Charlie had almost killed him. I wasn't a fan. His windpipe, which Charlie had crushed, still rasped with each word he spoke.

"It's mine!" Opal's voice grew louder. Kyle let out a cruel laugh and pulled the blanket so hard it nearly yanked Opal off her feet.

I was about to intercede, until I heard someone cry out, "Give it back, jackass!"

My brother was out of the hospital and back to his old self, though he was still making a recovery and trying to get used to his treatments. The way he moved, though, you wouldn't think he was sick at all.

Ez crossed the cellblock in minutes as he squared up with Kyle. "You've got two seconds to fuck off."

"Why? I thought we were having fun," Kyle teased. He pulled again on the blanket, and my heart cringed as I heard it rip. A huge hole ran up the side, ruining the quilt squares. "Oops. My bad."

"*No!*" Opal screeched, and she began sobbing.

Kyle tossed it back at her with a sneer. "Game's over, I guess."

Ezekiel socked Kyle across the face. He went sprawling to the floor with the force of Ez's punch. My brother had nearly knocked him out.

Kyle clambered clumsily to his feet, bunching his hands into fists. "You bitch-ass cripple. I'm gonna—"

"Bad idea," Charlie said. He stepped up behind Ez, and Kyle's eyes widened. He didn't bother to say anything else. The coward took off running, leaving the merperson cellblock and abandoning the fight.

Opal cried harder. Ez put a hand on her shoulder and said softly, "Don't worry, Opal. We can't get you a new one."

"You can't! It won't replace this one!" Opal wept, and she clutched the blanket to her chest like it was made of gold.

"I'm sure we can find something," Ez said, looking helpless.

"You don't understand." Opal sniffled. "It was my *daughter's!*"

Ez's mouth dropped open, and Charlie went rigid beside me. I was frozen in shock. Opal was younger than *me*. She had a kid? What... what had happened?

Ez and Charlie were still shell-shocked, so I decided to take action. "I can fix it, Opal," I offered. "Give it here."

"Can you?" Her eyes burned with hope. Oberi nosed her fingers, giving a soft nicker.

"Yes. A couple of stitches, and it'll be better in a jiffy."

Opal handed over the blanket, and I took it from her. "Let's go to the Arts & Crafts room."

Ez put his arm around Opal's shoulders and guided her behind us as we hurried to Arts & Crafts.

Professor Celosia took one look at Opal's tears and the torn blanket in my hands before she waved us through the door. She immediately gave me a needle and thread without us even having to fill out a form on what it was for. We sat on the floor cushions that were gathered around a window at the farthest corner of the Arts & Crafts room, and I got to work. The boys remained quiet as Opal wept, and I hand-stitched the pieces of the quilt back together.

Oberi bobbed her head. "Oberi likes your blanket. Says she appreciates the narwhals," I offered.

Opal gave a sad little noise. "It doesn't matter. It's ruined now."

"It's not. Never been a project that I couldn't patch up. I promise I'll make it good as new."

Ancestors, Kyle had really fucked it up, but I vowed to myself I would fix the blanket somehow, for Opal's sake.

The sadness in the air was so heavy as I worked. Ivy had told me months ago that his family— Opal's family— was really fucked up, and that she was in here because of them. I couldn't fathom how all of this was connected.

I glanced around the room. There was no one else in here. It felt lonely without Marcus in the corner working on his paintings. The gang had literally taken everything from him. But maybe it was best that we were alone, because Opal really seemed like she had stuff to get off her chest.

Ez was the first one who was brave enough to speak up. "What's your daughter's name?"

"Marina." Opal's lip wobbled. "She's three."

"That's a pretty name," Ez offered. "She's the same age my kid would've been."

"Re-really?" Opal wiped her nose. "I didn't know you—"

"Yeah. I got my girlfriend pregnant when we were sixteen," Ez said. "But she lost the kid, so... it wasn't meant to be, I guess."

If possible, Opal looked even more depressed. "I see. I hope you two can work it out, once you get out of here."

"That's not going to happen," Ez said immediately. "We were bad for each other. I've moved on. I'm never going back to that relationship."

"Oh." Opal looked down at her hands. "I've never had a boyfriend."

Ez was definitely confused, so Opal added, "It wasn't a one-night stand, or anything. Though I wish it was."

I had already guessed what was coming, but by the horrified expression on Ez's face, he'd just figured it out. Charlie, ever the silent and supportive bystander, remained by my side and let Opal say what she needed to.

"My mom died when I was really young," Opal explained. "My family has always been really chaotic. Drugs, alcohol... you name it. Ivy left as soon as he could. He tried to take me with him, but the vampires wouldn't have me... so I had nowhere else to go."

Opal shivered. "Marina... her father... he's also her grandfather."

I didn't understand, until I did. The realization was like a knife to the gut. Ancestors. It was worse than even I had imagined. The blood had drained from my brother's face, leaving him pale and horrified.

"My dad had always... but it got worse, as I got older." Opal was turning green, like this made her physically ill to talk about.

I couldn't imagine Opal's pain. What I'd endured, I'd only had to go through once. Opal had put up with years of abuse.

Charlie's hands quivered. I couldn't imagine how hard this was for him to listen to. He had difficult memories of his own trauma he had to deal with. I grabbed his hand and squeezed it. He instantly calmed at my touch.

"You don't have to explain your story to me," Ez insisted, and he grabbed Opal's hand. "You don't have to relive it."

I wanted to tell him to back off on the touching and give her some space. But Opal didn't seem uncomfortable at Ez's hand. Instead, she leaned into his grip. "I want to tell you everything. I want *someone* to know. I can't keep carrying this around alone."

"Okay. So go on."

Opal was totally fixated on Ez. It was like the two of them had forgotten Charlie and I were here as she continued. "I was so scared. I hid the pregnancy from my father as long as I could. When he found out, he tried to make me get an abortion, but by then, I was too far along."

Opal blinked rapidly. "Prom was a couple of weeks after I'd found out I was pregnant. I was so excited, because Ivy had sent me this beautiful dress from Chicago, and I really wanted to wear it. I just wanted *one night* of happiness and peace. I thought I'd be like Cinderella, you know, and some prince would come and sweep me off my feet, make me forget about my problems for a night."

Opal's voice grew volatile. "They were silly dreams. At the party, a couple of jocks cornered me. They didn't hurt me, but they tore my dress and pulled at my hair. I was so humiliated, I ran off. I couldn't stand up for myself back then, and I'd always been shy. By the time I was confident enough to go back out on the dance floor, I'd been gone for hours, and people wondered where I'd gone. Then, when we got back to school, those jerks told *everyone* I'd been gone for so long because I was sleeping with them. The rumor was pretty much confirmed in everyone's eyes once word got around that I was pregnant."

Opal wiped at her face again, while Ez's lip began to quiver. "That's why I didn't want to go to the Villain's Ball. Everyone made me out to be this huge slut who'd slept with a bunch of guys and got pregnant at prom, a whore who didn't even know who her father's daughter was. But that wasn't true. I never slept with any of those guys. They just threw my name out there so they could act like big shots. I didn't want that to happen again."

"What happened then?" Ez asked.

"My dad left me alone when I was pregnant. Didn't want to draw attention to himself," Opal said. "Then I had Marina, and she was just my whole world... I looked at her the second the nurse placed her on my chest and promised myself that no one would ever hurt her like they'd hurt me. I thought I had the chance to be happy."

Opal put a hand in front of her eyes. "After she was born, my dad came for me again, and I couldn't take it. I refused to allow him to hurt me one more time. This siren scream just burst out of me... his head exploded."

Charlie's jaw dropped, but Ez remained in control, thank the ancestors. He nodded along like Opal had said the most normal thing in the world. Opal shuddered. "I panicked. I tried calling Ivy, so we could clean up the mess and hide the body, but he was still so far away. He told me to wait, but I was so afraid that I tried hiding the evidence myself... and I got caught."

Opal hung her head. "They took Marina from me and put me on trial. My family has a bad reputation in the Atlantean court system, so I knew I wasn't getting off easy. They talked about executing me, or sending me to the Atlantean prison on a life sentence, but I was lucky enough to have a good criminal defense lawyer. She saved my life. She argued that I had a clean record before the incident and that I'd probably lost control of my powers by accident. She suggested the Institute... and the judge agreed."

"So what happened to Marina?" Ez asked solemnly.

"A stroke of good luck. She was placed with a good foster family, a nice couple with money. I know my child is being taken care of, at least, and that gives me peace of mind. Nobody in my family wanted to take her, and thank Atlantis for it, because I'd be losing my mind if I knew she was with any of them."

"The court system didn't find out about what your dad did?" Ez asked.

Opal shook her head. "The judge had heard the rumors about me at prom, and assumed that's where Marina came from. He didn't order a paternity test, and I didn't request one, because I didn't want people to know who Marina's father was and shame her for it. I did my best to save my daughter's respect, in the eyes of our people. I'd rather everyone think I was trash than know my child was a product of in— in—"

"You don't have to say it," Ez said, and he stroked his thumb along the back of her hand. "It's okay."

Opal took a heavy breath. "Getting my daughter back is dependent on the conditions of my release. If I graduate from the Institute, I'll get full custody. So I *have* to be good here, and leave the Institute with a clean record. So I can see my daughter again, and she can finally be back in my arms."

Opal wiped at her face. "I'm already losing so much time. I already have to explain to her where she came from, one day, and I don't know how to do that. Telling her I had to go to prison was hard enough. She didn't understand why I had to leave."

"She will one day," Ez said. "And she won't hold it against you."

"How can you be so sure?" Opal raised her eyes.

"Because I'm willing to bet that Marina is just like you, and you're the sweetest, kindest girl. You couldn't hate anyone, no matter what they did," Ez said. "And I know the way you talk about her that you love her. She knows it, too."

"I haven't even talked about this in group therapy." Opal ran a hand through her blue hair. "Though word has gotten around, somehow. Mad Dog knows. He's been torturing me about it ever since I got here. Thank Atlantis for Ivy, though. He drives him away."

"You don't have to worry about anyone bothering you ever again. If someone wants to hurt you, they're gonna have to go through me," Ez vowed.

Opal smiled for the first time. "You're adorable, but you can't fight off everyone."

"Why not?" Ez said lowly, like he wanted to try.

"I haven't seen my daughter since I've been sent here. I barely get to talk with her on the phone," Opal said. "That's why I need the blanket fixed. It's the only thing I have of hers the Institute allowed me to bring."

"And here it is," I said, tying off the last stitch. I handed it back to Opal. "Good as new, like I promised."

"Ava, it's perfect. I can barely tell it was torn," Opal said, peering at my neat stitches.

"See? There's nothing I can't fix," I said proudly. I stood up and tugged on Charlie's arm. It already felt like we were infringing on a very private moment, one that was meant for these two. "I'm really sorry to hear about everything that happened to you, Opal. I hope you can get your daughter back."

"I will, someday," Opal said. "Thanks for sticking up for me. And for fixing Marina's blanket."

"You're welcome. See you guys later."

Charlie and I left the Arts & Crafts room. As I took a glance back, I saw Opal and Ez curled up together on the floor cushions, cuddling and looking adorable as all fuck. Professor Celosia was acting like she hadn't seen them, ignoring the "no touching" rule so they could have a moment.

Well, good for them. I hoped Ez could help Opal heal.

We were quiet. By this time, it was around lunch, so Charlie and I naturally headed toward the cafeteria. I'd been hungry earlier, but now my appetite was depleted. Hearing about Opal's tragic life was traumatizing enough. I couldn't imagine living through it. Oberi followed behind us, unusually quiet.

"Do you think she'll be okay?" I asked Charlie as we approached the cafeteria.

"Yeah. She's got Ez," Charlie said. "He's always gonna be there for her."

I swallowed the lump in my throat.

Charlie changed the subject, because I don't think either of us could talk about Opal any longer. "So when do we check on the potion? Tonight?"

"The potion will take time to decipher the atomic makeup of the crystal," I said. "It should be ready in the morning."

"It'll take all night?" Charlie complained.

"I'm a master alchemist. My aunt trained me well, but I can't make potions work miracles," I told him crossly. "We're just going to have to wait and see."

Charlie gave an angry noise. "We don't have that kind of time."

"Would you relax? Ancestors, I thought I was the impatient one in the relationship."

Charlie's knuckles cracked. "There is no relationship because there is no us!"

Oberi stomped her hoof as hard as she could. She didn't mind if we bickered, because that was just Charlie and I, but she *hated it* when we fought.

"And who's fault is that? I'm not the one getting pegged by a succubus," I said snidely.

"I'm not getting— hell, I fucking hate you sometimes."

"I hate you *all* the time!" I stopped walking and faced him as we came to the entrance of the cafeteria. "But why should you care how I feel? You've got a new girlfriend now."

Charlie scoffed. "Scarlet is not my girlfriend. In fact, I'm hardly interested."

"You're interested enough; otherwise, you wouldn't have taken her out," I accused.

"So what?" Charlie threw his arms up. "We went on a date, and it wasn't anything special."

"Come on. We all know Scarlet's hot. Have you *seen* her ass?"

"*No!*"

"Okay, that was a stupid question, but you have to admit you've copped a feel."

"I have not!" Charlie yelled.

"Please. You can't expect me to believe you didn't sleep with her." I crossed my arms.

Conversation inside the cafeteria, which had been loud before, had died down. People had overheard us arguing and wanted to listen in on the prison's newest drama.

I didn't care who heard. I was too upset.

"We didn't do anything," Charlie growled. "We had breakfast, and we talked. That's all!"

"You don't have to lie to me. I know you have needs."

Charlie's mouth dropped open. "You're being overdramatic!"

"Says the man who can't control his temper to save his life— or our lives, really!"

He was off the rails lately, flying off the handle every which way and turn. Eddie had told me the Elf training session the other day hadn't gone well, but Charlie's people were depending on him. He had to do his best to keep it together.

Charlie's teeth gritted. "I don't have to explain myself to you. I'm single, you're single, and whoever I date— or whoever I sleep with— is none of your damn business!"

"Fine! You can fuck anyone you want, and you know what? So can I!" I screamed back.

Charlie let out a noise of rage and fisted his hands in his hair. "You're so difficult to get along with! *This* is why we broke up, because you take every little thing and blow it out of proportion!"

"What?" My mouth bobbed open. Had he really said that?

But he kept on going. Charlie seemed to be on a tirade as he ranted, "You know what I said. You're just a spoiled little rich girl who wants everyone to think that you give a shit, but deep down inside, you're just looking out for yourself. You pretend to care about everyone else because no one gives a fuck about you, just so you can feel like you matter!"

I didn't know someone could actually rip your heart in two. Or that it would keep beating afterwards. Because at that moment, I wanted it to stop.

Charlie! Oberi reared her head back, like she was shocked.

For the first time in my life, I was speechless. I couldn't think of anything to say back. Even the voices in my head were quiet, muttering Charlie's words over and over.

I couldn't think or breathe. All I could do was *feel.*

He'd really hurt me this time.

I think he knew it too, because his angry expression dropped, replaced with horror. "Pidge—"

I did my best to blink the tears away, grateful he couldn't see them. I stormed away before a sob could escape from my throat that he would hear. The tears were overwhelming me this time, and I couldn't make them stop.

I had to get away. Somewhere no one would see me cry.

The storage room that Ivy was using to build his secret nightclub was my first thought. Oberi trotted after me as I let myself in. By this time, I was bawling. I fell to the floor and curled up against the side of the stage, wishing the tears would stop but being unable to halt them.

I knew Charlie had been triggered by Opal's story. He was frustrated that he couldn't teach the Elves how to defend themselves, and that the potion was taking so long.

And maybe I'd been a bitch to him earlier, but seeing him with another girl had really twisted me up inside. I didn't want to care.

I did care. His words had gutted me.

Ava, Ava, Oberi said. She sank down, so she was lying across from me. *Don't heed what he said. His words were cruel, but he doesn't mean it.*

"I just want it to stop," I cried. "I should be doing something about this pain, not keep letting it get to me."

Tears are good. Crying is doing something about it. You are letting your feelings flow, so they don't get bottled up inside and ruin you.

I cast away my tears with the heel of my hand. "He wouldn't have said those things unless a small part of him believed it."

Oberi lifted my chin with her horn. *You are my Ava, and even if the world burns and Charlie goes down with it, you will still be my Ava.*

"But he needs you, too."

I am here for whichever of you needs me most. And right now, you need me more.

I sobbed into my hands. I heard the sound of the door opening and closing. I glanced up and saw Ivy, his skirt swishing as he hurried to sit down at my side.

"Oh, Ava." Ivy brushed my tears away. "I know it takes a lot to make you cry."

"It hasn't been the best day," I admitted.

"It's Charlie, isn't it? You got in another fight."

"Yeah." I didn't tell Ivy what Charlie had said, because I knew if I did, he'd rip Charlie's head off.

Ivy parted my hair back. "I'm sure he'll stop being a moron and come to his senses. And if you two can't work it out, I know a grave we can bury him in. Or some concrete shoes, if he'd like to take a swim in the lake."

A laugh bubbled up from my core. "You're the best, Ivy."

I noticed there was a bit of blood mottled around Ivy's nails. He didn't attempt to hide them as I asked, "What's that from?"

Ivy smirked. "Kyle might be sleeping with the fishes. Or he would be, if I didn't have to run off before I got caught."

"Ivy, that's so dangerous."

"Nobody saw me. He's gonna be breathing through a tube for a while, though."

"I take it you heard what happened, huh?" I asked.

"Yeah. Thanks for fixing Opal's blanket. It means everything to her," Ivy said, putting an arm around me. Ivy's skin was cool and smooth.

I huddled closer to him. "Opal's life was so sad."

"Everyone here has a sad story, precious. Some are just sadder than others," Ivy said.

"You were going to help Opal hide a body."

"Nothing I haven't done before."

"Ancestors, Ivy!"

"My dad was in the Italian mob. Half of them are vampires anyway, but you'd never know it. I told you my life wasn't all roses."

"Were you in the mob, too?"

"Not really. I helped them out with a few jobs, but who I was prevented them from accepting me."

"Because you're nonbinary."

"Yeah. They were looking for tough guys, and that wasn't me. I was too feminine for them to want to keep me around for long. I bounced back and forth between Chicago and Hawaii a lot. Mom didn't want me, and my dad didn't bother to know if I was dead or alive most days." Ivy wiped the rest of my tears away. "I'm guessing your folks don't know about what happened to you, either. Mine never found out. Or cared to ask."

I hadn't told him, but Ivy knew anyway. We just had that kind of connection. I looked up and asked, "You too, huh?"

Ivy gave a frown. "I got myself into a couple of bad places I couldn't escape once I was in 'em."

"Oh, no. That's terrible."

"My clients weren't the best people. I went home with a few guys I had no business being around but... I gotta eat, you know?"

I gave a heavy sigh and leaned against Ivy's chest. "Life sucks, Ivy."

"Only if you're a vampire."

I cracked a smile at his lame joke. "How many people do you think are at the Institute who don't deserve to be here?"

"Honestly? Most," Ivy said. "I was paying attention in Juvenile Justice— weird, right, because I never do— and Professor Jobe was saying that most prisoners end up behind bars because they didn't have enough resources or support back home. We had this group discussion, and almost everyone in class said if they had a stable home, or a better education, or good parents, they wouldn't have ended up here. I mean, some people belong in here— people like Mad Dog, and Naya. They come out of the womb bad. But most of us... maybe if things were different, we would've had a chance."

"I had the best upbringing I could've had, and I still turned out wrong," I said glumly, thinking of my parents.

"Maybe you're one of the bad ones," Ivy teased with a coy wink.

I scoffed. "Probably."

"I think a lot of us got dealt a bad hand. Then once we got started down the wrong path, we just... couldn't figure out how to get off."

I rubbed my eyes. I couldn't figure out how to fix my life anymore. "I don't know what to do, Ivy. I keep making the same mistakes."

"Happens to all of us," he insisted.

"Not like this. I'm just too emotional. I don't know if there's anything good left inside of me," I confessed. "I'm too much for Charlie to handle. That's why he keeps avoiding me. I destroy everything I touch, and I chase away everyone who gets too close. This proves it. I'm... I'm unloveable."

"Hey, hey," Ivy said, grabbing me before I could cry again. "Don't you let him make you think you're worthless, you hear me? You're a strong, beautiful person with a heart of gold, and you always have been. No matter what, you always got yourself, and you can't turn your back on the woman you want to become. *Nothing* can take that away from you, ya understand? And you're not unloveable. I love you, and your friends love you, and Oberi loves you. You got a whole team of people behind you, so fuck whatever Charlie said, you hear me?"

I cleared my throat and sniffed. "You're right. I want to feel better. Just... tell me how."

"I could tell you, but you're not gonna understand until you figure it out for yourself."

"You're always so brave, Ivy. I want to be like that."

A corner of Ivy's mouth raised. "I had to love myself, sweetheart, because it was damn obvious no one else was going to."

"Okay. Then show me how."

"I will. It's time you got your confidence back."

I blinked, and Ivy shook my shoulders encouragingly. "You know what? Chance said he's gonna bring Charlie down to the club tonight for the grand opening of The Devil's Playground," Ivy said mischievously. "Why don't we give Charlie an evening he'll remember?"

"What did you have in mind?"

Ivy grinned. "Revenge is my specialty, precious. Just follow my lead, and he'll live to regret ever letting you go."

"Ava, this is going too far."

My brother was complaining as he set up lights backstage at The Devil's Playground. It was opening night, and on the other side of the curtain, dozens of students with invite-only passes were getting ready to enjoy a night of drinking, dancing, and debauchery.

And I was the opening act.

Ivy had hired a bunch of girls, mostly succubi, to be exotic dancers for the club, and a couple of brawny vampires to act as security. He'd also hired a fae friend to cast illusions to keep the sound from escaping the club, along with a spell to hide the entrance from anyone who didn't have a pass. The dancing girls were to go on and continue the show after my act was finished.

This was my first performance in front of a live audience since I'd quit singing after Monica died. Underneath my silk green robe, I wore fewer clothes than I ever had, but I'd never felt so confident.

I'd managed to con my brother into helping me, though he refused to run the spotlight once he got it running, handing the job off to Opal. He clearly disapproved as I took a few steadying breaths backstage, wobbling in my knee-high leather boots that had a five-inch heel.

"Is he here?" Opal gushed, bouncing in place.

"Sitting in the front row with Chance," Ivy said in satisfaction. "His world is about to get knocked sideways."

Ivy wore identical boots to mine, with a green and black corset— Institute colors, of course— matching panties, and garter straps that held up fishnet leggings. He looked incredible.

My heart thudded wildly with the news that Charlie had arrived. He thought I was a spoiled little rich girl? Fine. Because I was getting *all* the money tonight.

Ivy twirled a feather boa around his neck as he faced me. "Ready to take back your power, precious?"

"I am *so* ready," I said sinisterly. I adjusted the headset microphone one more time. I hoped it didn't fall off with all the crazy moves I planned on breaking out.

"I can't watch this." My brother covered his eyes, while Opal let out an enthusiastic cheer.

"Remember, you are in total control," Ivy reminded me. "Make those dogs eat out of the palm of your glorious hand."

I nodded and began climbing the stairs to the catwalk. Once I was directly above the stage, I stepped onto a platform and wrapped my hand around the metal pole, taking my starting pose. No one would see me until the platform was lowered downward. It'd be a total surprise.

The curtains were drawn, and people screamed as the spotlight centered on Ivy. He began twirling around the stripper pole in the center of the stage like a master, twisting his body as if he was born to perform for a crowd. Ivy was a true artist with the pole. When he danced, everyone was captivated by the beautiful way his body moved.

We ruined our chances and got sentenced to hell
But I'm addicted to sin and have something to sell.
You think I'm a doll and want to play with my life
You can toy with me now, but only for a night

You can have it fast or easy, or you can take it slow
Just have that wallet ready, baby, or I'll tell you where to go.

Damn, Ivy could *sing*. We'd written this song in a rush for the club's opening, and only rehearsed it a few times with the DJ who was playing the song's instrumentals. Now that this was the real deal, he was belting out the lyrics like none other. Women— and men— both hollered in delight as he dipped down, showing his ass to the audience before grabbing the pole behind him and sinking down.

That was my cue. The bass thumped, the music pounded, and colored lights flashed everywhere. I felt like a goddess as the platform was lowered from the ceiling, hovering above the stage to the wild cheers of the audience.

My eyes scanned the crowd. I caught Kallie sitting with a group of fae girls at a table in the far corner, Alette on her shoulder.

Then I saw Charlie. There he was, having a beer with Chancey and waiting for the song to continue.

He thought he was here to support a friend. I was going to make him eat shit.

I shimmied my shoulders, then shouted, "This one goes out to the *asshole* who broke my heart!"

When Charlie recognized my voice, his expression went completely white. A wicked grin spread across my face as I spun around the pole and began to sing.

From the day I was born, I've always been a bad girl,
Stealing cars and breaking rules was my entire world
And if you're looking for a way to get inside,
Buckle up and hold on tight, because baby, it's a ride
Pin me up against the wall and grab me by the waist,
I can't say I won't be naughty, but damn, I'll like the taste.

I yanked at the tie on my green robe, and it fell off, revealing my outfit. It matched Ivy's, a green-and-black corset with garter straps and fishnets. I'd gone a little more daring on the panties— whereas Ivy's covered his ass, I was more or less just wearing a thong. The men in the crowd went absolutely nuts, giving wolf whistles.

With delight, I watched as Chancey leaned over to Charlie and hastily explained what was going on. Charlie's eyes got darker with every word. I grabbed the robe and tossed it to the crowd to the pleading demands of men.

And what do you know— it landed on Charlie's head. He flailed to yank it off, his hands trembling and his jaw still wide open as I continued my song.

Spoiled little rich girl who needs Daddy's credit card
We might be behind bars, but trust me, I can get you hard
These broke guys can't handle what they cannot see
The judge thought I was too damn wild, so my sentence set me free
But if you get me in handcuffs and read me all my rights,
You'll have me on my knees or any way you like.

The beat picked up, and I began my dance. I did a few dips and twists to the mounting enthusiasm of the audience before I wrapped one knee around the pole. I supported myself with one hand as the pole began spinning me around, and I switched tactics. Both of my legs clung to the pole as I began climbing it, higher and higher until I reached the top. I let myself go, hanging upside down with my arms out. My boobs nearly spilled out of my corset, until I steadied myself by grabbing the pole with two hands, extending my legs into the splits.

See? Ivy's dancing lessons had come in use after all.

"Holy shit, she is *flexible!*" some guy cried out.

"What I'd give to put her in any position!" another dude cried.

I wasn't even paying attention to Charlie's reaction anymore, because this was fun, and I was having the time of my life. I'd never felt more empowered as I made the pole my slave. I came down from the top of the pole and landed on my heels, giving a wink to the audience as I slowly slid down its length.

The platform was lowered to the stage floor. The crowd continued screaming insanely as I stepped down, and Ivy took his place beside me.

The platform rose back into the catwalk as Ivy and I duetted the chorus, melding our voices into a synchronized harmony.

My vices and my darkness I'll take to my grave
Because if given the chance I'll always misbehave
Addicted to the high of wanting sex and freedom
You'd better bow down, cause this prison is my kingdom
I'll be riding on top and screaming as I say it
I'm a bad bitch and don't you forget it!

We broke into a coordinated dance just as the beat dropped. The club was so loud that the floors shook. Thank the ancestors Ivy had put some good silencing wards on this place, because if he hadn't, the guards would hear us for sure.

But at that moment, I didn't care. I was free, and I didn't belong to Charlie, nor the Warden— not anybody. I was a powerful being who was fully in control of her life, and who had a body these men would die for. In this room, I held all the power— and all the attention. Ivy and I danced like we were one sexy being as the music swelled to a close, provoking us to take our final stance on the last beat.

The ground thundered as the act concluded. My chest heaved up and down as I struggled to catch my breath from the singing and the dancing. So much money was thrown onstage that I had trouble wading through it all. I couldn't put my heel down without stepping on a dollar. Ivy and I hastily collected the money as other dancers walked onstage to perform the rest of the night's entertainment.

Kallie cheered like a madwoman. I searched for Charlie and saw his back as he stormed out, punching the door open so he could leave.

Fucking jackpot.

I was still trying to catch my breath as I strode offstage. I took a seat beside Ivy, who'd planted himself on Chancey's lap and grabbed a cock-tail. Chancey had ordered drinks for us, and I took a long sip as the party continued around us. People flooded onto the dancefloor with their dates, grinding on each other to the music.

"You were spectacular, doll face. *Very* sexy," Chancey said as he clinked his glass against Ivy's.

"A toast!" Ivy cried out. "To the club's opening, and for Ava showing her ex that he ain't shit!"

I heartily agreed. I threw back my drink and chugged it in a few gulps before I asked Chancey, "You don't feel shitty for leading him into a trap?"

"Hey, he needs a wake-up call," Chancey said. "Besides, it was good to get a little payback for him whacking me in the face."

Everyone laughed, and Ivy ordered another round. Kallie had left the group of fae girls to come sit with us, giving me a high-five for my wicked revenge.

A dancer serving drinks had stopped at a nearby table. A warlock slapped her thigh and laughed.

The waitress let out a yelp. Ivy was instantly on his feet, calling over the bouncers. "Hey, *nobody* touches my girls, you got that?"

"Oh, yeah? What are you gonna do about it?" the warlock growled.

Ivy grabbed the loser by his neck and tossed him into the table. It collapsed. The warlock gaped, rubbing his shoulder and looking up at Ivy in fear. Before Ivy could pounce on him, a couple of bouncers grabbed the dude, pulling him out of the club.

"I gotta handle this," Ivy said with an eye roll. He got up from the table and hurried off to talk to the bouncer who was dragging off the jerk. Chancey followed him.

"I'd figured you were bringing a date," I said pointedly as I turned to Kallie. Marcus had gotten an invite, but it didn't look like he'd shown up.

Kallie knew exactly what I was talking about. She fiddled with her glass. "Marcus is ignoring me. It's pretty clear we're never going to get the happy ending I've been hoping for."

"You don't know that for sure," I objected.

"I do. Mates don't always end up together. It happens." She shrugged. "So... instead of pining away for him, why can't I be happy with someone else?"

"Are you saying you're looking for someone to fool around with tonight?"

Kallie grinned in a very fae-like, mischievous way. "I might be."

"Well, good." I looked around the club. "Maybe I'll do that, too."

"It should be easy for you. Half the guys in this club are looking at you like a snack," Kallie said.

Yeah, I had noticed. My little dance had gotten the attention of all the men in the club. None had come forward to flirt with me— yet— but I was certain it would only be a matter of time.

Alette fluttered on Kallie's shoulder. Since there were no prison guards around, Alette was free to roam. She'd been cooped up hiding in Kallie's room most days, so I was glad the little faekin was able to get out tonight. Even so, there were a couple of jealous glances from other sorceresses in the club who wanted Kallie's faekin all to themselves.

"You'd better be careful. Don't want anyone to steal her," I told Kallie.

"These bitches know better than to cross me," Kallie said, taking a sip of wine. "I'm an outcast, but I'm still the king's daughter."

"Aren't you worried someone will tell on you?"

"I'd rip them apart. She's the only one who makes me feel better most days," Kallie said solemnly, and she stroked Alette's fuzzy body with one finger. It was clear she was thinking of Marcus, and that wasn't an option in my book. I needed to find her a distraction— a good-looking one, preferably.

A slim shadow fell over our table. I scowled as I saw Scarlet looming over me. She was wearing red lingerie that revealed her tits, and sky-high heels that made her at least an inch taller. Her dark curls spilled around her red lips. She navigated her perky, perfect ass around me as she took a seat beside Kallie.

Ugh, *her*. She was the last person I wanted to see. She wasn't even a dancer. Why was she dressed like that?

"Hey, Ava," Scarlet swooned. "You were *amazing* on stage tonight. Do you think we could go somewhere more private so you could show me... you know... your moves?"

Her fingers danced up my arm, but I drew it back. "Thank you, but I'm not interested."

"Oh," Scarlet said, blinking. "My mistake. I thought you'd be into girls."

"Psh. I wish." It would be easier if I was attracted to women. They weren't as confusing as guys. Unfortunately, all I liked was dick.

Kallie, though, was jumping at the opportunity to get laid by anyone, and Scarlet was on the menu. She batted her eyelashes. "So... I take it you and Charlie aren't pursuing things further?" Kallie asked.

Scarlet let out a laugh that was so loud, it made the table next to us jump. "*Him?* Hell, no. It was the *worst* date I've ever been on."

"Really?" That was nice to hear. A devilish note of satisfaction balled in my gut and stayed there.

"Yes," Scarlet insisted. "I was totally coming on to him, and he kept rejecting me at every turn. I've never been on a date with someone so disinterested. I *had* to get out of there as soon as possible."

"You didn't have sex?" I asked, probably too quickly.

Scarlet laughed again. "No way. I'd rather date a toad than go out with Charlie a second time. Never again."

My entire body went cold. Wow. And I'd really thought...

Fuck. Now I felt like a real jackass, accusing him of what I had earlier.

Then I remembered how cruel he'd been, and the awful words he'd spoken to me. I straightened up and added, "Well, he never has much to say, anyhow."

Unless it's fucking mean.

"It's probably best that we didn't work out. Succubi have an unsatisfiable lust. Our need for sex can't be escaped," Scarlet said tiredly. "It's almost like a curse, being horny all the time."

"Maybe I can help you with that," Kallie offered, twirling a strand of hair around her finger. "That is, if you like blondes."

Scarlet's gaze flashed with desire. "Blondes are one of my favorites, actually."

Alette let out a *squee*. Kallie blushed as Scarlet grabbed her hand and pulled her up from the table. "You're a princess, right? I've never dated royalty before."

"Ex-princess, actually," Kallie said with a subdued giggle.

"No matter. I'm gonna make you feel like a queen."

Scarlet pulled Kallie toward the backstage. The moment the two of them had left me alone, someone slipped in to take their place.

"Oh, hey, Ghost," I said offhandedly as he plopped beside me. "Did you enjoy the show?"

"Yeah!" he said brightly. "I thought you looked great!"

Ghost's cheeks were pink, and he fidgeted in his chair. His voice came out in a nervous stutter as he asked, "So w-would you like to d-dance?"

Did Ghost have a crush on me? It was kind of adorable.

He held out a hand. I was impressed by his bravery, so I took his hand and smiled. "Sure. Let's go."

I had definitely made his night. He wore a huge, bright smile as he sang the words to the music. I found myself growing more cheerful with each passing second. Ghost was gangly, nerdy, and he didn't know how to dance, but I found his cutesy behavior very charming as we bounced up and down to the beat. Even better, he was respectful and kept his hands firmly on my hips as the beat thumped.

"I *love* that song," Ghost said as we left the dancefloor once it was over. "You're an incredible dancer."

"It was fun," I said, brushing my hair back with a laugh. Ghost was nice. I'd go out on a date with him, just to give him a chance, though I didn't think it'd go past that. I wanted to keep my options open, and my heart a little less broken, thank you very much.

"Would you like to— oops!" Ghost's words cut off as he accidentally bumped into a waitress carrying a tray of drinks. The drinks dumped all over his shirt, and the waitress scowled, going back to the bar.

"You okay?" I asked, pressing a hand over my mouth.

Ghost held out the bottom of his shirt. "Yeah. Oh, fiddlesticks. Better go clean this up."

I shook my head as Ghost ducked into the bathroom. I couldn't imagine how Ghost had lasted this long in fight club. He was more innocent than a church choir.

Then again, he *had* tried to break out of the prison, and almost achieved it, too. Kid had something in him.

"How was Ghost?" Ivy asked as I sauntered up to the bar. I was aware that multiple guys were staring at my ass as I ordered a cosmopolitan.

"He was okay," I said with a shrug. "But I'm not looking to tie myself down."

"Good girl!" Ivy praised. "You play the field. I'm gonna keep these drinks pouring, and the money flowing."

I was more than happy to play hostess. As the night went on, I talked to a couple more guys, and even danced with a few. Nobody gross or intimidating came up to me all night, which was good... although, I was certain that was because Ivy had told the biggest bouncer in the club to be my personal bodyguard as I made the rounds. As crazy as The Devil's Playground was, Ivy had made it safe, especially for women and his employees, and I couldn't be more grateful for that.

Though I was quickly getting bored. Ancestors, this was like being in high school again. None of these guys could hold my attention. Any attempt to communicate ended in one way, and one way only— with the guy muttering *uh huh* while latching his eyes on my boobs. Couldn't *any* of them hold a proper conversation?

Didn't have to worry about that with Charlie, I thought.

Shit, I wasn't supposed to be thinking about him, and yet he'd crept in anyway.

Screw him. I hoped he was sulking in his cell with a bruised ego and blue balls.

Even if he hadn't slept with Scarlet...

The club closed at nine thirty, because everyone had to be back for bed check by ten, and we couldn't risk anyone finding out about The Devil's Playground. As the club emptied out, Ivy and Chancey went behind the stage to count money.

"Hey, who threw this onstage?" Chancey chuckled. He held up a gigantic black phallic item that had to be bigger than my arm.

"Ancestors, it's a dildo," I choked out with a hiss.

"There's always one," Ivy said with a growl. "Some ass must've tossed it as a joke."

"Here, Ava. A souvenir to remember the night by," Chancey cracked as he slapped the dildo into my hand. "Use it well."

"What for? It's not gonna fit. It'd impale me if I tried," I cracked.

"Give it to Charlie. He always acts like he's got something up his ass," Chancey offered.

That made me snort. We counted the money— Ivy had made a small fortune— paid the dancers and the bouncers, then cleaned up the club.

We only had a couple of minutes to make it back to our cells before they were locked for the night, so we had to hustle. Chancey dipped into the angel cellblock once we passed it, leaving the two of us alone in the dark.

It had to be a funny sight— me running through the hallways in lingerie and knee-high boots, clutching a massive black dildo while Ivy hurdled behind. Both of us were buzzed by this point, and snickering due to the alcohol.

We'd almost made it to my room before the shine of a flashlight burst into our faces, and figures blocked our path. My stomach twisted as I saw two guards, carrying noxite guns and looking foul.

"We still got time," Ivy objected. "It's only five minutes to ten!"

"Drop your weapon!" the guard shouted. He didn't hesitate to point his gun straight at us.

Ivy threw an arm up and sank down, sinking his booty to the floor. I nearly died laughing.

"Not you," the guard snarled. "The girl! That item is contraband!"

"What, this?" I waved the dildo in the air. "I'm sorry, did you want to borrow it?"

The guard's face flushed, and Ivy howled. The guard clutched tighter to his gun. "You two are looking for a reason to piss me off."

"Hey, we had a deal. Twenty percent of the profits for you to look the other way, and to not tell the Warden," Ivy said. "You just earned yourself a nice, hefty payday. That is, if you can keep your mouth shut."

The guard scowled, and his friend shifted uncomfortably. "Fine. But our profit better be delivered by tomorrow."

"It'll be at the drop-off point before breakfast, promise," Ivy purred. "Can I count on my *special delivery* to be there like I asked?"

He had to be talking about the club's alcohol.

"Don't worry about it," the guard growled. "We'll hand it over next weekend— that is, if you keep your end of the bargain."

"I always do, sweet cheeks," Ivy hissed. "Now run along."

The guards sneered at us, but they left us alone. Ivy slung an arm around my shoulder, and we sang our song lowly on our way to my cellblock.

"You're amazing, Ivy. You controlled those guards no problem," I told him.

"I fuck everyone sooner or later," Ivy said with a careless laugh. "Whether that be actually screwing them, or screwing them over."

I snickered. This had been one of the best nights of my life. For the first time in months, I finally felt like myself again.

The old Ava wasn't coming back. But I could be someone different, someone *better*.

I couldn't wait to find myself again. And this time, I wasn't losing her.

Not for anyone.

It was fucked up. All of it. The Institute. The strip show. Marcus and the gang. It was *all* fucked up. And there was nothing I could do to stop the madness.

I tossed and turned all night. Ava's lyrics echoed in my mind, and I couldn't get the scent of her silky robe out of my head. The world spun around me just thinking about her standing on that stage, dancing and singing like that.

It wasn't that I had anything against dancers. But I sure as hell had something to say about that performance.

That dance hadn't been about Ava letting loose and having fun, and it certainly hadn't been about the money. She'd stood on that stage for one reason only— to piss me the fuck off.

"Spoiled little rich girl who needs Daddy's credit card. We might be behind bars, but trust me, I can get you hard."

I screwed up. I hadn't meant to say that stuff to Ava. Hell, I didn't even know *why* I'd called her a spoiled little rich girl. I didn't think it was true. Sure, her family grew up with money, but that wasn't her fault. She was here at the Institute, same as me. It was a far cry from *spoiled*. I'd called her difficult. Selfish. I'd even said she didn't *matter*.

That was the biggest lie I'd ever told in my life. Ava mattered. She always had, especially to me.

But that dance... the way Chancey described it... what she'd been wearing... those *lyrics*. Ava was taunting me— showing me just how much of a mistake I'd made. She wanted me to hurt the way I'd hurt her when that fucked up shit had come out of my mouth.

And it worked. I felt terrible.

I didn't know how long it took for me to finally drift off, but when I did, nightmares assaulted me. Images formed in my mind, which was weird, because I never dreamed with sight. I had no visual memories left to speak of. Even weirder, it didn't strike me as odd at the time. I just let the dream carry me naturally, letting it lead me to where it wanted me to go.

I PUSHED *a door open and stepped outside into the night air. The sky was dark, but the sidewalk was lit by streetlamps. The parking lot was nearly deserted. Ahead of me, cars whizzed by on the freeway.*

My heart raced, and I quickened my step. Something felt awfully wrong.

"What's the rush?" a girl beside me laughed. "We have all the time in the world."

I glanced at her. Her black curls and freckled nose were as familiar to me as my own features. I reached for her wrist, where she wore a green bracelet that matched my own red band. "Don't look now, Monica, but I think someone's following us."

Monica swung her head around and gasped. I didn't glance behind, but I knew there were two of them.

"I said don't look," I hissed.

Monica's voice shook. "Ava, they're getting closer."

I could see our car up ahead, parked in the shadows. My pulse quickened the closer we got, but it felt like a mile away.

We could make it. I knew we could.

"Hey," a man called from behind us. "We're looking for directions. Think you can help us?"

My whole body shook. Something told me they were looking for more than just directions. Monica and I walked faster, like we hadn't heard him.

"Hey, my friend asked you a question!" the second guy shouted. They were too close for us to escape, but we were going to try anyway.

"Run!" I shouted to Monica.

We broke into a sprint, and she headed to the driver's side of the vehicle. I reached for the passenger door handle, but before I could grab it, something tangled in my hair. My whole body yanked backward, and strong arms wrapped around my middle.

"Ava!" Monica screamed, but I barely heard her over the sound of my heart hammering in my ears.

I thrust my elbow backward, but it met nothing but air.

If only we had magic. I could burn this motherfucker if I had Fire.

But I didn't... I was too young. I couldn't defend myself.

"Get off me!" I screamed.

A van skidded to a halt beside us. Doors opened, and the man yanked me toward the van. I immediately knew what they were going to do to me, and I'd never felt more terrified in my life.

"No!" I shrieked. "Help! Somebody help!"

But there was no one.

"Let her go, you psycho!" Monica shouted. She jumped on his back, but he threw his shoulder back and tossed her off of him.

"Get in the van, you bitch," he growled as I continued to struggle.

"Get away from her!" Monica roared. She punched the guy across the mouth, and he swore.

I heard the sound of something click. Horror hit my gut when I looked over and saw a blade glisten in the light from the nearest streetlamp.

"Monica!" I screamed. I wanted her to run away. I wanted her to abandon me— save herself. I was nothing compared to her life. I'd die and be tortured if it meant that she could live. Take me instead, I wanted to scream.

But it was already too late. The guy thrust his blade forward, and it sank into Monica's gut.

Time seemed to slow as the world tilted on its axis. Monica went as still as a statue, her mouth hanging open and eyes wide in shock. She stumbled back a step and dropped her gaze to the knife protruding from *her abdomen. She yanked it out and stared at the blood-covered blade like it had come from another planet. She couldn't seem to process what had just happened. Blood poured out of the wound, and she collapsed.*

"No!" I cried out, so loudly that it seemed to shake the entire Earth.

"You idiot!" the guy holding me growled to the other. He must've been shocked, too, because his hold on me loosened.

I dropped to my knees and grabbed Monica, cradling her to my chest with one arm. I pressed my other hand to the wound, but blood poured through my fingers and soaked into my clothes. Monica gasped for breath.

"Monica, no!" I cried. Tears streamed down my cheeks as I stared down at her. "No, don't leave me! You can't!"

Her mouth bobbed, like she was trying to say something, but she couldn't get the words out. Her eyes glossed over, and I sobbed harder. She reached her hand toward me, like she needed to feel me, to make sure I was real.

Tires squealed nearby, and I heard familiar voices coming to my rescue— Mama and my grandmother. I didn't know how they'd found me, but they'd come a moment too late. I heard my mother scream, and the smell of ash filled the area as her powers ignited the men into flames.

"A-Ava," Monica rasped, before her hand went limp and fell to the ground at her side. Her head lolled back, and her eyes became like glass.

I knew then that I'd lost her.

"MONICA!" I screamed. I wrapped her tighter in my arms and pressed my face into her hair. I didn't care what the world did to me now, because nothing mattered anymore. I didn't know how to live without her, or even how it would be possible. She couldn't be gone. She couldn't.

But she was. Gone.

Forever.

And without her, I was lost.

I STARTLED AWAKE, my entire form dripping with sweat. I clutched my clothes as if I might find evidence of blood on them, but there wasn't any. It took a few moments for me to process it as a dream. When I did, I rolled over and buried my face into the pillow.

Hell, Ava, I thought. *I'm so sorry.*

I could relate to Ava's experience, because I'd experienced some-thing similar. My friend Marty had been shot in a drive-by shooting, and I'd held him when he died. But to see Ava's experience from her own eyes... it was horrifying. I never wanted to relive something like that *ever* again.

But how *had* I relieved it? It was Ava's memory, not my own.

What's wrong? Oberi's voice came through our bond. He'd stayed with Ava last night, but that was only on the other side of the wall. I could hear him clearly in my head.

Nothing. Bad dream, I told him. *Go back to sleep.*

It's past six. Time for breakfast.

I'm not hungry, I said.

Well, you're going to have to drag your pretty little ass out of bed sometime. Ava wants to meet you in the Lair pronto.

Oberi didn't give me a chance to respond. I felt our connection slip, like he'd rushed out of the cellblock. I was about to tell him to fuck off, before I realized the Lair meant only one thing.

The potion was ready.

I scrambled to get dressed. I swung by the cafeteria to sign in for breakfast, then grabbed a takeout sandwich and ate it on the way. I counted my steps across the prison yard and used my Earth magic to navigate through the trees. I couldn't hear my friends until I stepped into the Lair— courtesy of one of Kallie's illusions.

They were all here. Ava and Kallie spoke in low tones, and Marcus cleared his throat nearby. I felt for the couch Kallie always conjured and plopped down next to Marcus. He blew a breath. I could tell he was sulking.

"What's going on?" I asked.

"The potion's done," Marcus replied. "Ava was waiting for you to arrive before she told us what she found."

"I *meant* what's going on with you?" I said. Ava and Kallie were still whispering across the Lair, so I didn't think they'd heard.

"Me? Nothing," Marcus replied.

"Clearly," I stated flatly. "Trouble with your soulmate?"

Marcus scoffed. "You're one to talk. Ava had to send Oberi to get you. Couldn't even go get you herself."

I frowned. Yeah, I'd noticed.

"We all know Ava and I are screwed up," I said. "That's nothing new."

Marcus shifted on the couch. "Fine, you want to know what's new? Kallie's dating a *woman*."

I gaped. "But Kallie's bonded to you."

"Doesn't mean she can't screw someone else on the side," Marcus grumbled. "Ivy told me he saw her leave The Devil's Playground with Scarlet."

"Scarlet?" My jaw dropped. "If they left together, I can only imagine—"

"Please don't put those images in my head," Marcus begged. "Kallie's giving Ava *all* the details, I'm sure. I'm trying not to listen."

I sighed. "Man, I'm sorry."

"It's not your fault."

Yeah, it's yours, I thought. If Marcus and Kallie just got together already, they wouldn't have this problem. I knew he liked her, but he didn't have the courage to be with her.

But I guess I couldn't talk...

"It's *so* nice to not be single anymore," Kallie told Ava loudly, obviously rubbing her newest relationship in Marcus's face. "Scarlet and I *had* so much fun together last night."

Marcus bristled beside me.

"Charlie," Ava's voice broke through the Lair. "I'm glad you're here. We can finally get started."

Her voice was different— strained, in a way. Something was strange between us, and it wasn't the usual bullshit we struggled with. I picked up on it right away.

"Make it quick," Marcus said. "I have to check in with the Dead Men before class."

"I can try," Ava offered. "But what I found... this isn't going to be a quick conversation."

Oberi walked over to me and sat at my feet, his fur brushing against my ankle. I sighed. "We might as well get it over with. I don't think anything will surprise us."

Something tapped, like a pen against a clipboard. Ava cleared her throat. "I thought we were looking for something like noxite— native to Earth, but supernaturally enhanced. But the results show that this crystal doesn't even come from Earth."

My eyebrows shot up. I hadn't been expecting *that.*

"How would you even measure that?" Kallie asked.

"Isotope ratios," Ava said. "It's the same way scientists analyze rocks from space and know when they're looking at a meteorite."

"You think this crystal could be made from space material?" Marcus asked.

"It's *one* possibility, but that wouldn't explain its supernatural properties," Ava pointed out. "My best guess is that these crystals came from another spiritual realm."

"You're talking about hell," I stated.

Ava sucked a breath through her teeth. "It's the only thing that makes sense with these results. I mean, it *could've* come from the Blessed Haven, but why would any of the benevolent gods possess something so sinister? I think these crystals are being created or supplied by someone from the dark realm."

"That's impossible," Kallie said, like she was trying to convince herself of it. "How would the Warden get his hands on them?"

"The gods send us gifts all the time," Ava reminded her. "My mom owns a relic that was given to our people directly from the ancestors in our Ancestral Lands. It's not a stretch to think the Warden could be making a deal with a demon to get his hands on these."

"What kind of deal?" I asked.

Marcus shifted beside me. "We study demonic rituals in the Miriamic Coven. We're not supposed to perform them. They're more or less horror stories to keep us from making deals with demons, but I know anyone can do them. Demons usually want something like a piece of your life force or your magic."

"The Warden is already immortal, and I doubt he's giving up any of his magic," Ava said.

"I don't know what he's trading, but we can be sure it isn't good," Marcus replied.

"It doesn't matter what deal he's made," Kallie cut in. "He already has his hands on these crystals. What matters is stopping him from using them."

"It *does* matter," Marcus retorted. "Do you have any idea what we're up against if the Warden is getting help from another realm, let alone some demon in hell? This should terrify you."

"It does!" Kallie shouted. "So I'm going to focus on what we can do about it. What else do you know, Ava?"

"I discovered one other anomaly," Ava replied. "The frequency that these crystals vibrate... it's off the charts."

"That must be the ringing we heard," I said thoughtfully. "It's that frequency that made us sick. I'm certain of it."

"But why us?" Marcus wondered.

"We know demigods are capable of magic that's greater than even the most talented supernaturals," Ava said. "Magic itself vibrates, but demigods don't have to draw magic from an outside source. We're supposed to be able to create energy from nothing. What if *we* vibrate at a different frequency than everyone else?"

I pressed my lips together thoughtfully. "That makes sense. That's why the crystal only affects us, because its frequency interacts with ours. To anyone else, the vibration just passes through them— like a radio wave they can't tune into."

Kallie huffed. "And to us, that radio wave is like a dog whistle."

"Exactly," I stated. "Dogs can hear frequencies that humans can't. It must be like that with demigods. We can sense things others aren't able to— namely, these crystals— and it blocks our powers."

We sat in silence for a minute as we all absorbed the information. Marcus spoke first.

"Could we create something as a counter-frequency?" he suggested.

"You mean, to cancel the crystal out?" Ava sounded intrigued, but I detected a hint of worry in her tone. "It's something we'll have to look into."

"How long are we going to be able to hide what these crystals do to us in the meantime?" Marcus asked.

"As long as possible," I said. "We can't slip up. The second the Warden confirms we're demigods, he'll take us. It won't matter who your parents are."

"I know, I know. You've only mentioned that a million times." Marcus sighed. "I've gotta go talk to the Dead Men. Let me know what else you find out."

Kallie waited until Marcus was out of the Lair before announcing, "And *I* have a hot date. I'll see you guys later."

She was obviously avoiding having to walk back with him. It was awkward as all hell.

As Kallie left, I stood. Ava shuffled through her papers. I suspected it was to avoid talking to me. Beside me, Oberi wagged his tail, and it smacked into my leg.

He nudged his nose against my hip. *Go talk to her.*

Don't tell me what to do, I growled. But Oberi knew my heart better than I did. I *wanted* to talk to Ava. I just didn't know how to anymore. I dared to take the plunge.

I cleared my throat. "Ava?"

"I should burn these," she blurted. "I wrote all the results out on paper, but I should destroy them before anyone else finds them."

"Ava?" I repeated.

She continued speaking like she hadn't heard me. "But I might need to look back on them. I could add them to my Aunt Maddie's journal. I could—"

I grabbed Ava's shoulders, to steady her mind. I could feel her spiraling. I always knew when she was about to crack, and I couldn't help it. I ran to her when she was like that. It was an instinct built inside of me to catch her, and no matter what was between us or how we'd messed things up, I couldn't break that urge to protect her and make her feel safe again.

It'd never go away.

She leaned into me and began sobbing. "I can't, Charlie! I can't do it."

I stroked her hair as I held her. "I know this is hard, pidge."

The nickname slipped out and sent a pang through my heart, but Ava didn't seem to notice.

She drew away from me and sniffled. "No, you don't understand. I can't do this. I can't make something to counteract these crystals. I said I'd look into it because I didn't want Marcus and Kallie to feel hopeless, but I wouldn't even know where to start. I don't know a single earthly property or potion that'll counteract these crystals. And if there *was* some way to make something, we certainly don't have the resources at the Institute. We're stuck with these crystals, and if the Warden plants more of them on our professors, I don't know how long we can hold out."

"Let's hope his supply is limited," I said to soothe her, but it didn't seem to help.

"We don't know! We don't know enough about any of it. We're up against something I can't even comprehend, Charlie. I don't know where to go next."

I drew her into my arms again, and she sagged against me. This wasn't the Ava who had danced on the stripper pole last night, proclaiming her confidence to the world. She wasn't pissed at me right now— not like she ought to be. This was bigger than what was going on between us, and we both knew it.

"I'm sorry," I whispered.

"You don't have to apologize for the Warden."

"No, I don't. I'm sorry about everything else. I'm sorry about what I said to you. I'm sorry you're here at the Institute. I'm sorry about what happened to Monica."

Ava sniffled. "You don't have to be. That happened years ago."

"Not for me," I stated gently.

Ava pulled away from me. Her hands shook as she held my arms, as if trying to keep herself upright. "What do you mean?"

"Have you had any strange dreams lately?" I asked.

"Um, a few. I can't make sense of them. They're just noises and sensations. I can't see anything."

"That's because you're dreaming from *my* perspective," I told her, my voice trembling. There was once a time when I wanted to share everything with Ava-Marie, but not like this. I didn't want her to relive the traumas of my past.

"You dreamt of Monica?" she asked.

"Yeah," I admitted in a raspy voice.

"Ancestors, Charlie," she breathed. "I'm so sorry. You never should've seen that—"

"I've been through things like this before," I cut her off. "You don't have to apologize. It wasn't your fault."

Her voice came out small. "I haven't been able to convince myself of that."

"I don't want you to worry about what I'm experiencing," I said. "I just thought you'd want to know that maybe I'm starting to understand you better."

"But why?" she questioned. "Why are we having these dreams?"

It pained me to admit what I'd suspected aloud. "Maybe the more we stay apart, the more the bond drives us together."

Ava scoffed. "It's going to drive us mad."

"Oberi, any idea?" I asked him.

I would like to be excluded from this conversation, he stated bluntly.

"He knows," Ava accused. "He doesn't think we're ready to hear the answer."

I frowned. "Cryptic, as always. Oberi, can't you be of help *just once?*"

I've been helpful more than once, thank you very much. I believe I've already exceeded your expectations, he complained.

I scowled. "You're an ass."

Thank you very much, he replied proudly. I swore, he made it his life's goal to piss us off. Perhaps *he* was the one sending us the dreams.

Ava finally dropped her hands. "I don't know what to do about the dreams, Charlie."

"Me, either," I admitted. "I don't want you taking on my memories."

"Why? Are you hiding something?" she asked.

"No," I insisted. "You know what I've been through. Don't tell me you want to live through that."

She hesitated. "I'd rather not."

"Maybe they're happening because we're fighting," I thought. "If we can get along, hopefully they won't happen again."

"And how will we do that, Charlie?" Ava demanded. "We haven't had a decent conversation in... I don't know how long."

"We're having one now," I pointed out.

"Do I need to remind you of what you said the last time we spoke?" she questioned.

"No, ancestors. Please don't," I begged, running my hands through my hair. "I really *am* sorry about that. I didn't mean what I said."

"You sounded like you meant it at the time," she grumbled.

"I don't know what I meant. I was pissed, and I just said it to hurt you. It wasn't fair. You don't deserve that."

She paused several moments before speaking. "I... appreciate the apology. Thank you. And I'm sorry for the extreme reaction I had."

"Don't be sorry for your performance." The words spilled out of me before I realized what I was saying. I'd been so pissed about her song, but maybe it wasn't as bad as I thought. "You were hurt, and you channeled that pain into art. The song was actually really amazing. The fact that you took the time to write it... well, it shows you've come a long way since we first met."

My stomach twisted. I couldn't believe I was admitting this out loud.

"Oh," she said, like she'd expected me to fight back. "Um, thank you. It means a lot."

Silence stretched between us. We both stood there awkwardly, like we didn't know what to do next. Sure, we'd apologized, but we weren't *great*. There were plenty of harbored feelings still eating away at us both.

"We should get back," Ava finally said. "We don't want to be gone too long."

"Yeah," I agreed quickly. "Alistair's probably waiting for me in the library. I've got another braille lesson."

The tension in the air didn't seem to go away until long after Ava and I had gone our separate ways. Oberi had left with her, so I was alone. I stopped in the hall and leaned against the wall. I couldn't quite wrap my head around our conversation. We'd been civil, but something was still *off*.

I'd never admit it to myself, but I knew Ava and I belonged together. Nothing would ever feel *right* unless we got back together again.

But that was never going to happen, was it?

I forced myself to stand upright and make my way to the library. I got turned around a few times, but finally found my bearings when I passed the Villain's Den and heard the sound of the air hockey table whirring. From there, I could find my way to the library. I walked in to hear a group of people laughing in the corner. I made my way over to them.

"Do we get an invite to the wedding?" Alistair asked.

"Not so fast," Ez said.

"Yeah, we *just* started dating," a girl said. I was pretty certain it was Opal, but I didn't know her voice as well as the others.

"Things can move quickly when they're meant to be," Eddie pointed out.

"What's going on?" I asked as I found a chair and sat.

"Opal and Ez are dating," Alistair blurted.

"Congratulations. That's great," I said, sincerely happy for them. They made a really good couple.

Ez lowered his voice. "Hey, could we not announce it to the whole Institute? These people don't need to know who I care about. Too many inmates are willing to use that against you."

"I think they already know, Ez," I pointed out. "It's pretty obvious you and Opal share something special."

"Thanks," Opal said. "We do. It's not that we aren't proud of our relationship. We just... don't want each other getting hurt."

Alistair chuckled. "Still have a bunch of girls pining after you, Ez? I heard that center spread in the magazine was quite attractive."

"That's old news," Ez said. "Please don't make a big deal out of this. You and Eddie should think about being more discreet about things, too."

"Why?" Alistair demanded. "Because we're gay?"

Ez lowered his voice. "No, because Eddie's an Elf. He's already got a target on his back for that. If anyone wants to hurt him, they'll go after you."

Alistair scoffed. "I'd like to see them try."

Eddie didn't sound as confident. "That *is* a concern. Have we been that obvious?"

I chuckled. "Alistair can't stop talking about you. With his big mouth, I'm sure the whole school knows how he feels."

Alistair laughed. "Let 'em. I'm not afraid. If any of these suckers come after me, I'll show them what I'm made of."

Alistair wasn't taking this seriously, and it worried me. I lowered my voice. "And what if one of those *suckers* is the Warden?"

Alistair went completely silent. He had nothing to say about that.

"We should probably get going, Ez," Opal suggested. "I need to get some saltwater on my fins before swim class."

I waited for the couple to leave before I leaned over to Alistair and Eddie. "Ez and Opal are right, you guys. You don't want these inmates to know your weaknesses. Kallie and Marcus already got wrapped up in that kind of thing, and I couldn't stand to watch either of you end up hurt."

"What happened to Kallie and Marcus?" Eddie asked.

I froze. I didn't want to tell them about Marcus being part of the Dead Men, because I feared it would put them in danger. Alistair would want to help Marcus get out of the gang— which was impossible— and Eddie would be pissed that I was hanging around in fight club and getting my ass kicked every weekend to protect Marcus. The less they knew, the better.

"It doesn't matter," I said.

Alistair cracked his knuckles. "Who are these losers that hurt Kallie and Marcus? I'll take care of them."

"It's... complicated," I said.

"Dealing with your enemies is simple," Alistair retorted. "All you have to do is get rid of them. Boom. Problem solved."

"It's really not that easy—" I started, but I cut off.

Alistair was right. The way to solve our problems was to get rid of the enemy.

Not the Warden— we'd already discussed that. It'd be next to impossible to murder that man with our limited resources.

But the Dead Men Walking? I could do something about that.

I buzzed with energy all day, running scenarios through my head. Oberi met up with me after class.

I need to find Marcus, I told him.

I thought you were headed to your factory shift, Oberi said. *You'll be late.*

I have some time, I replied. *This is more important.*

Oberi huffed, but he dutifully pressed his nose to the floor. He sniffed around until he caught Marcus's scent. We found him in the Villain's Den with Rishi, working on homework. Thank the ancestors he was alone.

"You shouldn't be here," Marcus hissed. "If the Dead Men see me with you—"

"Then let's take a walk," I suggested.

"To give them more chances to spot us?" Marcus balked. "No, thank you."

"I don't want to be overheard," I said.

Marcus went silent for several beats. I must've intrigued him. After a long pause, he shuffled his papers and stood. He didn't say anything until we left the Villain's Den and were walking across the prison yard.

"What is it?" Marcus asked. "What's so important that you'll risk the Dead Men seeing us talking?"

"You don't have to worry about them anymore." I smiled.

"What do you mean? Of course I do."

"I found a solution to our problem."

"Okay. I'm listening."

"We have to get rid of Bones," I stated confidently. It would work.

"We have to—?" Marcus choked on his sentence. "Are you insane?"

"Think about it," I said. "Bones is the leader of your gang. The Dead Men answer to him. If he's gone, the gang crumbles—"

"Or someone else takes over," Marcus shot back.

"And who would that be?" I challenged. I'd met a handful of the Dead Men. None of them were smart enough or brave enough to take on Bones' role.

"I..." Marcus paused. "You might be right. Bones preys on the vulnerable. The rest of them are idiots, even Big G. They can't run an operation this complicated. No one else will be able to fill his shoes."

"Right. And once he's gone, the Dead Men will stop rigging the fights. We can pin the whole thing on Bones, and no one has to know you had anything to do with it. If he's gone, he won't be able to defend himself and turn it around on you."

"What if one of the Dead Men talk?" Marcus questioned.

"If they expose you, they expose themselves," I pointed out. "You weren't out there making deals with fighters to get them to throw their fights, were you?"

"No," Marcus admitted. "The other guys handled that. We all played our part."

"No one's going to talk, or they'll incriminate themselves," I assured him.

Marcus seemed hesitant. "How would we get rid of Bones, though?"

"Easy," I said with a smile. "How'd I get rid of Digger?"

Marcus stopped in his tracks. We must've been close to the siren pond, because the grass turned to sand beneath me.

"Ooh, I like this," Marcus said. "A tried and true method. Bones is already messing with nightshade, anyway. All we have to do is turn him in, and then he's the Warden's problem. Charlie, this could actually work."

"I know! We just have to find a way to tip off the guards without exposing ourselves," I added. "If anyone finds out we turned him in, we could—"

"Hey!" someone shouted from behind us.

I spun around. "What now?"

"Shit. It's Bones," Marcus hissed.

Speak of the devil. Bones stomped straight up to us. He must've been alone, because I didn't hear any other footsteps follow. His gang members must've been in class. "Does loyalty mean nothing to you, Little Drummer Boy? You've been warned more than once. I shouldn't have to remind you who you're dealing with."

"Loyalty means *everything* to me," Marcus insisted. "You should know that by now."

"No, it obviously doesn't," he growled. "Because this isn't the first time I've seen you hanging out with old friends."

"I swear," Marcus said. Papers rustled, and he shoved them at Bones. "Here are your bets for next week. I'm on your side."

Bones paused, like he was looking over the sheets. They rustled one more time, but he must've subconjured them, because I didn't hear them again. He sounded skeptical of Marcus. "You know what happens to traitors."

Marcus squeaked. I could only imagine the kind of punishment Bones had in mind. They'd already tried going after Kallie— even if none of the Dead Men remembered it. Sooner or later, they'd resort to torturing Marcus just to make an example out of him.

"Let it go, Bones," I warned. "Marcus and I aren't friends. I just needed help finding my way back to the building. I nearly fell in the siren lake."

It hurt to lie and say Marcus and I weren't friends, but I had to.

Bones laughed, like he was amused. "Poor blind kid. Can't even navigate campus. I'm shocked Captain lets you fight."

At least he was taking hits at me and not Marcus. I could handle it.

I smirked. "Yeah, it's unfortunate— unfortunate that I haven't met you in the ring yet. I'd love to kick your ass and show you what I'm made of."

"You keep threatening me, and you're gonna get your ass kicked right now," Bones growled.

I scoffed. "You want to try me? Be my guest. Winner gets Marcus?"

"Charlie, no—" Marcus started, but Bones was already stripping off his jacket. The fabric rustled as he tossed it aside.

"Winner gets to *live*," Bones snarled, before lunging at me.

Oberi barked, and Rishi yowled as Bones' fist cracked across the side of my face. Adrenaline shot through my system. The blow didn't even shock me anymore. In fact, I barely felt it. This was every other night for me, and I knew how to navigate my way around a warlock's punches. They didn't hit near as hard as shifters or vampires.

Bones threw another punch, but I felt the air whooshing past his fist. I ducked, then aimed my shoulder straight for his belly. I leapt and tackled him into the sand. Bones grabbed a fistful of sand and tossed it into my face. My eyes burned, but I squeezed them tightly shut. It's not like I needed them to fight.

I thrust my forearm into his neck, blocking off his windpipe. Rage boiled in my blood. After everything he'd done to Marcus, this fucker was going to pay.

Bones gasped for breath. He shoved his palm to my chest, and magic shot out of it so hard that I was blasted off of him. I flew several feet into the air and landed on my ass in the sand. My chest hurt like a motherfucker. For a second, it felt as if he'd shocked my heart with his battle orb.

My ears rang, but I could hear Oberi and Rishi howling nearby. Marcus shouted protests, but neither Bones nor I listened. The guards must've been too far away to see us, because no one stopped me. It didn't really matter, because they couldn't stop me even if they wanted to. I was taking this asshole down.

Bones ran for me, but I kicked up sand at the last second. He cursed as dirt entered his eyes. "Motherfucker!" he roared.

"You have no respect for the blind, my friend." I laughed. "Try fighting blind yourself."

I tangled my magic in his before he could react, and I yanked on it. His magic flowed into me. I could feel he was trying to conjure a battle orb, but nothing happened.

"What'd you do?!" he demanded.

"I don't know what you're talking about," I said innocently.

"I've already killed one guy in the ring," Bones threatened. "I'll kill you, too."

"With what weapon?" I taunted.

"You're a freak!" Bones shouted.

He lunged at me again, and we ended up in a scuffle on the ground. We both fought *dirty*— throwing fists into throats and sinking fingers into eye sockets. I could hardly keep track of which way his fist was flying as it connected with my skin in various places.

Was it insane that I enjoyed the pain? I was playing nice, to be honest, because I knew that in one swift move, I could end his life. But I didn't want to kill Bones— only teach him a lesson, and send him straight to Cellblock 9.

I was getting sick of this. I kicked him off of me and scrambled across the beach. With a twitch of my fingers, the air swept out of Bones' lungs.

"No—" he gasped, but the word was silenced immediately. I could feel him gasping for breath, but my magic resisted him.

I stepped forward, sneering. "I could suffocate you right here, right now."

I gave him just enough air so he could respond. "So do it," he rasped. "If you're so strong."

I scoffed. "You want me to stoop to your level? I'm nothing like you."

Bones chuckled. "And yet we're both here in the Institute. You're a bad guy, Charlie. Stop trying to convince yourself you're a hero."

My magic faltered for a second. Bones may not have the strength of a vampire, but he sure as hell knew where to hit me so it hurt.

Bones drew a breath, then shoved his knee into my balls. I gasped as pain riveted through my body. I couldn't help it when I sank to my knees. Nausea hit me so hard, I thought I was going to spew my guts.

"Charlie!" Marcus screamed, but he sounded distant.

"Huh," Bones said, like he was intrigued. "Guess you're not as bulletproof as you thought. I win."

I heard the sound of a pocketknife click open. Bones must've conjured it, though I didn't know how he'd smuggled it into the prison. I expected him to come for me, but he didn't. Instead, he turned toward Marcus.

"Your traitorous ass is going to pay," he growled.

Marcus screamed when he saw the blade. The memory of my dream flashed through my mind. I couldn't bear for Marcus to meet the same tragic fate that Monica had.

I leapt to my feet and threw myself at Bones. My hand connected with his shoulder. I couldn't make sense of the anger that bubbled through me at that moment. Magic sizzled in my chest, then just... exploded out of me. It wasn't my own. It belonged to Bones— his battle magic that I'd absorbed a minute ago.

The blast sent Bones spiraling through the air. His screams echoed through the prison yard. Then came the splash.

Horror swept through me. Bones had landed in the lake. It wasn't like when I'd tossed Mad Dog in there my first day here. Mad Dog was a vampire— nearly indestructible.

But Bones... he was siren food.

Bones' terrified screams cut through the prison yard, sending shivers down my spine. I heard the slap of fins on the surface, and the gurgle of Bones' cries before he was dragged under, the smell of blood against the water. It wasn't long before his shouts of pain became silent, and the water went still.

Marcus rushed over to me. I was so stunned, I couldn't move. We'd killed people during the battle in Forevermore, but that'd been *war*. We were just trying to stay alive, then.

This was different. This was personal. I couldn't believe what I'd done.

"I— I," I stammered. I'd wanted to get rid of Bones, but not like *that*.

"You did nothing wrong," Marcus insisted. "Bones' battle orb backfired on him. It was his own fault."

Marcus knew that wasn't true, but that was the story we had to go with.

My knees shook, and my voice came out hollow. "I need to see Captain."

"You're going to turn yourself in?" Marcus balked. "Bones did this to himself."

I wasn't sure I believed him. I had killed Bones, but I'd deal with that later. This fight wasn't over yet. I had one more thing to do to save Marcus.

"I need to go," I stated firmly. Then I just... took off.

I wasn't thinking. I just had to get out of there. I had to put an end to all of this. Oberi barked and raced after me.

I burst into Captain's office several minutes later. My chest heaved in heavy breaths. "I found him," I blurted.

I was met with nothing but silence. Oberi stepped into the room after me, and the door swung shut behind us. Then came the sound of Captain rising from his chair. He wasn't angry. If anything, his silence meant he was *amused*.

"I found the guy rigging your fights," I repeated.

Captain sounded both pleased and skeptical. "Is that so?"

He waited for an explanation. It spewed out of me. "It was Eugene Perry— or Bones, as you probably know him. He's been rigging fights for months, making deals with people."

Captain paced around the room. His footsteps were slow and ominous. "Bones is one of my best warlocks. You better be sure about this."

"I am," I stated confidently. "If you don't believe me, then check his stash. Your guards *do* know a spell to uncover everything a warlock has subconjured, don't they?"

"What is it you think I might find in Bones' stash?" Captain asked.

"Plans," I replied. "He's already got predictions for next week's fights."

"Well, I think I'll have to have a chat with Bones myself to confirm your theory," Captain said.

I scoffed. "Good luck. He's at the bottom of the siren lake. You'll be able to conjure whatever was in his stash, but he ain't talking, that's for sure."

Captain stopped in his tracks. "You're telling me that you found out who was rigging the fights, and you *disposed* of him for me?"

I cocked an eyebrow. "Wasn't that the deal?"

Captain burst into laughter. "I tell ya, boy. I didn't give you enough credit. Those sirens are ruthless. We'll be lucky if we find any remains at all!"

"Then you better start fishing now," I said coolly.

"I gotta say, I'm impressed. Assuming I can confirm your allegations, and the fights return to normal, you can consider yourself a free man, Bandit. You've done so well, you can take Chancey and Ghost with you, too."

"With all due respect, sir, I'm not the Blind Bandit anymore," I said.

Captain chuckled. "No, I suppose you're not. You're free to go, Charlie."

That was the most respect I'd seen from Captain in months. Apparently, the way to earn his respect was through murder. Oberi and I rushed out of his office as quickly as we could. As we walked down the hall, I felt Oberi's discomfort through our bond.

"What is it?" I asked aloud.

I wish you'd told me when you joined fight club.

"Please," I scoffed. "You knew the second I did. Ava and I talked about it all the time."

You still could've come to me directly, Oberi argued.

"You wouldn't have let me join," I reminded him. "You took Ava's side."

Maybe because I knew as well as Ava that it was no good for you, he retorted. *You figured it out eventually.*

"Yeah, I did, so why do you still have a stick up your ass about it?" I demanded. "Relax, Oberi. I'm out. I never have to go back to that sucky old gym again."

What about what you did to Bones? he asked.

"What are you now? The voice of my conscience?" I shot back. I heard voices down the hall and switched to speaking telepathically. *Bones messed with my friends. I had to do something! Or would you rather Kallie and Marcus get killed over this? I may have thrown him in the siren lake, but I didn't kill him. The sirens are to blame for that.*

Oberi was oddly quiet in response. Finally, he said, *You saved Marcus. You did the right thing.*

Hell, I hoped so. Because it didn't matter what I said out loud. Deep down, I couldn't shake the guilt twisting inside of me. I had committed plenty of crimes before, but I'd never done something like this.

The Institute had fucked with me and forced me to make decisions I didn't want to make. If I hadn't dealt with Bones, Marcus would be dead.

It didn't matter if you entered the Institute innocent or not. One way or another, it would make a villain out of you.

And sometimes, the villain became the murderer.

TWELVE

The Institute is making monsters out of you all.

The voices in my head were prodding this morning, but for once, I listened to them instead of ignoring them. They reflected my own internal musings so close that I was worried their thoughts were merging with my own.

A choice will soon be made, Ava.

You can't escape your own consequences.

What you are looking for is easily hidden.

"What are you trying to tell me?" I murmured.

It was then the voices became silent.

I couldn't decide if it was my intuition or my disorder talking to me. I should've been scared, but I wasn't. All I wanted to do was decipher the mystery of my own mind, because whatever the voices were saying, they seemed to be leading me somewhere important.

I passed Kallie and Scarlet making out in the corner, and I tried to ignore them. They were all over each other at all times of the day, to the point of shoving their relationship in everyone's face. It'd been cute at first, but it was starting to get annoying. Marcus had taken to pouting in the Arts & Crafts room whenever he wasn't in class, because he knew it was the one place where Scarlet and Kallie wouldn't show up.

He was starting to get on my nerves, too. If he was so bothered by

Kallie dating Scarlet, he should've spoken up sooner when he had the chance. It was his own fault he'd let her get away.

I lifted my gaze and saw Charlie walking toward me, Oberi bouncing at his side. I was determined to talk to him. I'd heard what had happened from Marcus, and had been looking for Charlie ever since. I rushed after him before he could find a way to get away from me.

"Charlie." I grabbed his arm. "How are you?"

He gave a noncommittal shrug. "Fine. Should I be any different?"

Something in this tone wasn't convincing. I couldn't give a shit Bones was dead. Like, honestly, who cared? But I cared about Charlie's feelings, and I knew for all his crimes, taking a life was something he'd never done before.

"Fine— Charlie, you *killed* someone!" I kept my voice low, but I was still afraid someone would overhear.

"So? I did what I had to," Charlie said roughly. "I have no regrets."

"But—"

"Just let it drop. It's better to pretend like nothing happened. That's the best way to keep your head down around here."

Charlie walked past me without a goodbye. Oberi skittered after him, growling a low complaint.

He was in denial about his feelings. This was going to bite him in the ass sooner rather than later.

But he'd done it to save Marcus. I knew if Charlie had no other choice, he wouldn't hesitate to kill somebody else, if it was to protect his friends. He hadn't even flinched when he nearly murdered Kyle in the Darke Games.

I worried this place was changing Charlie into a person I wouldn't recognize once we got out. *If* we got out.

Hardly anyone paid attention in Professor Hemlock's class. It was a dreary day, and though nobody talked, nobody listened either. Students doodled in their notebooks while Hemlock rattled on about portals all hour.

"What you must understand about portals is that there are multiple supernatural races, as well as magical creatures, that can make them," Hemlock began. "The fae are best known for their use of portals, but in some circumstances, angels can create them, too."

I lifted my head off the desk. Angels could create portals? What kind?

I wanted to ask, but Hemlock went into the next part of her lecture before I could raise my hand. "Now, different portals are capable of transporting different beings. Typically, a portal can only transport one individual at a time, though some portals are strong enough to transport multiple beings. Portals that can transport demons from hell, for instance, have to be much stronger than portals that can teleport supernaturals."

My hand was in the air this time before she could go on. "Could a portal transport... I don't know... a god?" I asked.

Hemlock blinked. "I'm not sure what you mean, Miss Mitoh."

"Like, if someone opened up a portal to hell, could a dark god pass through it, and come to Earth?" I asked.

"I don't believe so." Hemlock shook her head. "A god cannot go through the same portal a supernatural or a demon can. The type of power it would take to transport a god to Earth would be tremendous. I suppose the gods have come to Earth before, in various forms and incarnations, but if a dark god was trapped in hell by the other gods, they wouldn't be able to leave unless someone let them out."

The bell rang, and Hemlock dismissed us. I wanted to ask Hemlock more questions, but I thought it would be risky, so I gathered my things and left.

Coyote had come to me, and so had Whale Spirit. But they were benevolent gods, for the most part, and I bet they could go back and forth from the Ancestral Lands to Earth easily. Many of the dark gods, from stories I'd been told, were bound to hell because they'd been banished there by other deities.

What if the Warden hadn't made a deal with a demon? What if he'd made a deal with a *dark god*?

That was even scarier to think about.

Chancey sat on the stairs, working on a card trick. He was exactly the person I needed to talk to. His cards went flying everywhere as I plopped down beside him.

"Chancey, can I ask you a question?" I said.

He scowled and went to pick up the cards. "I'm a little busy, sweetheart."

"Cool. So can an angel open up a portal to a spiritual realm? Say, heaven or hell?"

His eyes flashed to the side. "Eh... you'd have to be really powerful," Chancey said with a shrug. "It's gotta be in your blood. Our ancient prophets in our holy book were said to be able to go back and forth to heaven. But I don't know anyone who could, in our time. Hell, though, that's a different story. It's easier to go down than up, if you get what I'm saying."

"I'm guessing you can't be an ordinary angel."

"No. Only our Deacons can make portals to hell, and talented ones at that. Those are the most powerful angels on our ruling council."

"So if a Deacon wished to go to hell, and they had the power, could they open up a portal to go there?" I questioned.

"It wouldn't be easy. The ritual requires materials that aren't easy to get your hands on, but I suppose if you *really* wanted to... but then, *why* would you want to?" He raised an eyebrow.

I clapped him on the shoulder. "This is perfect, Chancey, thank you."

He looked totally confused as I left him behind. I began scouring the school, on a mission to find my friends. I figured they had to be at lunch, but I actually found them standing on the edge of a huge crowd gathered outside the Warden's office.

"What's going on?" I asked as I pressed close to Charlie. Oberi licked my hand as a greeting. I scratched his fuzzy ears, and his tail wagged as I observed the gathering.

"They're taking new recruits for this year's Darke Games," Charlie said. "Ivy and Chancey already signed up."

"Yeah, and Alistair joined them," Marcus added.

"Along with Scarlet," Kallie pouted, crossing her arms. "She wants to break out of here and leave me behind."

I guess the new relationship wasn't coming up roses. I scowled. "Do these guys *want* to die?"

"I told them they didn't know what they were getting themselves into, but they seem to think the Darke Games are going to be a fun adventure with a chance to win a free ticket out of here," Charlie said.

"Reminds me of us," I grumbled.

"Reminds me of *you*," Charlie insisted. "You were the one who thought the Games were going to be a walk in the park."

I wrinkled my nose and stuck my tongue out at him, but Kallie grabbed my arm. "Never mind that. Ava, you've got that spark in your eye when you've found something."

"I did," I whispered. "Come with me."

We didn't go to the Lair— we'd been there too often lately, and I was worried if we kept slipping off, somebody would notice. We headed to the chapel instead. Oberi guarded the door, and Kallie scouted the room with her shifter senses. She gave the all-clear before I started speaking.

"I think the Warden is opening up portals to hell," I began. "And he's doing it on Darke Island."

"*What?*" Everyone asked at once. Out loud, the accusation sounded comical... but there was nothing funny about this.

I filled the others in on what I'd learned. By the time I was done, I was pacing up and down the pews. "I don't have any proof, but it makes sense. The Warden isn't just making deals with demonic beings to get his hands on the crystals. He's been to hell himself, and it's been more than once. I thought that portals to hell only opened on Darke Island once a year during the Games, and that's when the demons come out—"

I stopped pacing as a realization hit me. "Guys, what if the portals on Darke Island don't open up on their own during the Games? What if the Warden opens them *on purpose?*"

"I thought that the portals to hell opened up on Darke Island every December because they're on a magical leyline," Marcus said.

"I mean, they could, but what if that's the excuse?" I offered.

"What would be the point of that?" Kallie asked.

"To find demigods," Charlie said. "He's looking for people who are strong enough to beat them, people who show off their powers during the Games, so he knows who to target."

"You think so?" Kallie asked.

"That has to be the purpose of the Games," I insisted. "The Warden is watching us because he saw our performance, and knows we did well. We weren't really on his radar before we participated."

"That doesn't make any sense, though. He lets the winners go. They get their sentences erased," Marcus said.

There was a long silence. A mouse scuttled across the floor of the chapel, and Kallie asked, "Marcus... have you heard from anyone in Octavia Falls about Alice's return?"

Marcus' face slowly grew pale. "No, but... I don't really talk to anyone from home anyway, so I just assumed my cousin didn't want to speak with me. We weren't close before I came here. I mean, we're *distant* cousins— third cousins or something."

"Why *wouldn't* Alice contact you, Marcus? You saved her life in the Games. She'd want to check on you, make sure you were safe at the Institute, and we haven't heard anything back from her in months," Kallie said.

"Maybe she never made it back to Octavia Falls," I murmured. "Maybe *none* of them made it home. I bet they never left Darke Island."

"If they didn't go home, where did the Warden send them?" Kallie questioned.

"The Infernal Underground took them to test them for demigod powers," Charlie said.

"Exactly. And the Warden is putting the angel professors up to making excuses for their absence," I said. "Remember the Warden told Professor Cusak he needed to *get rid* of one of the succubus mothers that was questioning her daughter's disappearance? I bet anything that was Despona's mother!"

"So... does that mean we condemned Alice, Despona, Carson, and Wesley to be tortured?" Kallie asked hoarsely.

"We didn't know what they were doing. They were innocent. We were trying to do the right thing by giving them our win and setting them free," I pleaded.

"We gave up our Darke Games win for their team, so they could get out of the Institute and start a new life," Marcus said hollowly. "But in doing so, we cursed them to the Warden's experiments."

I closed my eyes as the heavy reality settled upon us. The guilt ate me alive, starting from my stomach and swelling over my soul. *Me doing the right thing always ended up with the wrong thing happening.* It was a theme of my life, and as hard as I'd been trying to escape it once I came here, I was cursed to be haunted by that fact. I could never win either way, whether I tried to do good or not, because what I got in the end would always be evil.

"If we had won, the Warden would've taken us, too, and experimented on us," Kallie said darkly. "It was them, or us. The Darke Games are a sham."

"Then we have to work hard to save Alice, and the others," Marcus insisted. "I'm not leaving my cousin to her doom."

"They have to be in Cellblock 9," I said. "The Warden is like a god here. He controls everything that happens on this property, but once they're off Darke Island, he faces consequences for his actions from the other supernatural races."

"I agree. It'd be easier for the Warden to hide them in a place where he has total control," Charlie said. "But we can't get down there without dooming ourselves. No one ever gets out of Cellblock 9, and with those crystals, the Warden could keep us there forever. We have to be smart if we want to break them out."

I nodded. "Agreed. And we have to tell Ivy and the rest of them they can't win the Darke Games, because otherwise, they'll be taken by the Underground, too."

"Oh great," Kallie grumbled. "They're gonna *love* that. They can't back out now that they signed up."

"So how do we get them out?" Charlie asked.

"We start with blueprints," I said. "Having a layout of the prison is a good place to start. We might be able to find a secret way in and out of Cellblock 9. I don't know where we could get them, though. They wouldn't be in the library. Students wouldn't be allowed access to them, because it'd be too easy to plan a way out."

"I still have access to the Warden's office from when I was with the Dead Men," Marcus said. "It's my last potion, though. Once I use it, it's done. Bones never gave me the recipe, and I don't know how to replicate it."

"Use it," Charlie said. "Alice and the others are in there because of us. We owe it to them to get them out."

Marcus gave a resolute nod. Kallie got up and gave a nervous glance out the door. "We can't skip lunch, they'll notice. Come on."

The cafeteria food seemed even blander than normal as we contemplated what horrible things Alice and her teammates could be going through right now. When we were done eating, we got up to return to class, but on our way out, a guard grabbed my arm.

By instinct, I tried to yank away. "Hey! Let me go!"

Charlie immediately moved to do something, but the guard growled, "You've got a call, Mitoh. It's your old man."

"Then let me go talk to him." I wrenched my arm away from the guard.

He sneered. Charlie shoved him out of the way— a risky move, but the guard didn't retaliate, only spat at our feet as we passed.

"Charlie, be careful," I murmured. I put a hand on his arm, trying to get him to calm down.

His shoulders hunched. "I don't like when people touch you."

"Well, neither do I." I frowned. "Thanks for defending me, though. See you guys later."

Oberi changed into a unicorn and trotted off after me. *You can't blame yourself for what happened to the other team*, she began.

I huffed. "Like Charlie can't blame himself for what happened to Bones? Face it, Oberi. We're all responsible."

She was quiet, then. The guard at the phone booth today was the same one who had cornered Ivy and I after our trip back from The Devil's Playground. "Farthest phone on the left," he said as I passed.

I picked up the phone. "Hel—"

"AVA-MARIE MITOH, I DID *NOT* SEND YOU TO PRISON SO YOU COULD BECOME A STRIPPER!!!"

I had to hold the receiver away from my ear. "How'd you find out about that?" I gaped.

"There was a video sent to my work email this morning, of *you* dressed *very inappropriately* doing *very inappropriate things*," Daddy hissed. "And now I have to scrub my eyeballs with bleach."

A *video?* That meant someone had snuck into the club and taken footage of me dancing. And instead of showing it to the Warden, they'd sent it straight off to my father, as if they'd known that would bother me more than an infraction would. Seriously, who would be that *petty?*

Daddy was still going on about it. "I can't believe you chose to— and those *lyrics!* Good to know those dance lessons I paid for were put to good use!"

"Ancestors, Daddy, you're ranting." I had no time for this. People were in danger, and my dad was more concerned about my one-time performance doing a striptease. "Don't you have more important things to do than scold me?"

"I canceled all my meetings. I'm not in the mood," Daddy grumbled. "I have to become accustomed to the fact that my little girl decided to become an exotic dancer."

I rolled my eyes. "I didn't take a *job.* Ivy just offered me the opportunity to dance on opening night, so I could get back at Charlie for acting like a major dick."

"Oh, ancestors, you're just like your mother." Daddy sounded horrified.

"What's that supposed to mean?" I threw up my hand.

Daddy ignored my question. His voice was tired as he mumbled, "Why are all my children obsessed with showing the world their underwear?"

"Hey, this is hypocritical," I pointed out. "You didn't get mad at Ez for doing the magazine shoot."

"Ez isn't dancing around a pole, singing provocative songs."

"I mean, he could. Ivy's got openings."

Daddy gave an annoyed sound, before he said reluctantly, "Anyway, this isn't why I called. I wanted to let you know your Uncle Jonah will be flying out to visit tomorrow. He wants to tell you the latest *news* from back home."

Daddy's words implied something different than their meaning. Had he found out something about the prison, something he couldn't tell me over these tapped phone lines? He'd promised to find information to get me and my friends out of here.

That had to be it. It was why he was sending someone to relay me information, because it looked suspicious if Daddy showed up and told me himself.

"Of course. I can't wait," I said. "And I'm sorry you saw that video, but I don't regret what I did. I made an empowered decision and all that."

"Empowered decision, my ass," Daddy mumbled. "Remember we agreed to *make good choices?*"

"Well, if we did, I forgot. Bye Daddy!"

I hung up the phone before he could lecture me further. No doubt right now he was having a meltdown at his desk. I passed the guard, and he smirked at me. He'd been listening in, the bastard.

"Tell the little freak I want double my pay," the guard said. "Or I report what I heard to the Warden."

"You'll get your money," I told him sourly. "As long as you keep your mouth shut."

The guard grinned and inclined his head. Though I was certain he'd keep his word, as long as Ivy shoved money at him, I wasn't so sure the Warden didn't know about the club already. I was certain the news had gotten back to him somehow. After all, he knew everything that went on in this place. But it worried me that he hadn't shut it down and thrown Ivy in Cellblock 9 for it. It meant the Warden thought he could use The Devil's Playground for his own purposes. I was certain he had people in there who were listening in for information, and that scared the hell out of me.

I was already late for class, and I figured the guards had told my teacher about the phone call, so I decided to skip the rest of it. I knew Ivy was in the mermaid pool this time of day. I headed down there and saw Opal swimming laps with him.

Ivy's mermaid tail was so beautiful. It was as sparkly as Opal's, and his scales were a variety of different colors, creating a shimmering rainbow underneath the water. I watched him jump out of the water and do a flip, waving his fin at me before he took a dive. Oberi changed into a narwhal, diving in to swim after them.

Ez sat on a pool chair, munching on Commissary snacks. I sat beside him and dug in his chip bag so I could have a few. Ivy swam up to the pool's edge.

"I heard you and Chancey joined the Darke Games," I said.

"Yeah, and according to Marcus, we signed up for nothing," Ivy bitched. "It's all a big scam."

"It's crazy to say, but the Darke Games aren't the worst you have to worry about right now," I said. "My dad just called to yell at me. Someone took a video of me dancing at the club and sent it to him."

"Dad *saw* that?" Ez's eyes widened. "Woah."

Ivy completely flipped shit. He slapped his tail against the water. "Dammit! I should've known someone wouldn't play by the rules. This puts the club at risk! We're going to have to body-search people now and make sure they aren't carrying any phones."

"The guards are also asking for more money, so you'd better cough up some cash if you want to keep the club a secret," I added.

Ivy groaned. "They'll get paid. That is, if they keep their end of the bargain. But I'm gonna need to find a way to bring in more capital. You want to dance again, Ava? The crowd loved you on opening night."

"No, thanks. It was fun, but that was a one-time deal," I said. "I got my kicks."

"You ruin me, precious." Ivy turned to Ez. "What about you, sweet peach? If I can't have Ava, I want her brother, and I *know* you can twerk."

Ez sighed heavily. "I'm gaining weight again. I have a medical exemption from the mines now, so they put me on secretary duty in the prison office. It's a lot easier, but I'm definitely losing my muscles."

"You look perfect the way you are. You're like my squishy teddy bear," Opal said with a giggle.

"Aw! That's the sweetest thing anyone's ever said to me!" Ez brightened.

Ivy tapped his chin. "I could *use* a body-positive dancer—" Ivy began, before he was cut off by a vicious cackle.

Naya was lounging on a pool chair nearby, wearing a swimsuit— but I don't know why, because I'd never seen her swim. I was pretty sure she hung out here just to show off to everyone how hot she thought she was.

"Nice to know there are *two* sluts in the family," Naya commented. "I hope your dear old *Daddy* appreciated the show."

My teeth clenched. *Naya.* Of course. She lived to torment me. I knew she was the one who'd sent the video to my dad. I didn't know how Naya had gotten her hands on it. She hadn't been invited to the club's opening. Ivy hated her. I bet one of her cronies snuck in a phone somehow and fed it back to her. And being the bitch she was, she'd emailed it to my dad.

"Nobody likes you, Naya. Just go away," Opal snapped.

"Shut up, Opal. We all know you're a chubby chaser," Naya spat at her. "After all, *someone's* gotta take care of your kid once you graduate from this—"

I called up a stream of water from the pool and sent it swirling straight at Naya. It soaked her from head to toe, ruining her hair. She screamed and jumped off the pool chair, completely drenched as I sprang to my feet.

Naya's nose wrinkled into a snarl. "You're going to pay for that, Mitoh."

"I'm waiting." I called a ball of Fire into my hand. Naya came at me with super speed and socked me in the gut. The hit sent me flying into the wall and knocked the wind out of me. I gasped for breath, but as Naya grabbed me by the neck and lifted me off the ground, I punched her in the face with a fist full of Fire. She let out a cry and clawed at her eyes, trying to get the embers off her skin.

I was about to jump on her back and start ripping her hair out before a couple of guards pulled us apart. "Break it up, girls," one demanded, pulling me off of Naya. The guards yanked us in two different directions, though I was still scrambling to get to her.

"She attacked me first! You all saw it!" Naya screeched.

"One of you stays, the other goes," the guard demanded. "If this isn't resolved in *five seconds*, both of you are going to the Warden!"

I froze, but Naya sneered and tossed her hair over her shoulder. "Whatever. I'm bored here anyway."

Naya retrieved her things from the pool lockers and strode out. The guards dispersed, but not before the one who'd grabbed me pointed a finger in my face. "This is your last warning, Mitoh. I was willing to look the other way when the Bandit was in fight club, but he's not fighting anymore, so your pretty little ass better start behaving, got it?"

"Got it," I growled, with more resentment than a promise.

The guard stalked off, and Oberi said, *You should've tossed Naya in the pool. I could've accidentally staked her with my horn.*

I scoffed. *Like that would work. People would start theorizing Charlie and I have an M.O. of disposing of people in bodies of water.*

Not an altogether awful assumption.

Ivy sneered. "Naya will get hers one day. Just you wait."

Ivy didn't make empty threats, so I was betting on that. Ivy and Opal had swim class, so Ez and I left the pool. Oberi hopped out and changed into a unicorn, trotting after us.

"I want to get some practice with magic," Ez said. "I was hoping we could go down to the Elementai greenroom together, and you could give me some tips."

"Sure." We walked to the Arboretum's waterfall with Oberi, and did some stretches to warm up.

"How are you doing with Water?" I asked.

"I'm getting better at it," Ez said. "I can do some small things now."

He hovered a ball of Water in the air, then whipped out a few small strands before freezing them to ice. It was far more than he'd ever done, but still, very short of being impressive. He was hardly a beginner.

But it was a lot of progress for my brother, and I was proud of him. I concentrated on summoning my Anichi magic, harnessing a white light to my palm. It was smaller than a golf ball and flickering out, barely glowing with the warmth it needed to stay alive.

As bad as Ez was at controlling Water, I was horrible at healing magic. I'd brought my brother back from certain death, but ever since, I hadn't been able to do so much as mend small injuries, though I'd been practicing nearly every day.

"I don't understand this," I said in frustration as the light in my palm flickered out. "My other magic is easy. Fire is passion and raw emotion, which I've got tons of, and Water is inner strength, which I can draw from, but I don't get the essence of healing magic. I don't know what quality I need to pull from that will make it so I can heal."

"Well, Anichi magic can do more than just heal," Ez said. "It can create light, make shields, turn you invisible, and even kill people, if you can reverse your healing magic to have the opposite effect."

"Kind of like the Warden's ability to overpower your life force." I tapped my chin. Mama was an incredible caster of Anichi magic. She could use it to manipulate the light particles around her and become invisible to the naked eye. I wanted to push my Anichi magic that far. "Ancestors, I'd love to become invisible. It'd sure do some good around here."

"Maybe you can only do it with one hand, like you can only cast Fire with your right and Water with your left," he suggested.

"Maybe." I didn't get this. I closed my eyes and tried to concentrate, willing the light particles in the room to form around me so I could disappear. I took deep breaths and tried to calm my mind, like I'd watched Mama do a million times before. I'd seen her vanish right before my eyes with ease. I should be able to do it, too.

I creaked open an eyelid. "Am I invisible yet?"

"I still see you clear as day."

I slumped my shoulders. "It's no use. I'm hopeless at it."

"You've never been one to give up." Ez raised an eyebrow.

"I can't even feel the magic inside of me. All that's inside is my Fire, and behind it, my Water. It's like my healing magic is buried so deep I can't access it," I complained.

"Have you talked to Mom about it?"

"Yeah, but she insists Anichi magic is something you have to feel from the *heart*. It can't necessarily be taught in a practical way." I crossed my arms. "Anichi magic is based on emotion, and to be honest, I've blocked off all my feelings lately."

"Well... how did you heal me?"

I scowled. "I didn't have any other choice at the time. It was either save you or let you die, and the second one wasn't an option."

"Then maybe you need to be pushed." He shrugged. "If you aren't allowing yourself to access your feelings, then you won't be able to harness them in order to perform Anichi magic, either."

"You think so?"

"Yes. My Water magic got loads better once I accepted my diagnosis. It didn't help me to keep denying that I was sick; it just blocked me. There's gotta be something you're not accepting, too."

I knew Ez was right. I tried to block everything out since Charlie and I had broken up. It'd been too much to feel... too overwhelming, too painful. I could only focus on so much at a time, and managing my bipolar was hard enough on a daily basis. Coupling that with accepting that I'd lost Charlie would make me lose my mind.

But you couldn't perform healing magic without emotion. It just didn't work. If I wanted to become a master at Anichi magic, I had to become fluent at facing, and working through, my feelings.

Not something at the top of my list of things I wanted to do. Being numb was easier.

Ez went back to juggling water balls in the air, and Oberi crept up behind me. *Your mother won't be able to help you in this regard. I've told you before your healing powers are more related to your demigod abilities than your Anichi ancestry,* Oberi insisted. *You're going about it the wrong way.*

"How so?" I asked her crossly.

You must find the source, and draw from it. From there, you will be unstoppable, Oberi said. *What is the source of healing magic, of its light? It is there where you must begin, at the very start of creation.*

I wasn't sure what Oberi was getting at, but her words were meant to guide me. If I wanted to discover how to heal on command, I had to understand where that power had come in the first place.

But what god, or goddess, could it be? There were hundreds, and not just from my own religion. I wasn't sure I could narrow it down to merely one. As a demigod, I could search for them, perhaps contact them, and ask them questions. It was merely a question of finding the right one.

Ez practiced for a little while longer, and I tried summoning balls of light until I developed a headache. I barely felt like I'd had the strength to stand. I'd been pushing myself too hard...

Or maybe I'd been pushing myself against what I wasn't willing to face yet.

"I'm going to lie down," I told Ez, rubbing my temple. I went back to my cell, and Oberi followed. I slipped into a pair of silk pajamas with soft shorts. Oberi changed into a husky and hopped onto my bed as I yanked up the covers.

Sleep, Ava, he said, lying over my feet. *All will be well.*

I wanted to. All I longed to do was to shut my eyes and block out the world for a while.

Though as darkness closed around me, there was an innate knowing in my soul that recognized sleep would be all but peaceful.

COLD. *I was so cold.*

I could feel the wet chunks of snow coat my thin jacket as they fell down from the sky. I'd been sitting here for so long my pants had frozen to the sidewalk, but I didn't have anywhere else to go. The shelter was full, like always, and the usual places I went to didn't have any room. I'd lost a bag of my stuff when some other guy had snuck up behind me and snatched it. I'd had a sleeping bag, a couple of chips, and some gloves. Treasures I couldn't afford to lose.

I thought about Marty. Our place hadn't been much, but it'd felt like home. I hadn't been able to pay the rent by myself once he was gone, and the landlords hadn't wasted any time in kicking me out— after they'd pawned all my stuff. All the people I thought were our friends turned me away when I showed up at their doorstep. They didn't want to get shot, too, and they figured I was bad news.

I almost wished the people who killed Marty would find me. I'd rather eat a bullet than continue to sit here and freeze to death.

I'd never felt so hungry. I couldn't remember the last time I had something to eat. This was the kind of hunger I hated, because I couldn't get used to it. Christmas music played down the street, and loneliness struck me.

Shit. I turned twenty-two today. Happy fucking birthday to me.

I was so unhappy. There was no one in this world who gave a damn about me.

And you know what? I could even live with that, if I had someone in this world to give a damn about. Forget being loved. I just wanted the opportunity to love someone else. To give a shit about somebody who wasn't myself.

But right now, the cold was almost worse than the constant abandon-

ment I felt. I knew if I was still here by morning, the cops would find another frozen corpse, and I hadn't survived this long just to die now.

I needed to get warm and get some food in me. If I survived the night, I could do anything. I'd find other guys to con with and other suckers to swindle. I just needed to get off these streets.

I heard the click of heels on the sidewalk. The footsteps slowed as they came in my direction. "You all right, sugar?"

Hope welled within me as I heard the voice of an older woman, probably someone in her forties. There weren't a lot of good people left in the world, but maybe someone had taken pity on me. I gave a shiver. "N-no."

A brush of wind swept by my face as the woman knelt down. I could smell her heavy perfume as she said, "A handsome thing like you shouldn't be sleeping out here all alone. What do you say, sugar? We can keep each other warm tonight."

I knew what she was asking for, but I didn't care. I'd give anything just so I wouldn't be so cold, or feel the hunger gnawing at my insides any longer.

I'd never been with a woman before, but the thought of sleeping in a warm bed again for the first time in more than a month was too tempting to say no to, and need overwhelmed my fear.

I nodded feebly and grabbed the woman's hand so she could help me up. I was so stiff I wanted to cry. She guided me forward, and we walked one block, then two.

I was so exhausted, but relief overcame my body as a sliding door opened and heat surrounded me. I couldn't express the intense tingles that surged over my body as the cold slowly began to drain away. It was nearly painful to experience.

The woman had an apartment building at one of the fancier places downtown. I could tell because the floors sounded like they were made of marble, and classical music played on the speakers overhead. We took an elevator up, and I heard the jingle of keys as the woman unlocked her apartment. Lights clicked on, and the woman asked, "When's the last time you had a hot meal?"

"I d-don't know." I was still shivering.

A microwave turned on, and the smell of something cooking filled the room. It nearly dropped me to my knees. She guided me to a chair, then placed a plate in front of me and put a fork into my hand.

I didn't know what she handed me to eat, and I didn't care, because I devoured it in seconds. I couldn't tell if it tasted good or not, because it was in my stomach by the time the food hit my mouth. When I was done eating, the woman guided me behind her. I heard her turn a faucet on, and steam filled the bathroom.

"I bet you're even more gorgeous underneath all that dirt," she said. "Take your time, baby."

Of course she wanted me to shower first. I probably looked like shit. I hadn't washed in over a week, and the last time I'd managed to get a shower at the local YMCA, a couple of my things had been lifted from my locker. I'd been too afraid to go back since.

She left the room, and I stripped out of my clothes. They practically peeled off my skin. The hot water made me relax, and I started sobbing in relief. This had been a close one this time, and I was damn tired of having close calls.

The bathroom door opened. "I've slipped into something comfortable, sugar. There's no need for you to get dressed. We ain't gonna need clothes."

I realized this could be my way out. There were other girls who'd want to take me home.

I could pawn myself out, just long enough to get enough resources so I could get back on my feet and find my own place.

Now that the immediate threat of freezing to death had passed, reality sunk in. Was I really doing this? I could leave now. She couldn't overpower me.

The thought of going back into that cold weather again instantly made me recoil. No. I wanted to stay inside, in a bed, just for one night.

If she lived in this fancy apartment complex, she was wealthy. That meant she had a couple of things I could steal. Just go in, do the job, and be out of here by morning. Her things would be gone before she had a chance to wake up.

I didn't know what I was doing, but I figured she had to like virgins, or at least inexperienced men, because she wouldn't have picked me up *otherwise. I couldn't see her, anyway, and that had to be one of the hardest parts, right?*

Maybe I could pretend like I loved her. I thought about the kind of girl that I'd like. She'd have long hair and smell really nice. Her skin would be soft, and she'd have a kind voice. She'd sing me to sleep as I laid my head on her lap. She'd be so small, I could wrap her in my arms and she'd fit just right.

Yeah, that's what I wanted more than anything. It wouldn't be so bad. I'd just play pretend, act like this woman was the imaginary dream girl I could never have, and it'd be over before I knew it.

I stepped out of the shower and dried off. When I opened the bathroom door, I heard the woman say, "Come here, sugar. We'll forget about our problems together."

My eyes shot open. I abruptly lunged upward in bed. Sunlight streamed in through my window, shining on the floor.

I'd slept the rest of the day away and hadn't woken up until the next morning, but the dream felt like it'd taken seconds. I pressed a hand over my mouth and did my best not to throw up, but even so, tears rolled down my cheeks.

He'd wanted the simplest things in life. A bed, a roof over his head, a *shower.*

I couldn't imagine the amount of lack he had, and how he'd managed to endure it for years on end. I'd experienced mere seconds, and it made me want to die.

I recalled how he'd devoured what had been placed in front of him. I'd refused food so many times, purposefully starved myself because I couldn't force myself to stomach anything.

I vowed never to turn down a meal again.

Oberi crawled forward on the bed and nudged my knee with his wet nose. *Ava?*

"How could people be so heartless, Oberi? I wouldn't treat my worst enemy that way." I wiped my face.

Oberi blinked at me. I hated this world. I hated it and everyone in it.

How he could have suffered so badly and no one did anything to help him, I could never understand.

"Pidge?" Charlie poked his head in. He'd felt something was wrong. He knew I'd experienced one of his memories.

I sniffed. "You just wanted to get warm. How could they be so cruel?"

Charlie came in and sat on the bed beside me, leaning against the wall. "Most people in the world aren't like you."

"I wish I had found you." I wiped at my face. "I would've taken you home and fed you and never let you leave."

Charlie gave a wry smile. "It would've been nice."

"How did you manage to keep fighting? I would've died of misery."

"I always had this sense in the back of my mind that I was fighting to get back to something," he said. "I didn't really know what it was, at the time, but now I do."

A forlorn question popped into my mind. "Why'd you pick Detroit?"

"I wasn't really thinking. It just seemed like the farthest I could get from California, and the easiest place to get away with committing crimes, because I knew that's all I was good for."

"Don't say that. I don't want you to think the way you did." I reached out and brushed a lock of hair out of his eyes.

I frowned. "Your hair is getting so long. Why are you letting it grow out?"

"You told me not to let anyone cut my hair but you."

My throat tightened up. His response was so innocent. "I'll trim it later, I promise."

Charlie cleared his throat. "I know I've been through some hard stuff, but what you had to go through was hard, too. None of it was easy for us."

My throat tightened again at the mention of Monica. Would she have died, if Charlie was there to stop us from running away? Would John have hurt me if Charlie was there to protect me?

I knew what the answer was before I had to ask, and it gutted me. Charlie wouldn't have gone hungry, grown up without love, if I was there. None of this had to happen, and yet it did, because we were forced apart.

"I feel like we were always supposed to be together, and the Elders robbed us of that when they sent you away," I said. "We should've grown up together. We could've been friends."

"At least we're friends now, right?"

"It's not enough." We both knew it.

Charlie took my hand. He didn't say anything, but he squeezed my fingers.

I rounded my shoulders and shivered. "How did you get over Marty?"

"I don't know. Maybe I haven't." He shrugged. "But it was pretty hard to grieve when I was trying so hard not to end up like him. I didn't have time to be sad about it when I was so busy trying to find food and a place to lay my head, and when I wasn't doing that, I was running from bullets. I didn't have space to miss him, so I just... shoved it down. Never forgot about him, though."

"I know if he could see you now, he'd be proud that you made it," I whispered.

"It doesn't matter. I'm right back in the same spot I was years ago. I'm alone in the world with no one to love." Charlie's voice was choked, and it hurt me.

"That's not true. Things *are* different now, because whatever happens, I will always love you."

It wasn't even a confession, just what was reality. I'd never stopped loving him. The breakup meant nothing. A thousand years could pass, and Charlie would always be the only one for me. My heart had already decided that.

Charlie completely froze. There was surprise in his eyes, like he hadn't been expecting to hear that. His entire body went stiff beside me. I swear, his hand in mine turned cold.

It was right then that Marcus knocked on the doorframe and leaned in. "Hey, Ava. A couple of guards told me your uncle is here to see you. He's waiting in the entry hall."

Of course. Way to ruin the moment.

I wiped my eyes again. "Coming."

I closed the door and got dressed. Charlie sat in silence as I disrobed, and Oberi waited for one of us to say something.

I didn't know what we were doing anymore, because the longer we were separated, the more and more pointless this seemed. When I'd slipped on my uniform, I opened the door, and Charlie stood.

"Marcus is sneaking into the Warden's office tonight," Charlie said abruptly. "I'll reach out to you once he's found something."

I suddenly felt very small. "Oh... okay."

Oberi's ears flattened in defeat as he led Charlie away. I counted the steps he took all the way down the cellblock, until he disappeared around the corner.

I'd laid it all out there, and he'd pushed me away. Again.

And yet, I couldn't feel sad about it. I didn't have any regrets about being brave. I was glad I told him how I felt. After everything he'd been through, he deserved to know someone loved him.

Uncle Jonah's towering frame was so comforting to see in a place like this. Several big guys threw nervous glances at him as they passed by. I ran forward and flung my arms around him. "It's great to see you!"

"Isn't it, though?" He hugged me back, lifting me off the ground by a few feet. "You look amazing, by the way. Very healthy."

"I've... actually been taking care of myself lately," I said, shocked to realize that it was true. "I've got some really good friends here."

"Friends are the best. They're just as good as family," he said. Uncle Jonah wrinkled his nose as he looked around the dusty entryway. "Is there anywhere— ugh— *less filthy* we can have a private conversation?"

"Not really, but... come on."

I led him to the balcony above the prison. I hadn't been up here since Charlie and I had broken up. It was physically painful to take these stairs and remember what had happened up here. But I wasn't sure where else we could talk that was safe besides the chapel and the Lair, and it felt like both of those were off limits.

"Finally, a nice view and a good breeze," he said. He sat backward and used his Yapluma power to hover in the air, like there was a chair there. He crossed his legs and said, "Sorry to say, it's not good news. But it's important, which is why I had to come."

"Did Daddy find something that can get us out of here?" I asked quickly.

"Yes and no," he stated slowly. "What your dad found is... complicated."

"How so?" My stomach dropped like a stone. I thought he'd found us a way out of here, but clearly, it wasn't that simple.

"Your dad found records of the experiments at the prison. *Recent* records, of prisoners who'd gone missing from the Institute, only to turn up dead a few months later," Uncle Jonah said.

"How'd he find them?" I asked.

"The old Elders left behind hundreds of files after the Hawkei Civil War was over. When Oleander was trying to take over the tribe, he was colluding with the Warden, we know that for certain," Uncle Jonah said. "He didn't have time to destroy them before he was killed. It's taken forever to go back through them, but we found files that directly referenced the Warden sending inmates to the Infernal Underground to be experimented on. Does that name mean anything to you?"

"Yes. We're investigating it right now," I said. "We thought it was a movement of people."

"It's not. The Underground is a place, some sort of experimental room," Uncle Jonah said. "Though it's well hidden. We never found out where it could be."

"What about Cellblock 9?" I asked.

"From the letters, we gathered the Underground was separate from Cellblock 9."

This changed everything. It meant we still had to find where the Warden had taken Alice and the others. We had to get our hands on those blueprints. It was more important than ever.

"Can Daddy use this evidence to get us out?" I asked.

"He tried. Your dad went to the United Supernatural Union with the files. It was this big court deal. It lasted days. But the Union was split, and they ended up ruling against the evidence and taking the Warden's side. The elementals, the fae, and the witches believed your dad, but the angels, mermaids, vampires, and Astromancers voted in the Warden's favor, and in a court of law, every Union member must agree that the defendant is guilty for the accused to be convicted."

"There have to be bodies on Darke Island," I insisted. "The people the Warden experimented on didn't just disappear."

"There were no hidden graves to be found, and as we couldn't tell them definitively where the Underground was, the Union took it as one big joke. Without physical evidence that went beyond the paperwork, your dad didn't have enough proof to overturn your sentence on the basis of cruel and unusual punishment."

"The Warden is never going to get what he deserves, so long as the angels are always going to vote in his favor!" I said.

"You see our problem." He frowned. "I don't see how we're going to get you out. All the evidence in the world isn't going to be enough to set you free, as long as the angels still have control of the Union's council."

"Isn't there anything Daddy can do?" My shoulders dropped.

"We can't try again. Your dad risked a lot going to the Union in the first place. They accused him of fabricating the evidence. There's more than his job on the line if he brings up another accusation against the Warden. He'll be tried for falsifying information, and we can't afford to have him locked up."

What Daddy had risked to try and get me out of here cut me to the core. My throat tightened, and I dropped my head. "You guys tried. That's what counts."

"Hey now, don't lose hope." Uncle Jonah fell back down to the ground and raised my chin. "The way I see it, you've got all the Fire in the world to fight the Warden. He doesn't stand a chance against you. Especially not with those sick dance moves!"

"Did you watch the video?" I snickered.

"Your mother, Auntie Imogen and I might've walked in when your dad was weeping on his desk," Jonah teased. "He's a big drama queen. Nice job, by the way! I'm *very* impressed."

I giggled. "Well, Ivy's a great teacher."

"I'd like to meet him," Jonah said in approval. "I think we'd get along splendidly."

"I'm certain you would." I smirked. "Though my performance was a one-night only show. Daddy said I'm just like Mama. I have no idea what he means."

"Oh, that," Jonah said coyly. "I know what he's referencing."

"What?"

"Well... let's just say your mom sought revenge when she and your dad broke up."

"Mama and Daddy broke up?" This was huge news to me.

"Oh, yeah, there was this big thing about it one year at college. They'd split up for months before they got back together," Jonah said, waving his hand. "It was very dramatic, but it all worked out. But not before your mom made your dad *pay* for dumping her."

"Woah, woah, woah, hold on," I said. "Daddy dumped *Mama?*"

The thought was absolutely insane. He was head over heels for the woman. I couldn't imagine him leaving her for any reason.

"Yep, and oooh, it was good," Jonah gushed. "I'm not going to spoil it, because I think your mom would tell the story better, but she ended up flashing her boobs to a city street *right in front of your dad* and getting a tattoo. It was a wild night, and that's not even the half of it!"

"Oh my ancestors!" I put a hand over my mouth and laughed. "She sounds like she was so much fun when she was younger!"

"We had some crazy times back then," Jonah said fondly. "Ask your mom about it. I believe it to be one of the shining moments of her existence."

"I guess we get it from her, Ez included."

"I mean, your grandpa's pretty proud about the magazine spread. He keeps going on about how Ez is keeping family tradition alive, seeing as how gramps won *Toaqua Today's* Rear of the Year Award back in the day."

I laughed. That was just like Grandpa Elliot— though I didn't want to see old pictures of him in the nude at any point in my lifetime.

Jonah's wide grin faltered. He came closer, and said, "By the way... there was something else I wanted to talk about."

His tone was so serious it made my heart stop. "What about?"

"Well, Ez is here on attempted murder charges. I know it's not because he wanted to beat up his ex's new boyfriend."

My eyes immediately watered. It took a lot not to turn away from him. "How long have you known?"

"You didn't come to stay with me all those years ago because you were fighting with your dad," he noted gently.

"And you never told anyone?"

"No. Josee and I had a discussion after you stayed with us, but nothing since."

I figured my cousin knew. She was one of those sharp people that caught on to everything. I swallowed down the lump in my throat and croaked out, "How?"

"I saw the signs, because I've been there myself."

"Really?" The admission was shocking. Uncle Jonah was so big, so strong. I couldn't imagine anyone doing to him what had been done to me.

"An old boyfriend, a really long time ago," he said heavily. "I've healed from it, but it's still... hard."

I nodded. "I'm so sorry."

He dropped his shoulders. "The thing is, if it can happen to me, it can happen to anyone. And I want you to know, whatever the details are, that it wasn't your fault."

My throat burned. "Do you think Mama and Daddy—?"

"I don't think they suspect anything, to be honest. I won't tell them, either. That's something you have to decide for yourself, if you want them to know."

I threw myself against his chest and squeezed him tight. "Thank you for letting me decide."

"You should always have a choice," Uncle Jonah said as he hugged me back. "No matter what you're going through, I will always support you."

"I love you so much for that." I pulled away. "Why didn't you turn him in?"

"Because it's your choice, not mine. I'm keeping a close eye on him, to make sure he doesn't go after any other girls... at least, not at the school." He gave a sad sigh. "There's only so much I can do in that aspect, because I can't be everywhere."

"How do you handle having John at Orenda Academy, knowing what he did?"

"I've requested not to have him in my classes," he said, mouth thin.

"I don't think I'd be able to look at him without blowing him to pieces. It's hard enough being in the same building with that monster. He reminds me of— well. The past is in the past, and all that."

The past was in the past. We'd all been through a lot. But maybe there was a chance for a better future. If my parents had split up and gotten back together, there might be hope for Charlie and me.

Uncle Jonah checked his watch. "I should probably get back. It was very dangerous coming here in the first place. I'm certain we're being watched back in Kinpago."

"What do you mean?" I asked.

"Your parents are dealing with a lot," he said regretfully. "Things at home are just as messy there as they are here. We've found vampire and angel spies hiding in the city. They're waiting to see what the tribe is going to do about the Elves, once they're found."

I'd seen the news. Things were getting worse between the supernatural races every day. "I'm scared. What if there's another war?"

"There's nothing wrong with being scared. We all are," he said. "What's important is what we do with that fear. Courage isn't a feeling. It's a choice. And you're brave enough to make the right decision, whatever happens."

It was reassuring that he had so much faith in me. I knew I could do anything, so long as the people I loved were behind me.

I said goodbye to Uncle Jonah, then left to go to class. I was anxious all day, and barely able to concentrate on anything my teachers were saying. I was so worried for Marcus— what he might find in the Warden's office, and what would happen to him if he got caught.

What if he came out with nothing? What would we do then?

We were supposed to meet up in Marcus' room at six o' clock. Time ticked by. He was late.

Kallie was nervous, chewing on her fingernails. "Where is he? He should've been here fifteen minutes ago."

Maybe he's curtains, and so are the rest of us, Oberi suggested.

"Oberi!" Charlie and I both scolded. Kallie couldn't hear him, but it wasn't like we needed to hear it, either. Rishi laid on the pillow and purred, like he knew there was nothing to worry about.

We all jumped as the door banged open. "I got them," Marcus said as he came flying into the room. He waved a bunch of papers above his head. "I wasn't seen."

My stomach twisted. "Do you think the Warden will notice they're gone?"

"These are just copies that I made. I didn't take the actual blueprints," Marcus said.

I took a breath. "I have to tell you guys something. The Underground is a place, not a movement like we thought."

Kallie nodded as I finished telling them what I'd learned. "If what your uncle said is true, the Underground could be on these blueprints. Let's have a look."

He placed the papers on his desk. We loomed over the blueprints. My eyes searched the papers, but my thoughts became frantic as I realized there was nothing here we didn't already know. In the basement level of the Institute, I saw the pool and Cellblock 9, but nothing else.

"This doesn't help us," I said, and I slammed my hands onto the table. "We know all these rooms are here already. There are no other rooms anywhere on this map."

"Well, if it's a secret, would it be on the blueprint?" Charlie asked.

"The fight club isn't on the blueprint, and that's a secret, too. I bet there are other hidden rooms," Kallie offered.

"It had to be built somehow. The Warden can't just make a room appear out of thin air, and he's too stuck up to get his own hands dirty building it," I said crossly.

"It could be an illusion," Marcus speculated.

Kallie shook her head. "Illusion rooms are difficult to maintain long-term, especially if you're using them to hide people. What if it's a cave tunnel, like the ones the Elves used to get to Forevermore?"

Charlie shook his head. "I already asked Eddie if there was a tunnel underneath the Institute, and he said no. The entire property was built on a huge slab of concrete, to prevent the patients from trying to dig their way out."

"Your Earth powers could move, or even destroy, the concrete," I pointed out.

"It would make a big mess, and it would take time," Charlie said.

"We'd get caught before I could make a tunnel large enough for us to leave."

"If the blueprints are useless to find the Underground, can we use them to escape?" Kallie asked.

"Escape how?" Marcus asked. "We know digging our way out isn't going to work, even with Charlie's Earth magic. And we can't get past the fence with those crystals buried there."

"We could use Charlie's Elven powers to escape somehow," I offered.

"And where would we go after that?" Charlie asked. "How are we supposed to find the other keys when we're running for our lives? We know there are keys on Darke Island, or at least close by. We'd have to leave the island to not get arrested again, and that would be pointless. Everything we need to save the Elves and stop the war is here."

"Let's go down to the basement and check anyway," I said. "Maybe there's a secret passageway or something."

There was nobody down at the pool when we got there, not even a guard, thank the ancestors. We started poking around, running our hands over the walls and floor. We searched for nearly a half hour and didn't get anywhere. As badly as I wanted to find some sort of gap in the stone, I didn't.

"I don't think there's a secret passage. My Earth powers would've found a break in the stone walls, and they're completely solid," Charlie said.

"What else can you sense?" I asked.

Charlie knelt to the floor and splayed his hand against the tile. "I can sense the pool, then the area where they hold fight club, and in the distance, Cellblock 9."

Charlie's eyebrows furrowed. "But everything else is just dirt and rock, and then underneath *that*, the slab of concrete the prison is built on. There are no hidden rooms underneath the asylum, as far as my magic can tell."

I threw my hands up and made an annoyed sound. "Ugh! If there's no tunnel underneath the Institute, and the Underground isn't in the basement, then where could it be? It must have a ward on it, and that's why we can't find it."

"Could the word *Underground* be a way to mislead people? What if it's actually in a tower, or in an abandoned classroom?" Kallie asked.

"Good luck finding it, then," Marcus said. "This place is huge. The Institute has tons of sealed off corridors they never bothered to renovate after they converted it to a prison. We'd have to bust into them to even take a look, and that would get us into trouble."

"Could the Underground be off prison property?" I speculated.

"I don't think so," Charlie said. "It's easier for the Warden to make people disappear when they're on campus. Once they're off Institute grounds, he can't hide them as easily."

"Could the Infernal Underground be in a section of Cellblock 9?" Marcus asked.

"No," I stated. "My uncle was sure that it wasn't."

Kallie began pacing in a circle. "There are six cellblocks at the prison for the main magical races, and Cellblock 9 for the worst of the worst, but what about Cellblocks 7 and 8? I've never even heard of them."

"The prison used to use Cellblocks 7 and 8 for the smaller supernatural races, people like Astromancers and hypnotists," Marcus said. "But they didn't send enough prisoners to the Institute to keep them running, so they shut those cellblocks down. They're not exactly sealed off like the other corridors in the prison, but we're not supposed to go down there, either."

"So, what if it's there, then?" Kallie asked. "It'd make sense if the Underground was in one of those abandoned cellblocks."

"That seems too out in the open. Cellblocks 7 and 8 aren't that far from the classrooms. Students would overhear them torturing people," I said.

"But it's the best place to start," Charlie said. "We don't have anything else to go on."

"At least we have places we can start," Marcus said. "It's better than nothing."

I wasn't sure. It felt like we were overlooking something. But there was no time to lose. We had to find Alice and the others, and get them out of there. It was the only way to make up for the mess we'd landed them in.

But once we found them, would they be the same? I could only hope that, wherever they were, the Warden's torture hadn't driven them to madness.

Or that we wouldn't suffer the same fate.

charlie
THIRTEEN

My head spun with all the information we'd learned about the Infernal Underground. It worried me that much of what we'd discovered was based on speculation, but something deep in my gut told me we were *right*. Ava talked about intuition, and how supernaturals had the power to access unexplained truths. I didn't have to know how to explain it. I just had to believe it. And I had to believe that one way or another, we would find the Underground and stop the Warden's sick experiments.

I just hoped we found it before it was too late.

"Did you find anything?" I whispered to Marcus on our way to therapy.

"You mean in Cellblocks 7 and 8?" he asked.

"Shh..." I hissed. "Do you want everyone to know you went poking around in there? Let's keep this under wraps, okay?"

He lowered his voice. "Kallie and I found nothing. Just empty rooms."

"Hell," I groaned. "This place could be anywhere."

"We're going to find it," Marcus promised. "We just need more time."

"I hope to the ancestors you're right." I sighed.

After a beat, Marcus asked, "Is something else on your mind?"

"Why would you say that?" My voice squeaked a little.

"You just seem... I don't know. A little distracted?"

I drew a deep breath and stopped at the bottom of the stairs that led to Professor Jaymin's office. "Ava told me she still loves me," I admitted.

"Wow, that's... wow," Marcus said.

"I'm sure she didn't mean it."

I mostly said it to convince myself, but it didn't matter. I didn't believe it. Ava *had* meant it. She still loved me. Maybe not in *that* way— but in a way that said she'd still lay down her life for mine. And hell, I'd do the same for her a million times over.

I didn't want to talk about it, though. Thinking about it— *confirming it*— was completely throwing me off.

Ava loved me. And I couldn't keep lying to myself by insisting I didn't feel the same way about her. So where did that leave us?

"Come on," I said as I gestured Marcus forward. We climbed the tower to Professor Jaymin's office.

I immediately froze when a sense of unease hit me. It was so strong I had to clutch the banister so I didn't fall down the stairs.

"I don't care what the punishment is," Ava growled from up ahead. "I *refuse* this treatment!"

Hell, it was *her* unease that had come through our bond. Something was up.

Charlie, get in here! Oberi barked in my mind.

I practically threw myself up the stairs, racing until I came to a stop inside Jaymin's office. "What's going on?"

"Miss Mitoh is refusing treatment," Jaymin sneered.

"Ava doesn't have to consent to this," Kallie argued.

I calmed down, and Oberi came to my side to guide me further into the room. *Ava's in one of her moods, isn't she?* I asked him.

She's upset, he replied, without explaining.

"Pidge, you have to take your meds," I said gently. "You know that."

"This isn't about my medication," Ava explained. "I take my meds religiously, day in and day out. This new *treatment* is a violation of student privacy. I've read the handbook! The Darke Institute is classified by the United Supernatural Union as a reform school. Under section twelve, paragraph three of the health code, a reform school under

Union law is only legally allowed to provide treatment that has been approved by our parents in writing or prescribed by a licensed physician, of which Jaymin is neither. My parents may have agreed to send me to group therapy, but they will never sign off on this if I don't want it!"

My brow furrowed the more she spoke. Ava sounded like she was about to go off on one of her social justice speeches, which meant she was pissed. I chose my words carefully. "What exactly is this new treatment?"

"A group of hypnotists are visiting the Institute this week to assist students in therapy," Jaymin explained, though she sounded irritated. "Our hope is that by uncovering your trauma, you may all be healed."

Jaymin's words sounded innocent enough, but her tone of voice suggested something otherwise. It was clear she had an ulterior motive.

"This treatment has to be optional," I pointed out. "Ava's right. The school can't require additional treatments without a doctor's orders, especially not hypnosis."

"Very well," Jaymin said curtly.

Her chair squeaked as she sat. She scribbled something on her clipboard. I was stunned silent that she had caved to the argument so easily. It was so unlike her.

"Although," she added, "I find it highly suspicious that Miss Mitoh— or any of you, for that matter— would reject such a highly respected form of therapy. Hypnosis has been scientifically proven to aid in the rehabilitation of mental illnesses."

I didn't know if that was true, but I didn't think Jaymin cared about the facts.

"Should you refuse, I'll have to assume you have something you don't want the hypnotists to discover," Jaymin continued in a condescending tone. She wasn't even trying to hide the fact that she was attempting to manipulate us. "Of course, anyone who refuses to see the hypnotists will be reported to the Warden. I'm sure he'd be very interested to learn you have something to conceal."

"I have nothing to hide," Ava insisted firmly. We all knew it was a lie, but she sounded damn convincing. "I just don't want someone else in my head. I have enough voices in there already. You should know plenty about that. Check your notes."

Jaymin huffed. "It sounds as if your interpretation of hypnosis is severely misguided, Miss Mitoh. No one will be entering your mind. Regardless, the choice is up to you. You either go through with the hypnosis session, or you answer to the Warden. Which will it be?"

"That's not a choice. That's an ultimatum," Ava snapped.

Jaymin didn't respond, but she must've been staring Ava down, waiting for her to break, because Oberi muttered in my mind, *Damn, that's one intense gaze, woman.*

Finally, Jaymin spoke. "Well, I have a hypnotist waiting downstairs for one of you. Somebody needs to go first. No other groups have refused yet. I'm sure the Warden would love to hear you four are the first."

We all went silent. We were scared to death of what the hypnotists might find. Considering they were hired by the Warden, I didn't trust their intentions. I'd bet anything he hired them to uncover our secrets and report back to the bastard. It was just like our therapy— just like the Darke Games and *everything else* in this prison designed to draw out demigods.

Oberi, are the hypnotists safe? I asked him.

Yes and no, he admitted. *They can open you to your subconscious, and they can't access anything you don't want them to. But you may not like what you find buried deep in your mind, Charlie. The danger is discovering not what you're hiding from them, but what you're hiding from yourself.*

"I'll do it," I blurted.

"Charlie, no!" Ava protested.

"Are you serious?" Marcus asked at the same time.

"Can't you see they're trying to manipulate us?" Ava asked.

"Of course they are," I said. "Just like everything else they do at this prison."

"*Reform school,*" Jaymin quickly corrected.

Ava grabbed my arm and yanked me toward her so she could whisper in my ear. "This could be dangerous, Charlie. Aren't you afraid of what they'll find?"

"Oberi seems to think it's safe," I whispered back.

I quickly turned to speaking my mind across our bond, because I didn't know how much Jaymin would hear. Ava hadn't been able to hear me before, but things were different between us lately. Maybe if I tried hard enough, she'd hear me. *If we don't do this, we confirm to them that we're hiding something. One of us needs to figure out how this works and report back. I have the most shit to uncover from my childhood. They'll have to dig through a lot of crap before they learn any of our secrets. Let me go in your place.*

She must've got the message, because she dropped my arm.

I straightened and repeated myself. "I'll do it."

Jaymin sounded far too pleased. "Very well. It's nice to see *one* of you volunteer. Perhaps this will give the rest of you time to think about joining the hypnotists over our next few sessions. Charlie, if you would head to the room at the bottom of the stairs, the procedure will begin. The rest of us will have a little *chat* while you're gone."

Chat, my ass, Oberi huffed. *You're gonna piss Ava off with your lecture.*

You should stay here with her, I told him. *Keep her from doing anything stupid.*

I left the room and headed down the stairs. The door at the bottom was already open, and a woman greeted me when I stepped inside. "Hello. I'm Dr. Trinity Hasan. You must be..."

She shuffled through her papers. "Marcus? Or Charlie?"

"Charlie," I stated. At least she sounded nice.

"Charlie, why don't you have a seat?" Trinity shut the door behind me.

I felt for a chair, but I nearly tripped over a sofa.

"You can lie down if you want," she offered as her chair squeaked across the floor. "Most people prefer it that way. It helps them relax."

I sank into the sofa and rested my head on a throw pillow. The sofa was really comfy, way better than the bed in my cell. Trinity must've been diffusing essential oils, because the scent of lavender surrounded me. Soft music played from speakers in the corner. Though unease rolled around in my gut, it was oddly easy to relax here. I knew it was nothing more than an illusion— a false sense of security designed by the Warden, and Trinity was nothing more than a pawn hand-picked by the Warden himself. She probably actually believed she was helping our rehabilitation.

"How does this work?" I asked.

"Hypnosis is a natural state of the mind," Trinity explained. "It's a trance-like state that you may have experienced many times. If you've ever been driving a car and zone out, only to suddenly realize you're almost home, you have experienced this."

"Well, I haven't, because I don't drive," I said awkwardly. "They don't usually give driver's licenses to blind guys."

Trinity cleared her throat, sounding a bit embarrassed. "I'm so sorry. Yes, of course that example wouldn't apply to you."

I shrugged. "It's okay."

"Um, to explain further," she floundered. "In this trance state, the conscious mind takes a backseat, and our subconscious mind is opened. Even non-magical people can perform hypnosis. However, with my magical abilities, I'm able to get you into a state of hypnosis faster, and amplify the clarity of your memories and visions. I can also access your subconscious in a limited capacity through psychic intuition. Finally, I'm a certified psychiatrist, so I can help you interpret these visions afterward. The whole session will take roughly an hour. Are you ready to begin?"

I settled deeper into the couch. "What exactly are we looking for in my subconscious?"

"That's up to you, Charlie," Trinity said. "Many students choose to leave themselves open to anything, so that their subconscious may show them the wounds that are most prevalent and need the most healing. Others choose to focus on one thing at a time, if they know what needs healing. However, setting an intention for the session doesn't always ensure a specific outcome. Sometimes, the harder you push to hide something from yourself, the more it will push back and show up, both in these sessions and in your external environment."

"I want to dive into my childhood," I said. Digging through that dumpster fire should be enough to keep us from uncovering more recent issues I didn't want her knowing about.

"Very well. Focus on the sound of my voice, and together, we will submerge deep into your subconscious."

Trinity's calm voice was soothing and could easily put me to sleep. She spoke along to the calm music, guiding me through a visualization of a waterfall. I pictured the sounds of birds in my head, imagining the spray of water from the waterfall and the hot sun on my skin.

When she said she could use her magic to put you into a trace quickly, she wasn't lying. All it took was imagining myself at that waterfall, and I was no longer in the counseling room anymore.

All sense of time seemed to fall away. I could still hear Trinity's voice off in the distance, but I couldn't quite process what she was saying, as I was returning to the past.

I REMEMBERED *the flashes of lightning against my bedroom walls. Thunder cracked outside my window. Though my night light usually scared the monsters away, they didn't seem to care tonight. They were coming for me, stomping just outside my window.*

The scent of fresh linen surrounded me, and I buried the teddy bear deeper into my nose. I squeezed my eyes shut tightly and pulled the blanket over my head. It was the only way to keep the monsters at bay. If they couldn't see me, they couldn't find me. At three years old, that kind of logic made all the sense in the world.

Please, please, please, don't let them get me, I begged.

I didn't know who I was begging or why. All I knew was that something was wrong— terribly wrong. A horrible sense of dread dropped in my stomach, worse than anything I'd ever felt before. Worse than when those scary men took me away from my mom... worse than anything. My heart raced so fast, and my whole body trembled. The only explanation I had for it was the monsters.

"Charlie! Charlie, you mustn't hide. I'm here for you."

The voice sounded so kind, very unlike a monster. I was brave, so I peeled back the covers to peek at the man who'd spoken. My eyes went wide when I saw a glowing eagle flying around my room, leaving trails of starlight behind. His feathers were blue, red, and green, painted with all kinds of pretty designs.

In my memory, the eagle was so mesmerizing. I wanted to reach out and touch it. The thunderstorm outside my windows was all but forgotten as I watched the eagle fly around my room. He swooped down, and before my eyes, the bird transformed into a man. He had dark skin and feathers twisted into his long braids. His eyes were bright yellow, like an eagle's, though they were welcoming.

"You're not a monster," I whispered.

He shook his head. "No. I am Eagle Spirit, the god of virtue. I am here to ask for your help, Charlie."

"I'm just a kid," I told him. "I can't help."

"Charlie, you are the only one who can help."

I glanced around the room, and thunder boomed louder than ever this time, shaking the walls. I sank deeper under the covers.

"H-help with w-what?" I asked.

"You will not comprehend what I'm about to say, but it's something you must hear, for you will remember when you are older," Eagle Spirit said. "Your soul has fragmented. It can be made whole again, but only if it is reunited here on Earth. But I'm afraid magic has interfered with the gods' will, and I fear your soul may forever be separated."

I didn't understand what the man was saying. "I'm scared," I whispered.

"I know," Eagle Spirit said gently. "But time is running out, and there is only one way to save her."

"Save... who?" I asked, my voice squeaking.

Eagle Spirit held out an inviting hand. "Come with me, child."

I hesitated, but Eagle Spirit seemed much nicer than the monsters I'd encountered before. Perhaps he could save me from the ones marching outside my window. I reached out for him. My fingers grazed nothing but air, but the second I touched him, the room spun around me. Eagle Spirit became solid beside me, and my hand clutched his. Darkness enveloped me, and the thunder immediately stopped. I saw nothing but the glow of Eagle Spirit's form. He gazed down at me with sadness in his eyes.

"I am so sorry, child. You are so young. You should not have to go through with this yet," he said gently.

"What's happening?" I questioned, glancing all around me.

Then I saw it. A bright light cut through the darkness. A woman screamed, and my heart boomed in my chest. I feared for her. She sounded frightened and in so much pain.

"No!" the woman screamed.

"Sophia, it's time to push!" another woman told her.

The darkness began to fade, and a scene formed around us. Eagle Spirit stood beside me in a bedroom with walls that reminded me of a cave. A woman lay panting on the bed, with several others surrounding her. Sweat covered her brow, and her legs were propped up beneath a blanket, so I couldn't see what the other women were looking at. A small white creature with big ears and giant blue eyes wept. Another animal that looked like a monkey with blue feathers moved about the room. I'd never seen anything like it.

Shadows formed in the dark corners of the room. The sight chilled me to the bone, and I took a step back. They were monsters. They were the ones causing this. I didn't know how I knew, but I could feel the darkness coming from them.

"It's okay," Eagle Spirit promised. I trusted him.

"She's still breeched!" the woman in the bed yelled. "Luana, you do anything! You take my life and put it into this baby's! You hear me?"

"Sophia, we're not—" one of the girls said, but she stopped when Sophia screamed again.

Something tugged at my heart, almost like I was in pain, experiencing all the fear that she was. It terrified me to my very core. Something deep inside me screamed to help this woman, as if she was my own mother.

I shook as I squeezed Eagle Spirit's hand. "She's scared! Help her!"

Eagle Spirit knelt to my level. He pushed my dark hair from my eyes. "I'm sorry, Charlie. I wish there was another way. A baby is about to be born, but she is losing this battle. The gods have done everything they can to save her, but even our magic has limits. There's one last spell we can try, but the only power strong enough to save the baby and her mother is a sacrifice— a sacrifice from you. Charlie, do you know what a sacrifice is?"

Tears stung my eyes, and I shook my head.

"It's when we give up something we care about to help someone else," Eagle Spirit explained. "You and this baby are connected. You must choose to give this baby a piece of yourself in order to save her. One day, I hope you understand why I am asking you to do this."

"No! Ancestors, please! Don't take her! Take me instead!" Sophia cried.

My heart twisted in my chest. The screams echoed in my ears, a pain I didn't quite understand.

I could feel the baby. I knew her fear and felt pain. She was slipping away.

I didn't know what all this meant. I was too small to really understand what death was. All I knew was that I'd do anything to save this baby, and if I didn't, she would die.

I said the first thing that popped into my head. "My eyes!" I cried to Eagle Spirit. "Give the baby my eyes!"

"Are you sure, Charlie?" Eagle Spirit asked.

"Yes!" I sobbed. "Save her. Take my eyes. I don't want them no more!"

"Very well." Eagle Spirit stood and placed his hand on my head.

"One more push, Sophia!" one of the women said.

The screams came to an abrupt halt, and the woman went limp on the bed. Tears streamed down my face, and I hiccupped. I feared that I'd made my decision too late.

Then I saw her. One of the women pulled the tiniest little baby from behind the blanket and held her up. She was so small, and though she was covered in goo, she was the prettiest baby I'd ever seen. She had a mess of black hair, and the biggest brown eyes.

My heart was instantly drawn to her, and I knew without a doubt that our souls were entwined, from now to the end of forever.

In the blink of an eye, the room disappeared from around me, but I heard the sound of the baby's first cry break through the darkness. I was so relieved to hear her voice, but at the same time, terror hit me like an ocean wave. I felt Eagle Spirit's hands upon me, but my eyesight was gone.

I was blind.

✑

I GASPED as the memory ended and I snapped back to reality. The sounds of music returned, and I smelled lavender. Trinity's chair squeaked as she shifted. I felt like I was going to be sick.

"D-did you see that?" I asked her nervously.

She let out a shaky breath. "No, but I sensed something... very profound. You've uncovered a significant memory."

"I... I don't know how I could've forgotten it," I whispered, more to myself than to her. "I must've thought it was a dream."

"You lost your eyesight to a very traumatic event," she said. "Perhaps even... something magical."

She sounded unsure, and I wasn't about to confirm it for her. If the Warden found out I gave up my sight for Ava, he could manipulate me to give up *anything* for her.

"It was frightening," I told her, just to give her *something*. I had to lie, but I couldn't spin my web too big. Surely, the Warden could uncover my medical records to confirm. "I woke up one morning and just... couldn't see."

"You don't know why this happened to you?" she asked.

"The vision was unclear," I lied. "All I know is that I was scared."

"Let's talk about that," she offered.

"What's there to talk about?" I asked. "I've lived my whole life blind. It's just how things are. I'm not bitter about it."

"Then perhaps we can talk about what you saw in your vision," she pressed.

"I'm *blind*," I reminded her. "I didn't *see* anything."

A shiver ran down my spine.

"Right." She scribbled something down, her pen scratching the paper. "Can you describe what you heard?"

"It didn't make sense. Just a lot of thunder," I told her. "There was a storm that night."

"Mm..." Trinity tapped her pen thoughtfully. "Do you remember where you were living at the time?"

"Some foster home. I wasn't there long."

She kept pressing for answers, but I kept everything vague. She knew the vision had frightened me, but she didn't know specifics. I didn't tell her anything the Warden couldn't already get his hands on.

"Can I go?" I asked after an endless string of questions.

"Yes, but Charlie... I encourage you to open yourself up to what this vision means. Your subconscious is trying to tell you something," she insisted.

"Hmph," I said, before leaving the room. I knew *exactly* what I was meant to learn, but I wasn't about to tell her that.

My body trembled as I left the room. I heard voices upstairs, but they didn't belong to any of my friends. It must've been Jaymin's next counseling group.

"Charlie!" Marcus called from a few paces away. I jumped, because I hadn't expected him to be there. "It's fine. It's just me, Marcus."

I relaxed. "I know it's you. I just..."

"You look like you've seen a ghost," Marcus said. "I-I mean *felt* a ghost. I mean—"

"I saw *something*," I told him.

"You mean... literally? You *saw* something."

I listened closely, and I heard footsteps down the hall. "Not here."

"Follow me." Marcus grabbed my arm and dragged me down the hall.

We didn't stop until we could no longer hear any footsteps. "What *happened* in there?"

I raked my fingers through my hair. "I don't know, man. I got hypnotized, and it fucked me up."

"How?" Marcus sounded worried.

I shook my head. "I can't even explain. It's about Ava."

"I'm listening."

I sighed. "I remembered something from when I was a kid. A Hawkei god came to me the night Ava was born. She was dying. The only way the gods could save her was with a spell that required a sacrifice."

Marcus' voice wavered. "What kind of sacrifice?"

"A sacrifice from me." My tone came out hollow. I still couldn't wrap my head around it. "Marcus, I gave up my sight so Ava could live."

The hall fell dead silent. I wasn't sure I believed it was true until I said it out loud. But the memory had been so real, so *fresh*— as if I'd just experienced it yesterday. I'd never known how I'd gone blind. It'd been a mystery to me for years. I figured I'd just had some kind of accident when I was little, and I'd forgotten about it.

Now I knew. It was all for her.

I broke down and told Marcus everything I'd seen in my vision. It was like if I said it out loud, I might be able to make sense of it. It still seemed surreal, though, even though I knew it'd actually happened.

"That's intense," Marcus finally said.

"I know. To think... our connection goes deeper than I ever thought."

"Are you going to tell her?" he asked.

"How can I?" I fell against the wall. "She'll blame herself."

"No, she won't," Marcus promised.

"She will," I argued. "Ava knows the shit I went through growing up. Once I was on my own, things got even worse, and a big reason for that was because I was blind. No one would employ me, so I had to turn to other methods to survive. Marcus, I dealt drugs and slept with women off the street just so I wouldn't freeze in the cold. None of that would've happened if I had been able to provide for myself. Believe me, Ava *will* blame herself for that. I don't know how I could ever put that burden on her."

"Ava should know. She has the right. She's your bonded partner," Marcus insisted.

"You can't tell her. It would destroy her to know. We can't say anything to her about this, because it would ruin her. *Promise me*, Marcus," I said.

Marcus was quiet, until he said, "I won't say anything. But I still think you should tell her the truth."

I frowned. "I just want to move past it. I'm sick of my past coming up all the time."

"You can't just *get over* stuff like this," Marcus said gently, like he knew far too well. It was pretty obvious he hadn't worked through his own shit.

"It's not that bad," I argued. "I don't regret giving up my sight for Ava. I know it made life hard, but I'd do it again a million times. I'm happy I gave up my sight for her."

"That may be true, but you're still bitter about your past," Marcus pointed out.

I crossed my arms. "I want to stop talking about it."

"That's not going to fix anything," he replied.

"Oh?" I questioned. "And you know that how?"

Marcus sighed. "There are ceremonies for this kind of thing in the

Miriamic Coven. We believe that shoving our emotions down will only make them fester. You have to face them and release what's holding you back."

"You've done one of these ceremonies?" I asked. I was getting a little irritated with him, because if anyone needed to face their past, it was Marcus. It wasn't his fault that his magic killed all those people, and he still blamed himself.

"Not yet," he admitted. "I'll get there. I'm just saying... if you want some help with this, I'm here for you."

"Oh," I said flatly. I suddenly felt bad for getting angry at him. He was only trying to help, and maybe I needed it.

"The best time to perform these ceremonies is on the full moon," Marcus said.

"That's this week," I remarked.

"Yeah, but we don't have to do it right away," he assured me. "Whenever you're ready."

I pondered his offer for a moment. "I don't know if I ever will be, but maybe I can try."

"Really?" Marcus asked, sounding shocked.

"It's not like I have anything better to do," I chuckled, but it came out stilted. I wasn't totally sure I was ready, but I knew if I put this off, it would never happen. "But only if you make me a deal."

"What kind of deal?" Marcus sounded skeptical.

"That you work through your shit, too."

"Charlie, I'm not ready—"

"You don't have to do this ceremony now," I told him. "Just... promise me you'll start figuring it out. If your people truly believe in exploring your emotions, then you've got to stop hiding them from yourself."

"I don't know how long it will take, but I can try," Marcus said.

I offered a light smile. "Then I guess we'll need to prepare for the full moon."

I TWISTED the threads of Ava's armband around in my fingers as I snuck toward the chapel later that week after my factory shift. Oberi led the way. The band had been a gift from Ava, one that I'd stashed away behind a drawer in my dresser when we'd broken up, because I couldn't bear to let it go. It was the first, and only, birthday present I'd ever gotten.

Marcus had said I would need something special to me for this ritual — something that represented what I'd been holding on to. I didn't have much of anything that was *special*. Hell, I'd lived most of my life out of garbage bags. But this? The armband was the most important thing I owned.

The halls were quiet, as it was almost curfew. Now that I was out of fight club, I didn't get special privileges to be out of bed after hours, but I'd arranged a pile of clothes under my blanket to make it look like I was sleeping. The guards never checked our cells that closely unless they had a reason, and I hadn't attracted any attention lately.

We chose the chapel because it was one of the most secluded areas on campus. The guards never patrolled this hall, since most students never bothered to come down here. The people in this place weren't exactly the religious type.

I slipped into the chapel and shut the door behind me. I could hear Marcus near the pulpit making clinking noises, though I didn't know what he was up to. Rishi meowed lightly, and Oberi panted as he guided me up the aisle.

"Are we ready?" I asked as I approached.

"I'm ready if you are," Marcus said. "The skies are clear tonight, and the moon is bright. It's the perfect night for this ceremony. You can sit."

I sat cross-legged across from him in front of the pews. Oberi lay next to me. The vast, expansive room made me a bit uneasy, but I knew we were alone. I shifted, though I couldn't find a comfortable position. "How does this work?"

"Did you bring something?" he asked.

I lifted the armband, and Marcus hesitated. "Ava gave that to you, didn't she?" he asked.

"Yeah," I replied sheepishly. "I guess I have more to let go of than I thought, huh? Will this work?"

"It's perfect. I just… didn't think you'd want to destroy that."

My eyebrows shot up. "You didn't say anything about destroying it."

"Oh, well…" Marcus floundered. "I meant to. We don't really have time for something else. Our rooms will be locked by the time we get back."

I sighed and ran my fingers over the bracelet. "I don't have anything else. I think… I think as special as this is to me, I need to let it go. Ava and I aren't dating anymore. I've accepted that we've broken up, but the rest of it… it's hard because we share a soul, and part of me has been hanging on to that. But I don't know if I can do that anymore."

You can't change it, Oberi said.

I scowled. *I asked you here for emotional support. I don't need your commentary.*

Oberi huffed.

I handed my bracelet to Marcus. "Let's do this."

"Okay," Marcus said. "I'll have you help me cleanse the space. There's a lot of history here in the chapel. I can feel it."

"Is it ghosts again?" I asked him.

He sounded uncertain. "Not ghosts, per se. Just an… odd feeling. The energy's weird. I don't like it. We need to cleanse the area with palo santo before we start. It's a Hawkei herb your tribe uses, so I think it makes sense we use it for your ceremony."

I heard the click of a lighter, then smelled the sweet scent of burning wood. I didn't know how Marcus always managed to have a lighter on him, considering inmates weren't even allowed *scissors*, but it was probably approved for spellwork in his warlock classes.

Marcus handed me a stick of palo santo. I walked around the room, filling it with the cleansing smoke. He did the same to the other side of the room. After a good fifteen minutes— because the room was *huge*— we met in front of the pews again.

"That should be good enough," Marcus said. "Take this."

I reached out, and Marcus placed a cup into my hands. "What's this?"

"It's water," he said. "First, I'm going to have you relax. Take as long as you need. When you're ready, you will whisper a prayer of forgiveness to the water and drink it. Your words have energy, and when spoken, you infuse this energy into the water."

"But I'm not a warlock," I pointed out.

"It doesn't matter," Marcus said. "This works with any intention. You remember the forgiveness prayer I taught you?"

I nodded. "Yeah."

Marcus pressed the lighter into my hand. "For the armband when you're ready. Let's begin."

A beautiful melody filled the chapel, played on a string instrument.

I tilted my head to the side. "What is that? A harp?"

"It's a lyre I found in the music room," Marcus said.

"Since when do you know how to play a lyre?" I asked him.

"You learn a lot when you hang out with band geeks through all of high school," Marcus said. "Don't worry about it. I'm here for you."

I closed my eyes and listened to the soothing music as Marcus ran his fingers over the strings. He spoke softly, guiding my breath slowly, until I began to calm down. I couldn't seem to sit still, so I stroked Oberi's fur with one hand. My mind raced, but Marcus had told me not to judge my thoughts— to just let them come as they pleased and observe them.

It wasn't easy. My past seemed to replay in my mind, and the cup of water shook in my hand. I didn't know if I would ever be ready to drink it. We were going to be sitting here all night.

"It's okay," Marcus said quietly, continuing his tune on the lyre. "Take all the time you need."

I drew a deep breath and nodded. *Ancestors, this is so uncomfortable.*

I noticed the thought slip through my mind, and I observed it with curiosity. Of course this was uncomfortable. What did I expect? But that didn't mean I should run from it. If I truly wanted to move on from my past, I had to embrace the discomfort.

"Under this full moon, I forgive my past," I said, repeating the prayer Marcus had taught me. "I release myself from the chains I have created out of my past experiences and the people I have come in contact with. I forgive myself of my past mistakes, and I welcome love into my heart now. I am at peace."

I drank the water, and I was surprised at how refreshing it felt. It was as if the words I said were even more powerful than I thought— like the water and the intention inside was permeating each cell in my body.

Marcus didn't say anything. He just kept playing the soothing melody. Beside me, Oberi curled his nose into my hand. He knew how hard this was for me.

I began to pick at the threads on Ava's bracelet, until the end of it untied. I ran my fingers through the threads, until they untwisted. I drew one thread from the braided tangle and flicked the lighter. The scent of the thread burning away met my nose.

"I forgive..." I choked up. Ancestors, this wasn't going to be easy. This shit sucked. "I choose to accept the life that I have lived. It is not my fault, or my parents' fault, that the Hawkei Elders took me away from Kinpago. Growing up the way I did... it taught me how to fend for myself, and to survive. I learned how to remain strong, even in the face of the toughest obstacles. That is one of the greatest advantages I can have if I'm to fulfill my prophecy."

The flames licked up to my fingers, and I dropped the thread. It must've burnt out before it reached the carpet, because Marcus didn't make any move to snuff it out.

I pulled apart the next thread and lit it. "I choose to forgive the Hawkei Elders for putting me into foster care. They saw me— a mixed-House child— as a threat, and were doing their best to protect the tribe. I do not have to agree with their methods, but their decision no longer has a hold over me."

The flames touched me again, and I dropped the thread, before moving on to the next one.

"I forgive my father and grandfather for never finding me. I go back and forth on whether they did everything they could to find me, or if they just left me to fend for myself, but dwelling on that won't change what happened. I choose to forgive them."

I lit the next thread. "I forgive Ava's father for sending me here to the Institute. For the longest time, I resented the man. But I spent so long trying to find a home, and if I never came here, I would still be searching—"

I paused as the confession hit me. I didn't even know I was going to say it before it came out. "It's not the Institute that's home. It's the people. If I never came here, I never would've found my true family."

Marcus choked up, and Oberi sniffed. For a moment, I'd forgotten that they were sitting there, listening to my confessions. Tears pricked at my eyes. I didn't realize how good it would feel to finally admit that. But my insides still twisted. I was holding back *so much* that wanted to come out. Names and memories flashed through my mind, as if each of them wanted to be released as well. It was so overwhelming, I didn't even know where to start. After being numb for so long, having any kind of emotion was too much.

I'm here for you, Oberi said kindly, like he could sense my panic. *We'll do this together.*

I nodded. I drew a wavered breath, then peeled another thread apart from the others. "I forgive the social care system and the endless string of foster parents who treated me like dirt. I do not agree with the way the system is run, and I can't condone the way I was treated, but I won't let it have power over me anymore. Everything I grew up with has shaped me into the man I am today. I know right from wrong, because I grew up with example after example of what *not* to be. I may be a criminal and a villain by the book, but I am a good person at heart."

The thread turned to ash, and I grabbed another. I swallowed the lump in my throat and continued. "I forgive the women who used me for sex. Truth is, I used them, too. I believe I deserved better than to pay for a warm bed and a full belly with my body, but it was a choice I made in a time of desperation when all I wanted was to survive. It's not something I ever have to do again, and I choose to let go of the fear that I will ever have to go back there."

Something broke inside of me then. To not only admit to myself that my days on the streets were over, but to *believe* it was profound. It wasn't that the Institute was better than the streets, but here I had a family—one that would be there for me long after we got out of this place. And heaven forbid if I lost them all, they were proof to me of the kind, generous hearts that lived in this cruel world. If I could find a family in a prison amongst criminals, I could find it anywhere.

"I forgive the gang that killed Marty," I said, but saying it felt like choking on needles.

Oberi started to stand when I gasped, but I placed a hand on his neck and guided him to lay down again. Tears spilled over my lids and streaked my cheeks, but I didn't wipe them away. Marcus and his people believed in feeling your emotions, and if I was going to finish this ceremony, that's exactly what I had to do. I couldn't speak as the thread burned, nor once it had turned to ash. All I could do was clutch my stomach and double over. Tears streamed from my eyes and landed on the carpet below me. I heaved for breath, though it didn't come. It was as if all the air had been sucked from the room, though I could still feel it with my magic. The air had gone nowhere, but I'd somehow detached from it as my crippling emotions overtook any sense of physical need.

Marcus stopped playing his harp, but I waved my hand at him, to tell him I would make it. I couldn't find the words, though.

"Ancestors, Marty!" I wailed. I didn't even realize when my vocabulary shifted, as if I was talking to a ghost. He wasn't here, and I'd never speak to him again, but hell, I had to say this out loud— even if Marty never got to hear it. "You always taught me to stay away from the wrong people. Why'd you have to get mixed up with them? You knew what they would do to you! You knew! And you... you died."

I hiccupped, and my whole body shook in sobs. "I'm so, *so* sorry. You shouldn't have died like that. I have spent so long going over that night in my head, wondering how I could've saved you, and I couldn't, Marty. And sitting here trying to change the past is useless. The only thing I can do is make sure it never happens to anyone I love ever again. You made a mistake getting involved with those guys, and they were wrong to kill you, but nothing I do will change it, and so I have to accept it. I choose to forgive it. You were there for me when no one else was, Marty, and I'll never forget that."

The chapel went silent, except for Marcus' music. After several beats, Oberi said, *That was beautiful, Charlie.*

My chest heaved as I sat up straighter. "I'm not done."

I had so much more baggage to release, but I felt immensely lighter already. I lit another string and gritted my teeth. "I forgive myself, for holding on to all of this for so damn long. It's done nothing but turn me bitter, and I can't keep going on like that. Anger has its place, but only if it's going to drive me to action. It has no place here— not in the past. I forgive myself for the criminal I've been. For so long, I thought I was a shitty person for stealing and conning people, and I just... *accepted* that I couldn't change that. But I did what I had to do to survive, and I'm not sorry about it. I choose to release myself of that shame, and to know that if I'm a villain, it's because *they* choose to see me that way. I don't fit into a box, and I don't play by other people's rules, but I don't have to make myself the bad guy. Hell, I murdered Bones, and if that makes me a bad guy in their book, so be it. But I saved a man's life in the process, and I'd do it all again in a heartbeat. So yeah, I forgive myself for doing what I have believed is right every moment of my life. I am not my mistakes, but I'll sure as hell start trying to learn from them."

My hands trembled as I lifted the final threads. I opened my mouth, but my breath caught. I squeezed my eyes shut tightly as the tears hit me like a flood. This one wasn't going to be easy. In fact, it was probably going to be the hardest one.

"I release the expectations that I have unfairly put upon Ava-Marie. The resentment I feel because she doesn't want to live life on my terms is crippling. I've searched my whole life for security, stability, and certainty, and I thought Ava could be that for me, but she can't. She wants adventure, and I don't, and I've felt so angry that she won't give that up for me. It's unfair. Ancestors, I want to be with her *so bad*, but I am so fucking scared that we're both going to get hurt. Everything I've ever had has left me, and so I can't rely on *faith* that Ava would stay. I'm so frightened of losing her that I thought it'd be easier to distance myself from her than love her."

Oberi stood, but he didn't say anything.

I continued. "The only thing I can be certain of is that I'm going to lose Ava-Marie one day, but I'm causing both of us more pain by staying away from her and trying to prevent it. That pain is already here. Ava may be difficult at times, but I'm the real mess. I love her so damn much that I've turned away from her. That's going to change. I forgive myself for the choices I've made. I cannot change them. But moving forward, I can no longer push her away."

My rib cage felt as if it was tearing apart, but I knew this would get worse before it got better. "I can't keep resisting my heart. Our souls are connected, and I can't turn away from that. I don't care if we're together or not. I will commit to everything we face together in the future. I will be there for her no matter what, through any obstacle, and I won't be a coward any longer and give up."

Sobs racked my chest, but I didn't resist them. I let them tear through me, because if something was going to tear me apart from the inside out, it's because it wanted to be let go.

"I know this is going to be hard," I cried. "I know there is going to be pain at the end. There's always pain. But it doesn't matter, because I want to be with her, and I'm making us suffer more by refusing to. So I forgive myself for letting her go, and I vow to make things right again."

You're going to tell her how you feel? Oberi asked.

I swallowed the lump in my throat. "I will. I can't keep going on like this— for either of our sakes. I have to be honest with her, and with myself. I love her."

As I dropped the final thread, I felt the weight in my chest lighten. Tears continued pouring out of my eyes, but I finally felt like I could wipe them away. Oberi pressed his head into my hand, and I scratched him behind the ears. That wasn't good enough, though. I wrapped my arms around his neck and pulled him into my lap, burying my face into his fur. Oberi pressed his forehead to my chest, and for the longest time, we just sat there. Not speaking— just feeling.

I didn't know how much time passed before I finally drew away from him, but I knew that for the first time in my life, I didn't feel so burdened. It wasn't completely gone, and maybe it never would be, but I finally felt like I could breathe.

Marcus stopped playing music and set his harp aside. "I'm proud of you, man."

I sniffled. "Is that it? Is it over?"

"Only you can say when it's done," Marcus said.

I wiped my nose. "I don't think I'll ever be done forgiving people, but right now I feel... pretty damn good. I mean, I feel really crappy, but there's this hope in my chest, and I just feel like everything's going to be okay."

"I hope you're right," Marcus said. "Your whole ceremony sounded really powerful."

"Thanks."

Marcus started gathering his things, then he handed me a blanket. "We're locked out of our dorms, so you might as well find a pew."

"Thanks but I think I'm good right here," I said. I lay down on the ground, using Oberi as a pillow. He curled into me, and I scratched him behind the ears.

You okay? I asked him.

I know how hard that was for you, he said. For once, he wasn't being a snarky asshole. He was genuine. *You're right that you never have to return to your past, Charlie. Because I'm here for you now. Even in death, nothing will ever change that.*

Thank you, Oberi. That means the world to me.

I snuggled into the blanket and closed my eyes. It struck me how familiar it was to sleep on the ground. But this was different. Though I was in a prison, and my conditions were less than ideal, I'd never slept so well in my life.

In the morning, I'd make things right again. I'd find Ava, and I'd tell her how I felt.

Everything would be as it was meant to be. I could hardly wait to take her in my arms.

She misses you, too, Oberi said, and I smiled. For the first time in a long while, things were looking up.

BANG!

I startled awake to the sound of a slamming door. Marcus gasped, and Rishi gave a squeak. I sat up, wondering what was going on.

Marcus rushed over to me and grabbed the back of my shirt, yanking me to my feet. He must've subconjured the blanket, because it disappeared from on top of me, leaving me cold.

"What time is it?" I asked.

"Sunrise," Marcus hissed. "Get behind the pews."

Marcus dragged me between a row of pews, and we ducked down low where we couldn't be seen. Oberi lay on his belly next to me, and Rishi scurried past me.

It's the Warden, Oberi told me. *I can smell him.*

I felt the blood drain from my face. *What's the Warden doing on this side of campus?*

Listen, Oberi said.

Footsteps approached. I held my breath, and my heart pounded. Marcus' breath wavered beside me.

"This is taking too long," the Warden's harsh voice filled the chapel. He was angry.

"We based our timeline on the assumption that the blood tests would reveal more hybrids," another man said. It was probably one of the angel professors, though I couldn't be sure. "We'll have to adjust."

"No," the Warden snapped as they passed by us. "There are more Elf hybrids in this prison. The prince is here— the seer foretold it. We need to find them by any means necessary."

"But sir, the blood tests confirmed—"

"Then the blood tests are imperfect!" the Warden roared. "I want them done again!"

"On every student in the school?" the man asked in a wavered tone. "That will take time. We only have so many tests left—"

"Then we test the strongest students first," the Warden demanded. "I want to be there this time, to oversee every blood draw. The hybrids won't slip through my grasp a second time."

"Who do you suggest we start with?"

Something smacked, and I was pretty certain the Warden had swatted the professor upside the head. "Use your brain, Gael."

"Uh oh," Marcus whispered, and his body tensed beside mine.

My stomach instantly knotted. Was he—?

"Ah-CHOO!" Marcus sneezed so loud, it could've woken the whole prison.

My whole body went rigid, but it was too late. Someone grabbed me by the back of the shirt and yanked me out from behind the pews. It happened so fast that my head spun. Oberi let out a deep growl.

"What do we have here?" the Warden asked, sounding amused.

He shoved me so hard that I fell flat on my face in the middle of the aisle. For a moment, I feared he would use his powers on me, like he had in Forevermore. I felt like I was back there, trembling in terror. Oberi barked.

"Please, sir! We were just—" Marcus started, but the Warden must've grabbed him, because he gasped. A second later, he landed on the ground next to me. Rishi yowled.

"Well, Professor Gael," the Warden said. "I think we just found our first subjects for the second round. I want them blood tested immediately."

Professor Gael's hands landed on me, and the angel began dragging me away. I struggled against his hold, but he was strong. Overpowering him would require some serious Elf magic I hadn't perfected yet.

Fuck!

"You can't do this!" I yelled. "We already got our results!"

The Warden just laughed. "You're forgetting who I am, Mister Wahkin. Make no mistake; whatever secrets you and your friends are hiding, I *will* uncover them."

Terror shook my body, because I knew I couldn't hide any longer. There was no way to con myself out of this one. The Warden was about to find out what I was.

And my secret would be the end of us all.

Ober barked loudly, but there was nothing he could do short of attacking the Warden. There was no use when angels could heal quickly.

Charlie! Oberi screamed in my mind.

My stomach hollowed as I realized there was no way I could tell Ava how I felt now. That would be cruel, because the second the Warden got those test results, I'd never see Ava again. Letting me go a second time after she knew the truth would break her apart.

It was over. I couldn't tell Ava I loved her, because I was headed straight to the Infernal Underground.

"Knock, knock." Kallie entered my cell early in the morning, holding out a drink from Commissary. "It's pumpkin spice season. Happy October."

"There's nothing in it, right?" I asked as I took it warily, sipping the coffee. I'd already gotten dressed for the day, and had a bunch of books spread out in front of me on the bed.

"Trust me, I watched the warlock who prepared it *very* closely. Your drink has no magical properties whatsoever, and as a bonus, it's decaf." Kallie took a drink. "Mine, however, is embedded with wolven herbs for my shifter strength. What are you working on?"

"Ivy let it slip to me that Charlie's lessons with the Elves haven't been going well," I muttered, turning a page. "I'm trying to figure out why they're having such a hard time performing magic."

"Simple, isn't it? They've been spoiled in Forevermore," Kallie said, sitting across from me.

"I know, but there has to be more to it. Even incompetent supernaturals can use *some* kind of magic."

"What does your intuition say?"

We'd been working on intuition all semester, meditating by the waterfall in the Elementai room. I was getting better at determining what my intuition wanted to say to me, but I still had trouble trusting my judgment.

"It says there's something we're missing," I stated. "The answer is right in front of us, but we're overlooking the obvious."

"That means it must lie with magic we already know," Kallie said. "Elves are similar to fae. What if they need to practice illusion magic first?"

"I guess, but how is that going to help them? They need to be able to overpower the guards and steal another supernatural's magic if they're going to escape." I finished off my coffee with another few chugs. I was on a mission this morning to figure this out.

"What about simultension?" Kallie asked. "There's a start."

I hadn't thought about simultension much since we'd used it in the Darke Games. It was the ability of supernaturals to meld their powers together, even across different races. We'd used it to beat monsters during the Games. "That could work. What if simultension is the best way to teach the Elves how to use their powers?" I speculated. "Start off slow, teaching them how to meld their magic with another supernatural's, *then* overpower it?"

Kallie smirked. "I am a genius."

"We have to tell Charlie!" I was so excited. This could be the key to getting the Elves out of here! I got up from my bed and ran to his dormitory next door. "Charlie?"

I poked my head in, but he wasn't in there. I began roaming the halls, wondering if he'd already gone down to breakfast. *Where was he?*

I did a mental search for Oberi. I felt him *somewhere* within the prison, but couldn't tell where he was, only that my Familiar was very worried.

Okay, I was starting to freak out a little. Kallie followed me as we roamed up and down the halls. "Charlie? Charlie! Has anyone seen him?"

People shook their heads as I asked, and my gut began to bottom out. He was never very far away. Even when he was mad at me, he was always nearby.

Kallie came closer as my breath started to quicken. I turned in place in the hallway, feeling faint. "Charlie! Where are you?"

"I'm right here."

Relief flooded into my veins as I watched Charlie approach, Oberi at his side. Marcus followed at a distance, his head down.

"Ancestors, you scared me." I hugged Charlie and kept a tight grip on his arms as I pulled away. "I thought something..."

My voice trailed off as I saw the tight look on his face. Something *had* happened. My hand brushed something. It dropped against my side when I saw a white bandage wrapped around his arm, the sleeve of his sweater pushed up.

"*No.*" I backed away, shaking my head. "No."

"They retested me. They took my blood this time. The Warden watched them do it," Charlie said heavily. "They're going to know I'm an Elf soon. The tests are more comprehensive, so it'll take longer, but he's going to know—"

"He *can't.*" My voice cracked. I refused to accept this as reality.

"There's no way to stop it now. I'm going to the Underground," Charlie said. "I have to get ready for whatever the Warden has in store."

I couldn't handle it. I hit the floor.

"Pidge!" Charlie instantly knelt by my side.

I was just *sobbing.* "You can't go," I pleaded. "You're my best friend."

He rubbed my back. "You're my best friend too, Ava."

I continued to cry, and Charlie lifted me up by the arms. "Come on. We gotta go somewhere private."

The music room, Oberi offered, and we went there. Kallie and Marcus didn't follow. Marcus held back tears and placed a hand over his mouth, while Kallie tried to console him. His eyes looked guilty. What had happened?

When we got to the music room, Oberi guided us to the piano bench. Charlie took my hands as I continued to weep.

"This is bullshit!" I burst. "I won't let them take you. I'll bust you out. I'll do whatever it takes— I'll even kill the Warden if I have to, I don't care about the consequences!"

"You can't do that," Charlie said in a concerned tone, like he knew I'd try. "It'll put your life in danger."

"Fuck it!" I yelled. "If they want to send you to the Underground, I'm going too! We'll be tortured together. I want to die *with* you!"

"Stop." Charlie wiped my tears away. "I don't want that."

I let out a very unladylike snort. "I haven't been one to listen, and I'm not going to start now, not when your life is in danger."

"This might not be a bad thing. If they take me to the Underground, I can find Alice and the others, and we could escape," Charlie offered.

He was trying to convince himself this wasn't a death sentence. "Charlie, they're going to torture you. The others aren't demigods, but you are, and more than that, you're the heir to the Elven throne. The Warden is going to figure that out eventually, and once he knows what you are—"

"It's all right." Charlie hugged me again, and I sagged against his body. What would I do when I lost *this*? I didn't think I could live without his presence, the light he gave me. A breakup was one thing. He was still around, in a place where I could see him, hear him, touch him if I wanted to.

I wouldn't make it without him. I knew that much.

Oberi sat at our feet, looking very lonesome. *I think we're over-looking one very crucial fact.*

I blinked as the realization set in. "If you're gone... who gets Oberi?"

"You, obviously," Charlie said. "If I'm not around, you need him to protect you at the prison."

"No! He has to go down to the Underground with you, to keep you alive until the rest of us can find you!" I insisted.

Charlie made a skeptical noise. "We haven't found many clues on the Underground, and each one has just led us to a dead end."

"We're close. I know we are," I insisted. "You'd just have to hold out long enough for us to locate where they took you."

"Like hell," Charlie growled. "You need to stay alive; that's my priority."

"Don't you understand that I don't care about living unless you're there!" I shouted. "I don't care if it's messed up, or unhealthy, or whatever other kind of crap people would say about it. Everyone on this planet can go to hell, as long as you and me—"

He cut me off. "*Listen to me.* Ava, you..."

His voice broke. "You're the best part of us. You're smarter than me, braver than me... hell, we're both prophesied to save the world, but I think you're gonna be the one to do it, because when you put your mind to something, you don't let anything stop you. I'm not like that. I can't keep fighting unless there's someone to fight for."

His voice dropped. "Sometimes, when I'm at my lowest point, I think that you're the only thing I like about myself."

"Charlie..." I whispered. How could I manage to tell him that I felt the same way?

He cleared his throat. "I've done a lot of stuff to reconcile myself to my past, and I've accepted my fate. I'm ready to move on, wherever I'm going. I haven't had a good life, that's for sure, but what's made it worth living is the friends I've made and the love I feel for you."

Charlie stuttered on the last line, like he realized he slipped up and said something he hadn't meant to. He went to say something more, but shut his mouth.

What more was there *to* say, anyhow? Everything was out in the open. It was stupid of us to keep pretending we didn't care about each other, because we did.

If only we had a few more days. I thought there was hope for us. I was certain we'd get back together again, if only we had the space to reconcile.

We ran out of time. The Warden took it from us.

We sat in silence for a moment, before Oberi shifted uncomfortably. *There is a solution, though it is unpleasant,* Oberi said slowly.

We said nothing, and Oberi went on. *Charlie is an Elf, which means he has the ability to break bonds. That means* any *bond.*

My mouth dropped open in horror. "You're not suggesting what I think you are."

What other option do we have? Oberi asked.

"Then it's simple," Charlie said. "I break my bond with you, and with Ava, then the both of you will be safe."

"Charlie, no," I protested.

I'm afraid you don't understand, Oberi said. *The two of your souls are so intertwined that you won't be able to control who I remain connected to. The connection you share is not an ordinary bond. The result of who I stay bonded to is completely up to chance.*

"Then who would you go with?" Charlie asked.

Oberi was quiet, before he said, *I believe I would remain bonded to whoever's connection with me was the strongest. It could go either way.*

I shuddered. The idea was abhorrent to me. Lose my bond to Charlie, and possibly to Oberi? A fate worse than death. I'd rather perish in the Underground at the hands of the Warden, as much as I hated the man.

Charlie, though, was contemplating it. I could see it on his face.

"Don't you do it, Charlie. I'll never forgive you," I threatened.

"What other choice do we have?" he said miserably. "This seems like the only way to make it fair."

"Nothing's fair at the Institute. That's why we have to play dirty," I snarled.

"Why can't you see that everything I've ever done is to protect you?" he said hopelessly.

"I'm a big girl. I can take care of myself," I demanded. "Don't break our bond. Just wait. There has to be another solution."

Charlie was still. I grabbed his hand. "Come on. We're going to the library. There has to be *some* kind of loophole."

I was damn determined to find some sort of law or rule that would make the Warden unable to take Charlie to the Underground, no matter what his blood status. Kallie and Marcus joined us, sifting through books and papers. I read the Institute's code of conduct three times and got nowhere. Marcus shuffled through pages in the international law book from the United Supernatural Union, and Kallie read illusion books, trying to find some sort of fae trick or contract that would get us out of this.

Charlie couldn't really help, so he just sat there. His fingers caressed my arm as I worked, or wandered around my thigh. He was looking for some kind of comfort, preparing himself for what he thought was inevitable.

I motivated myself as I worked. *I am Ava-Marie Mitoh. I am the firstborn of a great chief and the daughter of a powerful Chosen One. I will not be beaten by the Warden. I won't lose the man I love and allow him to be tortured and killed. This is within my power to stop.*

As time went on, though, my determination began to dwindle. By the end of the day, we were all back in the music room. I sat on the floor with my back against the wall, crying heavily. Whenever I shed one tear, there was another to come.

The Warden could take Charlie away at any moment, and we had nothing to stop him with. As clever as we all thought we were, we had no options.

"Let's just enjoy the rest of the night," Charlie offered. He sat next to me, Oberi splayed across his lap. "It's the last one we're gonna get together."

"We have to keep trying." I sniffed.

"Pidge, just let me have this. One small moment of happiness," Charlie begged.

The door opened. I didn't look up to see who it was, but the stereo in the music room clicked on, and a familiar song drifted out of it. A Latin ballad.

My brother stooped in front of me. He smiled and held out his hand. "Remember this?"

As if I could ever forget. Opal, Chancey, and Ivy stood in the doorway. They must've heard the news.

I didn't much feel like dancing, but Ez kept his hand suspended there. I took it and rose to my feet. He twirled me around, then pulled me into a tango hold. We began to move in unison, like we'd just done this routine yesterday instead of years ago.

Despite the misery I felt, a smile broke its way across my face. I remembered this dance. It'd been our favorite routine. I sang along to the words in Spanish, and Ez spun me around.

I was laughing by the end of it. Charlie smiled, like he loved to hear that sound. Our friends applauded in appreciation.

"Wow! You two can really rock a dancefloor," Ivy said in appreciation.

"We were champion ballroom dancers. Our Aunt Imogen and Uncle Jonah taught us very well," I said.

"Our dad made us quit because we won all the time, and he wanted to give the other kids a chance." Ez laughed.

"I never cared about winning. It was just for fun," I said. "I think that's why we did so well. Because we really loved what we did."

Ez walked over and hauled Charlie to his feet. "Come on, man. You've gotta get out there."

"I can't dance," Charlie argued.

"Have you ever tried?" Ez challenged. "I bet no one taught you in a way you could understand. You don't need to see to be able to dance. Here."

Ez placed one of Charlie's hands on my hip, then guided our hands together. Ez positioned our arms so they were tilted upward at a sharp angle. As the music changed, Ez said, "Okay, Charlie, take one step backward with your left leg. Ava will follow."

Charlie swallowed, like he was nervous. He did as Ez told him, and we moved together. Ez nodded in approval. "Next, step to the side with your right leg, then forward with your left leg, then back to the side with your left leg again. Simple box step. Easy."

A grin broke across Charlie's face as he followed the instructions fluidly. Ez clapped him on the back.

"See? You're dancing," Ez said. He reached out and spun Opal to his side, who gave a giggle.

Couples began pairing up; Chancey dipped Ivy to the music, while Kallie snapped at Marcus for stepping on her feet during a very awkward tango.

"Am I going to hit anything?" Charlie asked anxiously. The music changed to a romantic Latin ballad, and I felt him draw me closer.

"You won't. I promise," I said. "Everyone's giving us space."

"I can't believe I'm dancing," Charlie said as he spun me around.

"Of course you are," I said. "And you're amazing at it."

I taught Charlie a simple swing dance, before Ez said, "This stuff is for amateurs. Let's do swing lifts!"

"*Yes*," I agreed eagerly. "Those are the best."

"What are those?" Charlie asked curiously.

"You're going to want to hook your left arm around her waist, then bring her behind you and pass her to your other arm. The momentum should make the move simple. She basically curves around your body as you're lifting her," Ez instructed.

"I don't want to drop you," Charlie said.

"You won't," I insisted. "I trust you."

He was hesitant, but Oberi barked, *Do it, Charlie!*

His body tensed, but slowly relaxed as I drifted my fingers over his chest, waiting for him to make the right move. He hooked me around the waist and sent me flying around him.

Charlie could lift me easily. He was really strong, and I didn't weigh much anyway, so he could fling me around without much effort. I landed safely on his other arm and got back on my feet.

"Well done!" Ez said. "You two are naturals."

Opal kept falling out of Ez's arm when they did the lift, though he caught her each time. She fell against his chest and staggered on her feet.

"I'm getting dizzy!" Opal held her head and laughed.

"You'll get used to it," Ez told her. "Just takes practice."

Ivy and Chancey had mastered the lift as quickly as we had. Chancey spun Ivy around him like they weren't meant to do it, and I rolled my eyes.

"Show-offs," I taunted.

"Oh, goddess, I'm so sorry!" Marcus bumbled. He'd dropped Kallie on the floor while trying to lift her.

Kallie huffed a piece of hair out of her face. "I'm fine," she said as he helped her up. "It wasn't a big deal."

Charlie let out a small laugh under his breath, and his hand shifted from my hip to press into my back. We rocked back and forth, and everything felt perfect, a blissful moment tucked away for us in a dark world.

Dancing might've been something we enjoyed together... if we had time.

Oberi changed into a unicorn and walked to the stereo. She pressed her nose on a button and switched the song. It blasted hard metal music, and she began head banging to the beat. It was funny, watching a unicorn rock out.

"This is so much fun," Opal gushed over the noise. "We could start our own swinger's club!"

"Swing club, you mean," Ez corrected. "The former sounds like we're all hanging out to have group sex."

"I wouldn't mind," Ivy said coyly. Chancey grabbed him around the waist and tickled him.

We danced the rest of the night away, until it was nearly time for our cells to be closed for the night. The looming ten p.m. deadline seemed like a death sentence. Our friends left us alone as Charlie walked me back to my cell.

Every step was painful. I wanted that walk to go on forever. He stopped in front of my door, and I mustered up my best protests. "Let me stay with you. Just one more night. Please," I begged.

"I think it's better if we're not together when they come get me, and we don't know when that will be," Charlie said.

He knew I'd fight them, and he didn't want me getting involved. Tears rose to my eyes. "So this is goodbye?"

Charlie had a physical lump in his throat. "Ava, I..."

He bent forward and pressed his lips to my head. I felt him entwine a hand in my hair, and I thought I was dying.

"Don't..." The word suffocated in my throat as I felt him step away. I grasped for his arm, but his fingers fell away from mine, leaving me grasping for something that wasn't there.

Oberi let out an angry nicker and stomped her hoof. She went to go after him, but Charlie sharply turned.

"No, Oberi. Stay," Charlie commanded. He continued walking the other way, and Oberi bowed her head.

He wasn't going to stay in his cell. He'd camp out somewhere until they found him. At least he had the heart to hide, to not give in too early.

I watched him until he was out of my sight, then chasmed inward. What was I supposed to do? Go neatly inside my cell, pull the covers over my head and cry like a little princess that he'd been stolen from me?

Fuck no. There had to be some other way. Curfew was close, but I wasn't giving up.

I ran throughout the prison until I found someone I knew. Everyone else had already gone to bed. The only friend I discovered was Marcus, sitting inside the Villain's Den and looking dead inside, as if he didn't care if he got caught by the guards.

I scampered inside and stood before him. He took one look at me and visibly crumbled.

"Marcus," I wept. "Don't let me lose him."

His mouth became a thin line, and he straightened up. "Never.

Come on, Ava, let's go back to the library. There must be *something* we missed."

The library was closing when we got there. We only had enough time to grab a handful of books and check out. We raced back to my room, where we started going through the books we'd grabbed all over again.

"Dammit, I'm *not* going to let someone else die because of a mistake I made," Marcus hissed. "Fucking give me something!"

He yelled at the books, but obviously, there was no response. He furiously turned pages by moonlight, searching for an answer.

I was sprawled on the floor, papers scattered around me, and Oberi curled around my body. He was back in his husky form and nosing books my way.

I kept reading, but I found my eyes growing heavy. The grief and sadness I felt was just too much to push away. I couldn't handle it.

The next thing I knew, sunlight was streaming through my window. Oberi brushed hair out of my face with his nose, and I peeled myself up off the floor.

Fuck! How could I have fallen asleep at a time like this? I cursed myself for doing so.

Marcus looked exhausted. There were huge bags under his eyes, but a smile spread across his face as he shouted, "I think I got it!"

I started upward. "What did you find?"

Marcus panted as he opened the law book from the United Supernatural Union. "There's a loophole. The Warden can't prevent inmates from getting married at the Institute during their sentence."

I blinked. "Married? What do you mean?"

"By supernatural law, married inmates aren't allowed to be separated during their internment," Marcus said in a rush. "They have to be kept together. It's a law that was written for the benefit of mated partners, such as the fae. It's considered cruel and unusual punishment for inmates to be separated from their bonded partner if they're in the same institution, and since you and Charlie share a soul-bond, the law protects you as well."

"Does that even matter?" I asked. "Charlie's still part Elf."

"It *does* matter. You don't have any Elven blood. You're full-blooded

Hawkei, which means the Warden can't deport you to the Underground without a reason. He doesn't have one, because otherwise, he'd have sent you there by now. And if Charlie's spouse, a.k.a. *you*, are unable to be taken to the Underground, then he can't go, either. The Warden can't even send married inmates to Cellblock 9, or the adult penitentiary, without the spouse also being sentenced to the same place. He has to wait for their failure to graduate from the Institute in order to separate them."

My mouth went dry. "So if I want Charlie to stay..."

"You'll have to marry him, yes," Marcus said shortly. "There's no other option."

"But if that's the case, why don't Elves and Elf-hybrids just find random people to marry, so they don't get deported to the Underground, or wherever else the Warden sends them?" I asked.

"The law states that you have to have a *romantic history* with the person you're marrying, as well as evidence and witnesses," Marcus said. "You and Charlie dated for months before the Elves were even discovered. The Warden can't say your relationship is false. He admitted to it himself, when he threatened you last semester."

"But we're broken up now. The Warden knows about that," I pointed out.

"Doesn't matter. Say you had a change of heart, came to your senses and got married," Marcus said with a shrug. "Everyone at the prison knows you had a thing last semester. There are hundreds of witnesses who will confirm that you were a couple before this point. That's all the evidence you need."

"Is this enough?" I demanded. "The Warden runs this prison. I don't know if any of this matters without another supernatural entity getting involved."

"Darke Island falls under the United Supernatural Union's jurisdiction," Marcus said as he reached for a tome on Hawkei law. "If you get married on the island, the Warden *has* to honor your marriage, because it will be verified by the Union. Plus, you're the daughter of a chieftain, which means you have special privileges, and so does your husband. If the Warden, or any supernatural force outside the Hawkei tribe, attacks a member of a chieftain's family—"

"It would mean that he's declaring an act of war." I closed my eyes. "Of course. And if the Warden sent Charlie to the Underground, my dad would have to declare war on the angels for attacking his son-in-law, because that's his family. He'd be honor-bound to do it, and the rest of the Elementai Houses would have to back him up."

"We also know that the Union is split," Marcus added. "The angels, vampires, and mermaids are willing to help the Warden, but the elementals, the fae, and the witches aren't. If the Hawkei go to war, the witches will probably back them up, and the fae will be forced to pick a side."

"It'll start another war for sure," I said. "The Hawkei have seen what happened to the Elves. We elementals have been at the bottom of the supernatural hierarchy for a long time. We won't allow the other races to push us around any longer, because we know we'd probably go extinct next."

"Exactly. It sends the supernatural world into chaos at the wrong time, before the Warden wants it. He's not going to risk that, no matter how much he wants to experiment on Charlie." Marcus snapped the book shut. "So the only question that remains is if you're going to go through with it."

I looked at Oberi. He thumped his tail slowly on the floor and gave a doggy, wide-toothed grin. *I think you'd make a pretty bride.*

I cringed, then turned back to Marcus. "How do we even do this? We're at a prison."

"It's simple. There's a quick ceremony in the chapel, then some paperwork. Weddings can be performed by any professor at the Institute. It's part of their training in order to work for juvenile supernatural detention centers."

He scowled. "Though it's supposed to be done by the school's social worker."

I wrinkled my nose when I thought of Jaymin marrying us. She wouldn't do it— she was on the Warden's side. She'd refuse to perform the ceremony.

"Hemlock," I said, getting a burst of inspiration. "She'd do it."

"You'll have to change your name, to make it look legit," Marcus said.

"The Hawkei base their lineage on their mothers. It's tradition for the women of our tribe to keep our mother's names, and the men to change their surnames to ours. Not all Elementai do that, but I wanted to keep things that way when— *if*— I got married." I argued.

"The angels are a patriarchal society. If you don't change your name to Charlie's, the Warden will use it as evidence against you and say the marriage is fake," Marcus pointed out. "You gotta play by his rules if you're going to beat him."

I couldn't even keep my own *name*? But yet, it felt like a worthy sacrifice. I'd cut my heart out if it meant rescuing Charlie from this fate.

I hesitated a moment too long, and Marcus said, "Ava, this is the only way. If you want to save Charlie, we gotta do this now."

I jumped to my feet. I couldn't dawdle with the situation any longer. If I took any more time to think about it, I'd lose my nerve.

We had to find him. For all we knew, the Warden had taken him away by now. "Let's go. Grab those law books."

Marcus, Oberi and I charged down the hallway at a full-on sprint. We checked his room, but he wasn't in there. I began searching the hallways for Charlie, begging the ancestors that he hadn't been found yet.

"Hey!" Naya said nastily as I pushed her out of the way. She sprawled onto the floor, but I didn't stop to apologize. Screw her. Charlie's life was on the line.

Out of the way! Oberi snarled, and he snapped at the heels of a merman. *Wedding bells are ringing!*

"Do you have to put it like that?" I grumbled.

Well, I can't say I didn't imagine this moment differently, but at least it's happening, Oberi pointed out.

No shit. I'd never really put much thought into getting married. I'd had the normal daydreams most girls did, about what dress I'd pick, how it would feel when my father walked me down the aisle, what song we'd choose for our first dance, and the bliss I'd experience on my honeymoon.

I'd get none of that here. This wasn't how I wanted to get married. I wasn't even sure if I wanted this *at all*. The thought of binding myself permanently to anyone, no matter how much I loved them, made me afraid of the future. I loved my independence, and my freedom. I wanted to keep it.

But I wanted Charlie far more, and his life was worth any sacrifice I had to make.

"Where's Charlie?" I burst when I found Ivy and Chancey sitting in the cafeteria. I'd checked everywhere, and hadn't found him.

"I told him to hide out at The Devil's Playground," Ivy said. "They'd have a hard time locating him there."

Thank the ancestors for Ivy. I didn't stop to explain, just ran off. Chancey and Ivy followed us without having to be told what was up. I rushed to The Devil's Playground and flung the door open.

I didn't relax until I saw Charlie sitting on the floor, his back against the stage. He was safe. We could still pull this off.

A wolfish growl came from the corner, one that died when Kallie recognized who we were. She transformed from her wolf form back on to two legs. Kallie had been waiting there all night with him. Charlie could stop me from trying to protect him, but he couldn't stop her. She was a loyal friend.

Charlie jumped to his feet when he heard us coming. His form went rigid, but I called out, "It's us!"

The obvious fear on his face turned to rage when he heard my voice. "Pidge, why are you here?" he asked angrily. "I told you to stay out of it!"

"Never mind that." *Here it fucking goes.* I had imagined that this moment would be more romantic, but as I stopped in front of Charlie and looked up at him, my knees turned to water and my stomach flip-flopped inside of me. I was either going to be sick or fall into his arms, one or the other. I was brave, but this felt scarier than anything I'd ever done. I was glad he couldn't see me, for I was sure if we locked eyes, I would lose my courage.

"Well?" he fumed. "What is it?"

I took a deep breath. I tried not to let my voice waver as I said, "Marry me."

charlie

FIFTEEN

"**M**arry—" I practically choked. Ava couldn't be serious. "Pidge, what is this? A joke?"

It was cruel. I had hours at most before I was dragged off to the Infernal Underground and experimented on, and Ava was trying to be *funny*.

"Ugh, I'm sorry. Let me try again," Ava said. She squeezed my hands, and I felt her lower herself to the ground. Was she... *getting on one knee?* "Charlie Wahkin, will you marry me?"

I scowled and yanked on her arms. "Pidge, stop it. Stand up."

"I'm serious!" she insisted.

My heart stopped. No, she couldn't be. We weren't even dating.

But there was something in her tone that tugged at my heartstrings, something that made me want to hold her closer than I ever had before and say *hell yeah*.

But marrying Ava was nothing more than a fantasy. This wasn't a fairytale; it was a nightmare.

I was well aware that people were watching us, but it felt like Ava and I were alone. My heart began to race as I considered the real possibility of what she was saying. Of course I wanted to marry Ava someday. But that was never going to happen.

Something was wrong— *very* wrong.

"Pidge, did you take your meds this morning?" I asked gently.

"This isn't an episode, Charlie," she said. "I'm getting down on one knee and asking you to marry me. It's the only way to save you."

I reeled back a bit, though I didn't let her go. "Save me? There's a way—"

"Marcus and I found a loophole," Ava explained. "If we get married, the Warden can't separate us, by the United Supernatural Union's own law. If the Warden tries anything to hurt you, it'll be considered an act of war, since you'll be the son-in-law of the Water chief. A supernatural force can't attack a family member of a Hawkei chieftain without it being a declaration of war. *That's* why the Warden hasn't touched me yet. Please, Charlie. We *have* to do this. It's the only way to save your life."

I gaped, because I couldn't find the words. This wasn't how I pictured our wedding would go. I always imagined I would take Ava to a nice place— a garden or something— and propose *properly*. Hell, *I* was supposed to be the one down on my knees, begging for *her* hand in marriage. But that dream was long gone, ever since we broke up.

Ava's voice wavered. "Charlie, answer me. There's not much time left."

This is a bad idea, isn't it? I said to Oberi. Surely, he would back me up.

Actually, I'm with Ava on this one. It's the only way, he insisted.

Well, fuck.

It wasn't that I wanted to say no to Ava. I just didn't want to marry her now, under these circumstances.

But I didn't really have a choice.

Ava squeezed my hands, as if begging for me to answer. Everyone else had gone dead silent.

"I... yes?" It came out sounding more like a question, but Ava didn't seem to notice. She leapt to her feet and threw her arms around me.

"Thank the ancestors," she breathed, as if she'd been worried I'd say no. "We have to find Professor Hemlock right away. She can do the ceremony."

My stomach twisted, but my heart fluttered at the same time. My emotions warred inside of me, so much that it made my head spin. I woke up this morning expecting to end the day in the Infernal Underground. Instead, I was going to end it as a married man.

Ancestors, I couldn't believe it. This was fucking nuts.

Kallie squealed. "Oh, my gods! I can't believe you two are engaged!"

"The shortest engagement ever," Marcus added. "We need to get moving."

"You two go find Hemlock," Kallie said. "Marcus and I will meet you in the chapel in fifteen minutes."

Kallie and Marcus hurried out of the room. Chancey cleared his throat. "Um... anyone want to fill me in?"

"The Warden forced a second blood test," I told him. "He knows I'm part Elf."

"Getting married is the only way to keep Charlie from getting taken away," Ava said.

"And Hemlock can marry you two?" Chancey asked.

"She has the authority," Ava told him.

"Well, then what are we waiting for?" Chancey burst. "Go get her! We'll head to the chapel."

Ava grabbed my hand, and we rushed out of The Devil's Playground. I barely paid attention to where we were going, because my head spun. I should've been terrified about what was about to happen, but I'd be damned if I wasn't the happiest I'd been in my whole life. *I was marrying Ava-Marie Mitoh.* It didn't matter the circumstances. I was grinning like a fool.

We entered Hemlock's office. I heard her fae wings flutter from where she sat behind her desk. "Miss Mitoh?" she asked, sounding surprised.

Ava rushed toward her desk, dragging me behind her. "Professor Hemlock! It's an emergency."

Hemlock's chair squeaked as she stood. "Is someone hurt?"

"No, but they will be," Ava said.

"Miss Mitoh, is that a threat?" Hemlock gasped.

"No, it's— ancestors, how do I explain this?" Ava sighed. "We need you to marry us. Now."

Hemlock hesitated. "Miss Mitoh, have you been taking your medication?"

"Why does everyone keep asking me that?" Ava sounded annoyed.

"Surely a wedding can wait—" Hemlock started, but I cut her off. We didn't have time to discuss this. The Warden could be on his way right now.

"We can't," I said bluntly. I had no choice but to lay everything out on the table and hope we could trust her. It was the only way to get her to agree with this. "The Warden has ordered new blood tests— more accurate than the last. My grandfather was an Elf, and the second the results come back, the Warden is going to take me away. There's a place called the Infernal Underground where the Warden is conducting experiments on inmates. We've overheard him talking about it. He's going to take me there unless we do this *now*. He can't separate us if we're married, and he can't touch the family of a chieftain unless he wants to start a war."

Hemlock didn't say a word. I wasn't sure she was still standing there; she was so quiet.

"You have to believe us," Ava insisted. "We're not making this up. Even my father knows about the Underground—"

"No," Hemlock cut in. "I believe you."

The way she said it... it was like she already knew. Or at least suspected the Warden was up to no good.

"Then you have to help us!" Ava cried. "Please... save Charlie."

Hemlock began shuffling through papers. "You don't have to ask me twice, Miss Mitoh. I'll help you. I'll need to get the forms from the records office expedited."

"I thought we just had to sign papers," Ava said, sounding worried.

"You have to apply for a marriage license first and be approved," Hemlock explained. "Due to problems in the past, a psychological evaluation is required for students inside the Institute."

"How long will that take?" I demanded. We didn't have the time to wait for the paperwork, but the Warden wasn't going to honor our marriage unless it was official.

"Usually, it takes about a week," Hemlock said. "I'll have to backdate the application date."

"How does that help us with the psych eval?" Ava asked, sounding worried. "Jaymin would never—"

"Jaymin Vengier is not the only licensed professional in this place," Hemlock said, sneering at our counselor's name. "All professors are required to obtain a psychology certification before working here. With the amount of troubled students we encounter on a daily basis, we would never be employed without it. I'm fully qualified to approve your evaluation."

"You're saying you'll forge that, too?" I asked.

"We don't have time for a full evaluation," Hemlock pointed out. "And as far as I understand it, I see no signs of manipulation, mania, or otherwise from either of you. The final thing you need is witnesses."

"Kallie and Marcus," Ava said. "They're meeting us in the chapel."

"Go straight there," Hemlock instructed. "Take no detours. The Warden can't find you until this is done. I'll be there soon."

My heart hammered as we left the room. Oberi panted beside me as we rushed through the halls. He was obviously *thrilled.*

I, on the other hand, was terrified this might not happen. We were cutting this pretty fucking close. Every hall we took scared me more than the last— as if we might run straight into the Warden.

We turned a corner, and Ava and I plowed into a group of people. We stumbled back, and I nearly tripped over Oberi.

Watch it! Oberi growled.

"Ava!" Ez exclaimed. "You're engaged!"

"How did you—? Ugh, Chancey!" Ava cried.

"I hope you don't mind. I invited some guests," Chancey said proudly.

"I can't believe you're getting *married*!" Eddie squealed.

"I believe it," Alistair countered. "I can smell the hormones on these two. It was bound to happen."

"This is just so unexpected!" Opal gushed.

"Yeah, well, can we stop standing around talking about it?" I asked impatiently. "We're kind of in a hurry."

"Then it's good I was in the music room and grabbed *this*," Ez said.

Ava yanked backward, pulling on my arm. "Would you get that camera out of my face?"

"It's for the family!" Ez cried. "Mom and Dad won't want to miss this, and Alana will kill us if she doesn't get to watch the video."

"Ugh, fine," Ava groaned. "Come on."

We continued down the hall and slipped into the chapel unseen. Kallie and Marcus were already there. I heard them clinking glasses.

"Where's Hemlock?" Marcus asked.

"On her way," Ava replied.

"Ooh, where'd you get the booze?" Alistair asked.

Kallie giggled. "It's a fae illusion. It isn't real."

"I don't care," Alistair said. "Pour me a glass."

"Oh, and me!" Eddie added with a giggle.

Suddenly, everyone was asking for a glass of champagne. Ancestors, we hadn't even gotten married yet, and our friends were treating this like a party instead of life or death.

"Guys, stop," Ava complained, but no one heard her. The chatter was too loud.

"Kallie, did you put up all these decorations?" Ivy asked.

"I sure did," she said proudly. "It was an easy illusion, really. What do you think?"

As everyone gushed over the decorations, I leaned over to Ava. "What'd she do?"

"The chapel is decorated with white tulle and lace, and there are rose petals running up the aisle, all the way up to an arch. They're being completely over the top." Ava groaned, like she was less than pleased. She wasn't into this wedding at all.

That stung... but I knew Ava hadn't asked me to marry her because she *loved* me. She was just trying to save me from being deported out of here.

"They know this isn't a real wedding, right?" I asked.

Ava huffed. "They're acting like it is."

Kallie turned to us. "The decorations might be false, but there are a couple of things I wanted you to have for real. I found some tulle in the Arts & Crafts room, and I made you *this*."

Ava went speechless for a moment. "Uh... a veil?"

The fabric brushed my arm as Kallie placed it on Ava's head. "Yep. And I also made you these."

Something clinked as it dropped into Ava's hand. "*Rings?!*" Ava squeaked, like it was getting too overwhelming. "How did you make these?"

"If a fae's strong enough, they can create illusions that become reality," Kallie reminded us.

"Like your sofas you make in the Lair," I said. "But those fade as soon as you leave."

Kallie laughed. "A ring is a lot easier to make than a couch... and well, it helps when there are strong emotions behind the spell. These will never fade."

"Strong emotions?" Ava's tone became hard to read. I had no idea what she was thinking right now, and that in itself was crazy, because I was connected to her mind.

"Of course!" Kallie cried. "It's your wedding day. I'm happy for you, bitch! Now, let's get you two married."

Neither of us got a chance to respond before Ivy threw himself in front of us, practically knocking me into one of the pews. "Can I be the flower girl!? I've always wanted to be a flower girl."

"Um... sure?" I said. Everything was happening so fast. I barely had a chance to process it. My whole body was going numb.

"Oberi can be the ring bearer!" Opal suggested.

I'm on it, sister! Oberi sounded thrilled. He shifted into unicorn form, and the rings clinked as Kallie slid them onto Oberi's horn.

"This is perfect!" Kallie gushed.

"There's just one thing missing," Ivy said. "I didn't get to design a gown!"

Kallie gasped, like she just had a good idea. "Yes, of course! How could I miss that? I've got you covered. Ava, spin around."

"You're going to make her a dress with illusion magic?" I asked, my tone sounding hollow.

Ava stiffened next to me. Her aching emotions swelled like a powerful wave that was nearly out of control, ready to crash upon the shore and ruin whatever had the misfortune to be beneath it. It almost did me in.

"You sound upset," Marcus remarked.

Chancey chuckled. "I bet he's disappointed he can't feel it so he can rip it off of her later."

"Shut up," I growled, shoving him.

"No, Chancey has a point," Kallie said. "I'll make it solid, but it won't last like the rings—"

"*Stop!*" Ava screamed, and her shout echoed around the area. It'd become too much, and she finally cracked.

The chatter died down instantly.

"Okay, everyone. Listen up." Ava used that bossy tone she was so good at. "You're all acting like this is a real wedding, and you know what? It's not. We're here to save Charlie's life, and *that's* what matters to me. Not decorations, or some stupid dress. Can we stop acting like this is something to celebrate and just get it over with already?"

My heart sank. Ava was right, and I agreed with her, but it still hurt. This wasn't at all the way I pictured our wedding day would go... but I didn't have a choice. I couldn't give her a proper wedding even if I wanted to.

She didn't want to marry me anyway.

The chapel went dead silent. It was obvious everyone was disappointed, but what did they expect? Ava and I weren't together. This was an arrangement out of convenience, nothing more.

The doors burst open behind us, and Hemlock's heels clicked against the floor. "I got the paperwork. Let's get started."

Kallie clapped loudly. "Everyone in place!"

"Kallie!" Ava snapped.

Kallie leaned in and whispered, just low enough for the two of us to hear. "I know the wedding's a sham, but you at least have to play the part. The Warden will do anything to reverse this marriage. You need to make everyone believe it— even him."

Ava gave an annoyed sigh, like she knew Kallie was right. I just stood there for a second, unable to believe this was happening. Oberi nudged me in the ass with her horn.

"Ow!" I cried, rubbing my butt.

Let's get a move on, she snapped.

I heard the scuffle of shoes beside me and was nearly knocked over as someone slammed against my leg. "Come on, Eddie!" Alistair said.

"Where are we going?" Eddie asked.

"We need music!" Alistair's footsteps faded as he and Eddie climbed the stairs to the balcony, where the organ was.

Oberi pushed me again, so hard this time that I stumbled down the aisle. Hell, how was this even *happening*? It felt like a dream.

Or a nightmare.

Hemlock followed me to the altar. She grabbed my shoulders to show me where to stand. "Are you ready, Charlie?"

Hell no!

"I'm terrified, but... I love her," I admitted.

I felt something through our bond. Oberi had heard me say it, and she was happier than ever. Honestly, I couldn't believe I'd just admitted it out loud— to a professor, no less.

"I know you do," Hemlock replied, as if she knew it all along.

"But I don't think she feels the same way about me," I said. I hated how defeated my tone sounded. "I don't even know why we're doing this."

I didn't want Ava to marry me out of pity. The thought of her making such a great sacrifice for my benefit made me feel ill. I'd almost rather be dragged to the Underground.

"There's more to Ava than you realize," Hemlock said. "She wouldn't do this for anyone, Charlie. She *chose you.*"

I understood what Hemlock was saying immediately. Ava was giving me her freedom willingly, and that was the most precious thing to her. I wouldn't squander that gift.

"EVERYBODY READY!?" Alistair called down from the balcony.

"Ready!" Marcus shouted up to him as everyone shuffled into the pews.

Within moments, the chapel quieted. The horrible sound of clashing notes filled the room, blaring from the organ above me. Alistair obviously didn't know how to play the piano, but he was bound and determined to play *Canon in D*. He missed a bunch of notes, and the chords didn't work with the melody at all, but it loosely resembled the song.

My knees began to tremble as Ava stepped down the aisle. I could hear her footsteps coming toward me, but more than that, I *felt* her through our bond. The closer she came, the stronger the magic got. The bond seemed to strengthen with every step she took, and the magic flared through my body so hard and fast that I nearly fell over. Here we were, in a chapel and in our school uniforms, having a shotgun wedding to rival no other. I wasn't sure if I could go through with this.

Ancestors, I can't believe this is happening. Fuck! Ava telecommunicated through the bond. I didn't think she had intended for me to hear her thoughts.

It is, I said back. I felt her shock when she realized I'd heard her.

You weren't supposed to hear that, she said sheepishly.

Hell, she could say she didn't want to be with me all she wanted, but beneath the fear and anxiety, I felt her excitement. Something about this was intriguing to her, at least.

You're my fiancé, I said. *You don't have to hide anything from me.*

Ivy had to be walking down the aisle in front of Ava. I could feel the flower petals fluttering to the ground with my Air magic. Kallie must've gotten some from the Arts & Crafts room. When he reached the altar, Ivy threw the remainder of his flower petals in the air, and they rained down in front of me.

"Congratulations, ho." He laughed.

I scowled, but I turned my attention to Ava. The sound of her footsteps approaching sent a thrill through me, yet I was more terrified than I'd ever been. She reached me, and her raspberry scent surrounded my presence.

I reached for her hands, and she entwined her fingers with mine. When we touched, magic unlike anything I'd ever felt before ignited between us. Warmth swept over my body, and our bond became more powerful than ever. I could suddenly feel her heartbeat as if it were in my own chest. It synced with mine, pounding at a quick pace like a magical tune composed only for us. I swore her scent became even stronger, intoxicating me. Her voice in my head became louder than ever.

Did you feel that? she asked in my mind.

My fingers trembled in hers. *Yeah. That was weird.*

Ava and I remained silent as the music stopped, but one thing became very clear. Even though we weren't prepared for this, and we certainly weren't ready, we couldn't resist our bond. Our magic *wanted* this. It longed for this day since the moment we met— and it was here sooner than anyone could've anticipated.

"Dearly beloved," Hemlock said, her voice projecting across the chapel. "We are gathered here today to join Charlie Wahkin and Ava-Marie Mitoh in holy matrimony. Have the two of you prepared your vows?"

"Uh... um," I stammered. I didn't even know what to say. Ava and I weren't getting married because we were *in love*. We were marrying each other out of obligation. How could I tell her how I truly felt if I couldn't tell her I loved her?

"Yes, we have vows," Ava answered. She squeezed my hands, obviously noticing my unease. "I can go first."

"Very well," Hemlock said.

Ava drew a deep breath. I heard a soft sound as she took one of the rings from Oberi's horn and positioned it over my finger. "Charlie Wahkin, from the day I met you, I knew I would never stop hating you."

"That's romantic," I said with a scowl.

"Hear me out," she insisted. "I *thought* I knew how I felt about you, but then we were sentenced here, and things changed. I came to the Institute thinking I'd been sentenced to hell, but you've been by my side every day. What I thought was going to be hell turned out to be... something amazing. Incredible, even. This might not be the wedding of my dreams, but I've been unable to predict anything we've gone through since the moment we met. I've always been searching for adventure, but there's been no adventure greater than the one I've lived with you. I promise you from now on, you will never be alone. And so, I vow to follow you on all future adventures, because being with my worst enemy is the greatest adventure of all."

Ava slid the ring onto my finger. I didn't know if she meant any of it, but damn, it'd felt so sincere. Kallie had said we had to play the part, and Ava played it *very well*.

I swallowed the lump rising in my throat. "Hell, pidge."

Ava didn't say she loved me. We weren't ready for that yet, because if we did, this would become far too real. But somehow, in her own terms, she *had* said it. How could I follow *that*?

Say what's in your heart, Oberi encouraged. She nudged my

shoulder with the tip of her velvety nose, and I took the ring from her horn. I held Ava's hand and placed the ring on her finger.

I let out a wavered breath. "I hated you, too."

Ava snorted, and I couldn't help but laugh.

"I know. Shocker, right?" I chuckled. "I didn't know I could despise someone more than I hated you. But that hate turned into passion, and that terrified me. You wanted adventure I couldn't give, and I wanted security you couldn't promise. But I've come to realize that there's only one promise I truly need— and that's my promise to you. Ava-Marie, I vow to serve you as your bonded partner from now until the day we die, no matter how long that might be. I vow to hate you with the same intensity as the day we met, because no matter what happens, no one can take that from us."

I didn't know if Ava had spoken the truth, but I meant every word I said. I cared about her. I always had, and I always would. Making a permanent vow to stand by her forever didn't frighten me one bit, because it's what my soul had decided when I'd given up my sight for her long ago.

I'd given her my eyes. I was more than happy to give her my life.

Hemlock waited a moment before asking, "Charlie Wahkin, do you take Ava-Marie Mitoh to be your lawfully wedded wife, in sickness and in health, as long as you both shall live?"

I couldn't believe I was going to say this. My hands shook in Ava's as I answered with firm conviction. "I do."

"And Ava-Marie Mitoh, do you take Charlie Wahkin to be your lawfully wedded husband, in sickness and in health, as long as you both shall live?"

Ava paused. For a moment, I was terrified she was going to back out, and I felt unease flicker across our bond. A long moment passed in the chapel, and I heard a few people gasp to hold their breath.

Oh, *shit*. She wasn't going to do it. I was going to be left at the altar.

Then my heart trembled as Ava cleared her throat and said, "I do."

"Then by the power vested in me by the United Supernatural Union, I now pronounce you man and wife," Hemlock announced. "You may now kiss the bride."

We hesitated, and I felt Ava's unease through our bond. She was a free woman. She didn't want to get married. If she kissed me, it sealed the deal.

And yet Ava must've been willing to give that up for me. Otherwise, I'd be headed to the Underground right now.

Ava leaned into me, and I wrapped my arms around her waist. I hadn't kissed Ava in months, and my heart hammered in anticipation. An awkward silence passed, and the tension in the air was palpable.

Then her lips connected with mine, and all that tension fell away. My heart hammered, and my head spun. Every moment we'd shared prior— every word, every touch— came rushing back. I was suddenly reminded about all the reasons why I loved her.

I couldn't read Ava; she'd blocked me out. I didn't know if she felt the undeniable passion surging between us, but I sure as hell did, and it was enough to make my head start spinning.

Applause filled the chapel, and our friends screamed so loud that my ears rang.

Ava clung to me as she whispered, "I hate you so much."

"I hate *you* so fucking much," I replied breathlessly. I could feel her emotions now, as she'd opened back up again. She was *so relieved*.

"Get a room!" Chancey shouted.

"You have to sign the paperwork before it's official," Hemlock reminded us.

"Now. Let's sign it now," Ava insisted.

She grabbed my hand and led me over to a table. Papers rustled as Hemlock set the papers between us. Hemlock placed a pen in my hand.

"Right here," Ava said, guiding my hand to the signature line. I scribbled down my signature, then handed the pen to Ava.

"Kallie, Marcus!" Ava said in a rush. "We need witnesses. Sign, hurry."

Kallie and Marcus were at our side in an instant. They each signed their names, and I breathed a sigh of relief.

"It's done," Hemlock announced. "In the eyes of the United Supernatural Union, you are officially married—"

The doors of the chapel burst open, and Ava went rigid. My heart turned to stone in my chest. I didn't have to question who had just arrived.

"There he is! Get him!" The Warden's voice boomed across the chapel.

The guards' footsteps started up the aisle. A weight grew heavy in my chest and settled in my throat. They'd finally come for me.

Hemlock stepped in front of me, like she was willing to take a bullet for us. "Excuse me, Ophio. What exactly is going on?"

The Warden spoke smugly. "Charlie Wahkin is a liar and a criminal."

Hemlock scoffed. "Of course he is. Why else do you think he's at the Institute?"

"He's an *Elf!*" The Warden sneered.

"I fail to see how that makes him a liar," Hemlock said coolly. "Until a year ago, Mister Wahkin wasn't even aware magic existed. He grew up in the human foster care system, did he not? It's reasonable to assume he's unfamiliar with his lineage."

The Warden snarled, "I don't have to explain myself to you. I'm taking Wahkin."

"No you're not," Ava said proudly.

"*Excuse me?!*" The Warden boomed.

Our marriage license rustled as Ava grabbed it. She stomped forward and smacked the papers against the Warden's chest. He let out a low grunt.

"Charlie and I are married, which makes him the son-in-law of a Hawkei chief," Ava sneered. "You can't legally split us up, so if you're going to take him, you'll have to take *me*, too. But you don't want to incite a war just yet, do you? No... that would be too messy."

The following stunned silence was satisfying as hell. I could almost feel the Warden's disbelief radiating off him from here.

"I was fucking right. You can't touch him," Ava said smugly.

"This is a fraudulent marriage!" a woman screamed. I didn't realize someone else had entered the room with the Warden, but she sounded *pissed*.

"Jaymin, please." Hemlock sighed. "To the contrary, this marriage is entirely valid. I officiated it myself."

"Under Union law, inmates of the Darke Institute for Supernatural

Offenders must undergo a psychological eval before getting married," Jaymin seethed. "I performed no such evaluation."

"You're not the only qualified individual to do so," Hemlock snapped.

There was an obnoxious noise from Jaymin's throat. "I— I—" Jaymin stammered. "Ava's not fit to be married!"

"*I* beg to differ," Hemlock argued.

The Warden was obviously pissed. I could hear his heavy breath from here. He stomped toward Hemlock and spoke in a low, intimidating voice. "Tell me, Natasha, what's to keep me from firing you right now for such insubordination?"

Hemlock laughed. "Insubordination? Really, Ophio? I've been at the Institute for over twenty years. There's no alchemy professor in the world who could replace me. And I am well within my rights and certifications to approve the marriage application and officiate the ceremony. So what *insubordination*, exactly, are you referring to? Because whatever you think I've done wrong here, I'm sure the United Supernatural Union would disagree."

Holy shit. Hemlock was *bold*. She basically just told the Warden to tread carefully, because she was *not* a bitch to be messed with. I never thought I could love a professor more.

The Warden's breath became even shallower. He seemed on the verge of exploding. "You can only protect these students for so long, Natasha. Eventually, they *will* slip up, and I will have them."

He tossed the marriage license into the air, and I felt it flutter to the ground at Ava's feet. The Warden whirled around and stomped out of the room. Jaymin and the guards followed closely behind.

I breathed a sigh of relief, and my racing heart began to slow. I rushed to Ava's side, and she curled into me.

"Ancestors, Charlie, I was so scared," she breathed. "I thought he was going to take you away."

I kissed the top of her head. "Never."

Hemlock scooped our marriage license up from the ground, but everyone else remained frozen in stunned silence. "Congratulations on your marriage."

"Thank you," I replied.

"I must file this paperwork as soon as possible," Hemlock said. "For now, I suggest the two of you stay out of Doctor Taurus' way."

Her shoes clicked as she left the room.

Ava drew away from me and cleared her throat. "Thank the ancestors that's over."

Her tone was hollow. We were all shook from the Warden's sudden appearance.

Well, *almost* all of us.

"Let's celebrate!" Alistair suggested. He couldn't care less that the Warden stormed in here. He just wanted an excuse to party.

"We don't have to—" Ava started, but Ivy cut her off.

"I've got you covered," Ivy practically sang. "Drinks on me!"

"Hey, Hemlock *did* tell us to stay out of the Warden's sight," Chancey said slyly. "What better place than The Devil's Playground?"

Our friends started cheering, but it felt forced. They were trying to take our minds off the Warden. I felt jumpy and uneasy as we snuck toward the secret nightclub. I thought for sure the Warden would find some way to invalidate our marriage and take me away. But somehow, we made it to the club without being caught.

Ivy slipped behind the bar and started pouring drinks. "Let's have a toast! Shots all around."

My shoulders sagged. "Come on, guys. Let's not get too wild."

I knew how Ava got when she drank. Once she started drinking, she couldn't stop.

"But it's your wedding," Ez protested.

I scowled. I knew he was still holding that camera. "Do you really want your parents to see you getting wasted on video?"

"They've seen worse," Ez said with a laugh.

Ivy ignored my protests and kept passing around champagne. "A drink for the bride!"

I heard the glass clink against the counter, but I grabbed the drink before Ava could. Our hands brushed together as she reached for it.

"Pidge, we're not going to do this," I said.

"What do you mean?" She sounded offended. "Give me my drink, dammit."

Thank the ancestors everyone was chatting over one another, because nobody heard us. I slid the drink down the bar. "No."

Ava huffed. "You don't own me, asshole."

I smirked. "You took my last name, didn't you?"

"How *dare* you tell me what to do on my wedding day," she protested. "You don't control me."

I sighed. "Come on, Pidge. I was *joking*. Let's not start out our marriage with a fight."

"Why not? Seems fitting," she snapped.

I did my best to have patience. This was Ava, after all, and anyone who dealt with her needed a boatload of it. "Okay, look. I'm not trying to control you. I'm trying to *protect* you. Alcohol messes with your meds. You can do what you want, but we're married now. I'm responsible for keeping you safe and looking out for your welfare. I'm asking you not to do this, today of all days. Please."

Ava didn't say anything right away. To be honest, I didn't know what she was thinking, and I didn't dare try prying into her head right now.

"Fine," she finally said. "Whatever makes you happy."

Hell, she'd finally let me have my way on something. Was the world coming to an end?

"It's time to get this party started!" Ivy screamed.

Loud music boomed over the speakers.

"Come on, Ava!" Kallie cried. "Let's dance."

Ava groaned, like she didn't want to. Damn, I'd never seen that girl pass up dancing before. She must've been *really pissed* about this wedding. Kallie dragged Ava away, and she disappeared from my side.

Chancey nudged me. "Why so glum? You're the groom."

Before I had a chance to answer, Alistair cut in. "I'd be pissed too if I never got a bachelor party."

Ivy gasped, like the idea of missing my bachelor party was ludicrous. "That's *right*! What a shame. Well, there's never a time like the present!"

Ivy rushed around the bar and grabbed my arm.

I dug my heels in. "What the— where are we going?"

"On stage!" Ivy cried. "It wouldn't be a wedding without strippers."

"What kind of weddings have you *been* to?" I gaped.

Ivy didn't answer as he dragged me on stage. He guided me over to the pole and placed my hands on it.

"Stand there," Ivy instructed.

"What are you—?" I started.

The music changed, and Ivy called our friends on stage. "Come on, boys!"

Alistair laughed gleefully, and Eddie chuckled as they climbed on stage and surrounded me. Chancey reached past me to grab the stripper pole, and they all started dancing and grinding on me.

"I want in!" Ez cried. "Here, Opal. Keep recording."

Ez jumped onto the stage and started rubbing his ass on my leg. Marcus must've followed behind him, because he was suddenly next to all the guys, laughing in my ear.

Oh my fucking god. I was mortified. "This is *not* how I pictured my bachelor party at all."

My embarrassment lifted when I heard the sound of Ava's laughter below me— it was the first happy sound I'd heard from her all day. She cheered from below, "Work it! Mama and Daddy are going to love this. It's better than the last video they saw!"

"What a great way to introduce your new husband to your parents," I said sarcastically.

She continued giggling, and you know what? Fuck it. If it made her happy, I was happy.

Even if Ez was twerking so hard he was about to knock me over.

"I'll give 'em something to talk about," Alistair said. "Come on, Eddie."

The two spun away from me, toward the front of the stage. Alistair must've been using *Eddie* as a stripper pole, judging by our friends' applause.

"Go Alistair!" Opal yelled.

Eddie laughed the whole time, like he was having the time of his life. I bet he really liked whatever the hell Alistair was doing to him. Good thing I was blind, because I didn't want to watch.

"You call those dance moves?" Marcus challenged. "I'll show you dance moves."

Marcus reached for the pole, but he tripped and landed with a hard *slap* against the stage. He must've fallen right on his face, because he let out a pained noise.

"Okay, that's it," Kallie said. "You men don't know how to dance. Let me show you how it's done."

Kallie must've been really good, because everyone was hooting and hollering at her show. Soon, everyone was on stage, dancing and taking turns spinning around the pole. Even Oberi came on stage, clapping her hooves against the floor. There was so much going on that I thankfully got a chance to step back and sneak away.

Ivy kept the drinks coming, and my friends became tipsy over the next hour. Alistair and Chancey were taking shots, seeing who could drink each other under the table. I was certain Alistair was winning, because Chancey had fallen into a chair and broken it.

Opal gave noises of glee as Ez swept her around the dancefloor, and I was certain she was blushing as Ez whispered sweet nothings in her ear.

Their cutesy actions ate at me. I wished Ava and I could be that happy.

The guests were having more fun than the bride and the groom, that was for sure. Ava stayed away from me. She was with Kallie most of the time. I heard them dancing together somewhere near the stage.

Ava and I were the only two people who weren't wasted at our own wedding. I stayed at the bar most of the time and kept to myself, because I was still trying to process everything that had happened. I mean, I thought for sure I was going to die this morning, and now I was at my own wedding reception. Life at the Institute was just too crazy.

"This is so exciting!" Eddie babbled, already three glasses in. "My master is married, and our monarchy finally has a new queen! Maybe this will mean a new heir, and—"

"Eddie, *shut up*," I growled.

"Right away, sir!" Eddie hiccupped and gave a girly giggle.

Eddie couldn't hold his champagne for shit. What a lightweight.

I hoped Ava hadn't overheard, but I caught a slight pause across our bond. Hell. She had.

"Fuck," I grumbled. How close had she been standing to me when Eddie had been rambling?

"Eddie, new rule. No more talking about heirs," I stated flatly.

"Of course, sire!" His drunken salute slapped me on the side of the head, and I fell over. He hit harder than I thought.

"Oh, I'm so sorry!" Eddie clumsily reached for me to help me up, and he punched me by accident. This time, my head smacked the side of the bar.

"Ouch!" I rubbed my temple. "Can't you be more careful?"

"I've laid a hand on the grandson of the emperor! I must be punished!" Eddie wailed.

"Hey, that's *my* job!" Alistair complained. He stumbled into a barstool, and as it fell over, that hit me in the shin, too.

"Be careful of the royal jewels there, pal, the man's gonna need them on his wedding night," Chancey slurred, giving a childish giggle. As he staggered, he stepped on my hand.

"I'm going to kill you guys," I seethed. I half meant it.

"Would you all *please* stop beating up my husband?" Ava's sharp voice cut in, and I felt her hand on my arm as she helped me up. "The purpose of this wedding was to keep him in one piece, thanks."

Something changed within me when she called me her husband. It was a warm feeling, like one of possession and want. It was like I belonged to her. I never *belonged* to anyone before. Who wanted to claim me, anyhow?

Ava did. Maybe this marriage of convenience was more permanent than I thought. As she led me away from my tormentors, the upbeat music changed to a slow song.

"*Ooh,*" Eddie sang. "I know what this means."

I sighed. If they were going to put on another show— or beat me up again— I might just walk out. "What does it mean?"

"A slow dance, of course!" Alistair said.

"Yeah," Marcus piped up. "The bride and groom haven't had their first dance yet."

Someone shoved me, and I stumbled into Ava.

She groaned. "Guys, no. This isn't—"

"Come *on,*" Kallie begged. "It's your wedding reception. You have to dance."

Ava and I both hesitated. *Of course* I wanted to dance with her. All I wanted to do since the moment we broke up was hold her close. I hadn't had the chance until now.

But Ava didn't want this, and I wasn't going to push her. "If she doesn't want to, it's fine," I said.

"Mom and Dad will be disappointed if I don't get it on tape," Ez pressed.

Ava sighed, and my heartbeat skipped as she took a step closer. "Okay. One dance."

She took my hand and pulled me onto the dancefloor. I wrapped my arms around her waist, but I was more shocked than anything to be this close to her again. Her raspberry scent was intoxicating. My body was stiff as I guided her around in circles.

"Our friends are ridiculous," I said, to break the odd silence stretching between us.

Ava scoffed. "No kidding. We didn't *ask* for a reception."

I chuckled lightly. "We didn't ask for a marriage, either. Yet here we are."

"I know," she said, like she couldn't believe it. "I mean... you're my *husband*."

My heart fluttered when she called me her husband again. It still didn't feel real. I wasn't sure it ever would. As we spun around the dancefloor, the weight of everything that happened earlier finally hit me. Ava and I were *married*. I was standing here with her in my arms, instead of being experimented on by the Warden in the Infernal Underground. It was a miracle.

Without thinking about it, I pulled Ava closer, until her body was pressed against mine. Her head rested on my chest, and I couldn't help but think that was perfect. Emotions welled inside of me so strong that tears pricked at my eyes.

"I can't believe you did this for me," I whispered.

"Of course, Charlie. There was no question."

That warmed my heart more than she could ever know. Ava and I didn't say anything else as we danced. We spun past Oberi, who sat on the edge of the room with Rishi, Pig, and Alette. I swore I heard Oberi sniffling.

Our dance ended far too soon. I didn't want to let her go, but she dropped my hands the moment the long was over.

It nearly felt like another rejection. My heart was put back together only to fall apart all over again.

"I think it's time to wrap things up," Opal suggested. "We've been gone a long time, and people are going to start suspecting something if they can't find us."

Everyone around me groaned, but I spoke up. "Opal's right," I agreed. I didn't think Ava wanted to drag this out any longer, anyway. "It's time to go."

Ivy complained that we needed to keep the party going, but Chancey talked him out of it; we couldn't let the Warden find out about The Devil's Playground. We cleaned up quickly and headed back to our cellblocks, to the rousing chorus of *congratulations* from our friends.

Was there something to celebrate? I wasn't sure yet. Me not being deported, maybe. Wasn't sure about the rest.

Ava held my hand to guide me down the hall, but she came to an abrupt halt near our dorms. Oberi ran straight into me.

"What is it?" I asked.

"Our dorms!" Ava cried, sounding distressed. "Our doors are wide open, and everything's gone!"

The blood drained from my face. "Is the Warden screwing with us?"

"This isn't the Warden's doing." Hemlock's voice came from behind us. "It was mine."

We turned, and Ava gasped. "Where's all our stuff?"

"Consider it a wedding present," Hemlock said. "Come with me. I have something to show you."

I was really confused. How could stealing all our stuff be a *good* thing? But I was curious, too, so I held Ava's hand tightly as we followed Hemlock down the hall. She led us out of the Elementai cellblock and to a part of the prison I'd never been to before. A door creaked open.

"This is your new suite," Hemlock announced.

"A suite?" Ava asked, sounding confused.

"This is the Marital Wing of the school," Hemlock explained. "Married students are permitted to reside in the same dormitory. It's a privilege of being married. Welcome home."

I remembered hearing rumors about the *Conjugal Visit Wing* located in an older part of the school. It wasn't a cellblock, per se, as there weren't that many married students on campus. I'd thought it'd been a stupid joke, but apparently, this wing was real.

Ava gingerly stepped inside. "Oh, wow."

Oberi shifted into husky form and pushed past me, nearly knocking me on my ass. *This is great! No more switching rooms every night.*

"Is it... good?" I asked Ava.

"Charlie, it's twice the size of the other dorms. There are even two rooms!" Ava raved. "This one's got a couch—"

Mine! Oberi called as he jumped onto the couch. It creaked beneath his weight.

"And the other has... one... bed..." Ava trailed off, and my gut sank. We were married, but neither of us had considered that we'd have to sleep in the same *bed*.

"Is that going to be a problem?" Hemlock asked, as if to test us. No one could know this marriage was a sham.

"No, of course not," I said quickly— though it *totally* was.

"Very well," Hemlock replied. "Good luck to you both."

She left the room and shut the door behind her. Dread dropped in my stomach the moment she left.

"You're worried," Ava pointed out. She knew my discomfort immediately.

"They moved all my stuff," I complained. "I need order, or I can't find anything. I don't know where anything is. I'm going to be so lost here. I'm—"

Ava squeezed my hand, cutting me off. "It's okay, Charlie. You'll learn. *We'll* learn. Together."

I drew a deep breath. I appreciated Ava was here for me... but I still didn't like this.

Ava started moving around the room, and I heard furniture squeak. "What are you doing?" I asked.

"I'm checking to make sure it's safe," she said. "The Warden could've bugged the room before we arrived."

"I thought that technology doesn't work here," I pointed out.

"Ez's old camera works," she remarked as she continued inspecting the room. "But that's a piece of junk, and something like that would be difficult to hide. Mm... everything *looks* safe."

She began shuffling through her belongings. "And it looks like all our stuff is here, even my journal. Hemlock made sure our stuff got here safely."

"You can take the bed," I offered. I moved toward the couch and felt for Oberi. I slapped his butt so he'd move over.

Hey, this is my spot! Oberi said.

You can share the bed with Ava, I replied.

No, he insisted. *I refuse.*

Oberi immediately shifted into a unicorn. I heard the couch buckle underneath her massive weight, and she added, *Good luck moving me now.*

"Oberi!" I leaned down and began shoving her side. "Get off!"

Help! HELP! I'm being oppressed! Oberi screamed. She didn't budge an inch.

I wiped my sweaty brow. "It's no use. We're not moving a thousand-pound unicorn off the couch."

Excuse me, I weigh nine-hundred and ninety-eight pounds now, Oberi objected. *And this time, I'm keeping it off.*

"You're a conniving little shit," I snapped. I knew exactly what she was trying to pull.

Glad you noticed my new waistline!

Ava's voice was tentative. "You don't... *have* to sleep out here. I mean, the couch would be uncomfortable."

I turned to her. "It's fine. I've slept in worse conditions."

"I really don't mind," she promised. "We've slept beside each other before."

"Yeah, but that was before—" I cut off. *Before we broke up.*

I swallowed the lump in my throat as the obvious settled between us. "You didn't marry me to share a room. We got married out of convenience."

"You still deserve a good night's rest. Stop making it a big deal," she insisted. It was obvious she was starting to get annoyed.

"I don't want to complicate things," I argued. "We may be married, but we're not *together*. I know you only married me out of pity."

"*Pity?*" Ava repeated, like she couldn't believe I'd said it. "Charlie, I did what needed to be done to save your life."

"I know, and I'm really grateful for that, but you've already sacrificed enough for me."

"What do you mean?" she asked, sounding hurt.

I sighed. "I know this is hard for you. This wasn't planned, and it was sprung on us very quickly. You're a free spirit, but now that we're married, I've tied you down."

"You think you're a *weight* holding me down?" *Now* she sounded offended. Great.

"Well, we broke up," I reminded her. "You didn't want to be with me, and you were forced to marry me. I'm glad you saved me, pidge, but I know this is the last thing you wanted."

"How do you know what I feel?" she demanded.

I was getting irritated, too. I was just trying to communicate, and she was making it difficult. "You kept saying it all day. You didn't want the decorations or the party or any of it. I think it's safe to assume you didn't want to marry me, and why would you? It was our only option. It's not like we're really married."

"We're not really—" She gave a loud huff. "Well, I guess my signature on that paperwork meant nothing to you!"

We'd been married for a few hours and alone for five minutes, and we were already arguing. Should be expected, really.

"Of course it did!" I cried. "It meant you wanted to save me— not that you wanted to... to *be* with me."

"Stop it, Charlie," she insisted. "You can't stand there and act like you know how I feel. I was keeping it together all day because I thought *you* didn't want to marry *me*. I mean, the way you acted when I asked. It was a slap to the face! And the way you stood there when I was saying my vows... you were as stiff as a board! It was like this wedding was too much of a hassle to save you from the Underground. Ancestors, we might not be together, but I wanted to marry you to keep you with me. Don't you understand I would do *anything* to save you?"

There goes my attempt at communication. I'd been so guarded during this whole thing that Ava had no idea how I felt. I knew I wasn't the kind of guy who showed his emotions often, but I'd concealed them too well this time. She didn't have any clue that I still loved her.

Oberi sighed. *Can you* both *stop being dramatic and solve your problems so we can get to the good part?*

I ignored him. "Why didn't you say any of this earlier, pidge?"

"Because I don't know what to think!" Ava cried, like it was all too overwhelming. "You've barely said a word to me since we broke up. I have no idea how you feel anymore— or if you feel anything at all! You're a hard person to read. So forgive me if it felt a little weird walking down the aisle to a man who feels like a stranger!"

I hate giant misunderstandings, Oberi grumbled, like she was already tired of this.

And so was I. We'd been fighting for months, and it was time for us to find a way forward together. I didn't want us to have problems anymore. Maybe this was our chance— a way to get things *right* this time.

"Pidge—" I started, but Ava had already spun on her heel.

"Give me some space, Charlie," she stated. "I need a minute."

She fled from the room. I cringed as the door slammed behind her.

My heart sank. Ava and I might be legally married, but one thing was very clear. This relationship was already fucked.

ava-marie

SIXTEEN

Ugh. *Marriage.*

I seriously couldn't believe this guy. I gave up everything to be with Charlie, and here he was, lamenting that I only married him out of *pity*.

Ancestors, I won't bother to save your life next time.

He seriously had me miffed. I thought this wedding might've meant something to him, but guess fucking not. I could still hear his stupid words with his stupid voice rattling around in my head.

It meant you wanted to save me— not that you wanted to... to be with me.

The nerve of some people.

I was more or less wandering around. I needed to calm down before I turned into a giant sea monster and ripped his head off. Seriously, he was being ridiculous about this whole thing. It wasn't like this was the wedding I had envisioned, either. Sorry he didn't get what he wanted.

It was worse than that, though. It was like he was saying he didn't want *me*.

I felt huffy as I turned into the cafeteria. There were a couple hollers and some rattled applause— word must've gotten around. I gave a grim smile and waved to a couple of people, who shouted out congratulations as I passed.

Yeah, congrats, Ava. You married a big baby who detests you.

What a word. *Detests.* It spoke of an age-old feud, and that's exactly what it felt like between Charlie and me. A nightmarish cycle that never fucking ended.

There hadn't been food at my makeshift reception, only alcohol, so I found my friends at the end of a table having an early dinner— or was it a late lunch? Everyone was there, save for Eddie and Alistair... wonder where they'd run off to.

I slid next to Kallie, and she raised her eyebrows in surprise. "Hey. Thought you two would be enjoying yourselves."

"Honeymoon's over," I growled. I wish I *had* drunk something at the reception now. I'd held off for Charlie's sake, because he'd asked me to, and him looking out for me was kind of sexy, in a way. Now I just wanted to numb myself with alcohol.

"Did you guys get in another fight?" Opal asked in disapproval. Her lips tightened, like she couldn't believe we were bickering so quickly.

"Eh, they're like my grandparents. They're not happy unless they're arguing," Chancey added. He was holding his head. His hangover had already started, apparently.

"*He's* the one being a dick." I leaned against the table. I felt list-less. And depressed. Not how I'd imagined feeling on my wedding day.

"You guys could've smiled a little for the camera," Ez complained as he watched the video replay on the camera's small screen. "I didn't get hardly any good shots."

I sighed wearily. "Ez, please don't send them that video yet. I need to be the one to tell them."

Ez snorted. "Like I want to be the one to drop *that* bomb. Dad's gonna kill you."

I didn't even want to think about Daddy's upcoming reaction. It'd be a family legend for ages.

"How interesting is *your* life that you had an arranged marriage?" Ivy asked. He was sipping on a Styrofoam cup of tea, and appeared to be much better off than Chancey. Vampires burned through alcohol.

"It needs to stop being interesting! I want to be happy, for once!" I flung up my hands.

"Aren't you?" Marcus looked clueless. He cast a glance at Kallie, who shrugged.

"Happy that I'm married to a man who hates me? Are you guys nuts?" I asked. For the love of the Great Spirit, my heart was *breaking* right now. Did nobody see that?

Marcus frowned. "He doesn't hate you, Ava. Goddess, I don't know why you'd think that."

"Um, he just insinuated I married him out of pity, so there's that." I scowled.

"He's just being self-deprecating, like Charlie always is," Kallie added. "This is a big change for both of you, and it happened so fast. Give him some space to get adjusted. You're probably both still panicking."

Shit if that was true. My heart hadn't stopped pounding since the moment I'd said yes. I couldn't believe I'd taken an oath to be with Charlie forever, in front of the Great Spirit and all my friends. That meant something.

And I was no good at keeping promises. I always broke them. Shattering this promise was something that absolutely terrified me. My vows were important to me. I wanted to keep them... but how could I, if the person I'd sworn myself to didn't want me back?

"I can see you're spiraling," Ez said, and he leaned across the table to tug on my sleeve. "What's the real problem?"

My lip wobbled. I couldn't believe I was breaking down in front of all my friends like this, in the middle of the cafeteria, but I couldn't give a damn at the moment. "I married someone who doesn't love me."

There was a collective *aw* around the table, one that was broken when Marcus burst, "But that's just crazy! Charlie *does* love you, Ava."

"He does not," I insisted, and a tear broke out of my eye. I wiped it away and mumbled, "I told him I still loved him before all of this, and he didn't say *anything* back. He's been so distant through this whole thing. If he loved me, and this wedding was real, he would've shown *some* sort of emotion during the ceremony, or said something afterward that confirmed it was real."

I sniffed. "But it's not. It's a fake-ass marriage, one that's held together out of my duty to keep him alive."

"That's not true. Charlie's just a tough guy to read," Kallie said, and she put a hand on my back.

"Yeah," Chancey agreed. "I know Charlie. He's got his guard up, but he never lost his spark for you."

"You think so?" I wiped my eyes with the back of my sleeve.

"I mean, we all knew you guys would come back to each other eventually. We just didn't think it'd take this long," Chancey said.

Everyone around the table nodded. "It can't be that bad," I insisted.

"You two have really been dragging it on," Ivy drawled.

"Ivy," Opal scolded.

"What! The drama's intense," he said, taking a sip of his tea.

My shoulders dropped. "I don't know. Unless I hear it from him, I don't think I can believe it. And it's not like he'll ever tell me, so I guess this marriage really is a lie."

"That's not true!" Marcus yelled. "For the love of Mother Miriam, he gave up his sight so—"

Marcus abruptly shut his mouth. His face paled, as if he had a terrifying realization he said something he shouldn't. Everyone's mouth dropped open, and the table got *so quiet.*

I'd turned water to ice so many times in my life that I knew exactly how it felt when the magic left my fingers. That same sensation flooded over my entire body and froze me to the bench as my stomach bottomed out. "What... what did you just say?"

"Fuck," Marcus mumbled. He tore at his curls, and Rishi began meowing frantically underneath the table. "I wasn't supposed to— he's gonna be— shit."

I was over and across that table so fast a vampire couldn't catch me. I bunched my hands in Marcus' collar and began shaking him. "Marcus, *tell me.* What did he say!?"

Marcus squeezed out the words. "When Charlie went to the hypnotist... he remembered his past, before he lost his sight. Eagle Spirit came to him on the night of your birth and took him to your mom. Charlie saw dark spirits all around her, sent by evil gods, and their power was killing you as your mom was trying to give birth. You were *dying,* Ava. Eagle

Spirit said that the only way you'd survive is if Charlie sacrificed a piece of himself so you could live, and he decided to give up his sight. He was barely three years old, and he still chose to save you."

"Fuck," Ez mumbled under his breath, looking disturbed. He'd heard the story of my birth— everyone in my family had. It'd been a night that had long haunted my mother for ages. She'd always insisted that I shouldn't have survived, that something was supernatural about the day I was born. *Darkly* supernatural.

Now I knew why.

"So there. How can you say he doesn't love you?" Marcus rasped. "What bigger gift could someone give you? He always loved you, from the moment he first saw you. And you were the last thing he saw before he lost his sight forever. What else is love, if not that?"

I unfurled my fingers from Marcus' sweater and took a step back. Every breath I inhaled felt like a dagger shooting through my lungs. I was speechless. "I— I—"

Everyone looked *very* concerned. A couple of people went to stand, but before they could follow me, I turned on my heel and ran like hell.

I don't remember running from the cafeteria back to the cell. All I recall is throwing the door open, and Charlie taking a worried step back when he heard the doorknob smash against the brick wall.

You weren't gone long, Oberi remarked, still stuck on the couch.

Charlie had barely moved from the spot I'd left him standing in. I witnessed his body stiffen. He sensed there was something big that had changed between us.

A whimper escaped my lips as I staggered forward and threw my arms around him. I held him tighter than I knew I could as tears escaped my eyes and cascaded onto his front. "You gave me your eyes!" I wailed.

"Goddamn it, Marcus," Charlie growled under his breath as he clutched me to his chest. He folded his arms around me and rocked me back and forth as I wept uncontrollably against his chest.

You two obviously need a minute, Oberi said slowly. Oberi shifted into a husky. *While you work it out, I'm gonna get snacks. To the Commissary I go!*

I was crumbling to pieces, so once the door clicked closed behind Oberi, Charlie picked me up. My head fell against his shoulder and nestled there as he nudged the bedroom door shut behind us and sat down on the mattress.

I would've liked to be carried to the bed on my wedding night not crying buckets, but hey, beggars can't be choosers.

"What did Marcus tell you?" Charlie's voice got really soft, and his breath felt like velvet against my cheek.

"Everything." It felt really good cuddling him. "I owe you my life."

"Well, you got me back when you saved me from the Underground, so I guess we're even." He pressed his lips to the top of my head, and ancestors, a kiss from the gods couldn't feel better.

"How could you do such a thing? You were practically a baby," I said. "I shouldn't even be here, but I am because of you."

"I don't regret losing my sight, and even if I could remember what it was like, it was a worthy sacrifice to have you. Missing you in my life would've been real blindness, because I never would've seen what was truly important," he replied. "I knew I loved you right away, even when I was that little, before I could even comprehend what love was. I just... looked at you and knew I'd do anything to get the chance to love you."

It gave a whole new meaning to love at first sight. "But you missed out on so much. And so many terrible things happened to you because you were blind. You would've never suffered if you'd had your eyes."

"There's nothing more terrible than not having you in my life. If I hadn't saved you, things would've been different, but worse. Yeah, I would've had my eyes, but so what? I would've lived knowing a piece of my soul was missing, and it would've tormented me every day until the second I died. A life without you isn't a life, Ava; it's just living. And what does life mean if we can't be with the people we love?"

I still wasn't sure. The guilt I felt that he'd made such a sacrifice for me consumed me like a flame that began at my heart and caught fire outward. Charlie had been homeless, starving, taken advantage of and targeted his whole life because he was blind. And for what? For me?

"Yes, for you," he insisted. "And once I found out what I'd been waiting for, I was happy to do it."

He'd overheard what I was thinking. We were becoming so seamlessly connected. But I still couldn't understand his sacrifice.

I loved people— I felt it, knew the emotions, and knew that love was more than that, too. It was devotion, and promises, and yes, even sacri-fices. But underneath all that, I was struggling to understand what love *meant*. Because I still didn't comprehend how Charlie could love *me*, especially not that much.

"Would you do it for me?" he asked. The edge of the sentence was clipped. He worried that was the wrong thing to ask.

"Yes," I replied instantly. "In a heartbeat."

"Then is it really that hard to understand?"

"Yes. You're better than me. A purer soul," I insisted.

"What? That's not true."

"It is! You're a good person at heart, and I'm bad, and I didn't deserve what you did for me, not then or now," I said.

"I don't think it's up to you to decide if you deserved it— or me, either, I think. Who you were or what you were going to become didn't matter. I wanted you, I loved you, and here you are."

It sounded so simplistic, but how could it be? Wasn't love supposed to be complicated?

My voice wobbled. "I thought people judged with their eyes, but you taught me differently. It's like you see right through me, and know the real me instead of what's outside."

"You're easy for me to read, no matter how hard you try and hide it. I just can't believe it's hard for you to do the same with me. I figured how I truly feel is so obvious," he said.

"Even with a soul connection, it's hard to tell what you're thinking." I reached up and brushed a lock of hair out of his eyes. "You're so guarded all the time. And I know why you are, because you've been hurt, but even though I know that, it's still insanely difficult to get you to let me in."

"Then let me say it out loud. I was giddy when you asked me to marry you. There wasn't anything that could've made me happier than being in that chapel with you and sharing my vows. I just have such a hard time showing it, because I'm so afraid..."

"You don't want to lose anything else." I knew the feeling. I identi-fied with it, because we'd destroyed each other.

"Yes. But I've gotta get past that, because I want to be with you. I was almost over that fear. I was tired of us being apart. I was going to ask if we could try again…"

He sighed. "Then the second blood test happened, and I knew I was going to the Underground. I didn't have the heart to confess that I loved you right before I was taken away from you. That'd be so cruel."

"I wouldn't have let them take you," I promised. "I would've died preventing that. So you should've told me you loved me, so I could've gone down knowing that you did. I would've died with a smile on my face."

"I think it worked out better this way." Charlie pressed his forehead to mine, and the movement was blissful. He lay back on the bed, still holding me. Our legs tangled together like they always used to, and the way he held me against him was precious and tender.

This was everything I'd ever wanted since we'd broken up. Just his body pressing against mine felt so good. I closed my eyes and inhaled the scent of bergamot as my fingers caressed his shirt. I was dying to kiss him, but I knew once my lips touched his, we wouldn't be able to stop, and there were things we needed to talk about first.

"I wanted you too, Charlie. I wanted us back together the moment I walked away, but the memory of what happened in Forevermore held me back…" I took a breath, unable to escape the sounds that were filling my ears— the screams of dying Elves, the crackling of fire, the marching of the Warden's troops.

"I think we need to admit that Forevermore wasn't our fault. We aren't responsible for what happened to those people." His tone was broken, but a little flat. Time had created enough distance for us to see things clearly.

"Aren't we? We led the Warden there," I pointed out.

"The Warden was going to find Forevermore one way or another. He'd been looking for it for years. Who's to say my grandfather wouldn't have tried to break me out, and the Warden found out that way?" Charlie asked. "We can't take on the burden of a whole genocide. It isn't our fault that the Elves died."

"But now that we've revealed them, and they're back, it could start another war."

"War is coming. It always does," Charlie said in a tired way. "People are cruel and evil that way."

"Maybe we could've stopped it."

"No. I've only been at the Institute for a year, but I already know how the Warden works, because I met plenty of people just like him on the streets. He won't be satisfied with getting what he wants. He's just gonna want more and more. Forevermore was just the beginning."

I felt the edges of myself fraying when we discussed the Warden. The man was a travesty to this world, and he wanted to watch it fall while he stood over it with a grin. "We have to consider the power we have. We're demigods. We're dangerous, not just to each other, but to the world. We have to keep our powers in check."

"We can be together and not be a threat to the world," Charlie insisted. "Whether we're apart or together, bad things are still gonna happen. And I'm tired of facing them without you. It's breaking me apart."

I traced his jawline like it was a piece of art. "If we're going to fight... I want us to fight the world, and not each other. I'm prophesied to save the world, and I want to. At the same time, you'll do anything to save me. That got in the way when we were looking for the keys last semester."

"I just want to protect you. It feels like my purpose," Charlie confessed, somewhat longingly.

"We need to do things together. We're a team. We always have been," I said. "You can't just... defend me from the world and expect that I'll never get hurt. You've got to let me take the necessary risks, and in exchange, I'll be okay with you making the calls to keep me safe."

Charlie nodded. "I can agree to that."

"And I'm tired of all the miscommunication," I added with a frustrated sigh. "We never talk about stuff. We just assume and then end up arguing, and the pattern is getting old. We need to change it if this is going anywhere."

"That's going to be difficult," Charlie said. "Let's be honest, I just hide how I feel all the time, whether I'm aware of it or not."

"And I lie about how I feel because it's painful for me to be vulnerable, I know," I said. "But you're worth it. I want to change my bad habits for you because you deserve to be in a relationship with someone who's open. And you know what? So do I."

"It'll be hard admitting my feelings, or even showing them, because that feels like I'm making myself a target," Charlie said. "I'm not used to that."

"It won't be easy, when you've trained yourself to stay guarded to keep yourself safe," I agreed. I couldn't imagine how difficult it would be for him to break that behavior.

"But—" he added. "I want to give you everything. This isn't an easy thing to ask, but it's the right thing to do for us. I want to start trusting people more, including my friends. It'll be so much easier if I start with you, because I want you to know everything about me. I'm just... really scared to try."

"I need you to try," I begged. "You were so closed off to me when we found Forevermore. I tried to give you space, but it hurt so much when you didn't come to me about how you were coping. I wanted to help so badly, but I felt like I couldn't, because you weren't ready for me to be there for you."

"I thought my feelings would be a burden to you," he mumbled.

"What? Where'd you get that idea?" It was mind blowing to me.

"All a man wants is to make his woman happy, Ava. It tears me apart when you're upset, when you cry... whenever you're sad, I feel like I've failed," he confessed. "Burdening you with my unhappiness just made me think I was a bigger failure. It felt better to retreat from you and deal with it alone, because at least then, I wouldn't have to be disappointed in myself that I'd made you feel that way."

"You can't *make me* feel anything. I want to be there with you, through the good times and bad," I insisted. "I can deal with hard feelings, Charlie. Being bipolar, I do it all the time."

"Exactly! How can I put you through more shit than what you're already going through?" His body tightened. He was getting frustrated.

"You aren't putting me through anything if we face stuff side by side. In fact, it's actually *more* painful for me when you try to shield me from the world, because there's a disconnect. I don't feel close to you when you're hiding your emotions from me. It feels like you're pushing me away, because even though you want me, you don't trust me to still be here when you're falling apart," I said.

"Then why do you lie about how you feel?" Charlie asked. "Because you do it all the time."

I paused. The comparison was like looking in a mirror. "I want to protect people."

"And that's what I want to do for you. You can't blame me for wanting to shield you from myself. I get... destructive when I fall apart."

"I'm starting to realize that's wrong," I said slowly. "We don't need to protect each other from our feelings. We're strong enough to weather whatever comes through, because no matter how hard things get or how painful things feel, I still want us to be together the next morning. Running away hasn't done us any good."

"What if we fight, or what if we end up making it worse?"

"Charlie, I promise you that as a woman, there is nothing more painful for me to endure than knowing you're hurting, watching you suffer, but allowing you to walk away because you're not able to let me in," I said. "You talked about your purpose, but a big part of mine that I feel is right is the need to nurture you and love you through whatever storm you're facing. I know I can't always fix it, and I know I do the same thing time and time again. But we gotta be over that now. It's done. And if there's something that's bothering you, I need to hear about it, and I promise I'll do the same for you. It's what we deserve."

"You're asking me to take my walls down. I can do it, but it's not simple, you know," he said.

"Just let me love you, dammit!" I let out a choked laugh.

Charlie frowned. "The people who love me get hurt."

"I said the same thing when I met you, but you know what? I think it's the other way around, for both of us. The people that I love hurt me, and sometimes, that's what love is, you know? If it doesn't hurt, it wasn't real. I knew what we had was real the moment I no longer had you, because I felt like I was dying inside."

"Is this real?" Charlie asked in a whisper. "This... marriage we have."

"Yes. I want this to be a real marriage. I know I said it was all for show earlier, but that's because I wasn't sure of what you wanted."

"I want this for certain. I want you to be my wife."

I smiled. "I already am."

"So are you saying yes? That we're back together, that this is what we both want?" Charlie asked.

"Absolutely. I can't imagine wanting to be with anyone else. This is what I choose," I said sincerely.

Charlie was so quiet. I could tell he was holding back, so I said, "You know, we made an agreement to start talking about stuff. If we're married for real, we might as well start now."

He hesitated, but he didn't let his fear stop him from being vulnerable, and I was proud of him for that. "I just... I can't wrap my head around the idea that someone actually *loves me*, you know? Even when you say it, accepting it is... insane to me."

"I know you were abandoned, and I'm so sorry," I said. "I didn't help with that, either. But I can promise you that my love for you is stable. You aren't going to lose me. I'm not going anywhere."

"We're such different people, though, and we want different things. You need adventure, I need stability... how do we work that in?"

"I can be stable for you— that is, as long as my mind doesn't get in the way. Can't promise no more mood swings or bouts of psychosis." I scowled.

"I'm not talking about your bipolar. That doesn't scare me. The idea that we might be on different paths does. We got married really young because you wanted to protect me, and though this is a good thing, that is exchanging some of your freedom."

"We need to be on solid ground before I go off seeking adventure," I explained. "Travel is important to me, but so are you. I have my whole life ahead of me to explore. That part will come once we have a good foundation."

"You trust that you won't lose it by being with me?"

"I know you wouldn't take that away from me. That's all the reassurance I need."

Charlie rubbed my arm slowly. Ancestors, I nearly shivered at how good it felt. "Why'd we even break up in the first place? Seems stupid now."

"I don't know," I replied. "I think I figured... if you were with me, my prophecy would kill you. I knew the closer you were to me, the more danger you were in. So even if I wanted you, it didn't matter, because keeping you alive was more important than making sure we stayed together."

Charlie massaged my shoulder. "I think we agreed to split up because we wanted to keep each other safe. But I'm starting to realize we don't have much control over that, anyhow."

That much was true. When we died and how was up to the gods above, not us. We could choose our paths, but we couldn't decide everything. I fought against fate as much as anyone, but even I was beginning to understand the things I had power over and the things I didn't.

A few seconds of silence slipped by before Charlie whispered, "I'm sorry I took your key in the woods."

Agony invaded my senses. For the first time, I turned away from him and curled up on my side. "I don't want to talk about that."

"But we have to. It was fucked, Ava. I shouldn't have done it, even if my motives were to keep you safe."

That night in the forest had been one of my most beloved memories... and also one of the worst. Charlie and I had shared every feeling and touch underneath the shade of pine trees and the falling rain. I'd never felt more free or more loved.

But he'd soured it when he'd later revealed he'd used the moment to steal the key my mother had given me, in an attempt to destroy it so I wouldn't continue down the path of my prophecy. I knew he'd just been trying to protect me, so I wouldn't be at risk of what the prophecy said.

Yet he'd taken advantage of me when I was at my most vulnerable, at the worst possible moment he could. I wanted to forgive him for it, but it was hard to think he wouldn't do something like that again, because he proved he was capable.

"What can I do?" His voice was pleading. "I definitely screwed up."

Keeping my back to him felt wrong, so I faced him again, though I kept our legs separate. "I don't know," I replied. "I know you'd never force me to do anything, so it's not like I'm afraid of you. But since we're being honest, that's the worst thing you've ever done to me."

"You deserve to feel safe in that kind of situation," Charlie said. "I want to win your trust back. Tell me how."

"It's just going to take time," I said. "I can't be in the moment if I'm wondering if you've got ulterior motives—"

"There won't be any. Not ever again."

"Then I forgive you. I trust you won't do anything like that again."

"I won't," Charlie insisted. "I promise."

We were making a lot of promises today. Fear was welling up inside of me that we couldn't keep them.

That was just my ego talking. Yeah, I was afraid, but I loved Charlie more than I feared the future, and I had an inner knowing that things would work out as long as we stuck together. Call it my intuition— she'd never failed me yet.

Charlie's fingers moved from my shoulder to the ends of my hair. "I prayed for somebody like you to enter my life for the longest time. I never thought I'd actually find you, but you managed to show up at the perfect moment."

"I wish we could've had more time," I hushed. "You're why I believe in love. After I was raped, I didn't think I'd be able to feel that way about anyone. Then you came along, and it was like everything changed. Sometimes I think that if we'd always known each other, we could've kept each other safe."

"The past is behind us now. It's always going to sting, but we've got so many good years ahead that'll make up for the time we lost."

"You think so?" My heart lifted at the thought.

"With everything I have. I just *know* we're gonna grow old together." Charlie's voice got thick. "We'll get out of here, and we'll get a little cottage on the water. We'll sit on the porch, and you'll describe to me how the mist rolls in over the sea as morning comes, and I'll sing you to sleep every night."

"That sounds just like heaven."

"It will be. And to hell with the prophecy, you know? We either save the world, or we condemn it, but no matter what happens, we're there together. Even if the world caves in, I want to be the one who ends it with you."

His words cemented in me every feeling I'd ever have for him. I loved Charlie naturally. It wasn't like I needed to tell my heart to beat, or my lungs to breathe, and that's what it was like with him. He existed, and I cherished him.

My legs wound around his again, and he pulled me closer. I drifted my hands over his chest. "Can we act like we like each other now?"

"Definitely."

I buried my face in the crook of his neck. This was paradise for sure. My world was safe again now that Charlie was in it.

There wasn't a need to do anything or say something more. I think after a tumultuous past year, all either of us wanted to do was rest in the peace that we could be together again and not fight it. All the excuses I'd used to keep myself away from him seemed silly now, because what could be better than this?

"I just want to cuddle," Charlie said, and he kissed my forehead again.

"Me too." The bed felt so warm, even though the blankets were scratchy, and he smelled so good. I reached up and ran my fingertips over the stubble on his chin.

"By the way, I like your beard," I said, and I gave a little giggle. "It's sexy."

"Really? I didn't really notice it, to be honest. I just didn't care to shave it, because I was depressed."

"I think it looks hot, all short and scruffy."

"Then I'll keep it."

I was glad about that. The door creaked open as Oberi yelped, *I brought snacks!*

He jumped on the bed. Chips and candy went everywhere as Oberi dropped snack bags from his mouth and barked.

"Where'd you even get all these?" Charlie asked as he picked up a handful of cookies.

I'm a cute dog. People will give me whatever I want, he said with a wag of his tail. *Is everything all better yet?*

I laughed and scratched his ears. "Yes. Everything's perfect."

Ooh! I'm so happy! Oberi wiggled his way between us and snuggled us both. He licked our faces and pressed his snout to our cheeks. *Now we can be a family!*

"We are a family, officially," Charlie said. Then his expression slackened. His body went tense beside mine as he froze on the bed.

"What's wrong?" I sat up, immediately concerned. "Are you okay?"

Alarm spread through me as I watched his eyes water and his lip tremble. "I didn't realize... I *do* have a family now. You took my last name. We're married and everything."

"That's right!" A smile bloomed across my face immediately. "Charlie, we're your family!"

Yay! Oberi began jumping on the bed. *A real family!*

Charlie sniffed and used his sleeve to wipe at his eyelids. "I'm not alone."

"No. And you never have to be alone again, because you've got us," I said, throwing my arms around his shoulders. I squeezed him tight, because I wanted him to know I'd always be there.

Permanently, Oberi added.

"I want to show you every day that this is our forever," I said, and I stroked Charlie's hair back. "I'll do anything to prove that."

Yeah, that's why you held on to certain intimacy items for months, giving yourself false hope, Oberi clipped dryly.

"Oberi," I scolded. I was embarrassed he'd brought that up.

"What's he talking about?" Charlie asked.

"Ugh, this." I got off the bed and went to the next room. I ruffled through my bookbag, where I'd hidden something in one of the inside pockets. The foil packet crinkled as I took it out and walked back into the bedroom. "Remember those condoms my dad gave me the night of the Villain's Ball last year?"

"Yeah. I thought Marcus turned them into balloon animals," Charlie said.

"Don't pick on me, but I kept *one*," I said. "Just in case."

Charlie snickered. "How sentimental."

"Well, I wanted to be prepared in case something happened!" I said.

"That's sweet you were thinking of me," Charlie teased.

I threw the packet on the bedside table. "Anyway, it's kind of a stupid joke now, isn't it? Not like we ever used it."

"I still think it's weird that your *dad* was the one to buy them," Charlie said.

"My family is pretty open. It doesn't bother me to talk about that kind of stuff with my parents. They just want me to be safe." I shrugged. "My dad pretends I'm his innocent little princess, but he knows I'm a wild child."

"What tipped him off there? It's not like we have each other's names tattooed on our bodies," Charlie said sarcastically.

"That's true. What other bad decisions can we think of next?" I cracked.

"Wedding ring tattoos?" A sly grin had worked its way across Charlie's face.

"Ooh, yes!" I jumped right up. "Let's get them right now!"

"You being serious?" The smile hadn't left his face since he'd had the idea.

"Of course! Aren't you?"

"I think so. I want something I can't take off," Charlie said.

"Me too." I grabbed his hand and tugged him out of bed. "Let's find Marcus. Come on!"

We ran hand-in-hand through the hallways, and Oberi skipped after us. Elation ricocheted from one end of our bond to the other, and it made me feel like I was floating. I was so high on Charlie I didn't think I'd ever come down. The bliss I was experiencing had invaded my senses, and we shared that, bouncing off of each other's affection without a worry in the world.

We checked the Villain's Den first and found Marcus shaking one of the arcade machines as Rishi batted at the joystick. "Aw, man. It took my dollar!"

Of course. The Warden was always ripping people off.

"Bad luck," I said as I came up behind him.

Marcus turned. He saw Charlie and me holding hands and let out a relieved sigh. "Looks like you two worked things out."

"We did, and mostly because of you," Charlie said. "So thanks for telling my secret, I guess?"

"You're... welcome?" Marcus tilted his head, as if he wasn't sure whether to feel bad about being a bigmouth or not.

"And thanks again for finding the loophole," I said. "If you didn't, Charlie wouldn't be here."

"It wasn't a big deal," Marcus protested. "You guys are my friends. I'd do anything for you."

"In that case, we might have one more favor to ask," I said. "You still have that tattoo quill?"

"Hiding in my dorm," Marcus said with a knowing smile. "Let's go."

The walk to Marcus' dorm was short and brisk. Charlie stretched his hand out on the desk as Marcus got to work. The quill drifted carefully across his skin, inscribing today's date in a similar font to the one that was on his wrist— October 11.

It only took a few minutes, but even the tiny numbers that Marcus created were beautiful. It was truly amazing to watch him work.

When Marcus was done, Charlie slipped his ring back on his finger over the magical tattoo. "Your turn."

I plopped down in the seat and slammed my hand on the desk. The movement sent several paint bottles toppling off Marcus' desk. One splattered open on his pants, and Marcus growled, "Hey, watch it."

"Sorry. Too eager." I was literally bouncing in the chair. I couldn't wait. I slipped my ring off and placed it to the side as Marcus bent over my hand.

I studied the ring Kallie had given me. It was a thin, multi-row design of twisting black brambles that nearly looked like thorns, outlined with miniature black diamonds. Charlie's was similar to mine, a matching dark band with a line of black diamonds straight through the middle.

They were elaborately gorgeous. Kallie had put so much care into making these. Illusions became real when the caster put all their emotion into the magic. She really did love us.

"You're not drunk this time. Can't say it was a mistake," Charlie teased as Marcus drew the first number on my hand.

"I wasn't *that* drunk last time, either," I said. "That was just an excuse so you didn't know I liked you."

"And it was still obvious," Marcus commented as he finished off my tattoo. "We all knew you guys were meant to be together. I'm really happy for both of you."

His voice ached with something that pained me— like Marcus believed happiness was something he'd never get to have. I'd seen the look he'd snuck at Kallie when I was about to take my vows earlier today. I knew.

I grabbed his wrist. "Hey. You know not to give up, right? We didn't, and it was hard, but we found a way back to each other. So you don't give up either, okay?"

Marcus' grimace was lonesome. "Okay."

Charlie's stomach let out a grumble, and he put a hand over it. "Wow. Through all the excitement, I forgot we haven't eaten all day."

"I'm starving," I said. "Maybe there will be cake in the cafeteria."

"Oh yeah, the Warden cooked up a wedding cake just for us," Charlie said with a shake of his head.

"*Now* you two are dreaming," Marcus said as he started wiping the paint off his pants. "He's probably still fuming in his office."

"He's not gonna forget this," Charlie said warily. "We need to be careful."

"Screw him." I knew the Warden was probably off plotting his revenge, but that would have to wait for another day. Sticking it to the Warden was the best wedding present ever. Next time I was bummed out, I'd just remember how I'd wiped the smug-ass look off his face when I'd thrown my marriage contract at his fat head. That memory alone was worth the paperwork.

We said goodbye and left for the cafeteria. There wasn't cake, but they had pudding cups tonight, which was almost as good, and lasagna, which counted as wedding food because it was pasta. I fed Charlie off my fork and got sauce smeared all over his cheek, which I wiped off, and he nicked me two pudding cups instead of one, which we weren't supposed to do. Every laugh that burst out of him lifted my spirits.

This wasn't how I'd planned my wedding day, but the feelings were all perfect. The connection between us was so strong that it felt like a living, breathing thing.

Even the voices in my head seemed content. *This is so exciting.*

What a day.

Just look at him, Ava!

As we finished up dinner, I got this insane need to be alone with Charlie. I didn't know what it was, or why it came on all of a sudden. I just wanted him all to myself. The inmates surrounding us made me annoyed I had to share him, even though everyone was leaving us be.

Ugh, I ate too much, Oberi complained as we came back to our cell. *I gorge myself when I'm cheerful.*

"You must be in a good mood, then, because you choked down five slices," I said.

The couch is still mine. No take-backsies! Oberi hopped up onto the couch and rolled onto his back. Within seconds, he was snoring so loudly I could hear it across the room.

"Should we unpack our stuff?" Charlie felt for his suitcase, which was up against the wall.

"We can do that tomorrow," I said. "I just want to relax. The past few days have been stressful as hell."

"Me too, but we need stuff to sleep in."

A corner of my mouth upturned. "We don't need clothes."

Charlie paused. I felt him wavering somewhere between indecision and desperate want. "Are you sure...?"

"Yes. I want to remember what your skin feels like against mine."

"We don't have to." He reached out for me, and I took his arm.

"But we *can*. No one's stopping us, and we're not getting in our own way anymore," I said. "We're married. Let's enjoy it."

Charlie stayed silent. He wasn't blocking me out, so I felt his emotions converge against my own. He had desire, but he was... worried. I didn't like that.

"What's holding you back?"

His shoulders hunched. "Everything seems so good right now. I don't want to ruin it."

"We won't. Charlie, we've been through so much. Being together is our reward. I want us to have *all* the benefits of married life. Intimacy is a part of that."

He nodded slowly. "Okay. I'm willing to try."

I grabbed his hands and led him to the bedroom. Oberi's snacks were still all over. We moved them into the other room, and Charlie shut the door behind us. The way the lock *clicked* sent a shiver racing up my spine and all over my body.

Charlie's hands drifted down my arms, until they settled on my elbows. He leaned down to kiss me. His lips felt soft and tender against mine as we pressed together. Our kiss at the altar had felt tense with everyone watching, but now that we were alone, our walls could come down. I let my fingers run through his hair and over his scruff as he sucked and bit at my bottom lip. Our tongues melded together, and I moaned as I opened my mouth to let him in.

Charlie's hands grabbed my ass, and he lifted me upward. My legs wrapped around his hips as he carried me to the bed. His kiss went deeper, taking the very life from me as we lay back down on the bed. Charlie's hands went beneath the bottom of my sweater, and he pulled it off of me before cupping my breasts through the outside of my bra. I kicked off my shoes and yanked my socks off before Charlie's touch slowed me down, his fingertips trailing my ribs. He unbuttoned my skirt and slid it off before his mouth moved, lips pressing against the side of my neck, trailing down to my collarbone, stomach, and thighs. His fingers slipped underneath my bra to cradle my breast, and his fingers massaged my nipple delicately.

I was already getting lightheaded. I grabbed the edge of his sweater and yanked it over his head, admiring the way my hand splayed against his bare chest before I reached for the button on his pants. By this point, Charlie had unclipped my bra and tossed it aside so he could enjoy kissing my breasts. My back arched as he sucked on my nipple, his hand gripping my side.

He was waiting for me to give him some reassurance that this is what I truly wanted. But I wasn't lying about this. Every part of me wanted him right now, and I craved the sensations only he could give me. I grabbed his hand and moved it over my panties. His hand slipped underneath the fabric, and he teased me by running a finger over my center. I gave another moan, and Charlie ripped my panties off and tossed them to the floor.

Ancestors, all I wanted to do was be naked if it pleased him. He slipped his finger inside of me, and I whimpered with delight. I fiddled with the button on his pants before I finally got them unzipped, and I yanked them and his boxers down in one movement.

I missed the sight of his dick. He was so hard it nearly looked painful. Elation shot through my arm as I reached out to touch it, enjoying the feel of him in my hand.

"*Fuck*," Charlie ground out as I caressed him. His eyes fluttered closed for a moment. My head lolled backward as his finger dipped in and out of me, as his tongue danced along my breasts. I don't know how I managed, but somehow, I got the rest of Charlie's clothes off so he was just as exposed as I was.

Our heads hit the pillows as his lips ravaged my own, and I struggled to breathe as I was overcome with lust. His hands ran along my skin, and an overwhelming feeling of relief and happiness pressed down on me from the very heavens above. The emotion blazed in my chest, like someone had lit a fire in my heart and it was roaring out of control. It was so powerful that it made tears sting at my eyes.

"Do you feel that?" Charlie whispered. Goosebumps rose on my arms as he drifted a finger over my apex.

I let out a breathy sigh. "I think our soul is healing."

It was. The threads of our soul were binding back together. I thought what we'd done was irreparable, but as I was learning, nothing could damage the bond Charlie and I shared so terribly that it couldn't be reforged. We'd broken each other, but we could fix our relationship again. This was a brand new start for both of us, and I was enjoying every second of it.

But I wanted more. Touching him didn't satisfy the deep craving inside of me. There was a part of me I'd been too scared to give Charlie before, but I wasn't afraid anymore. I knew I could trust him, and that with him, I'd be safe always.

Excitement electrocuted my body when I realized the condom was still on the bedside table. While he was kissing me, my hand scrambled to reach for it. It'd been a joke before, but there was nothing funny about it now. Charlie had my soul, and he had my heart. I wanted him to make my body his, too.

Charlie withdrew from the kiss as he heard the foil packet. I gave it to him, and he said, "Do you think you're ready? The truth this time."

We'd been here before, but the emotions were so different. There wasn't any tension or reluctance, only trust. "Are *you* ready? Because I want us to be husband and wife in every sense of the word. I know I can give myself to you."

Charlie swallowed nervously. He didn't say anything out loud, but his thoughts echoed just as loudly as I heard him think, *Hell. What if I mess it up and scare her?*

"You won't scare me." I reached up and cupped both sides of his face. "You'd never hurt me. I choose to let you in. I choose you."

Charlie grasped my hand and kissed it. "Then let's do this together."

He put the packet back in my hand. I understood what he was asking right away. I ripped it open, then rolled the condom over him. He quivered, taking in a sharp breath.

I waited for him to get over me, but he said, "Let's try it on my side."

"Can we do that?" It's not like I knew how.

"Yeah. It's just a little different. Here."

Charlie faced me, then put an arm around me to pull me close. His hand ended up nestling on the back of my neck, and it felt good. His other hand he pressed on the small of my back, drawing me in as he slid one leg between mine, opening me up. The position felt like we were cuddling, and I loved it.

My heartbeat slammed against my chest as Charlie positioned himself. My breaths were shallow, but there wasn't a part of me that was afraid. I felt loose as water in Charlie's arms, and my hand naturally fell against his face as he slid into me slowly. Pleasure filled my senses, and I found tingles racing throughout my body as Charlie went deeper.

"Ava-Marie." I wasn't even aware he was fully inside of me until he let out a gasp of pleasure. I blinked, wiggling my hips.

It didn't even hurt. It felt *good.* I pressed down on him, and Charlie gave a quiet moan. I became obsessed with experiencing the fullness of him as he began to thrust. Pure bliss radiated throughout my body with each movement he made inside of me, and I began to float away.

Oh, ancestors, so *this* was what I'd been missing. It was incredible. The position we were in was sensual, and only allowed for gentle movement. As we were facing each other, I was able to look into his eyes as he lost himself in me. The tightening sensation at my core grew stronger with each stroke, and I found my breath quickening at the passionate expression he bore. Heat lingered on his skin, and my Fire magic absorbed the warmth, traveling downward to excite my apex. Pulses of electricity vibrated at my core, shooting outward until my entire form turned to putty in his hands, and he could mold me to any one of his desires.

"I love you so much," Charlie gasped, kissing my neck.

"I need you," I choked out, and a tear slipped down my cheek. "You're my Fire and Water, all wrapped into one."

"You're the earth I walk on and the air I breathe."

The way we wound around each other was flawless. It was like I'd been waiting for this moment all my life. Love built up in me so strong that I just couldn't hold back. I felt a small orgasm build and release, but the feeling was different than any other I'd had before. This one was more powerful, because the way we were connected felt so intense and spirited. I clutched his hair and gasped as I let myself go, and he thrust into me faster.

The two ends of our bond tangled and became one. I couldn't tell the difference between the two halves of our souls when we were making love. Sensations flooded from him to me and back again on an infinite loop, until I came to experience a great comfort of peace unlike anything I'd ever known. I kissed him as he continued to bury himself into my body, and as my lips met his, a surge of his thoughts spilled into my mind.

Hell, I want to get lost in her. He could barely get the words around the strong passion overtaking his senses.

His thoughts gave me inspiration. I wanted him to enjoy himself. He'd been with other women before, but that wasn't out of love. That was just performing to stay alive. I didn't want him to have to put in all the work. This wasn't his first time, but it'd be the first time he'd enjoy himself, that was for damn sure.

I twisted so my legs turned his body, and he lay on his back. I straddled him so that I was on top, and started to move my hips in a circle.

"What are you doing?" he whispered.

"Giving you the time of your life." I grabbed his wrists and pinned them above his head, sinking down deeper. Charlie let out a hiss and bit his lip. I took control and made my own rhythm, allowing the senses to fill me up. He wiggled one of his wrists free and reached out a hand to massage my clit as I moved on top of him. I went slow, not wanting to rush a single moment of pleasure.

I loved taking control of his body. In this situation, it was mine to master. I felt his excitement race across our bond, and it was heightened by my anticipation. I could feel him teetering on the edge, and I wanted to fly off it with him.

"Ava, I'm going t—" He gave another ragged groan.

"Come, Charlie. Do it now." I let go, and our orgasms collided as we came together. His was so strong it nearly made me see starlight. The feeling was like drifting downward from the heavens, seeing the world expanded out in front of you and knowing everything was yours to share with the person you loved. I forgot we were in a prison, because at that moment, we owned it all.

I caressed his face as we came down from our shared high. He wrapped his arms around me as we rolled over, pulling me under him. His body caged me in, making me feel secure. The feeling of floating gradually receded as I felt myself fully come back into my body.

Charlie was still kissing my neck. I combed my fingers through his hair and whispered, "You're my hero."

"If I'm a hero, then you're a goddess." Charlie slid off of me, but he didn't cease touching my face, my lips. "You seemed pretty comfortable."

"I was. It was a lot different than what I had expected."

"What did you think it was going to be?"

I didn't say anything, but an image of blood flashed across my mind, and Charlie flinched. "No, Ava. That's not what's supposed to happen."

"I heard it wasn't, but I didn't believe anyone."

"Well, you know now." Charlie brushed my hair back. "Does everything feel all right?"

"Yeah. Why?"

"Just checking." He got up and threw the condom away before he disappeared into the next room. He came back with a bottle of lotion and a snack.

"What are you doing?" I asked.

"Aftercare." Charlie handed me a package of cookies. "I'd give you water, but we don't have any."

He uncapped the lotion and began rubbing it on my back. It felt so relaxing.

"You just come up with this?" I asked.

"I considered it often, a long time ago back when we were together." Charlie worked on getting a knot out of my shoulder. "It was one of those scenarios I ran through in my head, trying to figure out what would make it best for you."

I nibbled on a cookie. "That is seriously so sweet."

"I figured it'd be one of those things that's important for us." Charlie massaged my entire back, my ankles and my feet while I had the rest of my snack. When he was finished, I was completely boneless on the bed and feeling totally blissed-out. Charlie covered me up with the blanket, wrapping it closely around me.

"Aw. You're tucking me in." I smiled.

"You should feel loved." Charlie slid in beside me and wrapped an arm around my front. I held on to it, kissing his fingers.

"I do. I really, really do."

I didn't think he had any idea how much this meant to me. This day had started out with so much fear, but I wasn't afraid of anything anymore. How could I be afraid when I felt this much joy?

Charlie was everything I wanted, and this marriage was a brand-new start for us. If this was just the beginning, I couldn't imagine how wonderful the rest of our lives would be.

I DIDN'T THINK I'd ever been happier. The rest of October felt like a dream. Charlie and I couldn't be kept apart. We spent every moment together when we weren't forced to go to class, writing songs or lounging in bed.

The security I felt from our relationship was the best part of it all. I had someone who loved me and took care of me, and I could do the same for him.

I woke up on Halloween morning to an empty spot beside me. I momentarily panicked, wondering where he'd gone, but my heart settled when I watched him walk in moments after I sat up.

"Hey. Where'd you go?" I asked.

"I just had to go to the infirmary before class," Charlie said.

"Are you okay?" I felt a thin icy veil of fear settle in around me.

"I'm fine. I got a prescription for birth control, since you can't be on it," Charlie said.

"They have that for guys?" I asked in surprise.

"Yeah. The Institute only prescribes them for married inmates, though," Charlie said. "It's magical. Don't really understand how it works, but if it does the job, I guess it doesn't matter."

"You'd do that for me?" So many guys would refuse to take birth control. They'd make their girlfriends do it.

"I'm doing it for us. We don't know if we want to start a family, and we definitely can't do that here," Charlie pointed out.

I was undecided on kids. That was a big step, and with how severe my bipolar was, I secretly feared what kind of mother I'd be. "But don't you want heirs?" My gut sank thinking of Charlie's stupid *obligation* to the throne.

"Gotta find the Elves first, and save them after that," Charlie said. "Not like we can have a baby running around the Institute, and I don't think either of us want to end up like Opal."

I got so sad thinking of her situation. Opal wouldn't get to see her daughter until after her release. It was so cruel to separate a parent and child like that, but the United Supernatural Union had their laws, and they couldn't be broken.

"It's just a pill. Not like it's permanent," Charlie added.

"It's permanent until we get the hell out of here, at least." I crawled out of bed and began rifling through the closet. "Do you still have your suit from the Villain's Ball?"

"Yeah, why?"

"It's a surprise. We're doing a group costume this year with Kallie and Marcus," I said. "Put it on."

Charlie and I got dressed. My high-heeled boots clicked on the floor as I led him to the Villain's Den. Halloween was the only time of year I could wear stilettos at the Institute, and by the ancestors, I was working them.

I spotted Marcus and Kallie near the couches. I stopped Charlie and put his hand on my arm. "Okay, now you can look."

Charlie laughed as he felt the arms of my costume. "What are you wearing?"

"A black leather pantsuit. We all are," I said. "We're *Charlie's Angels!*"

Kallie, Marcus and I struck karate poses. Oberi barked and wagged his tail. I blinked. "Uh, I know you can't see it, but we're all posing right now."

"Mine's a little small," Marcus complained, and he yanked at the side of the suit. Kallie's eyes were locked on the bulge in his leather pants.

"I'm guessing I'm Charlie?" My husband wore a playful smile, and it made my breath skip to see.

"Of course. We thought it'd cheer you up, since you're having so much trouble with teaching the Elves and all," Kallie said.

"And I've been working on my spy moves for weeks," Marcus said. He fumbled forward and did a cartwheel. He *tried* to end it in the splits, but he fell over and ended up ripping a giant hole in his crotch.

"Aw, man!" Marcus complained. "Now I've gotta go to class like this!"

"Nice dinosaur boxers." Kallie snickered.

"Nobody ever asks you what your favorite dinosaur is when you're an adult," Marcus grumbled resentfully.

I think I *look the best.* Oberi had insisted on being a pirate this year, and had donned a striped shirt with a matching skull and crossbones hat. Marcus had put Rishi in a taco costume, which was better than last year's pumpkin by far.

"Are we still having that Halloween party tonight?" Kallie asked me.

"Yep. The balcony at seven o'clock," I told her. "I can't wait."

"A party, huh?" Charlie poked my side, and I giggled.

"It's just a little thing with all our friends," I said, and I swatted his hand away. "Eddie wanted to have one. He's never celebrated Halloween."

Charlie frowned slightly. "I didn't realize. I should probably be paying more attention."

"Believe me, his costume is a riot. He went all out," Kallie said. "Let's go, Marcus, before Professor Mazur flips a nut about us being late."

Kallie picked up Rishi and headed out of the Villain's Den. Marcus waddled after her, holding his book bag in front of his pants.

We grabbed a quick breakfast, then Charlie walked me to Hemlock's class. I sat by Opal. Her face was painted with a variety of fake blood and dirt, and her clothes were ragged and ripped, like she'd just pulled herself out of a grave. Charlie pulled out my chair to help me in as I sat down— what a sweetheart.

"Nice costume," I said to Opal.

"Ez and I are zombies this year. What fun!" Opal grinned widely before Hemlock walked in. She had a Jack-O-Lantern pin on her cloak, but that was the only decoration she wore. She glanced at Charlie, looking him up and down.

"You'll want to sit in on this class, Mister Wahkin," Hemlock said. "It contains some very relevant information."

"I'm sorry, but I have to get to Criminal Justice," Charlie said.

"I'll give Professor Jobe an excuse for your absence," Hemlock stated. "Take a seat."

Charlie dragged a chair next to me and sat in it, because you didn't tell Hemlock no. She tapped the chalkboard with her pointer. "Calm down, everyone. I know it's Halloween and you're all very excited, but do your best to pay attention. We're covering new material today."

"Don't we do that every day?" Ghost complained. Someone tossed a paper ball, and it smacked him on the back of the head.

"Charming, Mister Walker, but that is the point of *school*." Hemlock scowled. "However, I think this lesson will be useful to some of you more than others, as we're studying twin flames."

Charlie stirred beside me, and my interest perked up. A lesson about people who shared a soul? That was literally our situation.

"Twin flames are the separate halves of one soul living in two different people," Hemlock began. "Twin flames are actually more common in the supernatural world than we realize. In fact, the Institute has its own twin flames in the case of Mister and Mrs. Wahkin."

I frowned. I didn't like how Hemlock was using us as her examples. I could feel everyone's eyes on Charlie and me as Hemlock continued her lecture. "Each supernatural culture has their own legends surrounding twin flames. In Miriamic lore, natural-born twins are considered to share a soul. In some cultures, twin flames are seen to be the sign of ultimate friendship between two platonic beings. Other races, such as the angels, don't believe in twin flames at all. In Hawkei society, it's usually thought to be a romantic connection. The Elementai believe that the person who is born first has their soul fractured at birth. The other half separates to go to someone else. The two halves are eventually united later within one Familiar, once both of the individuals come of age."

My Aunt Imogen had said something similar when Charlie and I had met, but before the idea could be confirmed, Hemlock went on. "However, this might not be the case. From what supernatural research has deduced, twin flames were split at the very beginning of creation, and are reunited during their mortal lives to complete some sort of divine mission. It is the objective of the twin flames to discover what their divine mission is, and work together to fulfill it on this Earth."

"Does that mean everyone has a twin soul?" Opal asked, raising her hand.

"No. Not everyone's soul is split," Hemlock said. "In fact, twin flames are particularly rare in fae culture, where we are destined to have soulmates. Uniting two souls through a magical bond is a very different connection than the one that exists between the halves of a singular soul, which is meant to be brought together and reunited at some point. There is a contract that is signed between these two different halves before birth to work together during their lives on Earth. Therefore, the bond that exists between these types of individuals is magnetic. It can't be denied once prompted."

"We sign contracts before birth?" Ghost questioned.

"Yes. In fact, it is believed that souls plan out their life paths and make agreements with other souls on the journey they want to take before they incarnate on the mortal plane," Hemlock said.

"So why isn't it happily-ever-after right away when twin flames meet?" Naya asked. I'd forgotten she was in this class, as she hardly ever paid attention or spoke up. Her biting comment had clearly been directed toward me, because she smirked as she said the words.

She was trying to be a bitch— everyone knew Charlie and I had problems in our past. I bet a lot of people thought our marriage wouldn't work out, including her. Screw them.

"The twin flame connection is *very* intense. It is one of the most powerful bonds the supernatural world has," Hemlock replied. "It's a balancing act of two different individuals. It's similar to looking in a mirror. A twin flame will challenge you, reveal all your flaws and push you to become the best version of yourself. It's not unusual for twin flames to be opposite in every way, and that kind of dynamic can be very difficult to manage."

Psh. She had that right. Charlie challenged me in all sorts of ways. No wonder we hadn't gotten along when we'd first met.

Oberi was unnaturally silent during the lecture. His ears remained perked, and he lay stiffly at our feet as Hemlock went on.

"Most people can't stand to be in that kind of energy at all times. A twin flame will provoke you to heal your deepest wounds and face your greatest fears. It's not unusual for twin flames to take separate paths after struggling to make their connection work," Hemlock said.

Charlie cringed, and I felt my stomach twist into knots. Did that mean we really were doomed?

"Ultimately, though, the twin flames who can endure the heat, so to speak, and remain committed to each other have very fulfilling and rewarding relationships," Hemlock stated.

I shot my hand into the air. "So do twin flames sign contracts with just each other, or can that be done between any number of souls?"

"This goes a bit more into theory than it does actual supernatural science," Hemlock said warily. "But, since you asked the question, we might as well discuss it. It is believed, among some academic circles, that before we are born, all of us make choices as to what we wish to experience in order to help our soul grow, and we sign spiritual contracts with other souls in order to fulfill our purpose and better the world. This goes beyond the concept of twin flames— the theory is we sign spiritual contracts with everyone in our lives, so that as we live on Earth, we can become a better society through the experiences of the collective soul population in the spiritual realm, even as we suffer through things such as pain or war."

I couldn't help but think of Kallie and Marcus. Did the four of us sign a spiritual contract before our birth that we'd all work to save the world together?

I had a brief thought about Monica. Had she agreed to die young? Had I agreed to *watch* her go through that, so I could grow and learn from the experience?

I wasn't so sure about that, and I didn't know how to feel about it. This stuff was way too complicated. But thinking about how I could've chosen my own path, instead of being a victim to suffer through whatever destiny decided, was somewhat comforting.

"Sounds like you'd be locked into a relationship for life without having any kind of control," Ghost said, and several people mumbled in agreement.

"Everyone is always their own person, Mister Walker, even twin flames," Hemlock said. "Contracts that are made in the spiritual realm before birth can be broken between all parties, just like contracts in the mortal world. Like most things in life, the twin flame connection is not determined by fate or destiny, but by our choices."

Hemlock put her pointer down. "I'm giving you the rest of the class period to work on your essays that are due next week, seeing as how *some of you* failed to turn in a first draft— or any sort of paper at all. Keep in mind that crayon drawings are not an acceptable substitute."

"I worked hard on that," I heard Jeffrey Johnson grumble behind us.

As people took out notebooks and pencils, I got up from my seat and took Charlie's hand. We strode up to the front of the classroom. I stood in front of Hemlock's desk as I asked, "Professor Hemlock, what you said about twin flames—"

"— Are we really at risk of taking separate paths?" Charlie blurted. He voiced aloud what I'd been thinking, and the anxiety that we both shared.

Hemlock gave us a kind smile. "Neither of you should be worried. I wouldn't have married you if I thought your relationship was doomed to failure. I believe that you two have a divine path to take together that was set by yourselves and the gods. What that is, I can't be sure, but your union is a crucial part of that. I married you on the pretense that I was doing what was best for both of you, and for the world."

"Thank you. That's good to hear," Charlie said.

I nearly let out a sigh of relief. Charlie and I had been through so much already. I couldn't imagine being separated from him after enduring our breakup. Another would be unimaginable.

I could tell Charlie was still thinking about what we'd learned when we left class later. It was a nice day, so we went to the prison yard to sit on the benches and enjoy the sunlight— which was rare on Darke Island. The yard was pretty deserted, considering vampire inmates could only come outside when there was thick cloud cover overhead.

"What Hemlock said about spiritual contracts is compelling. It's gotta be real," Charlie stated. "What do you think we signed up for?"

"Whatever we decided to do together, I want to see it through," I said, and I squeezed his hand. "Though I'd love to get some real answers on this whole twin flame thing."

"So what do you think it is in the case of our soul? Did it split when I was born, or were we already separated at the beginning of time?" Charlie asked.

"Why don't we ask Oberi?" I turned toward the dog.

Oberi huffed. *I'm not too sure about that. I believe that would be before my time.*

"Why not? Don't you have any idea what our divine path is, or what we're supposed to do?" I asked.

Not particularly. The answers should be in your prophecies, Oberi replied.

"You're super old, Oberi, and you came from the spiritual realm. At the very least, you must've been there when Charlie and I decided what our path would be before we were born," I argued.

Of course I was there, but it's not like I remember. That was years ago, he complained.

"Twenty or so years compared to the thousands you've been alive!" I shouted. "You can't say you have no idea."

Listen, Ava, there's a reason our memories are wiped clean when our souls incarnate on Earth. I recall some things, but not all, Oberi argued. *When I left the spiritual realm to find Charlie, and find you, my under-standing of the universe changed. I can no longer wrap my mind around things my spirit can. The answers are on the tip of my tongue, and yet, I can't explain them. I feel awful I can't help, but at the same time, my mortal brain doesn't comprehend the big picture. I can't give you the answers.*

"Why the hell not!" I threw my hands up.

Because the whole objective in this life is for your soul to grow and learn, and how do you learn anything when you have a cheat code? He shook his whole body, and his hat went flying off. *Oh no! My hat! Avaaaaa!*

I fixed the pirate hat and sighed. "Guess we're not getting any answers out of him."

"We should do what we can to keep studying twin flames," Charlie said. "I bet what Hemlock knew was only the beginning of what we can learn."

"I doubt we'd find that kind of information lying around the Institute."

"Well, what about your intuition? You've been working on it all semester. Let's start there."

That was a good idea. I made a mental note to meditate on it as soon as I had time.

We had to split up for our next class, so we didn't meet up again until it was time for lunch. I plopped on Charlie's lap immediately when I got to the cafeteria and saw he already had a plate made up for us. "Ooh, tamales."

"I know they're one of your favorites." Charlie nuzzled my nose, then kissed me. I heard an audible groan several spaces down as his lips pressed against mine.

"You guys are gross," Ez complained. "I don't want to watch my sister make out."

Didn't care. I hadn't gotten to kiss Charlie in months. I was making up for lost time.

"Hey, you two! I don't care if you're married. I've given you enough warnings about PDA," a guard snapped as he passed. "One more, and it's an infraction!"

I rolled my eyes and slid off Charlie's lap. These rules were really killing me.

Kallie had a new addition to her Halloween costume. It was a black leather collar with a metal loop hanging in the middle, a blue gem dangling from it.

I'm so jealous, Oberi preened as his eyes greedily observed the leather.

Marcus gripped his utensil tightly as he eyed the collar intensely. "What is *that*?" he asked in disgust.

"It was a present from Scarlet. I like it," Kallie replied.

"Don't you think it's inappropriate?" Marcus seethed.

"No. I'm a wolf. I can wear a collar," Kallie said defensively.

"Not a *sex collar*," Marcus hissed.

"Who's gonna stop me? You?" Kallie rebutted.

At the worst time ever, Scarlet walked in. Her boxer costume wasn't very original. She slid next to Kallie and nudged her. "Hey, hotness. Ready for our date tonight?"

Kallie bristled. "I'm sorry, but I already told you I can't come," she said. "I'm having a party with my friends."

Scarlet's nose crinkled. "Yeah. I forgot."

She leaned forward and put her chin in her hand as she locked her red eyes on a vampire across the room. "Could anyone introduce me to Zayne? I'd like to get to know him personally."

"Didn't he get sentenced here for a string of car robberies?" I asked.

"Yeah. I *love* a guy with some hot wheels," Scarlet purred. "They're so cool."

"I have a moped," Marcus offered. "It's cool."

Scarlet let out a mean snicker. "Wow. Could you be any more of a loser?"

Kallie's hands slammed on the table. "He is *not* a loser!" Kallie shouted.

"Okay, geez. I was only kidding," Scarlet said slowly. She stood up. "I've got to go train. See you around."

Scarlet swaggered off— in Zayne's direction, I noticed.

Marcus spoke quietly. "Thanks for sticking up for me. I know I'm a nobody."

"You're not," Kallie said immediately. "Don't listen to her."

The rest of lunch was rather awkward. I sent an intention across our bond to tell Charlie I needed to talk with Kallie. He made some excuse to get Marcus away once they were done eating. I waited for everyone else around us to leave before I turned to Kallie, who was staring at her plate rather listlessly. "What are you thinking about?"

"Homicide," Kallie said.

"Homi— *no*, I meant about Scarlet!"

"Oh." Kallie sighed and slumped forward. "She's cool, I guess."

"Not a promising response when you're talking about your girlfriend."

"We're barely dating," Kallie complained. "She's only around when she wants to have sex, which is great and all, but as far as romance goes, I feel like I'm being ignored."

"So is it better, sleeping with a girl over a guy?" I asked. I hoped I wasn't being invasive, but I was curious.

She shrugged. "I don't know. I've never been with a guy."

"Really? I thought that guy you were with back in Malovia—"

"Ew, no!" Kallie wrinkled her nose. "Don't even go there."

"So it's only been Scarlet," I said slowly. "Don't you guys cuddle or whatever after you're done?"

"No. She gets annoyed if I hang around, so I just... get my stuff and leave," Kallie said.

I thought about Charlie and me. We'd been messing around a lot after our first time, and every time we finished, he always made sure to take care of me by giving me lots of affection and getting whatever I needed. Imagining Kallie getting dressed and walking back to her dorm by herself after being in such a vulnerable position made me really sad. And angry at Scarlet.

"If you're not happy, you should break up," I offered. "You obviously want a real relationship, and Scarlet only wants one thing."

"I know. I'm trying to figure out how to break it to her easy," Kallie said. "Which is still complicated, because the only time I get with her is when we're alone in her cell, and she gets aggravated whenever I try to talk."

Kallie fiddled with her collar. "I *do* like this, though. I think I'll keep it."

"Maybe you can use it with someone else," I stated in an obvious way.

Her eyes were distant. "Yeah. Maybe."

She was still acting weird that night when we got together for the party. We waited until after dark so we could go stargazing. I stole a bunch of blankets from the laundry room after my shift, and Kallie stole popcorn from the cafeteria. Ez, Opal, Ivy, Chancey, Marcus, Kallie, Charlie and I sat on the balcony's stone floor and draped blankets around us as we admired the stars.

"I think that's Aquarius," Ivy said as he pointed upward at a constellation. Ivy's sexy kitten costume made him look great, but he was definitely pushing the rules of what was allowed.

Chancey had a sheet draped over himself with two eye holes cut in it.

"You put in a lot of effort," I remarked.

"At least I dressed up," he shot back at me.

"We're here!" a sing-song voice announced. I turned and pressed a hand to my mouth to hold in a giggle. Eddie was wearing an inflatable koala costume, and Alistair was dressed as a zookeeper. It was overtly ridiculous.

That night was nearly magical as we continued pointing out constellations and watching for meteorites. I couldn't help but describe it all to my husband.

"It's so gorgeous, Charlie," I said with a sigh. "The sky's a mixture of blue and black. There are so many stars— hundreds of them. You can see them clearly, because there's not much light pollution on Darke Island. The moon is a waxing crescent, and— oh wow, a shooting star!"

I watched it race across the sky, and Charlie said, "Make a wish."

"Hm... I wish..." I smiled as the thought crossed my mind. "I wish all of us could be like this forever."

"That's a perfect wish." Charlie kissed my cheek, and I swooned.

The stars looked so beautiful above us, and the sky was so wide and open, we might as well not be behind bars. Up here, surrounded by my friends, I'd never felt happier. I'd completely forgotten what it was like to be happy, as I hadn't in so long.

But happiness was warm, peaceful, and full of light. It was so much better than feeling the cold claws of misery creeping over you, and I knew that now. I was no longer used to the comfort of being sad, not since Charlie and I had married. I was really glad I wasn't in that space anymore.

Marcus' teeth chattered so loudly I could hear them across the balcony.

"You okay?" Kallie asked.

"G-great." Marcus crossed his arms, and Rishi meowed in his lap.

Everyone else had a buddy to keep them warm, but Marcus and Kallie were clearly sitting away from one another on purpose. Kallie scooted to where Marcus sat and said, "Here. I'm a shifter. I'm basically a walking heater."

Kallie hugged Marcus from behind, draping a blanket around both of them. Marcus stiffened, but he didn't make any attempt to pull away.

"I bet she just made his Halloween," Charlie said under his breath.

"Maybe next year he can be Red Riding Hood and she can be the Big Bad Wolf. I bet she'd love to eat him up," I whispered. Charlie laughed lowly.

"Aw, man, Oberi ate all the popcorn!" Ez complained. It was true—my Familiar's head was stuck far into the bag, and he was jumping around trying to get it off.

"I'll go get some more," I offered. We'd left an extra bag in our cell.

"I don't want you to go by yourself." Charlie didn't like me wandering around the Institute alone after dark.

"Then come along." Charlie and I untangled ourselves from each other's arms, got up and left the balcony. As we wandered down the black halls of the Institute, the cheeriness of the balcony left me, and I became overcome by a sense of eerie dread.

"I'm glad you came with me," I said in a low voice.

"No kidding. This place is creepy at night," Charlie muttered.

I had the thought we should turn around and go back, before I heard a low voice from the next hallway utter, "You shouldn't have come. This nearly exposes us all."

It was Hemlock. Her words caused me to stop dead in my tracks. I flung out an arm to stop Charlie. We pressed ourselves to the wall, waiting to hear who she was talking to.

A man's voice was low as he uttered, "The Infernal Underground must be stopped. I could wait no longer."

That was Professor Takahashi. I *knew* it was. Elation spread through me at the realization that my favorite counselor had returned. Did this mean no more Jaymin? Ancestors, I hoped so.

I was about to spring out and welcome him back, but Hemlock's fierce words made me pause. "The Underground is the only thing keeping Ophio distracted. It needs to remain functional, to keep his attention off our top priorities."

"I can't stand by and allow students to be ferried to the Underground. I took an oath to keep them safe, and as a guardian of this institution, so did you," Takahashi insisted.

Hemlock's tone was regretful as she said, "It is for the best. Sacrifices must be made for the greater good of us all."

It sounded like she was trying to convince herself, but Takahashi let out a harsh noise. "We can't keep allowing innocents to be taken to the Underground in exchange for buying Ava and the others more time."

"The discovery of the Elves has driven Ophio mad! We agreed that you needed to go into hiding until you discovered the *truth*," Hemlock said harshly.

"And I did."

"That doesn't mean it's safe to return."

"Ava and her friends should be informed. They need to prepare for what's coming," Takahashi responded gravely.

"They're not ready, Hiroto. They won't be for quite some time," Hemlock insisted. "We need to be patient if we're going to keep them safe. Ophio already has his eye on them. If he learns what you've discovered, they'll be in more danger than ever before."

"On this we disagree. The four of them— they're stronger than you realize."

"I don't doubt their heart. Only their ability to survive Ophio's wrath."

"Demigods are appearing all over the world, and of the ones I've seen, these four are the strongest. By keeping them in the dark, we're only prolonging the inevitable."

My eyebrows shot up, and Charlie stilled beside me. Takahashi knew we were demigods, and so did Hemlock. What else did they know?

Hemlock took a short sigh. "We'll discuss this in detail later. You need to remain *hidden*. I'll do what I can to ferry supplies to you, but I'm being watched as well. The gods be with you, Hiroto."

"And also with you." I heard the sound of retreating footsteps. I turned the corner and opened my mouth to say something. But the words died on my tongue as I realized Hemlock and Takahashi had both vanished. The hallway was completely empty, as if they were never there at all.

My blood ran cold. Professor Takahashi was *back*— but he was in hiding, and he knew something about the Underground. Whatever that knowledge was, Hemlock wanted to keep it from us.

We couldn't remain in the dark. Somehow, we had to learn exactly what Takahashi knew. Maybe he could help us save Alice and the others.

Or maybe he'd tell us exactly what we didn't want to hear. The only way to know was to find him.

SEVENTEEN

If anything was going to do me in inside this prison, it was Ava-Marie... my *wife*. The way my heart skipped a beat every time I heard her voice, and the surge of passion that came through our bond every time we touched, was unlike anything else. I could get lost in those nights we found ourselves tangled in the sheets— when I held her against my chest as we fell asleep.

The first time we slept together was like waking me to a lifetime of tender love and care I'd never experienced before. And giving that back to her? It was as if the elements had converged into one. The line between where Ava ended and I began was thin, and our soul was finally whole. If my heart gave out in any one of these moments, I'd die a happy man.

My fingers tangled in hers as we headed to breakfast one Saturday morning. We'd picked up shakes from Commissary on our way to the cafeteria. Oberi trotted alongside us, panting happily. Ava and I had groomed his husky fur together this morning while we wrote new lyrics. He'd drooled all over my knee. I didn't think Oberi had ever been happier.

Hell, I didn't think *any* of us had. I mean, Ava and I were writing *music* again.

Sure, the Warden was still conceiving secret plans, and the Underground was still operating. Odd things were happening inside the Institute, like how Professor Takahashi had returned— though we had yet to find him. But it didn't seem to matter what darkness and secrets were brewing inside the Institute, because whatever it was, Ava and I could handle it together.

We filled our plate, and Ava snagged a few extra bacon strips for Oberi. She led me over to our usual table, where our friends sat.

"*Somebody* looks happy today," Ivy remarked in a teasing tone.

"What's he talking about?" I asked.

Chancey chuckled. "We know the walk of shame when we see it."

My cheeks flamed. Ava and I had a wonderful morning, and it was the reason we were late to breakfast. But how could they tell? Could vampires sense it?

"Stop picking on my husband," Ava insisted playfully. She brushed her fingers through my hair, straightening the strands. *That's how Ivy knew*, I realized.

I scowled. "Pidge, you could've told me I had sex hair before we left the dorms."

"I didn't notice!" she cried.

"Or you *wanted* us to know," Kallie teased.

"Like you guys don't know we're doing it," Ava laughed. "We're married, for the ancestors' sake!"

"Yeah, and you won't let us forget it," Marcus cracked.

"What do you mean?" I demanded.

"Sir— I mean, Charlie," Eddie said. "You should see the shirt *your wife* is wearing today."

It was the weekend, so we weren't required to wear our uniforms. But Ava was just wearing a t-shirt. I'd felt it this morning when we cuddled. It wasn't anything special... or was it?

"Pidge, are you going to get yourself into trouble?" I asked.

"No!" she assured me. "It covers everything."

"And what's on it?" I questioned.

Ava sucked a breath, like she was embarrassed. "It says *Wifey for Lifey*."

I burst into laughter. It felt so good to laugh. "*That's* what you guys are concerned about?"

"You don't think it's... tacky?" Ava asked.

If anything, I found it hot as hell— all I wanted to do was take her back to our room and rip it off her.

Ava leaned into me and whispered, "You can do that later."

I smirked. The way my thoughts slipped through sometimes was starting to grow on me.

"Can you guys not talk about that in front of me?" Ez demanded. "She's my sister!"

"And I'm not a little kid anymore," Ava shot back. "Go suck a dick, Ez."

I'd already finished my shake, so I reached out to take a sip of Ava's. I nearly gagged the moment I tasted it. "Ancestors, how much peanut butter did you put into this?"

"As much as I could! I love peanut butter!" Ava exclaimed.

"This is *awful*! It tastes like I sucked off a peanut!" I shouted.

Chancey choked, and several people around me laughed. I heard Ava let out a *hmph* as Ez said, "All the Mitoh kids have a thing for peanut butter. It's our mom's fault."

"Yeah, Daddy thinks it's gross. He won't touch it," Ava added.

"That might be the only thing me and your dad ever agree on, because this is gross," I complained. "Talk about someone nutting in your mouth."

"The peanut jokes are a bit much," Ez complained.

I heard Ava take a sip, and I said, "Mm... peanut jizz!"

"Shut the fuck up!" Ava shouted, and she smacked my shoulder.

"If you guys keep talking about sex, I'm walking out," Ez threatened.

Ava bumped into me as she grabbed a grape from our plate and threw it at her brother. It bounced off of him and hit Alistair in the head.

Alistair gasped. "Food fight?"

"Woah, now," Chancey said. "You might want to sit back down."

"We can't get into trouble today," I agreed. "We have... practice."

The Elves hadn't had a chance to get together for weeks; not since the Warden blood tested me. I was certain the Warden was watching us even closer now, and it'd been hard to get us all together after the wedding. But we had to be willing to take risks. Today was one of them.

Ava had suggested we teach the Elves simultension first, so they could learn how to meld their powers with another supernatural. We needed to teach them the technique before we ran out of time and the Warden concocted another plan.

"Speaking of..." Eddie started. "We should get going soon. Everyone will be waiting for us."

"We'll go in batches," I suggested. "Who's on Hemlock duty today?"

We'd all been taking turns following Hemlock, hoping she would lead us to Professor Takahashi. So far, all our efforts had been a bust.

"Marcus and I can go," Kallie offered. "You don't need us anyway."

Our friends left the table one by one, until Ava and I were alone. We finished our food, then headed to The Devil's Playground together. When we arrived, the Elves were already there.

"It's easy," I heard Ivy say from the stage. "Just grab the pole right here... that's it!"

I frowned. "What's he up to now?"

Ava snickered. "He's teaching Soleil and Andrea how to dance."

I groaned. Those two girls had to be the most innocent Elves in this place. "He's corrupting them."

"Actually, they're doing really great," Ava praised.

"Like this?" one of the girls asked Ivy.

He clapped happily. "There you go!"

"Okay, okay!" I called. "Everyone off the stage. It's time to get serious."

"Boo!" Ivy called across the room.

I flipped him off, and he burst into laughter.

"Okay, ladies," Ivy said. "You heard the man."

Feet scuffled as everyone gathered near the bar. There weren't as many Elves here as there'd been before. Our numbers had dwindled by half, and that terrified me. It meant that for some of the Elves, it was already too late. I hoped this worked, because our last few sessions had been a disaster. If we didn't start teaching these kids something, they wouldn't make it through next semester. I hoped we could save the rest of them.

"Tell me you have something new for us," a kid named Leif said. His voice was distinct, and he was the loudest of all the Elves. He was obviously getting peeved at me that we hadn't made any progress.

I'd been trying to get them to siphon magic from other supernaturals all semester, but so far, Eddie and Reid were the only ones who could do it. We'd started too far above their pay grade, and we had to try something else. The Elves here could conjure their own illusions, but couldn't do much else.

"We have a theory," I said. "A good one. Ava and Kallie came up with it, and I think it may be the key to unlocking your powers."

"What is it?" a timid girl with a high-pitched voice asked. That must've been Lorie.

"It's called simultension," Ava said, stepping forward. "I learned about it my first semester, in Supernatural Behavior Science. My team and I used it to place second in the Darke Games."

"It's a magical technique that allows supernatural races to combine their powers," I explained. "It differs from Elf magic, in that both parties have to be willing participants."

"How does that help us?" Leif asked. "No guard is going to hand over their powers willingly."

"How's that any different from what we've been practicing?" Felicity added.

"Simultension is universal to all races," I pointed out. "It should be easier. But it's close enough to your powers that once you learn simultension, you'll gain a better understanding of your own magic. Eddie, would you like to help me demonstrate?"

Eddie scampered up to the front eagerly. "What do you need, Charlie?"

"An illusion," I said. "Can you create a pistol?"

"I can give it a try," he replied.

As Eddie formed the pistol with illusion magic, I infused my Air into the illusion. The weight of a pistol appeared in my hand, though it felt light as air. Eddie's illusion magic wasn't strong enough to make it solid. There were too many parts, and it was a complicated illusion. But combined with my Air magic, I was able to feel it in my hand.

I pointed the pistol at the ceiling and pulled the trigger. Air blasted out of the barrel, and concrete cracked.

Several Elves clapped, but Ivy gasped. "My ceiling!" he cried.

I winced. *Whoops.*

I ignored Ivy and continued my lesson. "Simultension is an artform. It requires creativity and imagination. Once you can meld your illusion magic with another supernatural, you will learn how to make their power your own."

"Who wants to give it a go?" Ava asked. "Samara? Can you make a goblet?"

"Sure," she said.

I heard the crackling of fire moments later.

"Well done," Ava said kindly. "I like how we made the flames part of the goblet itself. It would certainly keep your hot cocoa warm. How did it feel?"

"It was much easier to combine my powers with yours than to try taking them," Samara said. "I actually *felt* your powers. I've never done that before."

Good. We were making progress.

"Does anyone else want to try?" I asked.

"I'll give it a go," Felicity offered.

She stepped forward. We made a pop-up storybook of plants, with real flowers that grew out of the pages.

"Impressive," I told her as I stroked the sunflower's petals, before turning the page and smelling a rose. "Who's next?"

"I want to try," Reid spoke up.

"What do you say to a crown?" Ava suggested.

"Easy," Reid said confidently.

Ava giggled, then placed something upon my head. I shivered and reached up to feel a crown of ice and metal. It was heavy and solid. It seemed that combined with our magic, the Elves could create stronger illusions.

"This is great," I remarked. "Simultension seems easy for Elves."

"I've never done magic so seamlessly before," Felicity said.

"Then let's give everyone a shot," I offered. "Split into groups."

The Elves seemed excited, because they rushed into action. Ava and I walked around to observe, and she described to me what each team was doing.

"Ooh." She sounded impressed. "Chancey used his angel light, and Soleil formed it into the shape of a halo."

I snorted. "If angels come with halos, Chancey lost his ages ago."

Ava hummed as we continued around the room. She stopped dead in her tracks and grabbed my arm. Something whizzed by me, and a *crash* sounded.

"My favorite table!" Ivy cried.

What are you complaining about? Oberi cracked. *You've broken enough tables banging on them.*

I tried to hide my laughter. I mean, Oberi wasn't *wrong.*

"Alistair, please," Ava scolded. "Can we go easy on the battle orbs? It's practically filling the whole room."

"But that was impressive!" Alistair protested. "I've never created one so big."

"That's the beauty of simultension," I told him. "But you may not want to blow us all up in the process."

Alistair groaned, like I was being unfair. I just shook my head.

A screech tore through the room so loud that it made my head vibrate. I threw my hands over my ears, and the screaming stopped.

"Sorry!" Opal called. "Sorry, guys. It won't happen again."

I winced as the ringing in my ears faded. "What'd she do?"

"Opal and Andrea created a foghorn that used Opal's siren scream," Ava explained. "Thank the ancestors it wasn't stronger, or we'd be sitting under a pile of rubble."

"Yeah, we're going to have to set some safety rules," I said. "But I want them to learn how to defend themselves, so experimenting is a good thing."

"Wow! A *real* shield!" Ez cried. "How'd you do that, Alistair?"

"Magic, my friend," Alistair said proudly.

"Lorie made a really beautiful shield illusion," Ava told me. "Alistair combined his shield magic, and it became a solid sheet of metal."

My shoulders sagged in relief. For the first time, all the Elves were using magic. It was incredible.

We practiced for hours, until Alistair and Eddie started sparring against Chancey and Reid. A rogue battle orb nearly fried Oberi's tail. Ivy squealed and ducked behind the bar.

How dare you!? Oberi growled. *I just fluffed that this morning!*

"Calm down, Oberi," I insisted. "Guys, I think it's time to wrap it up. We've been gone for a while, and we've made good progress."

I was actually starting to believe the Elves would be able to escape the Institute soon if we kept this up.

"Plus, Oberi's getting pissed," Ava teased.

"Yeah, he's an old crank," I said. "You all did great today. You should be proud of yourselves."

The Elves started to leave, and I heard glasses clink onto the counter.

"You look wiped," Ivy remarked. "Need a drink?"

I hesitated. It was tiring teaching magic, but I wasn't going to drink unless Ava could, and she wouldn't. We didn't do that anymore.

"Do you have anything non-alcoholic?" I asked.

Ivy slid a glass across the counter. I sipped on a carbonated lemon-lime drink, before handing it to Ava. "Want to try?" I asked her.

"Mm..." Ava said. "It's good."

"There's more where that came from," Ivy offered. "Have a seat."

We sat beside each other on the barstools. We had time to kill, since we couldn't all leave at once or someone would notice.

"Is everything okay?" Ava asked Ivy. "You look down. Things are all right with you and Chancey?"

I could hear Chancey across the room, comparing muscles with Eddie. I bet Alistair was drinking that up.

"Yeah, everything's fine," Ivy assured us. "It's just... I've been hoping to ask you guys something."

"If it's about how to propose to Chancey, we're not much help," Ava cracked. "Charlie and I didn't really plan our wedding."

"No," Ivy said quickly. "It's, uh... more of a question for Oberi."

What? Me? Oberi perked up near my feet.

"Sure, we can translate," I said, though I was confused about what he could possibly say to Oberi.

"No one's paying attention to us," Ava said. "Ask away."

Ivy drew a long breath, like he wasn't sure how to word the question. "It's... embarrassing."

"You don't have to be embarrassed around us," I assured him. He was starting to worry me.

"I didn't even know you *could* get embarrassed," Ava added, sounding encouraging. "I mean, you're so confident about... everything."

"I know I come across that way," Ivy said. "But deep down, there's a lot that I hide. I'm still trying to find myself, you know?"

"In what way?" Ava asked curiously.

Ivy started wiping down the counter, probably just to give his hands something to do. His wet towel brushed my fingers, like he wasn't quite paying attention.

"It probably sounds dumb to you, but it's important to me," Ivy started. "It's about my pronouns."

"That's not dumb," I said. "Your identity is valid— whatever you decide."

Ivy sighed, like he had a heavy weight on his chest. "That's the thing. I *haven't* really decided yet. I mean, I know I tell people I'm okay with male pronouns, but it doesn't feel right. *They* feels better, but no one actually uses it, and I feel weird telling people to call me *they* when they've been using *he* as long as they've known me."

"It's not your job to make sure other people are comfortable," Ava pointed out.

"That's what I wanted to talk to Oberi about," Ivy admitted. "I hear you guys call Oberi *he* sometimes, and *she* other times. How do you decide which pronouns to use?"

Oberi pushed between Ava and me, placing his front paws on the counter. *Listen up, Ivy. You are a badass, and don't let anyone tell you differently. Regardless of your pronouns, you are amazing, you hear me? Only you get to decide who you truly are.*

Ava was quick to translate and repeated what Oberi said.

Ivy didn't say anything. I could tell this conversation was weighing heavily on him. I wondered how long he'd wanted to bring it up.

To answer your question, my gender changes when I shift. I have feminine forms and masculine forms, Oberi explained. *I'm a he when I'm a he, and a she when I'm a she.*

"Mm..." Ivy mused after Ava translated. "That makes a lot of sense."

Maybe you have different forms, too, Oberi suggested.

"I don't know," Ivy said. "I *could*. I'm intrigued."

"In a lot of indigenous cultures, including the Hawkei, we have something called Two-Spirit people. It's a broad term for LGBTQ people, but stems from the idea of a third gender role in our societies. Kind of like people who are considered to have a feminine and masculine spirit in one body," Ava explained. "That sounds like you."

"It could be," Ivy said reluctantly. "What do Two-Spirit people *do?*"

"They were super important to our tribe. They were often shamans and other kinds of religious and spiritual leaders, because they could see things from two different perspectives," Ava explained. "In indigenous society, we focus on what people *do* for our tribe rather than how they identify. Gender is fluid to the Hawkei."

"Maybe it's like that for your tribe, but my dad was really rigid on that kind of thing," Ivy said nervously. "He insisted men and women were different, that they think and do things differently, and people were either one or the other."

Well of course *men and women are different, but some of us just don't fit in either category, and can shift between the two,* Oberi said. *That's the gift of being like us. We all carry feminine and masculine energy inside, and while many people favor one over the other, some of us ride the middle.*

"Are you sure?" Ivy asked after Ava had translated. He sounded skeptical.

Yes. Gender isn't what you're born with, but who you feel you are and who you want to be. We are free to carve our own destinies and our own paths, and you are free to expand and create yourself in any way you desire, without the influence of others weighing you down.

I translated, and Ivy drummed his fingers against the table. "Would it be okay if you guys called me *she* today? Just to try it out? I'm thinking that today I might be a girl."

"Sure, Ivy," I told him— I mean, *her.*

The chatter faded as the last few people left the room. Chancey was the only one remaining.

"Everything okay over here?" Chancey asked. He must've sensed we were having a serious conversation.

Ivy didn't answer for a beat, so I spoke up. "Everything's fine. In fact, I think we should head to the Villain's Den for a game of foosball. What do you say? Guys against girls?"

"Sounds fun," Chancey said, without missing a beat.

I think you just made Ivy's day, Ava said through the bond. *She's beaming.*

Good, I replied. *If she's happy, then I'm happy.*

"So, you're a girl today?" Chancey asked Ivy curiously as we left The Devil's Playground. It was obvious Ivy had brought this up with Chancey before. He sounded really understanding about it.

"I'm trying it out," Ivy said timidly.

"I think it's hot," Chancey flirted.

Ava snorted. "Okay, *now* who needs a room?"

Ivy snickered. "We got one. This morning. *We* just know how to watch the time so we're not late for breakfast."

"Or it's over quickly," I cracked. "I like to take my time."

"Oh, believe me," Chancey replied. "This girl soaks up every minute."

Ivy snickered under her breath.

She's blushing so hard, Ava told me.

Are we embarrassing her? I asked.

No. I think she likes it.

Please, Oberi cut in. *I can smell the pheromones.*

We entered the Villain's Den and headed to the foosball table. "Guys on that side, girls on this side," Ava announced.

I started around the table, but I stopped dead in my tracks when a voice came from the corner.

"Girls? That vampire ain't a girl!" a guy accused.

"Vampire?" a deep voice mocked. It was Mad Dog. "He's not one of us. He's mermaid scum."

"I am too a vampire!" Ivy stammered.

It was weird to hear her sound so unsure. Usually, Ivy was always down for a fight, but this was definitely a soft spot.

"Watch it, Mad Dog," I warned. The chairs squeaked as he and his gang stood.

"Whatcha gonna do about it?" Mad Dog challenged. "You're out of fight club. No one's going to come to your rescue. We could beat your ass, and *you'd* end up in Cellblock 9."

Chancey just about lost it. He stripped off his jacket and shoved it into my hands, preparing for a brawl. "You really want to go?"

Mad Dog's entourage surrounded us, and a few of them ended up on the other side of Ivy. Oberi growled, but none of us moved.

I hesitated. I wanted to kick Mad Dog's ass, but we'd be in deep shit if we started a fight.

"You want to be called a girl? We'll treat you like one," one of Mad Dog's cronies cackled. "Come on, pretty lady. Show us what's under that little skirt of yours."

"Yeah," another chimed in. "Prove you're a girl. Show us what's between your legs!"

"You think *that's* how you treat a lady?" Ava snapped. "No wonder none of you are getting laid."

"You shut your mouth!" Mad Dog growled.

"Or what?" Ava asked boldly. "Show us how you *really* treat women. Go on, Mad Dog. Fucking hit me and see what happens."

The entire Villain's Den fell silent.

Ava scoffed. "That's what I thought."

"I won't hit a lady," Mad Dog said. "But I wouldn't mind going after her husband—"

"Ava! Charlie!" Kallie squealed as she entered the room. She rushed in so fast that I didn't think she realized what was going on.

Mad Dog cut off, and Kallie scoffed at him. "What are *you* looking at? Get lost, blood breath."

Kallie grabbed my arm, and she yanked me and Ava out of the room. Ivy and Chancey rushed behind us, and Oberi growled at Mad Dog as we left. I stumbled over Rishi and into Marcus when we reached the hall.

Ivy sounded dejected. "I *knew* this would fucking happen. It always does, every time I want to try. And you guys wonder why I stick with one thing."

"Don't listen to them," Ava pleaded. "You're trying to figure out who you are. You should be able to call yourself whatever—"

"No, it's fine." Ivy sighed. "We should just... go. Come on, Chance."

"Yeah. Thanks for breaking that up, Kallie," Chancey said.

"No problem," she said quickly, like she had more important things to discuss.

"We'll catch up with you later," I said to Ivy and Chancey. "Be careful out there, okay?"

"We will," Chancey promised, taking his coat back. "Let's go, babe."

Ava lowered her voice as their footsteps retreated. "Something's going on. Did you find Takahashi?"

Kallie cleared her throat. "Not here. Come on."

She led us down the hall to a secluded alcove. "Marcus and I found letters in Hemlock's desk," she whispered. "She concealed them with illusion magic, but I broke the spell."

My blood turned ice cold. There was something in Kallie's tone that worried me. "What did they say?"

Marcus audibly swallowed. "She's calling a secret meeting... with our parents."

"Our *what*?" Ava cried, so loud anyone down the hall could've heard her.

We couldn't have heard Marcus right. "She's calling a secret meeting with who?" I asked.

"Our parents," Kallie repeated. "Mine, Marcus', and Ava's. They're all coming here."

Ava gasped. "What for?"

I felt her unease through our bond. This couldn't be good.

"She's going to tell them we're demigods, and she's invited Professor Takahashi to be there," Kallie said.

"She can't do that," I hissed. "The Warden could find out."

"She has a secret illusion room," Kallie told us. "She mentions it in the letters. She can't leave the prison because she might be discovered, so she's bringing our parents here. She's going to duplicate herself with an illusion, like I did for us that time in the mines. She's practically a prisoner here herself, but she's found a way to hide it from the Warden. In a few weeks, our parents will be here. Whatever she says in that meeting could change the course of our future."

"And the prophecy," Ava breathed.

"So what do we do? Stop her?" I asked.

"No," Ava said firmly. "I want to hear what she has to say."

"What's so important that she thinks our parents need to know, but she and Takahashi are keeping us in the dark?" Kallie asked. "We're the subject of this meeting. Why don't we have the right to know what's going on in our own lives?"

"I don't know, but one thing's for sure. Hemlock has important information she's not sharing with us," Marcus pointed out. "There's only one thing we can do."

"Exactly," Ava agreed. "We're going to find out what Hemlock knows. When our parents get here, we'll be listening in on that meeting."

EIGHTEEN

The meeting was set to take place a few days before the start of the next Darke Games. Ivy, Chancey, Alistair and Scarlet were getting ready to participate, but as for me and my friends, we were concentrating on how to sneak into Hemlock's secret gathering without getting caught.

On Saturday evening the day of the meeting, we were pretty sure we had a good plan.

"Do you know where the room is for certain?" I'd asked Kallie the same question a million times, but it was a valid one— illusion rooms could move, you know.

"Yes. It's at the back of her classroom, concealed by a door that looks like a closet," Kallie said. "She has a million wards around the place."

"Which I can break," Marcus offered. "I've been practicing with them all semester, and I think I can sever them now, long enough so we can sneak in."

"And I'll put them back up again with my own magic once we're inside," Kallie stated. "Hopefully my magical signature will be strong enough that Hemlock won't notice it wasn't her own magic that put the wards up."

"If Marcus can break wards, we need to use it to get into the Warden's office," I said.

"This isn't like the Warden's office. We have to reinstate the ward if we don't want to get caught," Kallie pointed out. "I can replicate Hemlock's spell because hers is fae magic. The Warden's office is protected by something else— I'm not sure what. Besides, the point of this meeting is to overhear as much as we can, so even if Hemlock finds out we were there later, it doesn't matter, because she can't take back what we learned. If we get caught doesn't matter in the long run."

"But where are we going to hide in the room? We have no idea what it looks like," I said.

"We'll just have to find spots to conceal ourselves once we get in there," Charlie said.

I sighed. "I wished my healing powers were up to par. I could turn myself and the rest of us invisible with Anichi magic if I knew what I was doing."

Doesn't work that way... Oberi growled under the table.

"My mom can do it," I grumbled under my breath.

I've told you before, your powers aren't the same.

"We have illusion magic to hide us," Kallie said. "I say we go now."

We checked we weren't being followed before we ducked into Hemlock's classroom, which was completely empty.

"Come on." Kallie took us toward the door at the back of the room. Alette peaked her head out of Kallie's curtain of hair to watch.

Marcus held his breath as he splayed his hands over the doorway. "The ward is strong, but weaker than the one around the Warden's office. I should be able to break it. Stand back."

Magic swirled up Marcus' arms, and he transformed the wisps into a large battle orb. He tossed it into the air, and it exploded above our heads. I flinched at the loud sound.

Marcus winced. "Sorry, I had to transform the magic. This should be good enough. Let's go."

Kallie opened the door. "Get through," she hissed quickly. She shoved us in, and I came out on the other side of the doorway into a broad room. Kallie quickly recast the ward.

There was a circular table in the center of the room with eight chairs seated around it, along with a screen set up at the head of the room and a projector on a metal stand. The room was made of stone, with a high ceiling and stained-glass windows that let in false light. The ceiling was lined with thick wooden banisters and stone gargoyles perched along their length.

"This reminds me of the classrooms at Arcanea University," Kallie said, turning in place.

"It has to be made completely of magic. No way would something this large fit in a closet space at the back of Hemlock's class," I noted. My voice echoed around the room and bounced off the walls.

"What are we supposed to do? There's nowhere to hide," Marcus said anxiously. He nearly tripped over Rishi as he began pacing back and forth.

When Marcus picked him up, Rishi began yowling— *loudly*. The more Marcus tried to shush him, the louder he got.

"Marcus, why did you bring that damn cat?" Kallie snapped.

"Rishi goes everywhere with me!" Marcus all but wailed. "Ava and Charlie brought Oberi!"

Excuse me, I could provide valuable insight, here, Oberi stated.

Kallie cast a silencing charm with a sharp wave of her hand. Rishi blinked his wide eyes. He opened and closed his mouth, but no sound came out.

I looked around for a place where we could conceal ourselves. I knew there had to be something.

"The ceiling," I said quickly, pointing up. "We can hide on the banisters."

"I can get us up there," Charlie said.

Kallie and Alette fluttered upward, while Charlie levitated the rest of us up to the banisters with his Air magic. The banister we sat on was sturdy and supported our weight easily. It was wide enough that each of us could have our own space.

Not without bickering, though.

"Why does Charlie have the best seat? He's right above the table," Marcus asked. He scooted down to make room for Rishi, who was still gulping air trying to meow.

"Yeah, he should move to the end. He doesn't have to see," Kallie complained.

"I still need to hear!" he hissed, elbowing her aside.

I think you're all being petty, Oberi said. He'd hopped to his own bannister, and flattened himself to the top of it.

"Guys, shut up. There's plenty of room up here," I said. I was starting to freak out, knowing Hemlock could walk in at any time.

"What if they look up?" Marcus asked nervously.

"Here." Kallie wiggled her fingers, and a strangle tingle began to spread across my skin. I lifted my arm and saw that my skin and clothes had taken on the colors of my surroundings— like a chameleon. I could still make out the features of my friends, as well as the outlines of their bodies, but that's because I was close to them. Anyone more than six feet away would have a hard time distinguishing them from the rest of the ceiling.

"Our bodies will blend in with the background. The illusion will disguise us as long as we don't move too much," Kallie replied. "Just stay still until they leave, and they'll never know we're here."

Easy enough. We'd hidden just in time, because the door opened. I held my breath as I watched Professor Takahashi, as well as Professor Hemlock, stride in. They remained at the door as other people walked in to shake their hand.

A brunette woman strode confidently into the room, and a tall man followed behind. She had a badge on her hip attached to the waistband of her jeans. I bet that was Marcus' mother.

"Detective Taylor," Hemlock said, shaking her hand. "So glad you could make it."

"Call me Nadine. This is my husband, Lucas," Nadine said, stepping aside to introduce the man beside her. Marcus' dad was the same height as he was.

Hemlock clasped Lucas' hand graciously. "I apologize for the short notice, and for taking you away from your work. I know you were working on a story."

"The paper can wait. My son is more important," Lucas replied.

Takahashi was awfully quiet through all these introductions. He bowed slightly as Nadine and Lucas took their seats, but gave no other greeting.

The next people who entered the room caught my attention immediately. They were dressed in plain clothes, but walked with a sort of regality that betrayed exactly who they were.

King Ethan was muscular, dark-skinned, and had a stoic way about him. Jeez, Kallie's dad was *big*. The wolf shifter towered over everyone else in the room. I couldn't see anything in him that resembled Kallie.

In contrast, Kallie looked a lot like her mom. The older woman had beautiful red hair, and the same blazing spark in her green eyes that gave Kallie her ferociousness.

Hemlock hugged the king and queen as they came to her side. "Ethan, Emma. So nice to see the two of you again."

"We missed you," the queen replied, giving her a peck on the cheek. "It's been too long."

Hemlock stepped aside as the king released her from his embrace. "Your majesties, I'd like to introduce you to Mister and Mrs. Taylor."

"We've met before." Nadine smiled. Lucas gave the king a nod of acknowledgement.

"Indeed," King Ethan said. "Briefly, but we know each other."

"Yes. We helped them out of a rough spot a long time ago," Nadine said.

"What the fuck?" Kallie whispered. Marcus shrugged beside her, clearly stumped.

Our parents kept secrets like Ivy collected dollars on club nights. It was beyond annoying.

Mama and Daddy were the last to enter. Mama looked... worried. Her brow furrowed like it always did when she was concerned and didn't want to say it out loud. Daddy had a water canister attached to the side of his hip, I noticed. He hadn't come in here without ammunition.

"Please, take a seat," Takahashi said, and the sound of chairs scraping the floor filled the room as everyone sat down. There was a long moment of silence, filled with tension and distrustful glances.

They didn't know why they'd been asked to come here. But they knew it couldn't be anything good.

"I trust that all of us were able to enter the prison unseen?" Hemlock asked.

"Your portal was effective," Queen Emmaline said.

"Worked for us, too," Nadine said.

"Portals don't typically work on Institute property, but as it is close to the Darke Games and I am an instructor, I was able to open one on prison grounds without alerting the attention of the guards," Hemlock said. "I'm sorry I couldn't provide it for everyone, Mister and Mrs. Mitoh."

"Our son has medical issues. We came here under the guise that we're here to visit," Daddy spoke up.

"A good cover-up, so long as Doctor Taurus doesn't realize the rest of you are here," Hemlock replied.

"We plan to leave once this meeting is over," King Ethan replied. "It's difficult for us to be out of the country for too long without it going noticed, and the transition from giving the crown to my son is still on shaky ground."

Daddy scoffed. "You're not the only one with a nation to run. I'm surprised you took time out of your busy day to be here."

King Ethan sneered, but didn't bite back a comment. The queen stared at Daddy, as if trying to figure out what his deal was.

"I'm sorry to say we were unable to locate Cameron Wahkin. The Elves have followed Emperor Cassiel somewhere we don't know, and our best efforts to contact Charlie's family have been unsuccessful," Hemlock stated.

"I'm sorry, Charlie," I hushed, and I reached out to squeeze his hand.

"It's okay," Charlie whispered, but I heard the lie in his voice. Whatever anger he held toward his dad, he still wanted him to be here.

"Liam and I can act as Charlie's guardians," Mama said. "What did you bring us here for?"

Charlie's surprise was evident as he stiffened beside me, but Hemlock went on. "Professor Takahashi and I are a part of an organized group of elders called the Demigod Guardians," Hemlock explained. "Our numbers are few, but elite. Many years ago, both of us took an oath to join the Guardians in search of demigods, not to use them, but to protect them from those who would use their powers against the world. As all of you are aware, your children are demigods. And though we've done our best to conceal them, we are very certain that Doctor Taurus and his associates suspect, if not downright know, what your children truly are."

There was an uncomfortable shifting sound as people adjusted their seats, and Takahashi took the lead. "We are not sure of what Doctor Taurus is planning, or what he wishes to use your children for," Takahashi explained. "We've attempted to uncover his master plan for decades, but the Celestial Church continues to block us at every opportunity. We know he wants demigods, but what for or why still remains a mystery."

"What about the Infernal Underground?" Queen Emmaline asked. "You told us about it briefly when you reached out, but from the information you gave us, it seems you have nothing."

"We aren't completely certain of his operations in the Infernal Underground. If we were, we'd move to stop him immediately, but without the proper intelligence, we can't risk exposing ourselves for what might be an elaborate ruse," Hemlock said. "Doctor Taurus is cunning. If he wants to distract us, he has the means, and I don't believe the Underground is his master work."

"The Underground *is* real, though. You know it is, because students have gone missing," Nadine said.

"Yes. Elven students in particular, and anyone who the Warden suspects to be a demigod, are sent to the Underground," Takahashi confirmed. "Though what their fate is, none of us can be sure of."

"Has anyone come back from the Underground?" Mama asked.

"One," Hemlock said softly. "We managed to rescue one."

"Well, what happened to him?" Daddy demanded. "Why doesn't he tell you where the Underground is?"

Daddy must not be feeling well today. He was clearly in a mood and trying to provoke whoever would take the bait.

Hemlock didn't bite. "I'm afraid that Carson Forsberg is in no state to tell anyone anything," Hemlock said dryly. "Whatever happened to him in the Underground has left him mute and confused."

My chest tightened in fear. Carson had been one of Alice's teammates during the Darke Games. So the winners of the Darke Games *were* taken to the Underground.

"How did you rescue Carson if you weren't able to determine the Underground's location?" Lucas asked.

"He managed to escape the Underground on his own, though his mind is so rattled, he couldn't tell us how," Hemlock said. "It was a lucky thing that I found him before Doctor Taurus did. We've moved him to a safe place... unfortunately, the poor boy's in such a dire state, he'll most likely have to spend the rest of his life in a mental institution."

Hemlock sighed and placed a shaking hand to her temple. I squeezed Charlie's arm beside me, feeling horribly guilty. *We'd* done that by giving up our Darke Games win. What Carson was suffering through was our fault.

"Are you telling me that the Darke Games are some sort of elaborate ruse so the Warden of this prison can kidnap and experiment on whatever students he pleases?" Daddy seethed.

"That's what we've determined," Takahashi confirmed.

"This is bullshit! You encouraged our children to enter the Darke Games knowing if they won, they'd be sent directly to the Underground!" Daddy thundered.

"At that point, I wasn't aware that the winners of the Games were transported directly to the Underground. I had the hope that if your children won, the Guardians could swoop in and take them to a safe place upon their release, which is why I encouraged them to sign up," Takahashi responded.

He gave a dull sigh. "A very grave mistake."

"Mistake?! My daughter could be *dead*," Daddy seethed.

"We are unsure if the prisoners within the Underground are killed. Carson's survival speaks to the contrary," Hemlock said. "Let's not jump to conclusions."

Hemlock was right. If Carson had survived, it was probable his teammates had, too. After all, why let one live and kill off the others? I was all but certain that the Warden was holding Alice, Despona and Wesley against their will somewhere in the Underground. We just had to know where, so we could break them out.

"Why are our children still here if you have the ability to sneak them out?" Daddy asked. He wasn't letting up. "You got the other boy out with a portal, so use one to rescue ours."

"Carson Forsberg was a lucky opportunity. Doctor Taurus is watching your children at all times, and the United Supernatural Union has their eyes on them as well. Attempting to break them out of the Institute would be suicide. There is no rock Doctor Taurus would not overturn to find them," Hemlock said sharply.

King Ethan nodded. "My representative on the Union's council said as much."

"As did ours," Nadine added.

"As contradictory as it sounds, inside the Institute's walls is the safest place for all of them, even if they are under Doctor Taurus' thumb," Hemlock said. "If they were to escape the Institute, a manhunt would begin for them immediately, and there's no telling if all of them would survive the chase— or how many people they'd hurt in the attempt to get away."

Daddy let out an annoyed sound. "My Ava-Marie wouldn't hurt anyone."

"You believe she's incapable of great violence?" Hemlock raged. "Sir, I don't think you properly understand what you're *dealing with*."

Hemlock switched on the projector. Onscreen came a video of a busy town street. I recognized it as Octavia Falls, the witch city. The video was some sort of surveillance footage outside a shop. There were people all around Main Street. I'd never been there, but I knew enough about it to be sure that's what I was looking at.

Marcus let out a winded gasp and covered his eyes. Below us, Lucas turned his head away, but Nadine kept her eyes fixed on the screen... as if this had been the worst day of her life, and she still remembered every second.

"What's going on?" Charlie asked lowly. There was no sound, so he couldn't determine what was happening.

I didn't want to say anything out loud and trigger Marcus, so I thought, *It's a video of what Marcus did.*

Charlie got the message. He remained still beside me as I watched the reel play.

I spotted Marcus immediately. He was standing by a fountain, arguing with a blonde girl. Ancestors, that *had* to be Anya.

Marcus appeared angrier than I'd ever seen him. He went to turn away, but Anya grabbed his shoulders and spun him around. She shoved him backward, and said something harsh— I wasn't sure what it was, but it *definitely* got to Marcus, because he fisted his hands in his hair and screamed something back at her.

If it was anyone else, people would've just heard him shouting across the street. It would've been normal— a teenage couple's argument.

But it was Marcus. And he'd lost control. The camera shook as an explosion rocked the streets. Dust scattered upward, and debris cracked the screen of the camera.

Kallie was transfixed by the video, unable to look away from its horror. She put a hand over her mouth, stifling small sounds that broke from her throat.

When the smoke cleared, terror suffocated my lungs. Marcus had made a fucking crater in the street. The people standing around him were left in pieces. The fountain he'd been by was demolished, and water spurted everywhere. I tried not to gag as I observed the mangled bodies, the limbs missing torsos. On screen, Marcus let out a carnal scream that I couldn't hear, but that I *felt*. He ran throughout the streets, falling to his knees as he crawled through pools of blood. I could tell he was looking for Anya.

He wouldn't find her. There wasn't anything *left* to find.

Marcus had been open about the destruction of his crime, but I didn't really get it. Not until I saw it for myself.

Ancestors, how had he kept his sanity after all that? I couldn't imagine the type of pain he went through, dealing with the guilt day in and day out.

Hemlock spoke as the footage continued to play. Marcus continued to panic in the video while chaos rattled the streets of Octavia Falls. "Out of the four, Marcus is the meekest. He is the kindest, the least apt to anger, and he *still* managed to slaughter eleven people in one blow, in the blink of an eye." Hemlock snapped her fingers briskly. "One second of lost control. That's all it took for him. Can you imagine if Kallie were to lose her temper in such a way, or gods forbid, *Ava?* Those girls could level whole cities."

"Our children are not monsters to be contained and exterminated!" Queen Emmaline shouted. Her cheeks turned red with anger.

"Continuing to pretend they're harmless is ignorance!" Hemlock waved her hand at the screen, her voice rising in intensity. "As their parents, you fail to admit the obvious. These individuals are *dangerous*. I care about your children, I really do, but I have an obligation to protect the supernatural world. Even if it is from them. You're holding a bomb in your hands that could go off at any moment, all of you. And if you're not committed to learning how to contain it, then you're playing with fire."

Hemlock switched off the screen, and the horrible images went away. "You love your children, but they are weapons. This, you have to admit. And because they are weapons, there are people out there who will do whatever they can to use them."

Nadine and Lucas were extremely quiet. What could they say, really? They'd experienced the true devastation of Marcus' powers firsthand.

"So what can we do?" Daddy sounded so skeptical— like he didn't want to admit that I could possibly do the same thing Marcus had, even though I knew in my heart I could... and so much worse.

"All of you are voices of reason within your nations, and many of you are in places of power," Hemlock said. "You must use your power to stop Doctor Taurus at whatever cost, whatever he may be planning."

"You're asking us to incite a war," King Ethan stated.

"We are asking you to *stave off* war for as long as you can," Takahashi replied. "At least until the children are ready to fight."

"We need to make an alliance outside of Union control," Hemlock insisted. "The six of you need to agree to fight together. The Arcanea, the Hawkei, and the Miriamic Coven together would be a formidable force. It would at least cause Doctor Taurus to pause."

"It's not going to make him stop what he's doing," Daddy scoffed.

"No," Hemlock agreed. "But it will buy us some time so your children can graduate from the Institute. Then we can get them away from here once they do."

"That's over two years away. I'm not convinced he'll hold off that long," King Ethan said.

"We have no choice. The vampires and the angels are already making plans together after your treaty with them failed to go through last spring," Hemlock stated. "They're looking for more allies. Don't give them any options. If their forces remain small, they won't provoke the other races, and we can maintain some semblance of peace."

"The fae won't side with them. My son has already decided that," Ethan said. "We fought alongside them in the last war, but we won't do it again. That should be enough to make them pause."

"For how long?" Daddy's tone was harsh as he spat, "I regret sending my daughter here in the first place."

"So do I," King Ethan growled. "This was a mistake."

"With all due respect, Chief Mitoh, Ava would've ended up here one way or another. Her behavioral problems and— dare I say— addiction to causing trouble would've had the Hawkei court system sentencing her here eventually," Hemlock stated. "And my king, I beg you not to be offended when I say that the only other penalty Kalina would've received for her crimes was the noose, and you would've not executed your daughter."

"Marcus had to go here," Nadine said quietly. "The coven was calling for his head the moment he killed all those people, accident or not. I was worried the Burning Times were going to start all over again. Sending him to the Institute was the only way to keep him safe from the coven."

"And poor Charlie." Mama shook his head.

Hemlock sighed. "You understand my sentiments. This place saved him. As inept as this institution can be, the streets would've killed him. He didn't know any other way to live until he came here. So let's not deceive ourselves and think that this situation could've been avoided. They're here now, and damage control is the best we can do."

"What is this *really* about?" Daddy leaned against the table. "You didn't call us here to demand we unite. We would've done that anyway, to protect our children. What's the real fucking punchline?"

Hemlock glanced warily at Takahashi. The old counselor took a short breath as he removed his glasses and said, "Over the past seven months, I've taken a sabbatical from the Institute to investigate what's truly at stake."

"And what did you find?" Queen Emmaline asked.

"I began with Charlie's prophecy," Takahashi stated. "He is destined to lead the Elves to the Blessed Haven, their true home in the afterlife. It is his mission to unite the keys that open the Elven gate on Darke Island, so that the Elves may find a true home there. However, there are... consequences if he doesn't complete his mission."

"What kind of consequences?" Mama asked.

"The keys were lost centuries ago when they were stolen by the Unseelie fae, and after that, no one quite knows what happened to them. From what we can tell, the Elves who have died since the gate was closed are caught in a sort of in-between place between Earth and the afterlife," Takahashi said. "If those keys are not found and the gate to the Blessed Haven is not open, no Elf will ever enter the Blessed Haven. Their souls will be trapped forever in limbo, unable to rest in peace or reincarnate into new lives."

Charlie let out a choked noise beside me, and I felt my blood turn to ice.

"Are you telling me that the Elves that have died are *stuck*?" Queen Emmaline questioned.

"It's worse than that," Takahashi said. "The Elves were the first supernaturals, and therefore, each magical race shares a connection with them. Souls that aren't inherently Elven continue to pass back and forth from Earth to the afterlife, but it is a temporary state. If the Elves are not restored to the Blessed Haven, and their race dies out before the gate is opened, then *all* supernaturals will face the same fate of becoming bound to this in-between. Souls are energy. They cannot be destroyed, but neither will they be able to venture on to other spiritual planes of existence, or reincarnate into this one. After an eternity's passing, there's a worry that these souls will cease to exist at all."

"What about the gods?" Queen Emmaline insisted. "Surely they can do something."

"This is a great fight between the gods," Takahashi said. "The dark gods that populate the Eternal Torment— hell, as you all know it— don't wish for the gate to be opened. If souls are unable to journey to the Blessed Haven, they are able to be harvested. If a soul has a choice of being imprisoned in this in-between forever or servicing a dark god in hell, there are some who would take hell, and every soul that joins itself to dark forces increases hell's power."

"It can't end there. Ava's prophecy determines that she will be the one to decide what will happen to all magic. What does that mean?" Daddy asked.

"Our magic comes from spiritual sources— our gods, our connection to the afterlife, the Familiars that incarnate as our souls," Takahashi said. "If our connection to the Blessed Haven and our gods are lost, it would be a cataclysmic situation. There's no telling who would retain power over their magic, and who would not, who would survive and who would immediately perish."

"It's a similar situation to my wife's quest that we faced twenty years ago, but on a much grander scale," Ethan said.

"Yes. It's assumed that those who have sworn themselves to dark gods or who are channeling their power from the Eternal Torment would remain alive and in control of their magic," Takahashi said. "Which is exactly what we don't want."

"That's where Ava comes in," Hemlock said. "Whoever she decides to help, heaven or hell, will win. She will choose who keeps their magic and who does not."

I scoffed. I wouldn't choose to help out the dark gods. No fucking way.

"Why would the gods, ancestors, or anyone else choose Ava and put such a huge responsibility on her shoulders?" Daddy demanded. "This is a choice for a god to make, not a young girl."

"We don't know why, only that she was chosen," Takahashi said. "All of you sitting here have prophecies made about you that you fulfilled, and you did not understand the reasons you were picked until you completed your tasks. There's no reason to assume it'll be different for Ava, or for Charlie. All will unveil itself with the passage of time."

"And what does the Warden have to do with all of this?" Nadine asked. "Surely he has some idea this is all going on, and has a plan to work it to his advantage."

"That, we are unsure of," Takahashi replied. "But whatever he has in mind, we can be certain it isn't good, and that he needs a demigod to do it. He wouldn't be interested in your children otherwise."

"But he knows Ava is the key. That's why he's obsessed with her," Mama said.

"He most likely suspects, due to the wording of her prophecy, which he acquired through her phone conversations with her aunt. He knows she'll make the final decision on who wins, which is why he's so keen on bringing her under his control, if he can't sway her to his side," Takahashi confirmed.

There was a terrible bout of silence below us, one that was broken by the sound of Charlie's thoughts rattling inside my mind.

This is why your prophecy says that I'm meant to stop you, Charlie realized. *If you side with the Warden, you'll stop the Elves from going to the Blessed Haven.*

I would never do that, I insisted. *There isn't a force in heaven or hell that'll make me join him. You know how much I hate him.*

It didn't make any sense. The Warden was my worst enemy. I'd *never* help him. Why was it even a concern?

The quiet was shattered when Daddy said, "Well, to hell with the rest of you. I'm getting my daughter out of here, one way or another."

"I beg your pardon, but *your* child is the most dangerous out of all of them," Queen Emmaline spat. "She's the one who will choose what will happen to our magic, and forgive me when I say her track record isn't the best when it comes to making good decisions."

Daddy gave a cruel laugh. "Ava's never killed anyone. Your child is an *assassin.* She deserves to be here, and in my opinion, so do the boys. If they're such a danger to society, they should have life sentences at the adult penitentiary, not be allowed to roam free after graduation!"

"Don't talk about my son that way," Nadine threatened.

"Liam, that's enough. This is embarrassing," Mama hissed.

But his comments had gotten to Kallie's dad, because he shot to his feet. "Do you think *you* can make decisions about *my* daughter's future?" King Ethan roared. "I am a king!"

"And I am a chief!" Daddy's chair tipped backward onto the floor as he rapidly got to his feet.

King Ethan exploded into a massive white wolf with huge wings. He snarled and displayed his teeth, swinging his head back and forth as he pounced over the table and flew toward my dad. I gasped, but Daddy uncapped the water canister at his side. He fashioned it into a whip, which he smacked across the king's face. King Ethan went flying backward, and his massive weight broke the table as he landed on it. The wolf rolled back onto his feet, charging at Daddy once more.

Next thing I knew, water balls were flying everywhere. King Ethan prowled around my dad in a circle, snarling and swiping out his paws in order to knock my dad off his feet while Daddy kept him at bay with Water magic. They hadn't hurt each other yet, but they would.

I was ready to step in, but Charlie grabbed my shoulder firmly, to tell me to hold back.

"Gentlemen, please!" Hemlock shrieked, covering her head from a jet of icicles that cut off a chunk of her bun.

I couldn't believe our fathers were fighting like this. It was nuts. I nearly let out a scream when King Ethan reared on his back paws, preparing to crush Daddy underneath him, but a great magical shield welled up between the two of them and pushed them apart. The explosion sent Daddy flying against the wall, while King Ethan went rolling in the other direction.

I looked to the side. Lucas had cast the shield to split them apart. I could see the remnants of magic flickering at the end of his wand, which he'd pulled out of his jacket at the last moment.

"Break it up," Lucas said roughly, stomping toward them. His wand was at the ready, if either of them made another move.

The shield had hit the king so hard that it'd forced him back into his human body. He staggered to his feet and balled his hands into fists so he could duke it out with my dad hand-to-hand, but Lucas put a hand on his shoulder and held him back.

"You still owe me. Back down," Lucas said firmly. "Now's not the time to let our emotions get in the way."

The king backed off. Hm. Must've been one big favor the king owed Lucas.

Queen Emmaline stomped between my dad and King Ethan like a raging bull. "Would you two stop comparing dick sizes for *two* seconds so we can figure out how the hell we can help our children?"

"Go Mom," Kallie whispered beside me. Below us, her father scowled.

"Yes," Mama said, and her look was just as fiery. "Obviously, both of you are so used to being in charge that neither of you can put your egos aside for a moment, even for the sake of our daughters. If we're going to solve anything, we need to work together."

"But—" Daddy stammered.

"Liam, *sit down*," Mama barked.

The queen turned her blazing gaze on King Ethan, and I swear, he shrank an inch. Both my father and Kallie's dragged their feet back to their seats, acting like sad puppies who'd just been yelled at.

"By the gods, at least your wives have some sense," Hemlock grumbled as she fixed her hair. "May we *please* get back to the task at hand?"

"Emotions are high right now," Takahashi said, taking the counselor's role. "It's understandable, given the situation is upsetting, but there is a solution."

"Rishi," I heard Marcus hiss. He was floundering, trying to hold on to his cat. Rishi was clawing out of his arms, squirming to get away.

"Marcus, I swear to the gods—" Kallie growled.

Rishi bit Marcus' hand, and he gasped. "Ouch!" Marcus yelped, and he did it— he fucking dropped him.

That wasn't the worst part— Marcus lost his balance and went tumbling off the beam, screaming as he went. The illusion magic concealing us instantly broke as he and Rishi fell toward the table below. All the adults looked up, mouths dropping open as they watched Marcus careen downward.

I closed my eyes and looked away, but I didn't hear any impact. I dared to look down. Both Marcus and Rishi were hovering an inch above the broken table. Charlie had caught them at the last second. Charlie let them drop, and Marcus face-planted against the table.

Rishi ran to Nadine and Lucas. He rubbed his head against their legs, purring. Everyone stared at Marcus for a second, then looked upward at us.

Oh, ancestors, Hemlock looked madder than a twisted dick. "I suggest the rest of you get down here. *Now.*"

None of our parents looked happy. Great. Now we were in trouble.

"*They'll never know we're here,*" Charlie mocked as he floated us down. "Great job, guys."

"*I* didn't blow our cover," Kallie snarled back. She whirled on Charlie, but I got between them.

"You know what? It doesn't matter that we got caught, because we overheard everything we needed to know," I said, turning toward Takahashi. "Why weren't we informed?"

"Because you weren't ready," Takahashi said in a tired voice. "But I suppose there's nothing that can be done now."

"You said you have a plan," I said, and Marcus scrambled off the table to join us. "What is it?"

Takahashi opened his mouth, but Daddy stepped in front of me. "No. No, I don't care what it takes, you're going home, and you're getting away from these people."

"Excuse me?" I shouted. "I get you're overprotective and all, but *these people* are my *friends*, and I'm not leaving them for any reason. Yeah, they're kinda fucked up inside, but so am I. I'd do anything for them, and they'd do the same for me. So if you want to separate us, then good luck trying, because we aren't going anywhere."

Daddy frowned, but Mama came to the rescue. "We'd never split the four of you up. We of all people know how important friendship can be."

Mama shot a sharp look to Daddy, and he looked away guiltily. None of the other parents spoke up; they must've had similar opinions.

"Anyway." I sighed harshly. "So, the Elves are trapped, heaven's in danger and hell's about to take over. What do we do about it?"

"We train you to be ready. I have some understanding of demigod magic," Takahashi suggested. "I could teach you to use and control your powers in an effective way, to avoid another unfortunate situation such as Marcus' in the future, and to be ready to fight the Warden when it's time."

I was already in. We'd been floundering around all semester trying to learn our demigod powers. Takahashi's instruction could be valuable.

"Perfect. Let's get to work straight away," I said.

"I'm afraid that's not possible," Takahashi replied regretfully. "When I applied for my sabbatical, I agreed not to return to my position until the following year. If I return to the Institute now, it'll alert the Warden that I'm up to something. We must keep up the ruse that I'm still traveling. If he knows I'm here, there will be dire consequences."

Kallie's mouth dropped open. "You mean we have to put up with *her* for another semester?"

"Professor Vengier's position as counselor is temporary. She'll be gone by the end of December, and I'll return to campus in January," Takahashi said calmly. "We have to wait until then."

It was only two weeks, but with what was at stake, it seemed so far away.

Lucas put his hand on Marcus' shoulder. "I think all of us would like some time with our kids. This has been a lot to process."

"Agreed," King Ethan said. "Kalina, your mother and I wish to speak with you privately."

"What about?" Kallie's voice cracked.

"It's about you and your brother. Is there somewhere we can go?" her mother asked kindly.

Kallie nodded, but I could tell she was frightened. Whatever they wanted to say was super important.

"You may use my office," Hemlock said. She conjured a door, which materialized in the wall. "Doctor Taurus does not have access to it, and the two of you can leave back to Malovia through a portal there."

"Bye," I whispered as Kallie's parents escorted her out. She gave a short wave, but her complexion was pale. For as brave as she was, this conversation was freaking her out.

"Your family can have this room," Mama said kindly to Nadine. "My husband and I have to visit our son."

"And speak with our oldest," Daddy added grumpily. I wrinkled my nose.

"I will aid Takahashi in getting off campus unseen," Hemlock stated. "This room will remain open until the last person leaves."

She and Takahashi made way for the door, until she turned briskly and stated, "By the way, Ava, if you and your friends eavesdrop on me ever again, you will be extremely sorry. Don't make it a habit."

"Crystal clear, ma'am," I said with a salute.

Charlie nudged me as they walked out. *When are we going to tell your parents about... us?*

We'll take them back to our cell, and I'll break it to them easy, I replied. *Might as well tell them since they're here in person.*

I cleared my throat. "We should go back to my cell. Nobody will overhear us talk there."

"We?" Daddy said flatly.

"Yes, *we*," I said. No way I was telling them about all this without Charlie. "Let's go."

My parents followed Charlie and me out of the illusion room and back to our cell. Oberi skipped ahead of us, holding his tail high. I power-walked all the way back, hoping I wouldn't run into anyone who'd spill the beans before I could.

"This doesn't look like the Elementai cellblock," Mama said, looking around.

"They moved us," I stuttered. Shit, I was so nervous. "Almost there..."

"Mister and Mrs. Wahkin!"

My blood completely drained out of my body as I saw Professor Warbright round the corner, holding a file of sheet music and trying to wave us down.

Charlie stumbled, and his face went white. Warbright came bustling toward us. Mama's mouth dropped open slightly. Daddy narrowed his eyes, as if he wasn't sure if he'd heard him right.

Oh, fuck no. I tried to hasten my steps, but for an old chubby guy, Warbright was *fast*. "Mister and Mrs. Wahkin, wait!"

Ancestors, we were so fucking busted. I was forced to turn around and face Warbright as he came to a puffing stop beside us. I plastered on a smile as best I could. "Hello, Professor."

"I haven't seen you two in quite some time! I heard about your wedding!" Warbright beamed. He began vigorously shaking my hand, then Charlie's, as he said, "I want to offer both of you my congratulations on becoming husband and wife. It's always so wonderful when students here at the Institute make a life-long commitment."

I dared to glance over at the corner of my eyes. Mama had gone still with shock.

Daddy— oh ancestors, *Daddy*. I'd never seen him look so stone-cold. His hands shook at his sides as he stared Charlie down, eyes burning like he was imagining strangling him.

Your dad's looking at me, isn't he? Charlie asked across our bond.

Don't make a move. It felt like we were dealing with a wild crocodile and not my father. Thanks, Warbright, for blowing our secret.

Warbright turned toward my family. "Oh, you must be Ava's parents. How lovely. I'm certain you're very proud of your new son-in-law."

"Over the moon," Daddy seethed.

Mama did her best to salvage the situation. "We're happy to welcome Charlie to the family. If you don't mind, we were actually—"

"Oh, of course," Warbright said cheerily. "Important to get to know your relatives and all. Don't let me hold you up. Congratulations again, you little lovebirds!"

Warbright waddled away. *Awkward,* Oberi peeped, glancing between us.

Daddy sputtered. His face got red as he shouted, "What in the name of the ancestors is going on?!"

"Not here," I said through clenched teeth. I rounded on my heel and continued in the direction of our cell. Charlie stayed at my side, though Daddy didn't take his glare off of him for one second. I planted myself between the two of them, in case Daddy got any bright ideas to start swinging.

Once we were all inside our little apartment, I shut the door and let out a quick breath. "It's not what it looks like."

"But it is," Charlie added.

"And it's not," I finished. "It's... complicated."

"Exactly how long has this been going on?" Daddy yelled. "And why weren't we informed?"

"Lower your voice and give her a chance to tell us the truth," Mama scolded.

At least Mama was open to the idea. I braced myself and said, "We got married in October."

"Two months ago?!" Daddy yelped.

"I didn't say anything because I wanted to tell you in person," I begged. "I swear I was going to tell you guys everything over Christmas, when I got home. And... I kind of hoped you'd pay for Charlie to come back with me, because we're married now."

Daddy scowled. Mama pursed her lips.

"Honey, you can understand why we're confused," Mama said slowly. "The last thing we knew, you and Charlie were broken up. Now you're married. We don't understand what could've made you take such a big step."

"Were you coerced?" Daddy demanded. "Did *he* force you to do this?"

"Are you kidding me? You'd think I'd do that to her?" Charlie shouted. His rage exploded across our bond, and he took a few steps forward.

For fuck's sake, now *Charlie* was the one who was going to toss punches. The last thing I wanted— or needed— was my husband and father getting into a brawl, and that thought pushed me over the edge.

"Everybody needs to stop!" I said, and I put my hands over my ears. "You guys are gonna push me into a panic attack, and that's just going to make everything worse, so give me a minute to catch my breath!"

That made everyone pause. No one in this room liked it when I fell apart. It had devastating consequences for everybody.

"Let's sit down," Mama suggested, and she guided Daddy to the couch. Oberi hopped between them, and put his drooling mouth on Daddy's lap. Daddy frowned, but patted Oberi's head.

"Geez," I mumbled. I was burning up in here, so I unzipped my jacket and tossed it on the counter. Daddy's eyes got huge when he read the inscription on my t-shirt, and I looked down. The shirt I'd put on this morning literally said *I'm His Mrs.* and I didn't even realize. Oops.

It didn't help that my notebooks on the floor had *Ava-Marie Wahkin* written all over them in cursive with little tiny hearts everywhere.

And Charlie's prescription for birth control was still on the counter.

Fuck.

Charlie remained standing, leaning against the wall. He didn't like sitting when situations were this precarious.

I sighed and took a seat in the crappy armchair across from the couch. "The Warden was blood testing people for Elven ancestry, and sending the people who tested positive to the Underground. We tried to avoid the test as long as we could, but Charlie had to take it eventually. The Warden was going to send him to the Underground unless we stopped it. Marcus found a loophole— that married inmates at the Institute can't be separated. I'm the daughter of a chieftain, so if I married Charlie and the Warden kidnapped him to the Underground—"

"I'd have to declare war against the angels, as that would be an attack against a family member of mine," Daddy said, voice lightening with clarity.

"Exactly," I said. "We did the paperwork and the ceremony as quickly as we could. I had to marry him, to save Charlie's life."

"So this is all just one big misunderstanding," Daddy said in relief. "Once all this Elf business is taken care of, you can annul the marriage, and everything will go back to what it was."

Charlie was really getting irritated. He couldn't hold back his emotions through our bond even if he tried. I had to make this clear.

"Well, no," I said. "We got married to save Charlie from the Underground, but this is a *real* marriage. We realized we're important to each other, and we're in love. So we're going to stay together."

Daddy scoffed. "This is ridiculous. You're too young to be married."

"Bull crap! Mama was the same age as me when she married you!" I pointed out.

"That's different," Daddy stammered.

"How? By the ancestors, she was already pregnant with me by then. It's not like I'm carrying a kid around."

"Well—" Daddy grumbled.

Mama's voice was nervous as she asked, "Sweetie, don't take this the wrong way, but... you weren't cycling when you made this decision, were you?"

"Absolutely not. Hemlock was the one who married us. She wouldn't have done so if she thought I was in a manic state," I insisted. "I married Charlie of my own free will, because I wanted to."

Mama nodded. She believed me. "You have the authority to make your own decisions about your life." Mama leaned forward and grabbed my hand. "If this is what you want, we're behind you."

"Are you?" Charlie asked scathingly. "Are you really prepared to accept *me*?"

"Depends on your intentions," Daddy said before Mama could speak up.

"I know I'm not the best choice for your daughter," Charlie stated.

"I'm a convicted criminal, and I've done a hell of a lot more bad in my life than good. But the one thing I've done right is this marriage. I love my wife. And if you accept me or not, fine. Nothing's going to convince me to walk away. I don't need to earn the approval of anyone else, because I have her. And her happiness is what's important to me."

Oberi let out a loud whine and blinked at my parents with big black pupils. My dad looked totally guilty. *Good job, Oberi, laying on the puppy eyes.*

"You don't have to earn our approval," Mama said. "Family means everything to us. You know that, because you know Ava. Liam and I would never do anything to push our daughter away, and if she's married to you, then we'll consider you our son. There's nothing else you need to do to prove yourself to us."

Charlie relaxed a little. He wouldn't let himself believe Mama's words. But he wanted to, I could tell.

"The bottom line is, I love Charlie. He's my husband now, so he comes first," I stated. "And an annulment is out of the question, because we've already consummated the marriage, and we can't take that back."

Charlie moaned and slapped a hand to his face. He might think it was weird that I'd told my parents we'd had sex, but I didn't. They needed to know I was serious about him.

Daddy didn't look thrilled, but Mama gave me an encouraging smile. "You know your father and I are always ready to make our family bigger. There's plenty of love to go around, especially for you and Charlie."

I gave Daddy a pleading look, and he finally cracked. "If this is what you want, I'll accept it," Daddy finally said. "If my baby's happy, I'm happy."

"Thank you guys so much." I leaned in to give both of them a hug. "You have no idea how important this is to me."

"We might have an idea," Mama said with a twinkle in her eye. "Your father and I had quite the battle convincing our tribe that we should be together. I never wanted my children to have to fight for the right to be in love. And I always thought there was something special between you and Charlie from the beginning."

"I love you, Mama." I kissed her cheek, then pulled away. Daddy had become really quiet. I wished I could read his mind right now, because his expression puzzled me.

"We want what's best for you, and that includes a happy marriage," Mama said, stroking my hair back.

"As long as you're being safe," Daddy added.

"We are," I promised. "I wanted to be extra careful, after what happened with—"

I abruptly cut off when I realized what I was about to confess.

"What are you talking about, sweetie?" Mama's brow furrowed.

I bit my lip. The anticipation of diving off a cliff filled me, and I knew once I spoke up, there'd be no turning back.

Do you want to tell them? Charlie asked the question gently against my mind.

I think it's time. I was tired of hiding my past from everyone. It would've scared me to reveal my biggest secret to my parents before. After it'd happened, I'd sworn to myself they'd never know.

But I had Charlie here with me. That made me brave. I wouldn't be able to do this on my own.

"Do you... do you remember when I asked you if I could stay home my senior year?" I started. My throat got tight, and at the same time, my heartbeat raced in my chest.

"Yes. We found it so odd." Mama glanced at Daddy. "You loved school and cheerleading. But we know you missed Monica so much."

"I did, but that's not the only reason," I began. "There was that bonfire after Monica died that I went to. You probably forgot about it."

"I don't think so," Daddy said. "You seemed very upset when you came back home. We just thought you were grieving, so we let you have your space."

"But we knew something was off," Mama said.

So they had noticed something. I wasn't as good at covering shit up as I thought. "I'd just gotten back from the women's shelter."

"Why would you need to go there?" Mama asked.

"Because I had to get a rape kit done."

Ancestors, I'd never felt a silence like that in my life. It invaded my bones and completely ravaged me of any personal space. Mama leaned back against the couch and put a hand over her mouth— like she was fighting to keep her real reaction concealed. Daddy's face had gone completely white. My dad wasn't old, but I worried how this news would affect his health, because the words I'd spoken made him go gaunt.

I almost regretted telling them. They looked so hurt.

Charlie came over. He knelt by the armchair and took my hand. Oberi jumped off the couch to place his head on my lap, giving a tiny whimper.

"Oh, ancestors, Ava, what happened?" Mama had tears in her eyes. She leaned forward and grasped my other hand.

I had to blink rapidly to keep from crying myself. "I... it was John Smith. He got me alone in the woods, where he proceeded to do what he wanted to me. I didn't have my magic yet, so I couldn't fight back."

Mama dropped her head, like she'd been defeated. But where her reaction was subdued, Daddy completely lost it.

Daddy leapt right up. He began pacing around the room, his hands balled into shaking fists as he raged, "How dare that son-of-a-bitch violate *my daughter*! This bastard needs to be prosecuted to the fullest extent of the law! I'll kill him with my bare hands if I have to!"

I winced, and my husband stepped in. *"Please,"* Charlie pleaded. "We need to focus on Ava right now."

Daddy's face fell. Though I could tell it took him a great deal of self-control, he slowly sank back down on the couch, though this time, he was closer to Mama. "Okay. I'm listening."

"I'll never forget the woman at the shelter. Mia was so kind. I was just falling apart, and she was doing everything she could to help me," I blurted. "I was— dirty, and just covered in blood, and she remained so calm. I don't know how she did it."

"It's over now. You don't have to go through that ever again," Charlie said, and he squeezed my fingers.

Mama sharply grasped Daddy's arm. Recognition crossed her features, like she knew Mia's name. I didn't quite get the gesture, but Daddy nodded, telling her he understood.

"After I did the kit, I just... went home. I didn't know what else to do. I didn't say anything, didn't tell anyone." I was speaking too fast, like I had the habit to do. My bipolar was beginning to flare. I hoped they could understand what I was saying. "I think Josee guessed, and when Uncle Jonah visited a couple weeks ago, he told me he'd figured it out, but didn't say anything because he wanted me to be ready to talk..."

I gave a loud sniff. "I didn't say a word about it for two long years. It was like if I acted like it didn't happen, it'd go away. But it didn't. Then I got so close to Charlie so quickly, and he was the first person I told..." I wiped at my face.

"I'm glad you did, pidge. It helped you heal," Charlie said, and he rubbed my back with his free hand.

"It did." Ancestors, I couldn't keep the tears down now. They were overwhelming me. "After I said something to him about it, I felt like I had to tell my friends, then I really wanted to tell Ez—"

"Oh, ancestors. Ez." Daddy ran a hand through his hair. He looked *horrified*.

"He was just defending me," I told them. "Once Ez found out about the— the rape— he couldn't let John get away with what he'd done. But I still feel so bad about it, because he's at the Institute now."

"I shouldn't have been so hard on him," Daddy said quietly. "It's my fault he doesn't want to speak to me."

Mama had pressed a hand over her lips again. I wondered if she was trying to keep in a scream.

"You shouldn't feel bad about Ez coming to the Institute, pidge," Charlie said softly. "He just told me the other day he loves it here. Yeah, it's a prison, and it's kind of a shithole, but he wouldn't have met Opal if he hadn't come here, and the classes are better tailored to his magical skill level. He's happy."

"I guess so." I didn't know how anyone could be happy at the Institute... then again, I was happy here, and so was Charlie, so was it really that incredible that Ez was, too?

"But why'd you feel like you had to keep it a secret?" Daddy asked softly. "You could've told us."

"Because I was ashamed. I didn't want anyone to know, and who would believe me, anyway?" I asked. "I have a terrible criminal record. Everyone would just assume that I'm lying."

"But you have evidence," Mama insisted. "The kit—"

"Big deal." I gave a teary laugh that had no humor in it. "I'm already the laughingstock of the tribe. No matter how much evidence I have, I'm a criminal, so people will think that I deserved what I got. Worse, they'll say it was consensual, and that I waited so long to come forward proves it. There's no justice for me."

I dropped my head. "Besides. I'm the daughter of a chieftain. Stuff like this isn't supposed to happen to us."

"You didn't want to tell us because you were worried I'd lose my *job*?" Daddy's voice was aghast.

"Well, yes," I admitted.

"You could've come to us. We are always here for whatever you need," Mama insisted.

"You were the hardest people *to* tell. I respect you both so much, and I love you. I didn't want this to cause you any pain. Daddy had so many health issues the year before, and I didn't want him to be in the hospital again—"

"Don't worry about me." Daddy knelt in front of my chair. "I can handle scrutiny at work, and I've been dealing with my illness for years, but I will make any sacrifice to be sure you get whatever you need."

"I'm so sorry. I was so mean to you after it happened. I just didn't know what to do with my feelings," I sobbed.

"Don't worry about it," Daddy insisted. "You don't have to ask forgiveness for anything."

My tears finally dried. "At least you guys know now, and I don't have to hide it anymore."

"I'm sorry you went through such a terrible thing," Mama said gently. "We know it'll take time to heal, but we are here to help you through it, no matter what."

I had such great parents. I knew they'd stand by me. If I hadn't been so concerned about protecting them, I would've said something sooner.

"I just want you to know that you have options," Daddy said. "If you want to prosecute, you can."

"No," I said immediately. "He can't come to the Institute. I don't want him near me."

"Hell, send him here," Charlie said darkly. "He'll need a body bag when I get done with him. Problem solved."

"John won't be sent to the Institute," Mama said quickly. "His crime was an offense against another Hawkei, which means it'll be handled within the tribal system, and if convicted, he'll be sent to the Elementai prison on tribal land."

"Oh, he'll get convicted, all right," Daddy growled.

"But wasn't Ez's crime the same?" I asked.

"Your father had some pull with Ez. Your brother was to be put on trial and sent to the Elementai prison, but he convinced the other chieftains to send Ez to the Institute, as a favor to him and so he could be closer to you," Mama explained.

"And this bastard won't be so lucky," Daddy seethed. "He's going straight to the Hawkei penitentiary."

"It's Ava's choice," Charlie said firmly. "This has to be what she wants to do."

I remained quiet, pondering the possibility. I really wanted John to pay for what he'd done, and I thought the women of the world would be safer if he was behind bars, where he belonged.

At the same time, I didn't know if I could endure the humiliation of going through a trial if he ended up walking free.

"I need to think about it," I said. "I'm not ready yet."

"If you change your mind, I can fill out the paperwork at any time," Daddy promised. "It'll be a pleasure to prosecute this degenerate."

"Daddy, you can't do anything to go after him, even on your own," I said. "It needs to be my decision."

"Of course, peanut." Daddy leaned in to give me a tight hug. "I'll always do what's best for you."

Mama wiped her face before she cleared her throat. "Thank you, Charlie. For protecting her."

"Always. It's my purpose," he responded.

"How long are you guys staying?" I asked. I'd love it if my parents could visit again, even just for a little bit.

"We'll be here until the middle of the week. The Institute doctors wanted to go over a better treatment plan for Ez, and they thought it was best if we came here to discuss it," Mama said. "But we can't stay long, unfortunately. We're needed back in Kinpago."

"What's going on?" It sounded intense.

"We might as well tell you," Mama said. "You remember before you were sentenced to the Institute that your father and I kept getting called in for emergency council meetings."

"I figured you guys were trying to hide something," I said.

"We didn't want to worry you unless things were getting serious, but it looks like they are," Mama said. "Tensions are high in the supernatural world. The magical races are starting to make threats against each other."

"Threats?" Charlie asked.

"Potential declarations of war," Daddy clarified. "Nobody's been brave enough to pull the trigger yet, but things are getting heated. The other Hawkei chieftains want us to launch an offensive attack against the angels and vampires, before they attack us."

"Even Chieftess Vanessa?" I asked in surprise.

"Vanessa is a good person, and a great chieftess, but in times of war, the Fire tribe has always struck first," Mama said. "The other chieftains want the Elementai to get involved before an attack is launched, instead of attempting to stay out of it like we did last time. Your father and the Anichi tribe are the only Houses pushing to hold back."

There were five elemental Houses, for each of the five elements. I couldn't believe almost all of them wanted to go to war. The Hawkei didn't fight other supernatural races unless we were provoked.

But maybe they thought by striking first, they could save the lives of our own.

"Is there anything we can do?" I asked.

"You worry about your mental health and your prophecy. We can handle politics back in the tribe," Mama promised. "It'll be all right."

"And we want *both* of you home for Christmas," Daddy said. "I'll pay off the school. My son-in-law can't sit in a cold cell alone over the holidays."

Charlie looked like someone had knocked him upside the head. A huge smile brightened my face as I said, "Thanks, Daddy."

Mama stood up. "We're already late to see your brother. I hope he doesn't think we forgot about him."

"He's not the best keeper of time, anyway," I said with a laugh. "He might've forgotten."

Daddy frowned. He wasn't sure. This was the first time in nearly a year that he and my brother would be face-to-face, and they hadn't done anything but fight in between. I hoped everything went well.

We said goodbye to my parents. A huge weight fell off my shoulders as they left the room, and Oberi let out a snuff. *Well, the news about the wedding went better than expected.*

"I seriously thought I was gonna have to fist-fight your dad. I didn't know how I was going to do that without hurting him," Charlie said in a rush.

"Now he wants you to come over for the holidays. It's so weird." I giggled.

I can't wait! A whole Christmas ham for me! Oberi cheered.

"It *was* weird." Charlie's expression fell, and he reached out to grab my elbows. "I'm proud of you for telling them. I knew it was hard."

"It was, but keeping it a secret was harder," I replied. "Now I'm one step closer to recovering."

Charlie frowned. "When are we going to talk to Marcus and Kallie about the whole war thing?"

"Let's just wait until tomorrow." I shrugged. "Who knows how long their parents will keep them."

Charlie and I tried to relax the rest of the evening, then went looking for our friends the next morning. It was Sunday, so everyone was sleeping in, and the prison was pretty deserted.

We found Marcus and Kallie sitting on the bleachers in the empty prison yard. My stomach dropped when I realized that Kallie was curled up against Marcus, who had his arm around her.

Kallie was *crying*. Shit. What had happened? She never cried.

"Kallie!" I called out. She spotted us out of the corner of her eye and turned into Marcus' chest.

"What's going on?" I sat on the other side of her, and Charlie took a seat beside Marcus.

"Is it about your brother?" Charlie asked.

"Kind of, but I don't want to talk about it." Kallie sniffed.

"Is he okay?" I asked.

"He's fine. It's just... too much to understand." She hung her head.

Whatever they had told her must've shattered her world. Marcus said nothing, but he knew. His eyes were dark. He failed to elaborate as Kallie continued to squeeze his middle.

"Is there anything we can do?" Charlie asked.

"I just need some time to process." Kallie pulled away from Marcus and wiped at her eyes. "I'll tell you guys when I'm ready, I promise."

"Okay," I said. "We're here to help if you need us."

"I know." Kallie sniffed. She took a short sigh and said, "But we should talk about end-of-the-world stuff. My dad said things in Malovia are getting bad. It's a terrible time. They're still in the process of transitioning the crown from my parents to my brother and his mate. Kaz has got to deal with all this, and he hasn't even been on the throne a year."

"Ava's parents said the Hawkei chieftains are getting ready for war, too," Charlie said quietly.

At the base of the benches, Oberi sniffed a patch of large brown mushrooms. He licked his lips, which were drooling.

"Oberi, don't eat that," I scolded.

I didn't have breakfast, Oberi complained. *I'm hungry.*

I rolled my eyes. Oberi leaned down to lap the mushrooms up, taking down a giant one in a second.

Marcus shivered against the cold and rubbed his hands together. "Do you guys really think there's gonna be another war?"

An expanding tightness entered my chest— like I was having trouble breathing. I rubbed my throat as I added, "History is bound to repeat itself—"

"Oberi!" Charlie shouted as a coughing sound filled the air, and I looked down. Terror flooded my limbs as I watched Oberi stagger back and forth, gasping for breath.

The tightness in my chest suddenly became clear. That wasn't *me*, it was Oberi!

"Oh, ancestors!" Charlie and I both scrambled off the bench at the same time. We fell to our knees on the muddy ground. Oberi hacked as foam spittled at his mouth and dripped onto the ground. I watched his tongue turn blue as it lolled out of his mouth, the light slowly draining from his eyes.

"The mushrooms were poisonous!" I screamed.

"He's suffocating! Ava, we need a potion!" Charlie shouted.

I didn't even know the type of mushrooms he'd eaten. I could whip up an antidote in less than an hour— but it was already too late.

Oh, shit, Oberi gasped. *I guess I'll die.*

Oberi dropped to the ground. His paws convulsed for a second or two, and his body shook with tremors before going still completely. Oberi let out one last breath, and it whooshed out of his body as his lungs ceased to expand and his sight became distant.

I felt my connection to Oberi rip and tear. The effect was more painful than a dagger to the heart. The piece of Oberi that bound itself to me withered away, a fading beacon in a cold, dark world.

I struggled to hold on to my sense of self as everything I'd ever cared about— everything that had meant anything at all— turned into a bleak nothingness. I ceased to know who I was, to feel the ground, or even the heartbeat inside my own chest. My breaths became shallow, each inhale a stabbing blade that carved out my lungs. An effect like a cursed spell froze my organs, turning them to chilling stone. All I felt was a floating sensation that told me my Familiar was gone.

Without Oberi, I couldn't comprehend why life was worth living anymore. Why did I even bother existing? It's not like I mattered without my soul.

Charlie let out a sob, and tears trickled down my face as I reached out a shaking hand to feel Oberi's pelt. His body was already growing stiff and cold. I shook him, but the Familiar gave no sign of life. He had no pulse. The edge of our bond that connected to Oberi was lifeless, and his magic didn't respond when my own pushed against it.

I let out a shuddering wail. Our Familiar was gone.

Oberi was dead.

Everything had happened so fast that it felt like a dream. One second Oberi was beside us, and the next he was gone. I lost all feeling in my limbs as I shook his lifeless form. A weight crashed down on my lungs, and even with my Air magic, I couldn't be bothered to breathe. It was like I'd forgotten how.

This couldn't be happening. It had to be some sort of illusion. But I felt it through our bond, and I knew what had happened for sure.

Oberi had died.

No. I refused to believe it. This wasn't real.

"Charlie, do something!" Ava demanded. "Get these mushrooms out of Oberi! You have Earth magic."

"They're not plants, pidge," I snapped. "I can't control fungi any more than I can control animals."

"We have to do something!" Ava cried.

Fuck, we were both paralyzed. Our grief was so tremendous that it made us completely worthless to even try and reverse Oberi's fate.

Marcus leapt up from his seat. "We'll find Professor Woolly. He's an expert on mushrooms. He must know how to fix this."

Marcus was trying to give us hope, but I knew it was already too late. Kallie and Marcus' footsteps scrambled across the prison yard. Rishi meowed and raced behind them.

My hands trembled as I pulled Oberi into my lap. Tears streamed down my cheeks, and I pressed my face into his fur. Gently, Ava reached out for him. Her fingers brushed against my arm as she stroked his fur.

"He— he can't be..." Her tone wavered.

All the horror I felt twisting in my gut was amplified by her emotions. I felt them surge through me, then just wither away. Ava's connection to me faded, like a candle flame burning out.

This was worse than when we'd tore our bond apart when we broke up. Back then, I could still feel the edges of our soul reaching out for one another. Now... there was nothing. Without Oberi connecting us, the bond tying me to her was gone.

It was as if the earth had dropped out from beneath us, and the air had swept away. I was spinning through an empty vacuum, in a place where time didn't exist. Everything I knew to be true seemed to vanish in the blink of an eye, and all time and space lost its meaning. I forgot my name, or what I was even doing here.

The place in my heart where my soul should've been became empty and hollow. The chasm that opened inside of me was worse than any loneliness I'd ever felt, because I didn't even have my own *soul* to keep me company. Terror shook me to the bone.

I put an arm around Ava, just to make sure she was still there. Her presence was the only thing keeping me sane. I pressed my forehead to hers.

"I'm sorry, pidge," I whispered.

She sagged into me, and I placed a kiss on her head. The moment my lips touched her skin, she yanked away from me. "Hang on. If Oberi's dead, why are we still here?"

My stomach sank. I hadn't thought of that. Elementai couldn't survive without our Familiars, as our souls were tied to theirs. "Hell... we're going to die, too, aren't we?" I asked.

"We can't," Ava insisted. "There's a prophecy. We have to survive to fulfill it."

"Prophecies can be changed," I said in a rush, my heart pounding. "If Oberi dies, we die, right? How much time do we have?"

"It's usually fast, within minutes," Ava replied in a panic. "Days, at most... but maybe it'll be different with us, because we share a soul, too."

We wouldn't survive it. I already knew that. Our souls had become untethered the moment Oberi died.

We didn't have time to contemplate this. We could follow Oberi to the Ancestral Land within moments. There wasn't even time to grieve.

I took Ava's hand in mine. "Listen to me. There's an afterlife, right? So we just have to find each other there. I'll walk through hell and back to find you. I'll—"

How sweet. Oberi's thoughts cut through my mind. He stirred in my arms. Something twinged in my chest, rushing in to fill the emptiness that had been there moments before.

"Oberi!" Ava squealed.

Energy surged through our bond, and I didn't think I'd ever felt so *alive.* Air returned to my lungs, and I felt the solid ground beneath me. For a moment, Oberi's connection to us had been severed, but now it was back, stronger than ever.

I'd lost myself along with him in those few devastating moments, but when he returned, it was like I'd returned *with* him. It felt like rediscovering my identity and purpose all over again. The knowledge that I was Charlie Wahkin, heir to the Elven throne, husband to Ava-Marie, and demigod, flooded through me like my identity and soul were the one thing keeping me tethered to reality so I didn't lose my mind.

I gaped as Oberi pulled away from me. I heard him shake out his fur.

Welp, I'm never doing that again, he said, like this whole thing had been nothing more than a minor inconvenience.

"Oberi, what the hell?!" I demanded.

"What just happened?" Ava added.

I ate a mushroom, he stated flatly.

"We *know* that," I growled.

Oberi sniffed the air, as if looking for something else to eat. It was pissing me off how nonchalant he was being. He'd just *died,* and he didn't give a flying fuck!

It was quite the trip. He gave a bark, like it was some hilarious joke.

"How the hell did you come back?" I asked.

Ava spoke at the same time. "Did you go to the other side? What did you see there?"

Oberi continued sniffing. *Oh, gods, these mushrooms still smell amazing!*

Ava and I lunged for him at the same time. We grabbed him by the scruff and dragged him away from the mushroom patch. We weren't risking *that* again.

"Oberi!" Ava cried. "Get away from those mushrooms. Are you trying to kill yourself for the second time today?"

"You're going to tell us exactly what's going on," I ordered.

I don't really know, he admitted nonchalantly.

"Bullshit!" Ava said. "Don't give us that look."

"What look?" I asked her.

"He's flattening his ears to his head and looking at me with big eyes." She sighed. "It's not going to work, Oberi. You know more than you're telling us. That wasn't just a *trip*. You *died*. We felt it. But you came back. Tell us the truth."

Oberi let out a low whine. *I don't have* all *the answers. I didn't see anything on the other side. I don't think I was gone long enough. But I got this... feeling.*

"Like intuition?" I asked.

Yes, Oberi replied. *I just* knew *I was going to come back. And I know now that I always will... unless my Elementai die with me. I'm still a Familiar, so the rules still apply, I believe. So neither one of you get any bright ideas.*

"So, what? Mutabeecha can't be killed?" I asked. "Why weren't we aware of this?"

"Yeah, Oberi," Ava said accusingly. "I thought you said you could die."

Technically, I did die, Oberi pointed out. *And I'd die if my Elementai did.*

Ava gave an introspective noise. "We don't know a lot about mutabeecha to begin with, but they *must* reincarnate immediately whenever they die, as long as their Elementai live. How else can we explain him dying and coming back to life?"

"I don't know, but this is all really weird," I said with a shiver.

She paused for a moment. "This is good to know, but we're also a unique case. If one of us dies, could Oberi and the other person survive? Or would we *both* have to die for Oberi to die, too?"

I don't know, Oberi said. *Don't ask me, I'm just the dog.*

He sniffed around again and started in the direction of the mushrooms.

"Oberi!" I yelled, getting his attention. I stomped over to the mushrooms and squashed them under my feet. I didn't know if I'd gotten them all, but I think I'd made my point. "Could you pay attention for one second? You're an idiot for eating these mushrooms in the first place. You're not getting another helping!"

Oberi huffed. *They were delicious. You've ruined my breakfast!*

"We don't need to go testing any of these theories!" I raged. I couldn't believe he didn't see the problem. "Just because *you* came back to life doesn't mean you can cork off whenever you want. We don't know how this magic works."

"Charlie's right," Ava agreed. "We can't chance it again."

Oberi groaned. *By the ancestors, I'm fine!*

"You scared us to death!" Ava cried.

Oberi snorted. *You weren't the one who died, honey.*

"We're here, we're here!" Marcus yelled across the prison yard. I heard three sets of footsteps racing toward us.

"We found Professor Woolly," Marcus said in a panic as he skidded to a halt beside us. "He's gonna do his best, but can't make any promises."

Oberi walked up to Marcus and licked his hand, making a loud slurping sound.

Marcus sighed. "Oberi, not now. I'm trying to— *Oberi?*"

Oberi snickered in my mind. I was *not* amused.

"What's going on?" Kallie asked curiously.

I froze. How could we explain what had just happened?

We can't tell anyone, Ava insisted across our bond. *If the Warden finds out Oberi can't be killed, he'll want him— just like he wants us.*

Agreed, I replied firmly.

Professor Woolly sucked in a deep breath. He was obviously winded from running. "This is the Familiar in question? The one that ate the mushroom?"

"Yeah, but he was just..." Kallie trailed off.

"Well, it's obvious, isn't it?" Professor Woolly said in a jolly way. "This Familiar was playing a prank on you! They're quite intelligent creatures, really. He seems like a funny character. Aren't you, boy?"

Oberi panted and barked happily. *At least someone thinks so,* he said snidely.

"Who's a good boy?" Professor Woolly said. "Just don't give your Elementai too much trouble. Had you truly eaten those mushrooms, you'd be a goner for sure! No one has ever ingested a *macrulosa fungorum* and survived. They melt your organs from the inside out."

Oh, yes. I felt that as I was dying, but it's all better now, Oberi quipped.

My blood turned to ice.

"If they're so dangerous, why are they growing on prison property?" Ava asked.

"Oh, the guards spray the grounds every year, but Darke Island is their natural habitat, so one or two always manage to pop up on school grounds. The same goes for you, kitty," Professor Woolly said to Rishi. "Magical fae mushrooms grow around here, and they're very toxic."

"Rishi won't go anywhere near those, thank the Goddess," Marcus said.

Professor Woolly's tone brightened. "His name is Rishi? Like the mushroom! How creative."

"What? No. Like the— it's just a name," Marcus stammered. "It's not even spelled the same."

Professor Woolly ignored Marcus' response and walked over to the patch of mushrooms, which must've been in pieces after I stomped them. "Let's see, what do we have here? Ah, yes. Poisonous indeed. Thank you very much for bringing this to my attention. We'll have to eradicate them immediately. We can't have these growing in the prison yard. In the meantime, you'll want to take your animals back inside. Just the smell can be intoxicating to them. We wouldn't want to tempt them to eat a piece."

"Thank you, Professor," I said. All I wanted was to get Oberi far, far away. He licked his lips loudly, like he was ready for another serving of poison.

"Come on," Ava said, and we started back toward the building.

Kallie lowered her voice as we walked. "What just happened? Professor Woolly said Oberi would be dead if he ate one of those mushrooms. I saw him swallow it."

"Oberi came back," I said dryly. I still couldn't make sense of it.

"Back to life?" Marcus hissed.

"We don't really understand it," Ava said. "We're *certain* he died, so mutabeecha must reincarnate. This is weird, even for the supernatural community. We can't tell anyone."

"Cross my heart and hope to die," Marcus said.

"I won't tell a soul," Kallie agreed.

For the ancestors' sake, it was just a mushroom! Oberi bellowed.

"A *poisonous* mushroom," Ava shot back.

Okay, Mom, Oberi said sarcastically. *What are you going to do, ground me to my room?*

"If we have to," I said. "At least you'll be safe."

"What's going on?" Marcus asked.

I sighed. "Oberi's being a dick. He thinks it was no big deal."

I'm not going back to the room, Oberi insisted. *No way, no how. I'll spend the day with people who won't judge me for my life choices.*

"With who?" I challenged. "Rishi? He's a cat."

A non-judgmental cat, Oberi said matter-of-factly.

"We're not *judging* you, Oberi," Ava said gently. "We're worried. You made a big mistake. You can't just do whatever you want without consequences. What if you can only die and come back so many times, or—"

La la la la la, Oberi sang, ignoring us. *I don't need to be around over-dramatic pansies. You two are acting as if someone died.*

"You did!" we shouted.

For like, five seconds. By the gods, get over yourselves. Oberi sprinted ahead of us, and Rishi let out a meow as he raced behind him.

I sighed. "Oberi's acting like a child."

"We'll keep an eye on him," Marcus promised.

Oberi wasn't going to listen to us. The best thing we could do right now was give him some space. Ancestors, it really *was* like having a child.

Kallie and Marcus followed Oberi. Ava took my hand and led me down a separate hallway. She walked at a brisk pace, though I didn't know where we were going. Her hand shook in mine, and she gripped my fingers tighter than normal.

"It's going to be okay, pidge," I told her, squeezing her hand. "We got lucky."

"Yeah, *this time.*" Ava stopped abruptly before she dragged me into a nearby classroom. We couldn't talk about this stuff in the open.

The door clicked shut behind us. She sighed heavily once we were in private. "Shit. What if Oberi's lives are numbered? Legend says cats get nine lives, but I've never heard of one that came *back*. Maybe it's a story about mutabeecha. But we know nothing about them! If he's not going to take this seriously, he might push it too far. I mean, what's he going to do now that he *knows* he can come back? Ancestors, if it was me, I'd be delusional. I'd think it made me indestructible. Oberi's my Familiar. He has some of that in him. To think of what he'll do—"

I grabbed Ava's shoulders. "He'll come around. He's probably just embarrassed about the whole thing. That's why he's being such a jerk."

I didn't know where the suggestion came from. I might've picked up on Oberi's feelings, or I could've been making it up to soothe Ava.

Either way, it worked. Ava's shoulders fell, and she sighed. "You're right. Were we too hard on him?"

"No," I said immediately. "He fucking *died*. We have the right to be upset about that."

She stiffened. "I just... I can't stand the thought of losing either of you. And we almost—"

Ava choked up, and I wrapped her in my arms. "We didn't, though. Everyone's here. We're all okay."

Ava scoffed. "Yeah. For now."

I didn't like the way she said that.

"Charlie... what are we going to do if one of us dies?" Ava asked.

My guts sank. She was so blunt about it, and it sent daggers straight into my heart. "No one's going to die, pidge."

"Oberi did, though!" she cried. "We never know when our time might be. We need to be prepared if one of us is left alone with Oberi. We'll have to keep going, for his sake. Our lives are dangerous. I can accept my death, but I have to know that you two would be okay without me."

"Stop it, pidge," I growled. Just the thought of living without her, burying her before it was my time...

Ancestors. I couldn't even go there. I absolutely refused to. There was no greater fear I had.

"You're right. Our lives *are* dangerous. But that doesn't mean we have to be separated. If one of us dies, so do the rest of us. We'll all go together."

"But we didn't die when Oberi did," she argued. "That could mean—"

"Nothing's going to happen," I repeated sternly.

Ava had to believe me, because I wasn't willing to entertain any alternative. Ava would live just as long as I would, and we'd die together. That was it. Denial was the only safe option. To think anything else... it took me to a place I didn't want to go, turned me into someone I didn't dare to become.

I placed a kiss on the top of her head to distract her, and she melted into me. "We're safe right now. Oberi is safe. I may not know what's going to happen in the future, but I know that in this present moment, we're okay. Don't ask me to prepare to lose you, because I could never be prepared for something like that. If something like that *were* to happen, we'd deal with it. Right now, let's just celebrate the fact that Oberi survived."

Ava sagged against me. She must've noticed how this conversation weighed on me, because she spoke softly. "I'm glad Oberi lived. And you're right. That's something to celebrate."

I lifted her chin and pressed my lips to hers. Ancestors, she felt so good against me. It was torturous to think of living life without her, and all I wanted to do was savor this moment with her.

My dick hardened as she deepened the kiss. Ava and I had been fooling around as often as we could since we got married, and I still couldn't seem to get enough of her. My hands tangled in her hair, and my head spun as desire overtook my body. Warmth swelled through the bond as Ava's Fire rose to the surface. Without thinking about it, I cupped her ass and pressed my hips into her.

"Ooh," she sang as she drew away from me. "Is my husband trying to seduce me?"

"What would you say if I was?" I teased.

She snickered. "I'd say *hell yeah.*"

Ava grabbed my hand and began dragging me behind her.

"Where are we—?" I started. I heard a door click behind me. We fell into a giggling pile against the wall, and my eyebrows shot up. "A closet? Wow, we've been upgraded."

Ava wrapped her arms around my neck. "What? You don't think it's hot? You know I like being adventurous."

I chuckled. "Uh, I think you can feel how much I like it. I can get on board with this kind of adventure."

Ava fumbled with the button on my pants. The room must've been dark, because she moved like she couldn't see anything. It was adorable.

I grabbed her hands to stop her. "Here, pidge. Let me show you."

I guided her fingers against the button and undid my pants in one swift motion. Within moments, my bottoms were around my ankles.

She snickered playfully. "You're very talented."

"I have other talents," I said as I trailed kisses across her cheeks. My hands inched up her skirt, and I pushed her thong aside.

Her breath wavered. "Can you show me?"

"If the lady asks."

I placed a passionate kiss on Ava's lips before drawing away and spinning her around. She gasped as I pressed her against the closet door. My palm ran over her smooth ass, and I smacked her softly. It made a satisfying noise, and judging by the thrill that came through our bond, my wife was enjoying herself.

My heart pounded wildly as I reached between her legs and inserted a finger inside of her. She was *so* wet; it was insanely *sexual.* My one and only thought was to pleasure her. It was like my fucking drug to drive her wild.

Ava let out a soft moan.

"Keep making noises like that and this won't last long, pidge," I told her.

"What? Like this?" She moaned again.

"Ava," I warned.

She let out another sensual sound, and I lost it. I needed to be inside of her. *Now.*

I freed my dick from my underpants, then grabbed her hips and slid inside of her from behind. Ava gasped, and pleasure built as our desire for one another surged across the bond.

"Tell me I've been a bad girl," she said breathlessly.

I pressed her body against the doorway and thrust into her harder. Leaning down, I whispered in her ear. "You've been a bad girl, Ava-Marie."

"Oh, no," she feigned. "Are you going to punish me?"

"If you want me to," I whispered. I couldn't imagine truly punishing her, but I'd already learned that my wife was a bit of a masochist. If she wanted me to ravage her body, I'd be a fool to say no.

"I want you fuck me, Charlie," she said. "Fuck me like you never have before."

There was nothing I wanted more. "I always did like a challenge."

I lifted the hem of her shirt and pushed the fabric of her bra aside, pawing at her breasts like I was a wild animal and she was my next meal. She leaned her head into me, gasping. She apparently really liked it, so I pinched her nipples. She drew a sharp breath, and a thrill came across the bond so hard that I felt a tingle in my dick. Wow, Ava *really* liked this.

The air in the closet became hot and heavy as our powers flared. Fire and Water mixed with my Air to create a steaming sauna. The harder I pinched her nipples, the hotter the room got. If there was one thing I was good at, it was pleasing my wife.

Harder, Charlie, she begged. I didn't think she meant for it to slip through our mental connection, but I was happy to oblige.

I released one hand from her breast and slid two fingers inside of her, next to my dick. She became tighter, and my head reeled so fast I nearly lost my footing.

Ancestors, Ava thought. *You're going to make me come.*

That's the idea, pidge—

My thoughts cut off as the sound of a door opening met my ears. It was beyond the closet— out in the classroom. Ava and I both stilled.

Someone just came in, I thought across our bond.

Several voices filled the classroom, and I listened closely. I didn't recognize them.

"You're ruining my weekend," a guy complained. "Why do we have to have these stupid club meetings on Sunday?"

"If you could stay out of detention, we wouldn't have to keep rescheduling," a girl replied snidely.

"Let's stop fighting and get to work," another girl said. "The decorations for the Villain's Ball won't make themselves!"

My heart leapt, though I was pretty sure the feeling had come from Ava. She pressed down deeper on my dick, and it took everything in me not to gasp.

What is it? I asked.

It's hot, isn't it? Ava said. *It's so... naughty.*

We could get caught, I pointed out.

So? What are they going to do about it? It's not illegal to fuck my husband.

We'd been married for months, but my head still spun every time she called me her husband. When she said that, it didn't seem to matter that there were people on the other side of the door.

Hell, I hardly cared if they heard us. I just wanted to fuck my wife to the afterlife and back.

You're so damn incredible, pidge, I growled in her mind. *What kind of kinks are you getting me into?*

Well, what do you like? she teased.

This, I told her as I grabbed her hair and yanked on the strands, then thrust into her again.

She let out a low moan.

"Keep quiet, pidge," I whispered in her ear. "Or I'll have to punish you."

She moaned louder, but the decorating committee outside was arguing so loud that no one heard us. I spanked her ass, light enough that it barely made a sound, but hard enough that she felt it. Damn it, she was going to make me lose it.

Do it, she encouraged.

I couldn't contain myself any longer. I shoved Ava up against the door again, and I held on to her hips as I slammed into her. With every thrust, she let out a tiny moan. I could hear the door latch jiggling each time she moved against the wall. It was so fucking hot.

Ava gasped— loudly this time— and I felt her peak across the bond as I pulled her hair. One last thrust, and I was done for. We went spiraling into an orgasm together, so strong that I lost my balance and had to catch myself against the wall to stay upright. I emptied myself into her, feeling triumph as we came down from the high.

"Ancestors," Ava breathed. There were still people outside; I could hear them talking through the door.

That was so fucking dirty, I told her through our bond, so we wouldn't be heard. I yanked my pants up and sagged to the floor. I was so dizzy that I could hardly stand straight.

What are you doing? she asked.

I paused with my hands on my button. *Um... what should I be doing?*

Me. She snickered. *We're going to be here awhile.*

I smiled. *I'll need a few minutes. It's your turn.*

I grabbed Ava's hips and pulled her toward me, positioning her so that she straddled me. My hands cupped her ass as I brought her closer to my lips. She drew a surprised breath as my tongue grazed over her bud. Her sweet scent filled my nose, making my head spin. It was intoxicating.

An odd sensation tingled through my lips, and I realized it was coming through our bond. Ava was biting her lip *hard* to keep from crying out. Her passion pulsed through our bond, begging me for more. The sound of voices coming through the doorway only made my heart beat faster. It was exhilarating, thinking that we were doing this in a very public place and could get caught at any moment. Ava was doing her best to keep her noises quiet, but every whimper that escaped her mouth made me half wish someone *would* open this fucking closet, just so everyone could see that she was mine.

I inserted two fingers inside of her and continued working her clit with my tongue. She sagged against me, as if losing control of her limbs. I squeezed her perfect ass tighter to keep her upright. Ava sighed heavily, letting her pleasure escape, before rolling into another orgasm. An incredible feeling exploded through the bond as she contracted around my fingers. It was amazing.

Ava sank onto her knees, until she was straddling my dick. She wrapped her arms around me and rested her head on my shoulder. I felt more relaxed than ever as I stroked her hair.

"How was that?" I whispered.

She let out a blissful sigh. "Just about perfect... but I think we can do better."

An hour passed before the decorating committee finished their meeting— and Ava and I didn't stop the whole time. By the time we finished, we were pouring sweat and my hair stood straight up. I smoothed it down as we stepped out of the closet. The cool air in the classroom was in stark contrast to the heat of the closet. It instantly cooled me off.

Ava chuckled lightly. "Oh, boy."

"What is it?" I asked.

She straightened my shirt for me. "You look like you've just been fucked six ways from Sunday."

I ran my fingers through her hair. "Well, I have."

She laughed. "My parents are still visiting the Institute. We don't need them to see... you know what? On second thought, it might be funny if they saw us with sex hair."

My stomach dropped. "Your dad might kill me."

"Don't say that. Daddy will learn to love you the way I do."

"I hope not in the same way," I deadpanned.

She took my hand to lead me out of the room. "You know what I meant."

"We should probably go check on Oberi," I suggested. "I think he's had enough time to cool down."

"Let's hope so," she said sarcastically. "He acts like we were the dramatic ones, but he was the one putting on a three-act play earlier."

Ava and I started down the hall. We had to be near the infirmary when we heard angry voices around the corner. She grabbed me, and we stopped to listen.

"Can we not do this right now?" a male voice growled. It took me a moment to place the voice, before I realized it was Ez.

"Ez, we gotta talk." I recognized the voice of Ava's father— I didn't know voices well, but his was one that I always remembered.

"You don't want to hear what I have to say," Ez snapped.

"Of course I do," Liam insisted. "Your mother and I are leaving soon. I don't want to go home with this unresolved."

"That's the problem, Dad!" Ez yelled. "You think this can be resolved with a *conversation.* If you wanted to make things right, you should've started years ago!"

Liam sighed heavily, like he was trying to keep his composure. "I know you're upset—"

"No, Dad, I'm *hurt!*" Ez's voice cracked, and the hall went dead silent.

What should we do? Ava asked in my mind.

I don't know, I replied. *We might make it worse if we step in.*

Ava went to take a step forward, but I grabbed her arm and held her back. Whatever this was, it was between Ez and his dad, not us.

Liam cleared his throat. "You're hurt... by me?"

"Of course I am!" Ez raged. "Did you really not notice?"

"Whatever I did to you, I'm sorry—"

"Ancestors, you don't even know!" Ez exploded. "You can't even see why I'm pissed!"

"Then *tell me!*" Liam demanded.

"You want to know how I really feel, Dad?" Ez challenged. "You were never there for me."

"Of course I was—"

"*No!*" Ez yelled. "You don't get to tell me how I feel. You were hard on me growing up— way harder than you were on Ava, or Alana, or even Maverick! I needed your compassion, and all I got was your lectures. You let Ava get away with stealing *cars!* But when my condom broke, suddenly *I'm* the villain."

"I was trying to protect you!" Liam insisted.

Ez's tone wavered. He was on the verge of breaking down completely. "I didn't need you to protect me from anything. I needed your support! I was being safe, and doing the right thing, but even though what happened was an accident, you acted like a total hardass once I came to you with the news! I could've hidden it, but I didn't. I chose to trust you guys... and now I see that was a mistake. When Rosary got pregnant, I thought about running away with her. You weren't protecting me. You were pushing me away! And when she lost the baby, I— I—"

Ez couldn't finish. My heart broke for him. I didn't know what he was about to say, but it was evident how deeply devastated he was.

Ez's tone softened. "You let Ava get away with everything, but you were so strict with me. I did nothing wrong, and you treated me like I'd failed you!"

"Son, I'm so sorry," Liam said gently. "I always suspected you might've inherited my illness. I thought I was preparing you for the worst, because I knew how difficult it was going to be for you to face. And yeah, I was harder on you, because I wanted to prepare you for that. I hoped that if I toughened you up, you could face it easier, and stay strong."

"You can't *prepare* anyone for this disease. You just deal with it," Ez shot back. "Maybe if we'd all been honest and admitted that I wasn't healthy in the first place, I could've dealt with it better. I was really scared. I wanted someone to talk to, because I knew that something wasn't right with me. But I had to *pretend* to be healthy, and hold it all together because you know what? I'm the one who always does that. I'm the son who holds the family together. You get sick, or Ava fucks up, and I try to be the good kid who doesn't have any problems and can take care of everyone else, along with myself. But who was standing in *my* corner, huh?"

"I regret it, but I'm here for you now. I always have been. Can you ever forgive me?"

Ez scoffed. "You can't change the past, Dad."

"I can't, but I can try to correct the future," Liam said.

Ez gave a disgusted noise. "You know, the night I got arrested, you didn't even bother to ask *why*. You just came blazing in bitching about what a horrible kid I was—"

"I didn't mean anything I said that night," Liam said. "It was inexcusable, but I couldn't stand the thought—"

"Then you sent me off to the Institute without even a goodbye!" Ez cut him off without allowing him to explain. "I was *defending my sister,* and you treated me like some kind of criminal. You should've known me better than that. I would've never done what I did if I wasn't protecting the people I love. I wouldn't let myself get carried away by a jealous streak. And if you think that's true, then... I'm not really your son at all."

The longest pause I'd ever heard in my life stretched through the hall.

"I see that you're angry, and you have every right to be," Liam said. "I'll be here if you're ready to talk."

I'd never heard Ava's father speak in such an understanding tone. He knew he'd royally fucked up.

"Why bother?" Ez said bitterly. "Just take Ava home for Christmas. I'm staying at the Institute for the holidays."

"Ez, we all want you home."

"Well, I'd rather be alone. We have nothing to discuss."

Sharp footsteps started in our direction.

"Ezekiel," Liam called after him, but he sounded hopeless. His footsteps didn't follow.

Ez turned the corner where Ava and I were standing. He stopped in his tracks and sneered, "What are *you* doing here?"

"Ez," Ava said gently, like she wanted to help.

"Are you following me?" Ez accused.

"What? No!" Ava cried.

Ez started down the hall, stomping away from Ava and me. "Leave me alone."

"Ez, please!" Ava started after him, and I followed. "I want to help."

"*Help?*" Ez stopped again. "You're half the reason this is a problem in the first place! Do you know how hard it is to have a bipolar sibling? Everyone made everything about *you* all the time! I had to tiptoe around you, so you wouldn't break. Well, guess what? I was sick too! Hell, I wasn't even allowed to *be* sick, because that was *your* thing. You sucked up all the attention in the room, and there wasn't any left for anyone else. Nobody was ever worried if I was going to break!"

"Do you think we didn't care about you?" Ava asked. "Of course we did. Always, Ez."

"You're lying," he accused.

"Ez, please," I cut in. "Let us help."

"This has nothing to do with you," Ez growled. "Just go away, Ava. I don't want you around me anymore."

He stomped away, and we were too stunned to go after him.

"I've never seen Ez like this," Ava said in a hollow tone.

I reached out for her. She had her arms wrapped around her stomach, like she was trying to hold herself together. "I'm sorry, Ava. What he said must've really hurt."

She sighed. "Yeah, but he's hurting more. I just wish I could help."

She was downplaying it. I could feel the sting of his words through our bond. Ava felt responsible for Ez's pain now more than ever.

"You can't help him if he's not willing to accept it right now," I told her. "He'll come to you when he's ready."

"I hope so," she said in a sad tone. Her shoulders slumped when I wrapped an arm around her. We started walking, though we weren't headed anywhere in particular.

"Do you want to talk to your dad?" I asked.

"It'll just turn into another fight," Ava said with a sigh. "Daddy needs to focus on Ez right now. I've done enough."

I stroked her arm. "I'm here for you and your family, pidge. Whatever you need, just say so."

"I think we all just need some time," she admitted.

Chatter spilled into the hall, and the sounds of the air hockey table came from up ahead. I could hear Reid and Felicity arguing over their foosball game. A few other Elves laughed and joked with them.

"Let's go sit down," I suggested.

Ava led me into the Villain's Den. The room was so packed that we had to push past people to get inside. I heard our friends talking near the TV. It sounded like everyone we knew was there— except Ez and Opal. We didn't know where he'd run off to.

"I'm glad you and Scarlet broke up," I overheard Alistair say. "You were too good for her."

"Wait, back up. *What* happened?" Marcus asked— a bit too eagerly.

"It sounds like we got here just in time," Ava said in a brighter tone. She needed some gossip to take her mind off her family. Ava found us an empty spot on one of the couches. She guided me to it, then sat on my lap. Oberi padded over to us. I sensed his mood through our bond, and he seemed happier than earlier.

Kallie groaned. "It's not *that* big of a deal, guys. I just walked in on Scarlet and Zayne, okay?"

"Walked in on them... doing what?" Eddie asked innocently.

"You know," Ivy said coyly. "*It.*"

"Ooh," Eddie replied in realization, dragging the word out. "I'm sorry, Kallie."

"Don't be," she insisted. I detected both bitterness and relief in her tone. "Scarlet and I were bound to break up eventually. She was so jealous of—"

Kallie cut off, like she'd said too much. It implied everything. I'd bet anything Scarlet was jealous of Kallie's bond with Marcus.

"Alistair's right," Chancey added. "You're better off without Scarlet. She was a bitch in the ring—"

The sound of heavy boots entered the Villain's Den, and the room quieted within moments. The sudden shift of atmosphere was eerie. Ava stiffened from her spot on my lap, and my heart began to race. Whatever it was couldn't be good.

Guards, Ava said in my mind. *They look pissed.*

"All full-blooded Elves are to come with us immediately," a guard announced.

Reid cleared his throat from across the room. "Where are you taking us?"

"We're not taking questions," the guard sneered. "You can come with us the easy way, or the hard way."

They're taking them to the Underground! Ava panicked.

"We're not going anywhere with you," Reid snapped.

Before anyone else could move, an explosion sounded from the middle of the room... a battle orb.

"Hey!" Alistair cried.

Reid must've siphoned Alistair's powers. I was both proud of him and a little peeved, because the second Reid reacted, the room burst into chaos. Shouts filled the area, and magic whizzed by my head. A loud crash sounded, like the TV had been knocked off the wall. Several students screamed and fled the den. Rishi hissed loudly, and Oberi growled. I felt her shift into a unicorn, standing over Ava and me to defend us.

The click of noxite guns sounded. All I could think to do was protect Ava. I grabbed my wife and shoved her to the ground, throwing myself over her to protect her from rogue magic.

"Let go of me!" Felicity shrieked.

"Samara, get down!" I heard Leif shout.

"Stay away from my boyfri—" Alistair started, but he cut off at a whizzing sound. I was certain he'd been shot by a noxite dart.

"Hey, you fuckers!" Ivy snapped.

"Ives!" Chancey cried, but it was too late. Guns went off, and I heard both of their bodies hit the floor.

"Everybody on the ground!" a guard screamed, but no one listened.

"Master!" Eddie shouted across the room. My entire form froze as I heard him call for me. He gave a few choked sounds, like he was struggling to get away from someone.

"Charlie!" Ava cried, pushing against me. "Get up! We have to move. They're going for Eddie!"

Panic flooded through me. The second she said it, I was on my feet. I raced over to where I thought Eddie had been last. I sensed someone approaching with my magic. I gathered Air magic in my hands and blasted it outward. An *oof* sounded as the guard went flying backward.

At the same time, a sharp pinch shot through my leg. Oberi gave a loud neigh as she surged to help me, and I felt her place her body between me and the guards. I reached down and yanked a noxite dart from my skin. I'd been practicing all semester with noxite, and the diluted serum barely fazed me. My magic didn't even react to it now.

"Charlie, what do we do?" Eddie cried.

Fuck, I had to think fast. The Elves weren't ready to make a break for it, but if we didn't do something, the guards would take Eddie and the others to the Underground.

"We—" I started, but I hesitated too long.

"Don't touch Felicity!" Reid screamed.

I heard the sound of feathery wings flapping, and I knew he must've stolen an angel's wings. All his rage and anger must've made his powers stronger. But those wings were useless here in the Villain's Den. A blast of defensive magic shook the room, and several of us were blasted into the wall.

The air knocked out of my lungs, and I sank to the ground. I rolled over— straight into a puddle of warm, sticky liquid. I reached out, and my fingers grazed an unmoving body.

I realized with horror that the spell had killed one of the Elves.

I jumped back and scrambled to my feet. A woman's screams welled over the noise.

"You've killed Reid!" Felicity wailed. "How could you? You *monsters*! You—"

She cut off as another pair of footsteps entered the room. I swore I felt the air shift around him. The tension inside the Villain's Den was palpable.

I felt Ava's intense terror, and I knew exactly who'd entered. She feared one man more than any other.

The Warden, Ava told me through our bond. She stood across the room, and there was nothing she could do to come to my defense.

I swallowed the lump in my throat. Heavy footsteps sounded as the Warden crossed the room.

He barely even looked at Reid, Ava said. *He's coming toward you.*

I held my head high as the Warden approached. He stopped so close to me that I could feel his breath.

"Well, well, well." The Warden clicked his tongue. "If I had to guess, I'd say *you* were the instigator here, Mister Wahkin."

Every instinct told me to reach out and end this man right here. But his guards would finish the rest of us off. If I made a move, I damned us all. It tore me to shreds knowing there was nothing I could do.

"I was trying to protect my friends," I said through gritted teeth.

The Warden gave a light laugh, like he found it amusing. Then he leaned in and whispered for just me to hear. "You may think you're stronger than me, but one day, I will have you and Ava both. If you intercede again, perhaps that day will be today. I can't separate you, but if you attack *me*, the Warden of this school, I will have the full legal right to send you two wherever I like, and your tribe will be unable to do anything about it. Think long and hard about what you'd like to do."

Ava's terror came to me, and I knew she'd heard what he'd said through our bond. The Warden's threat was clear. If I kept fighting back, he'd take me and Ava both to Cellblock 9, or send us to the Underground itself. I had two choices. I could try to save Eddie and the other Elves and get them out of here, or I could keep Ava safe.

I already knew I'd failed at the first option. And no matter how many lives were at risk, I would never put Ava in danger. Not even for people I was responsible for... dear friends that I cared about. It was a gut-wrenching decision, but one I had to make.

All I could do was stand there as the Warden gave the order to take the Elves. Several guards pushed past me to get to Eddie, and horror twisted in my gut as I heard handcuffs clinking as he was dragged away.

"It will be all right, Charlie!" Eddie told me with terror in his tone. He went willingly, as did the others. No one wanted to risk anything after what happened to Reid. The eerie quiet in which the Elves moved gave me the shivers. They were being marched to their slaughter.

Hot, angry tears rose to my eyes. I'd kill the Warden right here and now if I thought I could get away with it. *Fuck him!*

"Good boy, Charlie," the Warden said in a condescending tone. "I see you'll do anything for your little wife."

He clapped me on the shoulder. It was nearly enough to make me bring this whole place tumbling down with my Earth magic. I would've, too, if Ava hadn't been here to be crushed beneath the rubble. My stomach twisted into impossible knots as the Warden left the room behind the guards and the Elves.

"Send a medic in for the ones who were shot," the Warden ordered someone, but it didn't sound like he gave a flying fuck about the students — just the protocol. "As for the others..."

He paused, and a shiver ran down my spine.

"Arrest them and take them back to their dorms."

ava-marie

TWENTY

eid's body was still oozing blood onto the carpet. The guards had blasted a hole in his chest so big you could see clear through to the other side. All around us, students screamed as they stepped over bodies and did their best to squeeze out the entrance as nurses from the infirmary hurried to treat the inmates who'd been shot with noxite.

Ivy, Chancey and Alistair lay limp on the floor. The noxite darts had knocked them out. I wanted to help them, but the medical staff would intercede, and right now, the Elves needed us more.

Charlie went to fight back, but guards wrenched his hands behind his back and slapped handcuffs on his wrists. I felt cold metal against my skin as the same was done to me. Kallie and Marcus were handcuffed too and hauled off in different directions. I called out for Oberi, who pawed her hoof like she was ready for a fight.

I'm going to break out of these noxite cuffs, I heard Charlie think, and I knew he could. *They're not getting away with this.*

Not yet, I told both him and Oberi. *We need to find Eddie. We can't risk getting in more trouble. If we fight back and make a scene, we'll lose our chance to figure out where they took the Elves.*

Oberi snorted, but she didn't make a move to attack as the guards yanked Charlie and me out of the Villain's Den. Out in the hall, the Warden continued barking orders.

"All students are to remain in their cells for the rest of the night," the Warden called out. "Anyone who is found wandering the Institute grounds will immediately be arrested and given a severe infraction. This is your only warning."

The Warden gave me a slick smile as the guards hauled us out of the room. He had us right where he wanted us.

Or at least, he thought he did. I damn sure wasn't giving up hope.

Charlie's body was stiff as the guards forced us back to our apartment and took our cuffs off, shoving us through the door. Once it shut behind us, the automatic lock clicked, sealing us in.

Oberi turned around to stand guard. It was like she wanted to be big right now, to protect us in case anything else came through. Unfortunately, it provided Charlie and I very little room to move.

"This is fucking perfect," Charlie growled.

"We can figure it out," I said calmly.

"Eddie and the other Elves could be dead by then!" Charlie shouted.

"We'll be able to rescue Eddie and the others if we can get to the Underground tonight."

"We still don't know where it is. What are we supposed to do when we find it, huh? We still have to escape the Institute once we do!"

"I don't *know*, Charlie! I need to think." I put a few fingers to my temple.

Charlie punched the brick wall, and his knuckles started bleeding. "I'm responsible for these people. They asked me to protect them, and I taught them everything I could, but my lessons backfired! Now they're in danger because of me!"

I could hear the tears in his voice, and as much as I longed to comfort him, that couldn't be my focus right now. Not if I wanted to save Eddie. I strode over to him and picked up his hand. As I brushed my fingers over his knuckles, they healed instantly.

I hadn't been able to mend many injuries since healing my brother, but what I did for Charlie felt effortless. I had no time to ponder about it. "I know this is a lot right now," I said, trying to keep my voice even. "But if we don't keep our heads, who's going to rescue them?"

"We can't do anything if we're stuck in here," Charlie protested.

"You're not helping," I growled through clenched teeth. "Go in the other room and calm down while I work on this."

Charlie swore under his breath, but he gathered himself enough that he managed to do as I asked. I grabbed at my hair and tried to think. I needed to review everything we'd already learned about the Underground. I had everything I needed to crack this case. I just had to be smart enough to put the pieces together.

Oberi hung her head low. *I am very sorry, dear one. My behavior this morning was out of the question. I should have been kinder. We all had such a terrifying experience, and I was trying to hide that with pride. I regret everything had to come to this.*

"Save your regret for later. Help me figure this out." We kept all the evidence we had for the Underground, as well as my journal, in a cardboard box underneath the couch, as we hadn't found a good place to hide it yet and the Lair was out of the question. I grabbed the box, then I took a huffy seat on the floor and started withdrawing the contents. I spread the blueprints out in front of me, as well as copies of the news articles we'd scanned about the Underground.

I examined them several times, but didn't notice anything I hadn't before. Oberi weaved her horn from side to side, just as confused about this whole thing as I was.

Hours passed, until I realized it had to be dark outside. I'd been investigating forever, and I was still going in the same circles I had been when we'd arrived. Charlie was awfully quiet in the bedroom, but the other side of our bond was about to go off like a powder keg. I couldn't keep asking him to be patient. I needed to give him some answers, so we could come up with a real plan.

This was getting me nowhere. I had to think outside the box. I'd been practicing with my intuition on and off, but Charlie and I had such a wild ride lately with everything going on between us, I hadn't taken the time recently to sit down and listen to what my spirit was telling me.

What had Hemlock said about intuition again? It'd been so long ago I couldn't remember, but I *had* to. A friend's life was in danger.

I crossed my legs under me as I closed my eyes. I took a few, calming breaths. *I need to find the Infernal Underground. I need to find the Infernal Underground.* The mantra I repeated melded against the symphony of ever-constant voices in my mind.

Long moments dragged on. I wasn't sure this was leading me anywhere. I didn't receive a spark of inspiration or any whisper of a clue.

Ancestors, please, I pleaded. *If we don't do this, Eddie will be killed. We can't let that happen.*

Again, there was a lapse. I wasn't sure how any of this tied together, but I knew that it *did*, somehow. We knew the Underground wasn't in the basement or in any of the abandoned cellblocks around the school. So why couldn't we locate it? It wasn't like there were many places left the Warden could hide it.

The Underground was concealed, but an operation that big had to have something hiding it. If it wasn't a building, then what was it? Was there a place on campus where no one would find a secret torture chamber?

It seemed impossible to conceal something that large. The Underground killed people; we knew that for a fact.

... Except the parents of the kids who went missing never found their remains. Where could the Warden possibly smuggle out and bury that many bodies without it being discovered? I didn't understand how the bodies of these tortured kids weren't being found...

That's because the bodies are being used to hide it.

The thought slammed into me and nearly knocked me off my seat. My mind raced to consider the possibilities. The Underground wasn't under the *school*. It couldn't be. We'd already decided that. But the prison grounds were huge— large enough to contain a small forest and a lake.

I checked the blueprints again. I saw that the concrete slab that was buried underneath the property to prevent students from escaping only went around the perimeter of the main building, not anywhere else on campus. There was plenty of space elsewhere the Underground could be.

So then, where? A random cellar in the ground somewhere in the woods?

That doesn't make sense. An inmate could find it if that was the case. The Warden needs something to sit on top of the Underground, to serve the ruse and pose as a distraction in case there's an investigation.

The Institute was made of two different buildings— the original asylum, which served as the school, and the chapel, which had been here before the asylum was built. Rooms had been added on to the asylum to make more room for more inmates, but the chapel had remained virtually untouched... except for one area, which had only expanded over time.

"Ancestors," I gasped. I rifled for the blueprints again, until I found one with the chapel on it. My eyes scanned the paper, and the realization hit me.

I took in a sharp breath, which halted when I heard the lock on my door jiggle. I jumped to my feet. Oberi stomped her hoof in warning. Charlie came flying in from the bedroom, ready to punch whoever came through that door.

I relaxed when Kallie slipped in. She was followed by Marcus, who had Rishi bundled up in his jacket.

"It's just Marcus and me," Kallie said, and Charlie unclenched his fists. "Nobody saw us."

"How'd you get out of your cells?" I asked.

"I've been able to unlock my cell door since they sentenced me here. It's how Marcus and I tried to escape during our first semester," Kallie said. "Vigilante skills come in handy around here."

"What about bed check?" Charlie asked.

"Kallie cast duplicates of us in case they look, but they won't hold up forever," Marcus said. "Please tell me you guys found something."

I clenched the blueprint of the chapel in my hands. "I've got it. I've fucking got it."

"You know where it is?" Charlie asked.

"The graveyard," I said breathlessly. "The Underground is below the graveyard."

There was a moment of silence, then Marcus slapped a hand to his forehead. "Shit. It's so obvious."

"How can you be sure?" Kallie argued.

"Because it's the perfect cover-up. The graveyard is where they bury all the students who die here," I explained. "If rumors about the Underground go mainstream and there's an investigation, no one is going to be bold enough to suggest digging up graves to look for it."

"You're right. Defiling graves would be sacrilege," Marcus confirmed. "And even if someone tried, there'd be a public uproar from the parents who have kids buried here. By the time it got handled, the Warden could clean up the evidence."

"So the cemetery itself serves as the ruse," Kallie said, crossing her arms. "Gotta admit, he's a clever one."

"Charlie and I know that chapel inside and out. If there was an entrance to the Underground there, we'd have found it by now, which means the Underground *has* to be beneath the cemetery," I insisted. "There's nowhere else on campus it could be."

"I bet if we go poking around in that graveyard, we'll find the entrance," Marcus said excitedly.

"Then let's get the hell out of here." Charlie was already halfway out the door. Kallie barely had time to cast duplicates in our place. Oberi shifted into a husky and charged after him as the rest of us followed.

The hallways were dark and intimidating on our way to the chapel. I was ready to throw a fireball at any minute, but we didn't see anyone on our way there.

"Where are all the guards?" Marcus asked.

"They must be getting ready for the Darke Games. They start tomorrow," Kallie replied.

"The Games are our only hope. The Warden and his lackeys are distracted," I said. "It'll buy us more time."

As we walked, I heard a couple of familiar voices coming from a door up ahead, arguing in hushed tones. I think it was an abandoned classroom.

"Wait a moment," I hissed. I pressed my face to the door and whispered, "Ivy?"

"Precious! Thank Atlantis!" he gasped on the other side.

"What are you guys doing in there?" I asked.

"The Warden had us brought here after we woke up from the

noxite," Alistair complained. "The nurses wanted us to pull out of the Darke Games because we don't have any magic at the moment, but he wouldn't allow it."

"What?" I spat. I couldn't believe this!

"Yeah! He's still making us compete even though our magic isn't back to normal!" Ivy screeched.

Ivy didn't get scared, but even I could hear the fear in his tone. He was terrified about going out there without his magic to protect him and the others.

"I can get you guys out," Kallie offered. "Just let me pick the lock."

"Won't do any good," Chancey added glumly. "He put tracking cuffs on us. He'll know if we break out the moment you open this door."

"I bet Scarlet ditches us the moment she has a chance," Alistair noted. "She's definitely going to consider us deadweight."

"Looks like we're being thrown to the wolves whether we can defend ourselves or not," Ivy said sourly. "And I thought I was too beautiful to die."

"Hide, Ivy," I insisted. "Stay out of sight until the Games are over, then they'll let you back into the prison. You just have to stay alive until the other teams kill the monsters."

"If one of them doesn't eat us first," Chancey grumbled.

"Where are you going?" Alistair asked. "Are you going to find Eddie?"

"We think we know where he is, but once we break him and the other Elves out, we have to figure out what to do with them," I said nervously. There were so many steps to this plan, and so many things that could go wrong.

"If you find Eddie and can get him off Institute grounds, we'll take care of them," Alistair promised. "Then *we* can get the Elves off the island and to safety before the Darke Games are over."

"That might actually work." It was the best— and only— plan we had.

"You guys should escape the Institute, too, and come with us," Chancey said. "We'll meet up in the woods and book it outta this joint."

My heart fell. "We can't, guys."

"Why the fuck not?" Ivy snarled.

"Because…" I didn't have time to tell them about the keys right now. "It's safer if you guys leave alone. But if we could go with you, we would. I promise."

I pressed a hand to the door, as if I could feel my friends on the other side of it. "Stay safe, guys. We'll do our best to make sure everyone comes out alive."

"Good luck, Ava," Ivy whispered.

I wanted to stay with them, but Charlie grabbed me and pulled me away. We couldn't linger where we weren't needed.

As we approached the door that led outside, Kallie said, "Even if we get them off the island, there's going to be a manhunt for the Elves. We're risking our own necks getting them out."

"We have to give them a chance," Charlie insisted. "I'm tired of the Warden pushing us around. Aren't you?"

Kallie's countenance was grim. I didn't know what was going to happen to us either once all this went down— or what would happen if we got caught— but we'd promised to see this through. Loyalty meant something to every single one of us. In a place like the Institute, it was all you had.

Once we made it outside, we stuck to the wall and avoided the spotlights on the guard towers that surveyed the prison yard. The spotlights ceased to survey the area around the chapel or the graveyard next to it. On another night, I'd think it was strange, but now I knew why.

The cemetery had a couple hundred headstones on the property, and it was surrounded by a metal fence. Inmates never came here, because there were better things to do in the prison yard. I'd never been here myself. Most of the headstones were crumbling into decay, as if the guards didn't bother to take care of them. Many headstones dated back to when the place was an asylum, but some were more recent. I noticed a couple graves from kids who'd died in the Darke Games last year by the entrance to the main gate.

After we'd slipped past the fence, Charlie knelt on the ground before a headstone and splayed his hand out.

"What do you feel?" I asked.

"There are a lot of bodies, buried about six feet deep," Charlie said. "But under that…"

Charlie cut off mid-sentence and pressed his hand deeper into the dirt. "There's some sort of structure underneath all the graves, about twenty feet down. It's huge... a kind of compound. My Earth magic didn't notice it before, because it just stopped looking once it got to the bodies. I didn't suspect there was anything else under them."

Victory rattled in my chest. "Let's get inside," I said.

I strode forward confidently. Oberi put his nose to the ground and sniffed as Rishi jumped from headstone to headstone. I took Charlie's hand and did my best to lead him around all the different graves.

We stopped in front of the mausoleum in the middle of the cemetery's property. It was a small, private building, built to house the resting place of one person. Two stone doors were chained up at the front of the monument, underneath a very grim and eerie looking gargoyle.

Hmm. Do you think the entrance could be in the big, scary, ominous and yet entirely obnoxious mausoleum? Oberi said sarcastically.

We approached the monument. It was old, at least a couple hundred years or so, but despite the moss and thorns that covered the mausoleum, it was still standing tall. I approached the doors and ran my hand over the lock holding them together.

"These chains are new," I murmured. They'd been put on recently. They hadn't even had enough time to rust in Darke Island's rainy weather.

Kallie approached a plaque attached to the side of the mausoleum. She brushed off the dirt and read aloud, *"Here lies Vincenzo Fillipo. Doctor, Scholar, Friend."*

"Ooh, I heard about him," Marcus blurted. "He was the crazy doctor who built the original asylum ages ago, then experimented on the patients. When he got caught, there was supposed to be a trial for his crimes, but he died before he could be brought to justice."

"Maybe he didn't die," Charlie said ominously. "Maybe he just faked his death as a way to continue his experiments."

"Only one way to find out." I put my hand to the chains, and they melted off. I struggled to push open the massive concrete doors of the mausoleum. Charlie and Marcus ran forward to help me. The boys opened the doors, which led to a darkened room. Oberi shifted into a husky, so he could follow us in.

I ignited my Fire and held it up to see. The mausoleum was bare, save for a plain stone coffin in the center of the room.

Marcus and Charlie went forward to move the coffin's stone slab off the top. Kallie rushed to help them. With her shifter strength, they budged the slab off the coffin, and it slid aside. Inside the coffin was not a body, but stairs that led downward.

"There it is," I whispered. The Infernal Underground... we'd found it.

TWENTY-ONE

I shivered as we descended the long staircase. Ava held my hand, and she shuddered as the area around us grew cold. I held my breath and listened closely for the sound of screams— for anything, really. I heard nothing but the soft pad of our own footsteps. It was eerie, and I feared we were already too late.

We reached the bottom of the stairs unharmed. The chilly air expanded into a long hallway, but the silence was deafening. The slight scent of something rotten touched my nose, but I couldn't be sure of what it was.

"That was too easy," I whispered. "Where are the wards? The spells?"

"Maybe the Warden doesn't need them," Ava replied. "He's arrogant enough to think he's concealed this place well enough."

"He needs the guards to do his dirty work," Kallie pointed out. "If he placed a ward around this place, they couldn't come and go."

Ava's hand shook in mine. "I can't see a thing."

"I'll use my witch light—" Marcus started, but he cut off with a gasp. He jumped backward and knocked straight into me. He hit me so hard that my hand slipped out of Ava's. I stumbled, and Rishi screeched when I stepped on his tail. His cry echoed down the long hall.

I caught myself on a ledge cut into the wall. Something tumbled from the ledge and landed with a loud *clunk* on the ground. My fingers grazed something long and hard. I picked it up and ran my hands over it, trying to make sense of it. My heart leapt to my throat when I realized what it was. I instantly dropped it and scurried a few steps back.

Bones.

My foot landed on top of the bones that had fallen from the wall. A sickening *crunch* sounded beneath my heel, and I knew instantly that I'd just crushed a skull.

My voice wavered. "Wh-what is this?"

Ava grabbed my shirt and pulled me farther away from the wall. She curled into me. "It's a crypt," she said in a shaky tone. "There's a long hallway, with endless doorways and holes in the walls between them."

"The holes were cut out for caskets," Marcus said thoughtfully.

"But instead of caskets, these people were left here to rot," Kallie snarled in disgust.

Oberi padded forward and sniffed the bones. *These bones have been here for a long time. Decades, at least.*

"Let's keep moving," Ava said.

She started forward and guided me through a doorway. Ava gasped when she saw what was inside. I reached out, and my fingers curled around a cold metal rod. My stomach dropped as I moved my hands over rod after rod, all lined up in rows from the floor to the ceiling.

"Cells," Ava said in a hollow tone, more to herself than to me. "This must be where the Warden has been holding people."

I continued down the row of cells, wondering how far they went.

Ava described the room for my benefit. "There's dry blood all over the floor. It's—"

Something wet squished under my shoe, and I slipped. I flung my arms out to grab on to the cell bars, but my hands met nothing as I went crashing to the ground.

"Charlie!" Marcus cried, racing over to me.

I landed on my back, and the liquid seeped into my shirt. My hands felt sticky as I lifted them from the floor.

"What the—?" I started, but I cut off when the horrifying realization hit me.

It was *blood*. Magic swirled out of the blood and tingled up my arms. It felt so familiar and similar to my own.

"Uh, it's not all *dry* blood," Marcus said. My stomach clenched as he helped me to my feet.

"You don't think…" Ava started.

"It's Elf blood," I said with certainty.

"How do you know?" Kallie asked.

I swallowed. "I can feel the magic with my Elf powers."

The room fell dead silent for a few beats. I didn't bother trying to clean up, because there was no time to waste. I continued moving around, hoping to find more clues. As I reached the end of the row of cells, I ran into a table. I reached out to feel what lay atop it when—

"Charlie, don't!" Ava cried, but it was already too late.

Pain shot through my palm as my flesh met the tip of a sharp blade. I winced and immediately felt warm blood spring from a deep cut. I'd touched a saw of some kind.

"Ah, fuck!" I growled. I curled my fingers tightly around the wound to slow the bleeding, but it only made it hurt like hell. I heard drops of blood splattering across the table. A flap of skin moved under my touch.

Ava hurried over to me. She grabbed my hand to inspect the cut. "Hold still!"

She pressed her palm into mine, and her warm healing magic swelled through me. The throbbing pain eased slowly. I breathed a sigh of relief when she dropped my hand.

"Don't touch anything else before I look at it, okay?" Ava suggested.

"Agreed," I said firmly.

Metal clinked as she picked up one of the items on the table. "Torture devices," she said thoughtfully. "They've been used recently. The Warden must be using them to get information. He tortured them before…"

Ava paused. We had no idea what happened to the Elves, and none of us were willing to jump to conclusions just yet.

"We need to figure out what he did with them," I said. "We might still have a chance."

"Then let's keep moving," Kallie suggested. "There have to be more clues somewhere."

Ava took my hand, and she guided me out of the room and down the hall. The next door creaked as she opened it. She stilled in the doorway the same time a putrid scent hit me. It smelled of mold and rotting flesh. My head began to spin, and I thought I might puke.

Oberi gagged. *Ew, I am* not *going in there. This place stinks!*

"That's making me sick!" Kallie cried.

I sniffed the rotten air. "What is that?"

"Mushrooms," Ava said, though she sounded curious. "There are rotten bits of wood everywhere, with really strange mushrooms all over them. The Warden's growing them for... something."

"Poison, you think?" I wondered aloud.

"I don't know," Ava admitted. "I don't recognize this fungus. It looks like red tentacles, with black spikes growing out of the stumps. I've never seen something like this used in potions."

Marcus pushed past us and stepped into the room.

"Marcus, don't!" Kallie protested, but I was certain he was already touching the mushrooms.

"It's devil's finger," he said nonchalantly. "I've seen it on the mushroom identification chart in Professor Woolly's classroom. It's supposed to be really rare."

I stepped forward and ran my fingers over one of the mushrooms. *Tentacles* was an accurate description. The tentacles bloomed from the center of the fungus, and I ran my fingers down them until I touched something hard. My head began to spin, and nausea twisted in my gut, but my curiosity got the better of me.

"Mm... what's that?" I asked thoughtfully.

Oberi came up beside me and nearly shoved me out of the way to get a good look. He sounded horrified. *Uh, Ava! You might want to come and look at this.*

Ava came to my side. "Oberi, what are you—? What *is* that?"

Ava's fingers brushed mine as she started digging into the fungus. She gasped as she pulled something out. "Ancestors, it's one of the crystals Jaymin had. No wonder we feel so sick in here!"

"The Warden is hiding the crystals inside fungus?" I asked. "Why would he do that?"

"I don't think he's hiding them here," Kallie said. "I think he's *growing* them."

"Devil's finger is believed to be connected straight to hell," Marcus said in a shaky tone.

"So these crystals are coming from hell," I stated.

"It actually makes a lot of sense," Ava pointed out. "We know these crystals didn't come from Earth. This fungus must act as a portal of some sort."

"Then let's destroy this room!" I cried. If this fungus was rare, and it was the only way the Warden was getting his hands on these crystals, we could burn his operation to the ground.

A crackling sound came from Ava's hand as she conjured fire. "You're right. We have to get rid of this."

"Wait!" Kallie protested. "We're not done here yet. If we burn this place down now, we may not find the Elves."

"Kallie's right," Marcus said. "We need to see what other clues we find first, before we burn all the evidence."

Ava huffed, like she wanted nothing more than to throw her fireball. I hated to admit it, but I agreed with Kallie and Marcus.

"We'll finish it off," I assured her. "But let's find Eddie first."

"Fine," Ava said. "But I'm burning this room to the ground before we leave."

"Let's get out of here," Marcus said quickly. "These crystals are giving me a splitting headache."

"Agreed," I said. I couldn't get out of there soon enough.

We left the room, and Ava opened the door across the hall. The moment we stepped inside, she sucked a breath and turned into me, like she couldn't bear to look.

I held Ava tightly in my arms. Water dripped onto my head from the ceiling.

"Oh my gods," Kallie whispered.

Everyone just stood there for several seconds, taking it all in. I wasn't sure if I wanted to know what they were seeing. Water splattered on my head again, and I reached up to wipe it out of my hair— but my fingers came away sticky. I reached toward the ceiling to figure out where it was coming from. My stomach bottomed out when my hand sank into something soft and squishy. Chains clinked, and I gasped when I realized what it was.

A body.

Wet innards spilled from the corpse suspended above me. Ava and I screamed as we jumped backward. The guts landed with a loud *splat* on the floor. I gagged, and Ava whimpered.

"What the hell is this place?" I demanded.

Kallie stepped past me and entered the room. Oberi followed her, sniffing the air. "The Warden has set up metal tables, like those you'd find in a morgue," Kallie told me. "There are blood stains on the floor and broken crystals everywhere."

"This is where they experimented on them," Ava said with certainty. "This is where he tried to uncover their demigod powers."

"How do you know?" I asked.

She swallowed audibly. "A pretty damn strong feeling."

"Do you think he could've experimented on Eddie?" I wondered.

"I don't think he had time," Ava replied. "Apart from this corpse, I don't see any fresh blood."

"This corpse is still fresh, though," Marcus said thoughtfully. He stepped around me to inspect the room with Kallie. "I'll bet anything this guy died earlier today."

My guts twisted so tightly that I could barely get the question out. "Is it anyone we know?"

Marcus swallowed audibly. "It's Tony. His body is hanging off hooks."

The Dangerous Dragon. I should've been sick to know what the Warden had done to him, but truth be told, I didn't care that Tony was dead. He'd hit Ava last semester, and I'd nearly killed him for it. At least he couldn't hurt her anymore.

"The Warden must've kept him prisoner for a long time," Ava said in a hollow tone.

"His test results showed he was part Elf," I reminded her. "I'm sure the Warden bled every bit of magic he could out of him."

"The Warden's experiments are failing," Kallie said from across the room. "These crystal bits are useless. I can't feel a thing within them."

"Maybe—" Marcus started, but he cut off when Oberi started to whine. "Hold on."

"You found something?" I asked, hoping it might lead us to the Elves.

There's something under this table, Oberi said.

Marcus gasped, and I heard something jingle. "It's from my coven," he rasped.

"What'd you find?" I questioned.

Marcus placed something into my hand. I ran my fingers over it to see it was a small star pendant attached to a chain.

"The five-pointed star represents the five types of witches in the Miriamic Coven," Marcus explained. "Alice wore a necklace like this during the Games."

"So she *was* down here," Ava said, sounding horrified.

Nausea slammed into me. We were right. The Warden had never sent Alice and her team home when they won the Darke Games. It was all a ruse to identify the strongest inmates and run experiments on them. I had been holding on to the last shred of hope we had that we'd been wrong, but this confirmed it. Guilt ate away at me with the confirmation, and my fingers curled into a fist around the necklace.

"This should've been us," I said in a hollow tone. "We gave up our win for Alice and her team. We should've been the ones to win and been experimented on down here. I thought we were saving them."

"We all did," Kallie said gently. I could hear the guilt in her tone. We all felt awful. This was our fault.

If you'd won, the Warden would have the demigods he wanted, Oberi pointed out. For once, he wasn't being snarky. He was trying to help, though it didn't make me feel any better about what Alice had gone through. *Who knows what would happen then?*

"Exactly," Ava replied. "We need to figure that out. Let's keep moving."

No one moved to leave the room, though. I was still trying to wrap my head around what happened there.

Oberi pushed his head against my hip. *Come on. We don't know how much time we have.*

I forced myself to move, and we continued down the hall. Ava tried the next door, but the doorknob didn't budge. Tingles spread across my skin.

Ava turned to Kallie. "You can pick this lock, right?"

"Hang on," I said. Before Kallie could answer, I stepped forward and splayed my hand over the door. Energy buzzed through me. "There's magic here— a ward of some sort. We aren't getting through. If we try, the Warden will be immediately alerted that we're here."

"Unless we break it," Marcus said. He strode up to the door and nudged me aside to inspect it. "Remember, I can break wards with my Curse Breaker powers. Usually, Curse Breakers can only work with witch powers, and *sometimes* fae powers, because their magic is so similar."

"But this is the Warden," Kallie said hopelessly. "You broke Hemlock's ward because she's fae, but this is angel magic."

"And we're demigods," Marcus pointed out. "If I can overpower his ward, I can break it."

"We can't reinstate the ward like I did to Hemlock's room," Kallie stated.

"Doesn't matter," Marcus said. "This is bigger than us. We need to figure out whatever he's hiding. At least if I break the ward, it buys us time. The Warden won't know we were down here until we're long gone."

"Do you think you can do it?" Ava sounded uncertain.

Marcus hesitated. He may be a demigod, but he had yet to truly embrace his powers. He constantly held himself back. I wasn't sure he could do this unless he believed in himself.

I placed a hand on his shoulder. "You can do this, Marcus. I believe in you. We all do."

He drew a deep breath, like he was trying to work up the courage. "Everybody stand back."

"Is it dangerous?" Kallie asked in a shaky breath.

"To break this, I have to transform the magic into something else," Marcus said thoughtfully. "It has to be similar to a ward, and wards are protection magic, so I could make a shield."

"Let's get to work, then," I stated.

I could hear Marcus rubbing his hands over the door. He drew several deep breaths, then began muttering to himself. "I've got this. I can do this. It's simple."

I knew the second Marcus began his spell, because I could feel the magic shifting around us. It was like an electrical current that made my hair stand on end. Something moved deep in the earth below us. I didn't think the girls felt it, and I wouldn't have either, if it wasn't for my Nivita magic.

Marcus groaned, like he was trying to lift twice his body weight. The spell was too much for him. The ground began to tremble, and I was certain this time everyone could feel it.

Ava grabbed on to me to steady herself. "What's going on?"

I don't like this, Oberi said in a shaky tone. Rishi meowed loudly.

"Marcus, you need to stop!" I cried.

"I'm almost there," he replied.

Kallie squealed as the ground began to shake more violently. I could hardly stay upright, and I had to steady myself against the wall. Dust rained down on us from above, and bones fell from their crevices in the stone wall and crashed to the floor. I could feel with my Earth magic that the entire Underground was losing its structural integrity.

I began to panic. I stumbled toward Marcus and yanked on his shoulder. "If you don't stop now, this whole place is going to cave in!"

"If I stop, we'll never get inside!" Marcus protested. He shoved his elbow into my chest, and I stumbled backward. I landed on the ground, and Kallie and Ava screamed as they fell over from the violent tremors.

"We'll die!" I shot back. Of fucking course, Marcus had to be brave *now*, when it could kill us.

"The Elves will die without us, if they haven't already," Marcus spat.

Aw, hell. He was right.

But this magic was too strong for him. I could sense it buzzing through him, rattling around his body and begging to escape. The shield he intended to make never came. If Marcus didn't bring this whole place down, this ward was going to kill him. I scrambled forward on my hands and knees and reached out for him again. The hall shook so hard that I couldn't find him.

"Marcus, let me help!" I screamed.

"Don't stop me," he begged.

"Quickly!" I cried, reaching out my hand. "Now that you've drawn out the ward, I can absorb the magic inside of you with my Elf powers. We have to do this together!"

A moment of hesitation passed, and Oberi whimpered from down the hall. I thought for certain this place would crumble, but Marcus grabbed my hand a moment later.

Magic shot up my arm so fast that I was blasted backward. My whole body flipped through the air, throwing me straight into the wall. My head knocked against the stone, and the wind left my chest. My body dropped to the ground, and my thoughts spun so fast I couldn't make sense of what happened.

"Charlie!" Ava's voice cut through my confusion. Her hands landed on my face, and she dragged me onto her lap. "You're okay. You have to be okay. It's over. Wake up, Charlie."

I groaned as I tried pushing myself upright. It took me a few moments to realize that the tremors had stopped. Pain throbbed through the back of my head, and nausea rolled in my gut. I thought I was going to hurl, but nothing came up.

"I'm sorry, Charlie," Marcus said in a shaking tone.

I ignored his apology, because only one thing mattered. "Did we do it?"

"Yes," Marcus answered, though he didn't sound particularly proud about it. "The ward is broken."

Ava helped me to my feet. I felt so unsteady that I had to hold on to her. I couldn't make heads or tails of my surroundings.

"Are you okay?" Kallie asked me.

"I feel like shit," I admitted. "Let's get this information and get out of here, because I don't know how much longer I can stay in this place." The disorientation frightened me a more than I'd admit.

Everyone moved quickly, and we hurried into the room. Ava stopped abruptly, and I ran into her. I grabbed her shoulders to steady myself, and I felt her tremble beneath my touch. I heard Marcus gag.

"What's wrong, pidge?" I demanded.

Ava swallowed audibly, and her tone became hollow. "There's a bulletin board behind the Warden's desk. He's pinned a pair of..." Ava sounded like she was going to be sick.

Kallie finished for her. "He's pinned a pair of Elf ears to the board."

My stomach bottomed out. "Fresh?"

"No. The color's drained from them," Kallie said. "But they seem oddly well preserved. It's sick."

"They're Uriel's," I realized in horror. Uriel had been half-vampire. That had to be why the ears were so well preserved. Uriel had been dragged to the Underground after being accused of the murder at the pool. The Warden had tortured him and sliced his ears off as some sort of souvenir. He was a *monster*.

"Guys, we have to get to work," Marcus said, snapping us all back to attention.

"I'll start at his desk," Ava said in a rush. "Marcus, you check those bookcases over there. Kallie, see if you can crack that safe. Whatever's in there must be important."

Kallie spoke confidently. "Looks like my vigilante days are about to pay off."

"Here, Charlie," Ava said. "Take a seat. You can help Kallie with the safe."

Ava guided me onto a chair. I was grateful to be sitting, because I was certain I'd hurl if I remained on my feet much longer.

Drawers squeaked as Ava started searching them. A heavy stack of papers slammed to the Warden's desk, and she began shuffling through them. Oberi hurried over to help her.

I turned to Kallie beside me. "How's this work?"

"Very precisely," she answered vaguely. "I'll show you."

Kallie guided my hand outward, and my fingers met cold metal located along one of the Warden's book cases. She had me place my ear to the side of the safe.

"I'm going to test each number on the dial," Kallie explained. "With the way the locking mechanism works, you'll hear a slight *tick* when we've reached a contact point where the lever inside will drop slightly. We'll need three numbers for the lever to fall completely into place and unlock the safe."

"That seems simple," I remarked.

Kallie chuckled lightly. "It takes practice for sure. Let's get to work."

Kallie started spinning the dial slowly. I held my breath, listening intently for the *tick* she mentioned. I couldn't hear a thing except for Ava and Marcus rifling through papers. Oberi's nails scratched the floor as he paced around nervously, and Rishi kept letting out hopeless *mews*.

Several long minutes passed before Kallie sucked a sharp breath. "There it was! I got the first number."

"Really? I didn't hear a thing," I said.

"Like I said, it takes practice," she replied.

Kallie kept working. She surprised me by finding the second number even faster than the first. At least fifteen minutes must've passed. My nausea was finally beginning to ease.

"Guys, I found something!" Ava cried at the same time I heard the lock disengage.

"I found something, too," Marcus said.

"The safe is open!" Kallie exclaimed.

"That's great!" Ava abandoned her papers and hurried over to us.

"What's inside?" Marcus asked eagerly.

"Let's see..." Kallie slowly opened the door, and the three of them gasped in unison.

I grabbed Ava's hand instinctually, as if I expected something dangerous. She didn't tense under my touch, though, and I quickly realized she wasn't frightened at all.

"It's a key," Ava said breathlessly.

My jaw dropped. "You mean one of the keys from your journal, the ones your Aunt Maddie drew from her visions? A key to the Elven gate?"

Ava's breath wavered as she stepped forward to take the key. "Exactly like one of those."

"It has angel wings on the end," Marcus said thoughtfully. "This must be the one the angels received when the keys were split up. How did the Warden get his hands on it?"

"I have no idea," Ava said. "But the Warden's power doesn't surprise me anymore. He has more resources than we could ever imagine. We need to decide what to do with this key. If the Warden finds it missing, he'll know we took it."

"I can make a duplicate," Kallie said. "A key's a simple illusion to turn solid. It won't hold its magic, so it can't open the gate, but if the

Warden checks to see if it's still in his safe, he won't know the difference."

"It should work," Marcus agreed. "I think Charlie should take this key."

I furrowed my brow. "Why me?"

"Because you're the only person without one," Marcus pointed out. "We'll get it back to the Lair with the other three as soon as we can, but if we ever need to split them up, Charlie should be in charge of this one."

"I agree," Ava said. She reached for my hand and placed the key in my palm. "We shouldn't be keeping the keys together, anyhow. Once we find a safer place for them, we'll each take one to keep an eye on."

"That sounds like the safest option," I agreed, though I didn't like the idea of being responsible for something so important. It made me really nervous.

I slipped the key into my pocket, while Kallie conjured a duplicate into the safe and sealed it back up. I turned to Ava. "What'd you find?"

"Evidence. A lot of it," Ava said. She hurried back toward the Warden's desk and began shuffling through the papers she'd been studying. The rest of us gathered around her. "Eddie and the others are still alive but... the Warden's notes say they were tortured. It sounds like he didn't get anything out of them before they were moved."

I was already certain Eddie had been tortured, but the confirmation made me ill. "Moved where?"

"There's several mentions in his records about some sort of concentration center," Ava said. "There's *this* document detailing the rights to land, signed by members of the United Supernatural Union. The Union gave the Warden land to set up a camp."

"What, like an internment camp?" I sneered.

"That's exactly what I'm thinking," Ava said. "I found a list of people, and *all* of them are identified as Elves."

"That's where they're taking the Elven inmates," I realized.

"Yes," Ava replied. "But it's more than that. There are names on here I've never heard before, and there are *way* more Elves at the camp than were captured in Forevermore."

"So they're rounding up any Elves that have been discovered and putting them in this camp," Kallie realized.

"Exactly," Ava said. "But the numbers are weird. It's like the Warden is sending more Elves to the camp than were ever at the Institute to begin with."

"He's forging the numbers," Marcus thought out loud.

"Why?" I wondered. "If he's already got authority over the camp—"

I cut off when I realized it.

"He can't run his experiments from the camp," I said. "He's sending off any Elves he's uninterested in and forging the numbers to keep the Union happy and to hide what he's doing here at the Underground. But he couldn't keep the Elf kids here forever."

"The Union might've been forcing his hand," Marcus theorized. "He ran out of time."

"But not everyone on the Union is corrupt and wants to hurt the Elves," Kallie protested. "My Uncle Theo is the fae representative for the Union, and he'd never let this happen."

"The Elementai representative wouldn't allow this to go on, either, or the Miriamic representative," Ava said. "The Warden's hiding things from certain Union members in order to please the angels and vampires; I'm sure of it."

"There's more," Marcus said in a gut-wrenching tone. He dropped a book onto the table, and it landed with a heavy *thud*. "The Warden's been learning dangerous spells. These spell books shouldn't even exist."

"Do I even want to know what kind of spells?" I asked.

Marcus drew a deep breath. "They're the kind of spells that summon demons and monsters. He's bookmarked pages and written notes in the margins— crossed out spells he couldn't perform and highlighted ones that worked. He's definitely been making deals with dark gods to get those crystals, but..." Marcus sucked a breath.

"But what?" Kallie prodded.

"One of these spells..." He hesitated, like it was hard to even think about. "It's a spell to open portals to hell."

"So the magical ley lines *are* a lie," I spat.

"Do you guys remember when we were fighting the malumuto demon in the Games?" Marcus asked. "I remember he said, *Who unleashed me?* The demon hadn't come here on his own. The Warden is forcing the monsters to come here. He's manufacturing the Games as a test of power. There's no threat to the island— it was him all along, framing it in a way to get students to sign up and show off their demigod powers. This proves it."

"The whole Institute is a lie," Kallie growled in disgust. "Rehabilitation, my ass. It's all a ploy to move kids through the system so he can find demigods—"

"HELP!" A young girl's scream tore down the hall.

I stilled momentarily. "There's someone here."

"Come on!" Ava grabbed my hand and yanked me out of the room.

More voices came as we raced down the hall.

"Please, don't!" a boy cried.

"Stop!" a girl screamed.

"They must be—" Ava cut off as we burst into a room at the end of the hall. An awful scent hit my nose, and I thought for certain we'd entered another room of mushrooms.

I didn't realize Ava had stopped moving, and I took a few more steps into the room. My foot caught on something, and I went tumbling to the ground, but the hard smack of the floor I expected never came. Instead, my arms sank into a pile of... something I couldn't place. I felt around to figure out what it was, and that's when I felt a pair of fingers on mine. A body landed on top of me, and my heart leapt.

"Help!" I yelled to my friends. The Warden had found us. His guards were tackling me!

Hands landed on my ankle, and my friends dragged me backward. I broke free of the body that had dragged me down.

"Go to hell!" I screamed as I leapt to my feet. I lifted my hands to fight back, but Ava grabbed my wrists.

"Stop, Charlie," she said gently. "They're not alive."

"They're not—" I cut off when I realized what she'd said.

Ancestors, the smell. It wasn't mushrooms. It was *corpses*. Honest to god, rotting corpses. A whole pile of them. And I'd fallen right into them. All the nausea I thought had passed came slamming into my gut again. I doubled over and gagged as bile shot up my throat.

Victim's screams continued to fill the room, but they were quieter now— like someone had turned down the volume on a radio. A shiver traveled down my spine.

I wiped my mouth. "What is this?"

Marcus' footsteps sounded as he paced around the room. "It's a residual haunting. Their cries are echoing through time. These voices are trapped because of the trauma that happened here."

"So no one's really here?" I asked.

"No living soul, at least," Kallie stated. She stepped closer to the pile of bodies, and I heard something squish as she began moving corpses aside.

"What are you doing?" Ava asked her.

"I'm trying to determine the cause of death," she replied.

Something smacked, like a corpse's hand landing on another's face. I winced.

"Oh, gods," Kallie gasped. "She died of bloodletting. And he was drowned. Where are her intestines—?"

"Kallie," I snapped. She was going to make me hurl again. "Can you not?"

"Dear Goddess!" Marcus screamed. The terror in his tone made my blood turn to ice. He raced across the room. I didn't realize how big the room was, until I heard him cross it. The pile of bodies had to be much bigger than I was imagining.

"What did you find?" Kallie asked.

"It's... it's Alice. Dear Goddess." Marcus' voice trembled. I heard bones clatter to the floor, like he'd been trying to lift her skeleton but it crumbled to pieces under his touch. "I'm so sorry, cousin."

So that was it, then. We were too late. If Alice was dead, Wesley and Despona were, too. We'd condemned them to their deaths.

Ava took my hand and led me across the room. She spoke curiously. "How do you know?"

Marcus hesitated. "I can just... feel it. I think it's my necromancy magic."

Kallie gasped, like she had an idea. "Marcus, your coven has psychometry, right? You can see the past of objects if you touch them, correct?"

"Some witches do," he admitted. "I'm not sure that I have it."

Kallie signed. "Damn. I was hoping we could get some answers from her bones."

Marcus sniffled, and I heard his sleeve rustle as he wiped his face. "I can't do that... but I have another idea. Help me rearrange these bones."

Bones clinked against the ground as Kallie and Marcus arranged the skeleton. When they finished, Marcus stepped back, but he stumbled over my foot. I caught him to keep him upright.

"Sorry," Marcus mumbled. "Everyone, get into a circle around Alice's bones. We're going to use my magic to summon her spirit."

"Is this safe?" Ava asked.

"Um... let's save our questions until the end," Marcus said quickly, and I heard him conjure a few items. "Ava, light these candles. I have to make two circles— one with fire, and one with salt."

Fire crackled as Ava ignited the candles, and salt scattered as Marcus poured it out on the floor. Then came a scratching sound, like writing being etched onto the concrete.

"What are you doing?" Kallie asked.

"I have to write protective sigils in chalk, so the spirit remains contained and doesn't get out of control," Marcus said.

"Is that a risk? It's Alice," Kallie said.

"We don't know what they put her through. Her spirit could be traumatized. She could hurt us even if she doesn't mean to." Marcus took a breath. "Okay, it's set up. Everyone join hands."

I took Ava's hand on one side and Marcus' on the other. He began muttering Latin words under his breath, and a chill traveled across my skin.

Clicking noises sounded, and it took me a moment to realize it was the bones. The skeleton rose from the ground and stumbled forward. I jumped back as the bones landed on me, as if the skeleton was lunging for attack. My fingers slipped out of Marcus', and I broke the circle. The skeleton dropped to the ground, as if it was a puppet that'd just been dropped.

I shuddered. "Holy hell, Marcus! A little warning, please."

Marcus sounded less than pleased. "Come here and finish the circle, or this won't work."

Warily, I stepped forward, feeling with the tip of my shoe so I wouldn't step on any bones. I felt Alice's skull and stopped in my tracks.

Marcus grabbed my hand and began muttering his spell again. The skeleton moved again, making rattling noises until it was standing in front of us.

"Alice," Marcus called out. "Are you here with us?"

"I'm here," a ghostly, ethereal female voice came through. "But I don't know how much time I have."

Ava squeezed my hand tightly and leaned over to whisper. "She's speaking through her skeleton. The protective sigils are keeping her inside the circle."

"Alice, I'm so sorry about what happened to you," Marcus said. "We need to prevent this from happening again to someone else. Is there anything you can tell us about the Warden that you learned when you were down here?"

"The Warden made a deal with the dark gods," Alice said. "It's how he's getting the crystals. The Warden wants to be the ruler of all supernaturals on Earth. He wants to control who gets magic and who doesn't. I overheard his whole plan while they were torturing me."

"What is his plan, exactly?" Kallie pressed.

"He'll funnel people to hell for the dark gods. In exchange, the dark gods will give him power," Alice explained. "He doesn't want people to be able to get to the Blessed Haven, because he wants himself and the angels to decide who gets what— who lives and who dies, who rests in peace and who is condemned."

"How do the demigods play into this?" Ava asked.

"He needs a demigod's power to find some sort of key," Alice said. "He spoke of a gate that he wished to open, and then destroy."

The Elven Gate, Oberi said.

"But that's not all," Alice continued. "He wishes to harness demigod power. He wants to put their power into the crystals so he can try and draw from it. He wants to become a demigod himself."

I gave a shudder. "Have any of his experiments been successful?"

"Not yet," Alice said. "Everyone he's experimented on so far has died, and the crystals always break every time he tries. You must not let him succeed. If he's able to harness demigod powers, he could gain enough magic to betray the dark gods. He intends to kill the gods we worship and become a supreme being himself. But there are whispers on the other side. The dark gods are manipulating him. They need him to start this war, in order to overthrow our gods and free the dark gods from hell. They will kill the Warden when that happens."

The skeleton creaked as Alice turned. "My reaper is here for me. My soul has been tied to this place, waiting to pass on the information I've learned. Now that you know it, I can leave the Underground and join my ancestors in Alora."

"Go in peace, Alice," Marcus told her. "We'll do what we can to save people with the knowledge you've given us."

A whoosh of air swept through the room, and Alice's skeleton crumbled to the ground. I smelled smoke as the candles went out. I knew her time with us was up, and I hoped she was finally at rest.

"We have to escape," Ava blurted. "If the Warden experiments on us and succeeds—"

"How do we keep him from hunting us down?" Kallie asked.

Their voices faded as I took several steps backward in shock. I could hardly wrap my head around everything Alice had just said. The Warden wished to use our powers to kill our gods... the Great Spirit, Mother Miriam, the Seven Gods... all of them. And when he did that, all hell would be unleashed.

Literally.

I took another step back. Something clinked beneath my feet, like the sound of metal on metal. My feet tangled in the shackles, and I fell over. As I landed, something snapped, and heavy metal teeth clamped around my ankle. I heard the crunch of bone. Pain shot up my leg, and a scream tore from my lungs so loud that it echoed through the room.

"Charlie!" Ava screamed. She rushed over to me, and her fingers curled around some sort of metal trap.

"His leg's broken," Kallie murmured as she knelt beside me.

I felt Marcus prop me up from behind. "Shit. He's about to pass out."

"They're down there!" a female voice came from down the hall. Hell, I knew that voice all too well. It was *Jaymin.*

Ava stilled. "Fuck! They've found us!"

Oberi shoved Ava aside. *Quickly! There's no time. We must hide the key.*

I was in too much pain to ask what the hell he was doing. Oberi used his paw to dig into my pocket, and I heard the key I'd put there *clink* onto the ground next to my hand. Oberi's tongue grazed my skin as he snatched up the key in his jaws and swallowed it.

Guards burst into the room. Screw the pain. I lifted my hands to blast them to motherfucking oblivion... but nothing came out. My magic rattled inside of me, but something was blocking it, keeping it in...

I realized in horror that it was the ward. All the disorientation I'd been feeling hadn't been from the blow to the head at all. It was because I could no longer use my magic to orient me.

"Guys, the power I absorbed from the ward backfired," I said weakly. "It's trapped all my natural magic inside of me. I can't do any spells."

Ava gave a whimper of terror at the same time Oberi whined. I couldn't fight back. All I could do was wait to be captured.

TWENTY-TWO

We'd never been so screwed in our entire lives.

Guards poured into the room and blocked the exit. Jaymin stood at the head of them, a stupid, shit-eating grin on her face like she knew she'd won.

She hadn't won shit. She didn't know how to play this game, and I had news for her; we were villains, and we *loved* fighting dirty.

Jaymin carried a pistol. Why the hell did she have a gun? Supernaturals didn't need them.

Unless she was counting on using it as a quicker way of killing us off than what her Nivita magic was capable of.

"What are you waiting for?" Jaymin cried. "Get them!"

The guards began shooting at us with their noxite guns. I created a huge wall of Fire that spanned up to the ceiling, burning the darts down to nothing but cinders before they even got close. The guards kept firing until their guns began clicking, signaling they were running out of bullets. I kept the wall of Fire up, fueling it as high as it could go so the guards couldn't reach us.

"Ava, you've gotta call the flames off." Charlie coughed, and I heard Kallie and Marcus gasping for air.

The heat was going to kill the others if I didn't tone it down, and I'd suffocate if the smoke continued to rise. I let the Fire wall fall. Now that their noxite guns were empty, the guards resorted to magic. A crackling sound filled the room as guards fired off battle orbs, elements, and spells. Kallie created a shield, and we ducked behind it as the spells let loose. Magic slammed against her shield, which vibrated with the force of the guards' spells.

"We're not getting out of here unless we can get these fucks out of the way!" Marcus yelled, shielding his head.

"I can take them down," Kallie promised. She conjured a bow with a quiver of magical arrows that glowed bright blue from her powers. She leaned around her shield and began firing them off at the guards. The arrows exploded on impact, turning guards to jelly and injuring whoever was standing close.

Oberi changed into a unicorn. She shot off bolts of Fire magic with her horn that was aimed at the guards, forcing them to sprint out of the way as her magic exploded.

Marcus sprang out from behind the shield. He shouted an incantation, something that sounded foreboding and ominous. Goosebumps rose over my skin as I watched the corpses and skeletons around the room rise with ghostly groans. They proceeded toward the guards with their arms stretched out, burying them in hordes and ripping out their throats with rotting teeth. Marcus kept the army of the dead going, a menacing green glow overtaking his eyes. Green necromancy magic wrapped up his arms, making the warlock appear all the dark demigod he was.

While Marcus kept the guards busy with the corpse army, I ducked outside Kallie's shield. I shot off blue fireballs at the vampire guards, who I knew would be the hardest to take down. I was quick, but with their super-speed, they were a lot faster, and I missed my targets often.

As he was directing the corpses to attack the guards, Marcus formed a battle orb in his hand. He sent it whizzing through the air the same time Rishi let out a vicious growl and jumped in front of it.

"Rishi!" Marcus yelped, but the cat wasn't hurt. It was like he'd intended to jump *into* the orb itself. The battle orb infused around

Rishi's form, until Rishi was inside of Marcus' magic, completely surrounded by the ball of sparks.

"Holy crap!" Marcus shouted, but he kept the spell going.

Rishi took off running, the battle orb swelling around him. He hissed and yowled as he bounced around the room like some kind of explosive, electrocuting whatever guards he came into contact with. Rishi was the companion of a demigod, which meant he was special. I didn't think any other cat in the Miriamic Coven could do what Rishi had just done.

Rishi raised his paw and swiped at a vampire guard in front of him. The guard was cut in half by the power of the battle orb, which reduced the vampire to nothing more than dust.

Ancestors, that was *cool.* I didn't know Rishi could do that!

Charlie sifted through the mound of bodies on the ground that Marcus hadn't summoned. I didn't know what he was looking for, until I saw that he'd grabbed a discarded dagger— probably one that had been used to torture the inmates. A guard let out a harsh string of orders, and Charlie flung it in that direction.

Unfortunately, Kallie was running by right at that time. The dagger that Charlie threw embedded in her calf, and I cringed as she let out a scream.

"Ow! What the fuck!" Kallie screamed. She ripped the knife out of her leg and tossed it. Her shifter healing powers mended the wound quickly, but if he had thrown it any higher, he could've really hurt her.

This is exactly what had happened in Forevermore. Charlie had panicked, become overwhelmed, and had shot spells off everywhere, hurting more Elves than guards. We couldn't afford more mistakes like that. He wanted to help, but in this situation, it was better if he stayed out of it.

I grabbed his shoulders and dragged him back behind the shield. "Charlie, you can't help! Stay down!"

"You need to worry about yourself, not about protecting me!" he demanded.

"You're hurt, you can't see, you don't have your powers, and you can't even sense where you are! It's irresponsible for you to interfere! Let us handle it!" I demanded.

An aggravated noise rose from Charlie's throat. Blood poured from his hurt leg, and he slapped the puddle. "Use my blood! At least then I'll be good for something!"

It was gruesome, but his words gave me an idea. I pulled the blood off the stone floor with my Water magic, then flung it in a stream over the shield. The blood got the attention of the vampire guards as it splattered against the wall, causing them to freeze. I took their momentary pause to summon a barrage of fireballs and blast them their way. By the time they knew the fireballs were coming, the guards were surrounded by my flames. I heard the dying gasps of vampires as my Fire caused them to greet their fate. Anyone I missed, Oberi killed with her horn.

Kallie, Marcus, Oberi and I kept the magic going, but no matter how many guards we took down, there always seemed like there were others to take their place. We'd already killed so many men, and yet more kept coming. We could mow down these guards all day, but if the Warden showed up, we were in trouble. We had to get out of here and off Institute grounds before he showed up. Jaymin remained out of the fight, as if we knew it was only a matter of time before she wore us down.

"Kallie, do it now!" Marcus screamed.

Out of the corner of my eye, I watched as Kallie went to snap her fingers. At the same time, a stray battle orb hit her, sinking into her gut. She let out a cry of pain and crumpled to the floor as her time magic vibrated outward.

The scene around me was like watching fast-forward on a television screen. Guards moved at a rate that was impossible for them to perform, even as vampires. The entire room around us turned into nothing but a blur, while the four of us, along with Oberi, were caught at a standstill. Rishi zoomed around the room in his battle orb until it exploded in the middle of the fight, dropping him to the floor. I turned in place, unsure of what was going on. Marcus failed to keep hold of the necromancy spell, and Kallie's bow dissolved out of her hands. I tried conjuring a fireball, but the magic flared up and died out in my palm in a manner of nanoseconds.

Then everything stopped, returning to normal speed once again. Total fear overwhelmed my senses as I realized we were surrounded...

and in captivity of the guards. One guard had slapped some sort of metal cuff on my wrist. It had a crystal in the middle like the ones we'd seen in the room that grew the devil's finger— the crystals that weakened a demigod's power and made us sick. A wave of nausea overwhelmed my senses, and a migraine began to blossom across my head as a familiar ringing sound echoed in my ears. I realized that all four of us were wearing similar cuffs.

I tried, but I couldn't access my magic with this cuff on me. Fuck, *fuck*! We were so screwed. Kallie's eyes went wide, as if she couldn't believe what she'd done.

My heart sank to the floor as I realized the truth. She hadn't stopped time. She'd *sped it up*. And because she had, we'd been unable to defend ourselves and had gotten caught.

Kallie tried snapping her fingers again, and she let out a whimper as time ceased to move to her command. A guard wrenched her arms behind her back so she couldn't move.

"Make sure the wolf can't escape," a guard barked at his lackeys. A couple of dragon shifter guards stormed forward, grabbing her arms.

"Get off me, you bastards!" Kallie cried, but even with her shifter strength, she couldn't escape two dragons.

Marcus attempted to wrench free in order to get to Kallie, but a guard slapped him across the face. His knees buckled at the blow as his head hung limply. Rishi yowled. He charged after the guy who'd hit Marcus, but a guard reached down and shoved him into a cat-sized cage he was carrying, locking it so Rishi couldn't break free.

Charlie had been forced to his feet by a guard, but his broken leg wouldn't support his weight. They didn't even bother putting cuffs on him, just held him tightly by the arms. They'd guessed, for whatever reason, his magic wasn't working at the moment.

Oberi tossed her mane and charged forward to help him, but one of the guards threw out a binding spell. She collapsed to the floor beside Charlie, her hooves bound by some sort of invisible force. She couldn't move, nor could she break the spell.

"It's in your best interest to stop resisting," Jaymin announced. "That is, if you want to keep your parents alive."

The guards parted. My heartbeat kicked into overtime as I watched a group of guards drag my parents into the room, shoving them to their knees. They were bound with noxite cuffs, and had probably been drugged with it, too. They didn't have any magic to spare. They were defenseless and unable to fight back.

"Don't listen to her. The four of you need to get out. Don't worry about us," Daddy demanded. He was in chief mode, using his authoritative tone to tell me to run. But how could I leave them here?

One of the guards punched Daddy across the face, and Mama gasped. I cringed, but Daddy spat blood onto the guard's boots and shot him a glare. "This is child's play. I've been through more than that in my day."

"You two have caused me enough trouble," Jaymin snarled at him. "Be silent."

"We should've never stopped searching for you until we found you," Mama growled. "It was a mistake to let you go."

"We all have regrets, Sophia," Jaymin replied coldly.

Jaymin's attention returned to me, and her voice dropped to a deadly tone. "Ava-Marie, if you or your friends make a move to harm us, your mother and father will be killed. It's best to do as I say."

Kallie hesitated and glanced at me.

Marcus whispered, "Ava, what do we do?"

I swallowed the lump in my throat as a thought crossed my mind. Had Kallie and Marcus' parents gotten off campus without being captured? What if they were being held somewhere, too? I knew we were all thinking the same thing as I observed the stricken look on my friends' faces. We had no idea who Jaymin was holding hostage. We could be killing off all our families if we made an effort to escape.

"Professor Vengier, why are you doing this?" Marcus asked in a wobbly tone.

"Her name isn't Vengier. That's Jaymin *Riske*," Daddy spat. "The war criminal."

I froze in shock. I'd heard of Jaymin Riske— everyone in the tribe had— but hadn't made the connection. She'd used child soldiers and committed terrible crimes during the Hawkei Civil War. I had no idea she was still alive. She hadn't been seen in over twenty years, and was rumored to be on the run. I couldn't believe she'd surfaced here, at the prison.

"Actually, I went back to my maiden name after my husband had an *unfortunate accident*," Jaymin replied simply. "So don't accuse me of being too dishonest."

My gut twisted with horror. "You killed him."

"He wasn't on board with the plan," Jaymin spat. "He was willing to do *anything* during the Hawkei Civil War to win, but he insisted getting involved in the affairs of other supernaturals went too far. It was so sad that tree crushed him, but if you're as dedicated to the cause as I am, you'll do whatever it takes to win. A sad liability I had to get rid of."

"You're a monster," Mama said, with all the hatred in the world.

"Don't you morons understand? If the Hawkei can align themselves with the angels, we can elevate the status of our race. We can preserve the line of the tribe, and what's more, *we* can decide the fate of other supernaturals. The Elementai will finally be one of the dominant magical races, instead of being forced to live at the bottom!" Jaymin ranted.

"The Warden isn't going to share power," I growled. "You're delusional if you think he'll let anyone have a say in how the world is run besides himself."

"Doctor Taurus is a visionary. I wouldn't expect you to understand," Jaymin said scathingly. "But we're not here to convince you to our side. Bring her to me."

"Ava—" Charlie cried, but he fell forward trying to get to me.

The guards forcibly dragged me to Jaymin. I didn't know how this could get worse.

Ava! Oberi's magic was so strong, it broke the bonds around her and set her free. She managed to get to her hooves. She charged forward, her horn down. She pointed it at Jaymin, aiming for the heart.

Jaymin whirled around and fired the gun. Both Charlie and I reeled backward as we felt the bullet sink in. My breath caught in my throat as Oberi went down, collapsing mid-gallop and sinking to the floor.

"*No!*" Charlie and I both screamed at the same time. Oberi changed into a husky mid-fall. Jaymin had shot him in the shoulder. Blood gushed from the wound.

Shock overtook my entire form as I watched my Familiar pant on the floor. Tears spilled out of my eyes as it sank in that she'd actually *shot* Oberi.

"I need to help him!" I screamed. I struggled against the guards, who yanked me back into place. Charlie managed to pull himself free, but the guards shoved him back down to the ground.

"I'll shoot your Familiar again if you don't comply," Jaymin threatened. "Don't make this harder than it has to be."

Oberi let out a few painful cries. He lay in a pool of his own blood. My poor dog was in so much pain.

Ava, don't worry about me, Oberi rasped. *I'll... regenerate even if she kills me.*

We don't know that for sure. I stopped struggling and went limp immediately. I wouldn't do anything to hurt Oberi, even if it meant doing what Jaymin said. I knew there was a possibility that he'd come back, but I didn't want to take that chance, or put him in more pain if Jaymin shot him again.

Charlie tried crawling in my direction, but a guard put a boot on his back and forced him to the floor.

"Let her go!" my mother screamed. I heard her and Daddy fighting against the guards that were keeping them on the floor, but neither of them broke free.

They were as powerless as the rest of us were. And now, with these terrible crystals attached to our bodies, we couldn't fight back even if we wanted to.

"Inferichite is highly effective at weakening demigods. It absorbs their power quite gradually," Jaymin said with glee. "Unfortunately, its side effects can be fatal, if the exposure period is too long. But you'll keep your life, if we manage to succeed."

One of the fae guards conjured a metal table. They forced me onto it, then fastened my ankles and wrists to leather binds that were attached to it.

A guard placed two inferichite crystals on either side of my head. Once they were laid upon the table, Jaymin began chanting a spell. "*Dii tenebrae, hanc potestatem sumite, ut ea uti possimus nostro. Dii tenebrae, hanc victimam haurite, ut nos delecti fiamus.*"

I wasn't proficient in Latin, but I knew enough to translate what she was saying. *Dark gods, take this power, so we may use it for our own. Dark gods, drain this victim, so we may become elite.*

At Jaymin's chant, a thin stream of magic connected from the crystals to both sides of my temple. The moment the magic from the inferichite latched on to my mind, I began to scream.

They were trying to funnel my powers into the inferichite. I couldn't let them take my magic. I fought against the inferichite with everything I had, but ancestors, it was painful. The inferichite had latched on to my organs and was attempting to forcibly rip the magic out. I screamed and wrenched against the binds holding me in place, twisting on the table as my body was forced to endure the worst pain I'd ever experienced. I thought I might pass out, but the inferichite forced me to remain conscious as it stripped me of every thought and sense of being about who I was. My Fire magic was eating me alive from the inside out, while my Water magic filled my lungs and made it hard to breathe. The only thing that remained hidden was my Anichi magic, which stubbornly remained out of my reach even as I begged it to heal me.

This is what the Hawkei Elders had tried to do to my aunt long ago. They'd tried to take her powers of prophecy by using the inferichite, and now, they were doing the same to me. Ancestors, I wanted it all to end, if this is what I had to endure. I would've gladly died there at that moment, just to be rid of the pain. I wanted to curl up and find a place to hide as the crystals began tearing me up inside, skin to bone until it felt like my entire form was in pieces, yet I was still whole.

Despite the ritual taking place, I didn't feel any magic leave me, just dissipate for a moment before returning. I realized that my powers weren't fueling the crystals. All the inferichite was doing was making my magic go in a loop, through the magic tendrils and into the crystals before they funneled back into my own body. Despite Jaymin's incantation, the inferichite couldn't hold on to my powers.

These dumb fucks. They had no idea how to use these crystals. Even in my inebriated state, I could figure that out.

But they weren't as smart as me. And their incompetence on how to use inferichite against a demigod properly was probably going to take my life.

"Stop it!" I heard Kallie plead. I think she was crying. I could barely make out the rest of the room as tears streamed out of my eyes and screams ripped out of my throat.

Charlie knew exactly what I was going through. His expression was overtaken by a visage of utter horror and disgust as he felt my magic being turned against me through our bond. He shook against the ground and tried to get up, although the guards held him down. Oberi moved his paws against the stone, trying to find the strength to fight back.

"Leave her alone! Stop torturing her like this!" Mama's voice was frantic as she pleaded with Jaymin to stop, but I knew it was a hopeless attempt at bargaining. Jaymin would do what she wanted with me, no matter what anyone said.

"I'll deal with the two of you later," Jaymin seethed. She grabbed my mother by the hair and threw her at Marcus' feet before a couple of guards did the same with Daddy. "For now, stay out of my way."

My throat went raw, and eventually, I stopped screaming. There was just no use in fighting against this kind of pain. Letting it happen would be easier. My body slackened against the table and began to convulse. Maybe I was finally nearing the end. I longed for it. I knew someday I'd make it out of here, though maybe not in the way I hoped... and I accepted that I probably wouldn't be walking out of the Underground. Ever. What Jaymin was doing to me wasn't reversible. It was permanent, and going back to who I was before was a lost cause now.

"Jaymin, she's dying," a guard said from far-off.

"Then we'll start on one of the others," Jaymin replied, but her voice was hesitant. She was worried about losing me.

"The Warden won't be pleased if we let this one die," the guard growled back. He sounded ready to intercede himself.

"We stick to the plan," Jaymin barked. "Go for the one with the broken leg."

Charlie couldn't go through this. It'd kill him, as it would surely kill me. But there wasn't much I could do as I heard them haul Charlie up and slam him onto another table. I heard the clinking of crystals as they were placed by his head, and Jaymin began her wicked chant again.

Charlie started wailing at the top of his lungs. I'd never heard him scream like not— not even when the Warden had drained his life energy in Forevermore. Ancestors, is that how I sounded? I could feel his pain through our bond, making my own torture seem twice as intense. Oberi whimpered from several feet away, giving soft noises that told me he'd die if they kept this up.

Somehow, the sound of Charlie's screams overpowered my own pain. It made me go mad with hatred for Jaymin, the Warden, and anyone who was involved with them. With each cry he let out, I felt my anger grow stronger. Uncontrollable rage began to fester in my chest until my whole body shook. They could do what they wanted with me, but my husband and my Familiar were *off limits*. The fury was intense, stronger than the magic of the crystals suppressing me, making me see nothing but red.

I'm going to make them suffer.

At my rage, I felt a huge well of energy rise up in me and burst outward through the tendrils that connected me to the stones. Both of the crystals shattered, sending fragments scattering and breaking the leather cuffs that held me in place.

The pain instantly died, and my body relaxed as it felt blissful freedom from the inferichite's hold. I heard Charlie gave a gasp, and there was another shattering noise— his crystals had broken, too. He collapsed off the table and rolled on the ground, curled up in pain.

I was no longer bound, so I could get off the table. But I didn't feel like I could. I had so little strength. My wrist shook. The cuff I wore still held my magic back. The outburst of energy had failed to break the over-sized piece of inferichite within the cuff itself, although it had shattered the smaller pieces used to torture Charlie and me.

Jaymin let out an enraged noise. She slammed her hands against the table, and it quaked at her touch. She'd been expecting something grand to happen and was sorely disappointed. "This isn't how it's supposed to work! The inferichite is supposed to anchor her powers, so *we* can take them for *ourselves*!" she screeched.

"We've never managed to transfer a demigod's power into inferichite before," the guard said. "We need more time to work on the girl."

"We've never had a *real* demigod before! All we've ever worked on is average supernaturals and the occasional prophet! This *should* work!" Jaymin screamed.

It's not going to work if you don't know how to use them, I thought weakly. Jaymin thought she could be all-powerful, but she lacked the knowledge to use the inferichite properly. She'd never get my powers into those crystals otherwise.

But I was damn sure she'd keep trying anyway. I wasn't sure how much longer I would hold up.

"Something's wrong with the ceremony," the guard argued. "If we take our time and learn what we did wrong, perhaps we'll be able to obtain her powers on the next attempt."

Jaymin took a moment to think, before she said, "Fine. We'll take Ava, and kill the rest. Capture her Familiar. Ava needs the dog to stay alive."

No. I heard the terrified screams of my friends and family as the guards went in for the kill. Even through my exhaustion and pain, I felt panic. If I didn't manage to get off this table and find a way to save them, my parents and my friends... Charlie, the love of my life... would *die*.

I'd rather burn in hell.

The guards moved in, but I rolled off the table. I couldn't access Fire, Water, or healing, but I still had my wit, and ancestors, it had to be enough to get us out of here. Before Jaymin could react, I grabbed the pistol she was holding and yanked it out of her hands. I pointed it at her and put my finger on the trigger.

"Stop!" Jaymin screeched. "Everyone freeze!"

Nobody dared to move. I took a couple of shaky steps backward. Everyone's eyes were on me, waiting to see what I would do.

Jaymin stared down the barrel of the gun with an arrogance she didn't bother to conceal. "What are you going to do with that, Ava? Do you even know how to use it?"

I swallowed. "All I have to do is point and pull this trigger."

"To kill me, yes," Jaymin responded dryly. "But I assure you, there are only five bullets left in that pistol. It's not enough to get you out of here."

She was right. Even if I managed to kill Jaymin and a few others, it was still too many for me to take down on my own with just one gun.

I was backed into a corner. There was nowhere for me to go.

My voice trembled as I said, "All right."

I put the pistol against the side of my head. Mama let out an ear-shattering scream. My friends started shouting things, but I didn't comprehend what they were saying. Daddy's face blanched of all color.

Charlie's eyes went wide. He had no idea what was going on, only knew that I must've done something insane.

Better he didn't know. He didn't need to see this.

"Don't come any closer," I warned. "I'm not fucking around."

I didn't know if this plan would work. But I'd use myself as a hostage if it meant saving the people I loved.

"You don't dare," Jaymin seethed, narrowing her eyes.

"Everyone always called me Crazy Ava-Marie, right?" I let out a hoarse, mad laugh, and I felt my eye twitch. "Let's see just how *crazy* I really am."

My voice had taken on some kind of deranged tone that I didn't recognize. It wasn't me, and yet... this was more *me* than I ever had been before. Jaymin had made a huge mistake. I was Ava-Marie Wahkin, and I refused to be cornered. And if I was, I'd fight. I'd fight like hell to get out, even if I had to kill myself to do it.

Now Jaymin looked scared. "Now, Ava, let's think about this."

"Fuck you!" I screamed. "You come any closer, I'll blow my brains out all over the fucking wall!"

Charlie looked like he was going to be sick as he realized exactly what I was doing. His emotions overpowered our bond, drowning me in nothing but panic, fear, and complete devastation.

"Ava, don't," he pleaded. "Please don't hurt yourself. I'm begging you, pidge. No matter what happens, stay alive for me. We can get through this. Don't pull that trigger."

"This is for the best." I swallowed as I tried to work up the courage. I didn't want to die, but I wanted my loved ones to live. I had to choose between the two, because I couldn't have both.

"If you go, I'm coming right after you," Charlie gasped.

"You'll find me again, Charlie, I promise." I don't know why I said it — seemed like a silly thing to say at the time— but it slipped out of my mouth anyway. It was some sort of promise we'd made to each other over and over again without ever saying it aloud, and we'd never broken it.

"You're my wife. Don't leave me," Charlie pleaded.

My heart broke inside my chest like fragile glass, and it hurt worse than the bullet would. I thought I'd found a way out of my miserable life, and that I could finally begin again with Charlie.

I'd been in denial. My darkness would never go away. But for as breakable as my heart was, my mind was made of stone, and I made a concrete decision on what had to be done. I hated that I was doing this to him, but if it meant saving his life... well, I'd be the craziest motherfucker that walked this Earth. Gambling with my own existence meant nothing if he could keep breathing.

Ava... stay, Oberi whined weakly. He tried to say more, and failed. The blood loss had weakened him, though I could tell by the look in his dark eyes that losing me was his greatest fear.

"Honey, calm down. Let's think through this," Daddy said. He was trying to be a chief, forcing himself to be the level-headed negotiator while Mama wept at his side.

"I'd do anything for my family, Daddy. It's time to prove it." I was holding a gun to my head, but I hadn't lost my nerve. If anything I'd done in my life felt right, it was this— putting myself on the line to protect them. There were five other people in this room that I cared about. Their lives were worth more than my own just by sheer statistics. If one person had to sacrifice their life to make sure five others survived, well, it didn't matter who or what I was.

But I wasn't going down unless I took Jaymin with me.

"Baby, we'll find another way out of this. Put the gun down." Mama was hysterical, begging me to stop what I was doing even as I was trying to save her life.

Blocking out her cries was the worst. It wasn't easy to ignore your mother when she was pleading with you not to kill yourself, but we were in a tough spot. I'd be damned if anyone was leaving in a body bag today but me and the shitheads that had cornered us.

Jaymin took a slow step in my direction. "Ava, don't do anything rash."

"Why not? You need me. *The Warden* needs me," I said. "And if I die, all his plans and the ways he wants to use me go to shit. I'm willing to bet that if you drag my body back to him, he'll put you in a grave before morning."

Jaymin's complexion paled, and I knew I was right.

"We can work something out," Jaymin replied. "I'm willing to negotiate."

Yeah, right. She'd kill everyone I cared about the minute I put this gun down. The voices in my head were screaming now, making it hard to hear anything anyone was saying. I couldn't even hear myself *think*.

"You're a shitty therapist, you know that? You never realized the worst thing about me," I spat at Jaymin. "I have monsters living inside of me, and you want to know what they're saying right now? That every single one of my enemies needs to be fucking dead, starting with you."

"You're hearing voices again, sweetie?" Mama whimpered.

"I never stopped, Mama. It's my blessing and my curse." My fingers trembled as I held the gun. The voices kept repeating, *do it, do it.*

"She's psychotic! We need to put her down," a guard cried out.

"No! The Warden wants her alive!" Jaymin screamed.

"Yeah, I bet he does," I growled. "He wants all of us to either die or fall in fucking line. Which is exactly why I'm giving him a big *fuck you* on my way out. I'm not gonna feel a damn thing. The voices made me numb a long time ago."

I felt completely unhinged as mania overtook me. At this point, any doctor would rule me insane, because there was nothing I wouldn't do to get my friends out of this situation. I was done wearing the mask I had to put on every fucking day, done pretending that I was a good little girl who had her shit together because she took all the right pills and said all the right things. This was the real Ava, and I was letting her loose for the first fucking time. She could do anything she wanted and change her mind at any moment, just because she felt like it, and right now, I felt like pulling this fucking trigger *just* to see what would happen. Ancestors, I was finally free. Nothing could hold me back now.

"This isn't one of your little mind games. This is real life," Jaymin sneered. She was losing her patience.

"I told you to stay back," I warned again as Jaymin approached. She didn't listen. I took a deep breath and tried to summon my courage.

"You don't have the stomach," Jaymin hissed, and she darted toward me.

I closed my eyes and hoped it wouldn't hurt— though I hardly cared if it did. I wasn't letting Jaymin take me back to the Warden. I pulled the trigger, and the gun went off. Jaymin connected with me a second before I did so, and the bullet ricocheted into the wall. The gun fell out of my hands and broke into several pieces on the stone floor. I shoved Jaymin away from me, and she fell on her back beside the pistol.

I heard Charlie let out a cry of grief. He thought I'd done it. I scrambled back to my feet, and felt my back hit the wall.

"She's okay!" Kallie hurriedly stated. Charlie trembled, giving sobs of relief.

"I've had enough of this," Jaymin snapped. "Guards, kill the rest of them, and drag her back to the Warden!"

The guards rushed toward me in a stampede of fury. Throughout it all, my anxiety and fear had gotten out of hand, and they were causing the magic inside of me to tremble. The inferichite had weakened my body, but my demigod powers were longing to break free. The inferichite had rerouted so much magic back into my body that it was difficult holding on to it all. For the most part, my demigod powers always remained submerged, hiding within me in case I ever needed to pull from them. The inferichite had brought it all up to the surface, and I needed somewhere to put it. It was like trying to stop a spell that was already in mid-cast; you just couldn't do it. The more I tried to push back against my magic and put it back where it belonged, the more it longed to ignite. I couldn't seem to put it back where it'd come from. It wanted a *release*. If I was going to constrain it at all, I had to perform a powerful spell, though I wasn't sure what kind. The voices inside my head raged, giving me direction.

You can stop this, Ava.

Just let your powers be free.

Become unbound, and let them see what a demigod can do.

My gaze locked with Marcus. I remembered the security footage I'd watched weeks ago... when he'd lost control of his magic.

It was then that a desperate idea formulated in my head. My demigod powers, which were churning within me and warring against the inferichite, were desperate to be unleashed.

I had shattered the smaller inferichite crystals. With a bigger outburst of energy, I could overpower the crystal in the cuff so I could get my magic back. But if I did that, I wouldn't have any control over it... and the force of magic that would have to swell out of me in order to do so would be cataclysmic.

My eyes caught a mysterious glow in the back of the room. A coyote prowled forward on all fours, remaining unseen by everyone but me. His eyes locked with my own as he waited for me to make an impossible choice.

I hadn't seen him in nearly a year, but I'd recognize the Koigni god anywhere. Coyote Spirit stared me down with a look that told me everything I needed to do.

"Ava," Charlie whimpered. Tears coursed down his face as he reached out for me.

My voice broke out in a whisper. "I love you, Charlie. I wish it didn't have to end this way. Take care of Oberi— he's all you've got now."

As my back hit the wall, I looked at Marcus again. The blood had drained from his face.

"Ava, don't do this," Marcus begged. He knew exactly what I was planning.

A tear slipped out of my eye, and my lip trembled. "I'm sorry."

My gaze caught Kallie's. She nodded once, a sign that she understood. I hoped her timing was good. She'd only have seconds.

The guards approached me with outstretched hands. I couldn't bear to look at Charlie, not even one last time, so my gaze locked on Jaymin's instead. I gritted my teeth and snarled, "I'll see you in hell."

My arms trembled as I closed my eyes and let my powers erupt.

My magic blasted outward in a massive explosion. A shockwave bloomed outward first, and the sound shattered every piece of inferichite in the room, including those in the cuffs that my friends wore. I heard the crystals break, and metal clinked as the cuffs fell off. The moment that happened, Kallie's shield went up, protecting everyone I loved as Fire bloomed out of my body in one giant inferno.

The explosion shook the walls and caused the ground underneath us to tremble. Jaymin herself was standing too close and was ripped apart by the blast. As the flames hit her, shock overcame her expression. Skin began melting off her flesh, and her muscles turned to liquid. She'd realized she'd lost. Her bones immediately disintegrated into dust at my

Fire, until all that was left of her were the remnants of ashes being swept away by the blast.

Bodies slammed against the wall at the force of my power. The rest of the guards went up in flames with Jaymin, consumed immediately by the blast.

It was almost beautiful, you know? Watching all those people disintegrate into nothing but smoke at my fingers, their ashes suspended upon the air, was the most mystifying thing I'd ever seen.

And I'd be lying if I said it wasn't satisfying as fuck. I took *joy* in what I did to Jaymin and her guards. In those few seconds, I felt better than victorious. I felt alive for the first time, and I gladly fed off their horrible deaths like it was the air I needed to breathe. I allowed myself to be evil, and I took pleasure in sending these shitheads straight to their maker.

Finally. I was done denying who I was. I was a villain, a monster, and I had accepted that without feeling the need to fight it anymore. I could go to my death in peace.

The explosion was so powerful that the ceiling crumbled inward. I heard the sound of petrified screams, then silence, as the Underground caved inward and buried everyone alive.

I lost control completely, and my magic rebounded. This wasn't like what had happened with Marcus— he'd let his magic loose when he'd killed those people in the square. I was trying to hold some of my power back, so I wouldn't break Kallie's shield. I needed to give the people I loved a chance to survive.

Because of it, my own magic backfired on me.

As the explosion erupted out of me, I literally felt my spirit be blasted backward out of my body. When my spirit soared through the air, I watched my corpse hit the ground. I realized that I could no longer feel my body anymore. I was floating in mid-air, not really myself, but yet, more *me* than I ever had been. My form felt ethereal... like a wisp of wind that could be blown away by the breeze, something stronger than I'd ever been when I was alive. I was suspended in the moment, unmoving, neither here nor there.

Coyote ran forward. When my spirit connected with his, I found myself bound to his form. I was attached to the Koigni god, my spirit riding upon his back as he ran through the caving tunnels. He darted up out of the collapsing Underground and into the sky, merging as one with the stars.

There was nothing else to do. I allowed myself to surrender as Coyote carried my half of my soul to the Ancestral Lands, leaving Charlie's half behind.

TWENTY-THREE

Agony tore through my body, as if a powerful monster had emerged from the depths of hell and ripped my torso in half with its jagged jaws. The deafening sound of rubble crashing around me and burying me alive seemed miles off. The throb of pain in my leg disappeared. All I felt was the excruciating break in my soul as Ava-Marie was ripped away.

"AVA!!!" I screamed, so loud that it could be heard over the sound of the cave-in.

Dust entered my lungs, and I began hacking. All I wanted was for the stones to hit me, to crush me beneath their massive weight. It would hurt a hell of a lot less.

But they didn't. Someone must've created a shield, because by the time the rumbling stopped, I was still alive. I didn't know how. If the rocks hadn't crushed me, the weight of losing one half of my soul should've.

And it just might.

That was how it worked in Hawkei culture. If your Familiar died— a piece of your soul— you weren't far behind.

And hell, I wanted to follow Ava wherever she went. I couldn't stand to live without her.

But I wanted to live. I wanted us *both* to live. She was my *wife*, and I didn't get enough time with her. We had prophecies to fulfill. This couldn't be the end. It just *couldn't*.

I refused to believe Ava was gone. She had to live. She *had* to.

I began crawling across the ground frantically. Screw the pain pulsing in my leg and the blood pooling beneath me. I had to get to Ava.

My hands met stone. I pulled myself upright, balancing on one leg while I tried to move rocks out of the way. Screams came from nearby, and someone barked orders, but I couldn't process what anyone said.

Charlie, she's already made her choice, Oberi whimpered beside me.

No. Just no.

"Charlie!" I thought I heard Marcus call my name, but I couldn't be sure. Hands landed on my shoulders, but I shoved them off.

"I have to get to her!" I yelled.

Marcus yanked me again. "Charlie, you can't! We're completely surrounded by rubble. We're trapped."

I lifted my hands. The Underground was built out of stone. My magic could handle it. "I'm getting through one way or another."

Nothing happened. My guts sank in horror as I realized my magic was still bound by the ward inside of me.

I grabbed Marcus by the collar. "Get this ward out of me! Now! I have to find Ava— she— she's—"

I choked up, and I couldn't finish my sentence. I wouldn't say it out loud. She wasn't gone. She would live.

I wouldn't accept any other reality.

"Ava's *what?*" Liam demanded. "What are you waiting for? Move these stones. You have Nivita magic!"

Liam didn't wait for an answer. He moved past me, and stones began falling to the ground as he tried to dig through the rubble.

"Chief Mitoh, stop!" Kallie cried. "This could all come down on us."

She sounded wiped out, like she was struggling to maintain her shield. The weight of holding the collapsed tunnel was draining all her energy.

Liam gasped, and I heard him stumble to the ground. He was ill and pumped full of noxite. Moving literal tons of rubble wasn't exactly in the cards for him.

"Liam!" Ava's mother scurried to his side.

Marcus yanked out of my grasp and turned to Sophia. "You have healing powers, don't you?"

"Yes," she said frantically. "But Jaymin used noxite on us. Without a spell to get rid of it, I can't—"

"I have an idea," Marcus said in a rush.

Liam groaned. "It better be a fucking good one."

Marcus grabbed my arm and forced me to sit on a huge boulder. I shoved him off of me. "This is a waste of time! We have to get to Ava *now!*"

"If you want to get to her, you'll listen to me," Marcus barked. "You're the only one who's got Nivita magic, which means you're the only one who can get us all out of here. I'm going to take the ward out of you and put it into Ava's mom. The magic can be used for any form of protection. I'll transform the spell to protect her from the noxite. She'll be able to heal you. You're not getting to Ava with a broken leg, so let us do this and you can reach her faster. Got it?"

Hell, Marcus had never taken charge a day in his life. It caught me off guard. But I had no choice but to listen to him, because he was right. As long as my leg was broken and I had no magic, I wasn't getting to Ava.

"This better fucking work," I growled.

Marcus grabbed my hand, and I heard Sophia approach.

"Quickly," she breathed.

Magic swirled within me, rising through my gut and out of my extremities. Something twisted in my stomach, and I doubled over and spewed bile across the ground. I heard Kallie gasp, though she tried to hide it.

When I came back up for air, I felt like I could breathe easier. My sense of balance returned, and I could feel the earth and air around me. Stone surrounded us at all angles, including overhead. If Kallie let her shield fall, we'd be crushed.

Finally, we could get fucking moving.

I started to get to my feet, but an ungodly pain shot up my leg, and I fell back onto the boulder.

Marcus caught me. "Slow down, Charlie. Sophia needs to heal you."

Ancestors, Marcus. This wasn't a fucking carnival. We didn't have time to *slow down*. This was my wife's fucking *life*.

"Don't you get it?" I screamed. "Ava is on the other side of this rubble. If we don't get to her soon—"

"We'll find her," Sophia assured me as she grabbed my leg. "I promise."

She could promise whatever she wanted, but I knew she was lying through her teeth. She didn't believe it herself. I could hear it in her voice.

"Hurry up," I demanded.

Warmth filled my leg, and the pain slowly subsided. I winced as I felt my bones knitting back together. My skin stretched, but I didn't let Sophia finish. The second I felt I could stand on two feet, I yanked away from her. Blood continued to trickle down my leg, but it meant nothing compared to Ava's injuries. My bone ached, because I didn't let Sophia heal it all the way, but I could walk. I'd take it.

I threw myself at the rocks and began moving them aside with my magic. Stone crushed, and dust rained down from overhead as I forced the rubble aside, creating a long tunnel in front of me. Kallie sighed in relief as I took over with my magic, keeping the stone in place so it wouldn't crush us. She was finally able to drop her shield. Oberi whined, and I felt his worry for Ava through our bond.

"Sophia, get to Oberi," I barked. She had to get that bullet out of him.

I heard Liam try to get up, but his wife yelled at him. "Liam, stop! I have to heal you, too."

Kallie, Marcus, and I scrambled through the rubble as fast as we could. My heart raced, and I feared I'd never find her. She'd been standing on this side of the room. We had to be close—

I moved another pile of rubble out of the way. Kallie gasped, and Marcus began to gag. I knew instantly that we'd found her.

I dropped to my knees and crawled forward, until my fingers met Ava's shoe. I ran my hands up her legs to feel for injuries. A warm, sticky liquid coated my palms. Blood seeped through my pants as I crawled closer to her. My hands touched her torso, and I began to weep when I felt the gooey sensation of her insides spilling from her abdomen.

Ancestors, she'd ripped herself apart...

"*Ava!*" I screamed in agony.

This couldn't be real. I was misinterpreting what I felt. It was an illusion. *Something.*

Hell, this was my fault. I couldn't do anything to fight back, and because of that, Ava had gotten hurt.

I pulled my wife's head into my lap. "Ava, please."

I reached out through our bond to communicate with her. She had to feel me. She had to come back to me.

But she didn't respond. Her half of our bond was empty... unresponsive.

I realized I'd never truly felt Ava be *gone* before. Even before I'd met her, her presence had always been there. Now there was an empty gap where her soul had been, like someone had carved a hole in the middle of my chest.

Maybe I was still fucked up from the inferichite, and that's why I couldn't feel her. I reached out to Oberi, and that connection remained solid as ever.

Fear took over me as I tried again. I thought I might hear her thoughts, feel her consciousness... something.

I felt nothing.

Marcus whimpered. "She... she's not breathing—"

"DON'T!" I yelled. "Don't say that. She'll— she'll be fine. Her mom can heal her."

Footsteps sounded, along with the pad of paws. Ava's parents rushed down the tunnel I'd created, followed by Oberi and Rishi. They reached the end, where I sat with Ava curled in my lap.

"Ancestors!" Liam cried.

Oberi whimpered loudly. *I can't believe she's gone. I'm a terrible Familiar. I... I should've protected her.*

Yeah, you should've, I growled. I couldn't sympathize. All I had in my heart was agony and blame. At the moment, I *hated him* right now for allowing this to happen to her. He should've kept her safe...

But that was my job. I'd failed her more than anyone.

Sophia must've gone still, because I didn't hear her at all.

"Heal her!" I demanded.

Sophia came to my side immediately. Her breath wavered, and several of her tears fell onto my arm. I felt Ava's body shift as Sophia placed her hand on the injuries. Several awful moments passed, but nothing happened.

"What are you waiting for?!" I cried.

Sophia drew away. "Her— her injuries are too extensive. I can't heal her without surgical intervention."

Fuck.

"You have to do something!" I screamed. "Magic *has* to fix this!"

"Charlie, I don't think you realize the extent of Ava's injuries," Sophia sobbed, though she tried to keep her voice strong. It was just too much for a mother to bear. "I can heal skin wounds and broken bones and burns, but without surgery, this—"

I shoved Sophia aside. If she said *surgery* one more time, I was going to fucking lose it. I pulled Ava into my arms and cradled her as I got my feet. My leg protested, as it hadn't fully healed, but I didn't give a damn.

Dirt rained down on our heads as I began shifting the stones to my command. I didn't even have to move my hands to make them get out of the way— they moved at my thoughts. I shoved them aside so hard that they were reduced to nothing but tightly compacted dirt. I formed a staircase upward through the earth overhead.

Something dislodged from the earth, but I couldn't control it. It rolled down my makeshift stairway, and Marcus yanked me out of the way so I wouldn't be crushed by it. Whatever it was, it was bigger than me.

"What the fuck was that?" I asked.

Marcus swallowed audibly. "A casket from the graveyard above us."

To hell with it. I pushed the last bit of dirt aside, until I felt a gust of air whip through the staircase. I moved as quickly as I could, carrying Ava from the Underground and into the cemetery. I used my magic to help me navigate around gravestones and out of the graveyard. The others rushed behind me, and we raced to the infirmary. Oberi guided me, giving loud barks so I knew which way to go.

The second I heard footsteps up ahead, I began screaming. "Help! We need a doctor! Somebody help!"

Nurses began yelling. I heard the sound of doors slamming, then wheels screeching as someone pulled a gurney down the hall.

"Call the Warden!" a nurse barked.

"I can't disturb him," another replied. "He's preparing for the Darke Games. They begin today."

A nurse reached for Ava's body and tried tugging her out of my arms. I knew I needed to hand her over to the doctors, but I couldn't let go of her. She was *my* Ava. I had to make sure she made it.

"Sir, we need to get her into surgery, *now!*" the nurse snapped.

"I'm going with her," I insisted.

"Not unless you're family—"

"*I'm her husband!*" I screamed. Tears began pouring from my eyes. The nurses must've noticed my desperation, because they didn't argue.

"Get her onto the gurney and come with us," one of them said.

"We're her parents," Liam said firmly.

"All of you, with us," another nurse demanded.

My arms were still frozen around Ava. The nurses had to yank her away from me to get her onto the gurney. I held her hand tightly as they rushed her into a private room. Everyone followed.

Ava's fingers were cold and limp in my hand. No matter how tightly I held on, she didn't squeeze back.

My head spun. I couldn't make sense of what was going on. So many doctors and nurses filled the room, and they yelled orders at one another. I heard the sound of machines being wheeled in, tubes hitting the floor, and medical supplies being unwrapped as a swarm of frantic activity burst out around me. It was overwhelming, and the worst part was, everyone sounded scared, even the doctors who were supposed to be in charge. If they were afraid...

All I could do was push Ava's hair out of her face and pray.

Fuck, I wasn't the kind of guy who prayed, but right now, I had no other options. *Please, ancestors. You can't take her from me. She has to make it. Let her stay.*

Suddenly, all action in the room stopped. I heard the medical staff collectively hold their breath.

I had the thought this couldn't be fucking real. Then a woman said softly, "There's no pulse."

My heart crumbled into a million pieces. The room went silent, and the nurses took a collective step back. For a moment, it felt like time had stopped. Kallie had to be fucking with it. But I heard the sound of breathing beside me, and I knew time was still moving forward. But I must've heard them wrong...

"Check again!" I screamed.

Nobody moved. It was like they hadn't even heard me. All I heard was Oberi's soft whimper beside me. No one spoke, but we all seemed to feel the same thing.

It was no use.

"Call it," a man said.

"Don't you fucking dare—" I started, but a woman was already speaking.

"Time of death, three thirty-three a.m."

Sophia began to wail, and Marcus and Kallie choked up beside me. Oberi nudged his wet nose into my hand. Ava's father gave a gasp of grief. I heard him stumble backward as he collapsed on the floor in shock.

"*No*, you fuckers!" I cried. "You have to do something. You have to try again. You have *magic*. Are you going to use it, or are you going to stand around like useless fucking idiots?!"

The nurses were already leaving the room. They ignored me.

"Are you her husband?" a man asked.

My head spun, but I managed to answer. "Yes."

He shoved a clipboard into my hands, and I took it before I knew what was happening. "We need your signature. You need to sign the death certificate, so we—"

Hell, no! I threw the clipboard onto the ground as complete fury exploded through me. I grabbed the man by the throat and shoved him up against the wall. Surgical tools fell from a nearby table and clattered to the ground.

"She's not gone!" I screamed as the man gasped for breath. "You're going to do whatever it takes to bring her back. Use surgery or potions or healing magic— I don't care! I'm not walking out of this room without my wife!"

The man clawed at my fingers and spoke in a strained tone. "Then you can... take her in a... body bag."

Rage flared through my veins, and I tightened my grip on his neck, until I felt the air leave his lungs completely.

"Charlie!" Kallie yelled. She yanked on me, but I siphoned her shifter strength so she couldn't move me. "Charlie, stop! You're gonna kill him!"

I didn't fucking care. Ava was *gone*. This fucker couldn't save her. He could perish with her for all I cared.

"Charlie!" Marcus yelled. I felt his hands on me, but he wasn't strong enough to drag me away.

Magic shocked my entire system, and I lost control of my body. I stumbled backward and landed flat on the floor. The ground seemed to tilt back and forth below me, and I realized Marcus had hit me with a stunning spell.

"Asshole," I growled at him.

"I had to," Marcus said.

I heard the doctor sink to the ground, then the scuffle of his feet as he hurried out of the room. I swore he muttered something about a *crazy fucker* and about calling security. Screw him. He was a lost cause anyway.

Kallie reached out and helped me to my feet as the spell wore off.

"I know this is... it's unbearable." Kallie's voice cracked. "But there's nothing that can be done."

"She's... she's in a better place now," Marcus added weakly.

Fuck him. She didn't belong anywhere that wasn't with me.

Nearby, Ava's parents sobbed. Oberi let out a long howl. He padded to the surgical table, and through our bond, I felt him weakly nose Ava's hand.

"If you believe in your culture, you'll accept that it's her time," Kallie said, and she choked back a sob. "The Great Spirit must've wanted her on the other side. He... he must've needed her."

"*No.* I need her more than he fucking does." My friends were just saying vapid, empty things that everyone said when somebody died. I knew they were trying to comfort me. None of it meant anything, because it couldn't fill this fucking void. I shoved past Kallie and returned to Ava's side. I lifted her hand, but her whole body was limp. Tears streamed from my eyes as I pressed a kiss to Ava's fingers.

"We'll give you some time to say your goodbyes, before we take the body to the morgue," a nurse stated quietly. The doctors and nurses shuffled out of the room, but their voices and footsteps seemed distant. I barely noticed they'd left.

Even through all of that, I waited for Ava to respond. I expected her to get up off that table right now, and yell at all of us that she was fine and we were being overdramatic. I wanted her to call me a stupid bastard and demand that I cart her down to Commissary to buy her chocolate, just because she wanted some and because she felt like bossing me around. All I wanted more than anything I'd ever wanted in my life— more than I wanted food when I was starving, or warmth when I'd been freezing to death— was to take her back to our cell, curl up in bed with her and hold her, so she could stroke back my hair and tell me this was all a bad dream.

She did none of those things. Because I realized... she was no longer here.

This *couldn't* be how this ended. We'd hardly been married for three months. It had been the most blissful part of my life, but it would never be enough. Ava and I had a life to live together. We had plans for when we left this place. Sure, we hadn't set anything concrete, but I always assumed we'd spend time traveling before we settled down and Ava dove into her anthropology work. I'd become a supernatural bounty hunter. And maybe, somewhere along the way, we'd start a family. We'd have kids. We'd piss each other off every day and make love every night and grow old together.

We couldn't have any of that in the Ancestral Lands.

Every moment of our future had been stolen from us. All the lessons we'd come here to learn had been ripped away. We had failed to fulfill the prophecies we were destined to achieve. This life meant nothing if we didn't get to live it. If this was the end, I didn't know why we'd been sent here in the first place.

I refused to believe this was it. We'd come here for a reason. The gods didn't create this realm for nothing, and our lives had meaning—

whether I knew what that meaning was or not. Ava-Marie's life mattered, and it was too soon for it to end.

I wouldn't live a life without her. I hadn't died yet, which meant it was possible I could survive without her. Oberi's portion of our soul continued to keep me alive. I realized, with a bout of horror, that I could live for decades with Oberi, and continue to exist even without Ava here. As we'd guessed, he only needed one of us to survive.

I didn't want to live without Ava-Marie. My half of our soul yearned for hers the way my chest yearned for air. I couldn't be without her. One way or another, we would be together— whether I had to die, or bring her back.

But Oberi needed one of us to survive himself. If I killed myself, I'd kill Oberi, and I wasn't going to do that.

I was going to bring Ava back. Call it intuition or desperation, but I knew deep within my soul that it could be done. Great Spirit be damned. He didn't own Ava-Marie. *I* was the one who shared a soul with her. *I* was the only one with a right to determine her fate.

"Ava-Marie is mine," I growled at Kallie. "The Great Spirit can't have her."

I stood at the head of Ava's gurney and rested my forehead on hers. Oberi whimpered as he climbed onto the gurney beside her. He splayed his paws over her chest, and his forehead came to meet mine, until all three of us were touching.

I prayed that Ava's chest would rise and fall... but she was completely still.

Everyone else had gone so silent that there might as well have not been anyone else in the room. There was just me, Ava, and our Familiar.

"Pidge," I whispered. "I know you're out there somewhere, and I hope to the Great Spirit you can hear me. I'm not letting you go. I can't. You're my love, in this life and the next, but I *will not* move on to the next life without living this one with you. I have never loved anyone the way I love you. In this life, I don't need to see, because you have been my eyes. I used to think all there was to life was surviving, but you showed me differently. You make me see the world in a way I never have before. If you're gone, I'll be shrouded in darkness forever. A year wasn't enough time with you. I don't care if it's selfish to want you for myself.

I'll damn the whole world if it means bringing you back. You're stubborn as hell, pidge. You're not going out this easily. I don't care how much the Great Spirit wants you. You're part of my soul, and I firmly believe there's no power greater than the love and connection we share. You're coming back to me. You have to—"

Sobs broke from my chest, and I could no longer find the words. Oberi nudged his wet nose into my face, and I cried even harder. I could feel his sorrow bleeding through the bond and sinking through my gut.

"Oberi, please," I begged. "There has to be something we can do— a ritual, magic. Something to bring her soul back to mine. We're not supposed to be separated like this."

Oberi drew a deep breath. An emotion I couldn't pinpoint broke through the sorrow. It was clearly something Oberi wasn't sure he wanted to share with me.

You know something, don't you? I accused through our bond. *Oberi, if there's anything we can do, we need to do it now.*

He was silent for a moment before guilt crossed our connection. *There is one thing,* he admitted solemnly. *But it's quite risky.*

"I don't care!" I growled, lifting my head. "Do it!"

You don't understand, Oberi replied. *My magic is not meant to be used in cases like this. Ava-Marie is gone. She's in the Ancestral Lands and at peace. If you rip her out of the afterlife and bring her back here, she's not going to come back the same.*

I don't care. Bring her back!

You don't understand the consequences. If I do this, I'm playing God, Oberi emphasized. *We don't die until it's our time, the time that we have decided and the time that is written. That is our fate. If Ava's dead, it's her time to go. If we bring her back, the timeline of destiny will be altered permanently. We'll be messing with her fate, and the fate of others.*

I don't believe that, I told him. *Her prophecy said otherwise. She isn't meant to die today. She needs to come back.*

This magic can only be done once, Oberi said. *But I cannot force Ava to return. She has to make a choice to come back. If she doesn't want to return to her mortal life, she'll remain in the Ancestral Lands, and I'll have used up all my magic. That means that if you die, Charlie, I can never bring you back.*

I don't give a fuck! I screamed in my mind. Why was Oberi being like this? Didn't he *want* Ava here with us?

One of you needs to remain alive to fulfill the prophecy, Oberi pointed out. *You were supposed to stop Ava from fulfilling hers. Now that she's not here, you can fulfill your piece without her getting in the way, and save the Elves.*

"Screw the prophecy!" I screamed out loud. "I'm not going to live without her. If Ava-Marie is gone for good, so am I. I'll kill myself to be with her!"

Several people in the room gasped loudly, and Marcus stepped in. "No, Charlie. You can't!"

"Of course I can!" I cried. "And I fucking will!"

"Don't think that way!" Marcus protested. "Do you have any idea what you're saying— any idea how much pain you're imposing upon yourself—?"

"I'm already in pain!" I yelled. "And I'll gladly kill myself to end it."

"This isn't the easy answer you think it is," Marcus snapped back.

"You don't know! You've never lost someone like I just did—"

"Yes, I *did!*" Marcus screamed. "I tried to end it, too. More than once. And it never goddamn worked. I didn't share a soul with Anya, but you better believe I know what the hell you're going through. I have enough experience to know that killing yourself isn't the answer. If the gods don't want it to happen, it won't."

My blood turned to ice. Marcus had never admitted he was suicidal before. But... knowing everything he'd gone through, I couldn't say I was surprised.

Kallie's soft footsteps approached. She sounded emotional as she said, "Marcus... I had no idea you went through that. I'm so sorry. I wish I could've been there for you then."

"It's not your fault," Marcus said.

"I'm just... *so* glad you're alive," Kallie told him, before turning to me. "And I'm glad *you're* here, Charlie. And I hope to the gods you stay. Ava's gone. We already lost her. We can't lose you, too. Please."

Fuck this. I refused to live in a world where the *gods* determined our fate. I was a goddamn demigod, and I was taking control over mine.

"Do it, Oberi," I commanded.

Are you sure? he asked. *We can never take this back.*

I'd never been more sure of anything in my life. *Yes.*

So be it.

Oberi climbed down from the gurney and took a step away from me. Something within our bond shifted, the way it felt when Oberi changed shape. But this was unlike anything I'd ever felt before. Instead of the intense Fire that came from her unicorn form, or the smooth Water energy I felt in her narwhal form, a calm, serene sensation settled in my stomach.

I heard the unfurl of feathers, and something soft and solid touched my arm. The warmth of Spirit energy brushed over me, similar to when Sophia healed my leg earlier. An image of a large white phoenix began to form in my mind. It was like each time I'd touched spirits before—first with my ancestors in the Lair, then with Whale Spirit in the hospital. When Oberi transformed into her Spirit form and touched me, I could *see* her standing before me in her ethereal form.

Oberi's phoenix form was magnificent. Her beautiful white wings stretched out in an awe-inspiring display. Beautiful white plumes of feathers grew from the top of her head, and long, narrow feathers formed a gorgeous white tail that drifted all the way to the ground. Spirit magic shimmered up and down her form, making her glow with crystalline power against the darkness.

Gasps traveled around the room as Ava's family and our friends took in Oberi's new form. My jaw dropped as I took in the incredible moment.

Oberi flapped her gorgeous wings, and I remained speechless as I watched her fly upward. I could hardly comprehend the beauty of her incredible form. She hovered above me, sending waves of air off her feathers. Spirit magic seemed to flow with her flight, and calm waves of energy washed over me.

Oberi began to hum a beautiful tune. By the Great Spirit, Oberi's song was incredible. She had me entranced.

Oberi ducked her beak. She pulled away from her chest with a single glowing feather, trapped in her mouth. She lowered her head, and the feather fell through the air. I reached out to feel it land lightly on Ava-Marie's chest.

A second voice joined in Oberi's tune, creating an enchanting melody. It was so quiet at first, I wasn't even sure I'd heard it or if I'd just made it up. It had to be Ava's voice, because there was no other in the universe that sounded so sweet.

Oberi leaned toward Ava, and a sight I never thought I'd witness began to form in front of me. Oberi's beak lightly touched Ava's forehead, where her third eye would be. Ava's spirit began to take shape in my mind. She wasn't totally solid, and she was more ethereal than anything, but ancestors, I could *see* Ava's spirit as it returned to her body. At first, all I could see was her face, but slowly, more and more of her body took shape, as if witnessing an artist draw out her spirit in real-time.

And that's what Ava-Marie was. A work of art.

I never had to see what another girl looked like, because if I had to make the perfect person for myself, this is what she would be. It had never been more clear to me than in that moment that Ava-Marie was *made for me*.

I couldn't do anything but stare down at my love. She was everything I could ever dream of. Tears streamed down my face, and I reached out for her.

"Welcome home, pidge," I whispered.

Ava-Marie's eyes shot open, and that was the last thing I saw before the image of her spirit swept out of my mind. Oberi's phoenix landed on the ground behind the gurney, and I heard the sound of her body collapse. Her spirit form disappeared from my vision. Oberi squawked, like the magic had been too strong.

Then the terrifying, ungodly sound of Ava's pained screams tore through the room.

My heart lurched. Horror struck as I realized what Ava had just returned to. Her body was broken and bleeding, and her insides were spilling from her abdomen.

I became a statue, because as much as I wanted to bring her back, I didn't realize how much agony it would cause her. *I'd* done this to her.

The sound of a door slamming open met my ears, and I heard Kallie yelling. "Help! We need a doctor!"

Footsteps sounded down the hall. I was vaguely aware of nurses rushing back into the room, but I remained rooted firmly in place. I didn't know what to do. Someone shoved me out of the way, and I snapped back to attention.

"Help her, please! My wife," I begged.

"How the hell did you resuscitate her?!" a doctor barked as hasty noises began filling the room.

No one responded. I think we were all in too much shock.

"Get the family out of here!" a woman cried. "I need anesthesia immediately."

"I'm staying," Sophia said firmly. "I'm a healer. I can help."

"She stays. Everyone else leaves," someone barked.

Ava's cries continued to fill the room. Terror spread through our bond, and I couldn't believe what I had done.

Hands landed on me, and several people dragged me out. I didn't fight back, but I couldn't seem to move by myself, either. Ava's screams continued to echo down the hall.

"Is she going to be all right?" I rasped as someone rushed past me.

"We don't know," the doctor said hastily. "Her injuries are extensive, and the surgery she's about to undergo is high-risk. I want you to be prepared that she might not make it."

My heart shattered into a million pieces as he rushed past me. All the hope I'd held on to, praying that she would survive, paled in comparison to the reality in front of me now. I could feel Ava's soul again, but our bond was still terribly weak. She was barely holding on.

"I…" Whatever I was about to say died in my throat. I immediately reached out to Oberi, who landed on my shoulder. Her soft weight pressed into me as she ruffled her feathers, giving me comfort.

What's going on? I thought she'd be okay, I said to my Familiar.

I told you, Charlie, Oberi said sadly. *We brought her soul back to a broken body. But now it's Ava's turn. She has to decide whether to stay, or go.*

My half of our soul became withered and cold. We'd brought Ava back from the dead. But that wasn't the same thing as saving her life.

Despite the miracle Oberi had just performed, Ava could still die anyway. I could lose her all over again.

I had chosen her in spite of the risks. Ava still had her own choice to make. Oberi and I had done everything we could. The choice for Ava to live or die was now in her hands.

I didn't know if she could hear me, but I spoke to her anyway. *I'll be waiting for you, pidge. I'll accept whatever you decide, because I love you that much. But if you can, please... come back to me.*

ava-marie
TWENTY-FOUR

When I woke up, I was flat on my back, staring up at a marvelous sky.

The colors overhead were brilliant. They were a mixture of orange, yellow, purple and pink, melding together in a delightful array— and above that was a pitch-black night, stars dotting the expanse in what had to be the millions. The two different skies seemed like layers, one on top of the other.

It was somehow day *and* night at the very same time. How incredible.

I didn't recall how I'd gotten here. One minute, I was riding on Coyote's back into the stars, and the next, I was flat on my ass in a place I didn't know.

I caught a streak of red and blue colors gleaming overheard, and the shape of a bushy tail at the edge of my vision.

"Hey, where are you going?" I called out. Coyote continued to sail away and into the gorgeous sky, vanishing from my sight.

So much for showing me around here. But... where was *here?*

I sat up. I'd been deposited into some kind of grassy plain. The long amber grass weaved in the slight breeze like waves on the ocean. I looked around. There was nothing but hills for as far as I could see, and mountains in the distance that were taller and more majestic than any I had ever witnessed. When I looked behind me, I saw the edge of a redwood forest, spanning outward with trees that were hundreds of feet tall. I saw rainbows, but they didn't arc like regular rainbows did. They twisted and spiraled in different directions, making all kinds of shapes in the sky, and moving up and down like they were actually *breathing*. The rainbows were alive, and I watched as an array of magical creatures flew around them. Dragons, pegasi, griffins, and other winged animals spun around the rainbows, the colors reflecting off their wings and spanning outward in hundreds of different directions.

Oh, *wow*. This had to be the Ancestral Lands. I was a bit stunned that I hadn't ended up in hell like I thought I would, but that surprise faded away as I was overtaken by how beautiful everything was.

The whole place reminded me of home, but Northern California wasn't as beautiful as the majesty I saw around me. The very *colors* seemed to be more vivid here, and the air smelled sweeter.

In the background of it all was the most mystical singing. The sound of bells, flutes and drums blended with harmonious voices, singing notes in the Hawkei language. I heard the intermingling of female song intertwining with the battle cries of men. I slowly stood to take it all in, turning in place as warmth embraced me from the skies above. The song was overwhelming, overcoming everything in my life that I'd been through until it didn't matter anymore. In this place, I was safe, and I was loved, and I was free to be myself. I didn't have to hide anymore. This place was a sanctuary for my soul to accept myself freely as I was.

As the song continued, I realized... holy fucking shit. The voices in my head were gone. *The voices were gone.*

I was finally out of my stupid brain! I gave a *whoop* and began to dance on the spot. The voices were history, and my bipolar was gone. I'd never have to deal with them again! Thank the ancestors, because I was over it.

A shape on the horizon caught my attention. I held my breath as I watched a grizzly bear lope across the planes. The bear approached at a slow pace, as if not to startle me. Peace came over me as I recognized one of my spirit guides approaching. The bear shifted, becoming a man.

It was my grandfather. It was weird how much he resembled my dad. I'd seen him in spirit form before when I summoned him during ceremonies, but here, he seemed solid. He wore a pair of jeans and a suit jacket thrown over a t-shirt. He looked like he was in his late forties.

Grandpa Liwanu put his hands in his pockets as he stood in front of me. "Welcome home, Ava."

"Grandpa." I put my arms around him and hugged him tightly, and I found that he *was* solid. Even more, I could feel the life energy that thrummed through him as vibrantly as my own spirit. I'd been longing to meet him— *really* meet him— my entire life, and now he was finally in my arms. It felt like a miracle.

"Is this really real?" I asked. I'd believed in the Ancestral Lands, but believing in something and actually living it were two completely different things.

"More real than anything you've ever experienced," Grandpa said. "We've been waiting for you."

"Why do I have a body?" I asked, gesturing to myself. "I thought I'd be a spirit."

In the Hawkei religion, we'd been taught that when we died, we fused and became one with our Familiars. Obviously, that had happened with my grandfather. But... my Familiar hadn't come with me, so I didn't think the same rules applied.

"You don't *need* a body, though you're new here, so it's the form your spirit has chosen to materialize in," Grandpa Liwanu explained. "You'll be able to simply inhabit the Ancestral Lands in spirit form once you get used to it."

"Where's Monica?" I asked, looking around.

"She'll be along. Come with me."

He changed back into a grizzly bear. I recognized his Familiar from photographs my dad had— this was Tatum. They truly had fused together, in the afterlife. I climbed onto the bear's back, and he took off in a jog throughout the plains.

When we reached the edge of the redwood forest, I disembarked from Tatum's back. The bear transformed back into my grandfather, and we started walking through the trees together.

"So are you permanently stuck like that? Changing back and forth between your Familiar and yourself?" I asked.

"We can split ourselves," Grandpa Liwanu explained. "On Earth, our Familiars were our souls, but we merge with them once we enter the Ancestral Lands. We can choose to separate these different parts, if we want to spend time with each other. Watch."

I was mesmerized as I observed Tatum step out of my grandfather's body as a spirit before he materialized as a fully-fledged bear. I reached out to stroke Tatum's ears and found that they were solid. "That's amazing."

"It's how it was always meant to be."

"Are there... other places?" I asked. "I've heard of other afterlives, but wasn't sure if this was truly the only one."

"There are many different planes of the Blessed Haven, same as there are many different levels of hell. You are in the Hawkei afterlife, though if you wish, you may visit the others," Grandpa Liwanu said.

I was already excited to start exploring new places, even though I had barely seen this one.

I spotted a small cottage up ahead in the middle of the trees. It didn't look like much, only one or two rooms, but the little windows and slanted roof made the whole thing look cozy.

"We'll be stopping here to rest. Your soul had a long journey to get here," Grandpa Liwanu explained. He proceeded toward the cottage door, but I stopped just outside of it.

"Grandpa? Are you... mad at me?" I wasn't nervous as I asked the question, but it still prodded at me anyway.

"Why would I be angry at you, *pawee*?"

He'd used the Hawkei word for *beloved little child*, and the term was so affectionate. It made me melt inside. "Well... I kind of blew myself up..."

"You did what you had to, to save the people you loved." Grandpa put a hand on my shoulder and stroked back my hair. "Why would I be angry at you for that?"

"Does anger even exist here?" I asked.

"Sometimes, though it's rare." My grandfather knocked on the door. I was momentarily shocked when I saw who opened it.

At first, I thought it was Ezekiel, and I wondered what had happened for him to end up here at the same time as me. But it wasn't my brother... this man's hair was shorter, and he had a more muscular build. He was the same age as me, though, and had that same lopsided smile that my brother always had.

The man grinned at me and said, "About time you showed up, niece."

This was my Uncle Ezra. He'd died shortly after I was born. His energy and presence were so similar to Ezekiel's. I immediately felt like I was at home. I grinned and flung my arms around him. Ezra's embrace was tight and welcoming, unlike my grandfather's, which had been so stiff and rigid.

"I can't believe you're actually here," I said, and I squeezed him even tighter.

"You've been a rascal, let me tell you," Uncle Ezra said, ruffling my hair. "You definitely kept my dad on his toes."

Grandpa Liwanu let out a *hmph* behind him. As Uncle Ezra stepped aside, I entered the cottage. It was sweet and comfortable here. A fire burned in the hearth, and Hawkei memorabilia lined the walls alongside wooden furniture.

A woman stood at the stove, cooking some sort of dish. When she turned around to greet me, I had to do a double-take. It was my Aunt Stevie— I knew she had to be— and she looked *so much* like Josee. They were nearly twins. It was mind blowing that I was actually meeting her birth parents, after hearing so much about them growing up.

Stevie was my age, too. She and my uncle had passed away so young.

"I'm happy you finally made it," Aunt Stevie said, and she gave a laugh. "I think it's great you arrived with a *bang*."

The joke made my lips twitch. Her weird sense of humor would make us get along just fine.

"Did you know I was coming?" I asked, tilting my head.

"Of course." Aunt Stevie stirred the pot. "Everyone has the date written that they'll die, Ava. We saw that you were about to show up and made sure to prepare for your arrival."

She took the pot off the stove and dumped the food into a dish. She served it as Uncle Ezra put out plates and silverware, and I sat down at the kitchen table. All my senses were still working— though I wasn't sure if I needed them— and damn, whatever she had made smelled *good*.

"What is it?" I asked.

"It's a casserole made of corn, squash, and beans. It's your uncle's favorite. He'll eat half of it himself, so get yours while you can," Aunt Stevie teased. Uncle Ezra wrapped a hand around her hips and tickled her middle while she beat him off with a dish cloth.

"Can we... eat here?" I asked. I didn't think spirits needed food.

"We don't have to eat, but we can for pleasure," Grandpa Liwanu said. "And the spiritual food here will nourish your spirit, now that you've made the transition from there to here."

I took a bite, and ancestors, I almost died again. It was just cooked vegetables, seasoned and donned with some kind of cheese, but it was far better than the most elaborate dish cooked at a five-star restaurant on Earth. Every bit was savory and satisfied the core of me. I cleaned my plate in minutes, and felt satisfied— not stuffed, but not hungry either. Uncle Ezra wolfed down his food— ancestors, so much like my brother— while Aunt Stevie had a modest helping.

My grandpa didn't eat, which didn't surprise me. He seemed like the kind of soul that stuck to the basics and didn't go out of his way to do things that were unnecessary.

"You look really good," I told Aunt Stevie. In life, she'd had the same disease my dad had, and had looked ill in so many of our pictures, even in the ones where it was obvious she was having a good time. She'd been sicker than my dad was, and had died from her illness shortly after Uncle Ezra passed away in the war.

It was weird thinking in those kinds of terms here. The same people that had *passed away* were sitting right here in front of me, eating food, talking and laughing like such a thing had never happened at all. Death seemed pointless and meaningless here.

"All diseases and illnesses are cured in the Ancestral Lands, but you already knew that," Aunt Stevie said with a shrug. "Sickness is an earthly thing that's meant to teach us lessons. There isn't much use for it here in the spirit realm."

"This is insane that it's all real," I said, looking between them all. "I... I can't really be dead, can I? I mean... I'm so young."

Uncle Ezra put a hand on my arm. "I know it's a lot to take in. I had the same reaction, too, when I first showed up."

"It can be more difficult for people like us to transition," Aunt Stevie said. "Since we didn't get a lot of time."

Her words seemed heavy on my frame, before the feeling flitted away in a moment. She was talking about *me*. I'd... died young.

What a crazy thought. On Earth, I'd felt invincible. Like I'd somehow live forever.

"Yeah," Uncle Ezra said, giving a somber nod. "But we'll get another go-round."

"What are you talking about?" I put my fork down and leaned forward.

"We're getting ready to reincarnate again," Uncle Ezra said. "We just chose our new parents yesterday."

"Reincarnation is real?" It was taught in the Hawkei religion, and Professor Hemlock had gone over it in her class, but getting information straight from the source was fascinating.

"It is, but you pick when you want to go back," Aunt Stevie said. "It's taken a long time to decide what lessons we wanted to learn and how we wanted to benefit other souls in our next lives."

"Because *someone* is picky," Uncle Ezra grumbled.

"I wanted something *interesting*!" Aunt Stevie complained.

"All this information about the afterlife seems so confusing," I said.

"Your spirit will remember it, after a while," Grandpa Liwanu said. "It takes time for your soul to recall all the information your past lives have learned before, in the Blessed Haven and on Earth."

"Are you guys twin flames?" I asked. "Like—"

The question fell away from my lips as I remembered. Charlie. He wasn't here.

Deep within my spirit was something absent. A missing piece. The other half of my soul wasn't complete. Even here in the Ancestral Lands, I wasn't made whole without him and Oberi.

It made me feel vacant in a way that the others weren't, and that emptiness tore through me, even though everything was safe here.

I had to force myself to put Charlie aside. I'd made my choice. A life for a life, and I'd been glad to make it. There was no turning back now.

"We're technically soul mates. Ezra and I have been together in almost every lifetime," Aunt Stevie explained. "We just signed our newest contract to be together in our next incarnation."

I looked down at my hands. "So... you're going to leave soon?"

"Oh, no, there are multiple versions of ourselves in the spiritual realm, and they all exist at the same time. Even once we reincarnate as other people, these versions of ourselves will still be here," Uncle Ezra said, gesturing between him and Stevie. "In fact, you can go talk to my warlock self that lived in the fifteen-hundreds if you head down to—"

"Wow, *really?*" I burst. "How's that even possible?"

"You can have multiple versions of yourself that exist at once, because time isn't a continual line," Aunt Stevie said. "Think of time kind of like a planet... like the world you came from. California and Malovia both exist at the same time, in different places, you just have to hop on a plane or take a portal to get there. So multiple versions of yourself can exist at once, just at different moments in time, because you are all one being— your higher self, which is your spirit name."

I'd never gotten my spirit name on Earth, despite going through multiple ceremonies, so I didn't really know who my higher self was supposed to be, or what she was supposed to be called. The idea seemed complicated, at first, but it really wasn't to me. It was sort of like what Oberi said about having different forms at different times. They were all *Oberi*, just not all at once.

I wish I could tell Kallie all of this. She'd have found this stuff about time interesting.

"Does that mean I can go meet other versions of my past self?" I asked Grandpa.

"If you wish, but I don't suggest it," Grandpa Liwanu said gruffly. "They don't make for good conversation."

"You just say that because all your other selves argued the whole time," Uncle Ezra stated. "*My* past selves were great."

"Ezra's selves all put together have the intelligence equivalent of an onion," Aunt Stevie teased.

"Hey, we know how to party! You can't say it wasn't a blast," Uncle Ezra argued.

"It *was* a fun time..." Aunt Stevie admitted reluctantly.

Hm. It'd be interesting to have a conversation with multiple versions of myself. Or a party, in Ezra's case.

Or maybe it wasn't a good idea. Me and all the past Avas would probably conspire to do something crazy here in heaven.

I could hardly wait.

Grandpa Liwanu stood from the table. "There's so much more to see. Ezra will show you around."

Aunt Stevie waved her hand. The dishes whisked away, as if they never existed at all. I followed my uncle outside, where his Familiar emerged from his body. It was Dyami, his thunderbird. The massive yellow bird was absolutely beautiful, with jolts of lightning racing up and down his feathers. I reached out a hand to stroke his cheek, and the thunderbird nuzzled against me tenderly.

"You're gonna love this," Uncle Ezra said. He climbed onto Dyami's back, then reached out a hand to pull me on in front of him. Dyami took off, electricity shooting off his wings. A warm wind brushed my hair back as we rose from the trees and into the multi-colored sky. The rainbows swelled around us, and I looked down to take it all in.

The Ancestral Lands went on forever, in every direction. The expanse was so massive that I didn't even know where the other planes of heaven could *be*, because this place went on forever.

Dyami sailed upward, out of the day and into the night, but he didn't stop there. He kept moving through the layers of sky until the land below us vanished completely and we were surrounded by nothing but galaxies.

We had no need to breathe. Dyami sailed through the stars, flying through space just as easily as he would anywhere else. My jaw dropped as we sailed past planets, blazing a trail through meteors and comets. I put my hand out and felt a tingling sensation as the stars around me skimmed over my fingers.

Eventually, Uncle Ezra pulled Dyami up. "Watch this," he said, with a hint of arrogance.

I looked down. Below us was a gigantic red star, at the very end of its life. The star burned hot, turning redder and redder until it suddenly exploded into a bright white supernova. The supernova shone outward with its incredible brilliance, beaming in a circle until the star began spiraling inward, turning into a small white neutron star. It glowed with a miniature light that was pale in comparison to the beaming supernova it had just been.

I was speechless. I couldn't believe I'd just observed the collapse of a *star*. Those took millions of years, and I'd seen it all in a matter of seconds. Like death, time didn't mean anything in the spiritual plane.

"Cool, right?" Uncle Ezra prodded. "I've seen like, dozens of them."

"Can we explore other planets, even if we're tied to the Ancestral Lands?" I asked him.

"Planets? Sweetheart, you can explore other *galaxies*," Uncle Ezra said. "The universe is always expanding, and there's always more to see. You could spend a literal eternity trying to see it all, and it would never happen. Whatever you want to observe, or study, it's here for you. All you have to do is make up your mind to go."

I nearly began shaking with all the possibilities. I'd always had a heart for adventure, but exploring Earth was like taking a vacation in your hometown compared to being able to watch stars collapse and visit far-off solar systems.

And that was just the capability of space. I hadn't even touched on what the Ancestral Lands themselves could do. Dyami swooped back down, heading toward the Ancestral Lands once more. We crossed the boundary of night and day, and Uncle Ezra steered the thunderbird toward a beach.

The sand was crystal white here and gleamed like diamonds, while the ocean itself was completely clear. I could see all the way through the water down to the depths of the coral reefs hundreds of feet below, and watch the incredible creatures that swam within. I spotted a kelpie herd, a hippocampus, several humpback whales, and even a sea serpent before Dyami came close to landing.

Ancestors, *the fish*. There were millions of them, and they made a rainbow just as intricate as the one in the sky as we drew near. Aunt Stevie waited by the shore of the ocean, waving up at us.

"Did you like that?" Aunt Stevie asked as I slid off Dyami.

"I *loved* it," I gushed. "Is there more?"

"Always," Aunt Stevie said. "You want to see?"

"Yes!" I hopped up and down.

Stevie called to the ocean, and a half-griffin, half-mermaid type creature swam up from the deep, pulling itself onto shore— a cypher. It was her Familiar, Nihoni.

Stevie gestured for me to get on. I climbed onto the cypher's back, and Nihoni began swimming out to sea. I nearly held my breath as she dove down, before I realized I didn't have to. Nihoni surged forward, and I held on to her slick feathers as her fin propelled us fiercely forward.

She swam for a long time. I wasn't sure where she was taking me, until I saw a drop-off in the sea ahead. Nihoni pulled up, allowing me to observe. At first, I thought it was some kind of underwater waterfall, until I realized it was much bigger than that. The drop-off was a sinkhole, over a thousand feet across and at least five hundred feet deep. The expanse was massive, making me feel as if I tried going down that hole, I'd be lost to the depths of the sea forever.

When Nihoni swam me back to shore, I was soaking wet. As I trod up the beach, I waved my hand by instinct, not realizing I was casting Toaqua magic. I dried myself off instantly. My magic worked even more effortlessly here than it had on Earth.

"Wow! That sinkhole was huge. It was marvelous to look at," I said.

"It's actually a portal to the merfolk afterlife," Aunt Stevie explained. "Once you enter it, you go *really fast,* until you're taken to their city. It's like riding an underground roller coaster."

I was ready to dive back down there and try it out, but Uncle Ezra grabbed my wrist. "Not so fast. You've gotta see the rest of this place yet."

My disappointment over rollercoaster portals was whisked away as they led me away from the shoreline. Their Familiars stayed behind to play on the beach. I heard conversation, and my interest piqued. We walked back into the trees, but it wasn't too long before they parted to make a clearing.

The clearing was filled with dozens of Hawkei. They wore deerskin clothes, and wore their hair braided with shell necklaces and earrings. The longhouses gathered around the area were made of cedar planks. There were hundreds of them, sitting among the trees in rows. Everywhere, people were weaving baskets, playing music, or working on building canoes to sail out onto the water. Their Familiars roamed throughout the area and lived beside them. Unicorns played games with foxes and wolves, while tigers and panthers rested with birds in the trees. Even ghastly creatures like manticores and cockatrices observed the tribe peacefully underneath the sway of the branches.

An overwhelming sense of serenity and rightness overcame me. This was the way my people always should've lived, in harmony. They finally had that here.

"We try to live as closely to the ancient ways as possible, here in the Ancestral Lands," Grandpa Liwanu said. "Though *someone* can't seem to give up the video games."

"You'll tear my console away from me when the Ancestral Lands themselves are gone," Uncle Ezra shot back.

I watched as a couple of children played in a puddle nearby, then ran away squealing from a snake. One thing struck me as I watched them. "What about all the kids?" I asked, gesturing to them.

"Children usually reincarnate very quickly, though they remain as children eternally here, if they died early in life," Grandpa Liwanu said. "Infants who pass away in the womb can reside here and wait for their families, but most of them return to be born to the same parents during a different pregnancy."

A fire roared in the middle of the camp, where people started to gather. Grandpa Liwanu gestured for me to follow, and we sat on the ground near the fire. An elder with long white hair sat at the head of the group, telling stories in the Hawkei language.

I leaned over to Aunt Stevie and whispered, "He looks old. I wasn't aware age was a thing here."

"It's not, really. Your spirit just acknowledges them on how you perceive them to look," she explained.

"So... Grandpa Liwanu looks older to me, but not to *everyone*," I said.

"Yep," she replied. "If you ask your great-grandfather, Liwanu looks like he's in his thirties, to him. Your spirit recognizes my spirit, and all that. It's what you're most comfortable with. But Ezra and I won't look old to anyone, since we came here early. You won't either."

I bet the old dude telling the story looked like a hot tamale to the elderly lady sitting next to him. She was eyeing him like they were still in high school.

The elder raised his hands, and everyone quieted down. "This is a very special moment for our people," he began. "Today, we celebrate as one of our own ascends."

"Ascends?" I whispered, but Grandpa Liwanu gently shushed me. Apparently, I was supposed to listen and not talk.

"In our world, death does not exist, because all our soul is meant to do is to return to the Great Spirit, and return to nature as it is, forever," the elder said. "To do so takes many lifetimes, and much wisdom. What we are meant for is to merge as one with the elements. I'm proud to say that a soul among us has achieved such a mighty goal."

He lifted his hand. A glowing ball of light approached, hovering toward the circle until it formulated into a man. He had a bare chest, with a long braid going down his back, and dark eyes that appeared deep with all the thoughts of the universe.

"Who's that?" I hushed to Aunt Stevie, who was probably more willing to answer questions than my stern grandfather.

"Sani is very old, and very wise," Stevie said, nodding at the man. "He has lived many, many lifetimes, more than most of us, and most of his lives have been Hawkei— most of *those* lives Koigni. He just finished his last life, and has learned everything his spirit needed to. Today is the day where he ascends."

I didn't get what was going on, but I didn't get the chance to ask more questions, because the elder said, "Let us send off our honored friend by giving praise to the gods of the Ancestral Lands."

Everyone in the circle started singing in Hawkei, even my grandfather. It was a happy song, full of joy and celebration. I began singing along, once I caught the rhythm and had memorized the short verse. The circle swayed back and forth as the elder stood, and Sani came forward.

"Sani, what element do you choose to merge your soul with?" the elder asked.

"The element of Fire," Sani replied in a deep tone.

"Very well," the elder said. "Step into the flames, and allow your spirit to meld with the power of Coyote Spirit."

Sani didn't hesitate, or even blink. He stepped into the bonfire, and I gasped. I watched as the flames became a multicolor array of blue, purple, red, orange, and green. They licked up his spirit, and Sani raised his hands to the sky. His soul morphed, until I could no longer see the man, but saw the outline of a person inside the flames. He began dancing with the fire, until the outline of the man dissolved and there was nothing but the flames licking up the logs— but I knew it was still him, moving the fire with the power of his magic and spirit. Applause and cheers rang over the area as Sani's spirit rested within the fire.

I didn't think you could cry in the spirit realm, but apparently you could if they were happy tears, because a few ran down my face. It'd been a beautiful moment. He'd *become* the fire, and in every fire that burned, in the spirit realm or on Earth, there he would be. He would never die. So long as there was fire in this universe, Sani would exist.

It was said in our stories of the Ancestral Lands that when people died, they, their Familiar, and their element merged as one, but I had never really gotten the last part. Now I understood.

"That was incredible," I whispered as people began to disperse.

"Yes. And his heat will warm his descendants, and he will be able to visit them in the flames whenever there is fire available," Grandpa Liwanu said. "One day, I hope to merge with Water, becoming the ocean and the waves wherever they may be. But that is still many lifetimes off."

A thought crossed my mind. "Can we visit people still left on Earth? Without ascending?" I asked.

Grandpa and Uncle Ezra glanced at each other. Aunt Stevie hesitated. "Yes," she admitted. "Though I wouldn't recommend going back right away."

"We can return for certain circumstances and manipulate things, but our power is limited," Uncle Ezra explained. "Spirit guides and a person's direct ancestors usually have the most influence to help someone who's still alive on Earth."

"Ezra helped me cross over, when I was dying," Stevie said fondly. "He took my hand during my last breath and led me here. I saw him in my hospital room the morning I passed away, though no one else could."

"So... even if I go back, they won't be able to see or hear me," I said.

"It would be extremely rare. The person would have to be gifted with magic that could hear and see spirits, and even then, it doesn't always work, especially if you're close with the person who's trying to talk to you," Uncle Ezra explained. "There are reasons we can't talk to our loved ones who are still on Earth. They have their path, and we have to let them learn from it, instead of just giving them all the answers. It wouldn't be fair, and they wouldn't learn what they needed to know, so they'd just have to reincarnate to learn the lesson all over again."

In the empty part of me, I'd hoped Marcus could perform some kind of ceremony to summon my spirit back so I could speak to Charlie again. I doubted now that the Great Spirit would let that happen. We'd been able to talk to Alice when Marcus had summoned her, but they hadn't been extremely close. Charlie and I were the same soul... living in two different places.

"It's really complicated, being dead," I said with a sigh.

"We don't really use the term *dead* here," Aunt Stevie said.

"I mean, *technically* people on Earth are more dead than we are," Uncle Ezra said. "You just don't see it that way until you're here."

I nodded. On Earth, people had bodies that got sick and deteriorated and grew old. They had limits on what they could do, even with magic. Here, anything was possible, and nothing could get in your way.

"I can't wait to start exploring it all," I said. "It's like miracles happen constantly here."

"I mean, all the amazing stuff is great at first, but sometimes, you just want to go home and eat junk food in front of the TV, even if it is heaven," Uncle Ezra said with a shrug. "It's really up to you what you want to do while you're here."

I couldn't imagine being bored enough here to just go watch TV. It was crazy.

"I just..." The void in me tightened. "I'm really glad all of you are here. But I wish Charlie was with me. And Oberi. That's the only thing that would make it better."

When Elementai died, they took their Familiars with them to the other side. I somewhat felt like the odd one out, being the only Hawkei without one.

"Your spirit will be made whole again," Grandpa Liwanu said kindly. "Twin flames can never be separated for long."

Uncle Ezra smacked my arm playfully. "Come on. You're still not done being shown around, and there's a lot more to take in."

I think he was just trying to distract me from Charlie, but I wanted to be distracted, because he wasn't here right now, so I got up. The three of them led me out of the village, and the dirt path changed into a silver brick road. The trees gave way to the plains again, and I noticed a skyline touching the clouds. They were leading me into some kind of glistening city, which was far off in the distance.

We started to come up on the other side of a hill. "So is this city a Hawkei city, or— OH MY GAWD!!!"

Conversation fell out of my mind, as the sight before me was extraordinary. The most blessed thing I'd ever seen came into view. It was better than the fucking supernova.

It was a *mall*. A goddamn beautiful mall, right smack in the middle of heaven. I was rendered completely speechless. Oh glory hallelujah.

Grandpa Liwanu shrugged, like he didn't see the big deal. "We don't need material things here, but you can create or have anything you want, so if you wish—"

I didn't hear the rest of what he said, because I *ran* full speed at the doors. Time didn't exist here, but I'd just come from Earth, and I hadn't seen the inside of a mall in two damn years. This was my eternal reward. I slammed against the glass doors and peered inside. Ancestors, there were dozens of stores, and lots of different restaurants, and right in the middle of it was a huge spa, right next to a dazzling fountain. People were scheduling spa treatments and getting their nails done right beside designer purse stores and fro-yo stands.

I could get a pedicure. I could spend as much money as I wanted and get as many outfits as I pleased. Ancestors, the *shoes*. I could buy so many shoes!

... But Charlie wouldn't be here to carry my bags, so was it even worth it?

That weird feeling came over me again, and I had to shove it down, but the empty hole remained. I stepped away from the door and wrapped my arms around my middle.

"You *can* go to the mall... later," Uncle Ezra said. "Right now, you have class."

"Ugh, I have to go to *school* in heaven, too?" I thought I'd earned the right to be done with it.

"You're never done learning," Aunt Stevie said. "None of us are."

"It's not your typical school," Uncle Ezra explained. "It's a school for you to learn about your life, to go over the lessons you experienced and understand why you went through the things you did."

So I'd finally get some answers on why my life had been so fucked up. *That* was going to be nice.

"You can also attend the school to learn how to be a spirit guide, if you so wish. I'll be one of your teachers, along with your other spirit guides. They're waiting for you there," Grandpa Liwanu explained.

I hoped this didn't take too long, because I was planning on getting a massage, stat. We left the mall (sadly) and started proceeding toward the city again, which is where I assumed the school was.

"Hey, Uncle Ez?" I asked.

"What is it, sweetheart?" he asked. He reached up to pluck a fruit off a nearby tree and started eating it along the path.

"Stevie died nearly a year after you did," I said. "How did you cope while waiting for her?"

He looked at Aunt Stevie, then reached out to take her hand. "It really wasn't that long to wait. Time moves differently here. It had been a year on Earth, but really, it felt like a few days here, by the time I went back to get her."

"Charlie and Oberi will arrive soon," Grandpa said. "Even if they live to be a hundred years, and then pass on, it will only seem like moments to you."

It might be a short time to me, but to Charlie... it would be anything but. "Is there like, a board or something I can check to see when they're supposed to die, and how?"

"It's actually more like a book," Stevie said. "You'll get access to it once you complete your orientation."

I wrinkled my nose. "Am I going to run into Jaymin in there?" It'd be a bitch if I'd blown myself up to get away from her, just to run into her again.

"Oh, no." Uncle Ezra laughed. "She's in the bad place. That particular incarnation of herself is, anyhow."

"It takes a lot to get banished from the Ancestral Lands," Stevie said with slight disgust. "Jaymin earned it."

All of us looked up when we saw the bright white light of a spirit orb descending. We had to stop along the path when the spirit orb hovered in front of us, forming into a man. The man wore shiny, silver armor and carried a long spear. He looked like a guard.

What the hell. I thought I was done with these assholes, but apparently, they had brutes even in heaven.

The guard spoke in a sharp, brusque voice. "Ava-Marie Wahkin, the Hawkei gods request your presence immediately. There is something that must be discussed. And you must come alone."

I looked at the faces of my family. Was this something that happened often?

By their expressions, apparently not.

"Best to go with them," Grandpa Liwanu said. "We'll be waiting for you when you're done."

"But..." I wanted to stay with them.

"No questions. Come with me." The guard reached out to grasp my wrist. Once the guard touched me, I found myself portaled from one place to another.

I stood in some kind of amphitheater. White light shone from above so brightly, I couldn't really see where I was. I turned on the spot, but the guard was already gone.

Voices came from all around me. The bright light faded, and my jaw dropped as I looked up. I'd been taken to some kind of court chamber, with rows upon rows of stone walls, like the inside of a carved-out mountain. On these platforms were all kinds of animals. There were bears, wolves, snakes, bison, horses, and so many more— literally thousands of them, in every species imaginable. If you asked me to name them all, there's no way I ever could. I spotted Whale Spirit, the goddess of Toaqua, along with Eagle Spirit, the god of Yapluma, standing along the lowest platform in their human forms.

There were more gods here than were listed in the Hawkei pantheon. My people didn't even know about them all.

One particular god was more familiar than the rest. Coyote Spirit prowled toward me on his paws, the only god who was on ground level with me.

"Coyote," I said as he looked at me. "What's going on?"

A special case, he said. *Since your death, we gathered to discuss the fate of your prophecy, and how it would change now that you are no longer able to fulfill it. But it seems there are other factors at play, for now we are here to help you decide your fate.*

I was about to ask him what he was talking about, until I felt myself being wrenched away from the Ancestral Lands.

It was a jarring experience, going from utter peace to complete devastation. Every awful emotion that I ever experienced flooded back in a singular suffocating stream. Grief, sadness, loss... it rammed into me with all the power of a tsunami, and I found myself drowning under the weight of that terrible typhoon.

No sooner did I register that I was on Earth again— *somehow*— than an agonizing pain tore through me. It felt like I'd been turned inside out. I let out an agonized scream, then another, and another. I felt the pressure of anesthetic fail to put me under as the sensation of scalpels and gloved hands tore through me.

"We're losing her!" I heard someone cry. Through the pain, I heard the sound of a heart monitor, slowly beeping until it went flatline.

The moment the heart monitor went flat, I found myself ripped from my body and dragged back to the spirit realm. I was once again standing in the middle of the amphitheater with the gods, and not in... whatever horrible place I had been.

I still held my stomach, although everything had ceased to hurt. There was no such thing as pain here in the Ancestral Lands, but I remembered exactly what it felt like, and the thought of experiencing that again made my spirit recoil inside and out. Pain was an earthly experience. It wasn't something that was supposed to happen in the afterlife.

Then, I heard a blissful voice coming from somewhere far off... Charlie's voice. *I'll be waiting for you, pidge. I'll accept whatever you decide, because I love you that much. But if you can, please... come back to me.*

His voice shook my soul to the core. I nearly dropped to my knees.

What the hell was going on? How could he communicate with me across realms? It was unfathomable, even with a soul bond.

"What was that?" I asked with a shudder. I had no idea what was going on.

Coyote paused. His ear twitched, as if he was listening to something. *It would seem Charlie and Oberi are doing their best to return you to your mortal life.*

I went completely still. "Can they do that?"

Before Oberi left, she was given a special kind of magic— a power she could only use once. She has used that power to attempt to restore your body and bring your soul back to Earth.

"They want me to come back?" I asked in a whisper.

It would seem so. Your body is in surgery right now, although your spirit is hesitant to return. Coyote shook out his fur. *This is a very rare occasion, even in the magical world. It appears that your soul connection to Charlie is what's enabling it to be possible. It's very difficult for a soul to reside in two different planes of reality; however, it can be done.* Coyote gave a little growl, like he was displeased.

"Is it going to work?" I felt my lip tremble.

That is up to you.

"Me?"

Yes. You alone have to make the choice if you wish to return to Earth to live a mortal life, or continue to stay here in the Ancestral Lands.

A voice cried out from above. *This is preposterous. She has seen the Ancestral Lands. She cannot be permitted to return!*

It was a badger, with green and silver lines running through his fur. He had to be Badger Spirit— the god of stubbornness.

This really wasn't his business, so I wished he'd just butt out. Voices from the other gods cried out, to say they agreed with Badger Spirit.

She is much more than an ordinary Elementai, as all of you know, Coyote barked viciously. *An exception must be made.*

Preposterous! Badger Spirit said. *You do not have the power to decide—*

She belongs to me! It is I who was there when she was formed, Coyote snarled, turning around to stare at Badger Spirit with bared teeth.

"And I," Whale Spirit said, coming forward in her human form. "We *are the gods who oversaw her creation. It is we who shall decide their fate, and we say, Ava will decide."*

This is a task for the Great Spirit, not us, Badger Spirit argued.

"But aren't you *all* the Great Spirit?" I protested.

Yes and no, Coyote admitted reluctantly. *The Great Spirit is a much greater power than we. I am the laugh in the Great Spirit's voice— Whale Spirit is the kindness of the Spirit's touch, Eagle Spirit the adventure that inspires us all. Each of us have different qualities of the Great Spirit, but even together, we cannot match the Great Spirit's power.*

"Well, let me meet the Great Spirit, then," I said.

The entire congregation broke out laughing. I didn't get what was so comical. Their harsh laughter rang over the rafters, inspiring anger to well up within me.

I bunched my hands into fists. "If I have a chance to go back to Charlie, and the Great Spirit says I can't, then I'm gonna kick his— or her— ass!"

Most of the gods gave offended gasps, but Coyote chuckled. *Are you offering to battle the master of creation?*

"Yeah! Just put me in the ring with him. Then he'll be sorry."

Don't be ridiculous, Badger Spirit said. *The Great Spirit would never allow that.*

"One of us must go to the Great Spirit in her stead," Eagle Spirit stated. *"That is the only way for us to agree."*

"We shall go, Coyote and I, and plead her case," Whale Spirit said. *"Then the matter will be settled."*

"If all of you are going to make the decision for me, then why am I even here?" I asked harshly.

"Be patient," Whale Spirit told me. *"We shall see what the Great Spirit says."*

Coyote and Whale Spirit disappeared on the spot. I started to pace the moment they were gone, while the gods above made conversation, watching me with eyes that felt greedy and keen.

Long moments passed. It felt like I was waiting around forever.

"What's taking them so long?" I barked at Eagle Spirit. I knew I was being disrespectful to a freaking god, but fuck.

"Have you truly considered the consequences if you return?" Eagle

Spirit asked me. *"You are leaving an eternal paradise for a world that is full of agony and pain."*

I huffed. Yeah, heaven was great. And to be honest, I didn't *really* want to leave. This place was wonderful. I wasn't up for leaving it to return to a body that was mentally ill— not to mention in pieces.

But I had a destiny to fulfill, and more than that, the other half of my soul was still back on Earth. I'd give up heaven to be with Charlie, for as wonderful as heaven was, my real paradise was with him and Oberi, wherever they were. If we were together, we could get through anything.

And I wouldn't abandon him to walk through life alone if there was any chance I could spare him that pain.

Eventually, Coyote and Whale Spirit returned. They didn't give me an answer right away, which pissed me the fuck off. The gods whispered amongst themselves, until eventually, Coyote and Whale Spirit turned back towards me.

The Great Spirit has decided that it will be your choice, Badger Spirit said, but he sounded pissed about it. *Make up your mind, girl. Be aware you cannot reverse this decision once you have chosen.*

"Then I want to go back," I said automatically.

Think carefully, Coyote reminded me. *Your body is in a very dire state. Even if you return, and attempt to survive, there's no guarantee you won't end up back here, with nothing to show for your decision to return but possible weeks or months of sheer pain.*

"I like taking risks. Makes things interesting."

The girl doesn't understand what she's asking for, Badger Spirit said.

"Then answer me this. Is the Blessed Haven still in danger? If I remain in the Ancestral Lands, will the Warden continue to try to take over heaven, summon the dark gods from hell, and rule Earth?" I asked.

There was silence. None of the gods responded, and I took that for my answer.

"Then if the Ancestral Lands and the rest of the spirit realm is in danger, it's my job to go back and protect it, even if I have to give all this up," I said firmly. "The Great Spirit chose me to decide what happens to the afterlife. No matter how much I have to go through to defend it, I'm going back."

You could go back only to make the wrong choice and damn us all,

Badger Spirit growled. *Your very presence on Earth is a risk. If you are here in the Ancestral Lands, we stand a better chance of survival!*

If that is her choice to return, then we will honor it, Coyote said harshly. *The Great Spirit chose her to fulfill her prophecy. She deserves a second chance to see it completed, and to make the choice to save our world, or damn it.*

"I promise that I'll do everything in my power to save the spirit realm once I return," I vowed to the gods. "I won't let the Warden decide who's fit for heaven or who's not."

Badger Spirit gave a dissatisfied noise. *Very well. We shall see if you keep your promise.*

Yeah, whatever. I'd show him.

Before you return, Coyote said. *There are two people you should meet.*

I couldn't imagine what could be more important than getting back to Charlie, but I figured I might as well humor him, as I didn't have much of a choice. Coyote indicated I should hop on his back again, and I clambered on. Coyote gave a bow to Whale Spirit, and only her, before he took off into the sky, and she inclined her head in kind. Soon, we were running along a stream of colors, soaring out of the open-air amphitheater as Coyote took me to who-knew where.

"Whale Spirit is pretty," I said, goading him on.

She is elaborate, Coyote replied. *I am quite fond of her.*

Hmph. The way Coyote had talked about my parents during my Darke Games run, Coyote acted like Fire and Water being together was some big joke, but he definitely had a thing for Whale Spirit. I didn't know who he was trying to fool.

Coyote flew me to another little house, this time a stone cottage that was anchored on the side of a deserted mountain. I slid off his back, and he remained off at a distance to watch me as I proceeded toward the house.

I knocked on the door. I didn't know if I was supposed to, but there wasn't anyone else out here to talk to.

The door opened. A tall, beautiful woman with red hair stood in the doorway. Behind her, a lovely girl with dark skin poured coffee into three cups that sat on the kitchen table.

They were both my age. They must've died young. I didn't recognize either of them.

But they knew me. "Ava. Come inside," the redhead said in a sultry tone.

I glanced back at Coyote, who didn't give me any sort of instruction. I entered the cottage. It was really hot in here— they both had to be Koigni. I was Fire, too, so I wasn't uncomfortable. The house was decorated in a modernist style— clean lines, everything black and white.

I sat down at the table, and they sat across from me. I took a sip of coffee, which I found to be a hazelnut latte. It was divine.

"Miranda makes the best coffee," the redhead said, taking the other woman's hand with a smile.

"Only because you make it sweet, Lindsey," Miranda responded, giving her a peck on the lips.

The names were familiar— I'd heard them before. "You were my mother's friends," I said. "You sacrificed yourself in the Hawkei Civil War. What you gave up was incredible."

"What we gave up was worth it to save the tribe," Lindsey said.

"And it enabled us to be together, so it all worked out in the end, as it always does," Miranda said, taking a sip of her coffee. "We've been waiting a long time to speak with you, Ava, and explain things. Maddie told us it would happen someday, when we were alive, but we never expected it would be like this."

"My aunt? Wait— you were the ones who wrote in my journal. It was *your* handwriting I couldn't recognize," I said.

"Yes. We're the ancestral guardians of your prophecy. Your Aunt Maddie tasked us with helping her decipher her visions of the future before we died, and now that we're ancestors, we're here on the other side to help you with your journey," Miranda replied. "We've been informed you've made the decision to go back."

"I did." I fiddled with my cup. "Do you think I'm making the right choice?"

"It doesn't matter what we think. What matters is the choice you make for yourself," Lindsey said. "If you really do want to go back, we're here to guide you on your path."

"What does that mean?" I asked.

"It was hard for us to get in contact with you when you were living on Earth," Miranda said. "We tried so hard to send you hints and give you clues to help you defeat the Warden, but what we can do even as ancestors is limited."

"Can you explain the rest of my prophecy, and tell me what the future holds now that I'm here with you in person?" I asked.

"We could if you remained here in the Ancestral Lands and chose to leave your prophecy behind you, but since you're returning, we can't do that. Telling you now could influence the outcome of the prophecy, and put the world, as well as the Blessed Haven, in danger," Lindsey said, shaking her head.

"Why can't you just give me the answers now? I don't understand," I said.

"We are magically bound to say nothing," Miranda said. "Prophecies are only fulfilled when the chosen one partakes in the journey and fulfills their destiny through their own choices and power. If we give you everything you need to learn on your own, the prophecy's magic will wane. Then the Blessed Haven *will* be destroyed."

I pondered what I had read in my journal, and remembered one of the lines from my prophecy. *She dances the line both dead and alive.*

"My aunt saw me resurrecting to fulfill my prophecy, didn't she?" I asked.

"She did," Lindsey admitted. "What you and Charlie share is powerful magic."

"Well damn, she could've told me!" I said.

"You wouldn't have taken the steps necessary to be here if you knew, so it would've never happened, and the prophecy's magic would break, as we said," Miranda insisted. "Giving you the answers changes the entire path of the future. There's no telling what course it could take, if we told you what's coming. Then the Warden will certainly win."

Well, no matter how curious I was, I wasn't letting him beat me that easily. "So if you can't give me the answers now, but can guide me on my journey, how are you planning on doing that?"

"We'll send you clues as you come along each point of your path, since your soul still has lessons to learn," Lindsey added. "Trust me; you'll know it's from us."

"How can I get in contact with you? You aren't my ancestors, so I can't communicate with you directly, and I don't think having a friend summon you would work more than once, if at all."

"Your mother has a very special compass in her possession," Miranda said. "Once you get back, ask her to give it to you. We'll be able to channel our energy and speak with you through it."

"We won't always be able to communicate with words, but the compass will show you what you need to do and where you need to go," Lindsey said. "When you use it, it won't always make sense. But be aware that the compass is always right. Follow it as best you can. That's all we can tell you."

I nodded. "Okay. Then I think I'm ready."

"You're very brave for going back," Miranda added. "I don't think I ever could. Not after being here. I've even put off reincarnating. I don't want anything to do with Earth for a long time."

"I'm not going back because I want to." I was going back because the world needed me.

And Charlie. He needed me. If he was calling me back, then my soul had to go. We were two parts of one being. I couldn't let us exist apart. It just wasn't right.

We stood from the table. When I opened the door to the cottage, Uncle Ezra, Aunt Stevie, and Grandpa Liwanu were waiting for me.

I guess they'd heard the news. They didn't look mad about it, though. If anything, my grandfather appeared proud as he puffed out his chest. "That's my girl. I knew you wouldn't give up the fight so easily."

"I'm going to miss all of you," I said, giving each of them tight hugs. It sucked that I had to leave already after meeting all of them.

"Ah, you'll be back in a minute," Uncle Ezra said with a wave in his hand. "Spirit-realm speaking. No telling how long you'll be down *there*."

Aunt Stevie stroked back my hair. Her tone was thick with emotion as she said, "Say hi to Josee once you see her, okay? Give her all our love."

"I will," I promised her. "First chance I get."

"We're always around her, though we know she can't see us," Uncle Ezra added. "Tell her that."

"She'll love to hear it." I paused. I looked around, waiting for the one person I longed the most to see. "... Will I get to say goodbye to Monica?"

Nobody said anything. I realized the truth.

"Monica didn't come to see me because she wanted me to go back. Didn't she?" I asked. "She knew I wouldn't return to Charlie if I saw her."

Lindsey gave me a soft smile.

I turned away. "She knows me too well."

"She wanted you to have these," Aunt Stevie said. In her hands materialized a bouquet of huge, bright pink flowers that looked like buttons. "They're Spirit Flowers, grown here by Monica's own Nivita magic. They'll always be in your soul. They never fade and never die. Whenever you think of them, she'll be nearby, and it'll always remind you how much she loves you."

I took the bouquet of flowers with a tear streaming down my face. At my touch, they dissolved, and I felt a warmth enter my spirit. "I knew she never left."

My loved ones parted. They bowed as Coyote proceeded up the path, walking in a straight line toward me. *The time approaches. You must return now, if you wish to go back. Is this still what you want?*

I remembered the awful pain. I almost changed my mind and told him no. The last thing I wanted to do was crawl back into that broken and sick body that I'd come from.

But Charlie was on the other side of it, and reaching him was more important than suffering through the agony.

I once said I'd do anything to get back to him. Time to prove it.

I nodded. Coyote Spirit reared up on his hind legs to touch his nose to the area between my eyes, and I gasped. My loved ones and the mountain range faded around me. I felt my spirit crumble into nothing more than ether as I went spiraling backward, leaving the paradise of the Ancestral Lands behind...

Retreating from the light and immersing myself into darkness once more.

charlie
TWENTY-FIVE

I wanted to cry... to scream... to do *anything*, really. But I didn't move, nor speak. All I could do was sit there, clutching the armrest of a leather chair. Oberi whined lowly from where he lay at my feet.

I sat in a private room in the hospital wing, waiting for Ava to emerge from surgery, but it felt as if I sat somewhere outside of time itself. I didn't know how much time had passed. Nothing seemed real. I'd let myself go completely numb, because if I dared myself to feel...

I couldn't fathom it.

The sound of the gunshot echoed over and over in my mind, and my hands shook. I'd been so afraid that Ava would pull the trigger— and she *had*. She'd brought the whole Underground down on herself to save the rest of us. My soul seemed to crumble all over again just thinking about it.

Perhaps this is what she truly wanted.

Had I made a mistake? What pain had I caused her by bringing her back? Could the doctors save her? Would she even *want* to return to me?

I couldn't bear to have these questions answered, because I feared the worst.

At least I was alone. I didn't need reassurances from Kallie and

Marcus, and I didn't care to face the grief from Ava's parents. Surely, they blamed me as much as I blamed myself.

The doctors had only allowed one person to wait for Ava in recovery. Everyone else sat in the waiting room. I needed to be here, so I'd know the second she was out of surgery.

Heavy footsteps sounded down the hall in a quick beat. Adrenaline shocked my system, and I snapped to attention. I shot to my feet the same time he burst through the door.

"Where is she?" the Warden demanded.

My hands curled into fists, and Air began to swirl around the room. I couldn't control myself. Oberi jumped to his feet beside me and growled. If the Warden thought he could lay a single hand on my pidge, he could burn in the fires of hell.

"What do you want with her?" I growled.

"Dr. Taurus," a nurse from out in the hall said gently. "If you're looking for Mrs. Wahkin, she's still in surgery. We can take you to her if you'd like."

The Warden paused for a beat, then spoke calmly. "Alert me once the doctors have finished. I'd like to speak with her *husband* first."

The door clicked shut. A shiver traveled down my spine, but I was done fearing this old fuck. He could experiment on me or kill me; it didn't really matter. Unless Ava made it out of surgery, I had nothing left to live for.

"It's over," the Warden stated firmly. "I know what you and your friends are."

"And?" I questioned coolly. "That doesn't help you unless you can do something about it. Jaymin proved tonight that you have no idea what the fuck you're doing."

"Jaymin was a loose cannon," the Warden snapped. "She was sloppy. It was a mistake to hire her. Her only use to me is her death. Ava-Marie murdered her, and that's grounds enough for me to lock her away for life. As an accessory to the murders that occurred tonight, you will also receive a life sentence, Mr. Wahkin."

Anger rushed into my chest to replace the numbness that had settled there. I was too fucked up with rage to take his threats seriously. I scoffed. "Is that the story you're going to tell everyone? And what proof do you have?"

"I know the four of you caused that cave-in," the Warden snarled. "Jaymin left me a message before she pursued you. I need no other proof."

I gritted my teeth. "The Union's going to want proof. And if all you have is testimony, you openly admit that you knew about the Underground. The Union will go snooping— and it'll be *all* the Union members, not just the ones you have in your pocket. They'll discover what you did down there. All the parents of missing kids will know what happened— all the torture and crimes you committed against every supernatural race. They'll show you no mercy. You'll receive the death sentence."

My tone became innocent— fake. "We're so sorry about what happened to our counselor. Jaymin was our therapist, the best we ever had, and she was really helping us reform. We'd just seen our Elf friends die and be dragged away. She knew how traumatic that would be, so she invited us to the graveyard for a midnight ritual under the moon. She was only trying to *help*. That's when the sinkhole happened. You know, these caves we mine— they're so unstable. We tried to save her, but it all just happened so fast."

The Warden blew heavy breaths. I was obviously really pissing him off. "You'll never convince anyone of that story. No one has sympathy for a convict like yourself."

"Oh, really? They'll believe *you* over the poor, blind orphan whose wife is on her deathbed?" I scoffed. "I can be just as manipulative as you, but believe me, I'm better at it."

"You can't tell your story if you're locked away in Cellblock 9," he threatened.

I let out a cold laugh. "You don't know what I've already said. You don't know what Ava's parents have seen. Or are you going to take *them* to Cellblock 9, too? The Union would be all over the investigation of a missing Hawkei chief. You want to play this game? We can play it. My wife is *dying*. I have nothing left to live for. As much as you try to make the rest of us believe you're the ultimate power here, you have your limits. So, no, I don't believe you'll be accusing us of murder anytime soon."

"You're not as clever as you think. I know what you are— *the emperor's legacy, his heir,*" he growled. "You're the last Elf in this prison. It has to be you."

My teeth gritted, and my eyebrow twitched, betraying me. If the Warden didn't know for sure what I was before, I'd just confirmed it for him.

"Then you know the wording of my prophecy," I stated dryly. "*It is his choice to damn the realm, or save us all.* I'll gladly damn every last soul in existence to destroy you."

The Warden chuckled, like he found my threats nothing more than amusing. "I'll get what I want from you first. All I need to do is perfect this spell, and use the inferichite to drain your powers. You have nowhere to go. Rest assured, Mr. Wahkin, as long as you are inside this prison, *I own you.* Demigods or not, you can't escape. You think because you're not locked in a cage in Cellblock 9 that means you're free?"

He laughed maniacally. "Mr. Wahkin, you're already locked in *my* cage. And I will drain every last bit of your power before you make it out of here."

He turned and strolled out of the room, slamming the door shut behind him.

Fuck him. I sank back into my chair and stroked Oberi's fur.

He's a real asshole, that guy, Oberi said.

"Yeah," I agreed. "But he doesn't know what kind of asshole *I* can be. The Warden thinks he won this battle, but I'll make damn sure he loses the war."

The door creaked open, and my spine straightened. I could hear Ava's father sobbing from the waiting room.

"Ava's strong," Sophia reassured him. "She'll fight for her life."

"Mr. Wahkin?" a kind female voice said, though I didn't recognize it. It had to be one of the doctors.

"Yes," I replied quickly.

"Your wife made it through surgery."

A heart rate monitor beeped. The wheels of a gurney squeaked as they brought Ava into the room. I nearly toppled over in relief. They transferred her onto the bed, and I immediately went to her side.

"Pidge," I breathed as I took her hand. She didn't squeeze back.

Poor pidge. She had to be so weak. Even so, her skin was warm, and I realized that was the most incredible feeling in all the universe.

Sobs broke from my chest, and I pressed my lips to the back of your hand. "I'm so glad you made it. I—"

I broke off when I reached for her face and felt a tube coming out of her mouth. My world shattered all over again. Ava wasn't awake. The hollowness inside seemed to expand. I hadn't noticed it before, because I was too numb to feel anything at all. Now, it was all too encompassing. Oberi whined solemnly.

The doctors and nurses moved around me, arranging tubes and electrical cords. I barely paid them any mind as my shaking fingers grazed across Ava's broken body. I took note of the bandages across her face and arms. A large cloth wrapped around her entire stomach. I feared touching her too roughly, because I knew her skin must be riddled with bruises.

My voice shook. "She's going to make it, right?"

"We can't say for sure," the doctor said slowly. "She's stable, but she's been put into a medically-induced coma. Ava-Marie's body needs time to heal. We'll be monitoring her twenty-four-seven..."

I barely heard the rest of what she said. The room swayed around me. Ava-Marie's body had made it through surgery, but her soul— my pidge— was nowhere to be found. She hadn't come back to me yet, and I didn't know how long it might take.

Hours must've passed. I sat at Ava's bedside, holding her cold fingers and waiting for her to wake. I must've fallen asleep, because I woke to the sound of static crackling overhead.

"Students of Darke Institute." The Warden's voice came over the ancient intercom system. "I regret to inform you that the Darke Games have been canceled, due to a tragedy that occurred in the early hours of this morning."

The intercom barely worked. All the magic inside the Institute interfered with the connection, and his words were difficult to make out. I wondered why he hadn't just called everyone to an assembly like he'd done before.

Then I realized— he was doing this for me. He wanted me to hear his speech. He wanted to show me he'd won.

"Around three a.m. this morning, a sinkhole formed in the school's graveyard," the Warden continued. "A group of students, along with their counselor, encountered the sinkhole at its untimely arrival. Our very own Professor Jaymin Vengier attempted to save her students, but she did not survive. Thirty-two guards rushed in to help, but they too perished. Three students survived with minor injuries; however, one of our own— Ava-Marie Wahkin— was severely injured."

He spoke her name intentionally. He wanted me to know that he could still hurt her.

"Jaymin did everything she could to save these students, and because of her, they made it out alive," the Warden continued. "She is a true hero. Our thoughts and prayers are with the families at this time."

Rage nearly took me over. What a manipulative bastard! People should know the truth about what really happened down there.

"Please be advised that the Institute is in no danger from the portals, as the threats posed during the Darke Games will be handled by residents of Shade Hills," he said.

Yeah fucking right. The Warden was opening those portals himself. There was no danger unless he said there was.

"The area near the graveyard is considered dangerous and off limits," the Warden continued. "Anyone found near the cemetery will be issued an infraction, for your own safety. We have no reason to believe the Institute grounds are in danger of a second sinkhole. You are all safe here. Have a good day."

The intercom hissed as his message came to an end. It was fitting, considering the snake he was.

I noticed he didn't mention Ava's parents. I wasn't sure what his plan was for them, but I didn't imagine it was anything good.

A light knock came at the door. "Charlie, how are you doing?" Sophia asked.

Feeling like shit, thanks for asking, I thought, but I didn't say that out loud. "Uh... I'm here," I said instead.

Liam's footsteps sounded behind Sophia. He stopped dead in his tracks. I could only imagine the horror he felt when he saw her. Ava had once told me her father had been hooked up to a breathing tube when he'd gotten sick and nearly died. He knew exactly what Ava was going through.

"Can we have a moment with her?" he asked gently.

I realized Ava's parents must've been waiting hours to see her. I stood, and Oberi followed me. "Yeah... sure."

I didn't want to leave Ava-Marie, but her parents deserved to see her. Besides, I had to check on Kallie and Marcus. I could hear them whispering lowly from the waiting room, but there were other voices, too.

I realized all our friends were there. It sounded like they were alone. I followed the sound of their voices, but they stopped dead when I entered the room.

"Charlie," Kallie said. "How's Ava?"

"She's... alive." The words tasted like ash.

"Mom says the doctors told her Ava's in a coma," Ez said softly. He sounded really broken up about everything.

"Yeah," I forced past the lump in my throat. "Medically-induced. Your parents are in there now, if you want to join them."

"I think I will. Thanks," Ez said before heading down the hall.

Ivy broke down into tears. "This *can't* be happening. I can't believe she'd—"

"Shh," Chancey said gently, and Ivy whimpered.

"At least the Warden released you from the Games," I said half-heartedly.

"He had no choice but to cancel the Games after the cave-in," Chancey told me. "If he let kids out of the Institute after that, there'd be an investigation. He's doing everything he can to cover his ass."

"Ava saved all of us," Ivy added with a sniffle. "The Warden planned on sending us into the Games with noxite still in our system. He wanted us dead, but she stopped those Games from happening."

"But everyone's okay, right?" I asked.

"Everyone but Eddie," Alistair replied sadly.

My stomach hollowed. I felt awful that we hadn't found Eddie. "There has to be something more we can do."

"We might still have a chance," Alistair said. "Kallie and Marcus told us everything. I can't believe you guys are demigods."

"I sometimes can't believe it either." I turned to Kallie and Marcus. "Have you heard from your parents? Did they make it off campus before...?"

"Yes," Kallie said. "Both of our parents are safe."

"We went to Hemlock," Marcus blurted.

My heart leapt a little. "Can she help us?"

Nobody answered for a beat, until Kallie spoke. "She's informing the Demigod Guardians of what happened. There's nothing else we can do. It's in their hands now."

My teeth gritted. "We have to do *something*. The Warden could reopen the Underground at any moment."

"He won't do that," Chancey said, sounding certain. "He has nowhere to hide it anymore."

"We don't know that. And what about the detention camp?" I challenged. "We don't know what he's doing to Eddie and the other Elves out there."

"What are we supposed to do?" Kallie asked. "We're trapped in here. We can't leave. We can't fight back."

"The Warden will *never* be held accountable for what he did!" I snapped, before lowering my voice. I didn't want to attract any attention from the staff. "We *have* to be powerful enough to get out of here."

"As long as the Warden has those crystals, we're not going anywhere," Kallie insisted. "All we can do right now is sit tight until Hemlock tells us what to do. This is out of our hands, Charlie."

"So we go through the motions and hope we survive," I growled. That wasn't good enough for me.

"We *have* to," Kallie said. "The Warden won't touch us right now, because he has nowhere to take us. We'll be safe until we can make a move."

"And how long will that take?" I demanded. I wanted to shake the earth, to bring this whole place to the ground. I wanted the Warden to *pay.* But even my demigod powers didn't stand a chance against the Institute, not with inferichite surrounding the property. The Warden had made sure of that.

Marcus placed a hand on my shoulder. "Focus on your wife, Charlie. We'll figure the rest out in time."

Time. Fuck that. Kallie had the power to manipulate time, and even that couldn't save us. We were totally screwed.

I raked my fingers through my hair. "Maybe you're right. I just need to focus on Ava right now." Honestly, I couldn't take anything else. "But I'm glad you're all okay."

I couldn't bring myself to mention Eddie. I was almost certain he was still alive, but I couldn't think about what they might be doing to him, or the other Elves, at the detention camps they'd been sent to. And there wasn't a damn thing I could do to stop it.

"I'm going to head back to Ava's room," I announced. "I need to be there when she wakes."

I'd already been away from her for too long.

I headed down the hall, but the sound of voices coming from Ava's room stopped me.

"You want to know what the last thing I said to Ava was?" Ez asked with a sniffle. He didn't wait for an answer before continuing. "I told her to leave me alone, that I didn't want her around me anymore. But I never thought she'd actually be *gone...*"

"She'll heal," Sophia said, though her tone wavered like she wasn't certain.

"I'm sorry for what I said in the hall, Dad," Ez added. "I didn't mean it—"

"Yes, you did," his father said. "And you were right. About all of it. You have nothing to apologize for. I hurt you, and you should be proud of yourself for how brave you were to stand up to me. I needed to hear it, so I can do better. I'm sorry I pushed you. I'm sorry I was hard on you. None of the lessons I tried to teach any one of you kids matters if it means you're no longer a part of my life. I love you and Ava both, Ezekiel. My kids are my life. My greatest hope is that this family stays together. We'll make it through this. All of us."

I heard the squeak of a chair, and I knew they had to be embracing.

"I love you, Dad," Ez said softly.

"I love you, too," Liam replied.

Footsteps approached the doorway, and I stood straighter. I didn't mean to eavesdrop. The door swung open, and Ez made a sound before nearly ramming into me.

"Charlie," he said. "Sorry, I didn't see you there."

"Didn't see you, either," I deadpanned. I knew he didn't need it, but I was fucking pissed at him right now. Ava had been crushed by what he'd said, and they hadn't made up before all of this. If she didn't recover—

I cut that thought off before it could go any further.

Ez sighed. "Look, Charlie. I'm sorry. More than sorry. There's nothing I can say, really. I was a total dick to Ava, and I wish I could take it all back."

He sounded so torn up, and my heart broke for him. I relaxed a little. "You couldn't have known what was going to happen," I said. "We all say stuff we regret when we're upset. I think Ava would just want you to be there when she wakes up, you know? She'll forgive you. I know she will."

"But she's not—" Ez choked up. "Charlie... what if she doesn't wake up?"

"She has to," I nearly growled. For him to suggest otherwise was fucked up.

Ez sniffled. "I love her so much, you know?"

Of course I knew. No one loved Ava as much as I did.

"I just wish she knew it," Ez said.

Then Ez hugged me. At first, I was caught so off guard that all I could do was freeze. I'd been hugged so few times in my life that it seemed unnatural. But when Ez hugged me, he embraced me like a brother. No one had ever hugged me like that before. It felt like we were actually family, and I realized... we were. So I hugged him back.

"She knows," I assured him. "I'm sure of it."

Ez cleared his throat, then backed away quickly, like he didn't want to make things too awkward. "Thanks, Charlie. I've gotta get back to Opal."

He rushed off down the hall before I could say anything else. I turned back to Ava's hospital room.

A familiar voice played quietly on TV. It was one of the newscasters who reported on the secret channel for supernaturals. This program was always playing in the Villain's Den. It was one of the few channels that actually came in on campus.

"Liam, turn it off," Sophia begged.

"We need to know what's going on out there. If the Union buys the Warden's story—" Liam said, but he cut off when I entered the room.

"Charlie," Sophia said, sounding relieved.

I shoved my hands in my pockets and stood near the door. It was the first time I had a chance to talk to Ava's parents since everything happened, and I didn't know what to say. All I could manage was, "How is she?"

"Not any better," Liam practically sneered. He didn't sound mad at me— just deeply hurt by the situation.

"Are you both all right?" I asked.

"We'll be okay," Sophia said gently.

I took a cautious step forward. "What happened last night? How did Jaymin capture you?"

"Hmph," Liam grumbled, but Sophia didn't seem bothered by the question.

"We extended our stay on the island so we could take you all home for winter break," she said. "We heard about the Elves being captured, and we were worried about Ava. We came to the Institute the moment we got the news, and we had the guards check your room. But you must've been gone by that time, because the guards started making excuses. We knew something bad had happened. We don't have cell phone service on the island, so we snuck to the payphones and called the Elders back in Kinpago. We were able to reach Chieftess Vanessa and tell her what was going on, but Jaymin captured us before we finished."

"She hit us with some nasty spells, too," Liam added.

"The chieftess must've heard you get captured, then," I said.

"She had to," Sophia confirmed. "I went back to the phone room this morning to update her, but the lines are down. They're saying it's because of the sinkhole, but I think Jaymin must've ordered someone to cut the lines last night."

"What are you going to do?" I asked desperately. "The Warden isn't willing to step on the Union's toes, because he knows he'll go down if he does. We can go to them. They'll have the upper hand."

"We plan on it," Liam stated. "As soon as we can get in touch with the Union, we'll—"

"Breaking news!" the TV blared.

"Turn it up," Sophia said quickly.

The volume grew as the broadcast began. "We have just received confirmation that a bombing has occurred on the southwest side of Celestial City, near the angels' governing headquarters. As of now, casualties are estimated in the hundreds, though reports are still coming in. Our sources say the origin of the attack is unknown, though witnesses confirm sightings of dragons flying above Celestial City minutes before the attack, ridden by Koigni riders..."

"*Fuck.* Dragons," Liam growled. "It was Vanessa. She hadn't heard from us, so she launched an attack."

"No. It can't be true," Sophia argued. "Vanessa wouldn't—"

"It *is* true, Soph. Vanessa was looking for a reason to make the first move. She didn't want the Hawkei to be a target like we were in the last war, and she wanted to get on the offense against the angels before they came for us," Liam said tiredly. "What else can we say? We knew this was coming eventually."

My blood ran cold. The next great war had started, and it was the tribe's fault.

Hell, what had we done?

Sophia gasped. "The kids, Liam! If the angels launch a counterattack on Kinpago—"

A chair skittered to the side as Liam stood up. "I won't let them get hurt," he stated firmly.

"You can't promise that!" she shouted. "Two of our children are in prison— one is lying in the intensive care unit. Alana and Maverick are alone and helpless."

"I'll go to them," Liam decided. "I'll make sure they get somewhere safe, then I'll return with them."

"You need to stay in Kinpago. The tribe's going to need you. You're the Toaqua chief," Sophia insisted. "You need to protect the tribe. You can't abandon them."

"I can't abandon my daughter, either," he raged.

"We have other children you need to protect. I'll stay here with Ava," Sophia said. "If we go to the Union now, it will divide them. The Hawkei attacked the angels first, so they're not going to believe what we know about the Warden."

"The angels might not, but we'll have others on our side," Liam said. "We have to tell them what we know."

"We'll go to the parents. Those who lost their children in the Underground deserve to know what happened. We'll get their support. But I *can't* leave." Sophia's voice cracked. "Ava needs treatment. I have to be here to heal her. If I don't, she may not make it..."

Their words seemed to disappear into the back of my mind. I was barely aware of Liam rushing out of the room, then Sophia saying something to me before she followed him. I couldn't make heads or tails of what had happened. It was all too much at once.

Was this part of Ava's prophecy? Was this the choice she'd had to make— to sacrifice herself and bring down the Underground? It had led to this attack. And I hadn't stopped her, so I was to blame. Hell, how many people were going to die for us? First in Forevermore, now in Celestial City. Even people at the Institute had died at our hand. Would the carnage ever end?

It didn't seem to matter, to be honest. Ava-Marie was lying in a coma. I could feel the void inside of me where her spirit should be. It seemed her fate was already sealed. Nothing mattered if she wasn't here.

But I couldn't give up on her yet. I held on to the hope that Ava-Marie would pull through. I'd heard her voice, seen her spirit return to her body.

Yet, why did her soul still feel so distant?

The rest of the night passed by in a blur, and one day bled into another. People came and went to visit Ava, but I barely heard the conversations going on around me. The news played constantly on TV, yet I couldn't work up the energy to pay attention. I caught bits and pieces. Supernatural societies were mobilizing to attack and defend each other. Refugees were fleeing their homes to avoid the bombings that were going on day in and day out. The Union was negotiating and forming alliances.

There were so many rumors, no one knew what to believe. Propaganda played on TV, painting the Hawkei as evil, since they'd been the first to attack.

Even if we exposed the Warden now, there'd be hordes of people who'd never believe us. I'd bet anything the Warden played a hand in the campaign against the Hawkei. The truth was hiding in plain sight, but who would believe it?

I realized then that the Warden didn't have to deal with Ava's parents if he could get other people to do it for him. They'd already made Liam out to be a sick, traumatized man who wanted justice for Ava's "accident." Now that the Hawkei had destroyed part of Celestial City, whatever the tribe could say to defend itself was basically worthless.

None of it mattered, though.

I never left Ava's side. I slept on the chair in her room and ate only when Sophia brought me takeout from the cafeteria. I forced the food down my throat and nearly gagged each time. It was the first time in my life when I didn't feel like eating. She brought me coffee every morning, but I just let it go cold. I couldn't stomach it.

More than once, I'd fallen asleep in the chair and woken to a blanket wrapped around my shoulders. Sophia hadn't left the hospital, either. I didn't think she knew what to do other than take care of me.

The Warden left me alone, thank the ancestors. Winter break had started, so I didn't have to go to class, though no one came to force me into factory shifts. I didn't know what the Warden was up to, but it must've been more important than worrying about keeping me in line. Or maybe he thought he could keep a closer eye on me if I stayed in Ava's room.

Whatever. All that mattered was being here when she woke up.

Sophia administered treatments, but her magic couldn't heal everything. All she could do was speed up the body's own healing processes, and if the body didn't want to heal itself... well, you were shit out of luck.

A week must've passed— a long, agonizing week without the other half of my soul. I didn't know how much longer we could wait. Ava's dad hadn't come back yet. I knew that nothing but total chaos and the need to protect his other children would keep him away from his first born, who was struggling to hold on to life. Whatever was going on in the supernatural world right now had to be absolute insanity.

The doctors removed Ava's tube to see if she could breathe on her own. I could hardly stomach the sounds coming from her mouth. She wasn't conscious, but I swore I heard her gagging like she was in pain. I wanted to crawl into her body and take her place, so she wouldn't have to feel the discomfort.

I prayed to every god I knew that she'd start improving, but judging by the deafening silence coming from the doctors, I knew things weren't looking good.

Oberi seemed calmer than ever— so calm, in fact, that sometimes I forgot he was there. He lay at the foot of Ava's bed most days, but that snarky attitude he usually had was just... gone. I was getting sick of it.

"Okay, Oberi," I snapped one day. We sat alone in Ava's room with nothing but the sound of the hospital machines to keep us company. "Speak up. What's going on? You know something, don't you? You're hiding something from me."

I'm not hiding anything, he promised, sounding genuine. *I just don't feel the need to speak.*

"You're acting like a psychopath," I accused. "Ava-Marie may not pull through, and you're just sitting there licking your paws like it's a Saturday afternoon at the spa."

Something twinged through the bond, and I swear to the ancestors it was the first thing I felt from him in a week. Oberi was *offended.*

You act like I'm not grieving, he shot back.

"Well, you aren't!" I cried. "Show some goddamn emotion, would you?"

I'm sad Ava's gone, but I'm also... at peace, he said gently.

I gaped. "At peace? How are you fine about all this? Do you not understand what's happening? Ava may never come back to us!"

I understand completely, Oberi said. *But I also understand that I cannot control the outcome. I don't need to worry about a problem that doesn't exist.*

"Doesn't *exist?!*" I shouted. "What are you saying? Ava no longer exists?"

Oberi remained calm. *It is only a problem if we make it one. I love Ava enough to accept whatever decision she makes. I'll be able to go on without her, because I know we'll be together again. Whether she decides to stay or go matters not. I will accept her choice either way. I trust that all will turn out exactly as it is meant to.*

His words shook me, and conflict swirled in my stomach. I didn't want to agree with him... but I had to.

Maybe Oberi was right. I'd had a week to process that Ava-Marie might be gone for good. I didn't want to put her through any more suffering. If Ava didn't want to return to me... well, I had to respect that and trust that she knew best.

And I had to trust Oberi when he said we would all be together again one day. Saying goodbye to Ava now didn't mean saying goodbye forever.

Yet my guts twisted knowing she didn't choose to come back to me. It was torture unlike any other. But that was my human brain talking. Deep down in my soul, I knew that Ava would never leave me.

I don't want to fight on your birthday, Oberi said quietly.

I furrowed my brow. "It's my birthday?"

I really *had* lost track of the days. It was nearly Christmas.

It is, Oberi replied. *Happy birthday, Charlie.*

Yeah, I thought bitterly. *Happy fucking birthday to me.*

A knock came at the door, and several people stepped inside. "Charlie?" Sophia said. "The doctors want to speak with us."

I stood up straight. "Is it good news?"

A woman drew a deep breath. "I'm afraid not, Mr. Wahkin. The truth is, Ava's not improving. Her mother's treatments have helped the surface injuries, but her chances of waking from the coma are low. With magic like this, we expected her to wake by now."

Sophia sniffled, sounding like she was trying to hold herself together. "I've done everything I can, but it's the body's choice to heal. I can't make her wake up."

My lungs felt as if they were collapsing. Even with my Air magic, I couldn't force myself to breathe. It was like a basilisk had wrapped itself around my middle and squeezed so hard my soul nearly left my body. "Wh-what are you saying?"

"Charlie... the machines are the only thing that's keeping her alive. It's time to talk about taking her off life support," the doctor said.

I couldn't believe what she was asking me to do. I staggered on my feet, and Oberi jumped down from Ava's bed to catch me. He didn't reach me in time, and I sank to my knees. One arm draped over Oberi's back, and I leaned into him.

"You're asking me to kill my wife," I spat.

Sophia spoke gently. "Charlie, they're asking us to do what's best for Ava. As her husband, it's your call to make."

My head spun. How could I possibly make that choice?

"You're her mother," I said. "What would you do?"

She took a moment to collect her thoughts, before she knelt beside me. "This wouldn't be the first time I'd been asked to make a difficult decision. Raising a bipolar child was hard. Ava meant everything to me, but sometimes, I had to make decisions that I could barely manage to stomach. But every time I did, I had to remember I needed to do what was best for *her,* and not what was best for myself. It's time for you to decide what you think she would've wanted, Charlie. Because this is no kind of life for her."

Oberi nudged me. *Let's think about what Ava would want.*

I drew a deep breath. I had to be brave and face this, no matter how hard it was. Ava would want that much from me, at least. I thought about Ava, being chained to this bed for the rest of her existence. She wouldn't get to go exploring, make potions, sing songs, or do any of the things she loved. This hospital bed would become her new prison, and she didn't deserve to be chained up like this.

I don't think she'd want to live on machines, I told Oberi in my mind. It hurt to say it, but it was the truth. Ava was all about adventure. She'd turn over in her grave if she knew I was keeping her body on life support. What a life that was...

She'd want me to respect her wishes, I told Oberi. *And as hard as it is to admit, I think I know what she's chosen. She would've come back to me by now if she wanted to. It's selfish to keep this going any longer. I want her to be at peace more than I want to be with her. I love her more than I need her.*

A shiver traveled down my spine when I realized the truth, as hard as it was to admit.

Then I guess we know what we have to do, Oberi said sadly. He may be at peace with any outcome, but it was clear he'd grieve it nonetheless. *Are you going to be okay with this?*

I have to be, I replied. *It's Ava's choice. I still have work to do with our prophecies, and I have to stay here and fulfill them for her. I'll die and return to her once I fix everything. If it was important enough for us to be together, she would've come back. It's not going to be easy, but I have to make the sacrifice to stay here.*

Ancestors, the decision tore me apart from the inside out. But I was willing to go through the agony if that's what Ava wanted.

I stood on shaky feet. "Ava chose the Ancestral Lands. I don't want her to keep suffering. I want to make this right."

"Very well," the doctor said. "We'll allow you time to say your goodbyes."

Tears pricked at my eyes, but it wasn't until the doctor left the room that I let them roll down my cheeks freely. Sophia approached me and pulled me into a motherly hug. I sagged against her.

"You're making the right choice, Charlie," she said, but I wasn't sure I believed her. "Ava will be at peace. We'll meet with her again in the Ancestral Lands."

I nodded and drew away. "I hope you're right."

The door creaked open again, and several pairs of footsteps entered. There must've been half a dozen. I suspected all my friends were here.

"I'll be right outside," Sophia said gently. "I'll call Liam. We'll... we'll do it once he arrives."

Ancestors, that could be mere hours from now. I had so little time to spend with her.

But I was fooling myself. Ava was already gone... she *had* been gone for a week now. It had just taken me that long to accept it.

"Oh, gods," Kallie choked out. "She looks *horrible.*"

I heard her sob, and it twisted me up inside. Kallie was tough. For her to act like that... I knew I must've been making the right decision.

I was grateful I was blind. I had no wish to have the image of Ava's broken body in my memory forever, as the last I'd ever see of her.

"Is it true?" Ez said. "The doctor just said—"

"It's true," I cut him off. I could barely keep my tone steady. "I'm just trying to honor her wishes."

"I... I can't believe this is it," Kallie whispered.

Hell, neither could I. This was too much. I didn't think I'd ever stop blaming myself for what was about to happen. I wanted to disappear... to just stop existing.

"She saved us, you know?" Marcus said.

"She died a hero," Alistair added softly. "I'll never forget what she gave up, trying to get Eddie back to us."

Opal sniffled. "I'm going to miss her. She was my first friend at the Institute."

I heard Ivy give a tearful huff, and he stomped toward me. "This is fucking bullshit. You *can't* do this, Charlie," Ivy argued. "The doctors have to keep trying!"

"Ivy, there's nothing—" I started, but he cut me off.

"*No!*" he shouted, and he shoved me backward. "There has to be *something*, goddammit, you hear me?! You can't give up on her!"

His words were like a knife through my gut. Was he right? Was I giving up on her... or was I giving her the future she wanted in the Ancestral Lands?

I tried to rationalize, even as instinct was fighting against me to keep her alive. "They've tried all the potions and healing magic they can, and it isn't enough. Ava... chose this. I can't hold her back from being at peace."

"She wouldn't *do* that! The Ava I know wouldn't give in!" Ivy yelled. "What kind of fucking husband are you, taking your wife's life away?"

I'd had a lot of people say some really shitty things to me in my life. But Ivy completely leveled me when he let those words fly out of his mouth. He knew how to hurt people, and nothing anyone had said or could say in the future would ever cut me like he just did.

"Ives, cut it out," Chancey snapped. "I know you're hurt. We're all losing Ava, but Charlie's losing the love of his life."

"I don't *want* to do this," I pleaded. "But I believe it's what Ava wants."

"I think so, too," Ez agreed. "We gotta let her go."

Ivy gave a few more gasping sobs, but said nothing more. I heard footsteps as our friends circled Ava's bed. Then the room fell silent. I wondered if they were waiting for me to say something, but what could I say? I'd only known Ava-Marie for a short while, yet everything I could possibly say about this woman would take a lifetime to share. She was my wife, the other half of my soul. Words just weren't enough in a time like this.

All I could do was take her hand in mine and let the tears come. I didn't care that all my friends were watching. I couldn't hold my grief back for anything.

Ancestors, I was going to miss her.

Marcus drew a breath, then the room filled with a beautiful tune. He began to sing O Holy Night... and it fucking shattered my heart. Somehow, Marcus always knew what you needed, even if you didn't know it yourself.

Kallie joined in, then Opal. I heard Ivy chime in on the third line, and eventually, Chancey and Alistair added their voices. Even Oberi began humming the harmony in my mind.

My chest racked with sobs as their voices filled the room. Ava would love it. It was so beautiful, and it was our last goodbye to her. We'd sing her off to sleep, so her soul could rest... and wait for me.

My heart swelled within my chest, and the hot tears became cool again. I realized as the song continued that my tears had transformed from sorrow to something akin to joy. I wasn't *happy* to be doing this, but I was less sad.

I was at peace.

And finally, Ava could be, too.

The song ended abruptly, and a gasp traveled around the room. My heart lurched in alarm, but it was quickly softened as a powerful energy filled my insides. It was like a bolt of lightning, flooding in to replace all the anguish. I felt... *alive*.

Ava's hand twitched in mine. I had to be imagining things.

Then the most beautiful sound filled the room— *Ava's* voice.

"I promised you'd never be alone again," my wife whispered. "Our adventure isn't over yet."

END OF BOOK THREE

Continue on to read a special excerpt from Book Four: *The Assassin's Destiny*.

HIDDEN LEGENDS

Read more from the Hidden Legends universe! Each Hidden Legends series takes place within the same world, but in separate and unique societies. Every series stands on its own, and they can be read in any order.

ELEMENTALS, DRAGONS, & MORE

Academy of Magical Creatures by Megan Linski & Alicia Rades

SHIFTERS, FAE, & SORCERESSES

University of Sorcery by Megan Linski

WITCHES, DEMONS, & REAPERS

College of Witchcraft by Alicia Rades

Never miss a new release! Join our newsletter at
hiddenlegendsbooks.com/fanclub/

THE ASSASSIN'S DESTINY
CHAPTER ONE

Charlie

If all the beauty in the world could be condensed into a single fragment of time, I experienced its entirety the moment my wife woke from her coma. Every laugh, every smile, every caress of a loved one's skin seemed to burst through and slam into my chest. I became so overwhelmed that I turned to a statue. I couldn't think, couldn't *breathe* as I took in the miraculous moment.

A week ago, Ava-Marie had died. The compound beneath the Institute's graveyard— where the Warden had been running his sick experiments on inmates— had come crashing down on her. She'd created an explosion to save us all and stop the Infernal Underground. But through her phoenix form, Oberi had brought Ava back to life, though it'd been Ava's choice for her soul to return or not.

My friends and I had come to the hospital to say our final goodbyes, but we didn't have to say goodbye after all. Ava-Marie was *awake*. She'd returned from the Ancestral Lands. I'd thought for certain she'd chosen to stay in the afterlife... but she'd come back to me.

"Gods, Ava! You're back," Kallie cried out before I had a chance to say anything.

The hospital room erupted into a chorus of thrilled voices, our friends' glee overlapping one another.

"Welcome back to the land of the living," Marcus said cheerfully, though his voice cracked with emotion.

"By Atlantis, it's a miracle!" Ivy cried. He shoved me aside and threw himself past me. I couldn't see what was happening, but I assumed he was hugging Ava. I stumbled to the side a step, though I didn't let go of her hand.

"We're so glad you're awake." Opal sobbed.

Ezekiel spoke quickly through tears. "Sis, I'm *so* sorry about what I said to you. I never should've treated you that way."

Chancey and Alistair spoke over one another. I couldn't process what anyone else said. The sounds were overwhelming, swelling over me like white noise. All I could do was stand there in shock. I didn't know what to say. A moment ago, I'd made the decision to take my wife off life support. The doctors were certain she wouldn't make it. Now, her soft voice and lively energy filled the room.

Thank the ancestors, she's here! Oberi's relieved tone cut through my mind. He sounded so happy.

"Guys," Ava pleaded in a hoarse but confident tone. She must've pushed at Ivy, because he finally peeled himself off of her and stepped back. "I'm awake. It's not that big of a deal."

The room went dead silent as we all took in her words. Ava had *no* idea what a miracle this was.

Ava struggled to speak. "Can I have a moment with Charlie?"

No one moved for a beat, until Kallie answered. "Yes. Of course."

Everyone shuffled out of the room, until Ava and I were alone with Oberi. I squeezed her hand tightly, and tears of relief sprang from my eyes.

"Pidge," I said breathlessly. I couldn't express myself in words. All I could do was lean down and squeeze her into a gentle hug.

Ava stilled in my arms. "Charlie, what's going on? You're acting like we haven't spoken in forever."

I choked back a sob as I drew away. Ava may be awake, but she wasn't fully healed yet. I had to be extra careful with her. She was so fragile.

"We... haven't," I spoke in a broken voice.

The weight of the situation must've hit Ava. Her fingers brushed the sheets. "Charlie, lay next to me."

Immediate hesitation overwhelmed me. I was terribly concerned I'd do something to set her back... make her fall into that coma again. "I can't. You're still hooked up to the machines, and I could hurt you, and—"

"You'll be careful. I need to feel you next to me. Please."

She tugged lightly on my arm. I pulled the covers back so I could crawl into the bed beside her. I made sure to feel where the medical tubes were so I didn't tear them out as I carefully maneuvered into the bed.

I was extremely careful with her as I looped my arm around her shoulders. She hadn't left this bed in over a week, and she'd just undergone serious surgery. I needed to be gentle. Ava rested her head on my chest, and when she did that, I felt the weight of the world lift from my shoulders.

I heard Oberi's nails click as he padded to the other side of the bed. I felt his fur as he laid his head next to Ava's hand. *Ava. I missed you, my dear love.*

Ava gave a tired sigh. "You're all acting like I've been out of it for an eternity," Ava said.

Sure felt like it. Oberi jumped onto the end of the bed and lay over our feet. I tried not to tremble, but I failed.

My wife was okay. This wasn't an illusion or a dream. The weight of her body in my arms was more real than anything I'd ever experienced.

Ancestors, it was exactly what I'd been praying to have for days. I thought I'd never get to experience a moment like this ever again. The gods had delivered just what I'd asked for.

I pressed my nose into her hair and inhaled her raspberry scent. I never wanted to let this woman go. She was *alive.* I thought I'd had bad luck my whole life from all the shit I'd been through, but I realized that I'd been saving all my lucky moments for her, so we could pull through this.

Ava sucked a breath, and I stilled. "Did I hurt you?" I asked.

"No," she assured me. "But I'm sore everywhere."

"I'm so sorry, pidge."

"It's not that bad, honest."

She was lying because she didn't want to upset me, but I knew what kind of pain she had to be in. She had blocked off her half of our bond, so I couldn't register her pain. She was trying to protect me in a moment where she was the breakable one. It was unfathomable.

"I love you." My trembling fingers delicately traced her face. "I thought I'd never get to have you again."

"I'm not going anywhere. Don't cry, Charlie." Ava wiped away tears from my eyes.

"I never wanted to let you go, but I thought it was the only choice—"

"I told you I'd never leave. Heaven and hell can't keep us apart," Ava said. "Death doesn't mean anything when you have a love like this."

That was the kind of thing people said in books and fairytales, but that was our reality. We had that once-in-a-lifetime kind of connection that couldn't be transgressed by any force. "I've been falling apart without you."

"You always had me. Even on the other side, I could feel you close."

"I couldn't feel you at *all*." I nearly suffocated on the words. "It broke me. You know you're my whole world, pidge. I didn't see the point in anything if you weren't here."

"It's all right now. We're together again, like it should be. It's going to stay that way."

Ancestors, I hoped so. I couldn't endure this a second time. It had nearly killed me the first time around.

Ava shifted against me. "Charlie... what happened?"

A lump rose to my throat. How could I begin to describe it all? The last week of my life had been like walking through ten layers of hell all at once.

But Ava had been the one to truly walk the afterlife. I had to be strong for her right now, because she needed me.

I swallowed. "You don't remember?"

She thought about it for a moment. "The details are fuzzy. I remember we found the Infernal Underground, and then... I remember Coyote Spirit. Charlie, I think I went to the Ancestral Lands."

I drew her closer. "You did," I told her. "I could feel it through our bond. Your spirit left."

"But I'm back now," Ava said simply. "Like I promised. I missed you."

"I thought I'd lost you for good," I admitted. "The doctors had lost hope. I thought you chose to stay in the Ancestral Lands."

"Never," Ava said. "I'd always come back to you, Charlie."

"I know you've promised me that before, but there are bigger things at stake here than us," I reminded her. "I thought I was honoring your decision to die."

"Honoring me how?" Ava sounded confused.

Ancestors, how could I have thought what I was doing was justified? Minutes ago, I thought I was doing the right thing. I'd been at peace with the decision. But now that I knew Ava had chosen to come back to me, it'd have been a terrible mistake. Guilt twisted in my gut.

"Ava, they... asked me to pull the plug," I spat out. I hoped she didn't hate me.

Ava snickered, though the sound turned to a whimper of pain. "*Pull the plug?* Ancestors, it's not like I was in a coma."

The air around me seemed to grow heavy. "Actually, Ava..."

She sucked in a breath, and my heart nearly shattered. "I was barely gone a day! It felt like..."

She trailed off as she tried calculating time in her mind. I wasn't sure how much she remembered.

"It might've felt that way in the Ancestral Land, but here, it's been a week," I told her. "They've been treating you with healing magic, and you weren't improving. Pidge, I don't know if you realize this, but you died. Twice, actually. Once in the Underground, and again on the operating table. Oberi used her power to bring you back."

Ava sagged against me as she pondered what I'd told her. She sounded thoughtful. "I remember the gods... Coyote Spirit and Whale Spirit... they said something about Oberi having a gift."

"She's a phoenix," I said, a hint of pride in my tone. "We found her Anichi form— her Spirit form. Part of her power is one shot at regeneration."

Ava's voice wavered. "And she... used it on me?"

Of course I did, Oberi replied. He nudged his nose between our legs affectionately. *I'd do anything for you, Ava.*

"Oberi, that's so sweet."

"It was your choice to come back, though," I explained. "We weren't sure it would work."

Ava brushed hair away from my eyes. "I'll always come back to you."

Her promise meant everything. I couldn't help it when tears began streaming from my face. I hugged her close, and she snuggled into me.

"Thank you, pidge," I whispered. "I don't know what I'd do without you."

"You don't have to worry about that, because I'm not going anywhere," she promised.

Her lips connected with mine, and all the anxiety twisting in my gut melted away. My heart surged, until it felt like I was floating on a cloud with her. Having her back meant the world, and nothing could ruin this moment.

Ava slid her hand beneath the covers, and her fingers grazed my waistband.

I drew away. "Uh... what are you doing?"

She giggled. "I'm horny."

She slid her hand inside my pants and wrapped her fingers around me. I didn't mind when she took initiative, but I wasn't comfortable doing this here.

I grabbed her hands to stop her. "We can't right now."

"Why not?" she asked.

"You're hurt. You've just been through major surgery, for one, and you're hooked up to all these machines," I said.

"So? You'll be gentle."

"Pidge," I sighed. I didn't think she truly understood how fragile she still was.

"Come *on*. I'm alive and all. We should celebrate! With sex," Ava pleaded.

"Maybe when we get out of here," I told her reluctantly. I was honestly too afraid to touch her at the moment. We could be intimate again when I wasn't worried about setting her health back.

"Ugh, fine. Cockblock," Ava complained, and she drew her hand out of my pants.

The door burst open then, and a pair of footsteps rushed into the room. "Ancestors, she's awake!" Ava's mother cried.

Good thing Ava had decided *not* to mess around, because her mom had almost caught us with Ava's hand down my pants. I permitted myself a small laugh. Humor felt weird after such a dark week, but I could laugh again, because Ava was going to be all right.

"Mama! You're okay!" Ava sounded so happy to see her. "And you're still at the Institute."

"I never left," Sophia said. "You needed treatments. I just called your father and told him— oh."

Her voice fell flat. I knew exactly what they'd talked about. She'd told him we'd decided to end life support. Liam had to be in utter agony.

"You better call him back," I said firmly.

"I won't be long," Sophia said in a rush.

She fled from the room to call her husband and tell him the good news. She must've left the door open behind her, because several pairs of footsteps approached. Slowly, our friends came back in, and the door clicked shut behind them.

I forced myself to climb off the bed. I didn't want to— felt like cutting myself in half, honestly— but I wanted to give Ava some space, just in case she wasn't being honest about wanting me next to her.

"How are you feeling?" Ez asked timidly.

"Uh... good?" Ava said, though it sounded like a question. I could only imagine the pain she was in. "What happened, exactly? I remember bits and pieces, but not all of it."

Your memories should return in time, Oberi told her. *Your spirit's just a bit shocked right now.*

"We found the Underground," Kallie said.

"Right, beneath the cemetery," Ava recalled. "And the Elves?"

"They weren't there," Marcus said sadly. "We found records that showed the Warden had already moved them to some camp on the island. But Jaymin showed up with guards, and you exploded the compound to save us all."

"That's when Coyote Spirit showed up and took me to the Ancestral Lands," Ava said, like she was starting to remember.

"What was it like?" Opal asked curiously.

"It was... amazing," Ava answered in a way that made me wonder why she'd ever want to leave. "It was so beautiful. I saw a supernova explode, and this underground water tunnel— ancestors, I met so many wonderful people. You'll never believe what they have there. *A mall!*"

Ez chuckled to lighten the mood. "I bet that made the decision to come back hard."

"Not at all, actually," Ava said, and my heart warmed. "Did I miss anything? Ancestors, how did the Darke Games go?"

"We didn't compete, thankfully," Alistair said. "You sort of saved us from that, too. They were canceled due to the *sinkhole.*"

"That's the story the Warden's going with, at least," Chancey added.

"I'm glad I brought that place to the ground," Ava said. "The Warden will have nowhere to host his experiments for now, and his inferichite crystal supply will be low, now that I buried the devil's finger that he gets them from."

She sounded so proud of herself, but we hadn't even gotten to the worst of the story. But no one spoke up to tell her about the mounting war, or how the Hawkei tribe bombed the angel city. It was too much information to drop on her right now, and we didn't want to set back her recovery.

"Wait a dick..." Ava said, like she just realized something. "You said it's been a week. What day is it, exactly?"

"The twenty-first," I said.

A long, dramatic silence stretched through the room as she absorbed what I'd said. Ava surprised me by breaking into sobs. "Ancestors, Charlie! It's your *birthday.*"

"Uh... yeah," I stated. I didn't get why she was so upset.

"This is horrible! We had a surprise party planned, and we *missed it!*" she cried. "I *ruined your birthday* with my surgery!"

"Pidge, don't say that," I insisted. I knelt by her bedside and took her hand. "Having you back is the best birthday present in all the world."

"But we... I got you a gift, and I wanted to bake a cake and *everything,*" she sobbed.

Ancestors, she was more worried about my birthday than the fact that she'd *died*. I couldn't give a flying fuck that my birthday was here. All I gave a damn about was my wife's well-being, and she was okay. That was the only celebration I needed.

"I don't mind. It will be all right," I promised.

"Not until you get your present," she demanded. "We can do that, at least. Marcus, do you still have it?"

"Yeah, of course." Marcus must've conjured something, because I heard a bag rustle.

Ava pulled her hand out of mine to wipe her tears. "Thank the Great Spirit. We all pitched in."

I reluctantly took the bag from Marcus, but I hesitated. My birthday was nothing special. We should be celebrating Ava right now.

Everyone's watching, Oberi told me. *Go ahead and open it.*

I opened the bag and dug through the tissue paper, until my fingers curled around a small square item. I ran my hand over it and found several buttons. It reminded me of the voice recorder I used for recording lectures in class.

"What is it?" I asked.

"It's a music player," Ava said. "I got one to match the headphones I bought you last semester. We've already downloaded a playlist for you, and a bunch of true crime podcasts."

"It only took a month with the Institute's shitty Internet," Alistair added playfully.

"I know you want to be a supernatural bounty hunter, so I thought you'd like to practice solving crimes by listening to the podcasts and trying to piece cases together," Ava rasped.

I choked up, and nearly broke down for the millionth time that day. Goddamn, it was such a thoughtful gift. Ava was the one person who actually supported my dreams and thought I could do whatever I wanted. Even lying all busted up in a hospital bed, she did her best to make things as amazing as she could for me. I didn't deserve this woman. "Thanks, guys. I really don't know what to say."

The door opened again, and I heard a barrage of voices coming down the hall. "I told the doctors she's awake," Sophia said as she entered the room. "They're coming to check on her."

Suddenly, the room became so crowded I could barely move.

"How is this possible?" a nurse asked.

"It isn't," one of the doctors answered.

"Everyone out!" someone barked. "She needs space."

Sophia placed a gentle hand on my shoulder. "They might need my healing powers. I've got this, Charlie. You can relax now. She's not going anywhere."

"Thanks," I said. In my heart, I knew Sophia was telling the truth. In my brain, I feared I might lose Ava again.

But if I wanted her to stay, I had to let the doctors fix her.

"It'll be okay, Charlie," Ava said, before she let out a short gasp, and she let her true feelings slip across our bond. I winced as I felt a small sting of agony ripple over my middle. I knew it had to be a hundred times worse from her point of view. I didn't want to leave, but her comfort was more important than mine, and she needed some pain relief.

"I'll be right outside the room," I told my wife before leaving. Oberi remained behind on the bed.

My friends went to the waiting room, while I sank into a chair right outside Ava's hospital room. I could hear the doctors unhooking Ava from the machines, but otherwise, the hall had gone silent. My head spun as I caught up with reality. Everything had happened so quickly.

I must've been sitting there a long time, because Marcus stopped by to ask if I wanted to go get food. I didn't, and I told my friends to go without me. Doctors came and went from Ava's room, until I was left in complete silence.

Footsteps sounded down the hall, though I didn't pay attention until someone said my name. "Charlie. I thought I'd find you here."

I stood, suddenly alert. "Uh..."

He reached out and shook my hand with a kind but firm grip. I hadn't been sure of his voice before, but his handshake was unmistakable.

"Professor Takahashi?" I asked.

"Yes. I have something for you. It can't wait."

Takahashi placed a hand on my shoulder. Something hard and flat touched my arm, and I realized he was holding a book. He guided me into the empty patient room across the hall. I went quickly, because whatever he had to say sounded important.

The door shut behind us. "What's going on? I thought you weren't supposed to return to the Institute yet. If the Warden sees you—"

"All is well," he promised. "I'm back on staff and preparing for the upcoming semester. I don't believe the Warden suspects me of anything, and I intend to keep it that way. The Demigod Guardians have run across information that you and your friends should know."

"If it's in that book, we need to hide it from the Warden," I insisted.

"The Warden should not suspect anything," Takashi assured me. "It's been right in front of us all along. This is a book of poetry— nursery rhymes and stories that are thought to be fables, all originating from supernatural societies. The book is widely available in the school's library. But there are some stories in here that have proven to hold truths, such as the Nivita legend from your own culture. The story told of a woman who died and became a tree."

"What does this have to do with demigods?" I asked.

"If that story is true, the others could be, too," Takahashi said. "We think we found a clue to the merfolk key that you and your friends will need to open the Elven Gate and fulfill your prophecy."

My heart surged with hope. "What's the story?"

"It's an old Atlantean story the sailors used to tell while at sea. It's called *The Assassin's Destiny*," Takahashi said. "It speaks of a woman assassin who stole *a treasure of the sea*. We believe that to be the merfolk key."

Takahashi began to narrate a verse aloud. It sounded like a poem.

"Into the dark she ran, with her treasure of the sea.
The key to her riches lies with the assassin's destiny."

Pages rustled as Takahashi closed the book. "We think this story is a treasure map that will lead us to where she hid it."

"This is great!" I cried. We already had four keys— after we stole the angel key from the Warden's safe— and already, we had a clue leading to another.

I pondered the words for a moment. "The assassin's destiny... what is that? Is this another prophecy?"

"It's likely," Takahashi said. "Which means—"

"It's about Kallie," I said simply. "She was an assassin in Malovia, before she was sentenced to the Institute. She's one of the demigods searching for the keys. So it must be her destiny to find it."

"We believe so," Takahashi agreed. "Which means that Kallie must be the one to decipher this. It is *her* prophecy, *her* destiny. She must connect with her origins and discover who this assassin was, in order to find where this mysterious woman hid the key."

"Maybe she already knows without realizing it," I said thoughtfully. "I'll tell her right away."

"Take the book," Takahashi offered, placing it into my hands. "Give it to Marcus. He can keep it in his stash."

"I will. Thank you so much."

"I know you're excited, but remember to keep your guard up," Takahashi told me. "I will see you in a few weeks' time, once our counseling sessions start up again. In the meantime, make sure to stay out of trouble."

That was always my prerogative, but with the people I hung around with, Takahashi was asking for the impossible.

I left the room buzzing with excitement. Ava-Marie was making a recovery, and we had a lead on the next key. All seemed right in the world.

When I entered Ava's hospital room, the doctors had cleared out.

"I found something about the keys," I said in a rush. "Well, Takahashi found it."

"We can talk about it when Kallie and Marcus get back," Ava said. "My mom just left to update my dad, and I don't have much time."

"Time for what?" I asked.

The bed creaked as Ava tried pushing herself upright. She groaned, and concern swelled over me. I tossed the book onto a chair and hurried to her bedside.

"The doctors unhooked me, but Mama won't let me get out of bed," Ava said. "She's *very* insistent I stay put so the doctors can observe me. They need to run more tests, and they don't know how long I'll be here.

But I *need* a shower. I feel so gross. Can you help me quick while Mama's gone?"

"Yeah, of course," I said. I'd do anything she wanted. I helped her sit up, then tossed the covers off her feet and guided them onto the floor.

Ava sagged against me. She was still so tired.

I frowned. "Pidge, you can hardly stand. Maybe this wasn't a good—"

Ava went to take a step, but she let go of me. My heart lurched as I felt her going down. I grabbed her tightly and caught her before she crashed to the floor. Ava clutched my shirt, and her body trembled. Oberi whimpered loudly.

"I'm okay. I can stand," Ava said, but something in her tone worried me.

"We need to get you back into bed. You're not well enough to be moving around," I argued.

"No, I've got this." She sounded frustrated as she put an arm around my neck. "Just support me, okay?"

I wished to carry her, but that's not what she wanted. So instead, I steadied her as she tried to take a step... only she didn't go anywhere.

My heart slammed against my rib cage. This wasn't right. "Pidge, what's wrong? What hurts?"

Ava's tone wavered. "It... it doesn't. That's the problem. I... I can't feel my legs."

The world seemed to stop spinning. I couldn't have heard her right.

"You can't...?" *Fuck!* My words trailed off.

Ava's panic ripped through the bond. I teetered on the verge of freak-out, but I didn't want to worry her further, so I shoved my emotions downward.

The door opened, and Sophia gasped when she saw me clutching Ava. "What are you doing?!" she cried. "Ava, I explicitly told you to stay in bed!"

I scooped Ava in my arms and set her on the bed. I'd gone numb all over, and my thoughts were completely blank. What was going on? We'd already been through so much... there couldn't be possibly more we had to endure, could there?

Oberi let out a low whine beside us, as if he knew this had been coming and wanted to protect us from it, but knew nothing he could do or say would help.

Ava's hands trembled, and her voice shook. "I just wanted a shower... Charlie, I don't understand. Wh-why can't I feel anything?"

I didn't have an answer to give her, and it tore me to fucking shreds. Sophia must've said something to Ava, but I didn't hear it. The whole infirmary seemed to turn upside down. I couldn't make sense of space or time.

A hand landed on my shoulder, and Sophia whispered softly, "Charlie... I need to talk with you privately."

Ancestors, I hoped she had an idea of what we could do to help Ava. I couldn't muster the strength to say anything as she pulled me into the hall. I raked my fingers through my hair. "Is she...?"

"While I was healing her, I discovered that some of the nerves in her spine were severely damaged at the base," Sophia said, her voice cracking. She sounded as if she was barely holding herself together. "The doctors and I did what we could to repair them, but even with my healing magic, we couldn't mend the worst of the damage."

My thoughts spun faster than a whirlwind. Most of the explosion had been concentrated around Ava's middle, as that's where her magic had blasted outward. But I didn't realize her spine had been injured, too. The doctors had never told me.

Then I realized why— because they didn't think Ava would ever recover enough for it to be important to mention.

"I'd seen the damage to her body, and I truly thought she wasn't going to make it. I didn't want to tell you and cause you more pain." Sophia sounded regretful. "But then she woke up. I was going to tell you both as soon as I came back to the room, but you already had her out of bed."

"So what do we need to do?" I asked. "Will she heal in time, or..."

Sophia sighed heavily. "I'm sorry to tell you this, Charlie. But Ava-Marie is never going to walk again."

Continue The Assassin's Destiny to submerge in the mystery of the merfolk key!

BONUS OFFERS

Find coloring pages, games, quizzes, and bonus content at hiddenlegends-books.com

Join *Orenda Academy of Magical Creatures* on Facebook for all things Hidden Legends!

Check out the *Prison for Supernatural Offenders Official Playlist* on Spotify!

Never miss a new release! Join our newsletter at hiddenlegendsbooks.com/fanclub/

About the Authors

Megan Linski (left) and Alicia Rades (right) are best friends and the authors of the Hidden Legends universe. Both are USA Today best-selling authors of young adult and new adult fiction. Megan Linski is a coffee connoisseur who enjoys ice skating, horseback riding, and shopping. Her stories feature themes of community and friendship while advocating for the rights of the disabled. Alicia Rades is a mother who loves baking cookies, reading tarot, and binge-watching Netflix. She has a passion for personal development and strives to incorporate emotional-empowerment themes into her books. Both girls love nature, animals, sexy romances, and eating cheese.